Moonshine

By the same author

Dance With Me
Out of Love
Past Mischief
Running Wild
Clouds Among the Stars

VICTORIA CLAYTON

Moonshine

HarperCollins*Publishers*

HarperCollins*Publishers*
77–85 Fulham Palace Road,
Hammersmith, London W6 8JB

www.**harpercollins**.co.uk

Published by HarperCollins*Publishers* 2004
1 3 5 7 9 8 6 4 2

A catalogue record for this book
is available from the British Library

ISBN 0 00 714343 5

Set in Sabon

Printed and bound in Great Britain by
Clays Ltd, St Ives plc

Remembering Constance Boyle,
my Irish grandmother.

Moonshine

ONE

The waves scattered the lights from the Swansea to Cork ferry as though tossing silver coins to the marine life of the Bristol Channel. The wind flung the contents of my stomach after them. I bitterly regretted the Battenberg cake.

'You don't look well, dear,' the motherly stewardess had said. 'Take my advice and have a little something to settle your insides. The crossing's going to be rough.'

Discouraging though this sounded, they were the first kind words that had been addressed to me all day. She had put down the plate before me and urged me to eat. It would have been impolite to refuse. Now my imagination was haunted by those lurid pink and yellow squares of cake, clad in wrinkled marzipan. As I pressed the cold iron of the ship's rail against my burning face a sense of monstrous ill-usage overwhelmed me and I groaned aloud.

'You poor thing! I've suffered from *mal de mer* myself and it's no fun. O death, where is thy sting? O grave, where thy victory?'

The voice was male, self-assured, amused. I suppose there is something comical about sea-sickness if you don't happen to be feeling it. I wanted neither the sympathy nor the teasing but nausea and faintness made flight impossible. I would have fallen if the stranger had not taken my arm.

'Steady! Come on, let's sit down.'

He half carried me to a row of benches. Naturally, at this hour of howling purgatorial darkness, they were empty.

'I feel awful!' I moaned. I would have added, 'The human race is despicable and life is a hideous pantomime,' if I had not, even in this moment of crisis, a disinclination to make myself utterly ridiculous.

1

'It's bad, I know. You just want to die.' He pushed me on to a seat and sat down beside me.

'I do!' I sobbed, the kindness in his voice encouraging me to give way to melodrama. 'You'd better let me throw myself in. It'll be the solution to every problem.'

'Not for me, it won't. People might think I pushed you overboard.'

'How like a man! It's got nothing to do with you. They'll think, quite rightly, that I couldn't stand another minute of this beastly boat going up and down, up and down. Oh, how I *hate* the sea!'

The man laughed. 'We haven't left the bay yet. Mumbles Head is over there, to the right. There's only a slight breeze and the water's as smooth as the proverbial mill-pond.'

I lifted my head. The lights of Swansea rose and fell most unpleasantly but the moon sent an unbroken path of beams across the water to meet them. The howling was all in my mind.

'I hate mill-ponds.' I continued to cry.

'That's right. Let it all out.' My self-appointed nurse patted my arm from time to time. 'Now.' He handed me his handkerchief. 'Have a good blow. Feeling better?'

I blew. 'I feel worse if anything.'

'The trick is not to register the motion of the ship. Don't, whatever you do, look at the rail. Keep your eyes fastened on something on board. A lifebelt, a noticeboard or a ventilation funnel. Or, even better, look at me.'

The light from the saloon window fell on the right side of his face. I saw someone reassuringly ordinary, fairish, with prominent ears. I could just make out a cheek creased in a smile.

'I suppose you're a journalist.' I was too tired to put as much venom into the accusation as I would have liked.

'My goodness, you know how to hit where it hurts! Do I look like a sot and a liar? Have I the appeal of a tramp with rotting gums and a leaky urinary tract?'

'You are, aren't you?' I persisted.

'I'm a literary agent. A pretty innocent game, on the whole. Are you a film star who wants to be alone?'

'Well . . . no and yes.'

I stared at him, trying to pierce the darkness and the bone, cortex and synapses that housed the impulses operational in lying. The last ten days had destroyed my trust in anyone I had not known from the baptismal font.

'What can I say to convince you?' He felt inside his coat. 'Wait a minute.' He stood up and searched his trouser pockets. 'Here we are. Car keys and useful torch attached. Present from a desperate godmother. At the time I thought it was a bit mean but now I'm grateful.'

He directed a pencil beam on to an open passport. I saw the photograph of a young man with a high forehead and bat-wing ears. Below this it said, *Literary Agent*.

'See?' He directed the light on to the white slot on the passport cover. The name was Christopher Random. 'That's me. I can show you my driving licence, if you'd like.'

'I believe you. I'm sorry I doubted. You've been extremely kind, Mr Random.'

'You can call me Kit.'

'I'm sure you've got more interesting things to do than sitting here with me.'

'I was about to have some supper. You ought to eat something.'

I shuddered at the idea of the cafeteria with its stuffy smell, smeary tables and bottles sticky with congealed ketchup. 'I can't go inside.'

'All right.' He stood up. 'Promise you won't do anything silly?'

'Like what?'

He paused. 'Like look at the waves.'

I closed my eyes. 'I promise.'

The crying had made me feel better, as it always does. I felt light-headed now, and immensely weary. For the past week and a half I had slept shallowly for no more than a couple of hours at a time before a sense of something being terribly wrong had dragged me back to consciousness. Now I sat in a state of apathy feeling the vibration of the engine through the slats of the bench, the slow chilling of my feet and fingers and the tip of my nose. The realization that I need do nothing for several hours as every second the boat took me further from home seemed like an extraordinary kindness for which I was inexpressibly grateful.

My thoughts wandered and revised my impressions of the day. There had been a long train journey. I had been gripped by an obsessive fear that I was being followed. The man sitting opposite me seemed to be watching me covertly from behind the open pages of his *Gardener's Weekly*. I became convinced that he was a newspaper reporter. After we passed Cheltenham he struck up a conversation with the woman next to him. He was a retired miner with silicosis. I saw again his eyes, mild, uncomplaining, his long upper lip and his patchily shaven chin as he talked about his passion for gladioli.

3

And then, as I dozed, it grew redder and more angular, with fierce eyes and bared teeth. It became my father's face.

I roused myself and pulled my jacket closer round me, for though it was July the breeze from the sea was freezing. A young couple sauntered past, arm-in-arm, gave me a curious glance and walked on. I fell again into a waking dream in which my father's face was constantly before me. His expression of ferocity as he threw down the newspaper at breakfast ten days before had lodged itself so securely in my memory that whenever I ceased to think actively it floated up from my subconscious to fill the vacuum.

We had been sitting in the dining room, a shrine to Victorian mahogany, brown leather and second-rate watercolours. There were always twelve chairs round the table and we had occupied the same places from the time my brother and I had left the nursery. As in a dentist's waiting room, we sat as far apart from one another as the arrangement allowed.

My father was a small man and, with characteristic perversity, had chosen to marry my mother, who at five feet eleven was seven inches taller than he. This had embarrassed me horribly as a child. It seemed to detract from the dignity of each and I was afraid that people might laugh at them. If my father was in a good humour with my mother, he called her 'Lanky'. Her name was actually Laetitia.

When I examined the photograph on my mother's dressing-table of my father in uniform as a young subaltern I could see he might once have been attractive. His hair had been thick and sandy, his brows well marked, his expression keen and pugnacious. Now he was largely bald so that clumps of hair sprouted above his ears in speckled tufts and his eyebrows were unruly. He bore a striking resemblance to a wire-haired fox terrier. He spoke in an aggressive, impatient manner and when he was angry the spaces between the thousands of freckles on his face became tomato red and the bridge of his short, hooked nose grew purple.

Of course he was going to find out.

When I had seen the newspaper neatly folded by his plate, placed there by our daily, Mrs Treadgold, I knew the moment of revelation had come. The story had been the third item on the television news the night before. I had switched it off with a fluttering heart and a sick feeling in my stomach as soon as I saw Burgo's face appear on the screen. Luckily my father considered television plebeian, so he never watched it. For the remainder of the evening I had sat in painful suspense by the telephone in the hall in case one of my father's cronies

4

at the Army and Navy Club should have seen the news and be stirred by curiosity to ring him up on the pretext of condoling with him. No one had. Perhaps they too were a little frightened of him.

I cannot explain why I was afraid of my father. I could not remember a time when I had not heard his approach with apprehension. Even when he was in a jovial mood, there was something combative in his voice and manner. And I knew how rapidly the joviality could turn to rage. I could be coldly analytical behind his back and sarcastic, even defiant, to his face, but none the less I dreaded his anger.

The moment had come. I had braced myself inwardly and pretended to be busy with the marmalade while he cut the rind from his bacon, buttered toast and poured himself a second cup of tea before picking up the newspaper. I heard the abrupt cessation of crunching as his eyes fell on the offending photograph. He had let out a sudden roar of fury that made me drop my knife.

'*What!* . . . No! . . . I don't believe it!' My father's voice, usually distressingly loud, had an ominous strangled sound. He clutched the edge of the table as though unseen hands were attempting to drag him away.

My heart, which had been pounding more or less continuously for the last few days, skipped a couple of beats. But I forced myself to look indifferently, even coldly, at him. We were alone in the dining room – my mother being an invalid now and Oliver unable to get up before noon. My father's small brown eyes were watering with shock and he was making a gobbling sound in his throat. I watched him, wondering with a frightening detachment if he were about to have a stroke. He threw his napkin to the floor, clapped his hands on to the arms of his chair, stood up, strode round the table to where I sat and prodded energetically at the front page of the *Daily Chronicle*.

'*Well?* Is there a *word* of truth in this?'

I stared up at him dumbly. He seemed to interpret my silence as denial.

'I want you' – my father was breathing heavily and his eyes were bulging and crazed with red lines – 'to tell me why anyone should . . . want to make up this dis*gust*ing farrago of lies.' I noticed with a detached part of my mind that a blob of spit had landed on the butter. I made a mental note of exactly where so I could scrape it off afterwards.

'Well? *Well?*' He tried to shout but violent emotion had divested him of strength. 'Are you going to give me some sort of . . . hah! . . . explanation?'

I stood up, perhaps subconsciously to give myself the advantage of height. I was three inches taller than he. I wiped my fingers slowly with my napkin while schooling my face into an expression of challenge and defiance. 'If you mean, have I been having an affair with Burgo Latimer, yes, I have.'

He landed a smack on my jaw that knocked me sideways and made my teeth rattle. 'Whore! *Bitch!* Shameless *whore!*'

I shut my eyes to prevent tears falling and though my cheek immediately began to throb I remained outwardly calm. I braced myself for a second blow but it did not come. Probably it was the undeniably proletarian flavour of domestic violence that saved me.

'By *Christ!*' he said at last. 'That ever a child of mine . . . behaving like a bitch on heat . . . common little *tart* . . . the dis*grace* . . . never live it down . . . sacrifices for my country . . . my own *daugh*ter . . . how am I going to hold up my head in the club?'

I knew it would be pointless to attempt an explanation. I let him rave uninterrupted to get it over with as soon as possible.

'I blame your mother,' he concluded, in a tone into which some of the bittersweetness of having been deceived and betrayed was beginning to trickle. 'She's filled your head with sentimental claptrap. I suppose you fancied Latimer was in *love* with you. I hope he was good enough in bed to justify compromising the first decent government we've had for years. Don't imagine you were the only one! He'll have had his leg over every party worker under forty. What *fools* women are!'

'You kept your word, I see.' Kit evolved from the darkness and stood before me, laden with bulky objects. 'Feeling better?' He dropped a pile of blankets on the bench beside me and proceeded to wrap me in them. A man in uniform approached with a tray.

'Just put it there. We'll help ourselves, thanks.' Kit put something into his hand and he slid away with a respectful murmur. 'Now.' Kit began to unwrap packages. 'Never let it be said that we English can't enjoy a picnic whatever the weather, even in the middle of the night on a ship trying to stand on its head. Cheese sandwich, madam? Or would you prefer cheese and pickle? Or there's cheese and egg, and, for the connoisseur, cheese and sausage.'

'I thought you said something about a mill-pond.' Suddenly I found I was even a little hungry.

'So I did when it was. As smooth as. But we've got out beyond the point now and it's blowing up. No' – as I turned my head to look – 'just take my word for it. Now have some hot coffee and if you eat up your sandwiches you can have a treat afterwards. I managed to commandeer the last two jam doughnuts. When in my extreme youth we had them for tea, Nanny used to wash them under the bathroom tap to get rid of the sugar because she feared for our tooth enamel. Ever since then, when things have looked on the bleak side, I've found there are few things more comforting than a dry, plump, sugary doughnut. Other men may hanker for *foie gras* but I thank God my tastes are more easily satisfied.'

Warm within my nest of blankets, with a strong breeze in my face, looking up at the stars while I ate the sandwiches and sipped the cooling coffee, I began to feel the truth of the saying that stuffing holds out a storm. It would be too much to say that I felt cheerful but while Kit was talking nonsense and when I was not thinking about Burgo I began to feel a little less miserable.

Ironically, it was entirely due to my father's passion for interfering with other people's lives that I had met Burgo.

By my own reckoning I had removed myself from my father's sphere of influence years before. As soon as I was capable of living independently (that is, the summer after I left school), I had spent three months living in a bed-sitter in Earls Court and working in an antique shop. That autumn I had enrolled at London University to read History of Art and after graduating I took a poorly paid but interesting job at Boswell's, one of the smaller auction houses. I shared a tiny house with two friends, Sarah and Jasmine, in an enchanting cul-de-sac near the river in Chelsea. To help pay the rent I spent some of my spare time writing articles for periodicals about things like embroidered textiles, fans, silhouettes and custard pots. For relaxation I was entertained by my share of the large, fluctuating collection of men friends about whom Sarah, Jasmine and I speculated endlessly over bottles of cheap wine in the intimacy of the shabby but pretty sitting room of 22 Paradise Row.

Jasmine was in love with a married man called Teddy Bayliss. Though Sarah and I had told her (until we were in danger of sounding like evangelists for the Divine Light through Abstinence and Purity) that this was asking for trouble and bound to make her miserable, it was impossible to be anything other than sympathetic when one saw her lovely face ravaged by grief. Naturally, after the first wild rapture of romance with Teddy had passed, all our predictions came true. There were long lonely evenings in thrall to the telephone, broken dates because of wifely comings and goings or the demands of his children, the misery of imagining him sitting by a Christmas tree unwrapping presents with his family while Jasmine sat in a suite at the Savoy, watching her mother drift into a gin haze. Though the trials of her situation were commonplace, even hackneyed, this did nothing to alleviate the unhappiness they created.

I could not understand the attraction. Jasmine was sweet-natured, gentle, generous and half-Chinese. Her waist-length hair was black and lustrous, her skin golden, her features childlike and enchanting. Teddy was middle-aged, had mean little eyes, scant hair, an under-sized chin, an oversized stomach and a self-conceit that seemed entirely unfounded. To see him treating Jasmine with a careless assurance that seemed to take her devotion for granted made us furious. We did everything we could think of to release her from the spell that made her blind to his ass's head – lecturing her as mentioned above, telling her that Teddy was a boring and pompous bastard, introducing her to nicer, more attractive men – but she remained enamoured.

Sarah, who owned the house in Paradise Row, and to whom Jasmine and I paid rent, had her own theory about this.

'Jazzy sees her father twice a year. He kisses her politely, gives her an inscrutable smile and a cheque and asks her to call him a cab. Ergo, she's looking for a father substitute.'

On the sole occasion Jasmine's father and I had met, he had shaken my hand and told me that Communism had been the end of civilization as far as China was concerned. Then he had whipped a book from his pocket and removed himself to the far end of the room to read. He held some diplomatic post at the embassy in Paris. It did not seem to me a position for which he was particularly well suited.

'But would you say that Teddy was exactly an ideal father figure? Having an affair with a girl half his age would seem to me to disqualify him from the start.'

'Don't be so literal, you fathead!' Sarah was a forthright girl, a barrister-in-training. She enjoyed polemic. 'Jazzy doesn't want a bloke smelling of pipe tobacco with slippers and a woolly waistcoat. She's looking for an authority figure to lead her through the maze of life and instruct her in every instance, including sex. Surely you know that all little girls have powerful sexual feelings about their fathers?'

I looked at Sarah's round brown eyes in her round face, framed by straight brown hair.

'I can say with absolute certainty that I never did.'

'You're afraid to admit it to yourself, that's all.'

'Afraid would be the word, all right.'

'Anyway,' Sarah continued with energy, 'Jazzy's still in many ways a child. She doesn't understand cause and effect. She refuses to take responsibility for her actions. Like a baby, she simply responds to the most pressing physical need.'

'I still don't see why that makes the repulsive, chinless, paunchy Teddy—'

'What a dunce you are! There's nothing special about Teddy except his age and his unavailability. She has to struggle to engage his attention. That feels familiar, therefore comforting. Those of us who've had reasonable relationships with our fathers can move on from there to seek men who satisfy our grown-up emotional and intellectual needs as equals.'

'So far we don't seem to have had much success.'

It was true that there were men of all kinds turning up on the front doorstep of Number 22 to take us severally out to lunch, dinner, the theatre, the cinema, exhibitions, home to meet their mothers, and sometimes to bed. But neither of us had so far met anyone who met all our requirements for more than a few months. Sarah had had a string of lawyer boyfriends who were unsatisfactory because they much preferred sex to arguing. My boyfriends tended to be artistic and unsatisfactory because they were self-absorbed, neurotic, unreliable, and always borrowing money. Once I had got as far as announcing an engagement in *The Times* before I came to my senses and called it off. The unpleasantness this engendered and my own deep regret for causing pain had put me off such conventional behaviour for good. After the tremors had ebbed I decided that if I met someone I wanted to marry I would do it at once and without more ceremony than the register office provided. No one had so far tempted me to put this plan into action.

None the less, it would be true to say that my life was continuing satisfactorily until one morning not long after the above conversation – 22 April 1978, to be precise – a telephone call from my father had come as a rude blast shattering the idyll.

TWO

'It's your mother. Broken her hip. You'd better come at once.'

'Poor thing! Is she in pain? How did it happen?'

'Fell down the library steps. Her own fault for frittering her life away with those damned stupid fairy tales.'

There was triumph in my father's voice. His reading matter was confined to the *Trout and Salmon Monthly* and the *Shooting Times*. He considered a taste for fiction evidence of bohemian depravity.

'I suppose it could have happened anywhere.'

'Stop arguing, Roberta! Your mother needs you. I'll tell Brough to meet the twelve-fifteen.'

Brough was valet, butler, gardener, handyman and driver. Due to a childhood illness that had resulted in a humped back, he was a tiny man, much shorter even than my father. Though he sat on several cushions, his view from behind the wheel of our Austin Princess was largely sky. My father regularly deducted the repair of wings, bumpers and headlamps from his wages, then lent him a subsistence to prevent him from starving. After twenty years of service, Brough was several thousand pounds in debt to my father. Because of this he seemed to feel he had no choice but to do my father's bidding, however unreasonable the task and the hour, and to put up with any amount of calumny in the process. Understandably Brough was a morose man, given to violent outbursts of temper when out of earshot of my father.

'I'll get a taxi from the station.'

'This is not the time to start throwing money about when I've the fruits of your mother's confounded carelessness to pay for. That damned clinic charges the earth.' Nor were reports of the general standards of hygiene of the Cutham Down Nursing Home

10

encouraging. But my father presumably thought it was worth paying for a superior sort of dirt.

'I'll come tomorrow on the ten-fifteen.'

'You'll come today, my girl, or I'll know the reason why!'

There followed an unpleasant exchange which bordered on a row. A compromise was reached and I went down to Sussex late that afternoon.

'How are you, Mummy?'

A temporary bedroom had been made of the morning room, ill chosen as such for it faced due north and was perpetually in shade.

My mother opened her eyes and sighed. 'Terrible. Can't sleep.'

'Were they kind to you in the nursing home?'

'They were *harri*dans.' Her voice was alarmingly weak but she managed to get a little emphasis on the last word. 'Ill mannered. Coarse and stupid. Like being nursed by a gang of Irish road-menders.'

'What a good thing you were able to come home early.'

'They said I ought to stay in at least until the stitches were taken out. But your father insisted on my being discharged. It's ninety pounds a day.'

Her skin was lined and greyish. Her gooseberry-green eyes were reproachful and her mouth quivered with resentment.

'Poor Mummy.' I bent to kiss her and stroke her once pretty, fair hair from her forehead. 'Does it hurt very much?'

'Don't pull me about.' She jerked her head away. 'You know how I hate it. It's perfect agony, if you want to know.'

I looked around the sickroom, noticing that the grey and white-striped paper was beginning to peel at the cornice, that the Turkey carpet had a hole in it and the bed on which my mother lay was propped up at one corner by a stack of books.

'This is such a dismal room.' I put an extra brightness into my voice to compensate. 'We must see what we can do to cheer it up. I've brought you some flowers.'

She looked at the bunch of exquisite pink and green-striped parrot tulips I held out, then turned her eyes away. 'I prefer to see flowers growing out of doors where Nature intended them.'

My eye travelled through the window to where Brough was hacking with uncontrolled fury at some spotted laurels, growing in a landscape of dank shrubbery and sour grass.

'I've brought you some chocolate. Walnut whips. Your favourite.'

My mother closed her eyes and screwed up her face. 'It's easy to

11

see you've never been ill. In the state I'm in, rich food is simply poison.'

'I've also brought the latest Jeanette Dickinson-Scott.'

'I expect I've already read it.' Her eyes opened. 'What's it called?'

I looked at the cover on which was a painting of a Regency belle in a low-cut purple dress, with powdered hair and a loo mask. '*Amazon in Lace*.'

'Who's in it?'

I flicked through the pages. 'Someone called Lady Araminta. And her guardian Lord Willoughby Savage. He's got sardonic eyebrows, long sensitive fingers and a jagged cicatrice from cheekbone to—'

'You may as well give it to me.' My mother's hand appeared from beneath the bed cover. When I looked in, half an hour later, she was reading hard and sucking the top of a walnut whip.

After that the days had crawled by at an invalid pace. There was plenty to do but only things of a most unrewarding kind. Cutham Down, once a village, now a small town, was in a part of Sussex that had a micro-climate of bitter east winds and exceptionally high rainfall. After my maternal great-grandfather had amassed a fortune bottling things in vinegar – 'Pickford's Pickles Perfectly Preserved' was the slogan – he had sold the factory and applied himself to the serious business of becoming a country squire. In the 1880s Cutham Hall had been a pleasing two-storey Georgian house with a separate stable block set in the middle of forty acres. This had not been grand enough to suit my great-grandfather's newly acquired notions of self-consequence so he had added a top storey and thrown out two wings, at once destroying the elegant façade and making the house unmanageably large.

Cutham Hall had ten bedrooms, most of which had not been slept in for decades, and a number of badly furnished rooms downstairs in which no one ever sat. My father lived in what he called his 'library', a room of mean proportions which housed the remains of the various hobbies that he had run through. There were drawers of butterflies and beetles pinned on to boards. There was a sad red squirrel with a crooked tail, his first and only attempt at taxidermy. In a cupboard were his guns and fishing rods. On the walls were photographs of meets at Cutham Hall from the period when he had been enthusiastic about hunting. No books, of course. He was really only interested in amusements that involved killing things.

Oliver and I spent most of our time in the kitchen where there was an ancient lumpy sofa by the Aga and a television, ostensibly 'for the servants'. We had no indoor servants unless Mrs Treadgold, our daily, counted as one. She had a twenty-eight-inch colour television in her tidy, warm, watertight bungalow and would have scorned to watch anything on our tiny flickering black-and-white set with its bent coat-hanger aerial.

For about three days after my return home, Mrs Treadgold and I diligently dusted and vacuumed the ancestral acres of mahogany and carpet. I could tell by the quantities of cobwebs and dead flies that they were unaccustomed to so much attention. Then, by tacit agreement, exhausted by labour that was as dreary as it was pointless, we closed the doors on the unused rooms and allowed them to sleep peacefully on beneath a fresh film of dust. I took over the cooking and shopping while Mrs Treadgold cleaned the few rooms we lived in. Between us we looked after my mother.

My chief duty was to keep her supplied with books and, as she read all day and half the night, I was constantly on the road between our house and the four libraries in the county to which she was a subscriber. Her taste was for romantic fiction. I had my name down for every novel that had the words 'love', 'heart', 'kiss', 'bride', 'sweet' or 'surrender' in the title.

'I've read this,' my mother said during the second week of my servitude, casting my latest offering aside. 'Don't you remember? You got it out last week.'

'Can't you read it again?'

'I know what happens in the end.'

'Of course you do. The handsome titled hero subdues the heroine's pride and spirit until she loves him so much she's prepared to let him do unutterably filthy things to her despite her natural disinclination. That's always going to be the ending. She's never going to go off with the good-natured wall-eyed coachman or decide she'd rather run a dress shop.'

But my mother affected not to be listening. 'You can ask Treadgold to bring my tea now. And tell her not to slop it in the saucer. That woman's so clumsy, she could get a job at the nursing home easily. You'd better go and see what Brough is doing. Now I'm lying here helpless I suppose the place is falling to rack and ruin.'

'It looks fine,' I lied. 'You mustn't worry about it. Just concentrate on getting better.'

My mother threw me a sidelong glance of annoyance. It occurred to me then that she much preferred lying in bed and being waited on to the unremitting slog of trying to run a large decaying house

13

with severely limited funds. I could sympathize with this. I went to see Brough as instructed.

The forty acres my great-grandfather had begun with had shrunk to four as parcels of land had been sold piecemeal during the last hundred years to prop up a pretentious style lived on an insufficient income. Most of the remaining acreage had been given over to shrubbery which required little attention. Brough had a comfortable arrangement in the greenhouse with a chair, a radio and a kettle by the stove where he sat for hours on end, no doubt brooding over his thralldom. On this occasion I found him actually out of doors, spraying something evil-smelling over hybrid tea roses of a hideous flaunting red.

'Wouldn't they look rather better if they had something growing between them?' I suggested, hoping to strike a note of fellowship with this remote, furious being. 'Perhaps some hardy geraniums or violas—'

'This is a rose-bed.' Brough's angry little eyes were contemptuous.

'Yes, but it needn't be *just* roses . . .'

'The Major wouldn't like it.'

The Major was my father.

'How do you know he wouldn't?'

'Because he told me. He said, "Brough, whatever you do, don't go planting anything between them roses. Over my dead body."'

One cannot call someone a liar without disagreeable consequences. I walked angrily away and set myself the task of weeding the stone urns on the terrace. A harvest of bittercress shot seeds into the cracks between the stones as I worked, there to take ineradicable root and, just as I finished, the handle of one of the urns dropped off and smashed, leaving two large holes through which the sandy earth trickled on to my shoes in a steady stream. I went indoors.

My brother Oliver, the fourth inmate of this unhappy house, threatened daily to shake the plentiful dust of home from his feet. He was twenty, nearly six years younger than me, and could certainly have done so without anyone objecting. I think my father might even have been willing to drive him to the station himself, had he been convinced that Oliver would board the train. Oliver was currently an aspiring novelist. He was working on something satirical about a Swiftian character who, like the fortunate Dean, was adored by two equally desirable women. Despite having completed a mere ten pages Oliver was convinced that this was to be his passport to success and a new life. I loved my brother dearly and to see him struggling

14

to maintain a fragile self-confidence was painful. I already knew the plot of *Sunbeams from Cucumbers* backwards and it seemed promising.

'It's all in the writing, you see,' he explained, lying full-length on the sofa after a lonely afternoon of creation, while I peeled potatoes for supper.

It was three weeks after my return and my mother had not yet managed to totter further than to the commode set up for her in the corner of the morning room. I was sinking into a lethargic despondency at the prospective length of my term of servitude.

'You know the saying "kill your darlings"?' Oliver went on. 'I think it was Hemingway who said it. Well, as soon as I write anything that seems any good, I have to destroy it immediately. So, naturally, it takes a while to get a page done.'

'You're sure you aren't taking it too literally?' I put the saucepan on to boil. 'I mean, if you only keep the bits that aren't any good, isn't that defeating the object?'

'It means you must cut out the showy, self-conscious passages.' Oliver licked out the bowl in which I had made a batter for apple fritters. School and the army had bred in my father a taste for nursery food which meant that solid English puddings, of the kind that require custard, were obligatory at lunch and supper. 'My problem is that to lose self-consciousness I have to be drunk. But not so drunk that I can't hold the pen. It's a delicate balance. You've no idea what a serious writer has to suffer.' As he said this at least twice a day I felt I was beginning to get a pretty good idea.

It was unfortunate that alcohol did not agree with Oliver. He had tried beer, whisky, wine, sherry, even crème de menthe, but they all made him wretchedly ill. He was a handsome boy with dark, almost black hair, a large, slightly bulging forehead, which gave him the appearance of a solemn child, a sensitive, girlish mouth and my mother's green eyes which, because of the drinking, were matched by his complexion. On bad days his skin was the colour of a leaf.

'I think this place is part of the trouble,' he went on to say as I cut corned beef into cubes for a hash. 'How can one be inspired when living in an atmosphere of intellectual aridity and Pecksniffian hypocrisy? That tosh Mother reads is atrophying her brain. She's so miserable with Father that she can't bear to live in the real world. I sometimes wonder where Father's getting his spiritual nourishment. I can't believe being beastly to his children and kicking Brough

15

around is quite enough even for a man with the mental acuity of a wood louse.'

'I can answer that as it happens. I drove into Worping this morning to see if Bowser's had any new romances and afterwards I stopped at the Kardomah for a cup of coffee. While I was there Father came in. That was strange enough but what made it even odder was that he was with a woman.'

'No!' Oliver swung his legs round to sit up, his green face lit by excitement. 'What was she like? And what did he say when he saw you?'

'I was sitting in the corner behind a sort of trellis screen covered with plastic ivy. I could see them quite clearly by peering between the leaves but he never knew I was there. I heard every word they said.'

'Go on!'

'She was asking him about Mother. Father said she'd do a lot better if she put some damned effort into it, instead of lolling about, filling her head with rubbish. He never let illness get him down, he said. If he had anything wrong with him he always went out for a brisk walk over the Downs and blew it away. I don't suppose a brisk walk would do Mother's broken hip any good at all.' I paused in the act of chopping onions to wipe my stinging eyes.

'Don't stop now!'

'She said something about being sure he was a brave man. He couldn't have done what he did in the war unless he'd been really courageous.'

'So he didn't tell her about being sent home with a bad case of Tobruk tummy to a desk job in Devizes. What was the woman like?'

'In her fifties, plump, hennaed hair, a lot of make-up and jewellery. Her name's Ruby. Not his usual type. Apparently they're having dinner on Friday at the Majestic in Brighton. She was quite excited and giggly about it. She must have had a sad life if dinner with our father is her idea of fun.'

Oliver gave a bitter laugh. 'So he's got a bit of rough on the side. How drearily unoriginal. I wonder if he pays her?'

'Actually I thought she was rather too good for him. She spoke kindly about Mother. She seemed concerned. And when Dad ticked her off for saying "serviette" – he's such a hideous snob – she looked crushed. I felt sorry for her.'

'The old bastard! And when I think what a fuss he made about Gaylene!' Gaylene was a girl who had worked the petrol pumps at a garage in a neighbouring village of whom Oliver had been much enamoured. 'He had the nerve to call her a draggle-tailed slut. I've a good mind to leave tomorrow!'

I seized the moment. 'I think you should, darling, though you know I'll miss you like anything. I'll ring David this minute and ask him if you can come and stay.' David was an ex-boyfriend of mine, with a flat in Pimlico, who had offered this boon when last I had discussed the problem of Oliver with him.

We sat up until one in the morning detailing plans for Oliver's escape. David professed himself willing to harbour the son of Hemingway, provided I would have dinner with him the following week. This was no hardship as I was still fond of David, though only in a sisterly way. I went to bed feeling glad that this depressing episode of my life would not be entirely unproductive of good after all.

When I knocked on Oliver's door the next morning, having got up at the ghastly hour of six to drive him to the station, there was no answer. I went in. The alarm clock was on its back in the farthest corner of the room and Oliver had both pillows over his head. He became almost violent when I tried to drag him out of bed. He came down to lunch in his dressing-gown and was bathed and dressed by four. By this time he had decided that as he'd had a brilliant idea for the novel he had better spend the rest of the day working and go up to London the following morning. This became the pattern for the next three days.

After that I cancelled the arrangement with David, except for the dinner as this would have seemed unattractively opportunistic. I tried to resign myself to the fact that I was powerless to help Oliver. The only good I could do him was to encourage him to go on writing. I made myself available for any amount of pep-talking and amateur psychotherapy. I bought him vitamin pills and sent him out for walks to catch whatever daylight was left. But all my efforts amounted to little. The novel proceeded at a rate of a couple of sentences a day. The truth was that Oliver was afraid to go. Some part of him clung desperately to home, hoping that even now he might be blessed by some vivifying drops from the fount of parental love.

'Mm . . . Kit?' I muttered thickly, my mouth crammed with doughnut. 'If you're a literary agent, I suppose you help novelists get published, do you? I mean, I happen to know someone who's written this absolutely brilliant book. It's practically finished, and I can

17

assure you it's quite exceptionally good, only he needs some professional help. You know, whom to send it to, what to say in the letter, perhaps even a friendly eye cast over the text and a few constructive hints?'

Kit was silent for a moment or two and something like a sigh escaped him. It occurred to me that probably a great many people had approached him with just such a request.

'It's a cheek to ask, I know,' I said humbly, 'and of course I'll pay you, but . . . Well, it's my brother, actually, and of course you'll think I'm prejudiced—'

'Your brother? In that case, the services of Roderick, Random and Co. are yours, willing and gratis.'

'Oh, how kind!' I felt a gush of enthusiasm for this stranger who had not only plucked me from the verge of shipwreck, warmed me and fed me but now offered to help rescue my darling brother with at least an appearance of eagerness. 'I don't know how to thank you. He'll be so grateful.'

'You can start by telling me your name.'

'Certainly. It's Bobbie.'

'Bobbie? Don't tell me, your parents wanted a boy.'

'It's a nickname. Not elegant, I know, but it's what everyone calls me.'

Except for Burgo. He disliked abbreviations. I had, he said, a perfectly good name that suited me perfectly.

'So what's the other bit?'

'Oh, let's not bother with formalities, as you said.'

'What a mistrustful girl you are. Who would have thought that beneath that angelically fair exterior there ticks such a suspicious mind?'

I stiffened and drew away from him. 'How do you know what colour my hair is? It was already dark when we left Swansea.'

'I was speaking poetically. Fair meaning pretty, you know. I hope you're pretty. I'm prepared to bet that you are. But I've no idea whether you're as blonde as a Viking or as dark as an Ethiopian.'

'I'm sorry.' I relaxed. 'Things have been . . . Lack of sleep is making me neurotic.'

'Actually the name Bobbie makes me think of someone with a pudding-basin haircut, red cheeks and a punishing serve. A sister to all men, always willing to make the cocoa, a jolly good sport.' I felt a tug on one side of my head. 'But your hair's long and you say it's fair. I'm awfully glad. I'll be happy to make the cocoa every time.'

18

'We'll have to do without it tonight. It must be at least ten o'clock.'

Kit shone the meagre beam of his torch on to the dial of his watch. 'Half past. Are you ready for your berth, Bobbie? Shall I escort you to the door or will that give rise to impertinent gossip, do you think?'

'I don't think I can face it. I went to look at my cabin when I came aboard. It's several floors down. Horribly claustrophobic. I booked too late to get a single berth. My bunkmate was jolly and friendly but smelt penetratingly of the stables. Apparently she's going to Ireland to buy horses. I'm not sure my stomach can stand being tossed about all night in a miasma of manure. Anyway, it's rather lovely up here and I'm not cold now.' And it was, in truth, lovely – if rough. The wind seemed to be blowing hard, or perhaps that was the motion of the ship, but the moon, three-quarters full, suffused the drifting clouds with silver. 'But you must go to bed. You've looked after me beautifully and I'm grateful. I shall be perfectly all right.'

'I'm not at all sleepy. Why don't you put your feet up and I'll tuck you in. Here, rest your head on my coat. Don't worry,' he said as I made noises of protest, 'the steward's keeping us under observation from the saloon window. He'll be the perfect chaperon. And as soon as I'm the least bit weary I shall leave you to it. Will it bother you if I smoke?'

'Not at all.'

The delicious smell of a Gauloise mingled with the tang of salt. The stars rolled languorously to and fro above my upturned face as the giant cradle rocked beneath me. It was strange to be lying with my head almost in the lap of a man I had known for two hours but at the same time it felt companionable. I began to relax. For ten days now I had slept patchily, always with a sense of foreboding. My rib cage stopped aching; my eyelids ceased to twitch.

'Marvellous, aren't they?' Kit blew out smoke. 'Impossible to believe they're indifferent to our joys and sorrows, isn't it?' I realized he was talking about the stars. 'There's one that's definitely winking at us. No wonder people make wishes by them.'

'If wishes were butter-cakes, beggars might bite,' I said drowsily. At least I thought I had said it, but it may just have been part of my dream.

19

THREE

Something brushed against my cheek.

'Sorry. I didn't mean to wake you.'

I opened my eyes. The sky had paled mysteriously. It took me a second or two to realize that this must be the dawn. I twisted my head and saw someone – Kit – looking down at me, smiling. Something hard pressed against my ear. I put up my hand. It was a coat button. I struggled to sit up, encumbered by blankets, my muscles unresponsive with cold. 'How long have I been asleep? What time is it?'

Kit looked at his watch, squinting in the grey light. 'Ten to five.'

'It can't be!'

'You were terribly tired.'

'I hope I didn't snore.'

'You were as quiet as a little cat. From time to time you purred and once you shouted "No!" quite fiercely. That woke me up.'

'Have you been here all night?'

He nodded.

'You must have been so uncomfortable. Really, you *should* have gone to bed.'

'I'm as stiff as an ironing board,' he admitted, 'but I managed to doze. I'm one of those lucky people who can get by on not much sleep. I'll just walk about a bit and I'll be fine. We'll be in Cork in less than an hour.'

'Cork!' I felt a rush of emotions, predominantly apprehension.

'Where did you think we were going?'

'Well, there of course. It's just that I've never been to Ireland before. And everything was arranged at the last minute. Oh, Lord, I can't move my fingers! And my neck's broken, I think.'

20

'Come on.' Kit pulled me up from the bench. 'We'll get our circulations going.'

We strolled about together until the blood had returned to our hands and feet. There were no other passengers on deck, only members of the crew who gave us particular looks and pointed smiles. Probably they assumed we were lovers who had preferred a romantic consummation beneath the stars to a struggle within the confines of a narrow bunk in a prosaic cabin. We stood at the stern rail, drank brown tea and ate tasteless white rolls filled with hard-boiled eggs and mayonnaise. We watched the sky blush with gleams of coral, salmon and rose. Slowly it flooded with gold.

'Lovely, isn't it?' said Kit. 'Doesn't it make you glad to be alive?'

'Mm . . . yes,' I said, more decidedly than I felt. Foam streamed in the wake of the ship. Gulls slid up and down the grey-green waves and quarrelled over the last crumbs of my breakfast. I wished the ship would sail on and never come to land.

'Now I can see for myself that you *are* fair,' Kit said. 'In at least two of the . . . let's see' – he counted on his fingers – 'six meanings of the word that I can think of immediately. Neither a marketplace nor good weather. Beautiful and with light-coloured hair, yes. And I'm willing to bet that you're just and impartial. But never mediocre.'

'Oh, don't! It was so lovely to forget about me. I must look a wreck. And of course I'm not impartial. No one is, however hard they may try to be.' I attempted to run my fingers through my hair but it was tangled by the wind.

'I'll comb it for you,' suggested Kit. The brightening rays of the sun shone through his ears, turning them crimson. His hair was curly and brown. His eyes were blue and intelligent. It was an appealing face, with its high forehead and good-humoured mouth. Not handsome but attractive.

'Certainly not. People will think I'm an escaped lunatic and you're my keeper.'

'I shan't mind if you don't. That steward hasn't taken his eyes off you since you woke up. You're putting colour into his drab existence. Can't you gibber a little and play with your lips? Where's your sense of civic duty?'

'I probably *am* a lunatic. Only a madwoman . . .'

I paused. Kit had been so sympathetic that I had been tempted to tell him something of my circumstances but then I thought better of it.

21

'Oh dear. That suspicious look again. You're as wary as a bird of paradise who's just spotted a woman in a rather dull hat.'

I laughed but said nothing.

Kit turned to lean his back against the rail so that he could look directly into my face. 'Forgive me if this is an impertinent question, but when we get into Cork will there be a husband or a boyfriend standing on the quay, counting the seconds?'

I thought of Burgo, imagined him with the collar of his coat turned up against the importunate July breezes, hands in pockets, frowning, impatient of delay, already running ahead in his mind, planning what we were going to do, where we were going to eat, make love. I felt a pang of desolation.

'No.'

'I see. Would it be presuming to ask where you're going to in such solitary splendour? I promise not to divulge the information to MI5.'

'I'm going to Galway. To Connemara.'

Kit whistled. 'Among the mountainy men? It's a wild sort of place and they're a strange, interesting breed. "To Hell or to Connaught", as they used to say. Meaning, of course, that there was little to choose between them.'

'Where's Connaught?'

'Where you're going. The ancient kingdom of the West. Where Cromwell sent the indigenous Irish after dispossessing them of their nice, fertile, well-drained lands in the east. Are you an accomplished Gaelic speaker?'

'Not a word. Will it matter?' I had a vision of myself shut away in some mountain fastness, in a household of eccentrics of whose culture and language I was entirely ignorant. Anthropologists would no doubt have delighted in the prospect. I found it alarming.

'Not at all. Despite the efforts of the Gaelic League and Sinn Fein to establish it as the first language, it's fiendishly difficult and the majority of Irish speak English. I just wondered if you were writing a book about the Gaeltacht or researching the dress code of the high kings or something like that.'

'I'm going to be housekeeper to a family named Macchuin.'

Kit whistled again. 'That's the last thing I'd have guessed. What do you know about them?'

'Almost nothing. I answered an advertisement in a newspaper. When I telephoned, the woman I spoke to said she was desperate for help. She engaged me on the spot.'

'And you accepted, just as impulsively?'

22

'All relevant questions, apart from how to get there, went out of my head. I needed to get away.'

'I hope you won't feel as urgent a need to get back. They might be dipsomaniacs, drug-smugglers, sexual psychopaths or an IRA stronghold, for all you know.'

'Perhaps all those things at once. Though we only talked for five minutes at the most I liked the impression I had of Mrs Macchuin. And I was flattered that she seemed so thrilled when I agreed to come.'

'Only someone absolutely hell-bent, neck-or-nothing, on escape would be encouraged by such enthusiasm. Are you impetuous, rash, devil-may-care by nature or are the bailiffs after you?' When I smiled but didn't say anything he went on, 'So what did this excitable woman say? Any kind of job description?'

'All I know is that there are three children between the ages of eight and sixteen, and six adults, one of whom is generally away. Mrs Macchuin sounded exhausted rather than excitable.'

'Worse and worse. Why is she exhausted, I wonder? Badly behaved children? Too little money? Or too much Mr Macchuin, perhaps.'

'I didn't ask. I was trying to think myself into a new role. The sort of person who does as she's told and doesn't ask questions. An efficient, invisible menial.'

'You'll never be that. Invisible, I mean. You don't look terribly efficient but here appearances may be deceptive.'

'I must admit my life so far hasn't really demanded efficiency. But it can only be a question of application.'

Kit sighed and shook his head. 'I see problems ahead.'

'It'll only be for six months or so. Then I'll go back to London, probably.'

'I wish you'd trust me.' He looked at me gravely. When I did not reply he pointed behind me and said quietly, 'Land ahoy.'

While we had been talking the ferry, unobserved by me, had been turning slowly. We were about to enter a wide channel bounded by distant promontories, perhaps a mile apart. I felt excited as I examined the low cliffs, half hidden in mist, trying to imagine my immediate future.

'Your first view of Ireland,' said Kit. 'It's such a beautiful country with the best people in the world, yet the most terrible things have happened here. Do you know anything of Irish history?'

'Not much.' I dredged my mind for facts. 'Um . . . Cromwell and the Siege of Drogheda. And there was the Battle of the Boyne.

James the Second. I think he lost. That's about all I can remember. Oh, and of course the IRA. I don't understand any of that. Why did they assassinate Airey Neave? Wasn't he trying to help the Irish?'

'Ah, that's a complicated one. You may as well forget your history lessons. Seen through Irish eyes, Ireland has suffered eight hundred years of merciless exploitation beneath the yoke of English imperialism. Make no mistake. We English are still the "Old Enemy".' I must have looked alarmed for he added, 'Don't worry. You won't be held accountable. They'll be charming to you. It's the British government and the army they hate. But you'd better acquaint yourself with some proper Irish history if you're going to make sense of the place. The Irish take enormous pride in their long struggle for national identity. Now they've joined the EEC things are looking up economically and a cultural change radiating from Dublin is gradually persuading the country people to abandon their inward-looking, backward-looking colonial complex, but essentially you've still got a population that is rural, conservative and poor.'

'I thought it was such a fertile country. Why is it poor?'

While Kit was talking, one part of my mind absorbed first impressions of my new country of residence, which I hoped would be something of an asylum. As we steamed into the mouth of the River Lee towards Cork Harbour I saw gentle hills, fields and farmsteads lit by a rosy light. Then the channel broadened and they receded into haze.

'Again that's not easy to say in a few words. During the second quarter of the nineteenth century conditions for the peasantry were tough but they were healthy and happy enough if one can believe the historians. Thackeray, in his Irish Sketch Book of 1842 described the Irish as being like the landscapes: "ragged, ruined and cheerful". But then they were struck by the worst disaster in Irish history: the Great Famine, when the potato crop failed four years in succession. Out of a population of eight million people one million died of starvation or disease. Two million, probably the brightest, most energetic ones, emigrated, mostly to England and North America. So much misery and loss is bound to have an effect on a nation's psychology. A sort of fatalism, a melancholy, that leads to inertia.'

'Oh yes, I see. But did we – the English I mean – do nothing to help?'

'Not enough, in my opinion. Certainly not enough in the opinion of the Irish. But there isn't enough time to explain exactly what happened. We're coming into Ringaskiddy. That's the ferry terminal. It's another two or three miles to Cork itself.'

The ship was turning as sharply as a large ferry can, which is not very, and we were moving at a sluggish pace towards land. The terminal was the usual noisy, busy, ugly conglomeration of warehouses, cranes, lorries and moored craft. Much too quickly it increased in size. The propellers reversed to reduce our speed to dead slow and we drifted towards the quay. Until this moment I had been lulled into a state of passivity by the knowledge that there was no alternative to idleness while the ship was in motion. Now anxiety returned with full force.

'I'd better go and get my things.'

'No hurry,' said Kit. 'Most of the passengers are still asleep. They'll take the cars off first.'

'All the better. I'll go before there's a crowd.'

'What's your cabin number? I'll fetch your cases for you.'

'No, really. You've already been kind beyond the call of duty. And I ought to wash my face and brush my teeth.'

'How are you getting to Connemara?'

'Train. Apparently it takes all day to go a hundred and fifty miles. I have to change twice. Then a bus from Galway to Kilmuree. But I shall have scenery to look at.' I tried to sound enthusiastic.

'I've a better idea. For the next few weeks I'm travelling round the country spreading light and hope among my lonely authors. Part business, part holiday. There's a delightful old boy on my list who lives near Westport. Writes books about geology. Sells about four a year but we like to diversify. He'll be thrilled to see me a few days early and I can drop you off at your destination.'

'You've got a car?'

'Picturesque though a high-perch phaeton is, I find it inconvenient. And too exposed to the elements.'

'I couldn't possibly ask you to change your arrangements.'

'But I can insist, truthfully, that I'm happy to do so.'

'I'm being met at the bus station.'

'All right. I'll drop you there.'

'But not until seven o'clock. In the evening, I mean.'

'We'll have a leisurely lunch on the way.'

It was too good an offer to refuse. I descended to collect my things. My cabin-mate was still asleep, lying on her back with her mouth open, snoring like a nest of wasps. The smell of horses had intensified. A wild creature with matted clown triangles of hair and smudged saucer eyes stared at me from the mirror.

'My word!' said Kit as I rejoined him on deck half an hour later.

25

'I was beginning to worry that you'd jumped ship. But it was worth the wait. You look glorious. That colour is marvellous with your skin and hair.'

I felt a stab of pain then, remembering Burgo saying the same thing, almost word for word, about the pale yellow linen dress I had put on.

'I don't want to give the Macchuins the impression that the steam-iron and I are unacquainted. My skirt not only bears all the signs of having been slept in but looks as though it might have been used as a picnic tablecloth as well.'

'I'm not so conceited as to suppose that you put it on for me.'

Kit's expression was non-committal but there was a slight sharpness in his tone. Had I sounded ungracious, I wondered?

'There's the old bus now.' He leaned over the rail and pointed to a red sports car being driven off the ramp and along the quay. The hood was down so we could see quite clearly a man in overalls behind the wheel, playing with the dashboard and flashing the headlamps. Kit watched with the sort of glazed impassioned look that mothers get when people bend to coo admiringly into the pram.

We were the first passengers to present ourselves at customs and were through it in no time. Kit's car gave a throaty roar at the first turn of the ignition key. My experience of cars was limited. In London I used buses and the underground. My father's ancient Austin Princess and my mother's battered Wolseley were my transport in the country. They rounded bends under protest and were rebellious when it came to starting. Kit's car seemed barely able to contain itself as we trundled through the streets of Ringaskiddy. It had a gravelly growl and made little menacing rushes at obstacles, like a lion on a leash.

'All the men are giving you envious looks,' I said. 'I don't know anything about cars. Is it something terrifically glamorous?'

'It's an Alfa Spider. But it isn't the car they're jealous of.'

Some men consider it only polite to keep up a steady trickle of compliments. I liked Kit and I was grateful to him, but I had no heart for the game. To flirt successfully you must believe yourself to be desirable. I was near to hating myself. Depression threatened. I pushed it away. I owed it to Kit to be a cheerful passenger.

The urban sprawl at the outskirts of Cork offered nothing particular to admire but the surrounding countryside made up for that. It was at once apparent why Ireland was called the Emerald Isle. It was not just emerald, though. Different tones of green – olive, apple, lime, grass, sage and chartreuse – reflected the sun with a glossy luxuriance. Even the light was green.

'That's Blarney,' said Kit, waving vaguely towards the west. I looked but saw only a church spire. He began to recite:

'There is a stone there that whoever kisses,
Oh, he never misses to grow eloquent.
'Tis he may clamber to a lady's chamber
Or become a member of Parliament.

'I know which I'd rather,' Kit went on. 'As Topsy said, I'm mighty wicked and I can't help it, but I lack the cold-blooded cynicism necessary to be a good politician.'

I glanced quickly at Kit's profile but it was a picture of perfect innocence.

'Look over there, to the north-west. The Boggeragh Mountains.'

I saw a series of massive heather-coloured triangles. We purred between stone walls that divided the land into tiny boulder-strewn fields while the trees laid blue and purple bars across the road, empty but for a few wandering sheep. Beside the road ran a sweetly purling river and seconds later we crossed it by means of a small hump-backed bridge.

'What wonderful names. This really is fairy-land.'

'Certainly it is. And you must be careful to keep on the right side of the good folk. They can be spiteful if crossed and they never forgive an injury.'

I examined Kit's face carefully for signs that he was teasing me. He must have felt my eyes upon him for he turned his head briefly and smiled. As we drove north through the small town of Mallow and on towards the Ballyhoura Hills, I watched the landscape unfolding into higher and ever more beautiful curves and angles, marvelling that I had been ignorant all my life of so much beauty lying in wait across a small sea.

I found myself wondering what Burgo would have thought of it. It occurred to me that in the twelve months that I had known him I had not once heard him comment, favourably or adversely, on the works of Nature. Had this been because our meetings had so often been snatched from commitments elsewhere, appointments with other people, and there had not been time to think about our surroundings? No, that wasn't it. Burgo had often been irritated by the shortcomings of the places we had been obliged to make use of. In fact he was highly conscious of his environment and of the way his presence changed things. Does that make him sound egotistic? Well, he was. Surprisingly, this had not stopped me loving him.

He was not, on the face of it, a vain man. I suppose his clothes must have been made for him because despite his height – he was six feet four inches – they fitted him perfectly. But I never heard him mention his tailor. His hair was straight, silvery fair, untidy. Probably he knew he was attractive to women so he never fussed about what he looked like, never looked in mirrors, was careless about mud and creases, did not seem to possess a comb. It was this confidence which had drawn me to him, which had been the fatal lure, I decided as I slid down in the car seat to escape the wind that whipped my hair into my eyes. Burgo's attitude was neither aggressive nor defensive. This must have been because his ego was never in danger. Other people's insecurity amused him. Possibly mine was what first attracted him. Certainly the occasion of our meeting had been unpropitious.

Dangerous though I knew it to be, a sense of ease and restfulness I had not felt for days tempted me to let my mind wander back to those first weeks of knowing him, when I had managed for the most part to live only for the moment; when only to think of him had lifted my despondent mood and made my heart race.

FOUR

Burgo and I had met five weeks after my return to Sussex to look after my mother. The encounter was preceded by a period of almost unrelieved dreariness. Despite visits from a physiotherapist, my mother had made no discernible progress. I had sub-let my room in Paradise Row so that Sarah could continue to pay the mortgage. I became supersensitive to the awfulness of Cutham Hall. When I walked into the house the smell of my father's cigar-smoke mixed with the rubbery smell from carpet underlay that was beginning to perish made me feel sick.

'It's the Conservative lunch on Wednesday,' my father had said at breakfast towards the end of the fifth week. 'As your mother refuses even to look at the wheelchair provided for her at enormous trouble and expense, you'll have to stand in.'

We were alone as usual so I knew he meant me, though he did not look up from his boiled egg. I cannot think quickly first thing in the morning. Irrelevant thoughts went through my mind. The wheelchair was on loan, gratis, from the Red Cross and had cost him only the telephone call I had made to order it and the cupful of petrol I had used when driving to pick it up.

'You don't mean you want me to go with you?'

'There isn't anyone else.'

'Well, thank you for such a flattering invitation but on Wednesday I'm taking the kitchen sofa covers into Worping for dry-cleaning, then I'm dropping the Wolseley at the garage to be serviced and while that's being done Oliver and I are going to the cinema. Mrs Treadgold's agreed to stay later to look after Mother.'

'You can do all that any day of the week. Your mother was

29

tremendously relieved when I said I'd take you. You don't want to set her back, do you?'

'Please!' said my mother later as I poured her a cup of tea the colour of white wine and buttered wafer-thin slices of toast. She had protested she was too weak to do her own buttering. 'Please, for my sake, go to that ghastly Conservative lunch with him. He has to have a woman on his arm. If he's on his own he feels as naked as going without trousers. He's threatening to make me go in the wheelchair. As if I could! If you knew the pain I'm in. All the time. It's relentless.'

'Honey or marmalade?'

'Marmalade. Sometimes I think I'm going to take all my painkillers at once and finish it for good. When your father starts hectoring me I absolutely make up my mind to do it. If he mentions this beastly lunch one more time, I shall.'

Brough, wearing his peaked cap and a cheap grey suit from the Co-op which was his chauffeur's uniform, drove us to the Carlton House Hotel in Worping where the lunch was to be held. I had offered to drive so that Brough would not have to kick his heels, throwing stones at seagulls, for two hours but my father was adamant that we should travel like important dignitaries in the back of the Austin Princess, hoping perhaps to excite envy and admiration in the breasts of his political brothers.

Attempting to reverse into a space before the hotel's porte cochère Brough crushed a plastic 'No Parking' sign and from the accompanying crunch of metal I guessed something had happened to the rear wing.

A man in a tail coat and striped trousers came running down the hotel steps. 'You can't park here. Didn't you see the sign? This space is reserved for the mayor and the brass hats.'

'I *am* a brass hat, as you put it,' said my father, getting out of the car.

At that moment the mayor's car drew alongside. It was of a size and magnificence to empty the rate-payers' pockets before anyone had even considered street lamps or drains, and all traffic came to a standstill.

'There *was* a time when the damned peasants knew their places,' said my father with feeling. 'I blame the Welfare State.' He strolled up the steps and disappeared into the hotel.

I saw that we had already drawn a crowd who were watching Brough's attempts to disengage the rear wheel (which had become

30

wedged against the kerb) with unconcealed amusement. 'I'd better go in,' I said. 'See if you can find a space in the car-park.'

I opened the car door in time to hear one of the witnesses to our humiliation say, 'Who *was* that pompous idiot?'

'That's Major Pickford-Norton,' said his companion. 'The sort of man the Conservative Party needs like a hole in the head. Blimpish, bloated with self-consequence—'

'Oh-ah-ha-a!' said another, whom I vaguely recognized. I think he had once been to our house for a shooting lunch. He threw me an embarrassed glance. 'Gentlemen, allow me to introduce you. This is Miss Roberta Pickford-Norton.'

There was an uncomfortable silence. None of this was my fault yet I felt myself blush with mortification.

'Miss Pickford-Norton,' said the one who had called my father a pompous idiot. 'I apologize for my unparliamentary language. Will you let me try to make amends by buying you a drink?'

He put his hand under my elbow and I found myself being borne upwards into the hotel foyer. He ushered me into the dining room, which was already nearly full. Several men and women surged towards him and began conversations, while others waved and tried to catch his eye.

'Hello, Lottie, how are you? Yes, I know, but you must excuse me for a moment. Good to see you, Herbert, talk later? Hello, Mrs Cholmondeley. No, I hadn't heard. Really? Let's talk about it after lunch.'

He tightened his grip on my elbow and steered me into a side room, which was comparatively empty.

'Just a minute.' He went away and reappeared almost immediately with two glasses of white wine. 'Now,' he said. 'I hope you like speeches and being bored to hell and drinking' – he sipped his wine and shuddered – 'something you could clean paintbrushes with because you're in for it now and no mistake. And in addition you've had to put up with my unforgivable rudeness. I wouldn't blame you if you wanted to stamp off in a rage. In fact' – wheeling round to look about him – 'if I weren't the most selfish of men that's exactly what I'd advise you to do. It's going to be unmitigated hell. But I hope you won't. If you can find it in your heart to forgive a blundering idiot – I mean me – I'd be grateful because I can see at a glance you're the only person here I want to talk to.' He grabbed a bowl of peanuts from a nearby table. 'You look hungry. Won't you celebrate a truce with a friendly nut?'

He had dark eyes that slanted upwards at the outer corners. Despite his repentant tone and the solemnity of his expression I could see he thought it was funny. My parents never found anything amusing and Oliver was usually in the toils of creative agony. My own sense of humour, having fallen into desuetude, revived. I took a few nuts to show there were no hard feelings.

'I forgive you,' I said. 'I'm not tactful myself. But you've confirmed my worst fears. I didn't want to come. I hate politics and I loathe politicians. Particularly Conservative ones.'

'I quite agree with you. About politicians, anyway. A worse lot of crooks, egomaniacs and shysters you'll never meet. Though I think the Labour Party's just as bad. Superficially they appear more altruistic but mostly it's cant. Individually they're just as greedy and dishonest. All politicians have had to cheat and connive and flatter to get their seats. Another nut?' I shook my head. 'However,' he went on, 'I like politics. I think it's exciting to feel you can change things for the better.'

'That would be satisfying, if you really thought you had. Improved things, I mean. But so often what politicians do seems to result in nothing more than manipulating statistics.' I looked at my watch. 'I only came to please my father. Perhaps he won't notice if I go away for an hour. I could creep back at the end when the worst is over.'

'That would be the wisest course.' He lifted his eyebrows. They were dark, in striking contrast to his white-blond hair. I thought of the hero of *Amazon in Lace*, Lord Willoughby Savage, whose sardonic eyebrows worked overtime. The absurdity of this thought made me smile. 'That's better,' he said. 'Clearly you have a forgiving nature. I wish I could come with you. It's years since I saw anything of the English seaside. We could have walked along the promenade and looked for shrimps and anemones in rock pools and I could have tried to impress you by skimming stones on the waves. Why don't we have tea—'

'Latimer! Dear chap!' A man with a large curved nose like a puffin's beak placed an arresting hand on my companion's shoulder. 'Well, well, well! This *is* a pleasure! Haven't seen you for, let me see, is it two years? Not since that polo match at Windsor. D'you still play?'

'No. I bust my arm and I've been too frightened to get on a horse since. Miss Pickford-Norton, meet Reginald Pratt.'

I held out my hand.

'How d'ye do?' Mr Pratt squeezed it briefly while giving me a quick measuring glance before dismissing me as someone of no importance. 'You know, Latimer, you shouldn't let a little thing like a broken arm put you off. Why don't you come down next weekend and join us for a bit of practice? You'd soon get your eye in again.'

'No, thanks. I never enjoyed it above half anyway. I only played to please my father-in-law. Do you like the game, Roberta?'

'I don't like team—' I began.

'How's the lovely Lady Anna?' Reginald Pratt interrupted. 'Why don't you bring her along to some of our constituency dos? Shame for her to be sitting at home on her own while you have all the fun.'

'She's in France. And she hates this kind of thing.'

'Oh. Pity. Still, no false modesty, Latimer!' Mr Pratt had edged round so that his back was turned towards me. 'You were a damned good player! Now, Leslie falls off every chukka, don't you, old boy?' He poked a finger into the ribs of the man who had come up to join us.

'I like that!' Leslie laughed until his face was pink. 'Who was it fell off last week and smashed his own bloody stick to matchwood, eh?'

I put down my glass and walked into the dining room.

'Roberta!' shouted my father as soon as he saw me. 'Come and meet Mrs Chandler-Harries.'

A middle-aged woman in a scarlet wool suit standing next to him was beckoning from across the room. I moved slowly between long tables decorated with arrangements of yellow spider chrysanthemums and blue napkins folded into mitres. Mrs Chandler-Harries seemed to have Reginald Pratt's share of chin. It swelled in rolls above her pearls and quivered as she talked. My father (the rat) cleared off at once.

'So *this* is Roberta.' Flecks of red lipstick had transferred themselves to her front teeth. 'Of course you won't remember an old woman like me.' She was right. She had hard, inquisitive eyes which travelled from the collar of my shirt to the toe of my shoe, pricing as they went. During the remainder of our conversation they trawled the crowd over my shoulder hoping to net bigger fish, returning only occasionally to my face. 'You went to dancing classes with my little Nancy.'

I remembered Nancy Chandler-Harries. A poisonous child with a squint, which she could not help, and a boastful manner, which she could.

'Nancy *will* laugh when I tell her I've run into you and where. She said wild horses wouldn't drag her along to a lunch at the Carlton House with a lot of old fuddy-duddies. But then Nancy is *so* popular and has so many demands on her time.'

I kept my face expressionless with some effort. 'How is Nancy?'

'She's engaged to be married to the most *char*ming boy. His family have the most *mar*vellous place in Hampshire. He'll inherit the title, of course. His family *adore* her. Of course, though naturally I'm prejudiced' – she gave a deprecating laugh which did not convince – 'I must say I think they're lucky to have her . . . winning ways . . . instinctive good taste . . . firm hand . . . poise . . . charm . . .' I stopped listening. I disapprove of violence under any circumstances but after this I could cheerfully have taken little Nancy outside and put out her lights for good.

There are moments when one becomes aware that one is alone in an unsympathetic world. I felt depressed to the depths of my being. I acknowledged that it must be my fault. It could hardly be the rest of the world's. Yet who could deny that Mrs Chandler-Harries was a complacent, insensitive . . . I realized she was looking at me expectantly.

'Sorry. What did you say?'

'Are you married or engaged?'

'Excuse me, I really must . . . before the speeches begin . . .'

I turned away and began to move towards the door. Someone clapped their hands for silence.

'Ladies and gentlemen!' Reginald Pratt was fiddling with a microphone. 'Before we partake of this veritable feast' – he waved a hand at the buffet table on which were stainless steel dishes of something sweltering beneath an apricot-coloured sauce: probably coronation chicken – 'first I must say a few words about our late lamented Member, Sir Vyvyan Pennell. We extend our sympathies to dear Lady Pennell.'

The applause that followed was lukewarm.

'Ghastly woman,' murmured the man standing next to me, to no one in particular.

'Sir Vyvyan did sterling work on our behalf and we shall all be the poorer for his sudden demise. That is to say . . .' Reginald Pratt made a snorting noise, unpleasantly amplified. '. . . we *would* be the poorer were it not for the fact that we're privileged to have in our new Member one who has done such . . . um . . . sterling work in the constituency of Hamforth East and comes to us as a new broom . . . blah . . . blah . . . blah.'

'Hear, hear!' came heartily from the audience.

Reginald continued to fumble through an obstacle course of clichés. I tried to get through the door but a large woman in a quilted waistcoat was leaning against it.

'We are fortunate,' Reginald Pratt continued, 'to have as our representative in Parliament a man who combines the gift of the gab with an ability to get to grips with any number of subjects, ranging from . . .' He consulted his notes. '. . . the need for more university places for the underprivileged to home ownership for council house tenants and—'

'What about inheritance tax!' someone called out.

'That is to say, taxation, of course and . . . and artesian wells for the Sudan—'

'Bugger the Sudan,' muttered a man in green tweeds to the woman in the quilted waistcoat. 'If you ask me this fellow's a damned Socialist.'

Mr Pratt realized that his audience was becoming restless. 'Well, you don't want a long speech from me—'

'Hear, hear!' cried the wits.

'Suffice it to say, I've known him a good while and there's no doubt he's an excellent chap and quite terrifyingly clever into the bargain. Ladies and gentlemen, Mr Burgo Latimer.'

The man who had fed me peanuts took Reginald's place at the microphone. He acknowledged the applause with a raised hand.

'Thank you, Reggie. I must begin by paying my own tribute to Sir Vyvyan, who, unlike most Members of Parliament, was not in love with the sound of his own voice . . .'

Roars of laughter greeted this.

'Too drunk to stand up,' muttered my neighbour.

'The man was an alcoholic,' said the woman in the quilted waistcoat. 'It said in his obituary he made his last speech in nineteen sixty-nine. God knows why he was paid a salary.'

'I can't claim such modest reserve,' continued the new MP for Worping. 'I intend to speak in the House on Friday on the subject of terrorism in Europe. The recent murder by the Red Brigades of the unfortunate Mr Aldo Moro, a crime as pointless as it was inhuman . . .'

Mr Burgo Latimer had his audience's attention immediately.

Everyone there was concerned about threats to civic order. He made a short, eloquent speech and looked thoroughly at home in his surroundings. He radiated confidence. The chest of every man listening seemed to swell with the certainty that they had their finger on life's pulse. Despite the stuffiness of the room every woman looked rejuvenated.

The applause afterwards was enthusiastic. The woman in the quilted waistcoat darted forward to secure her seat. I was through the door in a moment and breathing the salty air of freedom. I spent an enjoyable three-quarters of an hour in Worping's two antique shops, bought a cream jug which I could ill afford but which I was almost certain was Worcester, and ate a tomato and cheese roll, watching the breakers pounce like cats on to the shingle and attempt to claw the pebbles back into the sea.

I merged with the crowd as the lunch ended. My father was flushed with wine, coronation chicken and the sort of self-congratulatory, status-confirming conversation he enjoyed. He had not noticed my absence.

'Not a bad do, on the whole,' he said as we sped home. 'Though I'm not sure about the new chap. I don't like a politician to make jokes. Running the country's a serious business. You can be *too* clever.'

'Surely cleverness is always a good thing.'

'Not when it means you can't see the wood for the trees. Latimer's the kind of Conservative who wants to appeal to the lower orders with a lot of socialist-type reforms. Putting more money into state education. It won't wash. People don't want their taxes spent on reforms they're not going to benefit from.'

'If what you say is true, he obviously isn't that clever.'

'Well, he *thinks* he's clever. That's what I mean. It's the same thing.'

'Not at all. Everyone secretly thinks they're clever. But a few people really are.'

'I wish you wouldn't chop logic with me, Roberta. It's a damned unattractive trait in a woman.'

We travelled the rest of the way in silence. The telephone was ringing as I walked into the hall. I picked up the receiver. I was still angry but I attempted to sound even-tempered.

'Hello?'

'Roberta? This is Burgo Latimer. Will you have dinner with me tonight?'

'Dinner? I couldn't possibly—'

'Please don't say no. If I don't have a decent conversation with somebody human I may go mad. I've had all I can take of the burghers of Sussex. I'm beginning to wonder if there's anyone on this earth who feels remotely as I do about anything. It's a lonely feeling. Surely you know what I mean?'

I remembered liking his voice before, that hurried way of speaking, as though his mind was working furiously.

'Should you be a Conservative MP if you feel like that?'

'Can you think of a single job in which you don't have to put up with people whose company you don't enjoy?'

I thought of my own job. Of my boss, who was known to everyone as Dirty Dick because he was ineptly lecherous; of Marion in the antiquarian books department who was a poisonous gossip; of Sebastian in Musical Instruments who was morbidly touchy and difficult.

'How do you know we have anything in common? I don't suppose I said more than twenty words.'

'That's because I did all the talking. I want a chance to repair that. Besides, I knew be*fore* the twenty words. One does know these things.'

Was he right? It was true that I had felt disappointed to discover that he was, of all breeds of men, a 'scurvy politician', historically despised, universally mistrusted. I remembered that he also had a wife.

'I'm afraid I'd rather starve to death than set foot in the Carlton House Hotel again.'

'There you are! We *do* feel the same. I think you'll find where we're going the food will at least be all right.'

'You seem to presume your invitation's irresistible.'

'I'm hoping against hope.'

The truth was, I was not only lonely myself but also horribly bored. Oliver was dear to me but not much of a companion as he was asleep most of the time I was awake. My parents limited their communication to exchanges of practical information and complaints. Mrs Treadgold and I had a handful of conversational topics – my mother's progress or the lack of it; Mrs Treadgold's own health which was undermined by every germ, allergy and chronic disability to be found in her medical dictionary; and the previous night's television programmes – which we ran through dutifully each day. The friends of my childhood had left Sussex years ago and fled to London or abroad.

'Well . . . I don't know. It seems rather odd. We hardly know each other . . .'

'I'll pick you up at seven-thirty.'

FIVE

'You've missed some wonderful scenery,' said Kit.

I opened my eyes. I had been asleep.

'Where are we?'

'In the car-park of the pub where we're stopping for lunch. I'd better put the hood up. You never know in Ireland when it's going to rain.'

'But it's gloriously sunny.'

'That doesn't mean a thing. You'll see.'

While Kit fastened the canvas roof I took stock of our surroundings, yawning. The inn, which stood on the main street of a small village, was low, white-washed and charming. Behind it rose dark trees and, behind them, more mountains.

'Look at those mountains. That pair like raised eyebrows.'

'Rather as you might expect, they're called the Paps of Anu. She was a goddess of fertility.'

'Of course. I should have known. But, being a woman, it never occurred to me that they bore the remotest resemblance to breasts.'

'Can we men help behaving like children in a sweet shop when you women are so delicious and desirable?'

I examined myself in the rear-view mirror. Neither epithet could with truth have been applied to me. 'I'll need a little while in the Ladies' with soap and a comb to get the smuts off my face and my hair to lie down.'

'You go ahead. I'm going to nip across to that telephone kiosk to let my host know I'm about to descend on him.'

'Supposing he's away? Or he already has guests?' I still felt guilty about having disrupted Kit's plans.

'He never goes away. And the house is large and infinitely

38

accommodating. Don't worry. The Irish are tremendously relaxed about these things. Dean Swift once travelled into the country to have dinner with some friends at the house of a stranger. Swift was a difficult, acerbic sort of fellow, as I'm sure you know, and he grumbled all the way there, but he was so delighted with the welcome he received, the standard of cooking, the excellence of the cellar, the elegance of the house and the arrangements made for his comfort, that he stayed for six months. Ireland's changed since those days but the Irish themselves are as gregarious as ever.'

'I can't imagine many people I'd want to have to stay for six months. Certainly not someone as exacting and irritable as Swift.'

'I shall do my best to be neither of those things.'

Ten minutes later I emerged, much tidier, from the cloakroom to find Kit sitting at a table in the bar, smoking a Gauloise, a bottle of wine in a plastic paint bucket full of ice at his elbow. I sat beside him and took a sip of wine, which was not good but not bad either. The bar was fairly dark and despite the warmth outside a fire burned in the hearth. We were the only people there.

'This is lovely.' I meant not just the wine but the liberating feeling of being a stranger in an unknown land.

'I hope it's cold enough. The Irish mostly drink beer and whiskey. An ice bucket is an unknown quantity outside the big towns.'

'It doesn't matter. I think it's all charming.' I admired the artwork, several religious pictures in primary colours, a photograph of the Pope in a cardboard frame decorated with tinsel and a reproduction of Holman Hunt's *Light of the World*.

'T'ere ye are at last, madam.' A waiter came over to our table and winked at Kit. 'Worth waiting for, wasn't it? Madam's as lovely as a rose. And what'll you both be eating now? We've chicken or fish. But I'm t'inking the fish is a little past its best. I don't say it's off exactly but it's got a smell on it I shouldn't care to bring t'rough the house.'

It was the first time I had heard the famous brogue in its native setting: *th* pronounced as *t* and *s* preceding a consonant softened as in 'pasht its besht'. It was beguiling.

We decided on the chicken and I asked for a glass of water.

'I suspect the fish doesn't exist,' said Kit when he had gone. 'Only he wanted, in a true Irish spirit of hospitality, to have an alternative to offer us.'

'Really? How friendly and kind. Rather different from the English attitude, isn't it?'

'The Irish and the English have little in common. Except that neither nation is celebrated for its food. If I were you I'd have cheese instead of pudding. There isn't much you can do to ruin a piece of good Irish cheddar. The last time I ordered apple pie in a country pub it was brought to my table in its cardboard box to reassure me it wasn't a cheap homemade effort. The waitress kindly squirted the blob of cream from the aerosol can in front of me. You can understand it, really. When the majority of the population once lived on potatoes and buttermilk anything from a shop seems like luxury. The white tags on tea-bag strings are known as "wee glamours".'

'Not really?' I laughed. 'I think that's delightful.'

Kit smiled at me. 'I must say it's cheering to be with someone who's so ready to be pleased.'

'I expect I sound idiotic. It's just that recently things have been rather . . . difficult. This seems so different. It's a relief to have left it all behind.'

'You've had a bad time?'

'It was my own fault. One must expect to take the consequences if one behaves stupidly. But that's all in the past. Don't let's even think about it.'

'I wish you'd trust me.'

'It isn't that.' I stared hard at a picture of Christ standing on a hectic, crimson cloud. 'I don't want to tell you because . . .' I paused. 'The truth is I'm ashamed.'

'That sounds intriguing.' When I did not say anything he added, 'But I'm not to know why?'

I shook my head.

The waiter brought us a plate of sliced bread, already buttered, and my glass of water. Despite the glass being chipped and smeary I smiled and thanked him. He clapped his hand to his waistcoat pocket, roughly where his heart was. 'O-ho! She's a dazzler!' He gave Kit another wink. 'Yer t'e lucky man now,' he whispered mock-conspiratorially. 'They're saying in t'e kitchen t'e two of ye must be on yer honeymoon.'

'I wish we were,' said Kit.

'Arrah!' The waiter's voice was warmly sympathetic as he rested his hand on Kit's shoulder. 'She's keeping ye waiting, toying with ye like a cat wit' a mouse, but ye'll appreciate it all the more when she gives t'e green light. Bless ye both.' He hurried away.

I drank some of the water which was warm and swimming with specks of rust. I hoped it was rust. 'I've heard of Irish charm but I didn't expect to be flattered into a state of mild hysteria.'

'He's laying it on a bit thick.' Kit laughed. 'It's a national game, playing the stage Irishman to tourists: the rollicking, red-nosed loveable rogue; the lazy, boozy, belligerent, professional Celt. And there's something true in it as well. As a race the Irish are friendly, hospitable, good crack – that means company – and on the whole they do like to talk and get drunk. They prefer to say what they think will please, which I rather like. But there's often a degree of self-parody beneath all that passion and melancholy that can catch you unawares.'

'So I'm to disbelieve the flannel but take it as a gesture of good-will?'

'It's a game but it's quite good fun to play it.' Kit's eyes held mine expectantly. 'Though nothing's much fun for you at the moment, is it? I know I'm in danger of seeming offensively inquisitive but I wish you'd tell me what the problem is.'

'Oh, please, let's not talk about me. I'm heartily sick of the subject. And you'd be horribly bored, I promise you.'

Kit's expression became regretful. 'I've a confession to make,' he said. 'I hoped you'd trust me so I wouldn't have to. But I hate the feeling that I'm deceiving you. After I'd telephoned Phelim O'Rahilly – who, by the way, is raring to see me so you needn't feel guilty about my change of plan – I went into the village shop to buy a bar of chocolate to sustain us during this afternoon's drive. The English papers had just arrived. Even upside down I could see it was a good likeness.'

I suppose I must have developed something of a phobia about newspapers because I felt the blood drain from my face at the mere mention of the horrible things. My fragile pretence of light-heartedness crumbled. 'Oh,' I said, pressing my lips together to prevent them trembling.

'So, Miss Roberta Pickford-Norton, all hope of concealment is at an end. However, you are under no obligation to say anything.'

'But anything I do say may be used in evidence against me?'

Kit shook his head. 'Despite the inflammatory nature of the report-ing, it hasn't changed my view of you by one tittle or jot. I know what journalists are. And politicians.'

'Is it bad?'

41

Kit raised his eyebrows and widened his eyes.

Some instinct made me say, 'You bought it, didn't you? Let me see it.'

'You won't like it.'

'Hand it over.'

Kit drew the paper from under a cushion. It was one of the less reputable newspapers, though the distinction is fine.

The headline was: *Labour Backbenchers Demand Resignation of New Minister for Culture*. In smaller print was the caption: *War hero's daughter in love scandal*. The photograph beneath was of me driving out of the front gates of Cutham. I was looking straight at the camera, my eyes staring and my lips drawn back in a snarl. There was a caption beneath the photograph. *Roberta Pickford-Norton, 26, leaves ancestral home for Belgravia party*. Next to it was a studio photograph of a woman in a striped shirt and pearls, who leaned her chin on her hand and smiled into the lens. Beneath it, it said *Lady Anna Latimer, 35, daughter of the Earl of Bellinter*. I read the article.

Lady Anna, the minister's wife, has assured friends she will stand by her husband despite being devastated to discover he has been engaged in a year-long relationship with blonde bombshell, Pickford-Norton, whose father was decorated for bravery for his part in the battle for Tobruk in 1942. Slim, green-eyed, convent-educated siren, Pickford-Norton, is well-known in aristocratic circles for her wild behaviour and outspoken views. She told reporters, 'Who gives a **** about his wife? She's middle-aged and past it and anyway fidelity is a naff, middle-class thing.' The Labour Party is united in calling for Latimer's resignation but the Prime Minister, Margot Holland, who was clearly angry to find herself embroiled in scandal barely seven weeks after taking office, said in her statement yesterday, 'Burgo Latimer is a gifted, hard-working and conscientious member of the team, who has a great deal to contribute to the future of both the party and the country. This is muck-raking by the Opposition of the most discreditable kind.' Sources close to Pickford-Norton have denied she is pregnant by Latimer. Lady Anna, who is childless, is believed to have recently undergone the latest treatment for infertility: in-vitro fertilization. Continued Page Two.

I opened the paper to see a photograph of Burgo, striding along the pavement towards 10 Downing Street, looking preoccupied. I felt such a sense of loss, such a longing for him that I almost burst into tears.

'I don't want to read any more.'

I stood up and thrust the paper on to the fire. It burned brightly, then fell into the grate. Kit went to work with the poker to avert the burning down of the inn.

'Sorry,' I said dully. 'It was your paper. I ought to have asked.'

'You did the right thing. That's all it was fit for.'

'Most of it isn't true. I've never in my life said anything about Burgo's wife, even to him. What could I possibly say? I've never met Anna and Burgo hardly ever talked about her. I'm not remotely aristocratic. My father comes from a long line of undistinguished army officers and clergymen. Nor was I going to a party in Belgravia. I was going to the surgery to get some Valium. Not at all glamorous.' I tried, unsuccessfully, to laugh. 'My father wasn't decorated, nor was he a hero. I went to a Church of England school. Nothing's true. Except – except that I did have a love affair with Burgo. And I suppose that's all that matters.'

'Millions of people have affairs. Why should you be ashamed? My mother's had more lovers than birthdays and I don't believe my father minds a bit as long as nothing gets in the way of his own philandering.'

'Yes. Well, as you say, adultery is commonplace. But when you see your name in every newspaper, from broadsheet to gutter press, and you know that people the length and breadth of Britain are calling you a heartless, scheming whore, you feel profoundly hurt. It seems I've done something so terrible that anyone feels justified in saying the vilest things about me. Yesterday a well-known female columnist wrote an article deploring women who let down the sisterhood. She mentioned me by name, saying that in a few years my lifestyle would show on my face. Lying and cheating and fornicating would plough deep fissures from brow to chin, my body would become diseased from sexual excess and my hair would fall out from over-bleaching. While Lady Anna would deepen in beauty like a fading rose . . . It was rubbish from beginning to end but I can remember it almost word for word. Hatred was in every line. I'm frightened by so much hostility. I couldn't recognize myself in the woman she condemned. I feel I don't know who I am any more.'

To my dismay, my eyes filled with tears. Kit took my hand. It is wise to be wary when men offer brotherly comfort. It is generally a prelude to something far from brotherly. But Kit's grasp was warm and consoling. He neither squeezed nor stroked, he simply held my hand in his while I worked hard at being sensible, grown-up and self-controlled.

'Surely you don't plough fissures,' said Kit, after a while. 'You plough furrows, or lines perhaps, but fissures occur from hard surfaces splitting from weakness in their composition—' I may have looked reproachful for he interrupted himself to say, 'Sorry. It's the job, you see. You have to weigh every semicolon for sense and fitness. Something those journalists couldn't begin to do, even if they wanted to.'

'Probably it's just my pride that's been wounded.' I slid my hand away and tried to speak lightly. 'As a child I desperately wanted to be good, above all things. I spent hours on my knees begging God to make me heroic and saintly: a cross between Gladys Aylward and Thérèse de Lisieux. I longed to radiate seraphic purity.'

'I must say you don't strike me as being especially prim and proper. There's a light in your eye that I'd say was a warning to the faint-hearted.'

'Wholly misleading, in that case. I like to be in control of things, not luxuriating in sensuality.'

'Hm. Pity. Are you sure? When I look at this slender hand' – he picked up mine again and turned it over – 'I see the nails painted dark red, the skin smooth and white.' He tapped my ring. 'Emerald and diamonds, aren't they? Now my aunts – my father's sisters – whom I always think of as the embodiment of virtuous women, corseted by self-discipline, have strong square callused hands with nails cut savagely short, a little dirty from washing the dogs and digging up the herbaceous borders. They are strangers to hand cream. Ditto rings. Your hands are much more like my mother's, of whom, naturally, they strongly disapprove.'

I retrieved my hand. 'The ring belonged to my grandmother. I like beautiful things, perhaps more than I ought, but I'm not a hedonist. I don't believe that the pursuit of pleasure is the highest good.'

'What is, then?'

'I don't know. I suppose . . . behaving in a way which causes the least harm. One shouldn't be indifferent to the effect one's behaviour has on other people. It's impossible to talk of these things without sounding like a prig. What do you think?'

44

'I'm not so high-minded as you. I think if you enjoy yourself then you're less likely to be a burden and a nuisance and more likely to be amusing. If that's hedonism, then I approve of it.'

'I'm not high-minded at all. As I've demonstrated rather publicly.'

'So now you feel you're forever disqualified from sainthood?'

'It seems so.'

'So what's the real story? I don't believe you dragged a protesting, happily married man from the arms of his miserable, barren wife.'

'Apparently she's determined not to have children. One of the few things Burgo told me about her was that she dislikes them and is afraid of getting fat.'

'And do you think that's true?'

'Why shouldn't it be? It's not a particularly attractive attitude but it's perfectly rational.'

'Are men generally truthful when discussing their wives with their mistresses, do you think?'

'I suppose not. But Burgo's not quite like other men. Oh, I know people always say that when they think they're in love,' I added when I saw scepticism in Kit's blue eyes.

'Are you in love with him?'

'Who knows what love is? Mutual need? Desire? Vanity? Illusion? I wish I knew.'

'What's he like, then?'

What was Burgo really like? I wondered.

The landlord appeared at that moment with our food. The chicken had been boiled to an unappetizing grey, a match for the overcooked cabbage. I knew if I did not eat I would get a headache and feel faint by the evening but the newspaper article had killed my appetite.

'It's bad, but not that bad,' Kit said when I put my knife and fork together, having managed less than a quarter of what was on my plate. 'Surely you can get those potatoes down? Come along, I'll butter them for you and they'll taste better.' He unwrapped a square of butter, which had come in a foil packet with the rolls, and spread it over the vegetables as though I were a child. To please him I forced down a few more forkfuls. 'That's a good girl. Now eat that bit of chicken breast just to show you forgive me for upsetting you. I'm an ass and I'm really sorry.'

'You've been my absolute salvation.' I ate the chicken. 'I'm sorry to be so pathetic.'

'All right, so we're both thoroughly remorseful. Now, Scheherazade. If you wish to avoid strangulation, carry on with your tale.'

I began to tell Kit about Burgo.

SIX

'Why are you dressed like that?' Oliver had asked on the evening of the Conservative lunch at the Carlton House Hotel.

We were in the kitchen. I was wearing my mac buttoned to the neck while I washed up my mother's supper tray.

'I'm going out to dinner and I don't want to splash my dress. It's silk and even water marks it like crazy.'

'What's for supper?'

'It's called a navarin, but you'd better tell Father it's lamb stew or he won't eat it. It's a classic French dish. It's got peas and beans and turnips in it. It's delicious, honestly.'

'It doesn't sound it.'

'There's Brown Betty with gooseberries for pudding.'

'Oh, good. Custard or cream?'

'Cream.'

'Where're you going?'

I took off the mac and examined my reflection in the mirror by the back door. My hair is naturally wavy and resists all attempts to tame it. I had fastened it back from my face with two combs. My eyelashes are dark, luckily, but I had thickened them with mascara. I had painted my lips with a colour called Black Pansy which I had found in the village shop. The deep red made my mouth look sulky but was effective, I thought, with my skin, which is pale. I fished the pink plastic case from my bag and applied a little more for good measure.

All the time I had been washing my hair and putting varnish on my nails I had been conscious that my blood was circulating a little faster. It was a measure of how miserable being at home was making me, I told myself, if going out to dinner with a man

47

I knew nothing about, except that he had a job I rather despised and was married, could lift my spirits so dramatically. Not that the last was relevant. A Member of Parliament taking a single woman out to dinner in his own constituency could not afford the least breath of scandal. He would not dare to flirt with me. And even if he did, I was immune to his charms. Sarah and I had so often listed the reasons why it was certifiable madness to have anything to do with married men that we could have given public lectures on the subject.

'I don't know.'

'Who's taking you?'

'A man called Burgo Latimer. Our new MP.'

'Really? That sounds grim. What's he like?'

'He's a Conservative but he's not what you'd expect.'

'What's different about him?'

'I don't know, really. He isn't dull, anyway. There's the doorbell. Don't tell Father anything about it. He won't approve.'

'What shall I say? He's bound to give me the third degree if he thinks there's a mystery.'

'You're the novelist. Make it up.'

Burgo was standing with his back to me when I opened the door. I had forgotten how tall he was.

'Some good trees,' he said, turning, 'but if there's one plant I can't stand it's the spotted laurel. It makes me think of a dread contagion. And you've got so much of it.'

After his telephone call I had tried to remember his face but could only be sure about his eyes which I knew were dark brown and his hair which was straight and of that extreme fairness – a sort of white-blond – that generally one sees on small children. It had the same juvenile texture, soft and untidy, and was, I guessed, worn a fraction too long for the conventional tastes of his female acolytes. His nose was finely shaped with arched nostrils, his mouth full. It might have been considered a slightly effeminate face but for the eyes. They were sharp, amused, combative.

'We've practically got the National Collection of dingy shrubbery,' I said.

I followed him down the steps to where an enormous black car stood on the gravel.

I was relieved he hadn't expected to be invited in for drinks with my family. It seemed this was an opportunity to soft-soap the voters that he was willing to write off. Or perhaps he knew that even if he had snubbed my father, made a pass at my mother and taken an axe to the furniture, Cutham Hall would always be a staunchly Conservative household.

'You can starve a laurel,' I continued, 'leave it unpruned for years then hack it to the ground, but it's almost impossible to kill it. It's difficult to love something that can be thoroughly abused and taken for granted. You need a little uncertainty. The feeling that you have to nurse the guttering flame.'

'And this is so true of love between humans.'

A man in a real chauffeur's uniform, grey piped with blue, which would have made Brough horribly jealous, had rushed round the car to hold open the rear door nearest the steps. Burgo went round to the other side and slid in beside me.

'This is Simon,' said Burgo, when the driver returned to his seat. 'He drives me when I'm in Sussex. Miss Pickford-Norton.'

'Actually,' I said, 'I don't use the hyphen. I call myself Roberta Norton. Or, more often, Bobbie.'

'How democratic,' said Burgo.

'Pickford is my mother's maiden name. My father added it on when they married. It's a bit of a tongue-twister.'

Also I thought, but did not say, that it was an embarrassing piece of social climbing on my father's part. He liked to talk of the Pickfords of Cutham Hall as though they had lived there for centuries instead of barely a hundred years. And he kept quiet about the pickling.

'I like Roberta, though. Pretty and old-fashioned. Bobbie doesn't suit you at all. Step on it, Simon. We don't want to be late.'

Simon spun the wheels on the gravel and we shot away. The suspension was so good that one hardly noticed the potholes.

'Where are we going?'

'A place called Ladyfield. You won't have heard of it. It's about fifteen miles from here.'

Burgo leaned forward and closed the glass partition that separated the front from the back.

'Obviously you don't worry about appearing democratic.' I admired the acres of polished walnut and quilted leather. The back seat was the size of a generous sofa and you could have fitted a dining table and chairs into the space for our legs.

'Simon won't mind being excluded. He's thrilled to be asked to drive fast. He doesn't often get the chance.'

'I really meant, this is an opulent car.'

49

'It isn't mine. It belongs to Simon. He's a dedicated Conservative so he lets me have the use of it at a reasonable rate. It doesn't do me any harm to be conspicuous but the real reason I like it is because I can stretch my legs and sleep off the coronation chicken on my way back to London.' He extended them as he spoke and they were, indeed, unusually long. 'When Simon's not driving me about he makes a living ferrying brides to and from church at a stately crawl.'

This explained the powerfully sweet aroma of scent and hairspray that clung to the upholstery. I opened the window a fraction.

Burgo leaned forward and picked something from the floor. 'There you are. Confetti.' He handed me some scraps of silver paper, then swayed towards me as Simon took a tight bend at speed. The draught from the open window blew the tiny bell and the horseshoe from my hand. 'I find all sorts of things in here.' He looked in the ashtray and then felt along the edge of the seat. 'There you are.' He showed me a lace handkerchief, crumpled into a ball. 'It's still damp with tears. At least I hope it's tears. Once I found a garter. Another time a copy of *Tropic of Capricorn* with the spicier sections marked. Last week I found a photograph of a young man torn in two. Themes for a whole book of short stories.'

'Don't you ever drive yourself?'

'I don't have a licence. I gave up after the fifth attempt to pass my test. I offered the last man a bribe but he still refused to pass me. I found it reassuring, in a way, that he was incorruptible. My temperament isn't suited to driving. I get bored and my mind wanders. In London I take taxis. It's an opportunity to hear what people really think, talking to people who don't know I'm an MP. Naturally the cabbies all have strong views on politics and are usually much further to the right than I am.'

'My father seems to think you're practically a Marxist.'

'In theory I approve of some elements of Marxism but I disapprove of despotism, which is the only way you can implement it, humans being so unequal. History's shown us that Marxism and Fascism have a lot in common. Both systems rely on collective brainwashing to educate the populace and extreme brutality to crush rebellion. And that's positively my last word this evening about politics. You've told me unequivocally that you hate them and I've had enough of them today to satisfy the most ardent politicophile.'

'I like political history, though. Distance lends enchantment.'

'What do you really like?' He slid lower in his seat, folded his arms and turned his head to rest his chin on his left shoulder to look at me. 'What makes *you* want to get up in the morning?'

Meeting his eyes, observant, curious, humorous, I felt a moment of disquiet, almost alarm. What was I doing speeding through the countryside to an unknown destination with this man who was a stranger? Reality is so different from one's imagining. Getting dressed alone in my bedroom, I had felt excited and confident. Now Burgo was beside me, I felt oddly uncertain of myself and almost wished myself safely back in the gloomy dining room at Cutham.

'Well.' I looked down at the little heap of multicoloured confetti near his shoe and attempted to restore my composure by giving my attention fully to the question. 'Breakfast, for one thing. I usually wake up hungry. And extremes of weather. Not only sun but snow and wind, too. I even like wet days if it's a proper deluge. That's the only thing I don't like about living in London: you hardly notice the seasons, except as an inconvenience. Nature's confined to a few dusty plane trees growing out of holes in the pavement. I really love flowers and gardens. But London parks are too tidy. And I hate African marigolds.' Careful, I thought, you're starting to gabble. Don't let him see you're nervous. If only he'd stop looking at me. I put up my hand to check the combs in my hair, then was annoyed with myself for fidgeting. 'I'd always be willing to get up to see the first bud open of an oriental poppy called Cedric Morris. It's the most subtle shade of greyish pink.' Now you're sounding like a plant dictionary. Stupid, stupid. 'And I nearly always want to get up for work. I work for an auction house. I used to be in the antique textile department but last year I moved to porcelain. There's always the chance that something good's going to be brought in for valuation or to be sold. I can't often afford to bid for anything myself but just to see something beautiful – to touch it – gives me pleasure.'

'What do you call beautiful?'

'Practically anything that's eighteenth century. Ignoring the smells and the lack of antibiotics and dentistry, Angelica Kauffmann seems to me to have led the most enviable life. She was prodigiously talented and got to see most of the wonderful houses and gardens and exquisite furniture of the age.'

'Ah yes, she was a painter.'

'And absolutely on a par with the men. Sir Joshua Reynolds was a great admirer. Have you seen her work at Frogmore?'

'No. But I shall, now you've put me on to it. Do you paint?'

'In an amateur way. The need to earn a living is my excuse for not being better at it. But the truth is that I can't make up my mind what I like best. Textiles, fans and *objets de vertu* are passions but I'm equally besotted by porcelain, especially Chelsea and Longton Hall. As for early English walnut furniture . . .' I made a sound expressive of longing.

'Describe an average day.'

I told him about my job. Now I was on familiar territory I grew calmer. I felt a brief return of my London self. I was used to working with male colleagues, to being as much at ease with men as with women and confident that I knew what I was talking about most of the time. Burgo was a good listener. He gave me his whole attention and asked the right questions. I relaxed and wondered what had made me lose my nerve in that absurd way. It must be Cutham that disagreed with me.

'I like the idea of a life spent in pursuit of beauty,' Burgo said.

'Is that the impression I've given? Well, perhaps. Some people would think that superficial. Cold and selfish. And subjective, of course.'

'Only if they were thinking of beauty in its narrowest sense: the acquisition of fine objects. And even with material beauty, things must be honest, well conceived and well made to be beautiful. Keats said it succinctly enough in that wonderful sonnet. "Beauty is truth, truth beauty." Or was it the other way round? When we come to abstractions – goodness, truth, unselfishness, charity, justice, fortitude – in practice they're indivisible from one another and from beauty. I knew I'd like talking to you. You're an enthusiast and so am I. About different things but that doesn't matter. I like that dress. That *is* a subjective judgement. What do you call that colour?'

'I don't know. Pistachio, perhaps.'

'Your eyes are almost the same colour, a mixture of green and grey with that ring of gold round the iris. I've never seen anything like them.'

'I think you said your wife was in France? Is she on holiday?'

'She spends a lot of time in Provence. She has a *mas* there with a few acres of vines. She likes heat.'

'Does she make the wine herself?'

'No. She has someone to do it for her. She prefers to read and sunbathe and sleep. Sometimes she goes for walks or entertains. Anna is not an enthusiast.'

'It sounds a charmed life.' I wanted to ask more about her but was afraid of sounding inquisitive.

He turned his head away to examine a handsome old house as we flew past. 'I suppose it is. Are you married?'

'Not even engaged. I once was for a week, then thought better of it. The awfulness of breaking it off and hurting someone I was fond of taught me a lesson: not to go into these things without being one hundred per cent certain. But as one can't ever be that I may never get married. It seems such a terrible risk.'

'That's not the enthusiast talking. What about your parents?'

'What about them?'

'Happy marriage?'

'No.'

Burgo refrained from drawing the obvious conclusion, for which I was grateful. He continued to look out of the window. Trees overhung the road. Occasionally a flash of fire from the setting sun shot between the leaves and stung my eyes. I closed them to prevent them watering. A minute went by without either of us saying anything. The silence felt comfortable now, as though we had reached some sort of understanding. Perversely, this feeling of intimacy, as though the usual social rules need not apply, made me determined to break it.

'It's so kind of you to take me out and give me this treat. But you must let me pay my share.'

He continued to look out of the window. 'Are you afraid I shall call in the debt by demanding sexual favours?'

I kept my voice detached, though I was disconcerted. 'Not in the least. A man intent on paying for such things with dinner doesn't talk about his wife, unless of her imperfections.'

'So you're quite confident that what I want is your companionship for what would otherwise have been a lonely evening?'

'Perfectly confident. Isn't it possible for men and women to enjoy friendship with nothing else involved?'

Burgo did not reply but turned his head to look at me. It was not a flirtatious look. He did not smile or smoulder. There was no tenderness, no particular friendliness even. It was a look of simple interrogation, as though he wondered whether I meant him to give me a serious answer. I felt compelled to drop my eyes, conscious of a sudden acceleration of the heart.

'Here we are,' he said as Simon braked sharply and swung the car between a pair of iron gates.

'Where?'

'Ladyfield.'

53

An immaculately maintained drive was bordered on each side by a double row of limes. Beyond were park-like grounds dotted with stately trees.

'Is it a private house?'

'Yes.'

'Will there be other guests?'

'Eight more, I believe.'

I was almost annoyed to discover that we would be so well chaperoned. I had come near to making a fool of myself, thinking, as he had perhaps intended me to think because it amused him, that we would be having a cosy dinner *à deux* with the potential for advance and retreat that this implied. I caught his eye. He was smiling.

'Won't the people there think it odd? Thrusting a perfectly strange woman on them at the last minute, I mean?'

'You don't seem particularly strange to me.'

'You know what I mean.'

'Fleur won't mind at all. I ought to say she'll be delighted but that would be stretching it. I don't know that she's ever really delighted by people. She much prefers animals. This is where I stay when I'm in Sussex. When one of her guests rang to say she was ill, I told Fleur I'd invite you.'

'Is it her house?'

'Strictly speaking it's Dickie's. He's her husband. It's been in his family for a couple of generations.'

'They seem to have prospered.' I could not help comparing the grounds of Ladyfield with Cutham Hall, to the latter's disadvantage.

The lights of the house appeared through the trees. The drive curved round in a circle to end before an early Georgian house of soft red brick. Ladyfield must have been built at roughly the same time as Cutham Hall but had escaped Victorian revision. The light was fading but I could see a well-proportioned façade with a pedimented portico, pilasters and a balustrade at roof level ornamented with urns. The half-glazed front door stood open.

'Well?' Burgo asked as we stood on the drive after Simon had driven the car away. 'Like it?'

'It's enchanting!'

'Let's go in.'

The hall was painted a marvellous rich red, the perfect background for what seemed at a cursory glance to be good paintings. A cantilevered staircase curled round at the far end beneath a Venetian window. It was all quite grand but untidy. On the lovely, worn limestone floor a pair of gumboots stood beside a bowl containing pieces of meat. Beneath a side table was a dog basket from which trailed a filthy old blanket. A halter and a Newmarket rug were thrown over a chair. Burgo examined a pile of letters on the table. He picked up one and read it quickly, then threw it aside.

'Nothing that can't wait. Let's get a drink. Then I'll run up and change.'

We went into the drawing room. The walls were buff coloured and looked superb with the plasterwork, which was of a high quality and painted, in the correct manner, several shades of greyish-white. Burgo appeared at my side with a glass of something that fizzed.

'What are you looking at so intently?'

'Plasterwork's a particular weakness of mine.'

'Perhaps, after all, you are a strange woman.'

I stared at the painting above the fireplace. 'Isn't that a Turner?'

'Is it?'

'It's an early one. Before he was bitten by cosmic mysticism. But you can see the hand of the master.'

'You may be able to. I don't know enough about it.'

'Oh, I'm a novice myself when it comes to painting. That takes years and years of just looking.'

'You beast!' said a voice behind us. 'I've been waiting and waiting for you. And then you choose just the moment I dash out to the stable to arrive.'

A girl, younger than me, I guessed, had come into the drawing room. She walked up to Burgo, threw her arms round his neck and pulled down his head so she could kiss him on the mouth. Burgo disengaged himself from her embrace and held her wrist in one hand while he pulled her ear with the other.

'Roberta, this is Fleur,' said Burgo. 'My sister.'

'Hello.' Fleur gave me her hand. It was slightly sticky. 'Sorry I wasn't here to greet you. I've been drenching a colt. He's got worms.'

Fleur was small and slender. Her hair was brown, her face soft and round like a child's. Her eyes slanted up at the outer corners, like his, and had the same dark brilliance, but hers were vague and dreamy.

'Where is everybody? I thought we'd be the last to arrive.' Burgo poured a glass of champagne for his sister. She held the stem of the glass in a childish fist.

'They've all come. Dickie took them out to see the Temple to Hygeia.'

'Dickie's in the process of repairing an old folly,' Burgo said to me. 'Dedicated to the goddess of health and cleanliness. I'm going to change.'

Before I could ask: Why cleanliness? he had gone. There were noises in the hall and then people in evening dress came into the drawing room. I felt a little shy, not only because they were all unknown to me but also because I was certain they must wonder what I was doing there. But my diffidence was as nothing to my hostess's. She frowned, licked a finger and began to scrub at a mark on the skirt of her beaded dress.

'You must be Roberta.' A man with grizzled, receding hair shook my hand. He leaned upon a stick. 'I'm Dickie. Charmed to see you. Any friend of Burgo's . . . Can I give you a top-up?' I accepted his offer of more champagne. 'So nice of you to make up the numbers at the last minute,' he continued. 'It isn't everyone one can ask; *Homo sapiens* is a sensitive, thin-skinned creature.'

'Yes,' I said. Then, feeling my reply to be inadequate, I added, 'It certainly is!'

'Glad you agree with me!' The expression in his eyes above his half-moon spectacles was cordial. 'I must quickly do the rounds with the booze. Fleur darling, look after Roberta. Catch up with you later.'

He limped away. I watched him talking to his friends. He was affable, gave a pat on the arm here, a peck on the cheek there, his pinkish face suffused with pleasure. Fleur abandoned the scrubbing of her dress but kept her eyes on the carpet, her mouth unsmiling.

'Do tell me about your colt.' I had once been the proud possessor of a piebald with a large head and short legs and had been to enough gymkhanas and pony-club dances to be able to maintain a horsy conversation without making an idiot of myself.

Fleur's beautiful eyes met mine with sudden enthusiasm. 'He's nearly three and absolute heaven. Bright chestnut with white socks and a blaze. I've called him Kumara. It's the name of a Hindu god. He's got the most perfect action . . .'

While Fleur talked, the words coming quickly in a way that was already familiar to me, I speculated about what seemed a striking mismatch. What attractions, apart from a genial manner, had a man like Dickie for a lovely girl at least twenty years younger? He had a wonderful house and appeared to be well heeled, but Fleur did not seem the mercenary type.

'And I've already lunged him twice . . .'

There was something endearing about the grubby fingernails and a definite tidemark round the neck, half-hidden by the expensive dress.

'I've had a good offer for Kumara but nothing would persuade me to part with him. I love him best in all the world – after Burgo, naturally. But you can't equate people and animals, can you? I mean, Kumara looks to me for everything. I know that sounds rather sad and selfish, having to be important to something. But Burgo doesn't *need* me. He doesn't need anyone. That doesn't stop me loving him but it makes it rather one-sided.'

I looked across the room at Dickie, who was roaring with laughter at something he had just been told. He threw back his head and leaned more heavily on his stick to balance himself.

'Children need you, I suppose for the first few years, anyway,' I said.

Fleur's expression changed. Her fine brows drew together and she flushed. 'Probably they do.' She grew silent.

Obviously I had put my foot in it. I wondered what the trouble was? Perhaps Dickie was too much of an invalid to . . . I cast about for a change of subject. 'What sort of dogs do you have?'

'I've got three. Looby, a black Labrador, Lancelot who's a red setter and King Henry. He's a stray, a mixture of Alsatian and poodle, I think.'

Fleur told me the provenance of each dog, their likes and dislikes and particular charms. It ought to have been excruciatingly dull but actually I enjoyed Fleur's artless confiding style. It was like being with an old friend with whom no pretence is necessary.

'Darling, you haven't said a word to Benedict and you know how hurt he gets if you neglect him.' Dickie had his free hand on his wife's bare arm, caressing it discreetly with his thumb. 'Besides, I'm looking forward to talking to Roberta.'

'I don't think Benedict likes me at all. And I certainly don't like him.'

'Sweetie, he's crazy about you. Do your duty, there's a good girl.'

As she slouched off like a rebellious teenager Dickie gazed after her, love transforming his plain features into something pleasant to see. Then he turned back to me, smiling. 'I was watching you two. Fleur really likes you. She's no good at hiding her feelings, you know.'

'She's charming,' I said, meaning to please but meaning it, too.

Dickie lifted his upper lip and grinned like a dog. 'Isn't she wonderful? The first time I set eyes on her was at a garden party. Burgo was the guest of honour. It was in aid of somebody starving somewhere. It was hot and stuffy and the people were awfully stuffy too. Fleur was standing alone in the shade of a weeping willow. She took off her hat and shook out her hair. There was a band playing. One of those musicals. Te-tum, te-tum, te-tum.' Dickie hummed something unrecognizable. 'She started to dance, with her eyes closed, as though she was imagining herself far away. I said to myself, that's the girl I'm going to marry.' Dickie's face as he told me this story had become patchy with emotion. 'But I had to wait four years before she'd have me. She was only eighteen then and naturally she had other things on her mind besides marriage. And I was already a silly old buffer. I'm fifty this year – nearly thirty years older.'

I tried to look surprised.

'Yes, it's not so much May and September, more like February and November.'

I put a note of polite contradiction into my laugh.

'Actually . . .' He pulled a face. 'I bribed her into marrying me. I said she could have Stargazer as a wedding present. A horse, you know.' Dickie smiled, then looked solemn. 'People might think that was an ignoble thing to do: an older man taking advantage of youth and all that; but I knew I could look after her, d'you see? Her parents were dead and she only had Burgo to take care of her. He did his best – there's no better fellow – but he's a busy chap. I was in the fortunate position of inheriting money. My family were in soap. "You'll always love bath-night when you use Dreamlite,"' he sang, revealing a glimpse of pink plastic dental plate.

I remembered the commercial, one of the first television advertisement campaigns, featuring a girl wearing a tiara, false eyelashes and a pout, sitting in a bath and patting blobs of foam on to her carefully made-up face while a footman in livery, wearing a blindfold, held her bathrobe. Dreamlite, packaged in crested glossy gold paper but extremely cheap, had convinced the nation that there was pleasure and status to be had from an affordable soap. Now I understood why the Temple was dedicated to Hygeia.

'It was a clever piece of marketing.'

'Wasn't it! A simple message, easily understood. That was my father. He was a born businessman. He could have made a fortune selling dust for dining-room tables. It was the sorrow of his life that none of his children took after him. We're all as thick as fog. Ah, there's Mrs Harris to say that dinner's ready.'

A middle-aged woman dressed in black, presumably his housekeeper, had opened the double doors that led into the hall and was standing to the side of them, unsmiling, her eyes fixed on nothing.

'Come along, everyone,' called Dickie. 'Grub's up.'

I was, on the whole, pleased to find that I had not been placed next to Burgo. It seemed to confirm that I had been asked only to make up the numbers. If I was at all disappointed it was because he would have been more interesting to talk to than the orthopaedic surgeon on my right, who was accustomed to cut ice in his professional life and who shamelessly monopolized every subject we discussed. But the delight of finding myself in a beautiful room filled with wonderful furniture and scented with roses and lilies more than made up for my neighbour's shortcomings. On my left was a publisher. He dealt only with academic books so he was no use as far as Oliver was concerned. But he was intelligent and agreeable and we had fun talking to each other during our allotted courses. In fact we carried on talking to each other through the pudding and the cheese, though I was guiltily aware that the surgeon was waiting for me to turn back to him.

After that Fleur stood up and muttered something in an offhand way about coffee, which was the signal for the women to depart.

'Come on!' She grabbed my arm as soon as we were in the hall. 'I've got something to show you.' She led me to the kitchen quarters and opened the door of what appeared to be the boiler room. 'Look!' she said in a tone of deep feeling. 'Did you ever see anything more glorious?'

A large black dog – I ought to have said bitch – lay almost hidden beneath a heap of squeaking, squirming puppies. I bent to put my hand among the wriggling bodies. The puppies nibbled my fingers with velvet mouths. I stroked their backs and tickled their fat little paws. I picked one up. 'This is the first time I've held a puppy,' I confessed, kissing its wrinkled brow.

'You don't mean that!' Fleur's eyes were full of sympathy. 'You *poor* thing!'

'My father was bitten by one as a child. He's always hated all dogs since so we never had one.'

'How dreadful for you! I'm not going to let Looby have another litter. It's too difficult to find good homes.' She gave a gasp of excitement. 'Would you like a puppy?'

'I'd adore it but I'm living with my parents at the moment so it's quite impossible. But I'm flattered you think I could be trusted to look after it.'

'I can tell that sort of thing straight away. I'm hopeless socially – well, I don't need to tell you that. It's only too obvious. I hate pretending I like people when I don't. It seems to add insult to injury. To them, I mean. Often I don't like people who are perfectly worthy and decent and all that but they make me feel uncomfortable when they pretend things.'

'What sort of things?'

'Oh, that they aren't bored, that they're enjoying themselves, that they care about things just because they're supposed to. You know. Like this evening. All those women with fluty voices, praising each other, praising me, laughing at things that aren't amusing, making the effort to talk. Would it be *so* dreadful if we sat at the table in silence and thought our own thoughts?'

'I think it would quickly become embarrassing. And sometimes my thoughts aren't that interesting. Often I'd rather listen to some-one else's. But I agree it can be an appalling grind if you find someone unsympathetic.'

'You had that foul surgeon, Bernard Matthias. He calls me "young lady" and I know he disapproves of me. He thinks I'm gauche and rude and he's quite right. Burgo says I ought to grow up and play the game. He says it's self-indulgent to insist on being strictly truthful all the time. But when I try to put on an act, I start to feel peculiar. I can feel my face twitching and I get panicky and hot.'

'You're not the only one.' I put the puppy back into the basket. Its mother began to lick it painstakingly from nose to tail, remov-ing my scent. 'Sometimes I can't play the game either. At the Conservative lunch today I hated absolutely everyone in the room. Apart from your brother, of course. They seemed to me quite unrea-sonably pleased with themselves. But I expect I was in the mood to find fault.'

Fleur looked at me thoughtfully. Then she said, solemnly, 'Burgo was right. He said I'd like you. I was afraid you'd be grand and smart, but you aren't. At least, you look wonderful but you aren't at all *grande dame*.'

'Why don't you call me Bobbie?' I suggested. 'Nearly everyone does.'

Fleur considered. 'I like that. I once had a monkey called Bobbie.'

'Shouldn't we go back to the drawing room? Won't the other women be expecting you to give them coffee?'

'Mrs Harris always does that. Once I spilled it on the carpet and she had to spend ages getting it out. I think she's hoping I'll break my neck riding Stargazer and then she'll be able to console Dickie. She's crazy about him and thinks he's utterly wasted on me. She's quite right.'

'I've never seen a man so obviously in love with his wife.' I was being truthful. I would not have dared to equivocate with someone so passionately sincere as Fleur.

'Oh yes, he's in love with me but that doesn't mean to say I'm any good for him.' Fleur began to fiddle with the loop of a dog-lead that was hanging nearby. 'Often I think if I weren't quite, quite heartless I'd run away. After a while he'd get over it and he'd meet someone else – not Mrs Harris, she's much too boring – who'd be able to give him what he wanted.'

'What does he want?'

'What *do* men want?' She shrugged. 'A wife to run their house brilliantly, dazzle their friends, be nice to their mother? Luckily Dickie's mother died ages ago. And laugh at their jokes. I do when I remember but Dickie's jokes aren't very funny. Someone to be around when they're wanted and to disappear into the kitchen when not, although Mrs Harris would be furious if I ever tried to cook anything. And children, of course. Dickie would like children more than anything. Isn't it odd?'

'I can think of quite a few men who like children.'

'But they don't *yearn* for them as Dickie does. He adores looking after things. Sometimes I find him in here playing with the puppies and giving Looby extra biscuits though it isn't good for her to get fat. He goes round the estate feeding everything: birds, squirrels, foxes, badgers. It nearly kills me because I know what it means. He wants a baby to kiss and buy pretty things for and teach how to ride a bicycle and all that.' Fleur abandoned the lead and began to nibble a fingernail, a bar of pink across her pale cheeks. 'Poor Dickie, I suppose I'm just the meanest, most selfish person alive but' – she grimaced and shuddered – 'I just can't *bear* the idea—'

'I knew I'd find you here.' Dickie stood in the doorway. 'Come along, you bad girls. All the men are panting for the sight of the pair of you. You've made a hit with Matthias, Roberta. He asked me all about you.' Dickie winked at me. 'I thought I'd better warn you. Sound as a bell of course, no better fellow, but he does lack a sense of humour.'

'He's a horrible man,' said Fleur. 'He keeps his dogs outside in kennels all winter and he hunts.' It was clear there was no greater crime in Fleur's eyes.

Dickie laughed indulgently as he shepherded us back to the drawing room. 'He thinks of foxes as vermin, darling. It doesn't occur to him that it might be cruel. People's attitudes are mostly formed by their upbringing, you know.'

'Only stupid people's,' hissed Fleur.

As we entered the room several people turned smiling faces towards us. Fleur put her arm through mine and led me to stand with our backs to the room before a large landscape.

'Don't let's talk to them a second more than we can help. They're only being polite for Dickie's sake.'

'What a wonderful painting!' I was genuinely moved. 'It's a Claude, isn't it?'

'School of,' said a voice in my ear. It was the surgeon. 'Claude never painted pure landscape. He always put in figures from classical mythology. When we consider the different ways Claude and Poussin use reflected light . . .'

Fleur gave him a look of loathing and edged away but I was trapped for a quarter of an hour while he lectured me on Roman Renaissance art.

'Don't you think Elsheimer an important influence . . .' I attempted to turn the monologue to dialogue but the surgeon brushed aside my contribution by speaking louder and more emphatically.

I found myself swallowing yawns, my throat aching with the effort. It was now half past ten. I had spent an arduous day washing and ironing eight sheets, the same number of pillowcases and forty-two napkins. My father insisted on clean, starched napkins at breakfast, lunch and dinner. I had introduced paper ones one lunchtime during my first week at home and he had become plethoric with rage. I had persuaded Oliver to do without but, for once, my mother had sided with my father.

I turned my head discreetly as the surgeon gave me the benefit of his accumulated wisdom and stole a glance at the other guests. Burgo and I had not exchanged a word all evening. Whenever I had happened to glance in his direction he had been surrounded by women. Now he stood near the drawing-room door, holding a coffee cup, staring into its depths. A woman talked energetically to him, having seen off the competition. She was wearing an expensive-looking dress of bold magenta Fortuny-pleated silk, which looked good with her short black hair. She flashed her eyes and laughed frequently and, as far as I could tell, maintained a constant, face-aching expression of spirited gaiety. Watching her covertly over the surgeon's shoulder I saw Burgo strike a match to light her cigarette. She tossed him a look as smouldering as her cigarette end.

'When you take into account the importance of the inspiration of ancient Attica . . .' droned the surgeon.

I must have dropped into a waking doze for the next thing I heard was Burgo's voice.

'Sorry to deprive you of your audience, Matthias, but I promised Dickie I'd show Roberta the Temple of Hygeia,' said Burgo.

'Can't it wait, Latimer?' The surgeon looked huffy. 'You're interrupting a fascinating discussion. It isn't often I find a young lady so well informed.'

Burgo looked at me. I put as much entreaty into my eyes as good manners permitted.

'Sorry,' he said, 'Dickie was insistent.'

Fleur would have been disgusted, had she seen the departing smile I bestowed on Mr Matthias. She was sitting cross-legged on the floor, stroking the stomach of a small grey dog, ignoring a man who was squatting in front of her, trying to engage her attention. On our way out I glanced at the woman who had been talking so animatedly to Burgo. Her face was gloomy, her gaiety extinguished. She looked up and met my eye. There was something savage about the way she flung her cigarette into the fire.

SEVEN

'Poor woman!' Kit poured me another glass of wine as we waited for two cups of coffee at the inn near the border between Limerick and Clare. 'After applying herself sedulously all evening to the work she must have been annoyed to see you pocket the sweepstake. So you fell in love with him because he neglected you. Or was it because you saw him as a man of power surrounded by adoring women?'

'I wasn't in love with him then. We were still strangers, virtually.'

'But you were piqued by his indifference. You were in that state of pre-infatuation when the chosen one is supremely fascinating in all his, or her, words and deeds.'

'Perhaps. It had nothing to do with the old saw that power is an aphrodisiac. If he'd been a Labour politician it might have been slightly better. But until I got to know Burgo I was convinced that all politicians' souls had been traded in at an early age. And there isn't a species of male I dislike more than the Conservative toff. As it turned out, perhaps unfortunately for me, Burgo wasn't one of them. He loathes their craving for caste conformity. He's a Conservative because he thinks Socialism's hidebound by political theory and because he wants independence from the trade unions. The Labour Party has to wear its heart on its sleeve, however economically undesirable it might be to cripple industry in favour of handouts to the improvident. Burgo doesn't care about image. He thinks there are good men and monsters on both sides and all that matters is being effective.'

'In the light of what you say I'm glad I've never voted Tory. I shouldn't like to be so comprehensively despised by my elected representative. But no doubt the Labour and Liberal MPs are equally contemptuous of the great unnumbered. But to hell with politics. What I want to know is what happened when you went into the garden alone on a beautiful summer's night to view the Temple of Hygeia?'

'You can't really be interested. This is just therapy, isn't it?'

Kit laughed. 'Of course it's good for you to talk. But I'm honestly intrigued. Though you're trying to make it matter-of-fact your face and voice betray you.'

I smiled calmly but made a mental resolve that they should do so no longer. It was true that I was giving Kit an edited account of the beginning of my affair with Burgo but while I was talking I found I was reliving some of the sensations of a year ago, when all my ideas about myself, of the sort of person I was and what I was capable of doing and feeling, had been knocked for six.

'Now don't get cagey,' Kit continued. 'As I said, it's good for you to get things off that delightful chest. And I'm your ideal audience. A stranger you need never see again if you don't want to. I promise I'm not being polite. I make my living assessing the outpourings of professional pen-drivers. I do it because I dearly love a yarn. And my first requirement is total involvement in the tale. As soon as I'm aware that my mind has wandered to when I'm supposed to be picking up my shirts from the laundry or whether the dog's toenails need clipping, then the manuscript goes straight into the out tray. I'll let you know if you're boring me.'

'What sort of dog is it?'

'I haven't actually got one. It was merely an illustration.'

'Oh.' I was disappointed. 'I've always wanted a border collie. Or anything, really, that needs a home. But it wouldn't be fair to keep one in London, when I'm working all day.'

'You're temporizing. I want to hear about Mr Latimer, the answer to a suffragette's prayer. OK, you needn't shatter my nerves with explicit descriptions of a sexual kind if you don't want to – leave me leaning against the bedroom door – but get on with it, Bobbie. Your audience is agog.'

I got on.

'Should we ask her to come with us, do you think?' I asked Burgo as soon as we were in the hall.

'Who?'

'The woman in the magenta dress.'

'Is that what you call it? I thought it was purple.'

'She looked a little sorry to see you go.'

'We ran out of things to say to each other halfway through dinner. She's thankful to be rid of me.'

'You're not a very good liar, are you?' By this time we had walked the length of a passage and reached a door that led into the garden.

Burgo laughed. 'We had quite an interesting chat about the iniquitous doings of King Leopold in the Belgian Congo earlier on. But most of the conversation was about her. Her husband is a brute and a philanderer. And he drinks. Much as other husbands, in fact.'

'Are you those things?'

'I expect I would be if I spent much time being a husband. Anna is spared my uxorial shortcomings at least six months of the year. Look at that!'

The lawn shimmered with raindrops but the sky had cleared. The moon lay like a silver dish at the bottom of a large pond, quivering faintly as the wind breathed over the surface of the water. The shadows of the trees and hedges were knife-sharp.

'It's beautiful!' I said. 'And the scent!'

I could smell honeysuckle and roses and something else overwhelmingly sweet, perhaps jasmine. We strolled side by side, brushing against wet bushes that overhung the gravel path. The first lungfuls of fresh air banished any desire to yawn. The trunks of a stilt hedge laid shadow bars across our path. We entered a parterre of box, the squares filled with flowers, grey and lavender by moonlight. I ran my hand along the top of a hedge of rosemary, releasing a pungent scent which made me think of heat and Italy. And food.

'How can you be hungry?' asked Burgo when I confessed this. 'You've just eaten five courses.'

'That has nothing to do with it. With me hunger is connected with mood. I can't eat properly when I'm not enjoying myself. I barely tasted the soup or the beef Wellington when I was being harangued by the beastly surgeon about Stalinist purges. At home when things are miserable I go for days eating practically nothing.'

'I've got a bag of caramels. Will that do?'

'It would be heaven.' I took one from the packet he gave me. 'What a strange thing to have in one's dinner-jacket pocket.'

'I always carry sweets. For any children I may come across. I'm supposed to kiss them but I'd rather not. Their runny noses put me off. So I give them a sweet and they like it much better than being mauled by a strange man.'

'Are you being serious?'

'You're shocked by the cynical contrivances of a politician's every-day life?'

'I suppose I am.'

'Well, don't let that interfere with your enjoyment of the caramels.'

'I'm ashamed to say it isn't in the least. I haven't had a toffee for years. It may well be the most delicious thing I've ever eaten.'

'Does that mean you're particularly enjoying yourself?'

'Wouldn't you like to know?'

'So you *can* flirt.'

'Of course I can. But not with married men. It's a strict rule of mine.'

'And you've kept to it admirably. How wise you are, Roberta Pickford-Norton.'

'Perhaps that's going *too* far, but I'm not an absolute fool.'

He bowed gravely. 'I'm sure of that.'

We walked slowly. I ate another toffee. Epicurus was right to insist that man's principal duty was the pursuit of pleasure. We followed the path until it came to a narrow gap in a dense high hedge. He stood aside to let me go through. A square about half the size of the drawing room was filled with beds of roses. Behind them, forming one side of the square, was a small building with a pointed roof, upflung eaves and fretted windows in the oriental fashion.

'A China House!' I was thrilled. 'What a marvellous thing to find! I had no idea there was one in this part of the world. A wonderful example of *sharawadgi*!'

'What's that?'

'*Sharawadgi* is an eighteenth-century word. It means the first impression, the impact on the eye of something surprising and delightful. A shock of pleasure. In this century it's been revived with particular application to landscape gardening and garden architecture. It's a quasi-Chinese word made up by a European, no one quite knows who.'

'*Sharawadgi*,' Burgo repeated solemnly. 'I like that.'

'I don't know if I'm telling you something you already know, but England was tremendously influenced by the Chinese taste in gardening in the eighteenth century. It became known as the *anglais-chinois* style when it filtered through to the rest of Europe, finally ousting the Italian and Dutch fashions. But because the buildings were made of wood, most of them have decayed. This must be one of just a handful. Forgive the lecturing tone.'

'I like being told things. And I didn't know.'

'But how marvellous that Dickie has restored it. What a nice man he is. Can we go in?'

The door was stiff and Burgo had to be firm with it. The faint smell of new paint was quickly absorbed by the rose-scented air that accompanied us inside. Though the moonlight streamed in, the room was filled with gloomy shadows. As my eyes adjusted I made out a predictable set of garden furniture, a wicker sofa and two chairs grouped round a coffee table.

'This should be decorated with Chinese scenes of dragons and tigers, water lilies and fans, that sort of thing.' I walked about examining the room. 'And there should be scarlet screens and lacquered furniture. And really the garden ought to be Chinese as well, with a pond and a bridge.'

'You must tell Dickie. He'll be overjoyed to find that someone shares his enthusiasm. Fleur cares for nothing but her beloved animals. I'm sure he'd appreciate some help with the project.'

'Well, if you really think . . . I *could* make a few suggestions.'

'I realize I've no right to treat you like a social worker but I'd be grateful if that meant you'd see something of Fleur,' Burgo said. 'She has no women friends. She doesn't work so she has no colleagues either. Her shyness prevents her from taking part in charitable exercises like the Red Cross and so on. And the fact that she has no children separates her even more. I've seen how women support one another, and enjoy being with each other, despite the usual platitudes about women being catty, which of course are also true.'

So that was why he had invited me. For Fleur's sake. I ran my fingers over a section of white-washed tracery that I was almost certain was a stylized pagoda.

'She'll have children later on, won't she?'

'She and Dickie sleep in separate rooms. It was a condition she made when she married him.'

I was touched by this evidence of Dickie's devotion to Fleur. How many other men would have agreed to such a stipulation? I couldn't think of one.

'I'd be delighted to see Fleur again if she'd like it. What a good brother you are.'

'No, I'm extremely selfish. I found looking after Fleur a worry and a responsibility. So when Dickie wanted to marry her I encouraged her to accept him. Despite the horse I don't think she would have, if she hadn't wanted to please me. She's always valued my opinion more than it's worth. Now I can see they're neither of them particularly happy. But if you think that's why I asked you to come here tonight: to befriend Fleur, you're wrong.'

I turned from the window to which I had gravitated. I could see his face quite clearly now as he came to stand beside me. Until that moment he had not said a word to which the most captious guardian of morals could have taken exception. Neither overtly nor covertly had he sought to fascinate me. He had been as a brother. Now he looked at me calmly, with a suggestion of polite interrogation as though about to ask me whether I cared for touring abroad. He did not sigh sentimentally or attempt to take my hand.

Yet something threatened, like the shivering of a snowcap in response to an echo from the valley below, which sent me swiftly to the door.

'I must go home. I'm so glad . . . It's lovely. I'll talk to Dickie about it if I get the chance.'

I turned the handle but the door held fast. I pulled hard, struggling, almost panting with the effort to escape.

'Let me.' Burgo engaged energetically with the handle and the door gave way with a shudder. 'There you are. Deliverance.'

I thought I detected something like laughter or even derision in his eyes as he stood back to let me go through it before him. We walked back to the house. Burgo strolled beside me, his hands in his pockets, looking thoroughly relaxed.

Had he an ulterior purpose in taking me to see the China House? The situation had an air of contrivance about it. A cushioned sofa in a remote and romantic arbour, practically a love-nest . . . I accused myself of a chronic, spinsterish tendency to doubt men's motives. I had jumped at Burgo's invitation to go to see it and it had been my idea to look inside. Was I so cynical that I suspected that every man who found himself alone in the moonlight with a woman not actually hideous would try his luck with her? Well, yes. But after all, what had Burgo done? Precisely nothing. He might have been about to ask my opinion of his lunchtime speech. Or to confess to a troubled childhood. Damn the man! He could at least have made his intentions clear so that I could have apprised him swiftly and unequivocally of his mistake.

'So,' said Kit, finishing a cup of terrible coffee. 'He was damned if he did and damned if he didn't. You women don't know how lucky you are. Pity us poor blokes trying to interpret the signals from a girl who thinks she *might* fancy you if you make a sufficiently manly lunge, yet who might on the other hand want to scream the house down. I bet you've never been in the position of having to make the running. If you met a man you wouldn't mind a game of Irish whist with and he seemed a bit slow off the mark in taking you up, what would you do?'

'I'd assume he didn't like card games.'

'When a phrase has Irish in it, it usually means something not to be taken literally. Often it means the opposite, or it's describing something inferior as exaggeratedly superior. To have an Irish dinner means to have nothing to eat. An Irish nightingale is a frog. An Irish hurricane is what the navy call a flat calm. Irish curtains are cobwebs. Do you see? To throw Irish confetti is to chuck bricks at something.'

'Rather insulting to the Irish, isn't it?'

'For some reason it's been the common sport of nations to make a laughing stock of Paddy and Mick. But now the Irish are so powerful in the States, they can afford to ignore the banter.'

'So Irish whist means . . . oh, I see, sex. What you men can't seem to grasp is that a woman rarely thinks like that. Naturally, if she really liked a man she'd be prepared to scheme. She might try to run into him unexpectedly, or take up parachuting if that was his hobby. But she wouldn't be plotting to get his clothes off in record time. She'd be thinking about a love affair.'

'Men can be romantic, too,' Kit protested. 'But these days they're unlikely to wax warm about a woman who won't nail his hat to the ceiling pretty soon after meeting him.'

'You're ignoring the fact that plenty of men would be put off by a woman who made a blatant advance.'

'We'll conduct an experiment.' Kit summoned the landlord and took out his wallet. 'Make a blatant advance and let's see how I react.'

I prepared myself for argument. 'I really must insist on paying my share.' I put a five-pound note on the table.

'How kind.' Kit picked up the note and gave it to the landlord. 'That'll pay for my lunch too. But you needn't think you've bought me,' he added as we left the pub.

The landlord's wife, overhearing this, fixed her eyes on us with keen interest. As we drove away I looked back and saw her standing at the open door, staring after us.

'All right.' Kit accelerated with a growl from the engine as we came to a straight bit of road. 'Back to the story. You were stalking back to the house in high dudgeon because Burgo had – or possibly hadn't – tried to seduce you.'

'I'm sure you don't want to hear—'

'Will you get on with it!'

The moonlight must have been partly to blame for my confusion. It poured down upon the garden, washing the grass with silver. It was an enchanted place. A fountain splashed beside a statue of a naked woman with a pig at her feet. Or more likely a dog. A faint breeze swept over the lawns. Ghostly foxgloves waved their wands of ashen flowers, binding one with spells. As I passed beneath an arch I ducked to avoid the branch of a rose and a shower of scented petals dripped over me. It was impossible to be rational and wise on such a night as this.

'You remember that description of moonshine?' Burgo had stopped and was gazing upwards. 'Shakespeare, I think. Perhaps *A Midsummer Night's Dream*. You're supposed to be able to see a man with a lantern, a dog and a thorn-bush in the pattern made by the craters.'

The sky was spangled with stars. The melancholy face of the moon stared down open-mouthed, contemplating human folly. A shiver ran down my back. It may have been a petal.

I had to make an effort to speak. 'I think I just can.'

He was looking down at me, his pale hair gleaming, his face hidden by shadows. I felt again a sense of appalling danger but I almost didn't care.

'You're very quiet,' he said. 'What are you thinking about?'

The flowers – the garden – the intoxicating scent – the bliss of being alive on such a night as this, I wanted to cry. I longed to run and dance and lift my arms to Ch'ang-o, the Chinese goddess who stole her husband's drug of immortality and went to live in the moon to escape his wrath. But by a supreme effort at self-control I managed to keep my arms by my sides and walk on, a little faster.

'I was wondering how many hours it would take to mow so much grass.'

'No! Were you? What a practical girl you are, after all.'

I heard disbelief in his voice.

'Yes. I am.'

'I'll find Simon and we'll take you home. It must be nearly twelve.

71

As a prudent, sensible woman I expect you subscribe to the view that an hour before midnight is worth two after?'

'I most certainly do.'

'Nothing happened in the garden,' I informed Kit.

EIGHT

'So you managed to resist him,' said Kit. 'What's much more remarkable, almost incredible, in fact, is that he managed to resist *you.*'

We had left the town of Ennis behind us and were heading northeast. The wind had risen and snatched impatiently at the ends of the scarf I had resorted to winding round my head like a turban. I had no wish to arrive in Connemara looking like the thorn-bush on the moon. Ahead of us a lavender-grey cloud marred the exquisite blue of the sky.

I was used to Kit's flattery by now and continued to ignore it. 'I suppose even politicians, sex-crazed psychopaths though they are by reputation, draw the line at raping fellow guests at respectable dinner parties in the Home Counties.'

'Not often, I should say. Anyway, is Sussex a Home County?'

'Not quite. But you know what I mean. Is there any chance of a cup of tea, do you think? So much talking's made me thirsty.'

'We'll stop at the next town. On condition you go on with the story the moment your thirst is slaked. I absolutely must know what happened next. I identify closely with those Victorians who used to stop complete strangers in the street to ask if Little Nell was dead. It's quite as gripping as an episode of *The Old Curiosity Shop.*'

'You exaggerate my powers of narration. It's a trite tale that's often been told.'

'Now don't be bitter, Bobbie. It doesn't suit you.'

'I apologize for sounding stupidly melodramatic. I'm suffering badly from hurt pride, that's all. I mean, really, what an absolute idiot I've been! One small comfort is that by telling you – I haven't confided in a soul . . . well, only one other person apart from Oliver

73

– it's like reliving those days when Burgo and I were so entranced by each other. Now I remember why I was ready to risk my peace of mind, my self-respect, even my sanity for something that could never have a happy ending.'

'Is there a man or woman alive who hasn't taken a gamble and lost? Just because your unlucky speculation has been emblazoned in headlines the length and breadth of the country doesn't make it specially heinous. I gather his wife is not the vulnerable ingénue portrayed by the press. Nor, perhaps, a chaste Penelope working her fingers into calluses at her loom, until such time as her lord and master cared to drop in?'

'Burgo hardly ever talked about his marriage. I don't know if it was satisfactory or not. I assumed that it wasn't because he wanted *me* but I see now that was laughably naïve. I believed the truism that it's impossible for an outsider to break up a good marriage. I wonder what persuaded me to place reliance on that piece of sententious, simple-minded claptrap? Marriages are mutable, anarchic, boundless things and no two are alike.'

'What you seem to be forgetting is that things aren't quite over yet.'

'What do you mean?'

'Your running away is not necessarily an end. Perhaps it's just another part of it. Love affairs don't usually end with a neat severance. They gasp out their life in a slow, merciless suffocation of hopes and dreams.'

I felt a resurgence of optimism that a second later was dashed. 'Whatever our desires may be, it *is* over.'

Kit's silence told me that he was sceptical.

'What's that marvellous old building?' I pointed to a tall cylinder of stone with tiny windows and a pointed door standing in a field. I wanted to change my mood from high-flown pathos to something resembling cheerfulness.

'It's a tower house, like a small castle, you know, belonging to one of the lesser chieftains. Probably fifteenth or sixteenth century. The fortified enclosure running round it is called the bawn. There are lots of them all over Ireland.'

'What a lot you know.'

'Extensive reading is a requirement of the job. I'm no scholar, just a store of scraps of information. I never do anything with it. Too lazy. I'm a dreamer.'

How different from Burgo, I thought but did not say. As the car swooped over miles of more or less empty road the sky changed from blue to dove grey to pewter and the green of the Irish landscape became livid, the colour of brass. We drove through a succession of hamlets, which were usually single streets of small, dilapidated dwellings. There were broken windows patched with cardboard, and sections of roof covered with tarpaulins. The southwest seemed prosperous by comparison.

'What do people do here?' I asked. 'I mean, to earn a living.'

'Oh, they farm mostly: smallholdings not quite big enough to sustain the inevitably large families. Galway's coming up fast and there are good jobs there but the country people are reluctant to leave a way of life they've always known. You can understand it.'

'Oh yes. But the fields look so stony. There are great lumps of rock sticking out of them. Surely it must be difficult to plough?'

'Impossible in some places. The limestone pavements are famous for rare wild flowers – gentians, orchids, ferns – but of course you can't eat those. People used to grow potatoes by making what are called "lazy beds": scraping the earth into little heaps of a few square yards to get the required depth. In the good years when there was no frost or famine, the average Irish peasant ate fourteen pounds of potatoes a day.'

'You're making it up! No one could eat that many.'

'Truthfully. Many families existed on an exclusive diet of potatoes and buttermilk. And poteen, of course. That's home-brewed whiskey.'

'But surely on such an unvaried diet they'd be ill?'

'On the contrary, they were the healthiest people in Europe. Boiled potatoes and buttermilk provide all the nutritional needs of a full-grown labouring man. There were herrings and seaweed for those who lived near the coast.'

'But think of the terrible boredom of eating the same thing day in and day out!'

'Ah, but boredom is the luxury of affluence. You must remember that some of the country people were so poor their clothes were hardly more than rags. It's all about expectations, isn't it? They considered themselves as rich as kings if they could afford a pig or two, a cow and a few hens. All around them were living examples of what happened if you couldn't pay your rent. You were evicted and the roof was pulled off your houses. So you were forced to live in what were called scalpeens: hovels pieced together from a bit of corrugated iron here, an old door there, without windows, without chimneys even. Then you were too hungry, too cold, too miserable to be bored. When the potato blight destroyed your crops you and your children lay down in your hovels and died of starvation or typhus and your bodies were picked clean by foxes and crows.'

'And the landlords did nothing to help them?'

'What you must understand is that the vast majority of landowners were of English or Scots origin. They'd got their Irish estates through the land confiscations of the sixteenth and seventeenth centuries. Ireland was – still is, to some extent – two nations, divided not only by poverty and riches but also by religion, politics, language and culture. The bosses, the Protestant Anglo-Irish, saw the Catholic peasants as feckless, idle and dishonest. The old Irish naturally hated the usurpers, their masters.'

'Were they all – the bosses, I mean – callous and greedy?'

'There were some conscientious landlords. They waived rents and set up soup kitchens. But a lot of landowners had larger, more important estates in England. Some never set foot in Ireland. They didn't give a damn about the peasants who worked and starved to provide the rent money on which the landowners – in the old days anyway, before the eighteen eighties – grew fat. After the Great Famine years of eighteen forty-seven to eighteen forty-nine some landlords chartered ships to take their tenants to America to start a new life.'

'I suppose that was better than nothing?'

'It was cheaper to send them abroad than to pay for their keep in the workhouse. But the conditions on the boats were so bad that they were called coffin ships. At least half of them died on the journey.'

I tried to imagine what it must have been like: the ravaging of the flesh by hunger and cold and disease. Watching one's children suffer and being powerless to help them. Being uprooted from home and family, enduring appalling hardships to land in an alien place among alien people. Knowing that the prosperous world was indifferent to one's pain and grief. It made my own unhappiness seem contemptible. I resolved to say not another word of complaint about my own misfortunes.

'And now? What about British presence in Northern Ireland? Should we stay or go?'

'Ah! That's a hard one. And I've lectured you long enough.' Despite my assurance that I wanted to hear more, he changed the subject. 'See that ruin on the hill-top?' I looked obediently to my left. A row of Gothic arches stood proud against a Constable sky, smudged with shades of grey and indigo as clouds gathered. 'That's all that remains of a once magnificent Palladian mansion and a substantial demesne. That's just the folly, the eye-catcher, which no one could be bothered to blow up or burn down.'

'Where's the house?'

'Among those trees. I went to look at it last time I drove up here. It's nothing but walls and glassless windows now, and chimneys colonized by crows.'

'Oh, what a pity! There's a foul little bungalow slap-bang next to that exquisite stone gateway. And an electricity pylon on the other side. It should never have been allowed!'

'You can't expect the Irish to be exactly fond of the glory of the Ascendancy.'

'No. But beauty, no matter how degenerate its creator, is still precious, isn't it?'

'If it's a reminder of injustice and misery, it may no longer be beautiful.'

'Surely the making and preservation of fine buildings is one of the great consolations for man's sorrows?'

I must have allowed more indignation to appear in my tone than I had intended for Kit laughed and said, 'You're absolutely right. Don't be cross. I'm only trying to see the other point of view. Playing devil's advocate.'

'I'm not at all cross with *you*. How could I be when you've been so kind? What happened to the house and the family?'

'It was burned during the Troubles.' Kit paused to negotiate with an oncoming lorry for the left-hand side of the road. 'The family went to live in England. The people who live in that bungalow you so despise are the descendants of a long line of stewards who looked after them. They were very friendly and keen to show me round. Ironically, they were proud of the majestic ruins which they seemed to feel gave them a reflected status.'

'What was the point of it then? What good did it do to burn the house and presumably destroy the livelihoods of all the people connected with a working estate?'

'Good? No good at all, I should say. If you're going to get on in Ireland you must be prepared to abandon notions of cause and effect. Other things are more important, like love and generosity and good fellowship. And drink, of course.'

'It doesn't seem to me particularly loving or generous to burn someone's house down.'

'Ah, you'll understand in time. Logic's of no possible use to you here. Forget all about it and you'll be much happier.'

I wished I could be happy. I wished I could rid myself of a sense of loss that weighted my limbs with despair. But I reminded myself that my problems were trivial.

'What's up, Bobbie? Suddenly you look as though you've swallowed a bitter pill.'

I had taken it for granted that Kit's eyes would be on the road ahead. He might claim to be an idle dreamer, but in fact he was sharply observant.

'Oh, nothing.' I smiled. 'Just . . . I was wondering if my new employers have been reading the newspapers. They may well recognize me as a woman steeped in sin and hurl me out on my ear.'

'In that case you'll ring me from the nearest telephone box and I'll come and rescue you.'

This was reassuring. But I was conscious of getting deeper in Kit's debt. We stopped at a hotel in the town of Williamsbridge for tea. It was called, inaccurately, the Bellavista. The sitting-room windows looked across the car-park to the public lavatories. They had run out of sandwiches but there was cake, a sort of spiced bread called barmbrack. It was stodgy but I did my best to get some down, knowing that a few calories can do a lot for one's mood.

'I like to see you eat,' said Kit. 'It's depressing to see a girl squeeze the oil out of an olive before she downs it. My last girlfriend ate nothing but lettuce, poached fish and sorbet when I took her out to dinner but I'd find her standing by the open fridge at two o'clock in the morning guzzling a tub of chocolate ice cream. I fail to understand the rationale behind this peculiar eating pattern.'

'What was her name?'

'Fenella.'

'How old-fashioned and pretty. Were you very much in love with her?'

'I thought so at first. Then I discovered it was her face I was in love with, not her.'

'What did she look like?'

'She had marble-white skin, a hooked nose and bulging eyes. I know that doesn't sound alluring but there was a symmetry about her face and a kind of sculpted quality that I found fascinating. Her eyes were pale green, like the inside of a cucumber. She was cold, too, like a cucumber, and almost as immobile. At first I yearned to lie in her arms, like reclining on the bed of a fast-flowing stream. But after a while, I got chilly. That was when I fell out of love with her.'

'Was she dreadfully hurt?'

'Annoyed more than anything. Her mother gave her a lot of stick for parting company with me.'

'Her mother? How did she come into it?'

'She was a mink-wrapped, ruby-hung adding machine, totting up my credits, setting them against my debits.'

'The credits being? If that isn't an impossibly rude question?'

'An inheritance. A nice old house in Norfolk. An entrée into other nice old houses belonging to people she approved of.'

'I had no idea you were such an eligible *parti*.'

'I conceal it brilliantly, don't I?'

'Now don't fish. And the debits? Those *are* well hidden.'

'It's a little late to truckle, Miss Bobbie. Debits minimal, from Fenella's mother's point of view. An inability to take life seriously, a shocking inconstancy in matters of love, a face like an amiable schoolboy's and a strong dislike of scheming, snobbish mammas.'

'You said Fenella was your last girlfriend. Describe your present girlfriend, if you'd be so kind.'

'Situation vacant.'

'So you're looking for someone with a face like an El Greco saint, whose embrace is as cosy as thermal underwear and who loves fiercely but briefly. Preferably an orphan.'

'Oh no. I said I was inconstant in love. Now I want a woman about five feet six or seven, slender but not bony, whose hair is the colour of unsalted butter, with large, glowing eyes that vary in hue between neat scotch and seawater, who has a tendency to weep when she thinks no one's looking. She has a fascinating way of raising one eyebrow seductively and looking at you with a positively wicked gleam, while smiling as demurely as a postulant nun.'

'I think she sounds extremely irritating. I'd have nothing to do with her if I were you.'

'You aren't me. I shall have as much to do with her as I can possibly arrange.'

'But we know the fascination won't last long.'

'I have a feeling she's the exception that proves the rule.'

'You're obviously a case-hardened flirt.' I bit into the last piece of cake and smiled as I chewed to show I did not take him seriously.

'You're the girl of my dreams,' replied Kit, not smiling back.

'Oh, look! Rain!' I directed his attention to the window where plummeting water formed a curtain, obliterating the view of the public lavatories. 'What a mercy! Every single man who's been in there has waited until emerging into full view of the hotel to tuck in his shirt and zip up his trousers. Is there a law in this country against doing oneself up privately indoors?'

'But it's provided you with a conversational diversion. You needn't be afraid that I'm going to pounce, you know. I'm well aware you're still besotted with Mr Latimer. But, unlike you, I don't believe that you'll never get over it. I bet you think that from now on your life will be a sad round of charitable works and knitting hideous cardigans for your nephews and nieces.'

'I hope not. I hate it when the stitches get so tight you have to practically crowbar them off the needle.'

'Don't worry. Psychic wounds always heal eventually, even if there is some scar tissue left. People who pretend their hearts are broken really want an excuse not to have to risk themselves again on the merry-go-round of human relationships. Uncle Kit knows these things.'

He looked up as the waitress brought us the bill.

'I insist.' I snatched it up from the table.

'You see,' Kit explained to the waitress, 'I'm a kept man. My companion is fabulously rich and she takes me everywhere with her like a sort of pug-dog.'

The girl, who must have been about seventeen but was made up to look forty-five, was at first nonplussed. Then she melted under his friendly gaze and giggled.

'Is t'at *her* car t'en?' she asked, pointing through the window at the little red Alfa. 'I'd give anyt'ing to go for a drive in somet'ing like t'at. My boyfriend's a fishmonger and when we go out in his van I stink of fish for days after.'

'Like a mermaid,' said Kit. 'Your boyfriend's a lucky man.' His blue eyes seemed to dazzle as a ray of sunlight shot through the rain-glazed window.

She giggled again as she counted the money I had given her. 'I wouldn't go out wit' him but the other boys here only have bikes and I hate riding on crossbars. Your clothes get all anyhow. I want to go and work in Dublin but me mum won't let me.'

'You'd be a smash hit there.'

She looked at Kit doubtfully. 'Do ye t'ink so?'

'One glimpse of those eyes and they'd be hiring limousines to take you out.'

'Arrah, go on wit' you!' She twitched her shoulders and threw up her chin to show she could not be so easily taken in but her small, painted face was beaming. 'T'ank you, miss,' she added when I gave her a tip of fifty pence. 'T'at's very kind of ye. Enjoy yer ride now.' She gave Kit a last slaying glance over her shoulder as she went away.

'You're pretty much a smash hit yourself,' I said, getting up and putting on my mac.

'The Irish expect a little badinage. Talking's a national pastime. It's only good manners.'

As I checked my reflection for crumbs in the mirror over the fireplace I saw Kit whisper something to the waitress which made her blush with pleasure. She almost curtseyed when he gave her what looked like a five-pound note.

'Throat oiled and spirit soothed?' he asked as we got into the car.

'Thank you, yes. What a good Samaritan you are.'

'Could we have less of the distance-making gratitude? I *could* swamp you with thanks for lunch and tea, but I know how to accept gracefully.'

Opposite the entrance of the car-park was a shop that sold television sets. A small crowd had gathered on the pavement to stare at the rows of flickering screens, a bright point of interest in the dull, rain-soaked street. As we swept by I saw a man's face, striking in black and white, and was almost certain that it was Burgo's. I closed my eyes and swallowed down the sour taste that rose into my mouth, a combination of barmbrack and grief. For once Kit, who had been concentrating on the traffic, had noticed nothing.

'Now, my fair friend and fellow voyager,' he continued, 'as we embark on the last part of our journey, I want you to tell me what happened after the dinner party. You needn't look blank. You know perfectly well which dinner party I mean. The dinner party that ended in the China House with a general stand-off. I must find out what happened next.'

'I can't think why you're so keen to hear about it.'

'I told you. I've a passion for stories of any kind. And love stories are always the most enjoyable. Also I'm deeply interested in anything to do with you. Does that answer your question?'

81

I supposed it did. So, as we drove on through rain that fell in bathtubs rather than buckets and the road became narrow and winding and the land either side of it began to rear up into frowning black mountains capped with cloud, I went on with my tale.

NINE

'So what are your plans, Roberta?'

Simon's car was rushing through the darkness, the headlights making a silver tunnel of the overhanging branches. Burgo and I shared the capacious back seat, he lounging with his legs stretched out while I sat primly, knees together, clutching my evening bag.

'I haven't any. Not until my mother gets better.' I explained about the broken hip.

'It hardly seems fair to expect you to suspend your life indefinitely. Can't you get a nurse in?'

'Apparently there isn't enough money. My father's just had a line painted round the insides of the baths so we don't take too much hot water. It's just as though there's a war on.'

'I'm sorry. I hadn't realized things were so tight. In that case it was extremely generous of your father to make such a substantial contribution to party funds.'

'He hasn't! Well! That's the most ridiculous piece of swank—'

Just in time I realized that Burgo could not possibly be interested in our family travails. I suppressed my indignation. Outwardly that is. I stared unseeing into the bushes as they flashed past. I was simmering with rage. How dared my father tell Brough to change all the lightbulbs in the house to forty watts so that it was virtually impossible to read at night and then make extravagant donations to the Conservative Party merely to impress a lot of men who despised him anyway?

'Now you're angry.' Burgo sounded sympathetic.

'Not at all. It was a lovely evening. Thank you so much for inviting me.'

'I can almost hear the snorts of fury.'

'Do you have a busy day tomorrow?'

'Yes. Come on, Roberta. You needn't pretend. You're miserable and angry because you've been forced to live at home. You're home-sick for London and freedom and your job and who could blame you? You hate spending your days in the sickroom and your evenings washing up.'

'Yes,' I admitted. 'It's grim. I don't suppose a salt mine could be much worse.'

'Colder. And darker.'

I explained about the forty-watt bulbs. 'The worst thing about it is that I don't feel I'm doing any good,' I concluded. 'I could put up with it if I saw the least sign of improvement. My mother barely speaks to me and never gets any better. She seems to prefer Mrs Treadgold's company to mine. She's our daily. Though, heaven knows, my mother grumbles all the time about how clumsy she is. No matter how hard I try, tidying rooms, arranging flowers and so on, the entire place feels like a mausoleum for flies. When I planted some heliotrope in the urns on the terrace they went from a healthy green to brown in three days and died. I'm sure Brough watered them with weed-killer. He hates anyone to interfere with his pogrom against Nature.'

'Can't Mrs Threadbare do the nursing? It would save your father the cost of your keep.'

'Treadgold. He's actually talking about cutting down her hours. I think I might kill myself if he does.'

'You wouldn't consider jumping bail?'

'What, going away and leaving them to it?' I shook my head. 'I admit I've once or twice considered it. But I can't. I don't trust my father and my brother to look after my mother properly.'

'I thought you'd say that. You've a tender conscience.'

'Not particularly.'

'Do you think anyone would even ask me to devote myself to domestic vassalage? Of course not. Partly because I'm a man. And because they'd know I'd be useless. But just suppose for the sake of argument they did. I wouldn't dream of agreeing to do it. I might put up with boredom and discomfort and the suppression of my immediate pleasure for a brief period if it was in my own interest to do so. I endure things like today's lunch because that's part of my job, which is supremely important to me. You, on the other hand, put up with the lunch solely to please your father.'

'I did escape the major part of it.'

'True. That gives me hope for you. But most people are thoroughly selfish, Roberta, and if you don't make a fight for survival you'll be in danger of being trampled underfoot in the rush.'

'You make me sound feeble-minded and spineless. A doormat. I've always thought of myself as being someone who knew what she wanted and who went out to get it. But I hope not at other people's expense. I know that sounds revoltingly sanctimonious,' I added apologetically.

'That's quite right and proper and it's what we've all been taught. But the doing of it's so much harder than the theory would have it. If virtue is its own reward, it explains why there isn't much goodness in the human race. I'm like everyone else in that it gives me pleasure to do good to others. I'm happy to make the relevant telephone calls, write the necessary letters, have a word in someone's ear. I might even undertake an arduous journey or put myself through a whole evening of dreariness if it benefited someone who deserved my help. But these would be trivial privations. I should never throw away the things that make me what I am, the mainsprings of my happiness. My work, my love, my greater good.'

It occurred to me then that we might not be talking simply about the sacrifice of my *joie de vivre* to serfdom. Was there the suggestion that I might be giving up a valuable contribution to my happiness by withstanding his advances? Then I reminded myself that he had made none.

'Beware the man who begins by telling you that you've got life all wrong,' Kit interrupted. 'It's a prelude to him telling you how right you can get it if you'll only do exactly what he tells you. And before you can say "Family Planning Clinic" you're too busy sending him to heaven a dozen times a day to fret about a modus vivendi.'

'Should you be exposing your own sex as a band of cynical, intriguing libertines?'

'I'm not saying we're all the same. Or even that the new Minister for Culture is such a one. Merely remarking that there are some snakes out there, coiled seductively in the grass. Anyway, tell me how the evening ended.'

It had ended without incident. Simon, having satisfied his thirst for speed, drove us slowly over the thin gravel beneath the horse chestnuts that lined the drive and drew up by the front steps of Cutham Hall. The house was in darkness except for a faint light from the third storey where Oliver slept.

85

'Thank you for a marvellous evening.'

'It was angelic of you to come out at such short notice.'

As the interior light flashed on I grabbed my coat and hopped out rather quickly, conscious of Simon standing to attention, his hand on the open door. Then I turned and bent my head to look back into the car. 'I hope your meeting goes well tomorrow.'

He looked at me solemnly but again there was in his eyes something that made me suspect he might be laughing at me. 'Thanks. Goodnight, Roberta.'

'Goodnight.'

I smiled but probably, as my face was in shadow, he did not see me. I watched the red tail lights disappear among the deeper shadows of the chestnuts with feelings composed equally of relief and regret. Well, to be strictly truthful, there might have been a predominance of the latter. But, anyway, it hardly mattered. I was quite sure that the invitation would not be repeated.

Ten days passed in which I performed my duties with a lightened heart. Being reminded that there was fun to be had and that there were people who did not find me provoking (my mother), self-willed (my father), or bossy (Oliver) was good for my morale.

None the less it was a difficult time. Every day Oliver got up at tea-time and wrote feverishly during the night, covering pages of foolscap which the next morning I collected from the floor of his room where they lay in crumpled heaps round an empty waste-paper basket. I lent him money from my precious and dwindling fund to buy more paper. Also some biros to replace the fountain pen that leaked and was gradually staining his hands and face until he resembled an Ancient Briton decorated with woad.

My mother had been grumbling about the lumpiness of her mattress. I had a new one sent from Worping. Her complaints trebled, this time about its hardness. She sulked for a whole day when I gave her a piece of toast with her lunchtime consommé in an attempt to persuade her to eat something more nourishing than walnut whips and the violet creams that she devoured daily by the half-pound. The woman who owned the sweet shop had had to place an extra order with the wholesalers to keep up with demand. When the physiotherapist came my mother drew her sheet over her head and refused to speak to her.

'Poor old thing,' said the physiotherapist, whose name was Daphne, as I accompanied her to the front door. 'They get awkward, you know. We'll be the same, I dare say, when we're her age.'

'She's only fifty-one,' I said.

'Never!' Daphne riffled through a sheaf of notes. 'Well, goodness gracious, you're right! Dear, dear! And I'd thought she must be seventy-odd. She's such a bad colour! And her hair's that thin you can see her scalp.' This was true. The quantity of hair I brushed daily from her pillow could have stuffed the offending mattress. 'You'd better get the doctor to her.'

'She refuses to see one.'

Daphne tut-tutted as she manoeuvred her hips behind the wheel of her tiny car. 'Well, I don't know. Anyway, there's no point in my coming any more. Ta ta, love. I'd get someone in for definite.'

As I watched her chug down the drive, I wondered what I ought to do. I managed to catch my father by the front door, just as he was going out.

'There's nothing wrong with your mother that a bit of effort on her part wouldn't cure,' he said. 'It's all in the mind.'

'I'm not so sure. She still can't walk without help. Her hip ought to be healing faster than this.'

'What you know about the healing of fractures could be inscribed on a piece of lead shot. If you don't mind, I'd like to get off.' He tried to close the door but I hung on to it. 'Damn it, Roberta, let go! You'd like to warm the South Downs at my expense, I know.'

'The heating isn't on.'

He ran down the steps to prevent the rain from spoiling his shining brogues and spotting the nap of his suit. I wondered if he was going to meet Ruby. It was a favourite trick of Brough's to let out the clutch just as my father was stepping into the car, which caused it to jerk forward and him to fall on to the back seat with a yelp of protest. I could see from the grim satisfaction on Brough's face as he drove away that, though frequently played, this little joke was by no means stale.

'I'm *really* worried about Mother,' I said that evening.

My father, Oliver and I were sitting in the dining room, eating tapioca pudding. My father had removed three of the four bulbs belonging to the brass chandelier. The remaining bulb, high above our heads, only deepened the shadows cast by the giant sideboard and the enormous pseudo-Tudor court cupboard. More useful was a measure of dusty light which sneaked past the rhododendrons that crowded, like inquisitive passers-by, round the dining-room windows.

'Jam, please.' My father snapped his fingers in Oliver's direction. 'It's a magnificent colour.' Oliver stirred the jam and allowed a spoonful to plop back into the pot from a considerable height. Not surprisingly, he missed. 'Exactly the colour of a ruby, isn't it? *Ruby.*' He repeated the action with the same result.

'*When* you've finished smearing food over the table, perhaps you'll be good enough to let me have it,' barked my father. I felt like barking too. I had spent nearly an hour that morning polishing the beastly thing which seemed to expand as I laboured to the size of a tennis court.

'OK. No need to get waxy.' Oliver sent the jam-pot sliding across the couple of yards that separated them, leaving a long scratch.

'I am *not* waxy, as you call it.'

'I read a de*lic*ious book this afternoon.' Oliver rolled his eyes and pursed his lips, assuming the camp mannerisms he knew annoyed my father. 'Such lovely poetry. It's called *The Rubáiyát of Omar Khayyám.* Such an interesting word, isn't it? Arabic, I suppose. The *Ruby*-at.'

My father paused in the act of shovelling down his tapioca to regard Oliver suspiciously. 'If I didn't know you'd been after every scrubby little tart in the neighbourhood I'd be worried that you were queer.' He flung down his spoon, tossed his napkin to one side and stood up. 'I'll have my coffee in the library.' He walked off without bothering to shut the door, as though he were a rich milord with an extensive retinue.

'He's so stupid he never sees the point of anything.' Oliver was cross that his barbs had failed to lodge in our father's conscience.

'What do you think about Mother? She ought to be getting better by now. She looks at me sometimes in a way that's quite disconcerting. Huge, staring eyes. And she seems rather muddled.'

'Muddled?'

'This morning she complained that the toast smelt of electricity.'

'Women are never any good at science,' said Oliver with a complacency I felt was misplaced considering he had failed Physics O level twice. 'I refuse to believe Father and I have genes in common. I'm really the descendant of an itinerant minstrel and a gypsy princess who carelessly laid their baby beneath a blackberry bush. While they were canoodling among crow-flowers and long-purples an officious person discovered me and carried me off to Worping Cottage Hospital.'

I gave up trying to interest him in my own preoccupations. 'Help me with the supper things, will you?'

Oliver groaned. 'You're a slave-driver, you know, Bobbie. Men don't like to be bullied. You'll never get a husband if you go on like this.'

'I don't want one if it means I've got to wash up every night for two.'

'I've just had the most brilliant idea for my novel,' he pleaded. 'If I don't write it down at once I might forget it.'

'Make a quick note.'

'That won't do. Its brilliance is in the expression, not the naked fact. It's a question of atmosphere and mood. It's already beginning to fade as we speak. I must hurry or it will be gone for ever.'

I hesitated. Had Dorothy Wordsworth insisted that William put down his pen to help her sow the peas? I doubted it.

'Go on, then.' I gathered up the napkins to be washed.

'You're a dear darling, Bobbie. Will you get me some more paper tomorrow?'

'All right. But couldn't you write a bit smaller and on every line? It's getting rather expensive—' I was speaking to an empty room.

'Do you think my mother's getting a little . . . confused?' I asked Mrs Treadgold the next morning as we washed up the breakfast things together.

'How do you mean, dear?'

'Not making sense. It might be delayed shock from the fall, perhaps. Have you noticed her saying things that don't quite add up?'

'Can't say I have. Drat, there goes another.' She put down the cup she had been drying between hands like grappling-hooks and extracted the handle from the tea towel. I went to get the china glue from the drawer. 'The doctor says my arthuritis isn't going to get any better. He says I'll be a wheelchair case before much longer. But I'll still come in and do what I can, Roberta, don't you fear. Dolly Treadgold's never let anyone down yet. And, God willing, she never will.' She gave a shake of her head, her expression grim. 'Perhaps that idle good-for-nothing, Brough, could make a few of them wooden ramps to get my wheelchair over the steps. We could tie a feather duster to one wrist' – she waved what looked like an enviably flexible joint – 'and a wet cloth to the other.'

'Let's hope it won't come to that,' I murmured absently.

Mrs Treadgold's musculature was massive and she could have tossed the caber for the Highlands and Islands. She thought nothing of running up two flights with our ancient vacuum cleaner, which I struggled to lift out of the cupboard. On several occasions she had single-handedly pushed the Wolseley down the drive, with me in it, when it failed to start. I had long ceased to be alarmed when she described spasms, fevers, faints and racking torments that would long ago have carried off anyone less determined to pitch in, rally round, hold the fort and keep the flag flying.

'What's your ma been saying then?'

'Well, she told me the toast smelt of electricity.' I pulled a face expressive of something between amusement and alarm as I confessed this.

Mrs Treadgold slapped her hands against her aproned thighs, leaving damp palm prints. 'That's a funny thing! I was thinking the very same myself yesterday. Well, we can't both be wrong. You'd better have that toaster seen to.'

I abandoned the conversation.

TEN

On Saturday it rained without ceasing. This was doubly annoying because the rest of the country was having something close to a heat-wave and the newspapers were full of alarming stories about people being swept out to sea on lilos, dogs being suffocated in cars and the population being laid waste by the injurious effects of sunburn and heat-stroke. I was standing in the hall, staring through the window at the dripping laurels and wondering whether I had time to make a treacle tart for supper or whether it would have to be baked bananas again when the telephone rang. I picked it up at once. Nearly two weeks had gone by since the dinner party and I had heard nothing from Burgo. I had given up letting the thing ring six times before answering.

'Hello?'

'Hello, Roberta?' It wasn't Burgo. It was a much louder voice accompanied by noisy breathing. 'This is Dickie Sudborough speaking.'

It took me a second or two to make the connection. 'Dickie! Hello! It was a lovely party. I'd have written to say so but I haven't got your address. I did enjoy it.'

'Did you?' I imagined his pink, eager face crumpling, pleased. 'We were all so delighted to meet you. Now, look, Roberta, why I'm ringing you is this. Burgo says you were quite taken with my little temple and had some good ideas I ought to take on board.'

'Well . . . that's putting it rather strongly. I'm sure you have your own—'

Dickie interrupted me. 'I'm really keen to talk about it with you. What about coming here for lunch on Wednesday? No other visitors, just us. If that wouldn't be a bore?'

I hesitated. Perhaps Burgo had put Dickie up to this? I might arrive to find the scene reset for seduction. Even that Dickie and Fleur had been mysteriously called away.

'I'm not sure about Wednesday. I'm rather tied up . . .'

'Oh.' Either Dickie was a good actor or he was genuinely disappointed. 'I realize it's asking rather a lot. Particularly as Burgo will be in Leningrad so we can't offer him as an inducement. I expect I'm being awfully self-centred asking you but I was so bucked to think you admired my little folly—'

It was my turn to interrupt. 'Actually, I think I can rearrange things. I'd love to come.'

'You would? That's excellent. Shall we say twelve-thirty? Fleur will be so delighted.'

On Wednesday, having bribed Mrs Treadgold to look after my mother with the present of a scarf she had always admired, and left a breakfast tray loaded with orange juice, muesli, grated apple and vitamin pills across Oliver's sleeping stomach (which had a greenish hue too I noticed), I drove myself over to Ladyfield at the appointed time. My father had arranged to go up to town for the day so I dropped him off at the station, looking patrician and affluent in what I could have sworn was a new suit. Naturally he travelled first class.

Ladyfield looked even handsomer in sunlight. Its lovely red-brick front was bare of climbing plants but on each side of the front door was a box hedge enclosing carpets of silver artemisias. Dickie came limping out to greet me and kissed my cheek.

'This is good of you, Roberta.' He glanced at the Wolseley. 'My goodness, what a splendid old motor!'

Fleur ran out after him and flung her arms round me.

'Bobbie! How lovely! Have you changed your mind about the puppy?'

'I'm afraid not. My father . . .'

'Aren't fathers horrible! I hated mine. So did my mother. The minute he died she had all her skirts shortened and went down to the docks to get a tattoo. Oh, yes,' she added, seeing from my face that I only half believed her. 'She got the tattoo and a dose of something she hadn't bargained for, as well. Poor darling, it killed her.'

I looked at Dickie for confirmation.

'It's true,' said Dickie. 'Fleur's mother, poor woman, died of . . . of a most unpleasant contagious disease. But we don't talk about it more than we can help, do we darling?'

'I do,' Fleur said immediately. 'It was syphilis. I think people ought to know how dangerous sex can be. Fatal, in fact.'

'Only, darling, if you sleep with people who've already contracted it. And even then it's curable with penicillin. Your mother wouldn't accept there was anything wrong, that was the trouble.'

'She thought her hair was falling out because the hairdresser was too rough with it,' said Fleur. 'So she got me to wash it for her. I didn't mind but there was so little left in the end it was rather a waste of shampoo. When her nose dropped off we made her go to the doctor but it was too late by then.'

My eyes, which must have expressed the horror I felt, met Dickie's once more.

'You're exaggerating, Fleur. As usual. It was the septum, darling, not the whole nose. Anyway, you're upsetting Roberta.'

'Am I?' Fleur turned to me and gripped my arm. 'I'm sorry. I didn't want to do that. I like you and I know Burgo does too. In fact, I think . . . Ah, well, let's go and have lunch. I'm starving!'

My appetite was only briefly affected by Fleur's account of her mother's illness. The salmon was delicious, caught by Dickie's brother and sent down from Scotland the day before, the peas and tiny potatoes were from the garden, the cucumber from Dickie's own frames. We had tiny alpine strawberries and cream.

'How odd,' I said, tucking into my second helping of strawberries, 'to think that our house is only fifteen miles distant and yet it's the opposite of this place: dark and dismal and ugly, where nothing seems to thrive but laurel and every member of the household is either angry or depressed. Even the weather's better here. It was raining when I left home.'

'Is it really that bad?' Fleur paid attention to the conversation for the first time. She had been feeding bits of salmon to a cat under the table.

'It's terrible.' Because Fleur seemed interested I told her about my parents and Oliver, Mrs Treadgold and Brough.

'Perhaps there's a spell on the place,' suggested Fleur. 'Perhaps your father is a wizard.'

'Not a very good wizard, if so,' I said, 'or he'd conjure up some money.'

'He may have. He just isn't sharing it with the rest of you so he can keep you under his brutal thumb, poor, dejected and ill used, to satisfy his sadistic impulses.'

'Now, darling, I don't think you should speak so impolitely of Roberta's father,' said Dickie.

'It's quite all right,' I said. 'It's a most interesting theory.'

I guessed from Fleur's expression that she was half serious. Her childlike face was dreaming, her bony wrists bent at right angles as she propped her chin on her clasped hands.

'I wish I could do magic,' she said. 'I'd wish myself far away to an island covered with forest where I'd live like a savage, wearing a skirt of leaves, or perhaps nothing at all, and I'd eat nuts and berries and bird's eggs – never taking more than one from the nest, of course – and I'd tame a wild goat and drink her milk from a wooden bowl I'd carved from a tree.'

'How would you like cutting down the tree?' said Dickie in a humouring sort of voice. 'Remember how upset you were when I had those sycamores felled last year?'

'I wouldn't cut it down, silly.' Fleur was scornful. 'I'd just carve the bowl out of the trunk and leave the place to heal over. I'd have the cats and dogs and Stargazer with me, of course. And Burgo, natch. And you could come if you liked, Bobbie.'

Her exclusion of Dickie was pointed. He stirred sugar into his coffee, smiling. It was impossible to tell if his feelings were hurt.

'I'm not good at camping,' I said. 'I'd be nothing but a liability. I hate that dreadful ache you get in your hip joints from lying on hard ground. I frighten easily. I should spend all my time worrying what that peculiar rustling was, imagining a man with an axe creeping up on me – when I wasn't worrying whether that tickling sensation on my leg was a leaf or a scorpion. And I'm pretty bad-tempered without a proper night's sleep.'

Fleur looked annoyed. 'It isn't always night on an enchanted island.'

'Ah, no. But during the day I'd be hungry. I'm fond of nuts and berries but not invariably. And there wouldn't even be those in the winter. Bark and roots don't tempt me in the least. I'd rather stay here at Ladyfield. For me this is an enchanted place.'

Fleur scowled. 'What you really mean is that you're sorry for Dickie and you think I'm a pig. Well, you're right. I *am* a pig. But' – she shot him a glance of defiance – 'you shouldn't treat me like a child. Don't in*dulge* me all the time. Of course I know I behave badly. Why don't you tell me to shut up or at least look contemptuous? All right, take no notice. I'm being unreasonable again.' She brushed away a tear and made an effort to smile. 'Be careful, I might put a spell on you.'

She really was a strange girl. I guessed part of the trouble was that she *had* put a spell on poor Dickie. His adoration was patent. But unless you are extraordinarily vain (and Fleur, I thought, was unusually without vanity for such a good-looking girl) being adored quickly becomes irritating and guilt-inducing.

'Let's go into the garden straight after coffee and look at the Temple to Hygeia,' he suggested as though the conversation had not taken place.

'We'll go now,' Fleur stood up. 'We can take our coffee cups with us.'

'You'd better let me bring the tray, madam.' Mrs Harris, who had waited at table with admirable discretion, slid round the door with such alacrity I wondered if she had been listening. 'The pattern's been discontinued and it'd be a pity to spoil the set.'

'Ha, ha! Come now, Mrs Harris.' Dickie crinkled his face in pacifying smiles, his pale eyes kind and serene. 'What does a little broken china matter?'

'I haven't actually broken it yet.' Fleur's face was cold. 'But if I did that would be my business and no one else's.' She picked up the cat and left the room.

'Never mind, Mrs Harris.' Dickie began to get up, leaning heavily on the arms of his chair. 'Least said, soonest mended, eh?'

'Why don't I carry the tray?' I suggested.

'I'd best bring it myself, to be on the safe side,' she replied with a stiffening of her jaw. 'The path's quite uneven in places.'

I saw that she was jealous of her office so I did not press the point.

'Your stick, sir.' Mrs Harris handed it to him. 'What about leaving your coat, sir?' She brushed a crumb from the sleeve of his tweed jacket in a manner that was almost maternal. 'It's getting quite warm. You don't want to overheat.'

'Thank you, I shall be all right as I am.'

I could see from Mrs Harris's expression that she thought he was very much all right as he was. And, looking at him through her eyes, I saw that his affability, his presumption of power in his own kingdom and his courtliness in exercising that power was attractive. But to a girl like Fleur probably these things did not count.

'You'll beware, sir, where Billy's put that wet cement? We don't want you having a nasty accident.'

'I'll take care not to fall.' There might have been a little resentment in his tone and he seemed to stand up straighter as though encumbered by so much solicitude. 'Thank you, Mrs Harris,' he added in a softened tone. 'Where would we all be without you to take care of us, eh?'

A wave of colour ran over Mrs Harris's face. 'It's my pleasure, sir.' She began to clear the table, an expression of satisfaction curving her lips.

'A good woman,' muttered Dickie as we crossed the hall to the garden door. 'None better. But not always tactful. Damn! I wonder where Fleur's got to? I'm always afraid that when she flies into a pet she'll do something stupid on Stargazer. He's a wonderful animal but he gets a look in his eye . . .'

Dickie set the pace to the Temple, or the China House, which was how I thought of it. By daylight the garden had lost its mystery but was still lovely.

'What a fabulous rose!' I stopped to sniff at its tumbled raspberry petals revealing a glimpse of gold stamens. 'Oh, the scent! I wonder what it's called?'

'Souvenir du Docteur Jamain,' said Dickie, without stopping. 'French hybrid perpetual.'

'And this?' I cupped my hands round an exquisite quartered bloom of blush pink.

Dickie threw a glance over his shoulder. 'Queen of Denmark. An alba rose, probable parentage Maiden's Blush.'

I longed for information about the other roses that dropped showers of pink, yellow, white and crimson petals on the path as Dickie brushed hastily past but his anxiety was so manifest that it seemed cruel to detain him for a second. We came rushing through the gap in the hedge which surrounded the China House to find Fleur sitting on its front step, talking to a young man. When he saw us he stooped in a leisurely way to pick up a trowel and began to slap cement from a bucket on to a piece of ground marked out with string. This, obviously, was Billy. He had short hair, tipped blond, and a craggy sort of face, good-looking in an aggressively masculine way. He was shirtless, his back burnished by the sun. His legs revealed by cut-off jeans were muscular and his wrists were bound with leather straps. He cast me a look of interest that hardened into something more like approval.

'Arternoon, guv,' he said, in a high nasal voice that spoiled the tough, lion-tamer image.

Dickie was scarlet in the face. Beads of sweat sat on his forehead and his voice was not quite under his command for he was panting.

'Hello, Billy.' He looked at Fleur. 'There you are, darling. I wondered what had happened to you.'

'You look as if you're going to pass out.' Fleur sounded unsympathetic. 'Why don't you take off your coat? For heaven's sake, it's high summer and you're wearing a tie! I'm boiling!'

She pulled up her cotton jersey and hauled it over her head.

'Well, girls, if you don't mind, I think I will.'

Dickie leaned his stick against the steps and began to unknot his tie. I saw Billy looking at Fleur's breasts. Her nipples were prominent beneath her thin, not altogether clean T-shirt. Her armpits had tufts of dark hair. The gypsy look is not one I normally care for but on Fleur it seemed fine, even attractive in an earthy way. Billy's eyes narrowed and he licked his upper lip. I glanced at Dickie but he was still fighting his way out of his coat. Perspiration was damp on the back of my neck but I was disinclined to remove my jersey beneath Billy's lascivious gaze. Mrs Harris appeared with the coffee. I saw her eyes take in everything.

She put the tray on a table that stood outside the China House. 'I'll take that coat, sir, then you won't have to carry it back. You'd better put your shirt on, Billy,' she added sharply. 'It isn't decent in front of ladies.'

Billy looked at Dickie.

'Mrs Harris is always right.' Dickie smiled. 'We must do as we're bid.'

Billy showed by the contemptuous drooping of his eyelids precisely what he thought of the housekeeper. He put on his T-shirt and bent and stretched languidly over his task, pausing now and then to look at Fleur and sometimes at me. Once when I caught his eye he turned his back to the others and rested his free hand casually on his groin. I stared with cold dignity at a clump of delphiniums.

'Now, Roberta.' Dickie sank into a deckchair. 'Tell me honestly what you think.' He waved his hand at the China House.

'So far, excellent,' I said. I noticed that Fleur was amusing herself by chucking little stones into Billy's cement and that he was fishing them out and waving his trowel at her in mock anger.

'I've consulted pre-war photographs, though it was nearly a ruin then,' said Dickie. 'But outside, at least, it's as near as dammit to the original.'

'It's lovely. Did you know it was traditional to hang bells from the eaves, beneath the curled-up corners of the roof? So you get a tinkling sound whenever the wind blows. You could have a whingding at the apex. That's a sort of pinnacle. Something fanciful. Perhaps a crouching dragon with a long tail spiralling upwards?'

Dickie was thrilled by these suggestions and began to make notes on the back of an envelope. Fleur lobbed a stone that bounced on a bucket and struck Billy's thigh. He mimed a parody of spanking and she giggled. I heard him give a low growl. The little square of garden seemed to throb with dark primitive urges.

'You could paint the roof with a scale pattern, like a goldfish,' I continued, though my mind was not wholly on the subject. 'Scarlet, white and green would be appropriate colours. And you ought to reach it by crossing a little scarlet Chinese bridge across a square or circular pool. Strictly speaking, though these roses are lovely, if you want to be traditional the only flowers should be water lilies. Otherwise masses of ferns and rocks.'

'Roberta, you're absolutely right!' Dickie looked delighted. He turned to Fleur and just missed seeing her sticking out her tongue at Billy. 'Isn't it marvellous to have found someone who knows? Won't it be fun, darling? I'm determined we shall do the thing right. Now tell me, what should the bells be made of?'

'Anything you like. Often they were wooden but you could just as well have brass—'

I was interrupted by the sound of breaking china. 'Oh, bugger,' said Fleur. A pretty pink and gold Coalport tea cup lay in pieces on the gravel. 'Mrs Harris'll have a field day.' Then she giggled. 'It's your fault, Billy. You shouldn't make those ridiculous faces.'

Billy chuckled, an unpleasantly lubricious sound.

'Better pick up the pieces, darling,' said Dickie. 'Perhaps it can be mended. But be careful not to cut yourself—' It was too late. Fleur was sucking her thumb. The unselfconsciousness of the babyish pose was utterly charming and seductive. When she took it from her mouth drops of crimson fell on to the wet cement. 'Here's my hanky.' Dickie sounded alarmed. 'Put pressure on it and hold it above your head. We'll go in and get a plaster—'

'Don't fuss.' Fleur stood up. 'It's just a little cut. I was going to see Stargazer anyway. You stay and talk gardens with Bobbie.' She fluttered a hand at me. 'See you later.' Then she was gone through the gap in the hedge.

Billy put down his trowel. 'If you're going to put a pond in, is it any good me going on with the paving?'

'Well, no, I suppose not. You'd better leave all this for the time being and go and help Beddows with the grass.'

'I was thinking maybe I'd go and help Mrs Sudborough with the horse. She'll be a bit unhandy with that thumb.'

'Good idea. Off you go then.'

Billy gave me a last lecherous look, then strode from the garden. I gazed at Dickie's round pink face with his guileless eyes, snub nose and small mouth pursed up in an expression of whole-hearted enthusiasm and innocent pleasure and could have wept for him.

'I don't know though,' Kit interrupted. 'My sympathies are with the beauteous Fleur. Think how grim to be young and filled with the joys of spring and to be tied to a decrepit old buffer – however decent – incapable of gratifying one's appetites. Or did the dear old fellow wink an eye when the lickerish Billy put in a spell of overtime? If so, it was probably sensible of him.'

'A typically masculine reaction,' I said scornfully.

'Isn't that reassuring? I am after all a man.'

'For one thing, you talk as though Dickie's in his dotage. He's only fifty. And even if he were too old or too infirm to gratify anyone's appetite, as you so charmingly phrase it, you seem to assume that those appetites are important enough to justify Fleur sleeping with an ignorant lout for whom she cares nothing, and who doesn't give a fig for her. Are you telling me that men and women can't live entirely happily together without sex?'

'Yes.' Seeing that I looked indignant, he added, 'Well, you asked. With affection, yes, contentedly, possibly, but entirely happily? I doubt it. Not unless they're both over seventy.'

'You're entitled to your view, of course,' I said with a superior air.

Dickie lost no time in putting into practice my proposals for the China House. He was anxious to consult me on every detail and soon it was taken for granted that I would go over to Ladyfield for lunch or supper once or twice a week. It was wonderful to escape the dullness of Cutham for a few hours and the Sudboroughs' hospitality was never less than munificent. When the weather was good we ate on the terrace beneath a wisteria-covered pergola. When it was wet, in the dining room. Sometimes we had lunch in the China House. For a greedy person like me it was heaven to have straight from the garden tiny broad beans, carrots like baby's fingers, beetroot the size of olives and little purple artichokes to be eaten with a green mayonnaise and followed by tender noisettes of lamb or roast chicken with tarragon or skate with black butter. Mrs Harris's puddings were first class, too. I remember with particular fondness her omelette Rothschild, a wonderful concoction of nectarines, strawberries and kirsch baked inside a hot vanilla-flavoured froth of eggs.

Of course, the food was not the chief incentive for my visits to Ladyfield. I rapidly grew fond of both Fleur and Dickie and I thought they were often glad to have someone around with whom they were both . . . well, not intimate exactly, one cannot become that in a matter of weeks, but thoroughly relaxed. Three is only a crowd when two of the three are in love. Fleur told me she had never had a close female friend. At her smart and expensive school her farouche manners had not helped her to win popularity with staff or girls. Also she had hated tennis, dances and Radio Luxembourg and had been wholly uninterested in clothes, make-up and boys. Her experience of living as an outcast in an intensely conformist society had been enough to put her off other girls for good.

She excepted me from this comprehensive proscription, I divined, because her beloved brother had expressed a desire that we should be friends. For my part I found it easy to comply with Burgo's wishes. Fleur was honest and affectionate, which I appreciated, coming from a family who would have preferred to be grilled over hot coals than show one any tenderness. And she was extremely generous. I learned not to praise anything for I would find it on the back seat of my car when I reached home. Once she gave me her favourite dress when I admired it, another time it was a beautiful emerald ring which had belonged to her mother.

I returned the dress on the grounds that it was too short. The ring I gave back to Dickie who promised to put it for safe-keeping in the bank. But he insisted I keep the Mennecy silver-mounted snuff box painted on the lid with sprays of roses. I have it still and treasure it despite associations of guilt. When Fleur was riding (often with Billy, much to my regret) or walking the dogs, again accompanied by Billy as often as not, Dickie and I would talk about gardens and draw up plans for the China House.

Though I knew quite a bit about the history of gardening and could just about tell a *Lychnis* from a *Linaria*, I knew little about the practical side of horticulture, never having owned a garden. Discovering this, Dickie loaded my car after each visit with gardening books with which I cheered the hours at Cutham. I learned the comparative virtues of a Portland rose and a Bourbon, the pruning requirements of various groups of clematis, which Michaelmas daisies were resistant to mildew and to recognize the absolute desirability of a *Paeonia mlokosewitschii* however fleeting its flowering. Dickie and I spent happy hours among the flowerbeds, planting, weeding, staking and dead-heading until our hands and clothes were imbued with the scent of catmint, rosemary, bergamot and thyme. Those seven weeks – was it only seven? it seemed like an entire summer – were a delightful respite.

I had news of Burgo occasionally. He sent Fleur a scribbled post-card from Leningrad, then one from Moscow, after that from Kiev and finally from the South of France. She always showed me the cards, assuming that I would share her pleasure in reading them. His style was laconic. Something about the traffic or the hotel, the view or the heat. My apprehensions about Burgo dissolved as I began to forget what he was like in relation to me, and saw him instead through Fleur's eyes as an older brother, generally absent, preoccupied, wonderfully clever, sometimes impatient and unkind but just as often forbearing.

One evening – it was the beginning of August – Dickie rang to suggest a picnic in the garden of the China House. The cement was dry in the newly constructed lily pond and he wanted me to come and celebrate the turning on of the hose. I drove over to Ladyfield and walked out on to the terrace. Burgo was sitting at the table beneath the wisteria.

'Hello, Roberta.' He stood up as I approached. His hair, bleached whiter by foreign sunbeams, brushed against the dangling bronzed leaves. He was smiling. I had forgotten that he always looked as though he saw something amusing that was hidden from the rest of us. 'How delightful to see you again.'

He had the advantage, of course. He had known I was coming. As I felt the blood drain from my limbs and rush to my heart with a jolt that was thrilling to the point of being painful, I realized at once that I was in terrible trouble.

ELEVEN

'Have a drink.' Burgo poured me a glass of wine. 'Fleur's polishing Stargazer's hoofs and Dickie asked for twenty minutes' grace to get his hoses linked up.'

I sat down. The garden had grown dim and my ears were filled with a sound like rushing water. I picked up the glass and took several reviving sips. He was saying something but I could not understand it. I tried to pull myself together and fixed an expression on my face which I hoped was intelligent, or at least sensible.

Burgo's eyes were Fleur's shape exactly, slanted, sylphic. But his were darker and sharper. He was wearing a dark blue shirt, the sleeves rolled to the elbows, jeans that had once been khaki and were faded by the sun and scruffy navy espadrilles. The impact of his presence left me in no doubt that I had been deceiving myself if I thought I was interested in him only as Fleur's brother. He was saying something about England in summer. I forced myself to concentrate.

'It's perfect.' Burgo narrowed his eyes to look across the expanse of lawn down to where a pair of crinkle-crankle hornbeam hedges drew one's gaze to a statue of Flora and beyond that to where the beechwood began. 'I've longed for this.'

He leaned back in his chair to follow the progress of a house martin as it swooped over the grass, looking for insects. The wisteria's second flowering, nearly over now, dripped scent over our heads and bees foraged ceaselessly in the collapsing mauve blossoms.

'Have you?'

'Now, for a brief while, I can stop thinking,' said Burgo. He brushed back his hair from his forehead. 'I can breathe again. Allow myself to feel.' He turned his head sharply and looked at me.

I dropped my gaze immediately. I wished I could breathe. I drank

102

half my glass of wine in several swallows and stared fiercely at the grey teak of the table, mottled with silvery patches where wasps had tried to chew it.

'Cat got your tongue?' he asked.

'Only on loan. How was Provence?'

'Hot. Dry. Scorched to dust.' He glanced at the knot garden, swirls of box, germander and lavender, which surrounded the terrace. 'I much prefer the sound of blackbirds to cicadas.'

I was conscious of a feeling of gratification. I had no idea then that this was the beginning of a hateful process of keeping a tally. It took me weeks, months even, to recognize that in some secret, shamefaced part of my mind I was reckoning the score between Anna and me.

'How was Leningrad?'

'Beautiful but depressing. It confirmed all my assumptions about Communism.'

While he talked I examined a patch of violas flowering in a gap between paving stones at my feet. I came to know intimately the blushes and streaks of lilac on their primrose-coloured faces. Suddenly he was talking about my mother.

'Oh, it's kind of you to ask. She's no better, really. If anything, slightly worse. At least . . . physically she's the same but she seems rather confused.'

'What do you mean confused?'

I related the conversation about the toaster.

'I've known Cabinet Ministers who believed there were fairies at the bottom of the garden.'

'Lots of people don't have much grasp of science. I'm one of them. But she's said other things that bother me. Yesterday she refused to eat her potatoes because she said they were winking at her and it put her off. And when she talks she sometimes growls like a dog. She used to have a light, rather charming voice but these days she sounds like a sailor from Marseilles. In timbre, I mean. Of course, she speaks English.'

'Perhaps she's been lying down too long and isn't getting enough blood to the brain.'

'Perhaps. I wonder.' What a relief it would be if the explanation were so simple. These days a thread of anxiety about my mother ran through all my waking hours. Talking about my fears with someone who did not immediately dismiss them as nonsense was comforting. But of course he was being polite. The symptoms of my mother's illness could not be of interest. 'I'm sorry. It's a tedious subject: other people's sick relations.'

He made a motion with his hand, sweeping this aside. 'Has a doctor seen her recently?'

'In desperation I persuaded our GP to call but she shut her eyes and refused to speak to him. He went away very cross.'

'If the man's not up to dealing with a mildly difficult patient I'd go over his head and get a specialist in.'

'Do you think I should? But I don't know how. I thought one was supposed to ask to be referred.'

'Sometimes you have to cut corners. Leave it to me. I've got meetings all day tomorrow but I'll sort something out. Don't worry.'

It was as though the clouds had parted and a god had descended on suitable throne-bearing apparatus. But fear of disappointment made me tell myself he would have forgotten all about it even before I left Ladyfield to return to Cutham.

Aloud I said, 'That would be a greater kindness than I could ever repay.'

Burgo gave me a look I recognized, which seemed to ask if I intended to maintain the fiction that social punctilio had any part to play in our relationship. I felt the blood rush to my face.

'Here we are!' Dickie appeared round the corner of the house. 'Hello, Bobbie.' He hobbled round the table to kiss my cheek. 'The pool's filling nicely and Mrs Harris is setting out the grub. Exciting, isn't it? Of course Fleur doesn't care two straws for our little garden and we all know Burgo's mind is fixed on solving the troubles of the world. But you share my pleasure in our own little Utopia, eh?'

'I certainly do! I'm longing to see the pool with water in it.' I kissed Dickie with real affection. He was perhaps the nicest man I knew. And I was thankful to have a third person to ease the tension that continually threatened to take Burgo and me to a point beyond the bulwarks of propriety when we were alone. 'And I adore picnics.'

'It won't be a real picnic,' said Burgo. 'I saw Beddows and Billy carrying down a table and chairs. We shan't have to sit on rugs that smell of dogs, eating disintegrating Scotch eggs and drinking tepid tea.'

'At my age,' said Dickie, 'I like to be comfortable. And the leg doesn't take kindly to the hard ground. I agree there ought to be something primitive about a real picnic. But Mrs Harris has her standards and it makes her miserable to fall below them.'

'I once went to a smart entertainment which the hostess called a *dîner sur l'herbe,*' said Burgo. 'We were rowed out to an island in the ancestral lake by uniformed flunkeys. We ate lobster and swan from heirloom porcelain and silver and were entertained by a wind trio of hautboy, serpent and crumhorn. On the return journey the flunkey in charge of the picnic baskets, who had been keeping up his spirits with the lees of the bottles, upset the boat. The male guests had to dive to the bottom of the lake to fetch up priceless Sèvres and dishes hammered by Paul Storr. My dinner jacket shrank to the size of a baby's vest.'

Dickie and I laughed at this and I felt immediately reassured. What remained of my disquiet dissolved as we walked down to the China House.

'It's a funny thing,' said Dickie. 'I know so little about the Chinese except unpleasant practices like binding women's feet and the slow drip, drip of the Chinese water torture.'

'Don't forget Chinese burns,' I said.

'There you are! How can you reconcile these barbarisms with such a developed sense of beauty?'

'It's a question of obedience, perhaps,' suggested Burgo. 'A national concept of beauty depends on a conformity of ideas. I believe you can indoctrinate any race to do brutal things by convincing it that they're not outlandish practices but the norm.'

'I really don't think I could be persuaded to push bamboo shoots up anyone's fingernails,' Dickie protested. 'And I'm positive our dear Bobbie' – he patted me on the arm – 'is incapable of behaving barbarously.'

'I don't know,' I said. 'It would depend on what the pressures were. Supposing the only way you could save your own family from torture was to torture someone else's? Where would one's principles be then? It's easy to lose sight of the unreasonableness of demands when there isn't any reasonable behaviour to show them up.'

'Where would politicians be if people were able to resist psychological manipulation?' said Burgo.

'Now, you don't mean that, Burgo,' said Dickie. 'You'll give Bobbie the wrong impression altogether. She'll think you're not to be trusted.'

'She thinks that already.' He sent me a sideways glance and again I felt an electrifying sense of danger.

'Nonsense!' said Dickie.

We had reached the China House so I was saved the necessity of replying. We pushed through the narrow gap in the hedge that led into the little garden. Mrs Harris was laying the table that had been

105

set up on the grass in front of it. The pool contained an inch of water which had captured the hue of a robin's egg from the sky. Limestone boulders had replaced the rose-beds and already there were fronds of young ferns in the crevices.

'I wish Bobbie would come and live here with us,' said Fleur to Burgo as we ate lovage soufflé followed by turbot, then camembert and figs. 'We adore having her but she insists on going home, even though her parents are monsters of stinginess and selfishness.'

'Fleur!' protested Dickie. 'It's extremely rude to criticize Bobbie's parents.'

'I don't think they're as bad as that,' I said. 'If that's the impression I've given I was probably exaggerating in a bid for sympathy. The truth is, they should never have married. They're quite unsuited.'

'I can't think of many marriages that make the people in them feel better rather than worse,' said Fleur.

'Mine makes me feel heaps better,' Dickie said at once. 'It's the very best thing in my life.'

Fleur's cheeks took on a bright colour. Her eyes grew soft. 'That's kinder than I deserve.'

I was pleased by this evidence of Fleur's fondness for Dickie. Though I loved being with them I was often wounded on his behalf by Fleur's careless attitude. Particularly when I saw her with Billy.

'Marriage is a means to an end. One marries to have children, to secure property, continue a line, to simplify taxation,' said Burgo. 'Why people should yoke themselves together fiscally *and* expect to relish each other's maddening inconsistencies is more than I can understand.'

'There you go again, pretending to be cynical,' protested Dickie. 'It's learning to like people's maddening little ways because they're part of *them* that makes for love. The rest, fancying the cut of their jib, wanting to kiss them, is all very enjoyable but nothing to do with real love.'

Fleur dropped her head back and crammed a fig whole into her mouth. A trickle of juice ran down her chin. With her dark curling hair and slanting eyes she looked like a bacchante.

Poor Dickie. I had several times been up to Fleur's bedroom. It contained a double bed but the single pillow and the solitary bedside lamp beside a large photograph of Burgo confirmed the fact that Fleur slept alone. Bowls of water and biscuits and baskets took up much of the floor space. The counterpane was marked by fur-lined depressions, the furniture was scored with claw-marks and there was a distinct smell of tom-cat. It was hardly surprising that Dickie was keen to play down the importance of the physical side of marriage.

'I disagree.' Burgo spoke rapidly and waved a hand for emphasis, an elegant hand with long fingers like Fleur's, though cleaner and without bitten nails. 'It isn't cynical at all. I don't say there's no such thing as love. Of course there is, and it includes finding other people's idiosyncrasies enthralling, besides desiring them physically. It may even co-exist with marriage. But marriage is for other purposes and you shouldn't ask too much of it. It's like being disappointed that an aeroplane isn't a time machine. A plane is a superbly efficient method of getting about the globe fast. But to expect it to take you to the fourteenth century is unreasonable.'

'I don't see how you can separate things into different compartments like that,' Dickie objected. 'Marriage, if you spend any time together, can't be just a contract to give the income-tax man one in the eye. You'd be bound to have some pretty strong feelings about your spouse – though not necessarily all affirmative, I grant. Eskimos, Maoris, Choctaws; they all ceremonies of some kind. It's human nature for men and women to want to get together beside their very own cooking-pot in some sort of exclusive arrangement to keep the world at bay. And it's just what the doctor ordered when you're past your first youth: swapping the hurly-burly of the what's-it for the deep peace of the double bed and all that. Darby and Joan, Jack Sprat and his wife.' He stared up at the deepening sky seeking further illustration. 'Adam and Eve, you know.'

'They didn't have much choice.' Burgo smiled. 'As far as I remember they were the only two people there.'

Dickie laughed good-naturedly. 'You know what I mean. I'm no good at arguing. What do you think, Bobbie?'

'As the only unmarried person present obviously I can't speak from experience. I think probably my own idea of marriage is much more exacting than wanting to be taken to the fourteenth century. But if those hopes weren't fulfilled I suppose I'd try to persuade myself that a good marriage was whatever I had.'

'You'd risk settling for something thoroughly inferior by doing that,' said Burgo. 'But you might be right. Perhaps self-delusion is necessary for happiness.'

'Strike me purple and knock me down with an express train,' said Fleur. (This was one of Billy's favourite expressions.) 'I don't ever remember you agreeing with anyone before. You always say that unanimity makes for dull conversation.'

107

'On this occasion I reserve the right to contradict myself. Must you do that?'

Fleur was tossing scraps from our plates to Lancelot, her red setter, who was leaping to catch them, knocking against the table and making the knifes and forks rattle. She stopped at once.

'I like agreement,' said Dickie. 'It's pleasant and restful. I hate quarrelling.'

'Not agreeing with someone isn't the same as quarrelling.' Burgo leaned across the table to pour me a glass of red wine to accompany the camembert. 'Discussion – or argument if you like – is the proper way to get to the truth.'

'I don't know that I care about truth as much as all that.' Dickie cut himself a piece of camembert. 'I'd rather be comfortable and jolly any day. What do you say, Bobbie?'

I had the sensation – probably due to the heat and the wine and the pleasure of being in the garden – of having reached some plateau of happiness and the idea that if I remained exactly as I was and made no conscious mental effort in any direction I should be able to retain this for a while longer.

'I want . . . I want everything. Truth, beauty, comfort, jollity – I don't want to have to choose between things.'

'I agree.' Burgo took a fig and quartered it, exposing crimson flesh, crammed with pips. 'It's too perfect an evening to be serious about anything.'

Fleur began to laugh, though at what she would not say.

'I see now,' said Kit. 'It was the Garden of Eden. Ripeness and plenitude. Beauty and deceit. Fleur and Billy munching happily away at the fruits of the tree of knowledge without retribution. And slowly, steadily, resolutely the serpent was gliding towards you.'

'That makes it sound as though I couldn't help myself. I'm afraid that isn't true.'

'Well. We shall see. Go on.'

'I think I'll turn in.' Dickie groped for his stick and stood up. 'You'll forgive me, Bobbie, if I leave Burgo to do the honours. I was up at six watering the strawberries. Beddows always forgets.'

Moths dithered around the candles, repeatedly flopping down to the table as though scorched to death, only to revive minutes later to dash back into the flames. My head was spinning with the combination of wine and the scent of flowers and grass, intensified by night.

'I'll go home now,' I said as Dickie bent to kiss me. 'Thank you for a wonderful evening.'

'You can't go,' Fleur said to me. 'We're so happy. You'll spoil everything if you leave now. Remember that poem about the strawberries you used to tell me when I was little?' Fleur offered her cheek to Dickie but looked at Burgo. 'Something about a wood. Do say it again.'

'If I can remember it.

'The man in the wilderness asked of me,
How many strawberries grow in the sea?
I answered him as I thought good,
As many red herrings as grow in the wood.'

'What a relief!' said Fleur. 'It isn't meant to make sense. As a child I thought I must be stupid because I didn't understand it. There *are* some advantages to being grown up. I used to feel confused, like watching a film or a play in a foreign language. Now, though I don't often feel the same, I've some idea what the plot's supposed to be.'

'Ah, but then something extraordinary happens that turns logic on its head and again you're floundering.' Burgo's face was hidden in shadow. 'You think you know where you're going, what you want, what other people want of you. But then you read something, or see something, or meet someone who startles you out of your preconceptions and you're left bewildered.'

I got up. 'I really think I will go home.'

'We'll walk back to the house with you.' Burgo stood and began to put coffee cups and brandy glasses on to a tray.

Fleur put her hand on his sleeve. 'But you haven't seen inside the China House yet. He must, mustn't he, Bobbie?' She took a candlestick and went across the grass to the little pavilion. 'Look at the bells hanging from the roof.' Fleur tapped one so that it rang with a sweet shivering chime. 'Bobbie did drawings of them and Dickie got the blacksmith to make them. But come inside. That's the best bit, though it isn't finished yet.' She tried to open the door. 'Help me, will you? It still sticks a bit.'

Burgo applied pressure and opened it.

'See!' Fleur held the candlestick up high. 'There's the Chinese daybed. Bobbie designed it. Don't you love its little curly roof like an hysterical four-poster? It isn't finished yet. It's to have silk curtains and cushions embroidered with dragons. Someone Bobbie knows in

London's making them. It's costing a fortune but Dickie's adoring doing it—'

''Scuse me for butting in.' Billy's head and shoulders appeared round the door. 'Evening, all.' He nodded at me. 'Sorry to bother you, Mrs Sudborough, but Stargazer's leg is troubling him, like, and I was wondering if a bran poultice might do the trick.'

'I'll come at once.' Fleur was at the door in an instant. 'Bye, Bobbie.' She kissed me briefly. 'Burgo'll see you off. I'll ring.'

We were alone.

'We've had a lot of fun,' I said. 'Isn't the lantern a success?' I pointed to the wood and glass lamp in the shape of a pineapple. 'It's charming, isn't it?'

'Oh yes.' Burgo ignored the lantern.

'Don't you think Fleur's looking well?'

'Yes.'

'I'm so grateful to you for introducing me to them. I'm feeling enormously cheered up.'

'Good.' I thought I saw a suspicion of a smile.

'It must have been marvellous in Provence. I haven't been for ages. I once spent a month in a villa near St Rémy. We were students so we could barely afford to eat.'

'Really.'

'We had fish soup every day at a little café. I can still remember the taste of the *rouille* – you know, the hot peppery sauce that goes with it.'

'I know what *rouille* is.'

'Of course.' I felt a complete fool. A silence fell which I felt I must break at the cost of making more of an idiot of myself. 'Your wife must have been so pleased to have you to herself for a while.'

'We had people staying all the time.'

'Oh. Oh, how sad.'

'Why?'

'Well . . . because . . . I mean, you must miss each other and . . . and you know that saying about absence – La Rochefoucauld, wasn't it?' I laughed unnaturally. 'It usually is.'

'What did he say?'

'Oh, something about absence extinguishing little passions and increasing great ones, like the wind that blows out a candle but blows up a fire.' Another pause. 'So obviously, in your case, absence must be a good thing . . .' What on earth was I doing, talking about his marriage? It was an extraordinary impertinence.

110

'A good thing for us to live apart?'

'Yes . . . no . . . I don't know.'

I stared at him in hopeless confusion. He did nothing to help me. If he'd made the least attempt to flirt I could have made it quite clear that there was no possibility of anything between us. As it was, he was entirely cool and collected while I stammered and stuttered like a schoolgirl.

After a pause, Burgo said with a solemnity that might have concealed annoyance, or possibly amusement, 'It's kind of you to be concerned.'

'It's late. I'd better go home.'

'I'll see you to your car.'

'Don't bother, really. It'd be a bore for you. I can manage. Goodnight.'

In a moment I was through the door and the gap in the hedge and running along the path that led back to the house. Tricked by fitful beams of moonlight, I stumbled into flowerbeds, twisting my ankles and scratching myself on thorns and twigs. When I arrived, panting, within the area that was lit by the lamps each side of the garden door, I wondered what on earth I was doing, behaving like a child frightened by my own imagination. I walked round to the Wolseley, feeling indescribably foolish, and drove back to Cutham, thoroughly out of humour with myself.

The silent house welcomed me into its chill embrace with an exudation of floor-polish and damp. By the light of the dim bulb in the hall I saw there was a message by the telephone in Oliver's hand.

Jasmine rang. She says to call her the minute you get in no matter how late as she won't be able to sleep a wink until she has spoken to you. Is she as pretty as she is crazy?

111

TWELVE

'You mean he had you for a second time all to himself in that seductive little Chinese grot and he didn't make love to you? Or at least attempt it? Can he be flesh and blood?'

'Not every married man behaves like a fourth-former let out of school the minute he's alone with a girl not his wife.'

'That's just what you'd like to believe, my dear Bobbie. And now he's one of the powers in the land. It bodes ill for the country, that's all I can say.'

The telephone rang for a long time and I began to feel worried. Eventually someone lifted the receiver and I heard the sound of snuffling and rustling.

'Jasmine? Is that you? It's Bobbie.'

Several yawns and groans. 'What . . . Who . . . Oh, hello, darling. I was asleep . . .'

'I'm sorry. The message said to ring you at once. I'll telephone you in the morning.'

More yawning and sighing. 'No. Don't ring off. I'm dying to talk to you. Just let me gather my wits . . .' A long pause.

'Jazz? Are you still there?'

'Sorry. I'm awake now. You know how hopeless I am first thing in the morning.'

'Actually it's last thing at night. It's just after twelve.'

'No, really? Well, anyway, what the hell, it's all the same to me now. Teddy's left me!' She began to cry. I had a vision of tears shining in her coal-black eyes and spilling down her golden cheeks.

'Oh dear! Poor Jazz! I'm so sorry. You must feel wretched!'

'I'm going to kill myself. I just thought I'd say goodbye as you are my *very* best friend in all the world.'

'Thank you, but for God's sake don't do anything rash. Teddy isn't worth it. I understand how you feel but, believe me, this despair will pass.'

'You *don't* understand! You've never been agonizingly, sick-makingly in love with anyone ever, have you? You were a tiny bit fond of David and perhaps that Russian, whatever his name was, for a week or two, and that man with the Daimler Dart who had that collection of dreary old books.'

'Incunabula.'

'What?'

'That's what you call books that are pre fifteen hundred . . . Oh, never mind. I expect you're right. I've never been properly in love and I don't know what you're going through. But, dear Jazz, Teddy's made you so miserable so often. There are other men in the world. Nicer, more intelligent, more amusing men who aren't married. Better-looking men.'

'Teddy's the only man I'll *ever* love. No one else interests me in the slightest. I can't live without him. He only has to touch me and I feel faint with desire.'

I saw in my imagination Teddy's porcine eyes in which there was always a leer, heard his self-satisfied laugh, remembered his damp hands that found excuses to clutch at any girl young enough to be his daughter. The paunch and the shining scalp were perhaps just a question of taste.

'You think that now, but if you could only get through the first few miserable days you'd begin to see that he wasn't so perfect. Don't you think it's rather mean of him to treat the two women he's supposed to love, you and his wife, so badly and make you both so unhappy?'

'Lydia isn't unhappy a *bit*! She still doesn't know about me.'

'Hang on, I thought you'd insisted that he tell her. You said how much better you felt now the affair was out in the open.'

'Apparently he only said he'd told her to please me. He couldn't face telling her. That's why he's left me. Because he's afraid she won't let him see the children ever again. That's the sort of woman she is! She's bullied my poor darling Teddy, playing on his paternal feelings until he'd rather stay in a loveless, sexless marriage than desert his children. He's got *such* a strong sense of duty. It's one of the things I love about him.'

'Either that or he's a lying, two-timing bastard.'

This provoked such a wail of misery that I repented at once.

'It's a difficult situation for everyone,' I temporized. 'But remember that you're a beautiful, kind, funny, delightful girl whom any man would be lucky to have. They'll be falling over themselves to take you out once they know Teddy's off the scene and you won't have time to mourn the end of that particular affair.'

'What do you mean, funny?'

'Well, entertaining. You know, good to be with.'

'You mean I'm not brainy like you and Sarah.'

'No, not at all . . . I didn't . . .'

'Oh, don't worry. I know it's true. Sarah said her little brother's stick insect is more intelligent than I am.' Sarah could be extremely forthright. 'She says Teddy has the charisma of a senile skunk.' She wept again.

'Don't cry, Jazzy. Go back to bed and get some sleep. I'll ring you tomorrow to see how you are.'

'I shan't sleep a wink. Everything here reminds me of him.' I could not imagine why since Teddy rarely spent an evening at Paradise Row. I think he was conscious of Sarah's and my dislike of him. 'Bobbie darling, would your parents mind if I came to stay with you? I *long* to get away.'

'Oh. Well . . . it's a bit awkward with my mother being ill . . . and it's so horrible here I think it would only depress you even more. It depresses me.'

'You don't want me. Nobody wants me! I'm going to be alone for the rest of my life! I'm too boring and ugly and stupid . . .' The rest was drowned by sobs.

'All right, Jazzy, if you think it will make you feel better, of course you can come. I'd love to see you. But you mustn't mind if my father's bad-tempered. He's like that with everyone.'

'Of course I shan't mind. *My* father's not exactly a thrill on wheels. How many evening dresses should I bring, do you think? And do you have a pool? I've just bought the prettiest bikini . . .'

Before hanging up I advised her about sensible shoes, jerseys and mackintoshes and assured her that we would not be attending Cowes Week. In fact, I reflected as I climbed exhausted into bed, she would need nothing but jeans. The only social life I had enjoyed while living with my parents had been suspended, temporarily or permanently. I could not go to Ladyfield while there was any danger of meeting Burgo there. Jasmine's telephone call had been a timely reminder, if I had needed one, of the inadvisability of having anything to do with a married man. The greatest excitement I could offer Jasmine was a Viennese split at the Bib 'n' Tucker in Cutham High Street.

I thought a lot about Jazzy the following morning as I dawdled through the trivial round, the common task. Or was it the common round and trivial task? Anyway, I made soup and chicken liver pâté, scrubbed out the larder as Mrs Treadgold's back was playing her up again and she had a mysterious pain in her knees, and took out the rubbish, including a sackful of rejected paragraphs from the great work, *Sunlight and Cucumbers*. As I was returning from the dark little yard that housed the bins and coal I heard the telephone ring. It was Dickie.

'Bobbie, you've got to help me. If ever a man needed a friend it's now.' I could tell from his tone that the crisis was not of the life-and-death kind so I told him to hang on while I cradled the receiver under my chin and attempted to bandage with my handkerchief a finger dripping with blood. I had cut it on some broken glass in the dustbin.

'I will if I can,' I said cautiously when the flow had been stemmed.

'It's the Ladyfield Lawn Tennis Club's annual doubles thrash this afternoon. This year they're playing the Tideswell Parva team. It's a grim occasion but they've always had it here and I can't let them down. We've got a hard court *and* a grass court, you see, so what with the two courts at the village school just down the road and a grass court at the Rectory next door they can get through the whole tournament in one afternoon. I'd like to get rid of them both, really – the courts, that is – since neither Fleur nor I play. Ugly things with all that wire netting. If you've got children of course . . . Anyway, there's a certain obligation if you've got the only house of any size in the area to host these things. I'm sure you have the same problem.'

'Actually, when the vicar last asked us to have the fête my father said it was too much wear and tear on the grass. Luckily the vicar's never seen our balding, moss-ridden lawn. And the tennis court's got a forest of elders growing through the tarmac.'

'Really?' Good husbandry was second nature to Dickie and I could tell he was rather shocked. 'Well, the only thing that might operate in my favour is a spell of heavy rain but a cloudless day is forecast. Before the final match everyone converges on the top lawn for wine-cup and what's rather unattractively called a finger buffet. I feel obliged to join in as much as I can, which means consuming huge

115

amounts of sausage rolls and clapping like billy-o. Fleur always sneaks off and I don't blame her. But I feel that for both of us to duck out would look . . . well, snobbish, I suppose.'

'You want me to make a cake?'

'Heavens, no. There are ladies aplenty to provide scones and sausage rolls and whatnot.'

'You want me to come and be nice to people and hand the scones round?'

'Rather more than that, I'm afraid. The Ladyfield team is one short. I was wondering if you'd be angelic and stand in for the fellow who's most inconsiderately having a wisdom tooth out.'

'You want me to *play*?'

'We'd all be so grateful. The secretary's been scouring the countryside for a stand-in but so far no luck. I'd do it myself but with my leg . . . Somehow I feel in my bones you're a good player.'

'Never gamble so much as sixpence on those bones of yours. I'm extremely average and haven't played for at least two years.'

'Not to worry. They're all middle-aged to elderly, I promise you. Tennis clubs are rather *vieux jeu*, it seems. The young of Ladyfield prefer to go to the cinema or dance themselves into a stupor on amphetamines. I know for a fact that Dinwiddie – the man who's having his tooth extracted – is my senior by several years. It's just a bit of fun.'

'The only difficulty is that I've a friend coming to stay. I'm picking her up from the station at half past one. What time does the match start?'

'Two-thirty.'

'In that case I can just about make it, if you don't mind me bringing her.'

'Of course, of course! I'm so grateful. I always feel a responsibility to see that all goes well. Ridiculous, really, since I'm nothing to do with them. But somehow when it's in your garden . . .'

'Just don't expect too much, that's all.'

'You're a perfect angel, Bobbie dear.'

By the time I had dusted one of the spare bedrooms and made Jasmine's favourite pudding (profiteroles), my finger had swollen a little and was red. I just had time to puncture the choux buns to let the steam out and put them on a rack to cool before driving to the station to meet the train. Jazzy was not on it. The next train from London was not for another hour. I drove home, feeling a little anxious. There was a note by the telephone in Mrs Treadgold's writing. *Your friend rang to say she is not coming. She will ring you from the Isle of White. She says a million apology's for the change of plan.*

Before leaving for the station I had dug out my tennis racquet from the cupboard beneath the stairs and found that my old tennis skirt was grey from having been washed with someone else's socks. One of my gym shoes had a lace missing so I was obliged to tie it with a black one borrowed from Oliver. I dreaded the tournament but it was the least I could do for Dickie who had entertained me so frequently and lavishly. I had once been reserve in the school team and could usually get my second serve in. It was fortunate, I reflected heartlessly, that my opponents would be much older than me and handicapped by things like arthritis and spectacles.

Arriving at Ladyfield I was greeted on the drive by a man who must have been about sixty but whose calf muscles, below immaculate white shorts, bulged like grapefruits.

'You must be Miss Norton.' He shook my hand with an enthusiasm that made my cut finger throb. 'I'm Roderick Bender, your partner for the afternoon. We do appreciate you standing in at the last moment. Our captain was in considerable pain or he'd never have let us down like this. I know he'll be fed up at having to miss an opportunity to give the Tideswell Tigers a walloping. They've never beaten us yet.'

I smiled politely. 'I'm afraid I shall be a poor substitute. I'm rather rusty.'

'False modesty, I'm sure. Of course, no one's expecting you to be up to Dinwiddie's standard. He once played at Wimbledon, you know.' Before I could mutter some excuse, get back into my car and drive rapidly away, he gripped my elbow with fingers of steel and steered me across the lawn in the direction of the courts. 'Luckily, we've some time in hand before the others get here. We'll knock up together and see what sort of game you play before we decide on our strategy.'

'I don't think my game's sufficiently consistent to deserve a strategy.'

'Come, come! No defeatist talk, now, Miss Norton. Attitude's extremely important. We've got to put winning into the forefront of our brains and keep it there. Attack's the name of the game. Think slam, think smash, think victory!'

'Do call me Bobbie.'

'All right. And you can call me Roddy. Here we are. We've drawn hard. Less finesse required than on grass but it's an opportunity to display a bit of vim. It'll suit your game, I hope?'

I was about to say that as far as my game went the surface was immaterial but thought better of it. There was no point in rushing to embrace disaster. Roddy made minute adjustments to the net while I changed into gym shoes. There was a delay while I struggled with the zip of my racquet cover, which had become corroded by the damp endemic to Cutham. After a minute or two Roddy left the net and came to help. He wrestled with the obstinate zip for some time before saying, rather pink in the face, 'Dear me, this isn't a good beginning, is it?'

I humbly agreed that it wasn't.

'I'll go and see if any of the ladies have a spare you can borrow.' There was perceptible annoyance in the tilt of Roddy's head as he strode back to the house.

People in tennis whites began to drift in small groups across the lawn. I was delighted to see that no one was a day under sixty.

'Yoo-hoo!' hallooed a solidly built woman with fluffy grey curls as soon as she was in earshot. 'Lovely day, isn't it?'

I looked up obediently. I was disappointed to see that there was not a raincloud in sight. 'Lovely.'

'I'm Peggy Mountfichet. You must be a new member.'

'I'm Bobbie Norton. I'm just standing in for Mr Dinwiddie. He's gone to have a tooth out.'

'Three cheers!' chortled Mrs Mountfichet, hurling up her racquet and failing to catch it. 'Listen, folks,' she carolled to her team mates. 'Old Dinwidders isn't playing today.' She walked on to the court and flung off her cardigan, exposing sagging, liver-spotted arms from which I meanly took comfort. 'Don't think me unkind, dear, of course I'm sorry for anyone going to the dentist, but he takes it all so damned seriously you'd think we were playing for Great Britain instead of for the fun of it. This is Adrian Lightowler.' She indicated the stooped old man behind her who seemed to be having difficulty in opening a box of new balls.

'How do you do?' I watched Mr Lightowler's attempts to prise off the cellophane with palsied fingers, feeling further encouraged.

'You'll have to speak up, he's terribly deaf. Nearly eighty, you know. Wonderful for his age. How extraordinary!' Mrs Mountfichet looked about her. 'Where's Roddy Bender? In all the years I've played for Tideswell he's always been first on the court. Makes a point of it so he can pretend we've kept him waiting, the old so-and-so! Typical of men, dear, really, isn't it?' she added to me conversationally as she exchanged her Clark's Skips for a pair of plimsolls. 'Such babies, hating to lose. I've made fifty meringues, two dozen sausage rolls and a lemon mousse this morning besides turning out the airing cupboard and walking the dog. I bet Roddy's done nothing but blanco his shoes.'

'I'm afraid it's my fault he isn't here.' I confessed to the ignominious circumstances that had made Roddy break the habit of a lifetime.

'Don't you worry, dear. It's sweet of you to give up your valuable time to play with a lot of old crocks like us. Take my tip and be sure to get to the tea table early on. The meringues go in a winking. And don't, whatever you do, have any wine-cup until after the match. Mr Lowe-Budding makes it from lemonade and pomagne but Dickie always adds a bottle of brandy when he thinks no one's looking. He likes to jolly us up, you see; stop the men taking it so seriously. It's quite lethal. After one glass you won't be able to hit a thing.'

'Thanks for the warning.' I was really beginning to like this game old lady.

When Roddy reappeared he looked quite angry to find Mrs Mountfichet and Mr Lightowler already on the court, patting a ball gently back and forth to each other.

'Hello, Roddy,' she called. 'Who's a lucky boy then? You'll be the envy of the other men with such a beautiful partner.'

Roddy forbore to answer. 'This ought to be about the right weight.' He handed me a newish-looking racquet. 'Don't know about the grip, though.' It seemed to have been made for a gorilla's paw. I could hardly close my fingers round the handle. 'Never mind,' continued Roddy. 'You'll have to make the best of it. There isn't time to find another.'

'Hello, Bobbie my dear.' Dickie limped over to the umpire's chair. He looked smart in blazer and flannels and was carrying an official-looking clipboard. 'Lovely to see you. Let's make a start. The others have already begun their matches.'

'My partner and I haven't had a chance to warm up yet,' protested Roddy.

'Come on, you old fusspot!' said Mrs Mountfichet. 'You toss and I'll call.'

Mrs Mountfichet won the toss, to Roddy's evident displeasure.

'You'd better get up to the net as soon as you can,' he muttered to me. 'I'll stay back.'

I prepared myself to receive Mrs Mountfichet's serve. I repressed a smile as I saw Roddy bent double with a fiendish grin on his face, hopping from foot to foot, the silly old— Whang! The ball left Mrs Mountfichet's racquet at something near the speed of light and raised a cloud of chalk as it bounced on the line to thwack into the netting behind my head. I had not had time to lift my racquet.

'Sorry, dear,' she called. 'I don't think you were quite ready. We'll play that point again.'

'Good idea,' said Dickie breezily. 'All right, everyone? Play!'

This time I had my racquet lifted and my eye on the ball. It struck my racquet and knocked it clean from my hand, hurting my cut finger considerably.

'Sorry!' Mrs Mountfichet looked concerned. 'Do you want to play that point one more time?'

'For heaven's sake, let's get on,' snapped Roddy.

'Fifteen, love,' called Dickie.

Mrs Mountfichet changed sides and served to Roddy. He smacked it smartly back over the net and a pounding rally began during which he and Mrs Mountfichet whirled like dervishes and Mr Lightowler, standing at the net, volleyed like a champion without moving below the waist. The rally ended when I managed to hit the ball properly for the first time, unfortunately straight into the net.

'Thirty, love,' called Dickie with a suggestion of sympathy in his voice.

'Watch out for the top-spin Mountfichet always puts on her serve,' growled Roddy to me as I bent and grimaced into the sun.

I had no idea what to do about top-spin even if I recognized it. The ball skimmed the net by a millimetre and bounced short. I gave it a wallop. Somehow it came into contact with the wood and shot off sideways.

'Forty, love.' Dickie's voice was so sympathetic he sounded on the point of bursting into tears.

Mrs Mountfichet served to Roddy. He returned it with a punishing backhand, slicing it across court at a impossible angle, but Mr Lightowler stretched forth a sinewy arm and just popped it over the net.

'Yours!' bawled Roddy.

I rushed forward and in my enthusiasm scooped up a spoon's

worth of fine gravel, flinging it straight into Mr Lightowler's rheumy old eyes.

'Game,' Dickie almost whispered as we all converged to offer handkerchiefs.

Mrs Mountfichet fished and poked and prodded about in Mr Lightowler's eyes with ruthless efficiency until his sight was more or less restored. After that, every time I caught sight of his scarlet eyeballs blinking at me over the net, I felt a stab of guilt. None the less he managed to return every shot that came his way with tactical brilliance.

We had gathered quite a crowd of spectators now, who applauded almost every point and maintained a polite silence whenever I bungled a return. Roddy contrived to hang on to his serve by spinning about the court as though under attack from bees, intercepting any ball that was directed towards me. I was vastly encouraged when I managed to return one of Mr Lightowler's rather feeble serves, sending it down the line between our opponents. There was a storm of applause quite out of proportion to the skill of the shot. I felt bucked to discover that I had the sympathy of the crowd.

That, as it turned out, was my only moment of glory, but I did manage after that to whack the ball back over the net a few times only to see it driven practically through the tarmac by Mrs Mountfichet or directed cleverly just out of my reach by Mr Lightowler. They won the first set 6–2, owing to me losing both my service games.

'I'm terribly sorry,' I said to Roddy as we changed ends. 'I hadn't realized you were all so good or I'd never have agreed to play.'

'It's too late to think of that now,' said Roddy, rather ungraciously I thought. 'It'll be better if you stay back. Try to get the baseline shots and I'll cover the rest of the court.'

We got on better with this method and actually got to thirty all during my service game. Mr Lightowler sent up a high lob. Skipping energetically backwards to be sure of getting it, I slipped on the loose gravel and fell hard, grazing my elbow. The ball bounced two inches inside the baseline and, to add injury to insult, struck me on the chest. There was a murmur of concern from the spectators and a burst of laughter from several of the children so I could be certain I had looked a complete fool. Roddy bared his teeth at me.

I was tempted to throw down my racquet and walk off in a huff but a glance at Dickie's anxious face restored me to my senses.

'I'm absolutely fine,' I said in answer to his enquiry. 'Not a bit hurt.'

'Thirty, forty,' he murmured kindly.

My elbow was now throbbing every bit as painfully as my finger. I had a moment of mild success when I returned one of Peggy's ballistic backhand passes, though the impact jarred my arm from my wrist to my shoulder. I was running forward with a renewal of confidence to tackle what looked to be a fairly easy drop volley when Roddy yelled, 'Mine!' but just too late. My outflung racquet collided with his prow of a nose. He gave a howl of pain as the ball flew unhindered into the tramlines.

'Game.'

'I'm awfully sorry,' I said.

There was another flourishing of handkerchiefs. Poor Roddy's nose splashed his snow-white shirt with scarlet and the concerted mopping seemed to make it worse. A key was requested from the crowd and put down Roddy's shirt but did no good.

'Pinch his nostrils,' suggested Dickie.

'Ow-*how*!' protested Roddy as Mrs Mountfichet almost twisted his nose off his face.

After ten minutes of copious bloodshed it was agreed that he should go and lie down with an ice-pack.

'I'm so terribly sorry . . .' I began but Roddy was stalking away holding a towel to his face and affected not to hear me.

'That's put a spanner in the works,' said Mrs Mountfichet.

I hung my head.

'Damn shame,' said Mr Lightowler. 'I was just warming up.'

Dickie turned to address the audience. 'Perhaps someone would be good enough to stand in for Mr Bender. Just for a few games until the bleeding stops.'

'Good idea!' seconded Mrs Mountfichet. 'Come on, somebody,' she urged the watching crowd. 'Be a sport! It's only a bit of fun.'

The spectators blenched and shook their heads.

'I will,' said a voice from the crowd.

I experienced a frisson of horror as Burgo stepped on to the court. He was wearing white duck trousers, a red shirt that had faded to pink and his ancient espadrilles. On his face was an expression of great good humour. He had told me that he had meetings all day. Had I not been absolutely sure that he would be in London I would never have agreed to come to Ladyfield. I wondered how much he had witnessed of the exhibition I had made of myself. He must have seen me flat on my back in the dust.

'A round of applause, ladies and gentlemen, for our Member of Parliament, Mr Burgo Latimer,' said Dickie.

The crowd clapped and whistled, delighted that their entertainment was not to be cut short. I debated whether to faint or run away. Burgo was going to leap athletically round the court like a knight errant, demolishing the opposition, saving the day and completing my humiliation. Little did he know, I thought with savage satisfaction, that there was nothing I disliked so much as a show-off.

'Hello,' he said pleasantly as he strolled over to me, twirling Roddy's discarded racquet with a careless assurance. 'You seemed to be having such a good time that I couldn't resist the call to arms.'

'I suppose you're going to make mincemeat of all of us.'

'Hardly that. I haven't played for at least ten years. I can barely remember the rules. But it seems a pity for the match to fizzle out.'

I smiled coolly. At least it was an opportunity to impress the voters so his time would not be entirely wasted.

'Play!' called Dickie.

Mr Lightowler flipped a gentle serve over the net. Burgo hit it so far into the air that we all peered for what seemed like minutes into the sky until our eyes watered.

'I think it's gone into orbit,' giggled Mrs Mountfichet.

'Ouch!' Dickie rubbed his skull. 'Fifteen, love.'

Mr Lightowler served again. I slammed it back. It came flying over the net and Burgo took a swipe at it, missed, pirouetted on the spot, ran backwards, picked it up on the rim of his racquet and hurled it over the wire netting where it fell into the cheering crowd.

'Thirty, love.'

'Sorry,' Burgo said easily. 'I did warn you.'

After that I managed to place a few unremarkable shots and Burgo got in a spectacularly good return by what was clearly a fluke. He had a way of running up to the ball, seeming to hesitate and then either rescuing the point with extraordinary brilliance or losing it with such spectacular ineptitude that I became suspicious. Whether he hit it in or out the spectators began to enjoy themselves so much that they reached a state in which they found everything funny. The prevailing good humour was irresistible. Soon I was giggling helplessly. Mrs Mountfichet and Mr Lightowler made stern attempts to control themselves but that only made us laugh more. In the end they stopped playing seriously themselves, to the detraction of their game.

The match ran swiftly on to a final score of 6–2, 6–1, 6–3. The crowd revelled in it. That a Member of Parliament, an important man in the county, whose name was frequently in the newspapers, was prepared to make a cake of himself to save their tennis party was a marvellous thing and they loved him for it. When he came off the court they would willingly have carried him shoulder-high through the streets, had it been at all convenient.

The players and spectators converged on the tea table with enthusiasm to devour sandwiches, sausage rolls, cream horns, brandy snaps, meringues, plum cake, gingerbread and eclairs. I found I was extremely thirsty. The tea, stewing in a giant aluminium pot, was brown and bitter. I was no longer required as a player so I had a glass of wine-cup. Though it was the colour of marsh water with a flotsam of rapidly bruising fruit, it was refreshing, so I had a second. I felt suddenly light-headed and a little dizzy and resolved that it should be my last. Roddy Bender, his nose swollen and purple like an exotic fruit, loomed into view. By mutual consent we pretended not to have seen each other.

'I've saved you one of my specials.' Mrs Mountfichet handed me a plate on which two meringue halves were held together by cream and raspberries. 'You were a thoroughly good sport, dear. You mustn't worry about Roddy. Do him good to have his nose put out of joint.' She laughed heartily at her own joke. 'He's so competitive. Mr Latimer was a breath of fresh air.'

I looked across the lawn to where Burgo stood, surrounded by adoring women who were insisting he try their own particular contribution to the banquet. I saw he was charming them like birds to his hand. He looked both handsome and intelligent, a rare combination. His pale hair, slightly disordered after the game, and dégagé appearance contributed to a panache that made him extremely attractive. He seemed to have a sort of glow about him that had nothing to do with sunburn. It was the magnetism of complete self-assurance. I tore my thoughts away with difficulty and fastened them on what Mrs Mountfichet was telling me about her *Clematis viticella* 'Purpurea plena elegans'.

'Pruning group three, dear. Savage it in February. It's the only way to stop it flowering in a horrid tangle at the top.'

'I'll be certain to do that.'

'I doubt it, dear. You haven't heard a word I've been saying, have you?' She leaned closer and said, almost in my ear, 'He's very good-looking. If I were twenty years younger I think I'd be ready to throw my cap over the windmill. And Mr Mountfichet after it. But no doubt I'd be sorry later. A man with two women eager to tend to his needs is rather too comfortably circumstanced for his own good. Certainly for anyone else's.'

'Have some wine-cup, Mrs Mountfichet?' Burgo was beside us, holding a jug. 'Not exactly the milk of paradise but it has quite a kick.' He filled my glass despite my murmurs of protest.

Mrs Mountfichet shook her curls. 'Not for me, thanks. I've got to play again, thanks to you. You can crown the occasion by drawing the raffle if you'd be so kind. I'll just go and check that they've sold all the tickets.' She marched off.

'You've made a hit,' I said. 'I don't suppose that was all put on, was it? Being hopeless at tennis, I mean.'

Burgo looked injured. 'What do you mean, hopeless? I thought I played rather better than usual.'

'Remember, a liar needs a good memory.'

'You've got cream on your chin.'

I had to have recourse to the back of my hand, my handkerchief having been saturated with Roddy's blood.

'It's all over your cheek now,' said Burgo. 'Here, let me.'

He took a spotted bandanna from his pocket and dabbed at my chin with it. Something extraordinary happened to my knees. A second that seemed like an age passed before I looked down at my glass and drank its contents in three swallows.

Mrs Mountfichet was back. 'Come with me, Mr Latimer, and we'll do the draw now. Perhaps a little speech?'

While Burgo was encircled by the crowd I wandered about its perimeter and had another glass of wine-cup. How they lapped up his words and laughed at his jokes! I tried to listen to what he was saying but my mind fragmented, soared and swooped uncontrollably. The sun had ceased to scorch but gusts of heat rose from the parched turf and Dickie's beloved roses hung their heads, longing for the cool of evening.

'Hello, Bobbie.' It was Dickie. 'You look very happy.'

'Do I? So do you.' I wondered why I was laughing. 'What did you put in the wine-cup? I'm pretty sure if I flapped my arms hard enough I could fly.'

'I put in an extra bottle of cognac while you were coming off the courts. It's a relief that it's all gone so well. I feel I owe it to the old place to try to make these things a success. Don't know why I should care but I do.'

'Let me give you a hand with those.'

Dickie handed me the bag of old balls. 'Thanks. We always change them before the final match though there's nothing wrong with them. They're not heavy but a bit awkward with this damned leg. I thought I'd put them behind the screen in the China House for the time being. Really, I want an excuse to look at the ferns. I've been too busy getting the garden ready for the tennis to check they've been properly watered.'

We turned off along the path that led to the Chinese garden. Regal lilies with white, waxy throats and garnet streaks on the backs of their petals leaned over the rosemary hedge. Their powerful exhalations were like a drug, setting one's mind free to dream. Tortoiseshell butterflies fluttered like twists of coloured paper among the frothy stands of *Verbena bonariensis*.

The ferns were taking root and beginning to put out new fronds. The interior of the China House seemed velvety dark to our dilating pupils. I leaned against a bedpost while Dickie stowed the balls out of sight.

'The silk for the bed came this morning,' said Dickie. 'I'll pop back to the house and fetch it, shall I, so we can get an idea of how it's going to look?'

'Lovely,' I said, marvelling at the myriad emerald flecks that buzzed round the room everywhere I rested my eyes. When I closed them they were still there, swirling like clouds of gnats.

'I may be five minutes or so. I want to check that everyone's got what they need.'

'No hurry.'

After Dickie had gone I sat on the Chinese bed. The old counterpane that was its temporary covering was deliciously cool and soft. I removed my shoes and stretched out full length. The room revolved in time to the strange music inside my head, a combination of buzzing bees, singing birds and the pulse of my own blood. I heard Dickie come back. Felt the bed sink beneath his weight, felt his arm slide beneath my head that was as weak as a snapped stalk. Heard him say, 'My love, my love. Don't resist me any longer. This had to be.'

It was not Dickie. I knew this by a violent quiver of joy that ran from my burning forehead to my naked feet.

'Of course,' I murmured. 'But I . . . so terribly . . . didn't . . . want . . .'

'It's too late for regret. It always was.'

He was right. I had been a hypocrite, paying lip-service to propriety, trying to cheat myself into believing that my own sense of probity

126

could conquer selfish desire. From the moment we had stood in that hideous room at the Carlton House Hotel sharing a dish of stale peanuts I had known that it was only a matter of time before I became Burgo's lover. I gave myself up to the inevitable.

THIRTEEN

'Do look at those sheep.' I peered through slashing rain at bundles of grey and white wool crouching down beside rocks. 'They've got the most magnificent curling horns.'

'Remember what it says in the Bible about dividing the nations, the worthy from the unworthy? You'll never make a shepherdess if you can't tell sheep from goats.'

'You mean there are wild goats here? How romantic! We might be in Ancient Greece. Apart from the weather.'

'Those are the Maumturk Mountains.' Kit pointed to our left. 'And beyond them in the distance a group called the Twelve Bens.'

All around us were sombre mountains, water running down them in rills. At their feet the ground fell to the road in tracts of undulating green dotted with rocks and clumps of spiky grass.

'That's cotton grass,' said Kit. 'It means the ground's boggy. Thousands of years ago prehistoric man lived by slashing and burning the woodland that covered these parts. Eventually a layer of carbon formed that stopped the land from draining and thus the bog was created. When the woodland was all destroyed, the people who lived here could only get wood by digging up ancient trees from beneath the peat layers. Hence bog oak. A useful lesson for today.'

'I've seen furniture made from black bog oak but I'd no idea how it was formed.'

'So, during the game of tennis that so effectively demolished your defences, what was it, exactly, that you suspected? Are you unique among girls, do you think, in finding incompetence more disarming than proficiency?'

'I thought you were the expert on female psychology.'

'What was troubling you? Besides a sense of what you persist in seeing as impending moral collapse on your own part?'

'Don't you ever forget anything?'

'Not when it's a story.' Kit slowed to let a ewe and her lamb, their underbellies brown with mud, cross the road. 'Agents have to carry details in their heads. They're the long stop for major authorial blunders.'

'All right. Something made me think that he might be losing the game on purpose; that he was a much better player than he'd pretended. Then, in the excitement that followed, I didn't think anything more about it. But weeks later the suspicion resurfaced when I was returning some gumboots I'd borrowed to the downstairs cloakroom at Ladyfield. The walls are hung with old school photographs, mostly of Dickie at Harrow: the usual rows of blazered, boatered boys, plus photographs of Dickie in the First Eleven and the Second Fifteen. I'd never bothered to look at them properly but something must have registered subliminally because I spotted at once a photograph of Westminster School's Senior Tennis Team and guess who was sitting in the middle of the front row holding a large silver cup?' I waited politely for Kit to finish laughing before adding, 'Given that Burgo may not have played for a long time, is it possible for anyone's game to deteriorate so drastically?'

'I shouldn't think so. You either have good hand–eye co-ordination or not. Besides, Burgo had been keeping his athletic prowess honed playing polo, hadn't he?'

'My goodness, I hope your authors deserve you.'

'Did you take him properly to task?'

'No. I tried to forget about it. I suppose I didn't want to discover anything that made me trust him less. I wanted so badly to see him as perfect . . . and perfectly irresistible. In order to justify what we were doing I had to make myself believe he was the love of my life. And that I was of his.'

'And despite everything you still believe that.'

I did not answer. I was no longer capable of interpreting my own feelings.

'We've only ten miles to go until Kilmuree,' said Kit. 'Just tell me a little about the good times and I'll pretend the tale's been nicely rounded off. A sort of happy ever after that fades into oblivion. That's what we all want from a story. Physical consummation isn't enough. It wouldn't be enough for Elizabeth Bennet and Mr Darcy to climb between the sheets and indulge in erotic acts before going their separate ways. Or for Mr Rochester to take Jane Eyre through the *Kama Sutra*. The climax of a narrative is actually the moment when two people reveal themselves to each other by declaring a deeply felt, highly significant attachment.'

'It's strange that we get such vicarious pleasure from imagining other, wholly fictitious people falling in love. Is it just because we identify with one of them?'

'I don't see myself as Burgo Latimer. A public man, an orator, a manipulator of minds. Sorry if that sounds slanderous. Of course I'm jealous. In my mind he's as fantastical a being as the Minotaur. He's made you unhappy and left you to defend yourself.'

'I quite agree with you about happy endings. We want to leave them suspended in blissful communion. We don't want to be told afterwards how Jane and Mr Rochester remodelled Thornfield Hall in the style of William Burges. Or that Lady Catherine de Bourgh was catty about Elizabeth's taste in bedding begonias.'

'And I also want to know what happened to the lovely, feckless Jasmine. I realize her relationship with Teddy is a leitmotif of text-book adultery that runs parallel with your own love affair. Your audience is eager in anticipation.'

After Burgo and I became lovers, after those ten, perhaps fifteen minutes of intense physical pleasure, we lay in each other's arms waiting for our hearts to slow and for our minds to begin working.

Then I said, 'Dickie's coming back any minute.'

'I asked him to ring Simon for me, to tell him to bring the car round in half an hour. But he must have done that by now.' There was a brief silence, during which I tried to calm my breathing and focus my eyes. Burgo said, 'I'd better go.'

'Yes.'

'I'll always remember the way you look now.' He kissed me. 'All my life.'

We pulled our clothes on quickly, not speaking. I was terribly afraid now that someone would catch us in a state of undress, though only minutes before I would not have cared if the combined teams of the Ladyfield Lawn Tennis Club and the Tideswell Tigers had crowded into the China House to cheer us on.

'Goodbye, Roberta.' Burgo lifted my hand to kiss it.

'Goodbye.'

I watched him walk to the door and cross the little garden. I tried to tidy myself and the daybed. He must have met Dickie on the way.

I did my best to enthuse about the new silk for the daybed to please Dickie but I don't suppose I made much sense. I was trying to decide exactly what had happened, how it had happened and what the consequences would be. And I could not suppress a thrill of happiness. I wanted to grin with pleasure. Walking back through the garden I had forborne, with difficulty, to skip.

Dickie had politely pretended not to notice anything but had taken me into the cool, deserted drawing room and asked if I wouldn't like a little rest after my heroic performance on court. Through the window I could see the back of Burgo's head above the group that thronged about him on the lawn. When I insisted that I had to get back to Cutham Dickie had made me drink several cups of strong black coffee before conducting me to my car. Tipsy septuagenarians were packing their cars with tennis equipment and driving unsteadily away with two wheels in Dickie's penstemon border. I was astonished that the world managed to go on in its ordinary insipid way.

I had flown through the countryside on a super-powered cloud, survived dinner somehow, washed up and gone upstairs at the first possible moment so that I could be alone. Naturally after drinking so much coffee I had lain awake for hours, reliving the excitement of being in Burgo's arms, the protesting voices of sanity and prudence drowned by the singing of my effervescing blood.

The following day the weather conspired with a serious hangover to rub something of the bloom from my joy. Continuous drizzle cast a depressing grey light through all the rooms. The walls and floors seemed to sweat with damp. What was there, exactly, to be joyful about? I had had too much to drink and had made love in Dickie's garden with his brother-in-law, a man I hardly knew and might never see again. Perhaps Burgo took it for granted that he would bed a provincial voter or two whenever he ventured out of the capital. Probably these fleeting intimacies were the perks of a politician's life, a compensation for having to be charming to old ladies and committee bores. It could hardly matter that I always voted Labour.

He might tell his secretary to send the usual *douceur* of an expensive bunch of flowers, and she would know that he had once again been successful. She would be either indifferent to his behaviour or disapproving of it, but she would certainly despise me. Perhaps, the next time they were alone, Burgo would boast of his conquest to Dickie who, being a tolerant man, would smile and shake his head and mentally adjust his view of me, to my detriment. By the time Jazzy telephoned me from the Isle of Wight late the same afternoon, my mood had sunk from euphoria to bitter reproach, mostly directed towards myself.

'Bobbie? I've been dying to talk to you! You're the only person I can tell . . .' Jazzy's voice was tremulous. I pictured her face twisted with misery. 'You'll never guess . . . the most glorious thing.' My mental picture changed – with difficulty. It had been months since she had been anything like happy. 'He's left her!'

I did not need to ask who he and her were. I had once glimpsed Teddy Bayliss's wife, Lydia, at a party. She had hard eyes and a chin you could have struck a match on. Jazzy and I had invented a character for her so bad that between suffocating babies and experimenting on animals she would have had no time for Teddy's sexual requirements or his dry-cleaning.

'When? How? What's happened?'

'He says he's not going to be dictated to by anyone. She said he had to spend more time at home with her and the children. He says the children do nothing but squabble and leave wet towels on the bathroom floor. And they play pop music and have scruffy monosyllabic friends. She's a terrible cook and is always giving him takeaways. And she refuses to take his shirts to the laundry.' We were almost right then, about some things. 'And he hates her mother.'

'Jazzy— Of course I'm not defending her, but surely there must be something more than that? I mean, isn't that just family life? It doesn't sound quite enough to justify ending a marriage.'

'I thought you'd be the *one* person who'd understand.' Jazzy sounded hurt. 'I know you're terribly anti having affairs with married men but I thought you said you'd always be on my side, whatever.'

'Oh, I am. I am! But, Jazz, you have to be so sure that you and Teddy will be happy together.'

'We *will* be. Teddy says that no one in his whole life has understood him as I do. He says it's uncanny how alike we are, how we feel the same about everything that's important, how we can communicate without words. Honestly, it's true. Don't you remember, it all began when we met at that ghastly ball and discovered we both hated Latin-American music but loved Gershwin. And then we found that our favourite film was *Breakfast at Tiffany's* and our favourite place to stay was Raffles Hotel. Then we went on talking practically the whole evening, agreeing about absolutely everything. It was amazing.'

Poor darling Jazzy. So beautiful and so trusting. When I had once suggested that Teddy had simply had his eye on getting her into bed she had been wounded by my misanthropy.

'Well, if you're quite sure . . .'

'I'm utterly, totally, completely sure. As sure as anyone in the history of the world has ever been about anything. It's a synthingummy of minds and souls. And he says that making love to me is like eating pâté de foie gras to the sound of trumpets. Isn't that brilliant?'

'Perhaps it was when Sydney Smith said it.'

'Sydney who?

'Smith. A nineteenth-century cleric. He was describing heaven.'

'Oh.' A pause. 'Of course Teddy's so well read.' It would have been unkind to say that the metaphor was so well known that it had become almost hackneyed. Jazzy had been to dozens of expensive schools all over the world and learned little in any of them. 'And he says making love to Lydia is like waving an arm in a barn.'

I was repelled. 'If you give a woman four children you can hardly complain if there's some falling off from physical perfection.'

'No. I agree. It *was* naughty of him. I've decided I'm not going to say mean things about her any more or even *think* them if I can help. I'm desperately sorry for her, actually, and I feel quite haunted by the idea that at this moment she's going about her life unaware of the sword of Damo-what's-it that's about to fall. And the children . . . when I think of them . . .' For a moment the excitement went out of Jazzy's voice.

'What do you mean, "unaware"?'

'Teddy decided the best thing would be to avoid a confrontation when things might be said that couldn't be taken back. You know, to allow her to save face. He's doing his best to make it as easy for her as possible, which I agree with, one hundred per cent. I couldn't love him if he wasn't a *good* person. He's madly considerate of her feelings.'

'Oh, *mad*ly,' I said, with a sarcasm I instantly regretted. 'Of course it's a dreadful situation for everyone.'

'*Dread*ful. So he's left her a note. She's been away all week with the children visiting her mother. That was what prompted the row about him not doing enough with the family. But his mother-in-law is a complete bitch and is foul to Teddy. Lydia's getting back tomorrow.'

I imagined her arriving home exhausted after a long journey with squabbling children, planning what she would give them for supper, anticipating a hot bath and a glass of wine for herself after putting a load of dirty clothes into the washing machine. Pausing by the hall table to take Teddy's letter from the pile that would have accumulated during a week's absence. She would open it, expecting a reminder that the man was coming to service the boiler, only to discover that she was now a single parent and had become solely responsible for household maintenance.

'It's such *heaven* being alone with him,' sighed Jasmine. 'Knowing we don't have to hurry into bed to make the most of a few measly hours. I feel as though I've been given pure oxygen to breathe. I'm in love with the world and with everything in it: the island, the village, the spaghetti bolognese we had for lunch. It isn't a very good hotel but Teddy says we must economize now he's got two women to support and naturally I don't mind a bit. I'm even in love with the rather nasty cow-pat-green pillow-cases on the bed because we're together at last and can lu*xur*iate in each other.'

'It's marvellous to hear you so happy. How long do you expect to stay?'

'Oh, it's rather open-ended. Teddy's taken the whole week off. I never want to see London again. I wish we could hire a gypsy caravan and let the horse take us wherever it wanted to.'

'Mm, that does sound fun. But one of you'd need to know something about horses. Feeding, tacking up, grooming . . .'

'Oh, Bobbie, how typical of you to think of depressing, practical things.'

'Sorry. So what happens now? When she's finished snipping their wedding album into confetti and making a bonfire of his golf-clubs, what does she do next?'

'Teddy's going to ring her tomorrow to find out how she's taken it. I'm glad he's so thoughtful. It's one of the things I love about him.'

A quip about Teddy's extraordinary solicitude in abandoning his wife and children to abscond with a girl half his age darted into my mind but I suppressed it. 'I hope it goes all right,' I said. 'And that he deserves you.'

'I'm certainly going to do my best to deserve *him*. When I think of everything he's given up for me, it's really humbling. I've got to try and make it up to him somehow. I mean, sex isn't everything, is it?'

'Not for you, perhaps,' I said cautiously. 'I do think that for some men—'

'Oh, darling Bobbie, you're always so cynical. I *wish* Teddy had an identical twin so you could know what it was like to be adored by someone truly wonderful.' I remembered Teddy's pasty face and

134

crooked teeth in his rat-like mouth and felt nauseated. 'If I could I'd share him with you,' Jazzy went on. 'You've been the most marvellous friend to me through all the bad times and I'm so grateful.' I immediately felt guilty. 'Are things still awful at home? How's your mother?'

'Everything's the same except I've met some people who live nearby who've become good friends and I don't mind being here nearly so much.'

'Not a nice, handsome, eligible man with a vast bank balance?'

'No.'

'Ah well, darling. It'll happen one day. I'd better go and see what's happened to Teddy. I want our first night together as a proper couple to be sublime. I left him having a drink in the bar. The poor sweetie's had so much to worry him recently, he sometimes doesn't know quite when to stop.' This was the first time Teddy's obvious drink problem had been openly referred to by Jazzy. 'I'll ring you very soon. Try to be happy, dearest Bobbie.'

'You too.'

'Oh, I shall be in paradise, never fear.'

Five minutes after Jazzy had hung up the telephone rang again. It was Sarah, my other ex-housemate.

'Bobbie! Have you heard about Jazzy? She's gone off with that swine Bayliss. I tremble for her. A pig of pigs. An emperor of hogs.' Sarah was a bolder, more forthright person than I. She had been so outspoken about her dislike of Teddy that she and Jazzy had had a serious falling out from which their relationship had never quite recovered.

'She called me from the Isle of Wight just now.'

'How is the poor deluded girl?'

'Still deluded. But deliriously happy.'

'Silly fool!'

'I'm afraid so. But I keep hoping against hope that perhaps the benign influence of Jazzy will make Teddy a little less repulsive.'

'No chance. The man would have to have a complete personality refit to be tolerable. When I think of the tears she's shed over that worm, the crises, the sleepless nights, the chronic headaches and colds, the times she couldn't eat . . . She's like a walking bundle of sticks. God preserve us from married men.'

'Indeed,' I said. 'But even if he were single I don't think I'd like him.'

'He's an ignorant, talentless, priapic little runt.' Sarah was clever

135

and found most people irritatingly slow and feeble-minded but I knew she was genuinely fond of Jazzy. 'But being married gives a man an excuse to behave badly with a convenient let-out clause. He can be as selfish as he likes and blame family commitments. A single man can hardly rush round at midnight, poke you senseless, then bugger off without so much as a snack at the local caff or a decent conversation. I mean, when did Stinker Bayliss last take Jazzy out for a good hot dinner? Of course he says it's because he's afraid they'll be seen but I reckon he's as mean as hell.'

'Well, they're making up for it now.'

'I bet it's the cheapest place he could get a booking.'

'She did say it wasn't a particularly good hotel,' I admitted.

'There you are. I hope at least she'll tuck in now she's got the chance and get some ballast to withstand the next let-down.' Sarah was generously proportioned herself and scornful of delicate appetites.

'Perhaps it really will be all right. Who could know Jazzy and not love her?'

'Of course it isn't going to be all right! Honestly, Bobbie, have you been at the absinthe? There's nothing wrong with Jazzy. Except perhaps too few brain cells. But a skunk like Bayliss is incapable of loving anyone but himself. You know perfectly well there's nothing ahead but disaster.'

Lying in bed that night, trying to read by a bulb so dim that even the moths ignored its puny rays and instead crawled over the pages of my book, I thought of Teddy. I remembered his satisfied pig-like eyes and the way he stared at my bust when Jazzy's back was turned and wondered at the mysterious thing called love. And then, of course, I thought of Burgo who had hovered like a persistent phantom haunting my brain the entire day as I cooked, cleaned, fetched library books and ironed. His face had been on each of those forty-two napkins, swimming in the pea-pod soup, staring up from the cover of *Fear not, my Lovely* in place of the beetle-browed Lord Lucifer Twynge. I had rubbed Burgo's reflection from every dusty inch of the dining table.

Each time the doorbell rang I anticipated the florist's van and an insulting bunch of hybridized hothouse blooms to thank me for my readiness to accommodate his sexual needs. I had already decided to pass them on immediately to Mrs Treadgold. When another day passed without a bouquet to spurn or even the briefest note of thanks to rip to pieces I began to feel angry.

On the third day after the tennis party I opened the front door in response to a sustained imperative ring to find a strange man on the doorstop, flowerless but carrying a small black leather bag. He was lean and rangy with dark oiled hair swept straight back from a cliff-like brow and sharp aristocratic features.

'Miss Norton?' He handed me a card on which was written *Frederick Newmarch*, followed by a string of letters, among which I recognized FRCS. 'Burgo Latimer asked me to call. I've come to see your mother.' I opened my mouth but before I could think what I ought to say he was in the hall. He looked at me expectantly, impatience in his glittering grey eye. 'Just lead the way, Miss Norton. I'm sorry to hurry you but I'm operating in London at twelve.'

'Yes, of course.' I walked rapidly down the corridor that led from the hall to the morning room with the sensation that Frederick Newmarch was snapping at my heels. 'I hope . . . You mustn't mind if she isn't co-operative—'

'How old is your mother?'

'Fifty-one. But she looks much—'

'How long has she been unwell?'

'Oh, I suppose about three months. She broke her hip in April—'

'How's her appetite?'

'Poor, really, though she hasn't lost any weight. If anything she's put it on. But she does eat a lot of sweets.'

'Bowels?'

'A little constipated.'

'Does she complain of pain?'

'She says her arms and legs hurt sometimes.'

'But not specifically the hip?'

I paused by the door of the morning room. 'Not now, no. It seems to be a general all-over discomfort.'

'Is this her room? You needn't come in. I'll introduce myself.'

I was doubtful about his reception but Frederick Newmarch was evidently a man of steel and I was disinclined to argue with him. 'You mustn't mind if she's rather disagreeable. I think she's depressed—'

'Wait for me in the hall. I'll be ten to fifteen minutes.'

I sat on the chair by the telephone, wondering at a different kind of world in which one asked enormous favours from demi-gods and presumably returned them in kind. Burgo had not forgotten me. I was aware of a feeling of exultation that I could hardly account for.

When I heard Mr Newmarch's approaching footsteps echoing author-itatively from the encaustic tiles I leaped to attention.

'How did she—' I began.

'I've checked her over. I'll get a nurse to come this afternoon and take bloods to confirm my diagnosis. But it seems pretty straightfor-ward. Her heart's slow and there's severe myxoedema. She's had the problem some time, I imagine. The hospital ought to have picked it up.'

'Then it's nothing to do with her hip?'

'That seems to have healed all right although obviously I can't say for certain without an X-ray.' He looked at his watch. 'I must run.'

'What ought I to—'

'They'll put her on medication straight away and you should see a rapid improvement.'

'Really? Oh, this is so kind of you. I can't tell you how grate-ful—'

'You've got my number. Ring my secretary if you're worried about anything.'

He glared at the front door impeding his progress. I flung it open before he resorted to battering it down and called to his departing back, 'Thank you so much for coming . . .'

He jumped into his car and shot away. I opened the door of the morning room, expecting to have a book hurled at my head. My mother was lying back on her pillows, staring out of the window. She was a bad colour and, despite the jars of cream I rubbed in morning, noon and night, her skin was dry and flaky. Slowly she turned her head to look at me.

'I wish you'd wash my hair, Roberta.'

'Oh, certainly. With pleasure.' I had been trying for weeks to persuade her to let me but she had always said she was too tired. 'What did you think of Mr Newmarch?'

'It's exhausting to be pulled around.' Her gooseberry eyes were reproachful. It may have been my imagination but they seemed brighter already, such is the power of a good doctor who can inspire confidence. 'However, it was a relief to have a *gentleman* to consult. The working classes have such coarse responses. They don't under-stand how one *feels*.'

'He seems to think he knows what's wrong.'

'He was quite intelligent, I thought.'

'I couldn't tell. He didn't waste many words on me. He's amaz-ingly bossy.'

'Bossy, would you say? I'd call him . . . masterful.'

As I bent to rearrange the bedclothes my attention was caught by the jacket of the book on the bedside table and I was immediately struck by the resemblance of Mr Frederick Newmarch to Lord Lucifer Twynge.

The following afternoon as I was boiling sugar and water for a crème caramel Oliver put a tousled head round the kitchen door.

'Telephone for you.'

'Damn! I can't leave this. Ask them to ring back— No, wait a minute, it might be Jazzy. I'd better speak to her.'

'It's a bloke.'

I hesitated. Possibly it was Mr Newmarch, telephoning to know the result of the tests, in which case it would be ungrateful to put him to the trouble of calling back. 'Will you come and watch this like a hawk and take it off the heat the minute it goes brown?'

Oliver shambled across the kitchen, yawning. Even as I handed him the wooden spoon I made a mental note that his dressing-gown could do with a wash.

'Hello?'

'Roberta.'

It did not occur to me to pretend I did not recognize Burgo's voice. An odd sensation, something like pins and needles, spread to my extremities. 'Oh, hello! I must tell you, he was wonderful! It was so good of you to remember.'

'Who?'

'Mr Newmarch. He came to see my mother yesterday and sent someone to do a blood test. They telephoned me with the results today. Usually one waits a week only to find they've lost them. I'm astonished at the power of the Word. She's suffering from hypo-thyroidism. Apparently there's something called thyroxin which will make her better. I'm picking some pills up from the surgery this evening.'

'Good. He's a strange man. A cross between Rudolf Rassendyll and Alice's white rabbit. I bet he wakes regularly during the night just to see what time it is.'

'I don't know how you can speak so disrespectfully. To me he's the eighth wonder of the world and I'm ready to subscribe to a bust in marble. Who's Rudolf Rassendyll?'

'Don't you remember *The Prisoner of Zenda*? He was the gallant hero.'

'Oh yes. But it *was* kind of you to send him.'

'It's nice to be the recipient of so much gratitude, but that's not why I rang. I've been touring the North since I last saw you, making speeches and playing bingo with our senior citizens. I got back to London last night. I want to see you.'

'Well . . .' I tried to hang on to my determination to finish the affair before it had properly begun but from the moment I heard his voice the conviction had begun to weaken. 'I don't know. It would be lovely to see you but—'

'Come on, then. I'm in the call-box down the road. I'll find a suitable bush by the gate at the bottom of your drive and try to make myself invisible.'

My blood began to seethe as violently as the caramel. 'You're in Cutham Down?'

'Didn't I just say so?'

'Yes, but . . .'

'Hurry up.'

There was a buzzing sound. He had put down the receiver. I tore off my apron, dragged my fingers through my hair in front of the hall mirror and let myself out of the front door. I ran through the wood, which was quicker than following the curves of the drive, and then slowed as I drew near the gate. It would not do to arrive actually panting. I looked around but could see no one. For a moment I wondered if it might have been a cruel joke. Then a hand grabbed my arm and drew me into a stout laurel.

'You nearly made me scr—' The rest of what I had to say was lost as he kissed me long and hard.

'That's better,' he said as he let go at last. 'I've been longing for that. Not only that, of course.' He looked at my face. 'Just as I remembered it. Come here.' He held me tightly against him and then began to kiss me again, more gently. 'Oh dear! I was afraid it wouldn't be enough. Cold shower urgently required.' Obediently, the rain, which had held off for the last hour, began to fall and at once became a downpour, buffeting the leaves and releasing the scent of earth and mildew. 'But I told myself it would be better than nothing.' He kissed the top of my head as drops trickled down my face and tried to shelter me beneath his coat. 'And it is. We've got ten minutes before I have to drive back to London. This afternoon's meeting was cancelled so I seized the moment and leaped on a train. Simon's parked discreetly up the road. He's driving me straight back to town so I can be in the House by eight.'

'You don't mean you came all the way here just to . . . just to . . .?'

'Just to kiss you? Yes. Even *my* impatient ardour is deterred by the thought of making love in this benighted wood. Besides, there isn't time. Tell me, my love . . . are you my love?'

He looked at me intently.

I was, at that moment, incapable of lying. 'Yes. For good or ill, and I suppose it must be for ill.'

'Don't!' He held me tightly. 'I won't let anything hurt you. Trust me.'

So I did.

'I admit the man has talent,' said Kit. 'Despite my natural antipathy, I have to hand it to him. He knew you'd need a romantic gesture rather than a postcard and a box of chocolates.'

'You needn't tell me I was a gullible fool,' I said. 'I know it.'

'I didn't mean that. The thing is, you were already in love with him. He just had to break down your resistance. So there you were. At the beginning of an incandescent love affair. The die was cast.'

'Yes. Before then we were just playing. Although it was heady with romance, everything that occurred before that declaration in the laurels meant comparatively little. Afterwards it seemed to me that everything important – that is to say, my ideas about myself and other people, my presumptions about the future – was substantially changed. And pain was ever present, heightening the pleasure, a sort of fixative of experience.'

'You mean you felt guilty?'

'I'm ashamed to admit that for some time, several weeks, I didn't feel guilty at all. Anna seemed a hardly real figure in Burgo's life. He rarely mentioned her name. She seemed to have nothing at all to do with me. I assumed they had some sort of understanding. That's if I thought about her at all. At first I was so overwhelmed by feelings of . . . well, let's call it infatuation, that nothing else mattered. The pain came from excessive excitement. An overdose of adrenaline. Because we couldn't see each other often, the affair had to be carried on in my head. I must have been impossibly vague and unreachable. I drifted through the days that followed, cooking, cleaning, carrying trays in a dream, waiting for him to call, imagining what it would be like to see him again. Every minute of every hour I thought about him. When I got back to the house I found a ruined saucepan and a kitchen full of smoke. Oliver had left the bath running. He'd been so busy trying to mop up the bathroom floor with anything he could lay his hands on, including every clean towel in the linen cupboard and quite a few of the hated napkins I'd just ironed, he'd forgotten about the caramel. I didn't feel so much as a flicker of annoyance. America and Russia could have gone to war, Africa and India have starved, Sussex might have been submerged by a tidal wave and I wouldn't have given a damn. I only thought about Burgo. You see, I had never been in love before.'

'And once you'd had a taste of it, it went straight to your head like wine-cup.'

'I must be a sadly repressed sort of person.'

'I think you're perfectly adorable.'

I peered through the streaming window at banks of trees hanging over the road. Now the lower slopes of the mountains were clothed with green and looked more friendly, like parts of Italy. 'We must be near Kilmuree.'

'Four miles. I hope you brought an umbrella.'

'It never occurred to me. I was so desperate to get out of the house without the press spotting me that I've probably brought all the wrong things.'

'How did you manage it?'

'A friend helped me. Oddly enough, she came to interview me for a newspaper.'

'That sounds intriguing. You've just got time to tell me.'

FOURTEEN

Three days after Burgo's and my love affair became carrion for the nation to peck over for the juiciest bits, I was standing in the kitchen measuring spoons of Bengers into a pan of warm milk for my mother. She had given up eating proper food, complaining that everything made her feel sick, and existed on invalidish things like Slippery Elm and eggnog with brandy. And of course sweets by the bagful. I suppose she was trying to sweeten a life that had become sour. The current craving was for coffee fondants.

'Just a minute,' said Kit. 'I'm sorry to interrupt when you've just got going but I thought your mother had been restored to health months ago by the great Frederick Newmarch.'

'Oh, yes. I'd forgotten I hadn't told you about all that. The pills cured her hypothyroidism remarkably quickly. Her skin improved, her hair grew back, her voice lightened. Physically she looked better than I'd seen her for a long time. I planned to go back to London in September. Sarah said I could have my old room and my boss had agreed to have me back. And Burgo and I would be able to see more of each other, though we'd managed to meet most weeks in Sussex and occasionally I'd been able to get up to London for half a day. Of course, it was never enough. And that, I suppose, fanned the flames of passion.' I paused, wincing inwardly at this cold analysis of our love. But I had to try to detach myself. 'Anyway, I was telling you about my mother. Though she'd stopped grumbling about aches and pains, she refused to get dressed and wouldn't leave her room. And she wouldn't give up that beastly commode, though I knew she was capable of walking to the lavatory.

'Burgo got Frederick Newmarch to call again and *he* said that

143

there was nothing wrong with her as far as he could see but he thought she was seriously depressed. He advised a complete change, perhaps a holiday abroad. My father wouldn't take her. He only likes visiting war graves or battlefields: not the thing for lifting depression. So I went to the local travel agent for brochures about cheap places to go in France, my heart absolutely in my boots because I didn't want to be away from Burgo. Then my mother put paid to all that by deciding to get out of bed and go upstairs.

'It was the first time for nearly five months that she'd been outside her own room. It was a crazy thing to do. I was on my way to the Fisherman's Reel – the little pub where Burgo and I used to meet – my father was in London and Mrs Treadgold, who was supposed to be looking after her, was in the kitchen, listening to *The Archers*. Oliver was still in bed. Was it a coincidence that my mother chose one of the few moments when there was no one around to see or hear her? Anyway she managed, despite being as weak as water after lying so long in bed, to drag herself up to the top of the stairs and then fell down the entire flight, breaking an arm and a leg.'

'You think she did it deliberately?'

'I don't know. There was no reason for her to go upstairs. I was afraid that she'd meant to kill herself. I felt I hadn't been nearly nice enough. Of course the entire process began all over again. Two weeks in hospital, National Health this time, and heavens, did she complain! Then home, encased in plaster, to be looked after. She seemed to cheer up a bit then. If it hadn't been for Burgo it would have been me who was suicidal.

'I embarked on a new policy of calm endurance and tried even harder to please. I was so sorry for her. My father was cold to her, unsympathetic, whereas I was loved by this marvellous man . . . Anyway, the fractures mended, though it took ages. Another four months. By January she was more or less better. Just when I was thinking it might be possible to go back to London, she upset a pot of tea all over herself. She was burned from her neck to her waist. Back to hospital. Luckily, though the scalded area was large, it wasn't deep. She was home after a week. But the burn didn't heal. I think she picked off the new skin during the night.'

'Oh dear, you poor girl. Was it because she didn't want you to go away?'

'If I'd believed that it might have been easier in many ways. I'd have felt needed. No, she's always preferred Oliver. Though when he stopped being a gentle confiding little boy she withdrew from him too. I was always too independent and bossy. I know I am. I love making something good out of something hopeless. Once I grew old enough to be effective what affection she had for me waned almost completely. And now I was trying to make her well when she didn't want to be. What's more she saw all my attempts to make the house and garden more attractive as criticism. We were both to be pitied in the circumstances. I think she just enjoys lying in bed, being waited on, reading escapist novels and eating sweets, not having to go out into a world that holds no pleasure for her. I was simply a means to an end. All she needs is a more or less willing slave.'

'So you stayed.'

'I was afraid if I left she'd do something worse to herself. I don't know what I thought was going to happen in the future. That she might become bored with being an invalid. Or that Burgo might force the issue by deciding to divorce his wife so he could marry me. Yes, I suppose that's what I hoped. That he would take matters out of my hands and into his own. I was becoming increasingly dependent on him. He had become my happiness, my salvation. But, of course, that didn't happen. The Conservative Party stormed into power under the leadership of Margot Holland; she selected him to be her youngest minister and his face was splashed all over the newspapers. Someone saw the opportunity to make some cash. It sounds awfully squalid, doesn't it?'

'As far as I'm concerned, nothing that was associated with you could be squalid.'

'That's the kindest thing anyone's ever said to me.'

'I mean it. Don't cry, Bobbie. You don't want to mess up your face when you're about to meet these new people. Tell me about the journalist who found you this Irish job.'

'What a knight errant you are!' I sniffed. 'Fancy a man understanding the importance of mascara. All right, where was I? I remember, mixing Bengers for my mother with tears running down my face. Eating coffee fondants.'

'Go on.'

I wondered as I stirred and chewed and wept if I could outdo my mother in misery now. I might as well join the library myself and put in a regular order on my own behalf at the sweet shop.

Since the arrival of droves of reporters we had locked all the external doors and closed the shutters of the downstairs rooms. Brough had removed the pull from the bell and we had unplugged the telephone. My father complained bitterly about being compelled to live under a pall of darkness and was absent from breakfast until after dinner. Fortunately the morning room was always so gloomy and my mother's concentration on the written word so complete that she hardly noticed. Oliver was asleep during most of the day anyway so it made no difference to him. The only person who was actually having a good time as a result of my persecution by the Fourth Estate was Brough. He had never ceased to regret the end of the Second World War and was now in his element. He patrolled the grounds night and day with his shotgun, an expression of manic ferocity animating his usually sullen features.

Entombed in a dismal silence that was broken only by foolhardy reporters hammering on the windows and doors and rattling the letterbox until routed by Brough, I thought I might well be going mad. My sole outlook on the world was through one of the kitchen windows which opened on to the woodshed, coal bunker and dust-bin area. It seemed safe to leave this window unshuttered.

The coffee fondant was actually rather disgusting but I found my hand reaching automatically towards the bag for another when someone sprang up in front of me on the other side of the window. I yelled with shock and was about to turn and run when something familiar about her made me pause.

'Bobbie! It's me! Harriet Byng!' said the girl, putting her face close to the glass.

I undid the bolts of the back door. 'Quick! Come in!'

Harriet squealed as she saw Brough advancing, squinting down the barrel of his gun, his eyes inflamed with killer fury. After I had persuaded him to go and have a cup of tea and a biscuit to calm himself, I closed and rebolted the door and then examined my unexpected visitor.

I had met Harriet Byng at the wedding of her elder sister. Ophelia and I had been friends for some years. We had never been particularly close but we moved in the same circles in London and we liked the same kind of things. Ophelia was beautiful with huge blue eyes and silvery-blonde hair and had exquisite taste. I found her particular brand of hedonism and extreme single-mindedness intriguing. She could be entertaining or appallingly difficult but she was never dull. Other people complained that Ophelia was selfish and heartless but they had been proved wrong when she had succumbed to the charms of a good-looking but comparatively poor police inspector. I had been asked to the wedding a month ago and there met Harriet, one of Ophelia's three younger sisters. Harriet and I had had a long and interesting conversation about – among other things – the ideal lunatic asylum, the novels of Louise de Vilmorin and our favourite things to eat.

Harriet was quite unlike Ophelia, in looks as well as character. Her hair was long and straight and a rich dark brown. Her eyes were dark too and bright with intelligence. Her skin was pale and it was fascinating to watch the colour in her face come and go for Harriet was shy and blushed like a child. I thought her beauty bewitching, of a different order from anyone else's. Her ingenuous sweetness was not the least of her attractions and I was amused to observe that a tall, distinguished-looking older man had her under his eye most of the time. This turned out to be Rupert Wolvespurges, the artistic director of the English Opera House, and Harriet confided that they were in love.

'Oh, Bobbie!' Harriet hugged me tightly. 'How are you, you poor dear thing?'

These were the first words of sympathy that had been addressed to me since the scandalized world had been apprised of my affair with Burgo and they reduced me to a storm of sobbing. Harriet steered me to a chair and put on the kettle, then sat down next to me, holding my hand in hers until I had got over the worst.

'Gosh, I'm sorry,' I said. 'I don't suppose you've got a hanky? Mine are all upstairs.'

Harriet hadn't so I used the drying-up cloth which was anyway a more suitable size for the deluge that had been provoked by the sound of a friendly voice.

'It's all too silly,' I said. 'I don't know why I'm being such a baby.'

'I do,' said Harriet. 'It's really terrifying having those people harrying you, like hounds after a poor darling fox. You get the feeling they're going to rip you to pieces if they catch you. And they make up the most ridiculous stories about you and suddenly you find yourself wondering if they might be true. You get frightened that any minute you're going to go raving mad. After a while, though, you get used to it.' I remembered then that Harriet's father had only the year before been arrested for murder – wrongly, as it turned out. But for weeks stories and photographs of Harriet's remarkably handsome and interesting family had filled the gossip columns and one could scarcely pick up a magazine or newspaper without seeing one or all of their faces as they went into the fishmonger's or came out of a cinema. 'Honestly, though it's hard to believe, the reporters doorstepped us for so long that we actually got quite friendly with them. Some of them are perfectly nice people. It just takes a bit of getting used to.'

'I'm sure you're right. I've got to pull myself together. I haven't been sleeping and . . . It must have been so much worse for you with your father in prison.'

'That *was* truly awful.' Harriet shook her head as she thought about it, as though to rid herself of the memory. 'But, darling Bobbie, never mind the press for a minute. You can keep them outside and in the end they'll get fed up and it'll be yesterday's news. But what about you? Have you been able to see him?'

'No. If you mean Burgo.'

She squeezed my hand. 'You love him terribly?'

'Yes. Yes, I do.'

'And will he . . . is he going to leave his wife?'

'If he leaves her he's finished as a politician. Margot Holland can't have a disgraced minister in tow. As the first woman Prime Minister she's got to have higher standards, work harder and do everything much better than any man. She supports Burgo all the way, natu-rally: she wouldn't have appointed him Minister for Culture if she didn't think he'd do a brilliant job. He's only thirty-five and she's promoted him over the heads of several older and more likely candi-dates. Of course it's made him enemies.'

'People are envious of him, you mean?'

'Well, on the face of it he seems to have everything: brains, career, rich wife, willing mistress. The anti-Burgo faction is also largely anti-Holland, though that's more or less kept under wraps, of course. The scandal's given ammunition to those Conservatives who feel their manhood's threatened by having a female boss. As well as to the Labour Party, of course. The only chance Burgo's got of holding out against those who are baying for his blood is to be repentant and to persuade his wife to put on a public show of reconciliation with him. After that it depends on the tide of popular opinion. But plenty of politicians have had affairs and survived, provided they showed proper contrition and behaved themselves ever after.'

Harriet got up to make the tea. Keeping her back to me, she asked, 'Is that what he's going to do?'

'He's telephoned every day since the news broke. Each time he says he loves me and that he's going to give everything up for me.'

Harriet turned round. 'Oh, thank goodness! That's all right, then.'

I shook my head. 'He hasn't said it doesn't matter to him. That he doesn't *mind* giving it all up for me. I can hear in his voice what a wrench it is. He's always wanted this. He's terrifically ambitious; he wants to be able to change things. One of the things I love about him is his energy and the fact that it's channelled into real achievement. He doesn't care about status symbols, possessions, houses, cars, cellars filled with rare vintages. He doesn't care about winning. What thrills him is informing people, changing their opinions about things he thinks are important. Managing to get a bill read about reforming the laws on assisted suicide or doing something to help ex-prisoners buoys him up for days at a time.'

'I must admit it's not how I imagined politicians to be.' Harriet found some cups in the cupboard. 'I mean, they aren't usually very attractive people morally – or even physically. I saw Burgo on television yesterday. He looked pretty cracking.'

I had seen the piece of newsreel myself, of Burgo coming out of 10 Downing Street, looking stern, acknowledging the cameras with a nod and the coldest of smiles, walking quickly away. I had turned the set off after a few seconds because the pain of longing had been so intense.

I offered the coffee fondants to Harriet. 'Do have one. Or several. They're horribly sickly but I can't seem to manage proper food. It all tastes like ashes. Burgo's having to choose between two things he terribly wants and he thinks he'll choose me because I'm *just* about more important to him.'

'There you are then. You couldn't reasonably expect him not to care at all.'

'No, not that. But don't you see, if he left that world of power and influence and excitement, and we bought a semi in suburbia – neither of us has a bean, his wife has all the money – and he got a job in the Civil Service or presenting programmes on television, do you think I'd go on mattering that infinitesimal but crucial fraction more? We'd be bound to quarrel sometimes and perhaps the love-making would come to seem less exciting and I'd have to ask myself whether I was *still* more important than the job he'd always wanted, which was his for a few weeks and which he gave up for my sake. If I made a stupid remark or failed to sympathize properly, if I got tired and snappy, jealous, perhaps – after all, he's had one clandestine affair so what's to stop him having another? – every sigh, every

149

depressed look, every word that suggested he was becoming disillusioned would throw me into a blind panic. I lack the confidence to be sure I can be all in all to someone else.'

'You have to admire Wallis Simpson.'

'Ah, but he never wanted to be king. That's the difference.'

Harriet sipped her tea thoughtfully. 'I probably ought to urge you not to be a coward and to take on the challenge. But I'm so short of confidence myself I'm sure I'd feel just the same. People can't be everything to each other and they ought not to expect it. Actually, to be truthful, there isn't anything that matters to me even a thousandth part as much as Rupert, but then I'm not ambitious. And I've been crazy about him since I was old enough to spit.'

'You mean, you're childhood sweethearts? How romantic.'

'Not exactly. He says I was fat, grubby and toothless. But I've worshipped *him* all my life. Anyway, to revert to the jobs thing, although I enjoy my job it isn't what I really want to do for ever.' She grew pink. 'My secret desire is to be a poet. But if I had to choose between losing Rupert and never writing another poem, there'd be no contest. I suppose that means I'm not sufficiently serious about poetry. It's disillusioning.' Her eye fell on the fondants. I pushed the bag across. 'Rather more-ish, aren't they?'

'When are you getting married?'

Harriet blushed again. 'After he's finished directing *Lucia di Lammermoor*. But that's enough about me. It's you that matters now.'

'It's kind of you to come.' I was struck by a sudden thought. 'But why did you? Not that I'm not delighted to see a friendly face. But it's a long way to travel to console someone you've met only once before.'

Harriet turned a darker shade. 'Ah well, the truth is that I'm one of those inebriate vultures at your gate. I'm a reporter on the *Brixton Mercury*. I used to be the dogsbody but I've risen to deputy sub-editor – only because Rupert pulled strings. Oh, don't look like that.' I must have inadvertently assumed a look of distaste. 'Of course I'm not going to write a story about you. Or nothing that you don't dictate to me word for word. But my boss Mr Podmore asked me if knew you. He thinks I'm an ex-deb, which is quite untrue and that I know everyone with a double-barrelled surname. When I said that actually I did, he sent me out to get an exclusive interview. And I thought you might like a chance to put your own view to the world, via the *BM*. Of course our circulation's tiny but sometimes the national newspapers take things from the local ones. But if not, then I'll just say you were out. I promise you can trust me. I thought I might be able to help. I hope you're not cross?'

She looked so anxious that I couldn't help smiling. 'Of course I'm not cross. And I do trust you. You've already helped tremendously just by listening. But I don't know what I can tell the world that won't injure Burgo.'

'I could write a little piece about what a nice, sensitive, decent person you are. It seems to me that Lady Anna's getting all the favourable coverage at the moment.'

I had seen a wedding photograph of Burgo and Anna in one of the newspapers. She had looked quite different from my idea of her. When I had thought about her, which I did as little as I could possibly help, I had imagined someone tall, tanned and made-up; hard, perhaps even brassy. As a bride she had looked small, pale, elegant, her dress long-sleeved and high-necked, her only ornament a wreath of flowers that held the veil in place over her dark hair, which was swept back from her face. She was smiling into the camera and she looked so happy that I had immediately felt an acute sense of shame. I had reminded myself that the photograph was ten years old and that Anna and Burgo hadn't been lovers for some time. Or so he had said. For the first time I had wondered whether Burgo had intentionally misled me.

'Well, she *is* the innocent party. But if you make me out to be a vulnerable ingénue who spends her free time knitting blankets for earthquake victims and leading the hymn-singing at Sunday school it reflects badly on him, doesn't it? It's in his interest to have everyone believing I'm a wicked jade who cozens other women's gullible husbands into behaving badly.'

Harriet looked at me with solemn eyes. 'And you're prepared to let people think that of you? You really have got it bad.'

'I have. Also my pride revolts at the idea of attempting to justify myself. Why should I care what they say if it isn't true? I *do* care, of course. It stings like anything. But I'm going to fight against minding because it's pathetic to be upset by the disapproval of strangers who don't know anything about me.'

'OK, so you don't want me to do an article from your point of view. But if you don't mean to let Burgo give up his career for you, what *are* you going to do?'

'I'd like to get away, right away. Not only from the press. Every night at ten o'clock I plug in the telephone and Burgo rings me from a call-box and we have these dreadful conversations. At first hearing his voice is a huge relief. Then the misery starts. It's like seeing his shirt-tails and the soles of his shoes forever whisking round a corner. Never his face. Ever since we became lovers I've had this feeling that I was hanging on to tiny scraps of him. But I had a foolish hope that one day the crusts would become a feast. Now it's much worse, of course. We have to be extremely circumspect. Apparently newspapers tap telephone lines routinely. I suppose you knew that.'

'Not tuppenny-ha'penny papers like the *Brixton Mercury*. Only dailies with large circulations and big bank accounts.'

'He says how sorry he is. I say how sorry I am. He asks if I'm OK. I ask him how he is. We try to reassure each other that everything will be all right. He says how much he loves me, how important I am to him. He says he can't be happy without me. I tell him that he matters more to me than anyone has ever done. And that I never want to hurt him. He tells me to stay calm and be patient, that it will blow over and we'll be able to be together. I say I want to do what will be best for him. He gets agitated at that. I'm too weak to tell him that it's over, to refuse to have anything more to do with him. I know that would be the best thing. But I can't do it. I need to be able to detach myself a bit so I can be strong. I thought of going to stay with a girlfriend who lives in Rome. But I'm really too miserable to make a good guest. And there's a limit to how long you can park yourself on someone when you haven't any money. I need to work. Somewhere like Benghazi or Ecuador where they won't have heard of me.'

'I wonder . . .' Harriet said thoughtfully. 'Perhaps it's crazy, but I may know just the place. It's not as far away as South America, but does that matter? I was reading *The Times* on the train coming down, hoping to pick up tips on journalistic style, and I happened to see an ad in the personal columns that rather took my fancy: a request for a housekeeper. It had such a strange list of requirements – something about poetry and sausages – it sounded romantic and interesting. What a pity I left the paper on the train.'

'I've got a copy of *The Times* here.' I drew it out from behind the bread-bin. 'I was going to cut out the bits about Burgo and me before my father saw them. He gets furious about the holes in the pages

152

but at least I don't have to face him knowing he's read all that stuff about me being an insatiable scrofulous whore.'

Harriet scanned the personal columns. 'Here we are. Listen to this. *Housekeeper wanted, County Galway, Ireland. No previous experience necessary. Applicants must be clean, beardless, love poetry and animals, be able to cook sausages and possess a philosophical temperament.* Isn't it a peculiar list?'

'It seems rather haughty these days to question other people's washing habits,' I said. 'Still, it's no good standing on one's dignity when one's in a hole. And what about the beard? I believe there *are* women who have phobias about men with beards. Would many men apply for a job as housekeeper, do you think?'

'I wondered if it might be a pig farm. The sausages, I mean. I like sausages but I wouldn't want to eat them *all* the time. But the poetry sounded promising, I thought.'

I found myself indulging in a brief fantasy. I imagined a neat little house with an elderly couple or more likely a widow. An invalid, possibly, who wanted someone to read poetry to her. Rather particular and old-fashioned, viz. the prejudice against bearded men, but liking plain food. She had a poodle, perhaps, or a Pekinese which had to be taken for walks.

'I've never been to Ireland,' I said. 'But it might just be the answer to a prayer.'

'Now I see,' said Kit. 'Harriet sounds like a trouper.'

'I rang the number straight away. A woman answered.'

'What did she sound like?'

'Faint voice, slight Irish accent, younger than I expected. She asked me a few questions: could I drive? Did I mind living in an isolated place? Could I milk a cow?'

'Can you? Milk a cow, I mean?'

'No, but it can't be that difficult.'

'Mm. I wonder.'

'Anyway, she said I was the first person to answer the advertisement though she had put it into all the papers she could think of. Their last housekeeper had left suddenly, after a terrible row. They were absolutely desperate. Could I come at once?'

'Commendable honesty,' said Kit.

'I was encouraged to find that my future employer puts truth above self-interest. Also that she was not a fractious invalid. But *dis*couraged that no one else had even considered the job. Anyway, we agreed I'd be there as soon as public transport allowed. Harriet and I pored over train tables, then she went out to the call-box to book the cheapest available berth on the Swansea to Cork ferry.'

'Why not cross from Holyhead to Dún Laoghaire? Wouldn't it have been quicker?'

'We'd made the call to Galway from the house so in case anyone was tapping the line we thought it might be safer to take a slightly more circuitous route.'

'Luckily for me.'

'I'm the one who ought to be grateful. And I am.'

'Well, that's better than nothing, I suppose. Go on.'

'There's nothing much left to tell. I got Brough to drive me to Blackheath station the next morning. I was lying on the back seat, covered by a rug. The reporters banged on the windows when we got to the gates to get Brough to stop but he just put his foot down. I heard something like a scream as we accelerated away. I suppose if he'd caused serious injury it would've been in the papers.'

'How did your parents take your abrupt departure?'

'After the first burst of temper, my father seemed surprisingly amenable to my going. I gave him the telephone numbers of a couple of nursing agencies I'd been in touch with before the scandal broke, in the forlorn hope that I'd be able to get back to London. I expected him to kick up about the expense but he suddenly became astonishingly reasonable. He just said I'd better go and pack and he'd see to the business of finding a nurse. The sooner I went, he said, the sooner the lower classes would stop boozing and fornicating at his gates and littering the grounds with beer cans and crisp packets.'

'Fornicating? The press? Really?'

'No, of course not. He accuses everyone of alcoholism and lechery. When, in fact, he's the one the cap fits.'

'And your mother? What did she say?'

'She wanted to know who was going to fetch her library books. I assured her that I had made it clear to the agencies that the provision of reading matter was an essential part of the job, on a par with trays and baths. I had to order fresh supplies of nougat and toffee eclairs before I went. I hope Oliver will remember to collect them.'

'I suppose their indifference was wounding but it made it easier for you to go.'

'I didn't mind. I was relieved there wasn't a fuss. The only person who's going to miss me is Oliver. When I told him I was going away he said Cutham would be insupportable and – you mustn't think badly of him, it's just that he's exceptionally soft-hearted and affectionate – he wept.'

'I don't think the worse of a man for crying. I occasionally do myself.'

'Do you?' I smiled. This admission did much more to endear Kit to me than all his compliments. 'Anyway, I pointed out that he'd already spent seven years at Cutham without me when I was living in London but he said it was different now he was used to me being about the place. Naturally I was pleased to discover that he's so attached to me but it was an added complication. I do worry about him. He's so easily depressed. I can tell him to get his manuscript ready to send to you, can't I? That will cheer him up.'

'Oh, yes.' I thought I detected a note of resignation in Kit's voice but I knew I was in a state bordering on the neurotic and apt to see disapproval where there was none.

'So what did the Minister for Culture say when he heard you were emigrating to the wilds of Ireland?'

'I wish you wouldn't call him that. It sounds so . . . as though you disapprove of him.'

'I told you. I'm jealous. If I had a girl like you sighing her heart out for me . . .'

'Oh, don't! It makes me sound like a feeble victim. You've met me at my lowest point, that's all.' Despite my best intentions I felt my eyes fill. I was in that state where tears are so close to the surface that almost everything makes one cry. I could easily have wept to see a petal drop from a rose or a robin disappointed of a crumb. 'He doesn't know. I didn't plug in the telephone that last night at Cutham. I knew if he begged me not to I wouldn't have the strength to go away. I sat in the kitchen and tried to make a sensible list of things to pack and not to look at my watch. Oh, it was so *hard* when it got to ten o'clock.' I turned my head away from Kit to stare out of the window. I couldn't see a thing. 'I'm ashamed to be so watery.'

'My dear Bobbie, there isn't a man or woman alive who hasn't wept for love. Unless they're intolerably unfeeling and soulless, without an ounce of poetry in them.'

'I do like poetry but only when I read it to myself, by myself.' I attempted a smile. 'I hope my employer isn't a prolific amateur versifier looking for a captive audience.'

'She might be a reclusive genius. An Emily Dickinson.'

'She might, of course. What do you give for my chances?'

155

'Not much. Instead I'll give you the telephone number of where I'll be staying for the next few days. This is Kilmuree.'

A scattering of houses quickly became solid rows, which bordered each side of a tree-lined street that plummeted down a steep hill. As it was nearly half past seven the shops – all of which seemed to be the kind that sold kettles, mousetraps and nails – were closed and the small town was deserted.

I wrote down the number as Kit dictated it. 'You can't imagine how grateful I am. You've been so good to me and I feel so comforted knowing there's rescue at hand if the rhyme schemes are really hopeless.'

'You can express your gratitude with a kiss then. Quick, before we get to the bus station.'

It was the least I could do. To compensate for it being positioned chastely on his cheek I put some fervour into it. But when he turned his head towards me as though to kiss me on the lips, I said, 'Do look out! There aren't many lamp-posts as it is.' I pointed to a tired-looking building set back from the main street which had an apron of tarmac pierced by elder seedlings. 'Do you think that could be it? Where it says "Bus Éireann". Drop me here, would you? It'll save me having to explain who you are.'

'All right.' Kit drew in to the kerb. 'What a wrench this is! Can it really be less than twenty-four hours since we met?' He put his hand on my arm. His expression was serious. 'Can't I persuade you to give up this farcical scheme with the cows and the sausages and throw in your lot with me? On strictly celibate terms. I promise I won't attempt to poach Mr Latimer's preserve.'

Outside the rain gathered intensity and ricocheted in miniature fountains from the pavements before running in torrents down the hill. I felt a reluctance to get out of the little car, of which I had become strangely fond. For the last few miles I had been haunted by the spectre of supercilious strangers demanding a slavish application to uncongenial tasks. For a moment I was tempted to tell Kit to drive on fast, no matter what the consequences.

He put a hand on my arm. 'You really do need someone to look after you.'

These words checked my impulse to flee. I shook my head. 'I have to get on good terms with myself again by my own efforts. But thanks for the offer. Goodbye, Kit. I shan't forget how good you've been to me. I do hope we meet again.' I opened the door.

'You bet,' he said in his ordinary, cheerful voice. 'I'll get your cases out of the boot.'

'Don't. You'll get soaked. It's teeming.'

Kit insisted. I saw with regret the shoulders of his jacket become instantly dark with rain and his hair stick to his forehead. I seized the cases and ran.

FIFTEEN

The bus station was deserted apart from a friendly dog and a sleeping tramp. The ticket counter was shuttered. I put down my suitcases and sat on the cleanest bit of the bench that ran down one side of the waiting room. I saw Kit's car go past the door on its way to Westport and a disagreeable shiver of loneliness ran over me like a cold draught. The dog and I exchanged sniffs and words with mild enthusiasm. It was a large dog with a coat of long brown ringlets, like an apprentice perm. As five minutes became ten, I grew increasingly fond of the dog and less fond of the tramp who muttered in his sleep, broke wind several times and scratched his stomach with a grimy fist. I began to wish that I had thrown in my lot with Kit and faced the inevitable complications of such a course. When, three-quarters of an hour later, my thoughts were too wretched to be borne and the bench too hard for comfort, I rose and began to pace. This provoked the dog to bark. The tramp opened his eyes and sat up.

'Blood and wounds! Will you shut it now, you little devil, before I knock your dratted head off your body!' he commanded. He screwed his knuckles into his eyes then stared at me. 'Would your name be Miss Norton, by any chance? For Curraghcourt?'

'Yes. I'm Bobbie Norton.'

The tramp revealed a jumble of teeth. 'That's good! You're very welcome, miss! Timsy O'Leary is my name.' He pulled off a ragged cap to reveal a shock of mousy hair standing up above a seam of dirt made by the band of his headgear. 'I was sent to fetch you to the house.' He looked at the clock on the wall. 'Is that the time? The old one'll be cross as briars with you being so late.'

It would not do to fall out at the beginning of our relationship so I restrained my natural feeling of annoyance. 'Is this your dog? She seems . . . intelligent.'

'No-ho. She belongs to Miss Constance. Sure you might scrape all Ireland with a fine-toothed comb and you'll not find a better dog.' He bent down, supporting himself with his hands on his knees. 'Come here, Maria darling. Come to your uncle Timsy.' Maria barked defiantly in his face and ran from the waiting room. 'Well then, Miss Norton. We'd better be making tracks. The car's outside.'

We followed the dog into the street. I perceived from the unsteadiness of his gait and the smell of alcohol on his breath that Timsy O'Leary had been drinking. Or could this be part of the stage Irishman impersonation Kit had described? Was Timsy O'Leary actually sober and wearing clean underclothes beneath the beggar's outfit? Perhaps he had a consuming interest in Florentine Mannerist painters? I picked up my suitcases and followed him.

There was no car to be seen, only a strange-looking cart with two leather seats back to back and facing outwards over the wheels. A bedraggled-looking pony stood between the shafts. The rain was coming down in earnest and the poor thing hung its head with water trickling from its neck and sides.

'Up with you, miss,' said Timsy, grabbing my cases and chucking them into the bowels of the cart.

'Oh, but . . . this is . . . Where's the car?'

'Sure, 'tis right before your eyes. A fine old Irish outside car. There's many a museum would pay a lot of money for it. I gave it a polish till you'd be in danger of blindness with dazzlement if it weren't for the rain that's coming down in lakes to spoil it.'

I looked from Timsy's beaming face to the cart, the woodwork of which was sketchily coated with flakes of paint which any polishing would have instantly removed. Two boxes of sopping, yellowing cabbages were roped on to one seat. The other was covered by a heap of old sacks. 'You mean we're going in . . . this?' I had still enough innate optimism to hope this was the last act of the tragic Famine play and that there was something cheerful, four-wheeled and dry waiting round the corner.

'Don't be frightened, Miss Norton. You'll not find a better man to guide a horse than Timsy O'Leary should you traipse the whole of Connaught. Besides, the Cockatoo knows the way.'

'A parrot, do you mean?' I imagined us being led through the darkness by a white bird, beating its wings frantically against the merciless onslaught of rain and wind to stay on its course.

159

'No, Miss Norton.' Timsy seemed inordinately amused by what seemed to me a perfectly natural mistake. "Tis the pony's name.' He clapped a hand on the Cockatoo's streaming rump which made the wretched animal start and kick up his back legs. I put my foot on the step and Timsy gave me a violent push from behind that nearly threw me over into the cabbages.

'There's a fine bit of cover for your back.' Timsy grasped one of the sacks and knotted it about his neck and tucked two more into his belt to cover his knees. 'They'll keep you as dry as a nut in its shell.'

I picked up a piece of sodden hessian and wrapped it round my head, tying it under my chin. Timsy gave a hoot of approval.

'Faith, Miss Norton, ma'am, you make a picture that'd draw a fox out of his hole, though the hounds were gathered round it, dripping at the jaws.'

I acknowledged the compliment with a smile that felt tight-lipped. Timsy hopped up to the driving seat and Maria leaped up beside me. With a jerk that nearly threw me out on to the road and made Maria step up her barking to a deafening scream, we set off down the hill.

'Is it far to the house?' I asked.

'Nothing but a step. You could dance the whole way and not be out of breath.'

This was a relief. The steep incline of the street, the jolting motion of the cart and the slipperiness of the wet leather obliged me to hang on to the back of the driving seat with both hands to prevent myself from sliding off. Maria scrabbled with her claws and whined desperately. I gripped her collar and she managed to get a purchase by anchoring the front half of her body across my knees. When we began to go down the other side of the hill we were slightly better off though my hip soon began to ache from being jammed against the driving seat. Once we reached level ground I was able to relax a little and rearrange the sacking for maximum protection from the rain that dashed itself into my face and coursed in rivulets from every prominent point. Maria remained slung across my knees and I derived great comfort from the warmth of her body. From time to time she opened her toffee-brown eyes to stare into mine with what I interpreted as fellow feeling. We proceeded the length of Kilmuree's main street, nose to snout.

Soon the houses petered out and we were in the countryside. There were mountains, trees and black sheets of water aplenty but no houses.

As we trotted on through a narrowing valley that became more desolate with every twist and turn of the road I began to wonder at the
elasticity of the 'step'. Timsy O'Leary shook the reins and whistled
cheerfully, from time to time breaking off to laugh aloud at nothing
in particular as far as I could tell. It was marvellous how the man's
spirits kept up beneath the sluicing rain that penetrated the sacking
and my mackintosh within minutes. There were no fences, no tele-
graph poles, no cars, no carts even; nothing but grazing sheep and
flocks of crows to reassure me that Timsy, Maria, the Cockatoo and
I were not the only sentient beings on the planet.

I began to dream of a telephone-box. As I comforted myself with
the thought that in this wilderness of mountains and bogs the call-
box was unlikely to have been vandalized, the pony whinnied, pranced
between the shafts and stopped dead.

'Get on there, you spawn of the devil's arse!' said Timsy. 'Oh, I
beg your pardon, Miss Norton, I was forgetting meself and you the
most refined, delicatest lady that ever was. Sure I'd like to cut out
my tongue and lay it there in the road and drive over it—'

'What's the matter?' I interrupted brusquely, my temper soured by
the rain and the smell of cabbages. 'Why has the pony stopped?'

''Tis an ass lying in the road there like a corpse. The Cockatoo
cannot abide asses.'

I leaned over the side of the cart to penetrate the veils of rain.
'Why doesn't the donkey get up?'

'I'll be thrashing it till it does,' said Timsy with energy, seizing the
whip. Maria sprang from the cart and ran round to the pony's head,
yapping dementedly.

'You mustn't do any such thing,' I said, jumping down myself.
'Perhaps it's hurt.'

'Be careful, Miss Norton, ma'am. Those brutes kick like steam
hammers.'

We had kept a donkey in the paddock at Cutham as a companion for my pony so I was not particularly alarmed. Far from kicking, it was passive, barely twitching its ears as I approached. I soon
saw that the poor animal's back legs were tightly bound with ropes
that were attached to a heavy log.

'Have you a knife?' I called to Timsy. 'It's hopelessly tangled up.
I wonder if this was done deliberately? I can feel knots.'

'Faith, 'tis Michael McOstrich's jennet, I do believe.' Timsy had
got down to stand beside me. 'She's got a white star right between
the eyes. He's hobbled the creature. To stop her straying, you

understand. She'll be putting her foot through a loop and winding herself up.'

I was disgusted by what seemed to me nothing less than outright cruelty. 'Please give me your knife at once.'

'A knife is a thing I never carry.' Timsy adopted a moral rectitude that was wholly unconvincing. 'And Michael's a big fellow. He can knock a hole right through you so you can see the sky the other side. Better leave the creature and I'll take the pony round on the grass.'

'I'll say you had nothing to do with it if you're afraid of him.' I took my sponge bag from my suitcase and found my nail scissors. Water penetrated the folds of my clothes during this operation but I was too angry to care.

'Oh, Miss Norton!' Timsy protested as I set to work, much hampered by the thickness of the ropes, the smallness of the blades, the rain and the diminishing light. 'Will I take you back to Kilmuree now before Michael McOstrich finds out you've spoiled the best bit of rope this side of Galway?'

I said nothing, needing all my energy to saw through the wet strands. As the last thread was severed the donkey heaved herself to her feet. She shook herself, gave a delighted buck, then dashed away across the bog and disappeared into the gloaming.

'Oh, Jesus, Mary and Joseph!' Timsy's voice was agonized. 'When Michael's roused to anger his eyes glow like coals with the bellows blowing them up. We'll be putting all the bolts on the doors tonight. But I doubt they'll stand up to his fists.'

'Pooh!' I said, climbing back into the cart. 'I can't believe the RSPCA, or whatever the Irish equivalent is, tolerates this sort of thing. And if Mr McOstrich dares to threaten me I shall call the police.'

'Oh, no, I beg you,' Timsy groaned. 'Likely Michael will bring his brothers and they're nearly as big as he.'

'Oh, stuff his brothers!' I was too tired and wretched to care if the entire McOstrich clan should come knocking at the door to rend me limb from limb. In fact, I would be grateful.

Timsy was so affected by my foolhardiness that he ceased to whistle and laugh and we travelled on for a while with no accompaniment but the clopping of hoofs, the creaking of the cart and the occasional bleat and caw from the sheep and crows. The rain fell lighter now and the cabbages smelt stronger. The light was fading fast. I looked at my watch then held it to my ear. Discouraged by

162

the water which had dribbled between dial and glass it had stopped at eight o'clock, just as we left Kilmuree. I was on the point of asking Timsy the time before it occurred to me that time had become irrelevant. I sank into a state of miserable apathy. It was nearly dark before I glimpsed through the blur of moisture a trembling light. I fixed my eyes on it with feelings of hope and dread.

'Whoa there, Sir Cockatoo,' Timsy said as before long we drew up before a low sort of dwelling.

I could see at once why Mrs Macchuin had sounded despairing. It must have been the loneliest place in the universe. Light leaking between skimpily drawn curtains revealed some straggling leaves planted in whitewashed car tyres each side of the front door. Otherwise no attempt had been made with paths or trees or hedges or flowerbeds to graft the building on to the primeval landscape. The mean little porch might have sheltered a small child. But indoors, I reminded myself, it would be dry.

Timsy jumped down. 'Come on, Miss Norton, we'll have a taggeen to keep out the wet.'

'A taggeen?'

'A drop o' the best. The dust's got into my throat so my pipes are roaring like a chimney on fire.'

I doubted if there was a speck of dust to be found between here and Kilmuree. All was mud and bog and rock and water. 'Is this Curraghcourt?'

Timsy laughed. ''Tis McCarthy's place.' When I hesitated, uncomprehending, he added, 'A public house, ma'am.'

'A public house?' I must have sounded as evangelically abstemious as Katherine Hepburn in *The African Queen* before she is worked on by love and adventure. But Timsy was far from my idea of Humphrey Bogart. 'We can't stop here! We must get on to Curraghcourt. You said yourself we were late.'

'Arrah! 'Tis as cross as the devil with thorns in his shirt and stones in his shoes the old one'll be already. So we may as well hang back until the madness goes out of her.'

'Mr O'Leary, will you please get back into the cart and drive on!' I spoke with unusual firmness.

'No!' he replied with equal firmness.

'I shall be extremely upset if you don't.'

Timsy shook his head. 'I'm sorry for that, Miss Norton. And there's me thanking the good Lord for sending us a lady without equal for looks and with manners that'd make Cleopatra ashamed.

However, if you'll wait here I'll just step in and take a nip of something wholesome and I'll be out again quicker than a hen when she sees the cook coming.'

He opened the door of McCarthy's. 'God save all here!' he cried and for a moment the clamour of voices accompanied a bright light. Maria ran in after him. The door closed leaving me alone, apart from the pony, in the dripping darkness. After a minute or two I swallowed my pride, cast aside the sacks and followed Timsy in.

The pub rocked with noise and light. Eager faces pressed close to mine and I was swept forward to the bar by a peristaltic wave of shoulders and elbows. A glass of pale brown liquid was shoved into my hand. I took a cautious sip. I seemed to feel the shock in my little toes. I put the glass down and tried to look friendly and composed. I was the only woman there. The men stared at me, one or two with lascivious looks, but mostly they were curious or shy and when I met their gaze they looked away uneasily. Conversation was impossible as one half of the pub was singing a quite different song from the other half.

An aeon crawled by on its hands and knees. I stopped trying to look friendly quite quickly. The composure went the same way after fifteen minutes or so. The pub was gloomy and dirty, the wooden counter ringed with stains and crawling with flies. I grew first cold as the damp state of my clothing contrasted unpleasantly with the tremendous heat of the room, then hot as I began to steam. Not only was I anxious about the effect my unpunctuality would have on the temper of 'the old one' but I was also so horribly bored that the notion of climbing on to the bar and screaming myself sick actually began to seem a possibility. Just as I was contemplating running up the nearest mountain and flinging myself from the top, Timsy put down his glass, wiped his mouth with the back of his hand and threw up his chin as a signal to me to make for the door.

The fresh air was reviving. Also it had stopped raining and the moon was occasionally visible between swirling clouds. Timsy scrabbled ineffectually to climb into his seat but the numberless taggeens had gone to his legs. I flinched from contact with the seat of Timsy's trousers but a shove from below was the only way to get him on to the cart.

'Perhaps,' I said in a sarcastic, schoolmistressy tone when we were all seated, 'if it's all the same to you, we might get on to Curraghcourt.'

Timsy grabbed the reins and bellowed to the pony to get home 'as quick as you can shake the stardust from your darling little hoofs, my angel'. Some evil genius prompted him to take up the whip and lash the Cockatoo's back quarters. Maria and I exchanged sympathetic glances as the Cockatoo set off at a canter, bucking with his hind legs every few yards. I at least had hands to hold on with.

'Timsy!' I shouted. 'For God's sake, slow the pony down! We'll be shaken to pieces!'

Timsy yanked on the reins and attempted to stand up which resulted in him falling backwards into the cabbages. Moonlight flashed on the soles of his boots as he slithered sideways headfirst on to the road. The Cockatoo stopped immediately.

''Tis my back is broken.' Timsy began to sob.

'Nonsense!' I was unable to abandon the part of schoolmistress now I had got into it. 'Pull yourself together and let's get on but at a sensible speed.'

'If it isn't my back, 'tis my heart.' Timsy continued to weep. 'Ah, Kathleen! Kathleen, darling, will you not take pity on a poor misfortunate creature? Marry me, my beauty! Marry your own Timsy that loves you better than the king in his fine palace loves his crownded, diamonded queen!'

'Will you be *quiet*,' I said. 'You're frightening the pony with all that shouting. Now, either you get back on the box and drive the pony or *I* will.'

Timsy answered with a moan. Somehow I managed to coax him on to my seat. He lay across it at full stretch, flinging his arms and legs about so wildly that he was in danger of rolling off. Though I was tempted to leave him lying by the roadside I reminded myself that I had a duty to my employer so, at the expense of my fingernails, I fastened him by his waist and ankles to the bench with some rope I found beneath the seats. I climbed on to the box in a temper approaching savage. I instructed the Cockatoo, who had calmly cropped the grass at the roadside throughout this taxing operation, to walk on. He flicked back his ears and twisted his head to see who was in charge but when I shook the reins he broke into a trot. It was my first experience of driving an animal but in fact I was doing nothing more than preventing the reins from becoming tangled in the pony's legs, for the Cockatoo kept up a steady pace without another word from me for perhaps two miles while Timsy called on the stars above to persuade Kathleen to look favourably on his love.

'Is this right, Timsy?' I asked as the Cockatoo turned off the road into a thicket of trees.

'Right it is,' he moaned. 'Every damned yard, begging your pardon, is a yard nearer that terror of a woman who's as savage as a cage of ferrets downwind of a rabbit.'

I wondered whether he meant Kathleen or the mistress of the house. The moonlight showed me a long track that sloped steeply upwards. We approached a small house that looked quite pretty in a rambling sort of way and my heart lifted, but as we drew level I saw that planks were nailed over the windows and there was a hole in the roof. The Cockatoo kept up a good pace as we entered a wood. The track wound between the trees in almost total darkness and I shivered until my teeth chattered as the leaves dripped a freezing postscript to the rainstorm on to our heads. I had a brief glimpse of what might have been a pair of gateposts in a high wall and abruptly we seemed to have left the wood behind. A faltering light showed the remains of what had long ago been a garden. There were rows of small trees, perhaps an orchard, and the track had become a curving path without tarmac.

I turned round to ask: 'Is this Curraghcourt?'

'Begor, it is, it is,' Timsy murmured drowsily.

A stray beam glittered on something reflective and I saw a building of some kind clinging to the wall on my left. But this was also a ruin, hardly more than a broken frame containing splintered glass.

'Timsy! This can't be right! I don't believe the Cockatoo knows the way at all.'

For answer there came a snore. The Cockatoo trotted faster, ignoring my attempts to pull him up and soon we left the overgrown garden, the left-hand wheel scraping a gatepost in the opposite wall. The pony snorted with effort as the track inclined sharply to the brow of the hill. As we reached the top the moon sailed free from the clouds and I saw before me a steep drop that rolled down to a shadowy plain. From the floor of the valley, encircled by trees, rose the massive walls and lofty towers of a castle.

SIXTEEN

'Timsy! Wake up!'

We were careering downwards now, the weight of the cart pressing the Cockatoo into a canter. It seemed probable that the cart would be shaken to pieces for the track was rutted and strewn with stones. To prevent myself being thrown off I had to let go of the reins and hang on to the box with both hands. Maria had jumped out and was running ahead of us. A vision of her being crushed beneath our wheels and of the pony's legs being caught in the reins presented itself so clearly to my mind that I closed my eyes and gave myself up to providence.

As we reached level ground the Cockatoo, no doubt thinking of supper, broke into a gallop. I had never been so frightened in my life. Not until the cart ceased to bounce and throw itself wildly from side to side with terrifying creaks and thuds as though about to shatter into its component parts did I dare to look. We were rattling round a curve in the drive towards something that loomed like impenetrable rock. I hung on with one hand and clutched my head protectively with the other arm. The sound of the pony's hoofs changed briefly to a subdued thunder, then rang on stone. We had crossed a wooden bridge and were passing beneath an arch into a courtyard. The Cockatoo came to a standstill, his snorting and blowing echoing from the walls that I sensed rather than saw for it was very dark.

I sat still, waiting for the thumping of my heart and the trembling of my limbs to subside. It seemed scarcely possible that no one had heard us arrive. The Horsemen of the Apocalypse travelling full tilt could not have made more of a racket. A pale glimmer – one could not call it light, it was rather an alleviation of the enveloping gloom

167

– was detectable through a door in front of me that stood fractionally open. I stepped down from the cart, stiff and weak and conscious of my dishevelled state, certain that the reek of decomposing cabbage had transferred itself to my clothes.

I was about to make a search for a knocker or doorbell when I remembered Timsy. To my dismay the moon came from behind a cloud to show me that the rope was dangling loose and the seat was bare. I felt alarmed. He might have been seriously hurt. My first impulse was to run back the way we had come. A little thought persuaded me that without a torch, bandages, a stretcher and strong men to lift it I would only be wasting valuable time.

I stepped into the deep shadow of the doorway. My foot encountered something yielding, there was a low, bloodcurdling growl and sharp pincers gripped my ankle. I jumped back with a shout of surprise and pain. A pair of malevolent yellow eyes blinked up at me. A dog the size of a Shetland pony was stretched across the threshold. No one came in response to my cry. I wondered what to do. I was afraid to step over the dog but somehow I must make my presence, and Timsy's absence, known without delay.

The solution was unexpected. From above my head came stifled laughter. I looked up to receive a cataract of freezing water full in the face. Actually it was probably no more than a small jugful but the shock left me gasping. The dog, which had also received a wetting, lumbered to one side, leaving the entrance clear. I saw the iron handle of a doorbell and yanked it hard. Its relaxed response told me it was not working. I pushed open the door and went in.

I stood in a hall the size of a ballroom, my ankle throbbing and water dripping from my hair into my eyes. The room was deserted. Dark streaks of moisture ran down the massive pillars that supported the vaulted ceiling some forty feet above my head. Circular displays of swords, daggers and battle-axes decorated the panelled walls. Sixty or seventy feet away, at the far end of the hall, tattered battle standards hung from poles above a flight of stairs which divided to disappear in shadow. On one side of the staircase stood a sedan chair, on the other a suit of armour. The light from four enormous glass lanterns was reflected in a puddle in the centre of floorboards as black as bog oak. To my left was a huge stone fireplace containing a smouldering pyramid of ashes. Above it an enormous pair of antlers, far larger than any deer's head could have supported, persuaded me that I must have wandered into a fairy tale. I had not then heard of the Irish elk, a gigantic creature long extinct.

On my right, extending some fifteen feet in length, was a magnificent side table. I walked over to examine it, momentarily forgetful of Timsy. It was mahogany, eighteenth century at a guess, carved by a master in the style of William Kent. It was as fine as anything that had come up for auction at Boswell's. Dust lay on it as thick as felt. A bust of Shakespeare stood in the middle, a tiara perched on his marmoreal locks. Scattered down the table's length were books, newspapers, a vase of dead flowers, a tin of Vim, two blackened sausages on a plate and a bottle of nail varnish, its cap off and a drop of shining pink depending from the brush a millimetre from the precious surface of the table.

I screwed on the lid of the nail varnish before looking quickly at the dates of the newspapers. They were all several weeks old. I inspected the tiara. The setting was good and the stones emitted flashes of light like the real thing. But surely no one in their right minds would leave the front door open and several thousand pounds' worth of diamonds lying around in the hall?

'If you're thinking of stealing it,' said a voice behind me, 'you'll be wasting your time. It's paste.'

I moved away with an alacrity that must have looked guilty and turned to face my accuser. An old woman, a fairy Carabosse, was walking slowly towards me, leaning on two canes. Her spine was so crooked that her head was thrust forward and twisted a little to one side. Her hair was grey with two white wings springing from a high forehead. Her black clothes emphasized the emaciation of her frame. Her flesh seemed to have shrunk on her bones. But when she lifted her head to look me full in the face I saw that her eyes were not old. Not only were they unusually large, they were alight with challenge. She seemed to be all eyes, like a creature that lives in darkness, one of those translucent shrimps that is tossed about on the rolling currents of the ocean floor.

'Or perhaps you're a bailiff, come to distrain the family chattels?' Nor did she have an old woman's voice. It was clear and imperious, with no trace of the brogue. Her expression was proud and unpleasant. 'No job seems too sordid for women these days. I wonder how you like equality now you've got permission to slave like blacks all day and behave like prostitutes all night?'

I was taken aback to find myself on the receiving end of so much rudeness from a stranger, but perhaps there had been a mistake. 'My name's Bobbie Norton. I'm the new housekeeper.'

She narrowed her great cold eyes and took a step nearer to look at me more closely. I smelt cigarette smoke. The wings of her hair were touched with the gold of nicotine. 'Ah, yes. I was told there was another girl coming. You're English.' I could see from the increase of scorn in her expression that this was no recommendation. 'And you're late.'

'I was at the bus station punctually. Mr O'Leary was . . . taken ill on the journey. He fell off the cart and I'm afraid he may be injured. Someone ought to go and look for him.'

She made a derisive sound. 'Why don't you say he was drunk? I hate euphemisms. Why are you wet? It stopped raining hours ago.'

'Someone threw water over me when I was standing on the doorstep.'

'That would have been my grandchildren.'

She spoke as though it was a matter of complete indifference to her.

'That was after your dog bit me.'

'It is the dog's business to bite strangers.' Her eyes travelled slowly from my face down to my shoes. 'Your appearance does you no credit, Miss Norton. I particularly requested that the new girl should be clean.'

This made me angry but I assumed the cool hauteur I usually reserved for my father. 'Then you should have sent a clean cart. And a sober driver. And an umbrella.'

'If we are to get along together, Miss Norton, you had better understand that I do not expect to be answered back.'

I clenched my fists inside my pockets. 'And *I* don't expect to have water thrown over me by delinquent children. Nor to be bitten by a dangerous animal. As for being accused of stealing—'

'Your expectations are of no interest to me. I find you insolent, Miss Norton. I do not doubt that you are conceited. There remains the faint hope that you are not lazy.'

This was too much. I felt my face grow hot. 'If you'll allow me to use the telephone I'll ask a friend to come and pick me up at once.'

'A friend?' The sneer in her voice was galling. 'I suppose you mean a man. Young women these days are no better than common trollops.'

This shaft wounded me more deeply than she could possibly have guessed. 'That's a ridiculous generalization!' I was unable to contain my anger. 'Anyway, my morals are none of your business.'

So much for my resolve to be an invisible menial. That had gone by the board before I had even taken off my coat. But I absolutely refused to submit to insult. I was disconcerted to see something like a spark of humour flash into those lamp-like eyes. Or was it triumph because she had goaded me into losing my temper?

She stared hard at me for a moment or two in a manner I was prepared to resent but when she spoke her tone was no longer contemptuous. 'Well. Perhaps we've both been hasty. It might be better not to judge from first impressions. If I have offended you . . . I am sorry for it.'

I hesitated. My own feelings were not so easy to command. My cheeks were burning and my heart was beating hard.

'Maud? Is that you?'

I heard quick footsteps behind me and a young woman came into the hall.

'There you are! I wondered— Oh, hello! Are you Miss Norton? I'm so sorry I wasn't here to welcome you.' She took my hand and smiled. 'I'm Constance Macchuin. We spoke on the telephone.'

Her eyes were remarkable for thick dark lashes. Her eyebrows were dark too, and bushy, like a man's. She wore an old hacking jacket with bulging pockets and fraying lapels over a cotton print skirt and gumboots. She continued to smile at me while running her fingers through her brown curly fringe as if conscious of its untidiness. Then she tugged at her pony-tail from which wisps were escaping.

'You're not at all what I expected,' she continued. 'So young. And much too good-looking to be *our* housekeeper and . . . What am I talking about?' She laughed. 'I don't know what I expected . . .' Her voice trailed away. 'You look so cold!' She felt my sleeve. 'And you're wet!'

'Someone threw water over me when I was standing on the doorstep.'

'Oh *dear*!' Constance looked dismayed. 'How naughty of the children! Those murder holes were used to pour boiling oil or whatever was to hand, probably rendered mutton-fat, over our enemies in the old days. Though you'd think they'd have known better than come to the front door. Finn and I once soaked an aunt we particularly hated and we were sent to bed for a week. Finn made a great mistake telling the children about poor Aunt Lizzie. I'm sorry, Miss Norton, what must you think of us? Of *course* they must apologize and—'

'Oh, well . . . never mind,' I interrupted, seeing that her distress was genuine. She knocked her words together and breathed quickly

171

while rubbing her forehead with her fingers as though to smooth away a frown. 'Luckily it wasn't very much. I can understand that a murder hole and someone standing right underneath it was too good to resist. Besides, I'd already had one wetting. It rained quite hard after we left the bus station.'

'But . . . surely the Land-Rover . . .?' She looked at Maud.

I saw again the shimmer of mischief on the older woman's face, immediately suppressed. 'You were out enjoying yourself in the Morris and there was no petrol in the Land-Rover. I thought Miss Norton would appreciate an authentic Irish experience. I sent Timsy with the outside car.'

'You didn't! Oh, *Maud*! But I asked Timsy to siphon a gallon out of the tractor specially to go and meet Miss Norton! And now I think of it, you were there when I told him. And I was certainly *not* enjoying myself. Mrs Gogarty's son has gone to America and she begged me to call to stave off her terrible loneliness. I found the entire neighbourhood crammed into her sitting room, having a party.' She turned to me. 'What must you think of us? That old trap's only fit for a museum. We only keep it out of sentiment. And the Cockatoo is far from an ideal carriage horse. It's lucky you weren't injured. Where *is* Timsy?'

As though on cue the front door opened and Timsy shuffled in. He was muddy and dishevelled but, to my relief, in one piece. He put down my suitcases, made a bow in our direction, lost his balance and sat down hard, his legs sticking straight out in front of him.

'Timsy! What are you doing?' Constance went over to him and pulled at his coat. 'Get up! What will Miss Norton think of us?'

'Oh, Miss's a good sport. She'll think nothing of it. We had a grand time in the pub, didn't we?' He winked at me and raised an invisible cap in salute. Presumably the real thing was somewhere beside the track.

'So you've been drinking.' Maud looked at me. 'That explains your bad temper. It's not a good beginning, is it?'

'Oh, Maud!' said Constance crossly. 'That's wicked of you! Of course Miss Norton didn't want to go to that horrible McCarthy's.' She turned back to me. 'It's my fault. I forgot to fill the Land-Rover up when I was in Kilmuree yesterday. You must have been so uncomfortable! You must come upstairs at once and get into something dry and I'll bring you some tea. Or would you prefer whiskey?'

'No. Thank you. I – I'm not going to stay. I thought I'd telephone a friend of mine who's staying with friends not far from here—'

'You're angry with us and I don't blame you one bit. Please, let me try to make amends – I can't bear you to go away thinking so badly of us; really we aren't the monsters we seem . . . You've come such a long way and we need help so badly! Just wait till the morning and take a look at us by daylight, won't you?' She wrinkled her forehead into an expression of pleading and clasped her hands together beseechingly.

'Well . . .' I said slowly. Part of me wanted to flee this lunatic asylum now and for ever but another part, the voice of reason probably, said that the running must stop somewhere and the morning would be as good a time as any to come to a decision. Besides, I was dog tired.

'Good! I'll show you to your room. Maud, did you remember to ask Katty to air a bed in one of the best bedrooms?'

'Certainly not. Those are for guests. I imagine Miss Norton has come intending to do some work. I told Katty to prepare the west tower room.'

Constance picked up one of my suitcases. 'You know quite well those tower rooms aren't fit. Besides Miss Norton *is* a guest – a very welcome guest, too – and when did we last have anyone to stay? No one in their right minds . . . Oh, well, anyway, let's see. This way, Miss Norton.'

'Do call me Bobbie.' I picked up the other case and followed her to the foot of the stairs. I noticed that the suit of armour was lashed together with a skipping rope and a nylon stocking. A mouse sitting on its haunches in the shadow of the sedan chair stopped to wipe its paws over its face before running off.

'I will. And you must call me Constance, Connie or Con. Whatever you like.' She lowered her voice. 'Don't take any notice of Maud. She gets bored and likes to tease.'

As we walked up to the first landing where the staircase divided, I noticed a screwdriver, a half-eaten sausage, a hairdryer and some curls of orange peel deposited randomly on the steps.

'She has arthritis.' Constance panted a little for she had the heavier case. 'I suspect she's always in pain, though she never says anything. And her life hasn't been easy. Of course, it's sup*posed* to be a vale of tears, so we're told, but still I sometimes wonder why God didn't just make us happy and good instead of sending evil to tempt us. He must be awfully fed up by now with our sinning and bewailing and being petitioned all hours of the day and night for favours.' I probably looked cagey as the English generally do when God is mentioned. Constance stopped smiling. 'I haven't offended you, I hope? Father Deglan often ticks me off for being irreverent. But then nobody could be devout enough to please him.'

'I'm not offended at all,' I said. 'I don't go to church very often and I probably don't think about it as much as I should.'

'I'm practically lapsed myself. I make the children go to Mass most Sundays to please Father Deglan but Finn de*tests* religion and makes no bones about it. This is a shockingly ungodly household. Only Sissy, Katty and Pegeen go every Sunday through flood, storm, fire and earthquake.' Constance laughed. 'Maud's a Protestant so of course she's more wicked than any of us.'

I decided from this second reference to a shared childhood that Constance and Finn must be brother and sister. But who might Sissy, Katty and Pegeen be? Despite Constance's friendliness I was unsure of my status as an employee. It might seem impertinent to question Constance about members of her family so instead I asked, 'How old is the house?'

'The middle of it – the hall and the kitchen and the bedrooms above – is fifteenth century. The rest of it was added later. It's all built on the site of a much older castle. My ancestors came over from France in the twelfth century and managed to acquire twenty thousand acres of Connemara. Probably we stole it from someone else. Anyway, the land's all gone now. We've the demesne of ninety acres left and another hundred and twenty that's let to a farmer. And it's more than enough, actually: we can't look after what we've got. I'm ashamed of the garden. Occasionally I'm moved to pull up a weed but ten more always come up immediately. The flowerbeds are nothing more than hummocks in the grass now. Granny adored gardening. Of course she had men to help her, in those days. I remember her bringing in baskets of roses and those lovely blue things – not lupins but the same sort of shape. I can't remember what they're called.'

'Delphiniums?' For a moment I indulged a vision of gardening without Brough and his can of weed-killer before I remembered that I would probably be leaving Curraghcourt in the morning.

'Yes. Delphiniums. Anyway,' continued Constance, 'I was telling you about Maud. I do want you to forgive her, or at least understand what makes her so waspish. For one thing she used to be a beauty and they have a much harder time than the rest of us when their looks go. As Father Deglan often says – with a sort of pointedness I don't like at all – a woman's beauty is a snare framed by the

174

devil to lead men astray and gall and wormwood for herself when it fades. He means my reward's to come: because I'm not a beauty I shan't mind about wrinkles and grey hair. If you ask me, it's small consolation for being a maiden aunt.' She laughed. 'My sympathy goes out to those generations of spinsters expected to fetch shawls and fans for their more fortunate married sisters and be grateful. At least I can be sure there's more than enough here for me to do.'

Actually I thought Constance was pretty and certainly, with a decent haircut and more flattering clothes, perhaps a little dieting . . . I had no opportunity to contradict her disparagement of her own looks for she talked all the time, pausing only to draw breath.

'I must show you a photograph of Maud when she was young. She did the Season in England, you know, and was the most beautiful debutante of her year. I don't know why she married an Irishman. She was born and brought up in Cork but to listen to her talk you'd think she hated Ireland. Harry Crawley wasn't the most eligible of her suitors either – she was proposed to by an earl but Maud said he was so old he was almost dead – I suppose she must have fallen in love with him. But one doesn't think of Maud as being susceptible to the tender passions. Nor, by all accounts, was Harry a romantic figure. He *lived* for hunting. He fell on his head jumping a gate when Violet was eighteen and was brought back a lifeless corpse on a hurdle like Sir John Moore. Do you know the poem by Charles Wolfe?'

We had reached a dark corridor at the head of the stairs. Constance startled me by putting down my case, flinging up an arm and declaiming in a voice that throbbed with feeling:

'We buried him darkly at dead of night,
The sods with our bayonets turning,
By the struggling moonbeam's misty light . . .

'That's so beautiful, so evocative, isn't it?'
'Wonderful,' I enthused.
Constance dropped her arm. 'You really like poetry?'
'Yes. Well, not all poetry, of course. I like the Metaphysicals and Keats and Coleridge—'
'Oh, that's marvellous. I never dared to even hope . . . I put it into the advertisement but that was only to humour the children. Flavia said we must each make one condition so we could find

175

someone we'd all like. Of course it was Finn who put in the bit about a philosophical temperament. I thought that might put people off but he said on past showing anyone who'd even consider the job would be either too stupid or too deranged to— Oh, of course I didn't mean that *you* . . .' Constance put her hand on my arm. 'Bobbie, you *will* stay, won't you? I have such a strong feeling that we're going to be friends.'

It was difficult – impossible not to respond to such kindness. There was about Constance a beguiling candour that could not fail to attract. 'Well . . . perhaps tomorrow things will seem . . . Thank you for making me feel so welcome.'

'Welcome! And when I think of the soaking you had from the children and that dreadful trap and McCarthy's and the rain . . . What's funny?'

'I don't . . . know. So much has happened . . . It's exhaustion, probably . . . I feel quite hysterical . . .' I went off into another fit of laughter and this time Constance joined in.

'Timsy was right. You *are* a good sport. Give me that other case. You'll never manage it in that state.' She took it before I could protest and walked with buckling knees a little ahead of me. The corridor seemed to go on for ever. It was impossible to get any idea of the architecture or decoration, partly because the light was not good but also because stacked against the walls were chairs, tables, bookcases, cabinets, paintings, drawings and weaponry in no discernible order. 'What was I saying?' she threw over her shoulder. 'Oh, yes, Maud and Harry. Violet was just about to do the Season herself but when her father's will was read they found he was terribly in debt so she couldn't, after all.'

I was confused again. Violet was the daughter of Maud and Harry, then. But what relation were either to Constance?

'It turned out that a nasty little man Harry had been sleeping with had threatened to tell, so Harry had paid him thousands of pounds not to and that's why the Crawley estate was mortgaged down to the last paperclip. The minute Harry died the little beast squealed to the newspapers, so it was all for nothing.' I understood that Mrs Crawley's husband had been blackmailed because of his homosexuality. 'There was quite a scandal – it's still illegal in Ireland, of course – and Maud was deeply grateful to Finn for wanting to marry Violet.' So Violet was Finn's wife and Mrs Crawley was, therefore, his mother-in-law. 'Now, let's see.'

Constance threw open a door to our left and switched on the

light. A four-poster bed was buried beneath boxes of books, a heap of clothes, a stag's head and the top half of a pram.

'I must get round to clearing this up. How these things do move around so. I swear they're bewitched. Do you know that opera by Ravel: *L'Enfant et les Sortilèges*? When all the furniture comes alive and chases the horrid little boy who's been ill-using them? This won't do for you at all.'

She closed the door and opened the neighbouring room. It was jammed with teetering piles of canvas-and-steel stacking chairs.

'What on earth? Oh, goodness! These must be the wretched chairs we had for the poetry festival. No one could find them afterwards and there was such a row. We had to pay for them in the end. Finn was awfully angry about it. Really, the price the company charged, you'd think they were Chinese Chippendale.'

'Perhaps the hire company will take them back and reimburse you.'

'I doubt it. It was rather a long time ago. Now.' She opened a third door. '*This* looks better!'

I could not share her enthusiasm. It was true there was nothing on the bed except a mattress and a bag disgorging feathers that one might, in an optimistic mood, call a pillow. And the smell of damp that seemed to catch the back of my throat might be dispersed by lighting a fire in the grate of the undeniably fine marble fireplace. There was a beautiful serpentine-fronted mahogany chest of drawers that with some polishing would not have looked out of place in a Bond Street show room. But I was reluctant to spend the night with the stuffed racehorse. I could have slept in a stable with a live one if absolutely required to do so, but this dead one, its head hanging over the bed at an awkward angle due to the discharge of stuffing at its neck, with both eyes missing and cobwebs festooning its poor crumpled flanks, was an object of absolute repulsion.

I pointed to the ceiling. 'Do you think it might be dangerous . . .?'

'Oh dear, yes. Thank goodness you noticed!' The exquisite chandelier hung from plaster that bulged like a boil about to burst. 'There must be a leak. I'll get Timsy – he's really quite a good handyman when he's sober – to look at it in the morning.'

It did not look to me as though Timsy's skills had been much exercised. We returned to the landing.

'I'm afraid it'll have to be the west tower after all. Never mind. If we can only persuade you to stay, we'll soon fix you up with something better.' I followed Constance to the end of the corridor and up a spiral stone staircase. 'Be careful, some of the steps are worn. I'm sure you know that most spiral stairs wind clockwise so that the sword-arm is free coming down – to defend yourself against invaders, that is. But at Curraghcourt they all wind anti-clockwise. That's because most of the Macchuins are left-handed.' She paused and beamed down at me. 'Just a little local colour in case you're interested. I'm not actually – left-handed, I mean – but Finn is and Flurry and Flavia are too.'

'Flurry and Flavia?' I addressed Constance's ascending bottom interrogatively.

'My nephew and niece. Such darlings they are. Oh, I forgot, you'll be thinking them very bad. But most of the time they're quite good. Flurry's short for Florence. It's Finn's second name, too. He was teased about it at school for the English think it's a girl's name, and he wanted to call Flurry something safe like Henry or John but Violet insisted it was good for a boy to have to fight for respect.'

So Finn, who seemed to be the supreme authority at Curraghcourt, was the father of two children called Flavia and Florence, known as Flurry. I was beginning to get the hang of the family tree but there were still Sissy, Katty and Pegeen to be accounted for . . . and hadn't there been mention on the telephone of a third child? Suddenly I was so tired that I had a violent need to lay my head on something horizontal and give myself up to sleep.

Constance was panting with the effort of hauling up two suitcases. 'Why don't we take them up one at a time?' I suggested. Together, with her pulling and me pushing, we got the troublesome cases on to a small landing about the size of a telephone box.

'Here we are.' Constance fumbled with the handle. It turned without effect. 'Damn! I remember now. One of the screws is loose. Just a minute.' She dropped to her knees and felt around in the gloom. 'We're in luck! Here it is. I'll get Timsy to look at it in the morning.'

Once the screw had been inserted, the door opened easily enough. The room was, as one might expect in a round tower, perfectly circular. The small stone chimneypiece was curved but the straight backs of the wardrobe, the chest of drawers and the writing table stood at awkward angles to the walls. The bed, a narrow, crooked half-tester hung with brown curtains, occupied the centre of the room. Four curtainless lancet windows revealed the blackness of night. I detected an acrid smell that I could not immediately identify.

'What do you think?' Constance's eyes were fixed anxiously on my face.

'It will do beautifully, thank you.'

'I hope the bed's been properly aired.' Constance lifted the covers and put in a hand. 'Ah, yes, Katty's remembered the brick. Be careful when you get in. I've so often cracked a toe. There's your candle.' She pointed to the bedside table on which was a box of matches and a candlestick. 'The generator runs out of petrol sometimes. Quite often, actually. Towels.' She pointed to a towel horse that stood near the fire. 'I wonder, have I forgotten anything?' Frowning, she looked round the room. 'Oh yes, I must warn you. Don't, whatever you do, pull that.' She pointed to a rope that came down through a hole in the ceiling and disappeared through a corresponding hole in the floor. 'It rings the bell right at the top of the tower. In the old days the Macchuins rang it to raise the alarm when they saw the O'Flahertys coming over the hill armed to the teeth and lusting for blood. The peasants working in the fields ran like mad when they heard it to get inside before the drawbridge was raised. The bell's called Scornach Mór. It means "Big Throat".'

'Did the O'Flahertys ever manage to storm the castle?'

'Never! We're proud of that. There are some famous verses about the battles between the Macchuins and the O'Flahertys—'

'Oh, good,' I said quickly. 'So presumably the bell hasn't been rung for a very long time.'

'Actually, as recently as last year. I told you about the poetry festival – it wasn't altogether a success. The man who slept in this room thought it was a bell for the servants. Apparently he was expecting to be brought breakfast in bed.' She laughed. 'It seems funny now but at the time everyone was thrown into a panic, thinking we were being attacked by the IRA. The *Garda* and the entire fire brigade from Kilmuree rolled up within half an hour: it was a record turnout. Finn had to give them a hefty tip to make them go away. The poor poet left in a huff after Finn called him a drone and a parasite. You'd think Finn had never been young and foolish himself but I can remember lots of times . . .' Constance frowned. 'In Ireland poetry has done marvellous things. I really believe it's helped to fuse Gaelic and Anglo-Irish into a single tradition . . . You're yawning!'

I had pinched my nostrils till my eyes watered but I could not disguise the fact that weariness was stealing over my limbs and befogging my brain so that I was unable to understand what she was talking about.

'You poor thing! You must be *so* tired after your journey. You look quite white!'

179

'It's nothing. A long day . . . not much sleep last night on the boat . . .'

'I've been selfish. Talking far too much.' Constance looked contrite. 'You must go straight to bed and I'll bring up your supper on a tray.'

'Oh, no, really, that would be giving you too much trou-u—' I yawned again. '—ble.'

'*Not* at all. I'll just show you the bathroom and then I'll fetch you some nice hot soup. Well, I don't suppose it will be very nice because I made it and I'm Ireland's worst cook but I'll make sure it's hot. As the wind's in the south-west the stove's behaving itself at the moment.'

The bathroom was at the foot of the tower stairs. Bathrooms at Cutham Hall were not luxurious so I did not mind too much the acreage of chipped and cracked white tiles, the brown stains at the tap end of the bath, or even the fact that part of the lavatory seat was missing.

Constance saw me looking around for a bath plug. 'Here you are.' She handed me a round pebble. 'You have to stuff your flannel in the hole and then weigh it down with this. It keeps the water in just about long enough to wash.' I thought I had kept my expression politely neutral, but she said at once, 'I know what you're thinking. It *is* bloody hopeless, isn't it? I do try but I'm just not good at domestic things. Maud was so rude to the last housekeeper she gave in her notice. She said she preferred to starve than be insulted worse than a Turkoman. I don't know why Turkomans should be the recipients of rudeness but anyway . . . Naturally, we gave her a month's wages and she was extremely fat so I'm sure she *didn't* starve.'

'What was the quarrel about?'

'Maud accused Mrs Heaney – that was the housekeeper's name – of trying to poison us. We'd all had upset stomachs after a horrible supper of rabbit and turnips. Also she said Mrs Heaney was a sot and had been at the Château Margaux. I don't see how she *could* have for Finn keeps the key of the cellar and no one else is allowed to go down there on pain of having their throat cut ear to ear and their giblets pickled and hung from the battlements. I'd say it was the local poteen she was drinking. The final straw was when Maud said no wonder there were colonies of flies in the house because Mrs Heaney smelt like a tub of bad butter. She *did* have a peculiarly rancid smell, but of course Maud shouldn't have told her. Mrs Heaney made her exit at that point with the line about the Turkoman. Perhaps she took the bath plug in revenge.'

'How inventive of her. In the circumstances, I'd better have a quick bath before Mrs Crawley draws invidious comparisons in Mrs Heaney's favour.'

'Don't take any notice of the noises the water heater makes. It's never been known to blow up. I'll give you fifteen minutes before I bring supper.'

After Constance had gone I employed the patent plug method and was pleased to see steam cloud the tiles. As instructed I ignored the banging and shuddering of the heater and soon was seated up to my waist in brown but deliciously soft water, presumably straight from a bog. There was no soap but it would not do to be fussy. On returning to my room I found that Constance had lit the fire. A warm glow transfigured the rough stone walls while the delicious smell of burning turves overlaid the pungent atmosphere. It felt almost luxurious to climb, fairly clean and pretty nearly dry, into bed. The hot brick wrapped in a towel was gloriously comforting, as was the gentle hiss of flames. Constance returned with a bowl of soup that had a strange earthy flavour, some sweetish bread that was delicious, a hunk of dry cracked cheese and a packet of pink wafer biscuits, which were a little stale.

'It was all I could find,' Constance apologized. 'I roasted a chicken earlier but the children finished it. It had an unpleasant taste anyway. There was a little plastic tray underneath it which I only discovered after I'd cooked it.'

'This is fine. It's so kind of you to look after me. I promise I'll be better tomorrow.'

'I'd bring you supper in bed every night if you'd only stay. Finn'll be furious when he gets back from Dublin and finds Mrs Heaney gone.' Her face took on the anxious expression that, despite her readiness to laugh, seemed never far away. The master of the house was irascible, apparently. It would be a mistake to commit myself to staying until I had met him and decided for myself whether he was a man sorely pressed or a heartless tyrant.

Constance took the tray from me and put it on the bedside table. 'Won't you lie down and make yourself comfortable? Are you warm enough?'

I nodded drowsily and murmured my thanks once more.

'I haven't let you get a word in edgeways, I know. Finn's away so much and Maud's so . . . well, you've seen for yourself. I adore the children but of course they don't particularly want to talk to me. Anyway I worry sometimes that Flavia's too withdrawn. Flurry's a law unto himself, the darling. And Liddy's just what you'd expect

181

of a girl her age. As for Sissy, she's an original too, no doubt about it . . . and then there's Eugene.' I dimly perceived that she blushed. Flavia, Flurry, Sissy, Liddy, Eugene. The names seem to wheel in my head like a flock of birds. Constance's expression became eager, entreating. 'It would be so wonderful to have someone I could really talk to.'

I smiled and looked my gratitude. The feeling was quite sincere, but I was too exhausted to speak.

'Poor Bobbie.' She drew a chair near to my pillow and patted my arm. 'You're shattered, aren't you? Never mind, we'll talk more in the morning. Shall I recite "The Burial of Sir John Moore" through to the end? I always say poetry to myself before I go off to sleep. I find it banishes the little annoyances of the day.'

I closed my eyes to express assent.

'"Not a drum was heard, not a funeral note . . ."' Constance began in dramatic tones, but the rest was lost as a wave seemed to roll over me and drag me from the shore into the trackless deep that is dreamless sleep.

SEVENTEEN

It must have been nearly dawn when I woke. For a while I was adrift. I heard a sheep bleat distantly. I was not at home then. I opened my eyes. Dark, unfamiliar shapes advanced and receded as I tried to make sense of the perspectives of the room. As I began to knit impressions into thoughts the events of the previous day came back to me as a procession of dislocated images. Improbable as it seemed I was in a castle in the remotest part of Ireland. Immediately I was aware that the room was intolerably stuffy. It smelt of something penetratingly sour which came in waves whenever I turned restlessly between the sheets. Then I remembered Burgo and was gripped by pain.

I sat up, swung my legs over the edge of the bed and, remembering even in my misery the condition of the carpet, searched with my toes until I found my shoes. I stumbled to the window, pushed it open and took deep breaths of fresh air. The sky was dark, streaked faintly with pink. I stood for a while watching the stars fade as the horizon became a pencil-line of gold, trying not to feel or think until I was shivering so much that my jaws ached. Leaving the window open I returned to bed. Turning my face to a pillow that smelt like the lion house at the zoo I cried long and heartily.

From the moment Harriet had planted in my mind the idea of escaping to Ireland, I had had neither the time nor the opportunity to give myself up to grief. I had thought of Burgo frequently with longing, with tenderness, with anxiety, but I had not told myself that I had parted from the love of my life for ever. I had informed Kit that such was the case but I had not truly believed it. Now I had to say to myself, sternly, firmly, finally, that everything was over.

Until my affair with Burgo I had not believed in the alchemy of love. My romantic fantasies had featured men remote from the world's stain, indifferent to if not actually scornful of the establishment, devoted to a life of the intellect, with a passion for Hawksmoor perhaps, or Russian *objets de vertu*. In other words, they had to be like me but infinitely better, wiser, cleverer, nobler and possessed of encyclopaedic knowledge. They also had to be heterosexual, which was going against Nature, but I had continued to hope. A Tory politician, and one moreover not particularly interested in the decorative arts and without epicurean tastes, was so far from my imagining that I could only bow to love's transfiguring power.

From the moment we had declared our love in the rain-drenched laurel bushes of Cutham Hall I had realized that my proud presumption that I was in a position to dictate terms was an illusion. After that I had deliberately silenced all misgivings by losing myself in the absorbing happiness of the present. I had disobeyed every prompting of common sense to look out for myself. I had fooled myself to the top of my bent, as the saying is. I had crushed one illusion – that I knew what I was doing – with the weight of a thousand others.

After he had driven all the way from London to kiss me I had endured three days of waiting for the telephone to ring quite as meekly as that irritatingly humble Griselda whose knuckling under to her husband's tyranny had so infuriated me when we read about her in *The Canterbury Tales* at school. Now I had an inkling of what love was, my understanding of human nature seemed to have expanded a hundredfold. But probably that was an illusion too.

'Roberta.' I could hear voices in the background.

'Hello.'

Mrs Treadgold came into the hall. There must have been something in my voice that suggested intrigue for out of the corner of my eye I saw her pause and begin to poke the feather duster between the banisters.

'Can you pick me up from Blackheath station at twelve on Sunday morning?' He sounded preoccupied, businesslike.

'Yes.'

'I'll walk up to that little hump-backed bridge beyond the car-park and meet you there.'

'All right.'

'Goodbye.' He had put down the receiver.

I favoured Mrs Treadgold with a beatific smile. She, poor woman, had a job in hand for the staircase was floridly carved and filmed with the dust of ages. I floated away to peel potatoes, each one of which seemed to be surrounded by a shimmering mist.

Burgo was leaning on the bridge, looking down at the water when I drove up. I had thought of this moment almost every minute of every waking hour. I had planned to be poised, fluent and witty, but his actual presence was devastating to my composure. When he got into the car I felt suddenly so shy I could not look at him. Somehow I put the car into gear and found myself driving somewhere, anywhere. My mind was confused. How had it happened that I found myself in this extraordinarily intimate complicity with a man I hardly knew? He was so unfamiliar, so urbane, so blindingly fair, so . . . well . . . big. He filled the interior of the Wolseley, his head almost touching the ceiling, his knees brushing the dashboard. What was I doing having secret assignations with someone who could only bring me to harm? I was courting disaster. I felt almost sick with fright.

After we had driven a couple of miles in silence Burgo pointed to a lay-by ahead. 'Just pull up over there,' he said, like a driving instructor about to explain the intricacies of a three-point turn. I did as I was told. 'Turn the engine off.'

I obeyed, improvising a flight across the fields.

'Look at me, darling.'

With reluctance I turned my head and saw that the light of mockery in his eyes, the first thing that had attracted me to him at that ghastly lunch in the Carlton House Hotel, was absent. On this occasion I was grateful. He took my hand.

'Don't think me conceited when I say that I knew this was going to happen. Right from the beginning. I knew it *had* to happen. But even though I knew it I'm still astonished that now it has. The anticipation has only been months but it feels like half my life. I shall never be the same person again.'

With those words he ceased to be an intimidating stranger. He lifted my hand and kissed it. I had the fanciful idea that we were familiars wandering the earth who, despite every probability, had found each other. I forgot that words uttered as solemn truths at moments like these can be ridiculed or disowned in time to come. I forgot that lovers have thrilled to the bio-chemistry of physical attraction since they first crawled from primeval ponds. I believed that our love was decreed by a superior natural law, that it was irresistible and unalterable.

'Do you mind very much what sort of place we have lunch?' he asked.

'No. Anything will do.'

He rested his hand lightly on my knee. 'Let's go on then and see what we come to.'

There was no attempt to repeat the uncontrolled passion of our last meeting. How astute he was, how accurately he divined my feelings. It seemed to me a confirmation of the fitness of our relationship. It did not occur to me then that he was just good at reading other people's minds.

After a few miles of wooded lanes we crossed into Kent. Soon we saw a sign: '200 yards next left. The Fisherman's Reel. Good Food and Accommodation. Recommended.'

'It doesn't say by whom,' said Burgo. 'Never mind. We can drive on if it's horrible. I ought to have done some research. It's been a busy few days. On Thursday the last division was at five in the morning. I made a speech about the use of clear English in legal documents. I hope it was all right. I can't remember a word of what I said. I was thinking about you all the time.'

'Were you? I'm glad.'

'Are you, darling? You don't despise me for being so helplessly in love with you that I'm reduced to a dumb animal half the time?'

Naturally I did not. I turned to look at him.

'Mind the hedge,' he said.

The Fisherman's Reel was small, thatched, whitewashed and pretty with a duck-pond at its gate and apple trees in its orchard-like garden where hens pecked and cats lazed. Beyond the orchard a narrow river ran, brown and rippling beneath a tunnel of willows and elders. There were no other customers. We sat under the apple trees and drank a bottle of wine. The sun caressed the blistered table-top and my bare arms and played with the shadows on the long grass.

'You look like a visitation,' he said. 'The light's making a halo round your head and your hair's burning like fire. You ought to have a flaming sword. I can hardly look at you.' He took my hand and held on to it. 'Don't ascend on clouds of glory just yet.'

The waitress brought out a cloth, knives and forks and a jug of water. She banged the things down and told us what there was on the menu in a tone that suggested we were putting her to a great deal of trouble by requesting food. We ordered duck and green peas. It was surprisingly good: half a duck each, crisp outside, succulent within; roast potatoes; a mountain of peas that were sweet and not overcooked. I was so affected by nervous exhilaration that I ate everything. Burgo managed about half his. The waitress came out again to clear the plates. She looked at us with barely concealed hostility and asked us if we wanted pudding. With her pointed teeth and cold eyes she reminded me of a pike. Burgo praised the food and the prettiness of the place and asked her whether she was a native of Sussex.

To my surprise the woman unbent in response to his compliments. I suppose it was rare that good-looking young men bothered to be charming to her. She and her husband had bought the Fisherman's Reel three years ago, having run a public house in the East End for twenty years. Her name, Burgo discovered, was Mrs Slattery. Mr Slattery did the cooking while she saw to the housekeeping and accounting. It had been her husband's lifelong dream to move to the country but she missed the noise and bustle of town life. They were losing money due to the new bypass; there were not enough customers; she was bored. I noticed that though she continued to complain, the sour look left her face and she became animated, almost girlish.

'Now what will you have, madam?' She smiled at me for the first time. 'Bert makes a very nice bread-and-butter pudding. Or there's raspberries picked this morning.'

'Raspberries, please.' I smiled back at her but she was looking at Burgo.

'Bread-and-butter pudding sounds too good to be resisted,' he said. 'But if the raspberries are home-grown I'm going to have some of those as well.'

Mrs Slattery told him about Bert's vegetable patch and he looked as fascinated as though she had been revealing the secret of the construction of the pyramids.

'We'll have some of your best cognac with our coffee,' he said and Mrs Slattery hurried away, quite delighted with us.

'What a pity she doesn't know who you are,' I said. 'If she was a Labour supporter this morning, she'd be a Conservative now.'

'I don't suppose she bothers to vote. They'll be too busy to make a special trip into town. And she's the kind who thinks politicians are only concerned with feathering their own nests at her expense.' I was conscious of thinking much the same myself but I said nothing. 'The trouble is, we do so little for people like the Slatterys. They work hard so we can take a large slice of their profits to support the idle, the dishonest and the broken-backed. The tax threshold ought to be much higher than it is. Of course there's satisfaction to be got from doing a job well and leading a decent life and all that but they ought to have some kind of acknowledgement from the State. We support farmers when they have a bad year and we bail out certain flashy industries if the boss has the ear of a minister but people like the Slatterys, earning, I would guess, not much above subsistence level, have to soldier on unaided.'

I realized that his interest was genuine, that he had actually enjoyed talking to her. My own attitude to people like Mrs Slattery was regrettably self-centred, indifferent at best. I was too diffident or too lazy to try to break through barriers of dislike and resentment.

'Tell me, darling.' He took my hand again. 'I was wondering: *must* you go home tonight? Do you think your family could do without you for a few more hours?'

'I *could* telephone Oliver and tell him what I'd planned for supper,' I said with a coolness that belied the beating of my heart. 'Luckily my father insists we have something cold on Sundays "to save the servants". The fact that we haven't actually got any servants is immaterial.'

'Would you, darling? There's nothing I want more in the world than to spend the night with you.'

I had noticed a call-box several yards down the lane from the duck-pond. Fortunately Oliver answered. He was drowsy and inclined to protest at the idea of chopping beetroot into a bowl and folding gherkins and capers into mayonnaise but I promised that one evening next week I would drive him to the Nine Elms where there was a new barmaid who had taken his fancy. Oliver had yet to turn up on time to take his driving test, which negligence had frequently obliged me to play the part of Pandarus.

'I've taken a room,' said Burgo when I returned. '*The* room, I should say. Apparently Mrs Slattery's mother-in-law is in the other. She's bedridden and we're not to take any notice if she calls out in the night. Mrs Slattery says she's a wicked old woman who likes to cause trouble and make people traipse up and down with trays all day. It seems there's no love lost.'

'She has my sympathy. Actually, they both do.'

'You don't mind it not being a five-star hotel?'

'I much prefer this. Really. I don't actually like expensive hotels. Besides . . . we have to be careful, don't we?'

Burgo gazed at me reflectively. After a while he said, 'Roberta. You have *all* my love.'

I recalled these words and the look that accompanied them many times in the months that followed.

Over pudding and coffee – I ate most of his – we talked of ordinary things. Except that nothing was ordinary once we had shared it, it was transmuted to something precious, ineffaceable. Afterwards we drove down to the coast and walked along the beach, peered into rock pools, dug fossils from the cliff, played with a friendly dog. We watched yachts careering across the bay and dunlins and plovers probing the sand for worms and molluscs. We collected seaweed and shells. Burgo was impressed by my ability to identify a thick-lipped dog whelk and a wentletrap.

'Oliver and I used to spend part of the summer holiday with Aunt Cornelia who lived in Lyme Regis. Not really an aunt, but a distant cousin. She didn't like children. We were sent out to play immediately after breakfast and we weren't allowed to come back until six o'clock. Then we had to go straight to bed. Aunt Cornelia had been married to a professor of marine biology and his books were kept in our bedroom. I used to read Oliver to sleep with descriptions of shells and birds.'

'Tell me more about it. I like to imagine you as a child.'

'When the weather was good it was lovely. We spent our pocket money on food, mostly chips and sweets, and paddled and made sandcastles. But more often it rained and the wind from the sea was freezing. Oliver used to go blue. He was the thinnest child you've ever seen, with limbs like bamboo canes, swollen at the joints, and skin like biscuit porcelain. I used to take him into a promenade shelter and wrap him in newspapers from litter bins, tied on with string. Once we found a pair of knickers on the beach which Oliver put on over the top of his shorts. Aunt Cornelia carried them out to the dustbin between finger and thumb, smacked Oliver until he screamed and sent him to bed without any supper. We were awfully pleased, I regret to say, when shortly afterwards she was arrested for shoplifting and my father refused to speak to her ever again.'

'It doesn't sound a very happy childhood.'

'Oh, it was like most people's, I suppose. Good and bad. Nothing terrible. It's not that easy to be happy as a child, is it?'

'I think most people would say the opposite. No responsibilities, no worries about money, no fear of the future, no regrets, no knowledge of wickedness, sickness, death.'

'But children are made to dance to other people's tunes too much. The boredom and stupidity of school is agony. And then girls can be so beastly to one other. One feels the wounds of rejection and humiliation and failure so deeply. My pony was the best thing about my childhood, actually.'

'I know from Fleur that no man can hope to rival a horse in a girl's affections.'

'That's true, of course. But what you mean is that childhood's saving grace is living utterly in the moment. One's pleasures, when they come, are unmixed.'

'I'd like to recapture that childlike intensity of feeling so I could always remember this – being here with you – whenever I'm in a committee meeting or listening to a dull speech.' Burgo walked round in a circle, looking up at the sky while the breeze lifted his hair and ruffled his shirt. 'A cloudless sky. The sea burning my eyes with its sparkling. Seagulls; the grating of shingle beneath my feet. The pink of the inside of this shell' – he held it out towards me – 'is the colour of . . . what would you say? Roses? Flesh? Let's agree to be utterly irresponsible and live in the moment.'

I took the shell and put it in my pocket. 'We can try.'

We had tea in a café on the seafront of the nearest town. We bought toothbrushes, toothpaste and underwear. I bought a comb and Burgo bought a shirt. Then we drove back to the Fisherman's Reel. There were two other couples in the bar so we retreated to the orchard. Mrs Slattery came out with a cold bottle of Sancerre and cushions for our chairs. The setting sun warmed the top of my head and a cat sat on my knee. Burgo smoked a cigar while I ate crisps. I was so happy that I could not keep myself from smiling.

Despite the dropping temperature we ate outside. The soup was homemade tomato, the boiled potatoes and runner beans home-grown, the chicken one of Mrs Slattery's own. Burgo talked about what it was like to be a Member of Parliament. He described esoteric rules: no shaking of hands, for example, and no applauding. Approval was expressed by waving order papers, cheering or, if there was one, banging the table with one's hands. If you wanted to make a point during a division you had to put on a collapsible silk opera hat kept in the chamber specially for the purpose.

'It sounds just like a boys' public school, with arcane slang for Matron and tuck.'

'It's quite absurd, I agree. But there's so much about my life that's ridiculous. I can't think why I enjoy it so much. I often spend from breakfast to at least ten o'clock at night – sometimes the debate and voting goes on until dawn – at the House, tabling questions, attending meetings, dictating letters, researching in the library, meeting constituents. On Fridays I come down to Sussex and spend two days visiting schools, factories, housing projects, retirement homes, sitting through several hours of surgery, trying to put people's lives straight when they've gone so crooked that only emigration or a world war would do any good. Then there are lunches and dinners, parties, bazaars, fêtes – you name it, I'm supposed to be there.'

'Even tennis tournaments.'

'Ah, well, I must admit that wasn't in the line of duty. Don't be angry – I asked Fleur to let me know when you were next going to Ladyfield. I wasn't expecting it to be the next day but the minute she rang to tell me about the tournament, I arranged with my pair in the House to be away for the afternoon and hopped on to the next train. I know it sounds like wolfish behaviour but I was desperate. I knew you'd try to avoid meeting me. Are you furious?'

Was I? I disliked the idea that Fleur and Burgo had discussed me in such evidently frank terms, but the end was so entirely what I had myself desired that it would be hypocrisy to be annoyed. And had I not myself arranged a few hours ago to conduct Oliver to the Nine Elms so he could try to seduce the barmaid?

I laughed. 'I don't think I *can* be angry with you.'

'I should hate myself if I ever gave you real cause.'

'Remember, we said we were going to be irresponsible and live in the present? But would it be cheating if you went on telling me more about your life during the week? Just so I can imagine it tomorrow when you're back governing the nation and I'm sieving lumps out of custard. How depressingly our destinies have conformed to the stereotype. Wasn't it James the First who said that Parliament can do anything but make a man into a woman?'

'He was wrong. The laws about transsexuals are being amended to do just that.'

We sat outside, talking, holding hands discreetly beneath the table until the mosquitoes chewed our ankles and it grew dark. Inside the lounge bar was closed for redecorating so the snug was crowded.

'Want a nightcap?' Burgo asked. I shook my head, aware of many eyes upon us. 'Well, then . . . shall we go up?'

A man leaning against the counter made a great play of looking at his watch and then winked at Burgo.

'Goodnight, sir. Madam.' Mrs Slattery nodded at us from behind the bar. Her fishy eyes were curious, her smile conspiratorial. I wondered what there was about us that proclaimed so deafeningly that we were unmarried and in love. That is to say, not married to each other. A burst of raucous laughter accompanied us up the stairs.

The room was small with a sloping beamed ceiling and a floor with a gradient nearly as steep. It contained a bed, a wardrobe, a chair on which stood a table lamp and a minute triangular wash-basin in one corner. The curtains were faded and the furniture painted with a lurid green gloss, but everything was clean.

'I'm afraid they'll be amusing themselves at our expense for the rest of the evening,' I said as we surveyed each other across an expanse of white candlewick. 'I wonder why we're so conspicuous? I think it's your fault for being so tall.'

'Darling, don't you realize you'd be conspicuous anywhere? There isn't a man between eight and eighty who won't look at you and speculate what it would be like to hold you in his arms. It was the first thing I thought of that day at the Carlton House—'

There were several sharp raps from the other side of the wall.

'What was that?' I asked, startled.

Burgo dropped his voice. 'It must be Mrs Slattery's mother-in-law.'

I giggled and at once there was more knocking.

'The walls must be paper thin,' whispered Burgo. 'I'll close the window— E-ow!'

'Burgo! Oh, that must have hurt!' He had banged his head against one of the beams and fallen on his back, luckily on to the bed. I forgot to keep my voice down and the knocking was louder and more indignant than before.

'I think I've fractured my skull. The room's gone dark.'

'Let me see!' I leaned over him. 'Oh, you poor, poor darling! There's blood. Just a minute.' I edged my way round the bed to the washbasin and soaked the towel in cold water. 'Is it *absolute* agony?' I knelt on the bed beside him and dabbed tenderly at the tiny cut.

'Absolute.' He put his arms around me and pulled me down on top of him. 'There's only one cure for it. Now, my darling . . . now . . . now . . .'

There had followed a fusillade of knocking which, I am ashamed to say, we ignored.

I lay in my bed at Curraghcourt, tears sliding down my face, and wondered how I should ever get over it. Where was Burgo now? I imagined him lying awake in his flat in Lord North Street, thinking of me, trying to guess where I had gone – why I had gone. During

192

those terrible telephone conversations after the newspapers had got hold of the story I had tried to explain why I could not allow him to give up everything for me. He had accused me of pride. He had asked me if I loved him enough to put up with a few months of disapproval and misunderstanding. He had sworn that his love would not falter. Besides, he had added, though he would have to offer his resignation as Minister for Culture, he had friends in the constituency and he thought he might hold on to his seat. If we were discreet and he worked hard and behaved himself he might, after a few years out in the cold, be allowed to creep back into office. When I heard the determination in his voice I knew that whatever he might say about being ready to consider the world well lost for love, he was pinning all his hopes on being able to recover his position.

And why should I doubt that this would be so? Supposing it was only a question of waiting a while before we had everything we wished for? What was I doing, wilfully sacrificing all my happiness? And perhaps his? Suddenly I sat up in bed, threw back the covers and felt again for my shoes. I would get dressed immediately, ring for a taxi and begin the long, complicated journey home without delay. I would leave a note for Constance thanking her for her kindness, explaining that I was sorry to let her down but that circumstances beyond my control . . . From Paddington I would go straight to Lord North Street. It would be dark by then. The reporters would have gone home. The couple on the ground floor would let me in. I would run up the stairs, take the key from the Chinese jar, let myself into the flat. He would probably be out. I would get into bed to wait for him as I had done several times before. He would come in weary, sad. I would see in his eyes recognition, joy . . . Ah! I paused in the act of reaching for my dressing-gown. Supposing Burgo was thinking of me at this moment with feelings that included relief that I had taken matters into my own hands, that I had saved him from the infinitely painful business of ending it?

I guessed he would find it impossible to say the words that would break the ties between us. Burgo was like other men in that he shrank from emotional difficulties. In pursuing me he had not thought of his career, his wife, of what he might lose. Men are such simple creatures, motivated by lust, ambition, immediate gratification. Supposing his enemies were too much for him? He had brains, money, looks, charm. Many men were envious of him. He might not be able to win back what he had lost. He would try, I knew, to keep from me the knowledge that every day he regretted his sacrifice. But I would see through the pretence. As I grew wrinkled and grey-haired and my bust merged with my waist and my conversation became a dull reiteration of prejudices, he would look at me and ask himself if it had been worthwhile and I would know what he was thinking. Men do not love as women do. They may remain fond, as of an old dog or a comfortable pair of shoes, but fondness would not compensate for everything that Burgo had given up.

So I told myself for the thousandth time as I lay back in bed and pulled the covers over me once more. I was a coward. I could not endure the torture of seeing his love grow less day by day. But surely I did our love a disservice? It was not as the common run of loves. It was worth so much more than tawdry ambition. A politician's life was one of cynical manoeuvres, suppressing convictions, distorting the truth in order to catch the eye and ear of those who had crawled higher. As I pressed my hands to my temples I heard a soft thud which came from the direction of the window.

It was too dark to see into the shadows. I waited, still holding my breath. A faint scratching sound was followed by another thud. Something, or things, were creeping across the floor. I felt for the light switch, pressed it. Nothing happened. With shaking fingers I found the matches and lit the candle, holding it high. Five pairs of eyes gleamed, blinked. One pair headed back towards the window.

I let out my breath in a long slow sigh. Only someone as deprived of pets as I had been could have failed to recognize immediately that the overpowering smell in my room was that of tom-cats.

'Puss, puss!' I called.

They hesitated. One more courageous than the others advanced a step towards me before sitting down and washing his hind leg. 'Come here! Good pussy.' I patted the bedclothes. The brave one strolled over and the others watched to see what would be his fate. I scrabbled enticingly with my fingers on the eiderdown. After staring at my hand for some time he sprang and landed by my knees. Gently I stroked his ginger ears. He began to purr. I scratched him under his chin and he rolled over in ecstasy. A clinking sound drew my attention to the tray which Constance had left on the floor. The other cats were licking out the soup bowl and crunching up the pink wafer biscuits. A spat broke out over the cheese which was so hard I had been unable to eat it.

I got out of bed and divided the remains of my supper fairly between them, not forgetting the brave one. They gulped the scraps down as though they were starving. When they had finished the brave one leaped back on to the bed and washed briefly before curling up to sleep. Three jumped into the chair. One climbed the curtains of my bed to lie in the canopy. It was evident from the speed with which they made themselves at home that my room was in regular use as a cat's dormitory. While I observed them two more cats dropped over the window sill and, skirting me warily, made their way over to the tray to lick the empty dishes.

I went to the window to look out. Dawn had revealed, just a couple of feet below the sill, a sloping roof ending in a parapet. To my left a larger expanse of roof stretched away among chimney-pots, buttresses, gullies and turrets like a miniature village populated by cats. I counted six more. Some were sleeping; others contemplated the rising sun. Beyond the battlements the woodland, broken by brilliantly green fields, rolled away in gentle hills that in the far distance became black mountains, their peaks touched with tawny light. For a moment I had an intimation that my unhappiness, so overwhelming now, would ultimately, like all sorrows in every place, in every age, come to matter less than any one of those hills and trees, less even than a blade of grass. This was comforting.

I rescued my dressing-gown from beneath the slumbering brave one. He stirred and stretched out long skinny legs. His feet were unusually large, reminding me of lily-pads on stalks. I am not an expert on cats, or indeed any animal, but even I could see that there was something odd about this one. I stroked a soft striped paw. He gave half a purr then twitched it away, but not before I had been able to count seven toes.

EIGHTEEN

'Good morning, Bobbie! I hope you slept well. Are you feeling better?'

Constance was standing by the side table in the hall fidgeting with a jug of drooping scarlet poppies and magenta corn-cockles as I came down the stairs. Ears of wheat stuck out above the flowers. It was the sort of thing the ladies of the Cutham Down and District Flower Club might have entered for a competition entitled 'God Speed the Plough' or, if the president had literary leanings, 'Beldam Nature'.

'Oh, yes. Thank you.'

'I'm so glad.' She rubbed fretfully at the mahogany surface. 'It's a pity the flowers are half dead already. It's going to make an awful mess. What do you think of it?'

I walked over to the table and examined the arrangement. 'It's . . .' I groped for an adjective '. . . unpretentious. Artless, perhaps, is what I mean.'

'Do you *really* like it?' Constance asked doubtfully.

This, my first morning as a hireling and dependant, was not the moment for truth. 'It's certainly original. I should never have thought of including a raffia doll in a vase of flowers.'

'That's one of Sissy's fetishes, to protect the house from evil spirits.' Constance put her head on one side and looked thoughtfully at the collection of bent stalks from which petals were already drifting down. Next to the doll a spider was beginning a web between the stalks of stinging nettles. 'There's something lacking in my aesthetic sense, you know,' Constance continued. '*I* think it's perfectly hideous. Sissy's flower arrangements always make me feel as though I'm in a play by Eugene O'Neill. But if *you* admire it, it must be me that's wrong.'

I decided to forget the flowers. 'Shall I meet Sissy today?'

'Yes, but I don't know quite when. She's doing her exercises at the moment.'

'Is Sissy – I hope you won't think me inquisitive but I'm a little confused – is Sissy your sister?'

'I'm so stupid, I ought to have explained. And you *must* ask me anything you want to know. Sissy McGinty lives with us – has done for the last year, nearly – but she's no relation. You might say she's a friend of the family. Well . . .' Constance looked apprehensive. 'I may as well tell you the truth as you're bound to know sooner or later. She's Finn's mistress.'

I was silent as I digested this. So there was a *ménage à trois* at Curraghcourt. In my experience, emotions tended to run high in such a *mise en scène*, no matter how sophisticated the players.

'I hope you aren't shocked.' Constance regarded me anxiously. 'Although we don't share the same tastes in floral decoration, I'm fond of Sissy, though she isn't everybody's cup of tea. Naturally I realize that to those strictly brought up it may seem rather improper—'

'I'm not shocked at all,' I interrupted. 'How could I be? I know nothing of the circumstances and anyway it's none of my business.'

'It's awfully good of you not to mind,' said Constance, as though relieved. 'Father Deglan's always hauling me over the coals about Finn and Sissy, as if *I* could do anything. Naturally he disapproves of sex unless it's for babies – Father Deglan, I mean, Finn is definitely against babies – and even then he thinks it oughtn't to be enjoyed. But the Church is flying in the face of human nature, so I tell him. Besides, Sissy absolutely adores Finn and love can't be wrong, can it?'

'I honestly don't know,' I said. 'It's a question I've often asked myself.'

'What the Church won't allow is that love is involuntary. You can't turn it on and off like a tap.' Constance put her arm through mine. 'You must be starving. Come and have some breakfast.'

'Oh!' I cried on entering the dining room. 'Oh!'

The room was large and light, with four sash windows along one wall and a pair of French windows at the end. It was painted a hideous shade of brown and had ugly rep curtains of the same colour. Several paler rectangles marked the places where formerly paintings had protected the walls from turf smoke. The long table was cluttered with books, newspapers and dirty plates. But none of this was responsible for my gasp of astonishment. I turned on the spot, looking up. The ceiling was a glorious fantasy of flowers, leaves, scrolls and garlands. Above the magnificent marble chimney-piece were swags of plaster flowers and fruit. Roundels of birds and beasts decorated the walls, unfortunately covered with brown paint as was the frieze, a procession of griffins, centaurs, manticores and chimerae ridden and led by putti.

'This is absolutely wonderful!' I said. 'It must be the work of a master craftsman.'

'It is rather fine,' said Constance, going to a side table on which were several covered silver dishes, blackened by tarnish. Her gumboots made a flapping noise as she walked. 'Let me see if I can remember the name. Two brothers, Italian – or were they Swiss? La Franky-something. I've forgotten.'

'Not La Franchini!' I exclaimed.

'That's it.' Constance stared at me. 'How clever of you! How did you know?'

'It was my job: furniture and interior decoration, generally. I worked for one of the London auction houses. This is marvellous!' I walked round the room, my head back, my chin in the air. I stopped beneath a section of plaster which resembled the handiwork of a probationer nurse in Outpatients. 'But what's happened here? Is that an elephant? It's got five legs.'

'I think that's a tail. We had a burst pipe and the water came through the ceiling. It looked so awful afterwards that Sissy had a go with Polyfilla.'

I repressed a cry of anguish as I saw that six square feet of a masterpiece had been forever lost. The rest of the existing decoration was veiled with cobwebs, and glazed with fine cracks.

'We had a man from Hibernian Heritage here last year and he was quite angry when he saw that. He said we ought to have had it repaired by an expert. I didn't like to say that we hadn't any money. But we haven't, you know. Finn always gets a migraine whenever he does the accounts. The trouble is, Hibernian Heritage won't give us a grant unless we open Curraghcourt to the public. But how could we do that? Everywhere's such a mess. I showed him round and he admitted it was impossible. Now come and choose what you'd like.' Constance picked up a spoon and a plate. I joined her at the side table. 'There's scrambled egg. I don't advise that. I can never understand why it always goes grey when I cook it. Hello, Flurry, love. This is Miss Norton, our new housekeeper.'

A boy, round-faced with spectacles and black hair cut so short that it stuck up like the bristles of a brush, had entered the dining room. Grey flannel shorts revealed chubby knees encrusted with scabs. He came over to stand between us, giving me a darting glance before concentrating his gaze on a dish of rather pink sausages. 'You look much nicer than Mrs Heaney. But you won't stay so if you don't mind I shan't bother to talk to you.' He took the topmost plate from a large stack.

'That's *very* rude, Flurry,' Constance protested. 'Please shake hands with Miss Norton and say how pleased you are that she's come to help us.'

With his attention still on the sausages Flurry put out his hand and said in a monotone as though repeating a lesson, 'How do you do, Miss Norton? I'm Florence Finn Fitzgeorge Macchuin. How delightful to see you and I'm sorry you're going so soon.'

I took the hand and shook it. It felt damp and hot. The day was warm and he was wearing a grey wool jersey as well as a navy blazer. 'How do you do, Flurry?' I said. 'Please call me Bobbie. I hope to stay for a few weeks at least so it may be worth your while to exchange a few words now and then.'

'I'm so glad to hear that,' said Constance. 'Oh dear, what's this?' She kicked a bloody bone under the side table. 'Really, how disgusting!'

Flurry turned his eyes to my face and examined it carefully. I saw that one of his eyes was disfigured by an angry red stye. 'Mrs Heaney said no one who wasn't in league with the devil could stand living in a house with people who were all as mad as bullawawns and with an old woman with a tongue like a saw-mill. Perhaps you haven't met Granny yet?'

'I met Mrs Crawley last night.' I decided to dig myself deeper into the pit of lies. 'I liked her very much.'

'You did?' Flurry frowned and returned to the breakfast dishes. 'Aunt Connie?' He looked up at her. 'Did you cook these sausages?'

'I did, Flurry my boy. And I watched them like a mother her newborn baby. You won't tell me these are burned, surely?'

'No-o.' He sat down at the table and began to eat with steady concentration.

'What about some fried bread, Bobbie? It's good and crisp.' She demonstrated the truth of this by tapping with a spoon something I had identified as black pudding.

'Thank you.' I paused, embarrassed. 'But shouldn't I take my meals in the kitchen?'

'Mrs Heaney ate in the kitchen.' Flurry spoke with his mouth full and without taking his eyes from his plate. 'But Miss Macnulty, our nurse when we were babies, used to eat with us. Her teeth clicked. I expect you've got your own. I don't think you'll like Katty or Pegeen much and they're *always* in the kitchen. But then, if you liked Granny—'

'Of course you'll eat with us,' interrupted Constance. 'That's if you can stand our terribly bad manners. I want you to think of yourself as one of the family.' I noticed by the light of morning that Constance's deep-set eyes were a beautiful dark grey.

'That's kind of you,' I said. 'Well, then . . .' I inspected a dish that contained something dark and slimy, like squid cooked in ink. 'This looks interesting.'

'They're mushrooms. Sissy picked them this morning. I had to cook them so as not to hurt her feelings but I'm never sure if it's safe—'

'Don't eat them,' said Flurry. 'Not if you want to go on liking Granny. Or anyone.'

I settled for the fried bread and some shards of bacon, which splintered into fragments when I tried to cut it. To the left of my plate someone had written 'Kilroy was here' in the dust of the table. I tried to ignore a hairbrush, matted with hair, a few inches to my right. Opposite me Flurry sawed diligently at a sausage. The meat inside its shiny pink skin was raw. I hoped his immune system was well developed.

'Good morning, Flavia darling,' said Constance as a young girl came into the room, carrying an open book which she continued to read while walking to the table.

'Hello, Aunt Connie.' Flavia removed her eyes briefly from the page and offered a cheek to be kissed before sitting down. Propping her head on her hands, she continued to read.

'Darling, will you take notice for a moment? Bobbie, this is my niece, Flavia. Flavia, this is Miss Norton, who's come to help us.'

Flavia looked up with the unseeing eyes of someone whose imagination is busy far away. 'Hello,' she said vaguely before dropping them back on to her book. They were like her aunt's, deep-set and intelligent above good cheekbones. Her nose was snub, her mouth plump but her face promised beauty later. Her hair was long and curling and a wonderful chestnut brown.

Constance raised her eyebrows at me. 'I'm afraid the children's behaviour isn't always . . . I should do something about it but I'm rather hopeless at making people do things.'

I wondered why discipline should be the responsibility of an aunt. That Mr Macchuin was frequently absent I already knew, but presumably Violet – Mrs Macchuin – was usually at home. Perhaps, I speculated uneasily, Mrs Macchuin was as mad as a bullawawn, whatever that was.

'I can see specks of blood in this sausage, Aunt Connie,' said Flurry. 'Do you think it's all right?'

'Oh no, darling, how horrid. Don't eat it. I *am* sorry. I'll put them back in the pan.'

Constance took the dish of sausages from the side table and hurried out. Flurry continued to hold his knife and fork as though poised to eat and looked at the wall above my head. I offered him the rack of toast which was anaemic and leathery.

Flurry shook his head. 'I never eat toast.'

'Shall I cut you some bread?'

'Or bread.'

'Eggs?'

'No.'

'What do you eat?'

'Sausages.'

'You must eat something other than sausages.'

'No. Not now.'

'What, *nothing* else? What about at school?'

'When I went to boarding school I had so many detentions for not eating the food the teachers complained to the headmaster because they had to give up their free time to supervise me. I didn't like anything but the sausages. The school doctor said I was flabby and pale and it would be my own fault if I got ill. He said I ought to be beaten if I didn't eat what was on my plate.'

Flurry looked quickly at me and then back to the wall.

'That was rather unkind.'

'Yes. I wrote to my father and he came to see me. He was angry.'

'With you?'

Flurry shook his head. 'He took me away. I go to the Williamsbridge school now as a day boy. But I can still only eat sausages. I take a lunchbox.' I did not need to ask what the lunchbox contained. He looked at me consideringly. 'Can *you* cook sausages?'

'Yes. I think so. No one's ever complained.'

Flurry's expression became hopeful. 'It would be good if you could. Aunt Connie usually burns them black. Today was different but they still weren't right. Sometimes when we haven't got a housekeeper Sissy does the cooking and that's worse. Last time she cooked them with lavender.' Flurry made a face. 'E-ugh!' Then he added, 'I forgot. Aunt Connie says I'm not to say when I don't like things.'

'If it's just a question of food I hope you'll tell me.' When he said nothing but continued to sit staring into space with his knife and fork pointing at the ceiling I said, 'I'm looking forward to meeting Sissy.'

He gave me a blank look. 'I expect she's still doing her exercises.' Flurry stood up and went to the French windows. 'Yes. There she is.'

I abandoned the bacon and fried bread and joined him. Beyond a flagged terrace a large expanse of roughly mown grass was divided by two sheets of water bordered by stone kerbs. These ponds or, more accurately, canals ran at right angles from the house and stretched away into the distance. Between them were straggling, misshapen yews. A woman was cartwheeling expertly down the muddy path beneath the yews. Her long dark hair flopped up and down like a flag tugged by an intermittent breeze. She was naked.

'Can you cartwheel?' asked Flurry.

'Not very well.'

'I'm hopeless at games. Granny says I'm as fat as a flawn. Do you think I'm fat?'

'Well . . . no. Perhaps well covered.'

'You think I'm fat.' Flurry spoke in a tone that brooked no argument. He folded his arms behind his back and stood legs apart, watching Sissy as she came cartwheeling along the outside of one of the canals towards us. His manner was a combination of naïve schoolboy and elder statesman. 'What *is* a flawn?'

'It's an old-fashioned sort of pudding, like a custard.'

'E-ugh!' Flurry made a face. 'I hate custard! Do all girls look like Sissy with no clothes on?'

She was quite close to us now and as she revolved, arms and legs in perfect conformation at ninety degrees, no detail of her anatomy was left to our imaginations.

'Pretty much,' I said.

'E-ugh!' said Flurry again.

I wondered whether I ought to say something about the beauty of the naked human form but decided I wasn't up to it so early in the day. Sissy stood upright and stretched her hands above her head. Even through the filthy glass and across the twenty or so yards that separated us, I could see she was doing some deep breathing. Her rib cage expanded and contracted like bellows and her buttocks quivered with tension. Suddenly she sprang into the air. For a moment I thought she was going to dive headfirst into the turf but at the last moment she tucked herself into a ball and did a forward somersault, without touching the ground.

'Gosh!' I was deeply impressed. 'I wish I could do that.'

'Sissy used to be in a circus. She was a trapeze artist.'

'Really? How fascinating!'

'It is and it isn't. I've got rather blazered about it now.'

'Blasé?' I suggested.

'That's it.'

'Circuses are cruel,' said a voice behind us.

I turned to look at Flavia but she continued to read with her back to us.

'Flavia doesn't like animals being made to do tricks,' mouthed Flurry. 'She's bats about them.'

'What are you bats about?' I asked. 'Apart from sausages.'

'I'm not *bats* about them,' explained Flurry with dignity, folding his arms and looking at me over the top of his spectacles. 'I just happen to like them rather a lot. I happen also to like engines.'

'You want to be an engine driver, do you mean?'

'No.' Flurry's tone was contemptuous. 'Not drive them. Make them. Also I like building bridges and things. Have you ever heard of a man called Isambard Kingdom Brunel?'

'Yes, of course. Everyone's heard of him.'

'I don't know why you say everyone. Sissy hadn't.'

'Oh.'

'Or Katty. Or Pegeen.'

'Ah . . . well,' I temporized, 'when I said everyone I really meant men. They're more interested in engineering.' I reminded myself of my commitment to feminism. 'Though women can be excellent engineers, too, you know. There was, um . . . Caroline Herschel. She was an astronomer who constructed her own telescopes. And, er—'

'I want to be like Brunel. I'm building a railway in the garden. Timsy's helping me.' Flurry made a face. 'Only he's always drunk.' He looked hopeful again. 'Can you saw wood?'

'I never have but I don't see why not. It can't be difficult.'

'It's easy.' Flurry looked important. 'I'd do it myself but I haven't the time. I need a lot of sleepers, you see. You could be my second-in-command.'

I was genuinely flattered. 'I'd like that. But I'll have to see to the housekeeping first, you know.'

Flurry looked round the room. 'I can't see there's anything much to do.'

'Tell me, Flurry. Why did you pour water over me last night? It *was* you, wasn't it?'

Flurry looked away from me but a gleam of fun showed briefly on his face. I was reminded immediately of his grandmother. 'We didn't mean it for you. We thought you were Father Deglan. It was only a tooth-mugful. When the Jay Hoover Witnesses came we let them have a whole bucket. I'm sorry you caught it. Tell you what.' He burrowed in his pocket and brought out a handful of fluff-coated treasures. 'You can borrow my penknife for a day and then we'll be quits.'

I was tempted to say that I would forgive him without such a sacrifice but I guessed that it was a question of honour. I took the knife. 'Thank you.'

'Pax?'

'Pax.'

'Here we are.' Constance came in with a plate of sausages. 'I let them sizzle over the hottest part of the stove. They're bound to be cooked through now.'

Flurry looked at the blackened, shrivelled objects and sighed.

'Hadn't you better show me the kitchen?' I said to Constance. 'I'm beginning to feel I'm here under false pretences.'

The door opened and a man in a purple robe took a step into the room. I had time to register a pale face and brown shoulder-length hair before his eyes met mine with a look of surprise that changed to one of dismay. He turned swiftly round and went out again.

'That's Eugene,' Constance explained. 'I forgot to warn him you'd arrived. He'll feel shy about meeting you for the first time in his dressing-gown. He's so sensitive.'

I was reassured by this explanation. I had been afraid he had recognized me. Constance was clearly unaware of my notoriety but it could only be a matter of time before she came across a newspaper with my photograph in it. From what she had told me about her brother it seemed this was not an orthodox household. But double standards everywhere mean that an adulterous man is seen as a bit of a gay dog while an adulterous woman is a predatory slut. Besides, those monstrous lies had made me out to be a cross between

Messalina and an expensive whore. A sound between a cry and a moan interrupted my thoughts.

'What is it, darling?' Constance bent to put her arms round Flavia's shaking shoulders.

'Otter's dead!' wailed Flavia, pressing her face to the pages of her book. 'They've killed him! They've nailed his body to the gibbet with all the other poor animals. I loved Otter best of all!' She broke into racking sobs.

'It's only a story, sweetheart.' Constance stroked and soothed. 'It isn't real.'

'It's real to me!' protested Flavia jerkily through bursts of tears. 'I can see – his head lolling and his eyes – covered with dust and his – beautiful – coat streaked with blood!'

I picked up the book. It was B. B.'s *Down the Bright Stream*.

'Never mind, darling,' Constance continued. 'I expect the poor little otter went straight to heaven and was much happier there with as many buckets of fish as he could eat and a really lovely warm, dry nest . . . It's not a nest, is it? A warm, dry holt—'

'You don't *know* that! He's – dead and I can't – bear to read the book again – *ever* – and I loved him so *much*.' She clenched her fists. 'I hate people. I *hate* them!'

While Flavia wept and Constance stroked her and made soothing noises I read the offending passage. 'It *is* sad,' I said. 'It makes me want to cry and I don't know the rest of the story. It's awful that people want to kill beautiful animals and birds, isn't it?'

'*Awful*!' Flavia's voice trembled with feeling. 'But you ate bacon just now. That was Muriel. She was such a *good* pig. I used to say hello to her sometimes and she'd let me scratch her back. She looked after her piglets beautifully and didn't roll on *any* of them and her reward was that Mr Rafferty cut – cut her—' Flavia choked and was silenced briefly by a further flood of tears.

'I'm sorry,' I said, meaning it. 'I won't eat any more bacon now I know she was a friend of yours.'

Flavia regarded me suspiciously. 'Or pork chops from the freezer?'

'No.'

'Or pig's cheek?'

'Certainly *not*,' I said with perhaps unnecessary force.

Flavia's eyes still flowed. 'And what about the fish in heaven? Fish feel pain, too. They don't want to be put in buckets and torn apart by sharp teeth.'

205

'Probably animals and people don't need to eat once they're in heaven,' I suggested.

'I don't believe there is such a place, anyway,' said Flavia darkly, no longer actually sobbing but tense with woe. 'I think God is *cruel* making animals suffer and die!'

'*Darling*.' Constance sounded shocked. 'You mustn't think that. God's world is a good world and He loves us always, even if—'

'I don't care if He does or not! I don't *want* Him to love me! I don't think I even believe in him any more.'

'Flavia! You don't mean that. You mustn't lose faith, darling. God is infinitely wise and you can be sure, even when things seem tragic, it's all part of God's great plan for our salvation—'

'You can think that if you like but I don't want to be part of the plan of someone who makes everything die. I *hate* His plan! I think it's a very *bad* plan. And anyway, if you're so sure it's a good plan why were you asking Father Deglan the other day how God could possibly think it was all right to let children be born into families where the fathers were drunk and the mothers worn out with having babies and there wasn't enough money to feed them properly?'

'Well, I didn't mean—'

'I heard you say that it was obvious that God was male. And when Father Deglan ticked you off for blasphemy you said you thought the Pope was a silly old man with no idea what people's lives were really like.'

'I shouldn't have said those things, least of all to Father Deglan. It was extremely discourteous and I'm ashamed of myself. I just lost my temper—'

'And you said what happened to Mummy made you doubt there *is* a benevolent God. Benevolent means good and kind; I looked it up. So you shouldn't tell me off for saying just what you think yourself, should you!' Flavia ended on a note of triumph.

'Ah! But I . . . it really isn't a question of . . . You shouldn't listen to conversations not intended for you to hear. People sometimes say things in the heat of the moment they don't mean. Of course I *do* believe in God but from time to time . . . This is all too much first thing in the morning,' Constance concluded lamely. 'Let's just get on with the day and try to be as good and kind to each other as we can. Leave that horrid book and go and have a lovely ride on the Cockatoo.'

'The Cockatoo's got a friction burn from the head collar not being put on properly. Timsy shouldn't be allowed to drive him. I suppose that's all part of God's super plan according to Father Deglan: to make my pony's shoulder hurt like hell!'

'Try not to swear, darling, it shocks people and you're too young.'

I made a mental note that the word hell was considered swearing at Curraghcourt. In my own vocabulary it counted for little more than emphasis.

Flavia stood up, her face scarlet with passion. 'I'm going outside to swear *lots* and I'm going to put this book on Timsy's bonfire and burn it to ashes, then I'm going to pray to the devil to make all gamekeepers suffer for ever and ever!'

'All right, if that will make you feel better. Though not the praying to the devil, darling. It's wrong to wish ill to anyone. And then you'd better find your holiday work. I'm going to have to bone up on the maths. It looked incomprehensible—'

Constance sighed as the door slammed. 'I don't think I handled that awfully well.'

After what Kit had told me I should not have been surprised that in Ireland God and the devil seemed to figure so largely in the mental landscapes of its inhabitants. My life in London had been entirely secular and at Cutham, though there was intermittent church-going of a restrained Protestant kind, it was mainly *pour encourager les autres* – what my father called 'setting an example', as though the locals noticed or cared what we did, except to laugh at us behind our backs. My parents considered it bad form to discuss religion and anything like evangelical fervour would have been thought certifiable lunacy. I found this Irish willingness to thrash out spiritual matters refreshing.

'What *I* want to know,' said Flurry, whose eyes, large behind his spectacles, had been flicking from face to face during the discussion, 'is how did God make the world in six days if we revolved from tiny cells over jillions of years? I've been reading about trilobites and spirogyra in one of Dad's books.'

Constance and I looked at each other helplessly.

'The best thing you can do,' said Constance at last, 'is to make a list of questions and give it to Daddy when he comes home.'

'Can't girls understand that sort of thing?' asked Flurry. 'When Dad said he was surrounded by a pack of incompetent females you got angry and said women were just as clever as men, in fact much, much cleverer.'

'I wish you and Flavia wouldn't eavesdrop on conversations not intended for your ears!' Constance, who had remained marvellously

207

calm until this point, suddenly became heated. She rubbed her forehead until her brow grew red. 'How can I get anything done when I'm continually catechized by beastly little children who fling my most casual utterances in my face and demand to know exactly what I meant by them?'

Flurry smiled for the first time. 'Dad said when you're in a temper you remind him of an egg-bound hen. He's good at describing people, *I* think.'

'Well, of all the . . .' Constance began to laugh. 'All right, darling, don't let's quarrel on the first day of the holidays. You go and get on with your railway. Or, even better, make a start on your homework. *Please* let's make a resolve these holidays not to leave it until the last minute. I really can't stand the strain of having to stay up till four in the morning to finish it. I'm going to wash up.'

'If you'll tell me where the sink is,' I said, 'I'll do it. It's what I'm here for.'

Constance looked at me. 'I'd better show you the kitchen. This is the moment I've been dreading.'

NINETEEN

Together we loaded an antiquated trolley with the breakfast things and Constance pushed it, one wheel wailing like a hysterical child, into the hall. Behind the sedan chair was the entrance to an ill-lit passageway.

'Look out!' cried Constance, too late.

'Bloody h— Blow!' I said with remarkable self-control.

I had walked into a chain that hung down into the stairwell. The end of it had been fastened into a knot the size of a man's fist which dangled at the exact height of my hairline.

'I'm terribly sorry! I ought to have warned you. Are you hurt?'

I felt my forehead. 'No blood.'

'I must get Timsy to take that stupid chain down. It used to be for hoisting up baskets of turves for the bedroom fires. We never use it now. I do hope your head isn't hurting *too* much.'

'Not at all.' I was lying again. It was throbbing and I was certain there would be a bruise.

'We've all got used to dodging it, that's the trouble. The man from Hibernian Heritage said some swear words I'd never heard before. Not that I mind swearing a bit myself but the children get into trouble at school if they do. Father Matthew and the sisters are neurotic about any kind of expletive. One child was sent home for saying "shite". I know it's not pretty but it *is* just a word. Finn's language is sometimes awful and I occasionally say "bugger" myself.' Constance looked defiant.

'So the children go to a convent?'

'All schools in Ireland are run by the Church, if that's what you mean. If you ask me, there's too much emphasis on religion and not enough on foreign languages, but then no one ever does – ask me,

209

I mean. It's a mistake to be born a woman in this country. We're supposed to get equal pay now we're in the EEC but what's the use of that if women have to give up their jobs when they marry?'

'Have to by law, you mean?'

While Constance was talking she was manoeuvring the trolley along the passage which sloped steeply downwards. The light from the occasional electric bulb was supplemented by candles stuck in their own grease. At every step the unevenness of the flagstones threatened to dash the mountains of plates and cups to the floor.

'No, not by law but by custom, which is even more binding in a way. There never was a more doggedly reactionary animal than the Irish male. I tell you, women in Ireland get a raw deal.'

By this point in the conversation we had reached the kitchen, which lay at the end of the tunnel. I saw at once why Constance had been reluctant to introduce me to it. It was housed in what must have been the castle's undercroft, which meant that the large vaulted space was broken up by a great many picturesque but thoroughly inconvenient pillars. Also the semicircular windows were high up in the walls so it was impossible to see out and the nether regions were extremely gloomy. It resembled nothing so much as a dungeon.

A table took up most of the centre of the room. Its surface was scattered with the collection of heterogeneous objects I had come to expect. I wondered what part the accordion played in the preparation of food. A sullen fire smouldered in a cavernous inglenook, its smoke mingling with the noxious steam that issued from a blackened pot suspended above the turves. Huddled round the hearth were three figures, reminding me forcibly of a certain blasted heath. Despite the screeching and clattering of the trolley no one seemed to notice our arrival.

'Hello, everyone,' said Constance. 'Bobbie, this is Pegeen and this is Katty.'

Constance spoke in the rallying tones of a kindergarten teacher faced with stubbornly unsociable children. The two women stood up unsteadily and nodded untidy heads by way of greeting. Pegeen was, I thought, the prettier of the two. Katty had fierce little eyes and a hooked nose. 'This is Miss Norton.'

'Bobbie, please!' I smiled, hoping to ingratiate myself with my team.

'*Good* morning, Miss Norton,' said Timsy, who completed the

210

group of cave-dwellers. He touched his cap and raised the cup he was holding by way of salutation. 'I hope you'll be recovered now after that terrible journey. God save us, there never was a storm like it! There was lightning and thunder, as though the devil was smiting his anvil. It was all I could do to keep the pony going forward and he lame and Miss Norton hollering with fright.'

At this account of my suffering the two women smiled, Pegeen exposing a solitary tooth in the middle of her upper jaw which detracted considerably from her looks.

'I wasn't afraid at all,' I said indignantly. 'At least, not until we got to the top of the hill. And I don't believe there *was* any lightning.'

Timsy winked. 'Well, girls, did you ever see such a fine young lady before? There isn't a film shtar to match her, in my opinion.'

The two women examined me through the smoke. 'Is it film stars, Timsy, you old fibber?' screeched Pegeen, whose every sibilant was a piercing whistle. 'Why, bless her, she's so handsome the saints themselves couldn't compare with her!'

'She looks delicate, though.' Katty was evidently not disposed to follow Pegeen and Timsy's lead and attempt to turn my head with blatant flattery. 'I doubt she'll manage the work.'

'Is it delicate?' whistled Pegeen. 'I'd say a poff of wind could knock her down and a blade of grass run her through!'

Katty smiled as though the idea pleased her. They sat down again in ramshackle wooden chairs that looked as though they had been hammered together by a toddler in a tantrum. A bell jangled somewhere in the shadows.

'That'll be Maud wanting her breakfast,' said Constance. 'I've already laid the tray. Just the tea and the toast to do.'

While Constance rushed to boil the kettle and cut slices of bread, the others watched me covertly over the rims of their cups from which they took noisy sips.

'I'll make the tea,' I said.

'Oh, would you? Thanks. Just one teaspoonful of leaves. She hates it strong. And a thin slice of lemon on a saucer.' A column of smoke rose from the toaster. 'Oh, damn this blasted thing! It burns it every time!'

Constance seized a knife and began scraping carbon into the sink. I searched along the shelf of labelled canisters and opened the one marked *Tea*. It contained pieces of string. I eventually found the tea in a jar marked *Sago*.

'Where are the lemons?' I addressed the three round the fire in a general way as I took the teapot to the kettle to warm it.

'Is it lemons?' whistled Pegeen. 'Sure we have none.'

''Twas the last I used to clean the teapot.' Katty threw up her long chin with an assumption of virtue that was misplaced for the teapot, though made of silver, was dark brown with tarnish and tannin.

The bell rang again, violently.

'That's grand.' Constance took the teapot from me and picked up the tray. 'I'd better run up with this before she breaks the wire entirely.' She looked at me apologetically. 'Do you feel you could bear to start with the washing up?'

'Of course.'

'Thanks. Then I can get on with lunch. I thought we'd have a nice stew. Well, actually, we always have stew. Katty and Pegeen, would you do the bedrooms, please?'

Katty and Pegeen exchanged glances. 'Sure we'll be delighted, Miss Connie, just the second we're finished with our tea.' Timsy poked the fire leisurely until it shot out sparks and they all stared at it intently.

'Very well.' Constance composed her face into an expression of calm reasonableness but I saw she was rattled by this display of intransigence, which I suspected was put on for my benefit. 'I'll fetch the vegetables when I've seen to Mrs Crawley.'

After she had gone the three round the fire whispered and chuckled and glanced several times in my direction. I saw Katty tip something into her cup from a black bottle that stood upon the hearth. Pegeen and Timsy did the same and drank whatever it was with grunts of satisfaction. Whenever any of them happened to catch my eye they nodded and grinned. I realized that this silken obduracy was just the first round of a bitter contest. I went to the sink. After a prolonged hunt I found an ancient holey cloth, a bar of carbolic soap and a bottle of Parazone. When I had scrubbed and bleached the bowl, the sink, the taps, the draining board and the cloth I felt ready to begin. I washed steadily through the crockery we had brought from the dining room and was just beginning on the plates from the kitchen table when Constance returned.

'Sorry I've been so long. I got waylaid by Sissy. She wanted me to watch her walking up and down the garden steps on her hands. An impressive but not a useful accomplishment. I can't find the potatoes, Timsy.'

'Is it potatoes, Miss Connie?' He shook his head soulfully. 'I regret

212

to be obliged to tell you that Turlough McGurn sold the last potato just as I came panting up to the door like a whipped pony. But he had plenty of cabbages plucked that moment out of the fields with the dew like diamonds still on them. I brought them back with Missy last night.'

'You might have told me before I went to look for them. And why didn't you get potatoes from somewhere else? All the shops can't have sold out.'

'I swear, Miss Connie, on the soul of me brother that died these twenty years ago and me mother saw him go to God dressed all in white like a cloud of feathers at a goose plucking, there isn't a potato to be had this side of Galway.'

I had to admit that though I had not forgiven Timsy for the horrors of the previous night's journey I liked to hear him speak. The musical inflection of his voice and the soft *t*s and *s*s combined with the free use of metaphor gave the English language a literary richness rarely heard in its country of origin.

'You mean you forgot them.' Constance frowned. 'I'm very cross with you, Timsy. How can I make a stew without potatoes?'

Timsy winked at me as soon as Constance turned her back.

Katty got to her feet. 'I'll get them cans from the pantry. Sure potatoes are sweeter from a can and clean already.'

Constance sighed. 'It does seem ridiculous to be eating everything out of tins when we live in the depths of the country.'

I made no comment but put vegetables on my mental list. I had already decided to drive to Kilmuree at the earliest opportunity, in the pony and trap if necessary, to buy some rudimentary cleaning materials. The smell of carbolic soap was unpleasantly enduring. I smiled to myself as I added a washing-up brush to the list, thinking of Flora Poste.

'You can't think how glad I am to see you look happy,' Constance murmured. 'It's all too ghastly, I know.'

'What about those beds?' I whispered back.

Katty had returned to the fireside where silence had again fallen, broken only by the idle stirrings of Timsy's poker.

'It's too bad, isn't it?' said Constance. 'I'd never get a job as a sergeant major or a headmistress. Thank goodness! What could be more awful? I'm simply not good at marshalling troops. But it mustn't go on. All right!' Constance advanced on them, clapping her hands. 'Off you go and do something.'

'I'll just take a drop more tea.' Katty picked up the black bottle.

'I've a thirst like a camel's. Pegeen, give us your cup. 'Twill put some red into your cheeks for you're as pale as though Death himself was outside the door.' They both crossed themselves.

I gave them one minute. 'Right.' I turned from the sink and consulted my watch. 'It's half past ten. Katty and Pegeen, I want every bedroom in use dusted and vacuumed and the beds made. In exactly one hour I'm coming to inspect them.' They stared at me, round-eyed. Pegeen made as though to get up but Katty put a detaining hand on her arm. 'Timsy?' My voice was regrettably loud and bossy. 'What are your jobs for the morning?'

'Well now, missy.' He took a swig of tea and wiped his mouth on his sleeve. 'If it stays dry I'm cutting turves.'

'Right. Off you go.' They remained frozen to their seats. Katty permitted herself a derisive smile and this goaded me into action. I swooped down on the black bottle, snatched it up and walked over to the sink. 'If there's any more time-wasting, I'm going to pour whatever this is down the plug-hole.' I unscrewed the cap and began to tilt the bottle. There were gasps of consternation.

'Oh, missy!' said Timsy. 'You wouldn't do that! That's medicine for my back. My spine's as cracked in pieces as an old jar that's been rolled down Croagh Patrick!'

I tipped it further and a few drops of brown liquid that reeked of bonfires splashed into the sink. There was a swell of muttered protest.

'All right, all right!' Timsy sprang up. 'We're going.' He gave a sideways twitch to his head. 'I shouldn't like to be in your shoes, missy, if the master catches you pouring away good drink now! Waste is something he cannot abide and he's got a temper like a bear that's been woken out of his winter sleep by a swarm of bees.'

I had noticed a cupboard to the right of the sink which had a key in its lock. 'Until I'm satisfied that the work's been properly done this goes away.' I put the bottle into the cupboard, turned the key, then dropped it into the pocket of my jeans.

With faces that expressed their outraged feelings Timsy and the two women left the kitchen.

'Well done!' Constance was admiring. 'I'd never have thought of that.'

'It's too soon for congratulation. I can see I've got a fight on my hands. They don't like me or respect me because I'm English. Isn't that right?'

'Well . . . it's partly because you're young and beautiful and capable and clever and not at all like poor Mrs Heaney who was none of those things.'

'Go on, admit it. In their eyes I'm a reincarnation of Oliver Cromwell.'

'There *is* still a little anti-English feeling, I'm afraid, among some of the country people.'

'Probably it's justified, if half of what I've been told is true. But we'll have to work towards some kind of truce if I'm going to do my job properly. I suppose that's poteen in the bottle?'

'Timsy lives on the stuff. I don't think any of them are ever entirely sober. I can't imagine what their stomachs can be like. I've tried it occasionally. It takes the skin off the roof of your mouth.'

'We'll see what effect a period of abstinence has. Where does Timsy get it?'

'Lonnie Flanagan has a shebeen at Kilmuree.'

'That must be at least ten miles.'

'Twelve and a half.'

'We mustn't let Timsy have the keys of the car or Land-Rover. And we must stop him using the outside car. I know, we'll lock the harness up with the bottle.'

'Bobbie! There'll be a mutiny!'

'Supposing you threatened to sack them?'

'I couldn't! They've worked for us all their lives. They're part of the family. I'd as soon think of sacking the children or Maud.'

Though this un-English attitude was inconvenient, I was charmed by it. 'Does this loyalty work both ways?'

'You mean, would they walk out? Never. Their parents worked here for my grandparents. Curraghcourt is in their blood.'

'Well, then. That makes us even. Let me try it my way, Constance. I can see it's difficult for you. I'll take the consequences.'

'You're a brave woman.'

'No. But I don't like to fail when I've set my mind to something.'

'You're really going to stay? You'll never know how re*lieved* I am. Honestly, it's like a great weight being lifted off me.' Constance frowned and then smoothed her forehead as was her habit. 'To tell you the truth, I think I've been a bit depressed lately. Quite honestly, unless I'm reading or listening to poetry, my stomach is churning with worry practically the whole time. But what a fool I am! I don't want to put you off.'

'No fear of that.' I continued to wash up while Constance picked

215

up a tin of potatoes and absent-mindedly rolled it about between her hands, staring into the middle distance.

'These days I find that things that wouldn't bother me in the ordinary way – silly little things like how I'm going to get the iron mould out of Flurry's school shirts, whether I ought to get in the sweep, what to cook for supper – seem monumental and insurmountable. Yesterday I stood in the barn and bawled my eyes out just because the rats had got into the chicken pellets again. I've begun to wonder if I'm going mad.' Constance frowned again. 'That reminds me, I must go and check that Timsy remembered to milk Siobhan. She gets mastitis if he forgets.'

'You don't seem in the least mad to me. Just overburdened.'

Constance smiled at me. 'Bless you for that.'

As soon as she had gone I finished the washing up and started cleaning the kitchen. It was possible to wipe swathes through the dirt, like those television advertisements for cleaning powders. While I worked I thought about Burgo and wondered if he was thinking about me.

Once more I was overwhelmed by misery and uncertainty. Had I selfishly added to his troubles by my flight? Supposing he thought I had committed some desperate act, even killed myself? Was he at this moment ringing hospitals and visiting morgues, steeling himself to examine smashed bodies picked up from motorways or weed-wrapped corpses fished from rivers? No, of course not. I rubbed hard at an unyielding, slightly sinister dark red stain. Burgo knew me better than that. Besides, by now he would probably have received my letter posted for me by Mrs Treadgold, saying that I was safe and well and had left the country.

But wouldn't it be reasonable to ring him, just once, so I could fortify myself by hearing his voice? I might also allow myself to say that I loved him. Though he knew that well enough. And I was sure of his love. Wasn't I? I wrung the cloth vigorously under the tap to strangle doubt. Or was it – oh, hateful, humiliating question, which I had not dared to put squarely to myself until now – was it all about sex? If peculiar medical circumstances – a weak heart, a rare gynaecological disease – made it impossible for me to make love again would Burgo still want to spend the rest of his life with me? No, came the answer, swift and sure. He might hang dutifully around for a while but sooner or later he would drift away. But was there a man alive who would not do the same? Supposing the boot was on the other foot and Burgo became impotent? Sex was a thrilling aspect of our relationship but it was not the reason I loved him. I would have despised myself for leaving him for such a cause. I plunged the cloth into boiling water and pummelled it clean with the stick end of the mop. Did men ever really love anyone but themselves? I exchanged the cloth for a scrubbing brush.

Burgo had, as far as I knew, spent every minute of his spare time with me since that ridiculous tennis tournament. On the few nights I could get away from Cutham I would wait for him in his flat in Lord North Street until the voting finished at one, two or three in the morning. He always woke me, apologizing for the urgency of his desire. He had cut down his Christmas holiday in Provence from a month to two weeks and had spent those fourteen illicit days staying at the Fisherman's Reel so we could see each other for at least a small part of every day.

It was during that brief period of holiday that Burgo first spoke of divorce. Of course I had thought about it but I had decided that no circumstances could justify raising the subject myself.

'This situation is so hard on you,' he had said as we sat in the snug sharing a bottle of wine before supper. 'I suppose the decent thing all round would be to ask Anna for a divorce.' For a moment the room seemed to grow dim as terror and joy clouded my vision. 'It won't be easy,' he had added. 'Anna likes the arrangement as it is.'

'She must realize that something's changed,' I said, attempting to speak lightly. 'The fact that you've cut short the time you usually spend with her, for one thing. And I suppose you are not the same?' I would rather have been stretched to six feet six on the rack than ask him if they still made love.

'If Anna noticed a difference in me she'd put it down to pressures of work.' He smiled, I thought rather affectionately. 'She's not the suspicious kind. Her childhood's cocooned her against self-doubt. All her life she's had exactly what she wanted. Including me.' Burgo was building a pyramid of beer mats but paused for a moment to look at me. 'She does love me, you know. Does that sound horribly conceited?'

I felt a tightening of my stomach muscles. 'No, but it makes things more difficult, doesn't it?'

'What I mean is, some people might think we spend so much time apart because we're indifferent to each other. That's not the case. Until I met you I thought no woman could ever mean as much to me as Anna. I actually believed that our ability to be apart for long periods without damaging our relationship was a sign that we were perfectly matched. I've never wanted a Darby and Joan set-up: taking each other for granted; having to talk about trivia to conceal our boredom from each other. Anna is eccentric – some might say egocentric – but she's never dull.'

I was thankful that he had returned to his beer-mat construction so he did not see my face. Jealousy flared and burned hot, turning my insides to water. For one insane moment I wanted to ask him what the hell, if he was so well suited, did he think he was doing in the Fisherman's Reel with me? He had pursued me without encouragement despite being perfectly satisfied, it now appeared, with his wife. It shows how little I knew of men that I found this behaviour illogical.

Whenever I had allowed myself to think of Burgo and Anna I had imagined an early passion cooled to something lukewarm, perhaps to indifference bordering on dislike. He had told me during our first meeting that he thought her beautiful. I had managed to keep insecurity at bay by telling myself that certain kinds of beauty were cold and unengaging. But his admission that he never found her dull threw me into a ferment of self-doubt. Presumably he had not so far been bored by me because our time together had been constantly interrupted by the demands of Cutham and his job.

But my idea of earthly paradise was to spend as much time with Burgo as I possibly could. I had fantasized about us buying a cottage in the country, Kent perhaps, or Essex. We would be short of money to begin with. I would continue to work. We would both commute daily. While he sat late in the House I would undertake all those wifely tasks like ironing his shirts and digging the garden and cooking and . . . Vague ideas of making chutney, growing cucumbers and remodelling my winter coat were jumbled together in my mind, accompanied by a sense of blissful satisfaction that I would be doing those things for him, for us. And when he came home, I would have thought it nothing short of perfect happiness to discuss with him the trifling concerns of the day which he dismissed as boring. A Darby and Joan set-up sounded like heaven to me. I had schooled my expression into impassivity and after another glass of wine my pulse had returned more or less to normal. But those few sentences of Burgo's were imprinted in my mind, never afterwards to be far from my thoughts.

On that last day at Cutham, as I stood by the front door waiting for Brough to bring round the car to take me to the station, I had yielded to impulse and called Burgo's flat. I had been quite certain he would be out but foolishly I had wanted to picture the telephone ringing in the hall on the bookcase beneath the print of Charles I. When the receiver had been picked up after one ring and Burgo had said, 'Hello?' my face had burned with the shock. There had been a pause during which I had been unable to speak. Then he had said, 'Roberta! It's you, isn't it? For God's sake! I'm going mad, not seeing you, not knowing what you're thinking—'

I had jammed the receiver back on its rest and unplugged the telephone. I knew if he asked me again to go away with him I would agree. So I had left without saying goodbye.

But just a minute, said the other voice in my head during this infernal internal dialogue, that isn't true. I stopped scrubbing the table for a moment and stood cradling the brush in my hands. What had made me put down the receiver without speaking was the terror that he might listen once again to my sensible, unselfish argument and say, in tones of thinly disguised relief, that perhaps after all it would be a good thing if I went away for a while, that we ought to give ourselves time to think about what would be best for both of us. Then indeed I might have had to be dragged from the river or scraped from the motorway.

'"Lord, what fools these mortals be!"' I said aloud, practically raising smoke from the scarred oak as I launched myself savagely yet again at the unpleasant stain.

'Is it the table you're talking to?' said a voice immediately behind me, making me jump.

I knew at once who it was because of the long, dark, slightly ragged hair, though now she was the right way up and fully clothed. It was an unusual outfit for a sunny weekday morning. She wore a long crimson velvet dress that revealed most of her breasts. Her head was garlanded, Ophelia-like, with flowers. She was less than five feet tall, not beautiful but in an odd way extremely attractive. She had a small face, olive-skinned with black eyes rimmed with kohl, a short, flattened nose and a long upper lip. When she put her head slightly on one side and regarded me with solemn unblinking eyes she reminded me of a charming monkey.

'I was talking to myself.' I smiled and held out my hand. 'How do you do? I'm Bobbie Norton. The new housekeeper. And you're Sissy. I was admiring your athleticism from the dining-room window.'

Ignoring my hand, she screwed her face into a fearsome scowl and walked round me, examining me from every angle. 'Housekeeper? Pooh! You don't look as though you could mend a stocking without you'd have to lie down after.'

'I may not be able to turn cartwheels but I'm not as feeble as that.'

'You're English.' She sounded gratified by the discovery. 'He won't like that.'

'Who won't?'

'Finn. He doesn't like the English. He says they're double-dealing.'

I looked her squarely in the eye. 'Perfidious is the term generally used.'

Before I had any idea of her intention she had seized a clump of my hair and twisted it until it hurt. I minded the pain a great deal less than the fact that her hands were filthy. 'Don't do that!' I said, pulling away.

'And he doesn't like blondes. He says they're frivolous. Trouble-makers.' She put her head on the other side and stared at me, then wrinkled her small nose in disgust.

'Does he, indeed?' I felt thoroughly ruffled by this mistreatment. 'Well, if he doesn't interfere with my prejudices I shan't trouble myself about his.'

Sissy flared her nostrils and stood arms akimbo. 'You've a fine way of talking. Finn doesn't like clever women. He says they rattle on too much. Now me, I can be quiet for hours. He likes that.'

'Look here,' I said, exasperated. 'I don't care what Mr Macchuin thinks. I'm here to look after the house. I'm not interested in winning his liking or admiration.'

'No?' Sissy sounded doubtful. 'You're not going to fall in love with him?'

'Certainly not. I particularly dislike bad-tempered, opinionated men who neglect their wives and children and keep . . .' I had been going to say mistresses openly in the same house but restrained myself. 'And anyway I don't expect I shall see much of him so this is all irrelevant.'

'You swear by Mary, Mother of God, virgin of virgins?'

'Certainly!'

Sissy flashed splendid white teeth in a wide smile. 'In that case, you and I are going to get along just fine. *Fáilte!* Welcome to Curraghcourt.'

TWENTY

When, at the end of a long day, I reviewed my achievements, I was not entirely dissatisfied. There had been failures and even near disasters but successes, too. When I went upstairs to make my inspection of the bedrooms I found Katty and Pegeen on the landing, leaning on brooms and gossiping in Gaelic. I was quite sure that they were talking about me and that it was uncomplimentary. But I praised the making of the beds and the transference of fluff, flies and soot from one surface to another more than they deserved.

'I've always heard that the women of Galway are excellent housekeepers.' I take the view that a lie for a good cause is permissible.

'Is it excellent?' said Pegeen. 'Why, there's none in the world can beat them!'

I presented her with a rag tied to the end of a long cane. 'Would you take down those cobwebs, please?' I pointed to the webs, blackened by the dirt of ages, which hung like petticoat frills above our heads.

'Them creatures can cover a house faster than you could say *níor bhlas sé an biadh nach mblasfaidh an bás*,' observed Katty sulkily, folding her arms and looking grim.

I affected not to notice the sulking. 'What does that mean?'

She smacked her lips. 'It means: "He has not tasted food who will not also taste death."'

This was irrefutable. Pegeen twirled the stick feebly above her head, complaining of a headache but at least she was compliant. When I asked Katty to vacuum the carpets, however, I met with a check.

'The devil's in those machines,' declared Katty, taking a step back from the antique cleaner I had discovered in a cupboard. It looked like an exhibit from the Science Museum but when I plugged it in it made a roar like a football crowd and sucked up several inches of the tattered red runner.

'The electric makes a reeling in my head like a *fodheen mara*. 'Tis brushes we use,' Pegeen said sibilantly. She held up a broom head with a handful of broken bristles like the stubble on an old man's chin.

'Nonsense!' I said. 'If the electricity was travelling up to your heads you'd be dead.'

'We buried Mary O'Donovan two weeks ago,' Pegeen said with the triumph of one clinching an argument. ''Twas one of them vacuum cleaners she was using when she fell to the floor, white as a mushroom, and spoke not another word.'

Katty's face darkened. 'Mary O'Donovan promised me her best dress years gone by and didn't her sister wear it on Sunday, bold as a paycock drawing the eyes of all with its tail? 'Tis a tail all the men in Kilmuree are very familiar with, that's certain.' She and Pegeen held their sides and cackled at the wittiness of this slur on Mary O'Donovan's sister's reputation.

'What's funny?' Constance appeared with two trays stacked precariously. 'I should enjoy a joke. Maud's not in the best of humours. As for Violet . . .' She sighed and left the sentence unfinished.

'I hope we aren't disturbing them?' I raised my voice above the din while Katty and Pegeen made a pantomime of gasping for breath between fresh peals of laughter.

'Maud's in the bath and Violet, poor darling, nothing disturbs.'

I made a few passes with the machine up and down the landing. The runner rose in response to the terrific suction and fell away behind, miraculously clean.

I felt I had given an adequate demonstration of its innocuous nature. 'Come along, Pegeen.'

Pegeen approached it with a sidling motion. 'God save us, the perspiration is on me like the dew.'

I took a tray from Constance. 'We'll go down and start lunch. I think they'll get on better without an audience,' I said as soon as we were out of earshot. 'It's like a play by Beckett. That feeling of wild inconsequence. It's a sort of game, isn't it? I must say I enjoy it.'

'You do?' Constance paused at the bend in the stairs and looked at me, amazed.

'Honestly. It's so different from what I've been used to. I've been looking after my mother at home. There isn't a great deal of laughter. And there's a lot of tiresome respectability: the keeping up of appearances.'

'That would most assuredly be beyond us. Who's looking after your mother now?'

'I don't actually know. That reminds me, if you don't mind I'd like to ring home. I left rather suddenly.'

'Go ahead.' We had reached the hall by this time. 'The telephone's in here.' Constance opened the door of the sedan chair. 'This was Maud's idea and I must say it was one of her better ones. It means you're relatively private. I'll be in the kitchen. Take your time.'

I stepped into the chair and closed the door. There was a surprising amount of room, presumably to accommodate hooped skirts. The inside was quilted in yellow silk, sadly rotting. It smelt strongly of cigarettes and . . . I sniffed . . . Ô de Lancôme. I recognized the scent because I sometimes used it myself. I wondered who sat in this original call-box heavily perfumed and – I counted eleven cigarette ends in the ashtray – chain-smoking? Not Constance, surely. With her un-made-up gleaming skin and shining hair she was an advertisement for the benefits of fresh air and pink lungs. Nor, I thought, Sissy, who might smoke but was more likely to use something like patchouli. It seemed too young a scent for Maud. Perhaps the mysterious, reclusive Violet, whom nothing could disturb?

I rang the operator and asked for a person-to-person call to Cutham Hall. I had instructed Oliver to plug the telephone back in an hour or so after my departure for Ireland, in case I needed to ring home urgently.

'Oliver? It's me.'

'Oh, hello, Bobs. Where are you?'

'Discretion, remember? I told you where I was going and I'm there now.'

'Oh, yes. I'd forgotten. Somewhere in Ire—'

'Shush, you clot! I explained to you about phone-tapping.'

'Yes. Sorry.' Oliver dropped his voice to a whisper. 'I wasn't thinking straight. I've only just got up.'

'Whispering won't make any difference to anyone listening in. It just means *I* can't hear you.'

'You needn't get waxy.'

'I'm perfectly calm. How is everything? Are the reporters still there?'

'They left the same day you did. Everyone knows you've gone away, I don't know how.'

223

'I may have been spotted at the railway station. It doesn't matter. No one knows I'm here.'

'There wasn't anything about you in today's paper. I think you've gone the way of the dodo.' He laughed. 'A quaint old bird of distant memory.'

Aware that my sense of humour had not been exercised much recently, I forced myself to laugh too. 'I'm glad you're no longer being hounded because of me. I hope you're not *too* depressed.'

'Not a bit!'

'Oh! Good. How's Mother? Has Father found a nurse?'

'Yes. Her name's Ruby and she's a terrific cook. Last night for supper we had a chocolate meringue thing with marshmallows and jam.'

'Just a minute. Did you say Ruby?'

'Yes. Nothing to look at, but a nice motherly creature. Father seems to have taken to her amazingly. I actually heard him call her "dear" and, as I say, she cooks a treat. For lunch we had gammon and pineapple followed by chocolate chip ice cream with toffee sauce—'

'Oliver! Do you realize Father's brought in his' – I dropped my voice automatically – 'mistress to look after Mother!'

'Now who's whispering? What did you say? You needn't worry about Mother. She and Ruby like just the same kind of books and they're getting through sacks of sweets together.'

'What's Father doing?'

'He's in the library as usual. But you wouldn't believe what a good mood he's in. Yesterday he gave me a *fiver* to go down to the pub after dinner. He said not to hurry back.'

'So you aren't lonely?'

'Well, no. Ruby's got this niece. She's already popped in twice to see her aunt. Her name's Sherilee. She's the spit of Marilyn Monroe only with smaller tits and a tighter arse.'

'Oliver! For God's sake.'

'What? What's the matter?'

'Don't talk about women like that. It makes you sound inadequate.'

'I'm only repeating Sherilee's description of herself.'

'I see. Well, I'm glad you're enjoying yourself.'

'Oh yes. You needn't worry about me.'

'Anybody ring for me?'

I heard a rustle of paper. 'Yes. Jasmine. And Sarah. She says to ring her urgently. And someone called Fleur. She sounded rather sexy.'

'Is that all?'

'No, hang on.' More rustling. 'A bloke called David. Isn't he the chap with the flat in Pimlico?'

'Yes. No one else?'

'Not that I know of.'

My heart gave a lurch of disappointment, which was ridiculous. Had I not expressly forbidden Burgo to try to find me?

'Fine. Are you keeping up with the writing regime?' Before I left Oliver and I had worked out a timetable which meant he could fit in at least four hours a day of concentrated work. 'I've had an extraordinary piece of luck. I've met a literary agent who's prepared to look at your novel and give you an in-depth critique.'

'Oh, terrific. Look, I'd better go and get dressed. Sherilee's popping in for lunch and Ruby's making honey-roasted pork chops, followed by banana splits.'

'I hope you're remembering to clean your teeth. Has Ruby got shares in Tate and Lyle?'

'I haven't any idea.' Oliver sounded puzzled. 'I only met her the day before yesterday.'

'Never mind. It was just a feeble joke.'

'I don't get it.'

'I'll ring again soon. Don't neglect the novel. Give Mother my love and look after her and be nice to Mrs Treadgold. And if anyone asks about me—'

'What? There's the doorbell. It'll be Sherilee. Grrrr! Bye.'

I sat in the sedan chair, waiting for the operator to ring back with the cost of the call, more out of charity with my brother than I would have believed possible ten minutes before. But much more disturbing than any dissatisfaction I might feel with Oliver was the news that my father had imported his paramour to look after my mother. I checked this thought immediately. Considering my own behaviour with Burgo it was hypocritical to call Ruby names. But I was surprisingly upset by the discovery. It seemed to discount my mother so thoroughly and so callously. Apparently *ménages à trois* were all the rage.

'Oh, damn!' I said aloud. 'Damn, damn, *damn*!'

A face half hidden by enormous sunglasses peered in at the side window, giving me a fright. I opened the door and was overwhelmed by fresh waves of Ô. The face was surrounded by brown curly hair, inexpertly streaked with blonde. The mouth, painted crimson, was sulky.

'If you're going to hog the phone all the time we'll have to come to an arrangement.'

She was unnaturally thin. Her limbs, visible beyond a tiny orange dress of some shiny synthetic stuff, were little more than skin and bones. Her teeth seemed too large for her face and her chin, beneath a layer of white pancake make-up, was spotty.

I stepped out of the chair. 'Hello. I'm Bobbie.'

The blank stare of the spectacles was trained on my face then lowered to my jersey. 'Is that from Next?'

'No. Actually it's Peruvian, from a shop called Inca.'

'In London?'

'Yes. The bottom end of Sloane Street.'

'It's fabulous.' Her lenses moved to my earrings. 'Those are amazing! Where did you get them?'

'A little shop in Beauchamp Place. I can't remember the name. They aren't real . . .'

'Where's Beauchamp Place?'

'Just down the road from Harrods . . .'

'Harrods! I've never ever been to London!' It was a cry of anguish. 'I've only been to Dublin twice!'

'Ah, well. London's a wonderful place but like any big city it only glitters at the centre. There are some extremely scruffy parts.'

'I wouldn't care about that. Anything would be better than living in this place where everyone looks like refugees and the most interesting conversations happen between sheep.'

'But it's so beautiful! Mountains and trees and lakes. And this marvellous house!'

'We're so poor!' The girl sighed and fiddled with a plastic bracelet on her wrist, which was hardly thicker than a stick of rhubarb. 'It's so dull! I'm so bored!'

My pity was stirred. The mask of white, the dark spectacles and lipstick concealed the face of a child.

'I think I know how you feel.'

She removed the sunglasses and fastened extraordinary eyes, inherited from Maud, on mine. 'How could you? You've never had to live in a peat bog.'

'Before I went to live in London—'

'You actually *lived* there? How old were you?'

'Eighteen. I went to university in London. But before then I was

226

either at home in the most unimaginably gloomy place or I was stuck at boarding school in a forest of purple rhododendrons, which was even worse. Our uniform was purple and grey and so were our hands and faces and knees because it was always so cold.'

'Life's so foul when you're a kid. Not that I am any more, of course,' she added.

'You look very grown up to me.' I was becoming adept at the fib *juste*.

'I'm eighteen.'

I did not believe her. 'I suppose you're Flurry and Flavia's big sister.'

'Yes. I'm Liddy.' She shivered and fidgeted again with the bracelet, then twirled a lock of hair. Her elbow was a sharp point of bone.

'I'm the new housekeeper.'

'I thought you must be. But you don't look like one.'

'What do housekeepers look like?'

'Mrs Heaney had a beard. Long enough to curl. And there were often hairs in the food. It was very off-putting.' She shivered again.

'It's cold here, isn't it? The damp I expect. Have you had any breakfast?'

'I never eat breakfast. I'm planning to become a model.'

'Really? I think you'll find the interesting conversations remain with the sheep.'

Liddy smiled again. 'Yes, but it's the only thing I can think of doing to get away from here.'

'I can think of plenty of other things.'

'What?' She looked at me eagerly, her smudged lips parted.

'Let's talk about it later. I must go and help Constance with lunch.'

Liddy followed me to the kitchen. 'It'll be stew again. I *hate* stew! Aunt Connie's the most terrible cook. But that's good because I'm not tempted to eat much.'

'Morning, Liddy.' Constance was struggling to undo the string of a large newspaper parcel. 'I think the butcher's boy is a frustrated boy scout. He must be the knot champion of Ireland.' Liddy picked up a knife from the floor and silently handed it to her. 'Oh, thanks, sweetheart. That's better.' She unwrapped the meat. 'Blast the man! Why does he always send me so much fat and sinew?'

'Because he knows you won't complain, I suppose.' Liddy hurled herself into Timsy's chair and stretched out her hands and feet to warm them. 'Where's everybody gone? I don't usually get a sight of the fire.'

Constance smiled at me. 'Bobbie electrified them into activity.'

'Not literally, I hope.' I looked at the contents of the newspaper. 'Do you think that meat's quite fresh?'

Constance bent to sniff it. 'It has got a bit of a kick to it. But that'll go when it's been cooked. I could put in some curry powder.'

Liddy groaned.

I prodded the meat with the point of the knife. 'By the time you've trimmed the gristle there won't be much left.'

'Ought I to cut those tubey bits out? I usually just put the whole lot straight in with the potatoes. Luckily there are plenty of cabbages to make up for the shortfall.'

I decided to risk being considered intolerably interfering. 'Why don't you let me make lunch?'

Constance clutched my arm. '*Would* you? I'd be *so* grateful!'

'It's what I'm here for, after all.'

'Yippee!' said Liddy. 'I mean,' she drawled, 'thank God!'

Lunch was, surprisingly, a success. But cooking it had been a baptism of fire. In the fridge I found a packet of sausages, a pound of butter, five eggs, a plastic lemon, a box of processed cheese triangles, a bag of oranges going soft and half a bottle of Liebfraumilch. The larder was stacked with tins. I gathered together tinned tomatoes, tinned spinach, a tin of consommé and a bottle of mushroom ketchup with which to make soup.

The stove was a cast-iron, soot-caked range with two large circular plates on top. To get food hotter than a slow simmer you had to lift off one of the plates with a hook. Fire leaped through the hole and brought the contents of the pan to a violent boil in seconds. A glass of wine which I threw into the soup to cheer up the tinned taste set the whole thing alight with flames that rolled across the surface of the liquid like Milton's description of hell and which nearly took off my eyebrows. There seemed no way of cooking between these two extremes.

'You must teach me how to make this marvellous soup,' Constance had said, looking down the dining table to where I sat at the foot. 'Isn't it absolutely de*lic*ious, Maud?'

Maud had come downstairs in response to the gong. She looked haggard as though she had not slept well. I noticed that her hands were misshapen and she held her spoon with difficulty. The moment she had finished her soup she lit a cigarette.

'It hardly merits such enthusiasm.' She turned her great amethyst-coloured eyes to me. 'But I have eaten much worse in this house.'

'I think it's lovely.' Flavia, who was sitting next to me, looked up from the book, now spotted with soup, that was hidden on her knee. 'I was dreading the stew.'

Maud looked across the table at Flavia. 'I hope the subject matter is something improving. That will go a little way to make up for the extreme discourtesy of reading at the table. Also the deceit. It is good manners to make intelligent and amusing conversation.'

A silence fell immediately. I searched about for a topic. I was about to volunteer a remark about the glorious plasterwork but remembered in time that Maud's generation regarded comments on one's house and possessions as an impertinence. Perhaps I might say something about the current situation in Iran? But I really knew nothing about Ayatollah Khomeini except that he seemed to be thoroughly unpleasant. This view, though probably shared by everyone in the world who did not happen to be Muslim, hardly amounted to intelligent conversation. Then I wondered if it became me to speak before I had been spoken to. I felt, not for the first time, the awkwardness of my situation. The constraints of being a stranger were compounded by being also a paid servant while Constance treated me as a welcome guest. I felt like one of those tropical fish that swim on the surface and have half an eye adapted for seeing in air and half for seeing under water.

'I wonder how the preparations for the Pope's visit—' began Constance, but she was interrupted by the entrance of the pale long-haired man I had seen briefly at breakfast.

This time he advanced into the room, inclined his head gracefully in the direction of Maud and Constance and came round the table to where I was sitting. I was aware at once of a smell of mustiness with overtones of stale sweat.

'How do you do? I am Eugene Devlin.'

'I'm Bobbie Norton.'

Mr Devlin touched the back of my hand with his small red mouth. '*Enchanté.*'

He was a tall man, beginning to run to fat. He wore a green frock-coat and an embroidered waistcoat, which were much too tight. His legs, by contrast, encased in stockings and satin breeches, were slender to the point of skinniness. His face was large and pale and his eyes bulged, creating dark shadows beneath them. His hair was fastened back with a black bow. I was reminded of Prince Florizel, a little further into the fairy story when the romance was beginning to wear off.

229

'What delightful happenstance brings you to the mists and mountains of the ancient kingdom of Connaught?'

'Must you talk like a bad translation of a French play?' asked Maud.

'I saw the advertisement in a newspaper,' I explained.

Mr Devlin pressed two fingers to the bridge of his nose and looked pained. 'The newspapers are not the least part of the horrid distemper of mediocrity that has engulfed the modern world. Television sets, motor cars, aeroplanes polluting the air we breathe. However, in this case' – he bowed to me – 'we have been the beneficiaries.'

'Our television doesn't get much chance to pollute the air,' said Liddy gloomily. 'The reception's so hopeless it isn't worth watching. It's those sodding mountains.'

'Don't swear, darling. It isn't clever,' said Constance, going over to the sideboard and ladling out a bowl of soup for Eugene.

'Who wants to be clever, for God's sake?' replied her niece.

Eugene looked reprovingly at Liddy. 'Those mountains you curse so inelegantly, my child, keep the wicked world at bay. That reminds me of a poem I wrote after reading an account of the battle of the Boyne.' He took a deep breath and began to recite.

'Heavenward coiled the smoke of battle
Darkening the plain and frightening the cattle
While all around grim-visaged mountains steep
Cursed England's pitiless pride and the sheep . . .'

There was much more in this style. The rhyme schemes were unexceptionable. I repressed a smile as I remembered conversations with Kit. I thought of Burgo and how he would enjoy the eccentricities of Curraghcourt. Then I wished I hadn't, for the now familiar misery trotted obediently back to heel like a well-trained dog. I tried to distract myself by watching covertly everyone else's reactions to Eugene's performance.

Liddy continued to eat her soup, while drumming her fingers loudly on the table and affecting deafness. Flavia fastened her eyes on her book while Flurry found the centre of gravity of each of his eating implements in turn by balancing them on his finger. Maud said, 'Faugh!' and continued to smoke her cigarette with her eyes closed as though she wished to shut out the sight of Eugene standing in the attitude of a wine waiter, his napkin over one arm, the other hand thrust out as though bearing an invisible tray. Constance hovered at his elbow, holding the plate of soup. I waited with poised spoon and tried to finish my mouthful of bread but it was so stale that the crunching brought Eugene's protuberant eyes immediately to my face.

'You must eat, Eugene,' said Constance when his memory faltered. She put the soup in front of him, took a piece of bread from the basket, broke it into bite-sized pieces and buttered them for him. 'You missed breakfast. It isn't good to fast when you expend so much intellectual energy.'

Maud, her eyes still closed, opened her mouth in silent, mirthless laughter.

'I confess I failed to notice the omission.' Eugene sat down next to Constance and smiled his thanks. 'When one's head is in the clouds the exigencies of the body are as the buzzings of a gnat.'

Eugene's grubby lace jabot dangled perilously near his soup. His coat was sadly out at elbows. His appearance was of a piece with the room. I enjoyed myself, briefly, imagining we were all in a satire by Sheridan. When Flavia looked up I asked her, in a low voice, what she was reading.

'*The Incredible Journey,*' she replied.

I remembered with dismay the story of two dogs and a cat who undergo appalling suffering during their cross-country wanderings. I had been furious with the author when she had permitted the loyal old bull terrier to die within sight of home and happiness. I wondered whether I should say something to Flavia about the unhappiness in store. But perhaps I should not interfere. Surely it was her mother's place to protect her daughter? Where was Violet? Could she really be locked up in an attic with some Irish version of Grace Poole to curb her most savage lunatic excesses?

The door opened. It was not Violet who came in, however, but Sissy.

'I'm late again.' Her upper lip glistened with sweat, her hair hung in matted clumps, her red velvet dress was sprinkled with burrs and grass seed. Her breasts were heaving above the tight bodice.

'Evidently your mother did not teach you punctuality.' Maud's eyes were open and alight with the pleasure of a call to arms. 'She was too busy telling fortunes. Or stealing babies from prams.'

Sissy laughed, wrinkling up her monkey face. 'Why would she when she had a baby every summer for ten years till Dadda went off with the woman in the bicycle shop? 'Twas more likely she'd put some of us into other folk's prams.'

Maud looked angry at this failure of her barb to lodge. 'How do you account for your appearance? Have you been tumbling in the hay with a pedlar?'

'Ah, Maudie, you know I like your son-in-law too well to look at another man. 'Twas a butterfly that caught me fancy. Through brake and briar it led me till I was tired with running and me heart was lepping out of me breast.' Sissy laid a filthy hand on that near-naked part of her anatomy.

'I de*test* being called Maudie.'

'But I like to be friendly,' Sissy explained charmingly and threw herself into the empty chair next to Flurry whom she proceeded to pet and kiss.

'Don't!' Flurry protested, smoothing his hair and wiping his spectacles on his napkin.

Constance insisted on helping me to clear the soup plates and bring in the main course, a bastardized version of *salade niçoise* with potatoes, tuna, hard-boiled eggs, tinned beans and mayonnaise. Sausages, of course, for Flurry. The mayonnaise was an odd colour. I had made it with the dregs of a bottle of what looked like olive oil which was all I could find in the larder. I hoped it was merely a coincidence when Timsy complained a few days later that he could not find the lubricant he put on his boots to keep out the wet.

'This salad's really good,' said Liddy. I was pleased to see that she tucked in with enthusiasm.

'It just shows, my girl, how your palate has been mistreated.' Maud seemed to excuse herself from the obligation to make intelligent and amusing conversation. 'But it *is* an improvement on the boiled ligaments and withered tubers your aunt provides. Though the mayonnaise has a peculiar taste.' She was like a ballista, the device invented by the Romans for firing off arrows with terrific thrust in quick succession.

I looked apologetically at Constance but her eyes, usually vague and wandering, were fixed on Eugene.

'How did the writing go this morning?' she asked him.

'I struggled with a stanza and got it out fairly well in the end.'

'Eugene is writing a ballad about Deirdre's lament for the sons of Usnach,' Constance explained to me.

'How interesting,' I said.

Eugene bowed in my direction, dipping his jabot into the mayonnaise. I was uncertain whether I ought to bow back. In the end I contented myself with a slight nod.

'Not for us.' Flurry waved half a sausage on the end of his fork then looked abashed as he caught his aunt's eye.

'Have you published much?' I asked Eugene.

'He fears the corrupting taint of commerce,' Constance answered for Eugene. 'But I think it's a shame.' She smiled at him to dispel any suggestion of criticism. 'It would do people so much good to read his work. And he could always refuse to take the money.' Of course he could, I thought, if he were completely deranged. 'Poetry inspires the higher, nobler instincts,' Constance continued. 'It softens men's hearts and calls them to brotherhood.'

'Dear me, yes,' said Maud. 'One can imagine the IRA reading Eugene's little rhymes about inconstant moons and decaying buds, bursting into tears and throwing away their detonators.'

This sarcasm seemed to go beyond the point of what was permissible. I glanced anxiously at Eugene but he was gazing, one finger on his lips, at the bowl of rotting fruit in the middle of the table, perhaps polishing a metaphor.

'What are the main themes of the ballad?' I asked him. I was too ashamed to display my ignorance by asking who was Deirdre.

He waved large, white hands, blotched with ink. 'Disenchantment. The realization that love is merely the blinding idealization of another person. The rift in the lute.'

A cloud of tiny flies rose from the brown, liquefying mass in the fruit bowl and the light of inspiration leaped into Eugene's prominent eyes.

'Would you be an angel and read some of it to us before dinner?' asked Constance, with such sweetness that I at once regretted my cynicism. 'Bobbie adores poetry.'

Eugene looked at me with approval.

'I should love that,' I murmured.

'You are either a liar or a fool,' said Maud.

Eugene rewarded me with a sad smile. 'I hope you like our Irish poets?'

'Oh, yes.' I struggled to think of one. 'Um . . . Louis MacNeice.'

Eugene frowned. 'You admire him? Really? I have always considered him sadly out of tune with what it means to be Irish.' He put on what I was already able to recognize as his reciting face: flared nostrils, the inner corners of his eyebrows lifted above his nose to make a circumflex of pained surprise at the treachery of the world ranged so meanly against him. '"Ireland is a gallery of fake tapestries. Inbred soul and climatic maleficence. Drug-dull fatalism." Sentiments I cannot echo.'

'I particularly like W. B. Yeats,' I said hastily.

'Ah-h-h. *Yes!*' I saw I was on safer ground. 'Our greatest poet, without doubt. But he himself pronounced it Yeets you know, to rhyme with Keats. Willie Yeats: a genius, a colossus. *He* knew what it was to love and be rejected.

'O heart! O heart! If she'd but turn her head,
You'd know the folly of being comforted.'

I perceived that Eugene was like a poor street fiddler who knows only one tune. Thanks to Maud Gonne, Yeats was practically a bottomless pit on the subject of unrequited love and Eugene did his best to plumb it. Constance looked deeply engaged and I tried to imitate her. Everyone else reverted to their former occupations of drumming fingers, reading, balancing knives and forks and closing their eyes. Except for Sissy, who listened with eyes filled with tears, leaving me in no doubt that she had her proper share of Irish sympathy and sensibility.

Pudding was tinned raspberries, evaporated milk and meringues. I had made the meringues the size of ping-pong balls because of lack of time. It was not by any stretch of imagination a lunch to be proud of but its enthusiastic reception was gratifying after the indifference with which my efforts had been met at Cutham Hall. I began to make plans.

TWENTY-ONE

'It's all so awful, I know,' said Constance as we sat with cups of tea at the kitchen table, late that afternoon. 'You've worked so hard. I don't know how to thank you.'

'No need,' I said. 'Truthfully, I've enjoyed myself. I've always loved putting things right . . . That is,' I collected myself, 'putting my own stamp on things. I'm terribly bossy though I'm aware it's unattractive. Also I get great pleasure from simple things, like cleaning this, for example.' I admired yet again the exquisite George I teapot, now reflecting the light in shooting points from its gleaming sides. 'This is quite a valuable piece, you know.'

'Is it? I don't think I even knew it was silver. It's been brown as long as I can remember.' She looked round the kitchen. 'It all looks so different already. What a good idea to get rid of those old hams. I'd got so used to them being there that I never saw them.' Five ancient pig legs, thick with dust, the colour of bog oak and so hard even the flies had given them up, had been hanging from the rafters. 'Timsy was supposed to cure them with saltpetre and whiskey but I think he must have drunk it because the few slices we had off them were tainted.'

We looked towards the fireplace where Timsy, Pegeen and Katty were enjoying their tea. The black bottle was back on the hearth. The 'girls', as they were generally referred to though they were both in their thirties, had worked surprisingly well and I thought they had earned it. Katty and I had turned out the pantry and the still room, rejecting anything with a bloom of fur or a rank smell – about three-quarters of the contents – washing the shelves and saturating the insides of the fridge with bicarbonate of soda. Pegeen had scrubbed the floors throughout the service quarters, which comprised, besides

235

the kitchen and the pantry, a still room, a game larder, a dairy and a storeroom for china and glass.

Each time I asked them to do something they exchanged remarks in Gaelic which I was certain were insulting. They wanted me to know that I was an oppressive English tyrant and that my ways of doing things were not a patch on the good old-fashioned Irish ways. Katty was visibly angry when I made her throw away the milk in the cream pans and scald them with boiling water to remove the rancid grease adhering to their rims on which flies fed greedily. But because I was keeper of the black bottle they did as I asked them. Now they sat with their skirts rolled up over their knees, roasting their thighs.

Timsy's intention was to subdue me with Irish charm, consisting of extravagant compliments. This did not improve the girls' opinion of me. Pegeen began by joining in the praise but she soon grew jealous. With every pretty speech from Timsy in my favour Katty's hooked nose, spotted with soot, seemed to curve further down to meet her pointed chin, wrinkling her mouth and dark moustache. I had asked Timsy to cut back the bushes that crowded the high windows of the basement area, which were actually at ground level. Each time I looked up his teeth were bared in a grin as he leered at me through the filthy glass. Now shafts of light penetrated the Tartarean gloom.

'Oh damn!' said Constance suddenly. 'Is this Thursday?'

'I think it may be.' I did some calculations. 'Yes.'

'Oh, bother! Father Deglan comes for dinner every Thursday. Your first proper evening with us. What a nuisance!'

'Does it matter? Would you rather I ate in the kitchen? I don't mind at all.'

'I wouldn't dream of it! No, it's just he's a bit outspoken, and what with Maud . . . I'd have liked you to get used to us before suffering the full onslaught. He's really a very good man but he's fiery by nature. Brimstone is in that man's nostrils. He'd have been a good general or perhaps a buccaneer. He was put into the seminary at the age of eight and he didn't have the heart to disappoint his parents.'

'That was admirable of him. I doubt if I'd be so unselfish. One's whole life thrown away to please someone else's whim.'

'It's much more than a whim. Every Catholic mother dreams that her son may become a priest, and not only in the hope of pleasing God. Priests have power and often they come from poor families that have none. That part of it suits him. If he's not lecturing me about Finn and Sissy, it's about the children not attending Sunday afternoon service. What's the good of making them sit in a church if their minds and hearts are mutinous?'

'No good at all.'

'Father Deglan gets furious and tells me I'm unfit to have the care of them. Then he tries to bully the children about saying their prayers but it only makes them hate him.'

'Doesn't Violet – Mrs Macchuin – have a view on this?' My curiosity about the mysterious Violet had grown to the point that I decided to risk being thought rudely inquisitive. A dish of something called stirabout, which looked like thin porridge, had been prepared for her at lunchtime and carried upstairs by Pegeen. But there had been no other sign of Violet's existence.

'Who knows what poor Violet thinks about anything? I usually go and see her about this time with a cup of tea. Why don't you come with me?'

I made a fresh pot of tea and Constance carried the tray. We went up to the second floor of the castle. It must have been on the same level as my tower room for I saw through one of the windows that the three bowls of meat – Constance's erstwhile stew – that I had put out on the roof a little earlier were surrounded by crouching cats.

'This is Violet's room.' Constance opened a door at the end of a long corridor.

The smell of disinfectant made me sneeze. The only light in the room came from several candles, including one in a little red glass pot, burning before a statue of the Virgin Mary. On each side of the shrine was a window. The curtains were drawn tightly together to block out all natural light. I peered into the choking gloom and made out a bed. On it lay a body. Constance tiptoed to the bedside and I followed her.

'Hello, Violet,' she whispered. 'It's Constance. How are you, darling? And here's Bobbie who's come to see you.'

Now my vision was beginning to adjust to the darkness I saw an expressionless face with closed eyes and dark hair carefully fanned out over the pillow. Above the bedclothes her hands were neatly crossed on her chest as though she were an effigy on a tomb. Only the slight stirring of the sheet stretched tightly across her body belied the appearance of death.

'How do you do, Mrs Macchuin?' I touched the hand that lay uppermost. Its warmth was unexpected. I was even more startled when the lips parted to utter a faint sound, something between a hum and a grunt. Her mouth opened and closed several times like a baby making sucking motions in its sleep.

'Are you thirsty, sweetheart?' said Constance. 'We've brought you a lovely cup of tea.'

It was pathetic to see the way the head lolled helplessly as Constance took two pillows from the chair next to the bed and propped up the lifeless body. She poured the tea, added a generous amount of milk and put the liquid to her own lips to test the temperature. A box of bendable straws stood on the bedside table beneath a picture of Christ with his heart exposed and bleeding. Constance put one end into the slack mouth and slowly the pale liquid was drawn up. I watched in silence as the cup was consumed. Sometimes there was a fit of gasping as liquid entered the windpipe. Constance patted the frail bony shoulders until it subsided.

'Another one, darling?'

The protrusion of the tip of Violet's tongue initiated a repeat of the process.

'Good girl! Would you like to stay sitting up or lie down again?'

Again the half-human, half-animal grunt.

'That means down. I think.'

Constance took the pillows away and with great tenderness arranged the lank hair as before and repositioned the crossed hands over the bedclothes. She kissed the smooth forehead. 'Father Deglan's coming to dinner tonight, Violet. I've warned Bobbie to take no notice of his outbursts. D'you remember the arguments you and he used to have? Sometimes I was frightened you were going to start rolling on the carpet pulling each other's hair out. Remember the time you accused him of having turned you into a pagan? You said he'd put you off God entirely. God was a sadistic bully, you said. You made him weep with temper!'

A slight ripple of movement ran over the mask-like face.

Above the bed was a crucifix and on every wall were pictures of Jesus or Mary, their faces dolorous, their hands supplicating. A glass stoop of holy water hung by the door.

'Well, Violet dear,' Constance patted the lifeless hand, 'we'd better go now and leave you in peace. Pegeen'll bring you some stirabout in a little while. God bless you.' She took great care to shut the door noiselessly behind her. 'I'll never get used to it,' she said as we retraced our steps down to the kitchen. 'Violet was so full of life. Sometimes even now, I half think she's pretending, that she might suddenly sit up and say, "Ha ha! Fooled you, Con!" Then she'll swing her legs over the side of the bed and light a cigarette and tease me as she always used to. We used to get on all right but she was much more sophisticated. A sweet, affectionate girl and high-spirited. I was always shy but Violet adored being the centre of attention. She did everything to extremes – never missed a day's hunting – sometimes she'd ride all day and then drive for four hours to Dublin for a party afterwards. She was never tired and I don't remember her ever being ill before she had the stroke.'

'How long has she been like this?'

'She was thirty-two when it happened. That was four years ago. She was on the ferry crossing to England. Apparently the friends she was with were trying to lower one of the lifeboats without the crew noticing. Violet was lookout. It was her idea and typical of one of her games. Suddenly she was lying on the deck making odd noises. She's never said a word – nothing you'd recognize – from that day to this.'

I was unable to find an adequate expression of the shock and pity I felt. 'Is there no hope? What do her doctors say?'

'After a brief spell in hospital she spent two years in a convent outside Dublin. The nuns looked after her beautifully but they were old ladies and it got too much for them. Young girls aren't so keen to take the veil these days. When the convent closed Finn had her brought back here.'

'Has she made any sort of improvement?'

'If anything she's gone backwards. When I used to visit her in the hospital, she'd open her eyes. Now she never does.'

By now we had reached the hall. 'Does she have to be so far away from everyone else?' I asked.

Constance turned her head as though to make sure that no one was listening. 'To tell you the truth, it's Maud that wants her shut away. She insists Violet needs absolute quiet. To be fair, Dr Duffy and the nuns have backed her up. Dr Duffy says a sudden shock might actually kill Violet. But . . .' Constance looked over her shoulder again as we descended the passage to the basement. 'Really, Maud can't bear the sight of her. She used to be so proud of her pretty, vivacious daughter. Maud's arthritis is so bad now she can't get up to the top floor to visit Violet. The fact is she doesn't want to. It's not that Maud doesn't care. I know she'd give her own right hand to have Violet as she once was but as it is she'd rather not be reminded. You can understand it.'

239

I realized that Constance was pleading Maud's case. 'Well, yes. I suppose so. It's impossible to know how one would feel in such a situation.'

'It is, indeed. I always try to have a little talk with Violet each day. And I read her some poetry. Sometimes I think she can understand me but other times I'm not so sure.'

'Is it necessary to keep her in semi-darkness? I thought stroke patients were supposed to be stimulated.'

'I've heard that, too. But I wouldn't want to be responsible for another stroke that might end her life. You may call it cowardice, for that's what it is. Dr Duffy visits her once a month. He always says to carry on as we are. He says Violet's brain's most likely damaged beyond repair.'

I tried to imagine what it might be like to be conscious and imprisoned in a helpless body. 'Do the children go to see her?'

'Flavia goes though I sometimes wish she wouldn't: she's always so miserable afterwards. Liddy and Flurry hardly ever. They don't know what to say. They feel awkward. You mustn't think they're hard-hearted.'

'Of course I don't think that. It must be terribly distressing for them.'

'I'm so glad you understand. If they *do* try to talk to their mother Pegeen tells them to hush. We take it in turns to feed Violet but Pegeen's more devoted than anyone. It was she who put the statue and the candles and the religious pictures there. Maud would go mad if she knew. Being Anglo-Irish, of course she despises papacy.'

'I see.' I longed to ask if Mr Macchuin visited his wife but I did not dare.

'Finn goes up there most days when he's at home,' said Constance as though reading my thoughts. 'He takes up papers to read and spends an hour or so with her.'

I supposed it was unreasonable to expect more from a man who had brought his mistress to live in the same house as his children while his wife lay comatose in the attic. I decided to say nothing more on the subject in case Constance should divine my disapproval. It was none of my business and I would confine my thoughts to my job which was, most immediately, to prepare dinner for nine people.

But as I made a hollandaise to go with a piece of salmon I had taken from the freezer and was thawing in a pan of water, opened yet more tins of potatoes, peas and spinach and stirred pineapple chunks into sherry and evaporated milk – which was as horrid as it

240

sounds but everyone had second helpings – I could not prevent images recurring in my mind of Violet's face, white against a whiter pillow, of her body quietly drawing breath in a silent, darkened room, the seconds expanding to hours as a life that was not a life continued relentlessly, joylessly, perhaps agonizingly, towards death.

'Sarah?'

'Bobbie! Thank God! Just a minute, let me shut the front door and get rid of my bag. I've just this second walked in.' I heard the door slam and then a creak. In my mind's eye I saw Sarah flinging her considerable weight into the little papier mâché and mother-of-pearl chair beside the telephone in the tiny hallway of Paradise Row. 'I've been *crazy* with worry. Where are you? You were so bloody mysterious I started to think "leaving the country" might be a metaphor for the bare bodkin or chucking yourself in the Thames.' Sarah and I had spoken briefly on the telephone a few times since Burgo and I had first made the headlines but I had been obliged to be extremely circumspect. 'Why haven't you been in touch sooner? Are you all right?'

'Yes, I'm fine. Really. I've been so busy since I got here this is the first moment I've had to call you.'

'You *sound* OK. Are you eating?'

'Quite well, really, considering how awful the food is.'

'Where's "here"?'

'Ireland.'

'Ireland? What the hell are you doing there? I expected you to say Guatemala.'

'Why?'

'I don't know. Because it's one of those places people go when they want to get away from everything.'

'You're thinking of Ferdinand Lopez.' Sarah and I shared a passion for the novels of Anthony Trollope. 'That was fiction.'

'If you ask me, the whole ridiculous mess seems like fiction to me. I'd have put ten years' salary on your being the *last* person in the world to get tangled up with a married man. And a Tory politician! I've always admired you for seeing through all the flattery and attention you got because you were good-looking. I really thought you had your head screwed on. When I read that article in the *Daily Globe* I was convinced it must be an elaborate joke. All this time you've been carrying on with that – that true-blue shit and you never breathed a word! How could you be so *stu*pid!'

I felt a little wounded by the mixture of scorn and incredulity in Sarah's voice but I remembered that her inability to be hypocritical and disguise her feelings was a quality I valued. She was fiercely loyal and I had no doubt that she had been genuinely worried. Also she would have been hurt because I had not confided in her.

'I didn't say anything because we had to be so careful. Nobody knew except Oliver. I told him because he sometimes answers the telephone at home. But I didn't tell another soul.'

'Because you knew it was a bloody moronic thing to do! You knew anyone who cared tuppence about you would say you were behaving like a gibbering jelly-brain!' The words were harsh but I could hear that she was a little mollified to discover she was not the only one who had been kept in the dark. 'Well, I suppose one oughtn't to be surprised at anything, really. But after all we both said to Jazz about Teddy, it does seem incredible.'

'I can't defend myself.'

'I suppose you fell *in love*.' Her tone was sarcastic.

'It must have been that.'

'Oh, all right. I've no right to lecture you. I'm sorry, Bobbie. And you must be going through hell. Put my bad temper down to the fact that I've been so worried about you. You're the best friend I've ever had, Bobbie, and I'd do anything to help you.'

'I know that.'

'So you're dotty about this man.'

'Yes.'

'You must be. I have to admit,' she added in a more sympathetic tone, 'he's got something, bastard though he is. Charisma, a journalist would call it. He almost managed to win me round. Only remembering how wretched you sounded the other day – that and a firmly entrenched distrust of the male sex – stopped me from actually liking him. Of course that's his job, isn't it, winning people over to his way of thinking?'

I was thankful I was seated in the sedan chair as my stomach seemed to plummet to my feet, like being in an express lift. 'You've seen him? When? Where?'

'He came here, to Paradise Row. Yesterday. He wanted to know where you were. He seemed pretty cut up.'

I felt such a rush of love for Burgo that I almost decided on the spot to ring for a taxi. 'Was he upset?'

'I got the impression he usually gets his own way about things,' continued Sarah. 'He likes to be the one to call the tune.'

'What did he say?'

'He said he knew from what you'd told him that I was a good friend and he was going to assume that I'd have your interests at heart. He was going to tell me the truth. I don't know why I always immediately mistrust people when they say that; I suppose because it suggests that generally they don't. Anyway, the long and short of it is he's willing to divorce his wife and give up everything for you. He thinks being harassed by the press and your family has driven you into a state of temporary insanity. Not quite how he put it but that was the gist.'

'Oh, Sarah!'

'What?' When I did not reply she said, 'If you're so crazy about him, what's stopping you from taking up his offer?'

'I don't *want* him to give up everything. I *do* love him. I don't want to be the destruction of everything he's worked and planned for. I hate the idea of dragging him down into disgrace and obscurity. Surely you can understand that? And if I did I'd always be afraid afterwards that I wasn't good enough, clever enough, kind enough, pretty enough. Enough.'

'I see,' said Sarah and was briefly silent. Then she said, 'Do you know, I don't quite buy it. I mean, I'm sure you think you feel that but . . . I don't know, I'm no expert on matters of the heart but I think there's something here that doesn't quite add up.' I knew that contrary to her assertion Sarah did consider herself to be something of an expert on the human psyche. I imagined the expression in her round brown eyes becoming intense as she assumed her favourite role of Seeker after Truth. I also knew that quite often Sarah was spot on and therefore I was prepared to listen to her. 'It's true, he *did* harp on about how ready he was to cut himself off from all that made his life worth living to throw in his lot with you. I didn't quite pick that up at the time but now I remember I was left with the feeling that he was prepared to go through fire and water in order to call you his own. Now, I can appreciate that divorce is a nasty business and it's a shame if you've been successful to have to creep down to the bottom of the ladder again, but the way he talked about it you'd think he was going to be torn to pieces, like Orpheus by the women of Thrace. It might have been more graceful if he'd concentrated a little more on his concern for you.'

'He's ambitious. It's not a crime – in my eyes anyway.'

'No. Nor in mine, actually. All right, so he's your average self-centred man, only more so. But there's something else that really *is* odd. In this situation every other woman I know anything about would just fall into his arms and let the future take care of itself. I mean, that's one of the things I object to about adultery: the way it falsifies feelings. Forbidden fruit and all that. Generally the mistress, at least if she's single, gets so fed up with being side-lined that she'll do *any*thing to get him out of his wife's arms. Now you're putting yourself to considerable inconvenience to do the opposite.'

'I've told you why.'

'And very pretty, selfless telling it makes.' I flinched at this but allowed her to carry on. 'I think it may be darker than that, old thing.' I braced myself for the broadside that was coming. Sarah frequently prefaced her home truths by 'old thing' to soften the blow. 'This man has power. He's an authority figure. No . . .' she added as I started to speak, 'I'm not going to give you the old chestnut about power being an aphrodisiac. I think this has something to do with your father. We needn't go into details but let's just say it isn't the happiest of parent–child relationships, is it? *I* think when you took up with Burgo Latimer you wanted a father figure to whom you could submit without compromising your integrity and who would give you in return the love and admiration your pa has always withheld.'

'Honestly, Sarah, you're making this up as you go along.'

'Of course I am. That's what inductive reasoning is. I'm putting two and two together and making five. But I might be right. *You* know, consciously or subconsciously, that your father hates you because you've struggled from an early age to escape his control over you. Not only over your mind but your body. Naturally you won't let him do the one thing he desires above all else which is to have sex with you— No, hear me out,' as I attempted to protest. 'Your father's the sort of man that thinks women are only good for one thing. Of course you know you're right to resist this but none the less the refusal puts you into a state of conflict because you experience all the guilt every child feels when it disappoints its parent. But Burgo Latimer also treats you with brute selfishness, creating an emotional climate you recognize and therefore feel comfortable with, subordinating your needs to his own, making you grateful for what crumbs of attention he can spare from his work and his legitimate lover. But because he's *not* your father you can gratify his sexual demands and thereby receive the affection and approval you crave.'

I leaned sideways to rest my temple and cheek against the cool glass of the sedan chair window. 'Sarah, if you knew how ghastly this makes me feel you wouldn't go on.'

'Aha!' said Sarah triumphantly. 'We all know that the truth hurts, don't we? Well,' she continued in a milder tone, 'I won't go on then. I don't want to make you more miserable than you already are. I'll just conclude by saying that I think *that's* why you've left him. Because your instinct to survive – which I trust you'll listen to – tells you that the love affair between you and Latimer will eventually stultify all possibilities of growth and happiness. *He*'d be all right, dictating terms, exacting obedience and submission in return for his grand gesture, but you'd be locked into a child-like passivity, always having to be grateful, trying to please, giving up your right to autonomy for as long as you lived together. And because of your pa you know exactly what that feels like and you want it like a hole in the head. It's not *his* sacrifice you're anxious to prevent, but your *own*.'

'Oh God!' I said feebly. 'I'm incapable of even beginning to argue with you. If I was confused before, now I'm practically deranged.'

'Nonsense! You've got sense and you've got guts. I have complete faith in you to get over it.'

I felt absurdly grateful for this sudden declaration of confidence. 'Really? You don't despise me utterly, then?'

'Of course not! You're the sanest woman I know. The first person I'd turn to in a crisis. This is just a blip on the chart. And in the end you'll be stronger for all this. We all know about suffering unto truth. Now, tell me what gives in Ireland?'

'I've taken a job as housekeeper in a rather run-down castle in Connemara.'

'Never!' Sarah was silent while she digested this. 'You're not having me on?'

'I promise you. I've taken a short break between turning centuries-old food out of cockroach-infested cupboards and cooking dinner in order to ring you.'

Sarah was intrigued and by the time I had described Curraghcourt and its inhabitants and my first day as housekeeper I had managed to recover a degree of calm. Sarah's enthusiasm for the project and her ability to see why I might find it therapeutic encouraged me to think that for the time being at least I was in the right place. We said goodbye with our old feelings of affection and sympathy more or less restored.

* * *

When Constance and I entered the drawing room, hot and tired from our labours, Eugene ceased to pace with his arms folded behind his back. 'Ah, Constance! You have been detained by duties connected with your role as chatelaine, I am certain.'

'Are we late?' she said. 'I'm so sorry.'

Gracefully he waved away her apology and turned to me. 'A beautiful evening, Miss Norton.'

'So it is.' The drawing room, like the dining room, faced south and so looked down the canals. Having been immured in the kitchen for the last two hours, I had not noticed that the sky was campanula blue, finely threaded with cloud.

'I've been wandering in the woods all afternoon. Such sweet softness in the air, the light shot through with rainbow hues. I rested against a log and as I watched a lone bird hovering above my head I was reminded of the romance of Liadain and Curithir: lovers destined never to be united. It has inspired a new poem. I shall share it with you this evening. Also an accompanying tune which I shall play to you on my psaltery.'

Constance brought me a glass of white wine. To Eugene she gave a glass containing a brown liquid with something floating in it.

'It is a special brew Constance makes me,' he explained. 'To soothe my throat before a recitation. Madeira laced with honey and the yolk of an egg.' He sipped, with the air of a man conscientiously doing his duty while Constance and I looked on admiringly. 'Exactly right. I am nearly ready to begin. But I find I am a little warm after my exertions.'

'I'll get your fan.' Constance was at the door in a trice.

'I fear it is in my room.'

'I won't be a minute.'

With a convulsive movement Eugene swallowed the yolk whole, looking so exactly like a frog that I had to cough into my hand to hide a smile. 'I trust you have spent the day pleasantly, Miss Norton?'

'Do call me Bobbie.'

Eugene pointed his left foot and bowed over it in acknowledgement. At the ends of his spindly legs were muddy shoes, high heeled with tattered rosettes on the toes. 'I should be honoured if you would address me as Eugene.'

I nearly bowed back before I thought how silly I would look. 'I have enjoyed myself, though naturally I've been busy cooking and cleaning—'

Eugene raised a hand in protest. 'Let us not contaminate our minds with horrid images of toiling and moiling in the dirt. A young lady of your obvious cultivation of mind ought to have been gliding across a lake in an elegant barque beneath a silken awning, reading Homer. If there must be such a sordid thing as housework I prefer to think of you flitting about the house scattering a shimmering fairy dust that makes all it touches clean and bright.'

Constance, very much out of breath, returned with the fan.

'My good angel!'

Eugene waved it before his face and massaged his throat while Constance and I sat down next to each other on one of a pair of sofas beside the fireplace, raising puffs of dust. The sofas, inspired by Hepplewhite, were upholstered in lovely old grass-green lustring that was falling into holes. Constance hunched her shoulders, clasped her hands together beneath her chin and prepared to be transported.

My own experience of poetry readings did not lead me to suppose that pleasure was forthcoming. Writing and reading verse require quite different skills.

'*Tá sé in am di TEACHT!*' Eugene boomed suddenly, startling me.

'That's the title,' Constance explained in a low voice. 'It means something like "It is time for her to come". Eugene is writing in Gaelic at the moment. I must admit I find it extremely difficult, but the sound conveys a great deal of the sense. You can tune in to it with your subconscious.'

This was an unexpected boon. In order to give my subconscious free rein, I was almost bound not to listen.

Eugene threw back his head and flung up his hands as though he had a gun at his back. '*Ró-dhéaNACH!*' he cried.

That was almost the last word I heard for my attention was drawn by this action to several pieces of string that ran from the ceiling, presumably to guide the drips when it rained down to a large pan. The plasterwork was nearly as good as the dining room but not, I thought, by the La Franchini brothers. I had not had time to tackle the drawing room but my spirits lifted as I saw wonderful Irish Georgian furniture waiting, beneath piles of magazines, old socks, dead flowers, dirty glasses, toffee papers, apple cores and ashtrays brimming with cigarette ends, to be brought to life. What might it cost, I wondered, to have the plasterwork repaired? Unfortunately the roof must be put right first to keep out the rain and I knew from the bills at Cutham that this would be prohibitive.

Leading off the drawing room was the library. Constance had

already explained that this room was set aside for her brother's sole use. Borrowings had to be authorized and woe to him who had the temerity to sit in it. Even from the threshold it was obvious that though the library was dusty it was less disordered than the rest of the house. The large desk was bare of papers; the grate was swept clean; the books were neatly arranged; there were no remains of food or objects out of place. It told me little about its owner, except to reinforce the impression I already had of someone selfish and uncongenial.

Without warning Eugene distracted me from my thoughts by uttering a high nasal howl over several notes like a counter tenor. Then his voice sank again to its former style of delivery, resonant and portentous with something of a Gielgudian tremor in it. Behind his head birds wheeled in a sky that was beginning to lose its brightness. Flurry approached the window and put his face against the glass to look in at us, compressing his features into amorphous shapes like snails' feet. He waved the saw he was carrying and beckoned to me to come into the garden. I shook my head slightly and changed this to a rhythmic nodding for Eugene's eyes flashed at once to my face. When I dared to look again at the window only the condensed breath from Flurry's mouth and nose remained.

After another long minute of recitation during which Eugene minced about the room wearing an expression of agony as though his shoes were filled with dried peas, he stopped to pick up his psaltery. This was a lyre-shaped instrument with three strings. He plucked them with a large goose feather, making a hideous twanging noise. He had to concentrate to do this and I was free to let my eyes roam.

The drawing room was magnificent, a double cube with a wonderful marble chimneypiece. The walls were hung with yellow damask, the stretchers and nails hidden by a gilded fillet. But the damask was faded and spotted with damp, the fillet missing in places, the chimneypiece stained brown by smoke. It was a crying shame to see it crumbling before one's eyes. I could do little to halt the decay in the brief time I expected to be at Curraghcourt but I would get to work tomorrow on the furniture with duster and beeswax. That oyster veneered chest-on-stand required expert repair which was beyond my capability but I could do something about the pair of gilded consoles with marble tops. A solution of vinegar would clean up the marble and once the day-to-day housework was running smoothly I might find time to do something about the textiles. The curtains needed repair and that wonderful old carpet, Savonnerie most likely, was in a shocking state—

'*Tá CEOBHRAN ag teacht!*' cried Eugene.

He seemed to be coming to some sort of climax. He had put down the psaltery and stood with one hand on his hip, the other pointing downwards to something that lay at his feet. His tone was reproachful, as though his favourite spaniel had disgraced herself on the carpet. Constance explained to me afterwards that it had been a touching scene of reconciliation during which the hero had forgiven his faithless sweetheart and renewed his vows of love as she lay on her deathbed. I felt rather let down by my subconscious.

'*A stór! A stór!*' Eugene sank to his knees. '*Ní bheidh mé I bhfad!*' He dropped his chin to his chest.

It seemed it was over, to the thorough misery of all the characters. I looked at Constance. Her eyes were bright with unshed tears. Then I realized that the drama and possibly the tragedy were here in the drawing room. Constance was in love with Eugene. I did not waste much time wondering how such an intelligent, sweet-natured girl could fall in love with a Narcissus who looked like a frog. I had already learned that love defies reason.

Eugene rose and dusted off his knees.

Constance sprang up. 'Oh, thank you, thank you! I'm almost lost for words, it was so moving!'

Eugene nodded gravely, then looked at me.

'It was extremely . . . stimulating.'

Eugene frowned. 'I hope not *too* stimulating. It is after all a lament.'

'Well, yes. It was stimulating and tragic at the same time.'

'You think so?' Eugene seemed gratified. He stood for a while in profile, holding his chin, his stomach outlined by a beam of sunlight, lost in thought.

'Perhaps,' murmured Constance, her beautiful eyes soft with love, 'another poem . . .?'

I leaped up. 'The salmon!'

Constance seemed disappointed but looked hungrily at Eugene. 'If you're not too shattered by today's performance, tomorrow we might . . .?'

Eugene bowed. 'There can be no ill effect that solitude and sleep will not ameliorate. Salmon, you say?' His eyes bulged with what looked to me like unpoetical greed.

Constance looked at her watch. 'Father Deglan will be here soon.

I ought to warn you, Bobbie, he's a terrible old traditionalist, polit-ically as well as spiritually. He thinks de Valera was second only to God. Never mind that the man knew nothing about economics and kept Ireland in the dark ages for forty years. Father Deglan'll be bringing all last week's newspapers. We're too far away for the paper boy to cycle so we're always a week behind with the world. It's not a satisfactory arrangement because he cuts out the articles that have anything to do with the Church and it always happens that anything I'm interested in is on the back of them. He always brings the *Daily Mail* as well as the Irish papers so you'll have some idea of what's happening in England.'

'Oh, good,' I said, wondering where I had left the scissors. I hoped it would not be necessary to reduce Father Deglan's newspapers to unreadable shreds.

TWENTY-TWO

'Well, Constance, me girl,' roared a voice from the hall. 'You'd better be making Finn pay for new guttering if he won't contribute to Church funds. I'm wetter than a drowned man!'

'Oh, Father Deglan, I'm so sorry.' Constance ran ahead of me to greet him. 'Those naughty . . . drainpipes,' she finished feebly. 'You must come and get warm by the drawing-room fire. Though it's supposed to be summer we decided to light it as there's a little damp in the air.'

This had been my idea and Constance had been amenable to this, as to all my suggestions. There was apparently no shortage of turves, provided Timsy could be persuaded to dig them out of the ground, so it seemed imperative to me to have fires every day in all the principal rooms to bring the indoor temperature up to something tolerable and to do battle with the damp that was destroying the contents of Curraghcourt and the fabric of the building as well. Throughout the house the walls and ceilings were spotted with black, the floorboards and skirting boards were spongy, the curtains and carpets were falling apart, and everywhere smelt of decay.

'Now, Father.' Constance tucked her hand into his arm and turned him to face me. 'You must meet the greatest piece of good fortune I've had for a long time. This is Miss Bobbie Norton, who's been sent by my fairy godmother to put everything right.'

'My dear Constance!' Father Deglan frowned and wiped his forehead with his handkerchief. 'There's only one source of good things and one provider of help in times of trouble and you know well who it is, though you like to talk like a heathen.'

I had expected an ascetic with a pinched, disapproving mouth and cold, sin-seeking eyes. Father Deglan was ruddy, shining and fat, with

251

a crop of greasy, grey curls. He had a large corky nose from which water dripped. One of his eyes had a cast in it so that it gazed into the distance, unfocused and dreaming. Only his good eye met my expectations. It was sharp, intelligent and appraising.

I put out my hand. 'How do you do? I'm the new housekeeper.'

'How are you, Miss Norton?' He took my hand and crushed it. 'Your reputation has electrified Kilmuree already. They were right about the voice anyway.'

'Now, Father,' said Constance crossly. 'I won't have you being unkind to Bobbie. I like her English accent.'

'It's certainly a rest for my ears' – Maud was coming slowly down the stairs – 'after listening to the mangle you peasants make of a civilized language.'

'I'll not give you the satisfaction of rising to your insults, Maud Crawley. Rather call me a peasant than a liar or a thief. Is it civilized you call that sharp manner of speaking, like a shower of stones? Aye, if civilization means arrogance and pride of assumption. If civilization means to steal land and let the rightful owners starve without lifting a hand to help them. But, thank the Lord' – he came closer to peer at me with an eye that could have peeled varnish – 'you're not as painted as I was expecting.'

'Don't be offended, Bobbie.' Constance smiled at me. 'He speaks so often to God that he's apt to look down on us plain mortals.'

'Arrah, Constance, you've no reverence in you, not at all.'

'I'm not offended,' I said. 'Let me relieve you of those.' I indicated the dripping bundle of newspapers that was slipping from beneath Father Deglan's arm. 'I'll dry them out in the kitchen.'

He shot me another piercing glance before relinquishing them and going into the drawing room with Constance and Maud.

'We got him!' Flavia and Flurry came running into the kitchen as I was struggling with a fish kettle filled with near boiling water, a cumbersome and dangerous piece of equipment.

'So I saw. Let's hope he doesn't catch cold from his wetting and get pneumonia.'

'You don't mean it?' Flavia asked anxiously. 'Old Mrs Canty *died* from pneumonia.'

'Oh, I'm sure he'll be all right. But perhaps you shouldn't do it again.'

'Well!' I saw that Flavia was alarmed. 'He shouldn't be so strict and nosy. He always asks me how often I've prayed and what I've been praying for and it's *priv*ate! Dad never asks me that sort of thing and he's my *real* father! But I don't want Father Deglan to die.'

'Dad's too busy to ask questions,' said Flurry. 'Besides, he isn't interested. And anyway there are worse things than being dead. Mrs O'Kelly told Pegeen Mummy would be better dead. I heard her.'

'She *wouldn't*! That's a wicked thing to say and I don't want her to die *ever*!' Flavia's eyes filled and her chest began to heave. Maria, who had followed me slavishly around all day because I had given her some stewing meat for breakfast, whined in sympathy before returning her eyes to my face. 'At least I can hold Mummy's hand and sometimes I know she wants to talk to me but she's looking for the words.'

'I can't help what other people say,' declared Flurry. 'Don't cry, Flav, it's a waste of time. You said you'd help me sawing. I need six hundred more sleepers.'

But Flavia had left the room, head down.

'What can't be cured must be injured,' Flurry said philosophically.

'You mean endured.'

'Yes. Will you help me tomorrow?'

'Certainly, if there's time. But I want to go to Kilmuree for provisions.'

'You mean food and things? Can I come?'

'If I can borrow the Land-Rover, you may. In fact, I'd like your company.'

Flurry regarded me solemnly. 'You aren't going to get soppy, are you?'

I laughed. 'I hope not.'

'Good. Only women like to get into stews about things.'

'Stews?'

'Yes. They get soppy or mad as fire over tiny things that men don't notice.'

I had a sudden insight. 'Is that what your father says?'

'Yes.'

'Mm. I wouldn't be afraid of a little emotion occasionally. Feelings are important.'

'How are they?'

'Well, they can be enjoyable. And sometimes they're a guide to the truth. When you can't reason things out sometimes you can just feel what's right.' I saw that Flurry had lost interest. He was trying, with grubby fingers, to make a pyramid with the chunks of butter I had cut up for the hollandaise sauce. I removed them. 'Where are

Katty, Pegeen and Timsy? I haven't seen them for a couple of hours.'

Constance had told me that every evening she cooked and cleared away dinner single-handed as by that time the girls and Timsy were too drunk to be of use. The Protestant work ethic that was part of my social conditioning revolted against this laxity. I had made up my mind that such anarchy would no longer be tolerated, so after visiting Violet I had locked up the black bottle again to give them time to sober up. No protest had been made from Timsy and Pegeen. Katty had been busy lighting a pipe and had merely given me a malevolent look. Their tea break had already lasted over an hour.

'They're drunk in the apple store,' replied Flurry. 'Timsy found Sissy's homemade wine. Dad said it was probably poisonous. He told her to throw it away. What was that you said?'

'Nothing. It was a bad word and Father Deglan would be disgusted if he heard you repeat it. Well, we must manage without them.'

'I don't like the sound of we.'

'You want help with the sleepers, don't you? Just dry those plates for me, would you?'

Flurry obligingly took the cloth and began to polish some rather beautiful plates with deep blue borders and fine gilding which I had found in the storeroom.

'What are you doing?' he asked presently as I cut sections from Father Deglan's newspapers and put them in the fire.

'Some bits are too wet to keep,' I said, falling immediately by the wayside in the pursuance of truth.

Some of the Irish papers had photographs of Burgo and me. Father Deglan had given me several penetrating looks. When he saw me in the better light of the drawing room he would undoubtedly recognize me. I ought to have taken Constance into my confidence from the beginning. But I had been reluctant to make a bad first impression.

'What's that?' Flurry stirred something in a bowl. 'It looks horrible.'

'Sardine pâté. I found dozens of tins in the pantry.'

Maria's golden eyes loomed from the semi-darkness of the floor and a string of saliva dropped from her jaws. I gave her a taste of sardine, hoping it would put her off, but she licked her lips greedily and resumed her intense watchfulness of my face.

'Dr Duffy said sardines would help Granny's bones. Only they don't seem to. Sometimes I hear her groan when she doesn't know I'm listening. But she never lets on it hurts. And if anyone asks her

254

how she is, she gets into a bate. Why does she? I don't mind people knowing if I feel sick or anything.'

'Some people can't bear to be pitied. Perhaps it's courage. Or good manners. I don't know your grandmother well enough to say. I'll do the toast while you go and tell everyone dinner's ready. Then come back, please, and help me carry things in.'

'That'll be worth another two sleepers if I do.'

'Done.'

'How are the plans going for the Holy Father's visit?' asked Constance. She turned to me. 'The whole country's in a fever of excitement about the Pope's visit at the end of September. He's actually coming to Galway after Dublin. Everyone's having the day off and new clothes for the whole family and Eddy Murphy, the hairdresser in Kilmuree, says he's already booked solid for two weeks before the visit with women having perms and sets. As though the Holy Father will see them in the crowd that's going to be there.'

'Gosh!' I said, trying to imagine the population of, say, Yorkshire, getting into a fluster about a visit from the Archbishop of Canterbury. But then he was, through no fault of his own, so familiar and accessible and so lacking in mystery that the man in the street was thoroughly bored by the whole idea of him.

'I was going to speak to you about that,' said Father Deglan. 'We're getting up a subscription fund to hire three coaches to take us from Kilmuree to Galway Racecourse. Will you make a contribution, Constance?' It was hardly a question.

'Certainly,' replied Constance. 'Put me down for five pounds.'

'Thank you, my child.' Father Deglan's good eye went round the table. 'Anyone else?'

Eugene was absorbed by the chandelier from which hung veils of spiders' webs. I made a mental note to cajole the children into helping me wash each lustre and polish it to its original brilliance.

'Come now, Florence, my boy.' Father Deglan smiled indulgently. 'You've some pocket money to spare for a good cause, I'm certain.'

'No,' said Flurry. 'I need it all for my railway.'

'That's very selfish. Surely you want to help those less fortunate than yourself have the joyful experience of seeing the Holy Father?'

'No,' said Flurry again.

'Tsk, tsk!' Father Deglan began a lecture but abandoned it, seeing that Flurry's eyes were shut and he had his fingers in his ears. 'Well, well. We must forgive the lad, I suppose, as he isn't quite like the rest of us. Phyllida!' The indulgence was wiped from his face as he saw that she was examining her face in the back of a newly polished spoon. Under my direction every piece of flatware and every salt and pepper pot and candlestick had been cleaned that afternoon. 'You had better set an example to your little brother.'

Liddy blew out her breath through closed lips like a horse. 'Oh, all *right*. Fifty pee is all I can spare. And it's no good trying to bully me because I won't even give that if you do.'

Father Deglan frowned. 'I'm disappointed in you, girl. Now, my little Flavia, what are *you* going to—'

He looked astonished when Flavia leaped to her feet, crying 'No! No! *No!*'

The cause of her anguish was made clear a moment later when she hurled the book she had been reading under the table to the farthest corner of the room. 'Poor, *poor* Bodger!' she cried before bursting into tears and running out. It seemed that the starving and grievously wounded bull terrier had met his fate at the end of his incredible journey.

'These children become more like savages every day,' said Maud. 'But then it's hardly surprising, being brought up in this benighted country. It was a black day for Ireland when we repealed the penal laws.'

The spirit of mischief was in her eyes and Father Deglan rushed to take up the challenge. He leaned over the table to glare at her. 'It's a poor heart that does not leap up at the thought of Ireland free from its Protestant oppressors.'

'Pooh!' Mrs Crawley flung down her fork and picked up her cigarette case. She smoked unashamedly not only between courses but during them as well. The necklace of huge amethysts she wore was outshone by her eyes which seemed to catch up all the light in the room. 'It's we who've made something of this country. While you were preaching hell and damnation we were building fine houses and running the country. You kept the peasants in a state of guilt and repression and penury while we gave them employment and set standards and showed them what hard work was. The Irish would still be living in hovels up to their necks in mud if it weren't for us Protestants.'

'That hasn't always been the case, Maud,' said Constance in her usual gentle manner. 'The Ascendancy had nothing to do with the building of this house.'

'Exactly,' said Maud. 'We'd have knocked it down and built an elegant Palladian mansion instead of this draughty, pseudo-mediaeval monstrosity.'

This was not only unkind of Maud, it was also inaccurate. The mediaeval parts of the house were genuine and of course she knew it but liked to be perverse whenever possible. Perhaps it was an analgesic for pain. Also, though I was as fond as anyone of Palladian architecture, I admired the heterogeneous style of Curraghcourt, the elegant eighteenth-century front with its charming Gothick windows and battlements which had been wrapped round the earlier, sterner parts.

'I like it here,' said Flurry. 'I never want to live anywhere else. Miss McFadden, our history teacher, says Ireland'll never be united till all the Protestants have gone back to England and Scotland where they belong.'

Father Deglan's chin glistened with sardine oil and he looked triumphant.

'It's very wrong of Miss McFadden to say that.' Constance was indignant. 'She's supposed to be educating you, not airing her prejudices.'

'Don't worry, Aunt Con,' replied Flurry calmly. 'I don't often listen.'

'It's your father's fault for sending you to that appalling Catholic school,' said Maud. 'Those simpletons think the Pope has a direct line to God. With the Virgin Mary as telephone operator.'

'Blasphemer!' said Father Deglan.

Maud puffed smoke into his eyes. 'Bog-trotter!'

I found this style of conversation fascinating. Everyone had some passionate conviction about which they were prickly and they did not hesitate to champion their pet loves or hates despite the general readiness to fly off the handle at the least sign of opposition. I thoroughly enjoyed this fanaticism as a contrast to the usual English phlegm. I was disturbed, though, to find Father Deglan's good eye frequently trained on me with a look that was suspicious and even disapproving, while his weak eye, which was paler in colour, wandered about the tablecloth among the salts and peppers as though seeking extenuating circumstances.

'Don't take any notice of us, Bobbie,' said Constance. 'Though there's always bickering and taking sides in this house, it's only talk. We don't mean it.'

'I mean every word I say,' said Maud.

I brought in the next course. Maria, who had been sleeping on my foot, followed me faithfully until she was given the remains of the pâté. Constance insisted on helping though I was perfectly happy in my role of cook-general. It was not so different from Cutham, after all, except that everyone at Curraghcourt was touchingly grateful.

'God save all here,' said Sissy, bursting in halfway through the salmon. She seemed incapable of coming through a door quietly. Maria flew round the room, barking. 'Good evening, Father.' Sissy made a sort of half-curtsey in his direction.

'Good evening, my child.' I could tell from the way Father Deglan winked his eyes and thrust out his lower lip as he took in Sissy's appearance that he was having to draw on his reserves of Christian charity to smile paternally upon her.

'I suppose you tumbled into a bog.' Maud put a good deal of venom into her voice. 'That would account for the state of your clothes.'

Sissy threw herself into the chair next to mine. 'As it happens, 'twas addled eggs I was looking for, to make a cure for birth fever. I found a blackbird's nest with five. And a dead mouse full of maggots. They're good for cleaning the pus in wounds.'

Eugene closed his eyes and pressed his napkin to his lips.

'I know nothing of eggs but certainly your brain is addled,' said Maud.

Sissy looked as though she had not only tumbled into a bog but stayed in it for some time. The whites of her eyes sparkled in her dirty little face. She was strangely dressed for dinner in the country. I knew something about historical costume. She was wearing a doublet and trunk-hose with short canions in the style of James I's time but Sissy's doublet was made of polyester instead of velvet or silk and the slashing and pinking was crude. Beneath her dishevelled hair which was woven with twigs was a collar edged with machine lace. I wondered if she intended to go to a fancy-dress party later. Sissy examined the table, which had been subject to a preliminary polish and was now free from dust and dirt.

''Twas here this morning.' She looked at me. 'Is it you that's taken my hairbrush?'

If I had not known better I might have had my head turned by the praise heaped upon my ordinary little dinner. I doubt if Escoffier himself had ever been so complimented. Even Father Deglan, who subjected me to more searching glances and deeper frowns with each passing moment, paused in the consumption of tinned fruit cocktail and the meringues left from lunch to say, 'No doubt it was in London that you got the knowledge of cookery. 'Tis well known there's no shortage of good things to eat in *that* city.'

It was clear that for him there was little to choose between Sodom, Gomorrah and Knightsbridge.

'I know your face from somewhere,' said Father Deglan as I gave him a cup of coffee in the drawing room after dinner. 'What is your Christian name again?'

'Bobbie.'

''Tis not what your parents baptized you?' He closed his weak eye to focus the other more keenly.

'It's a nickname.'

I left it to Constance to offer him milk and sugar and slid unobtrusively from the drawing room.

'Jazzy? It's Bobbie.'

'Bobbie, *darling*!' The receiver seemed to vibrate with her enthusiasm. 'I'm so thrilled it's you! When Teddy showed me that article in the *Daily Spectacle* I said it couldn't *possibly* be my best friend in all the world. It had to be someone like you with the same name. I said I knew you'd *never* have an affair with a married man. Teddy called me a dear little idiot but I didn't mind. I like him to tease me. Oh, but anyway, there was a picture of you in the *Scrutiniser* in that black dress you used to lend me so I knew then it *was* you. But why've you never *said* anything? I must admit I am a teeny bit hurt.'

'I'm sorry, Jazzy. We had to be discreet, you see. Burgo's position, and his wife . . . I know after all I've said about married men I must seem like a hypocrite but, well, I found him attractive and . . . I don't know how to explain.'

'Oh, I can understand all *that*! I thought he looked dishy. But why's everyone so interested? Is he someone important? I didn't quite gather who he was.'

'He's just been given a seat in the Cabinet.'

'Is that that new restaurant in the Fulham Road?'

'No, he's been made a minister.'

'Like a vicar, d'you mean?'

'No. He's an MP. And now he's a member of the government.'

'Oh.' I could tell that for Jasmine this rated low. 'So, you sneaky thing, all this while you've been lecturing me you've been having it away with this – this married minister person.'

'I've behaved badly, Jazzy, I know.'

'Darling, I forgive you. Just don't do it again.'

'I think I can safely promise you I won't.'

'So where are you now? Have you eloped with Mr Dreamboat?'

'No. I've left him.'

'*What?* Why? Where *are* you?'

'In Connemara.'

'Is that in Italy?

'It's in the West of Ireland. I'm housekeeper to a charming family.' I thought of Maud. 'Most of them are charming, anyway.'

'How pe*cul*iar! What on earth are you doing? But first you must tell me all about this yummy man.'

'I will, soon, but not now. I've got to go and do the washing up and tidy the kitchen.'

'You haven't been sold as a white slave and you don't like to tell me because the slave-driver's there in the room with you? Just answer yes or no and I'll understand.'

'No. I really am all right. I just wanted to give you my number here and when I've got more time we'll have a really good talk. Is everything all right with you and Teddy?'

For the last ten months Teddy and Jasmine had been living in a rented house in Mayfair. Jasmine had sold all the jewellery her father had given her, which had raised a large amount of cash, and they had lived high, employing a Filipino couple to look after them, taking expensive holidays and going to restaurants and nightclubs. I had seen Jasmine only rarely, when I had gone up to London to meet Burgo, but we had kept in touch by telephone.

'We're still madly in love, if that's what you mean. But we've run out of money, which is a bit of a bugger. Teddy's having to go in to work more and we're about to move into the country. I've never lived anywhere but cities but I expect I shall like it. As long as there aren't cows. I've always been rather frightened of them. It's their horns.'

'There probably will be cows but they'll be tucked safely away in fields.'

'Oh, good. I'll ring you up the minute I know where we're going to be. I'm simply dying to hear all about *him*.'

I dictated the Curraghcourt number several times until Jasmine had got it right. We exchanged verbal pledges of fond friendship and then rang off. I returned to the kitchen. Katty and Pegeen were in their chairs, legs stretched out in front of them, feet rolled outwards, snoring. Timsy was spread-eagled in front of the fire, his head among the drifts of ashes. Elsewhere it lay like a sprinkling of powder over every surface I had scrubbed earlier that day. After washing up and putting everything away, I sat down at the table. While holding a cloth soaked in vinegar to my forehead – I had forgotten to dodge the dangling chain and had bruised my bruise painfully – I checked the newspapers again for mention of my name. I was in the process of trimming a brief reference from one of the gossip columns when a hand fell on my shoulder, making me start.

'I know now who you are.' Father Deglan continued to hold my arm with one hand while with the other he pointed to the article lying on the table which I had just cut out from the *Globe*. It contained a photograph of me coming out of the front door of the Fisherman's Reel. 'I never forget a face. Oh, woman! I wonder you've the temerity to come among decent people after the things that have been said of you! Committing lewd acts with fornicators! Have you no care for your soul? Remember the sixth Commandment: thou shalt not commit ADULTERY!'

Pegeen opened her eyes and lifted her head to stare at us. We must have made a strikingly biblical composition with me cowering in my chair and Father Deglan, a patriarchal figure in his black soutane, speaking in a voice of thunder, one hand raised heavenward in remonstrance. Pegeen sighed, rolled up her eyes and fell back into slumber.

Despite my instant determination that I would resist anything like a scolding with every fibre of my being I felt hot blood rise to my eyebrows. 'I don't think you can know anything about it. And if we're going to quote from the Bible I remember it says: "Judge not, that ye be not judged", which seems sound advice to me.'

'"All wickedness is but little to the wickedness of a woman." That also is written in the Bible. Daughter, your impenitence, your determination to walk in darkness, to cleave to the ways of debauchery and immodesty, your hardness of heart is a greater sin even than the sins of impurity you have committed.' He tightened his grip on my shoulder until I winced and his good eye bored alternately into both of mine. 'Clothe yourself once more in innocence. Wash out your sins in the blood of the Lamb! Jesus said I am not come to call the righteous but sinners to repentance! The price of a virtuous woman is above—'

'Just a minute,' I interrupted, standing up to shake myself free of his hand. 'For one thing, you shouldn't believe everything you read in newspapers. Most of it is lies. And for another I'm not a member

261

of your Church and you've no right to lecture me. My conscience is my own business.'

'You're a proud, unregenerate creature! As to what you say about the papers, I'm willing to grant that they're a lot of lying inebriates. That's as may be. But though you may not be of my flock I've the welfare of Constance and the little ones to think of.'

'I resent your suggestion that I'm in some way unfit for the company of children.' I was angry now. 'I'm guilty of nothing except perhaps loving unwisely.'

Father Deglan pointed again to the article. 'You've lured a man from his lawful wife and brought them both to trouble and despair. Is that the work of love? I'd call it the destruction of the sacrament of matrimony. The work of the devil.'

'Yes. Well.' I felt exhausted suddenly. It had been a long day. 'Of course you can tell Constance whatever you please. But before you damn me to boiling pitch in perpetuity you ought to ask yourself whether my being here might not do her and the children more good than harm.' I felt my chin tremble and tears of vexation and weariness gather.

Perhaps he saw them for his belligerent, ugly face softened a little. He paused, then nodded. 'There's something in that. Constance is sorely put upon. I saw this evening how she liked having you here. And though you assert your right to be answerable to none I take it as a sign of grace that you've removed yourself from the path of temptation and come to a better place where, if it please God, you may see the error of your ways. Resist the devil and he will flee from thee.' He put his face so close to mine that I was forced to lean back. He smelt strongly of sardines. 'Christ said to the woman taken in adultery, "Go and sin no more." I'll say nothing to Constance if you'll give me your word that you'll tell her yourself.'

We looked at each with mutual dislike.

'I was planning to tell her anyway.'

'Your promise, daughter.' Father Deglan's good eye was flinty while his filmy eye had the abstracted gaze of a philosopher. 'I won't leave without that.'

'Oh, all right,' I said at last, with ill grace.

'Meanwhile, I'll pray for you, my child, night and day, that you may be saved from eternal punishment.'

This was annoying but most of the fight had gone out of me. I summoned what strength I had left to keep up a brave front. 'That's kind of you but you needn't put yourself to so much trouble. I don't believe in hell.'

He put a fat forefinger practically on my nose. 'Obstinacy is a sin against the Holy Spirit.'

'I may not believe in him either. I haven't yet made up my mind.'

Father Deglan made a hissing noise like a tyre going down. 'Oh, my girl, you've a rebellious heart and a tongue to match—'

'Now, Father, stop bullying Bobbie.' Constance came into the kitchen with the tray of coffee cups. 'She isn't one of your congregation and it's very naughty of you. Your taxi's outside and it's time you were going.'

Constance took him firmly by the arm and led him into the hall. I heard his voice raised in protest and then the front door slam.

'Constance,' I said, when she returned. 'I've got something to tell you.'

TWENTY-THREE

Late the next morning Flurry, Liddy, Maria and I jolted along the two miles of track that led from Curraghcourt to the outside world. We had left Katty and Pegeen, who were suffering from bad hangovers, to work their way through a list of tasks. Timsy had not, so far, put in an appearance. Constance was in charge of feeding those who remained behind with the macaroni, tuna and baked bean pie I had assembled earlier. Speaking for myself, I was glad to be lunching out.

I had invited Flavia to join us but she said she had begun a new book about rabbits called *Watership Down* and besides she was usually sick in cars and always in the Land-Rover. I remembered the story well.

'It isn't altogether a happy book,' I warned her.

Flavia became pale. 'You don't mean . . . I don't think I can bear any more sadness. I haven't got over' – she bit her lip while tears welled – 'poor Bodger!' She had rushed from the kitchen overcome by a renewal of grief.

'Of course, it's no good hoping they'll have *Vogue* at the newsagent's,' sighed Liddy. 'You can get it sometimes in Galway but that's thirty miles. Mind that pothole!'

I did mind it but a little late and Flurry received a blow to his chin from being thrown forward on to the dashboard.

'Sorry. I haven't quite got the hang of driving this thing. It seems a little unresponsive.'

'Dad says there's something wrong with the brakes.' Flurry rubbed his chin. 'Can you stop a minute? I think I'll get in the back with Maria.'

The road to Kilmuree was smoother but narrow. There were

264

passing places which were barely wide enough to accommodate both the Land-Rover and the tractors and lorries which came the other way. Sheep, ignorant of the inefficacy of our brakes, were inclined to wander out in front of us. While I concentrated on not running over them or us into bogs, Liddy grumbled about the unremitting dullness of the scenery, the frumpishness of every dress shop in Ireland apart from Brown Thomas in Dublin (which she had managed to visit only three times in her life), and the awfulness of Ireland generally.

'Honestly, I can't agree with you.' I swerved to avoid a sheep lying in the middle of the road. 'Just look at those great mountains against those racing clouds. They're almost black in this light and the grass is swirling in brilliant shades of green, just like malachite.'

'It's going to rain,' Liddy replied unmoved. 'I suppose you bought that coat in London.'

'Yes. From Woolland's, a big department store at the top of Sloane Street. It's pretty ancient, though.'

'I think it's wonderful.' She fingered my sleeve. 'Why's it so soft?'

'It's part cashmere.'

'Cashmere!' Liddy groaned. 'I've only got my school coat. It's dark green Harris tweed: so scratchy you could de-fuzz your legs with it. And this old Burberry that used to be Mummy's. It stinks of fags and damp. The downstairs cloakroom's growing mushrooms on the walls.'

'At your age I didn't possess even a decent mac. Only my school raincoat. Navy gabardine and completely hideous. I had to wear it over my evening dress to my first proper grown-up ball.'

'Not really!'

'It was raining and my mother insisted. I screwed it up and hid it behind a chair in the cloakroom. All the other girls had borrowed their mothers' fur wraps and evening coats. That raincoat was a badge of shame. I wanted to go home straight away.'

'What was your dress like?'

'Grey tulle, with a full skirt and fake pearls sewn on to the bodice. I'd made it myself. I'd just been to a performance of *Swan Lake* and was mightily inspired by the cygnet costumes.'

'I don't know, it might have been rather pretty. Did you like the ball?'

'At first I hated it. I felt so shy. I hadn't grown up with those kind of people. They were much more cultivated than the hunting, shooting and fishing types my parents knew. I spent the first few dances

265

standing by the fire with a superior expression on my face, repelling all conversational overtures, trying not to look as though I was dying from loneliness.'

'What were the other girls' dresses like?'

'One of the girls looked marvellous in a strapless sheath of black satin. I thought it was the height of chic. Suddenly my dress, which had thrilled me so much when I'd put it on, seemed childish and silly. This girl was dancing with a man with long, straight black hair, parted in the middle, a sort of Aubrey Beardsley type. He looked aloof and bored and to my eyes immensely sophisticated. He was the best-looking man in the room. The *only* good-looking one actually. The rest were all either ancient or weedy.'

'I know what you mean,' sighed Liddy. 'Men are *such* a disappointment.'

'When this paragon of masculine beauty walked over to me and asked me to dance I almost fainted with shock. Also I'd been getting dreadfully hot standing by the fire but I hadn't wanted to draw attention to myself by moving away. My hands were pools of stickiness.'

'Poor you!' said Liddy with kind condescension. 'What was he like to dance with?'

'He was a wonderful dancer and incredibly easy to follow. He squashed my few pathetic attempts at conversation. Didn't speak, didn't smile, didn't look at me. But I was enraptured because he was so handsome. I know it's proof of baseness of character to put so much emphasis on appearance.'

Liddy dropped her tone of weary woman of the world. 'Did he try to kiss you?' she asked.

'No. I'd have been pretty alarmed if he had. I was completely inexperienced. We danced for hours, whirling about in heaven. At least it would have been heaven but for the fact that after a while I needed to pee. I'd no idea how to excuse myself gracefully. Telling this demi-god that I had to go to the lav seemed beyond impossibility. Eventually, when I was terrified my bladder was going to burst, I said I had something in my eye. I fled before he could offer to help.'

Liddy giggled. 'You took a risk, letting go of the only decent man there.'

'I had to, I was in agony. One of the girls in the cloakroom said to me, "Bad luck on getting landed with Orlando Weeks. I wouldn't dance with him if he was the last man on earth."'

'What a giveaway! She was jealous as hell.'

266

'Yes, but I was too dim to realize that at the time. I was astonished. I knew nothing whatsoever about him. Not even, until that moment, his name. But I was utterly smitten and already imagining myself married to him with four children with straight black hair and eyelashes as long as paintbrushes. Did I mention the eyelashes?'

'I was picturing someone more brutally male.'

'Ah. Well, anyway, I asked her what she meant, and she said, "Orlando Weeks is a dreadful creep and my father says I'm to have nothing to do with him. He takes drugs and things and he's queer." I had no idea what a queer was but of course I wasn't going to admit it. I'd concluded from my father's frequent homophobic rages that queers were men who were keen on flowers, cats and their mothers. I couldn't see anything wrong with that.'

'Dad told me about homosexual men. When I was thirteen he called me into the library and gave me a lecture about the facts of life. And abortions and venereal disease. He said he didn't want me to grow up thinking babies were found in the strawberry patch. He said that men were thoroughly irresponsible when it came to sex and that I had better be armed with knowledge. It was jolly embarrassing and I could see Dad was embarrassed too though he pretended not to be. He started off leaning against his desk as though we were just having a chat but when he got to the bit about . . . you know, what penises are for, he started to walk about and looked awfully stern. He said a young girl had to be careful not to be taken advantage of and getting pregnant was easier than falling off a log.' Liddy giggled. 'Afterwards I heard him tell Aunt Connie that he'd rather be flogged at the cart's tail than go through that again.'

Of course Mr Macchuin had been right to give Liddy the unvarnished facts but I took exception to his assumption that men were, as of right, predatory and that women had better look out for themselves. Naturally he judged by his own standards.

'Granny says sex before marriage is only for girls without breeding because they aren't expected to produce an heir to anything. She's such a snob. I'm going to do as I please about that,' Liddy added defiantly. 'Anyway, what I want to know is what happened next. When you left the cloakroom, I mean.'

'Orlando was standing by the door, waiting for me, looking moody and quite irresistible. He said, "Do you want to dance again? We may as well. There's another hour till supper." I felt as thrilled as though he had asked me to marry him. Just as I was about to fly away in his arms my host came up and said Brough, our driver, had arrived and was waiting to take me home. It was only eleven o'clock!'

'God! *Quelle horreur!* Parents are the *end*!'

'Orlando kissed my hand and said, "Goodnight then," and walked off. I floated out to the car on a cloud and was borne away in a dream because of the kiss. I was nearly home before I realized that my future husband and the father of my children didn't know my telephone number or even my name.'

'What are you two giggling about?' Flurry called through the little cracked window in the partition between the front and the back of the Land-Rover. 'You're making Maria bark in my ear.'

'Is that how it ended? Did you ever see him again?'

'No. Someone told me years later that he was living with an ancient margrave – that's a sort of German prince – in Morocco. Of course he'd forgotten me even before Brough had driven me home. The entire thing was the romantic projection of a rather lonely schoolgirl.'

Liddy sighed. 'I'd rather have *some* kind of romance, however made-up, than exist in this awful boring way where nothing *ever* happens. Who did you fall in love with next?'

'That'll have to be for another day. This must be Kilmuree.'

The town looked quite different when dry and lit by the occasional burst of sunlight. The small, square, shabby houses, some of them brightly painted, had a gay, almost holiday air. We left the Land-Rover in gear on the practically vertical main street and extracted Flurry from among ropes, sacks, and empty crates. He staggered at first, his tie under one ear, his spectacles crooked.

'It's like being bounced on a potato riddler in the back,' he complained. 'I can't see straight and Maria's barking's done something to my brain.'

I was struck by the contrast in appearance between Flurry and a group of boys roughly the same age lurking beside a cigarette machine in jeans and football jerseys. 'Why are you wearing your school uniform?' I asked. 'I thought it was the summer holidays.'

'I like to put on the same thing each day,' he explained with dignity. 'It saves thinking.'

'You wouldn't be more comfortable without your tie?'

'No, I wouldn't. I'd wonder why it felt loose round my neck and that would be bothering. I'm going in here.' He disappeared into an ironmonger's shop.

'Dad took him to see a doctor in London,' Liddy said as we walked together along the pavement, 'and *he* said Flurry was mildly – what's

268

the word? – autistic. His IQ's incredibly high but he likes to do things in patterns. I don't understand it but Dad said not to tease him about it. Luckily everyone's so batty in Ireland it hardly shows that Flurry's odd. Of course he didn't take *me* to London,' she added resentfully.

'Tell you what,' I said. 'Why don't you come and stay with me when I go back to England? I live in a tiny house but it's right in the heart of Chelsea and we've a camp-bed and you could share my room for a week—'

Liddy's scream drew the eyes of the street. 'You don't mean it! Oh, Christ!' She flung her arms round my neck. 'Please, please, *please* mean it!'

I disengaged myself sufficiently to look in Liddy's eyes that were shining with excitement. 'I mean it. I faithfully promise that you shall come and stay with me in London.'

'Could we *possibly* go to Harrods?'

'Certainly.'

'Will you take me to Bond Street?'

'Every day, if you like.'

'I'm so *hap*py.' Liddy spoke with emotion. 'You're an *an*gel. Would you help me get a job in London so I needn't go home? It needn't be modelling at first. I could be a waitress or a shop assistant.'

'Let's talk about that another time. There are things like A levels and university to be considered. Your career—'

'I don't care about a career. I just want to have decent clothes and go to good restaurants and be taken out by gorgeous men.'

'All right. But just this minute I've got to think about a week's worth of breakfasts, lunches and dinners. Where's the greengrocer's?'

Liddy tucked her hand under my elbow and with her on one arm and the basket I had borrowed from the still room on the other I proceeded down the declivitous street, greatly to the inconvenience of the other pedestrians. Being the provider of pleasure is a delightful feeling. Liddy smiled and giggled and the sun shone and had it not been for constant nagging thoughts of Burgo I would have thoroughly enjoyed myself.

We ordered large quantities of vegetables, meat, groceries and cleaning agents. The shopkeepers knew Liddy, of course, and we were treated like royalty. Chairs were dusted and cups of tea offered. The greengrocer's was the strangest of its kind I had yet encountered. There were hardly any vegetables in it, except the plastic ones making a display in the window, a few sacks of potatoes and carrots and several boxes of yellow cabbages. When I picked up a carrot

269

and managed to bend its leafy end to its muddy tip without break-ing it, Turlough McGurn, whose shop it was, informed me that these particular carrots were kept solely for the tinkers' horses. Those destined for Curraghcourt were even at that moment being plucked from the ground and would be delivered to the castle before we reached it ourselves. A tentative enquiry about celeriac, chicory, French beans, mushrooms, tomatoes, peppers, courgettes and, at Flavia's request, several pounds of oranges received the immediate assurance that the identical articles would be supplied along with the carrots. It seemed simpler for the whole order to be sent at the same time. The greengrocer bowed us to the door, swearing that such was our radiant beauty it would seem as though the sun had set the minute we departed.

Sean Rafferty, the butcher, said he would need time to prepare the particular cuts I had requested. He could tell I was a lady of un-rivalled judgement and taste, accustomed only to the best and I must never be tempted, therefore, to patronize Dermot McBride's shop where the meat was more closely related to a donkey than the donkey's own mother. He would deliver my order himself. We were to receive the best joints that money could buy, dispatched at breakneck speed.

In the chemist's, while Liddy examined the revolving stand of hair-slides and earrings, I selected soap, bath salts, several rolls of decent lavatory paper and a giant bottle of hand cream. I also bought eye ointment for Flurry's stye, flea powder and some pastilles to burn to counteract the smell of cats in my bedroom. After this we called at the ironmonger's where I bought a bath plug and a padlock for the kitchen cupboard. Flurry was still there, choosing nuts and bolts with single-minded purpose.

While Liddy explored the garish delights of Lulu's Hat Box I crossed the road to inspect the national dailies on the counter of the newsagent's. When, the night before, I had told Constance about the scandal attached to me, she had listened with a face that was first amazed then sorrowful.

'I think I may have read something about it last week,' she said. 'But I usually skip anything to do with politicians. This country's drowning in politics and it all means so little in the end, just excuses for men to fight one another. But go on, Bobbie, I'm listening.'

Though I had recounted the facts in a bright, dry style Constance's soft grey eyes were soon swimming in commiseration.

'You *poor* darling! You must be missing him so much! And you've given him up! I call that *noble*.'

'I'm sorry to tell you that it wasn't nobility at all. Self-preservation.' I explained my reasoning and was sufficiently detached to notice that a little of Sarah's argument had crept into my tale.

'But how will it be for him?' asked Constance, her sympathetic nature rushing to embrace the woes even of a stranger. 'He's clearly unhappy with his wife.'

I shook my head. 'I don't think he is, though. I just assumed that he must be. He told me he hadn't had an affair during ten years of marriage and I quite believe he was telling the truth. He's not a confirmed womanizer. I have to face the fact that in many ways his wife is perfect for him. She leaves him free to live his life as he likes. I know I'd want rather more than that. I'm not sure . . .' I paused for a moment as I thought. 'I really wonder if Burgo is the sort of man who wants to live with a woman at all. A love affair; brief, highly charged meetings, the thrill of love-making when passion is heightened by approaching separation – corny but exciting: I think that all suits him terribly well. It dovetails nicely with a demanding, high-pressured job. It's a neat diversion from the serious business of achievement. Not too time-consuming.'

'You make him sound rather . . . superficial,' Constance said with an air of apology.

I wanted to protest against this accusation. Though possibly doomed, it had been a magnificent, tragic, once-in-a-lifetime love affair. It had to have been worth taking risks for. Our great passion had been a *force majeure* which justified the betrayal of Anna. But had I not just condemned him out of my own mouth?

'I don't know what to think any more. I feel so confused. I hope you don't think, now you know, that I'm a bad character. A scarlet woman.'

Constance had laughed and placed a broad hand with nibbled cuticles on my arm. 'Of course I don't think any the worse of you. Good heavens, no! You've got things out of proportion, Bobbie. I know very well that love is unpredictable. You've been badly hurt. No one can hear terrible things said about themselves without minding but you must put those wicked lies out of your mind. My sanity depends on your remaining at Curraghcourt.'

I felt much better after confiding in Constance. But though I knew she was right about rising above the calumnies of the press I had a perverse desire to know what was being written about Burgo and me. I looked quickly through the Irish papers in the shop and could find nothing in any of them about either of us. Absurdly, I felt

271

something bordering on disappointment, as though yet another link with Burgo had been broken. It had been five days since we had last spoken. I had almost looked forward to seeing a photograph of him. The English papers were not yet in, the woman behind the till informed me. But, to be sure, the news in the *Irish Times* was every bit as good. To placate her I ordered next month's issues of *Vogue, Harpers & Queen* and the *Tatler*.

The children and I had lunch in Katy's Kauldron. The chips had the texture of cotton-wool and the sausages swam in grease but I remembered the macaroni and was grateful.

'"Anyone who had a heart, pom-pom,"' crooned Liddy as we drove home. She was apparently in the best of spirits as she pinged the elastic of a bracelet of red plastic hearts she had bought from Lulu's Hat Box. '"Would look at me, pom-pom, and know that I le-e-erve yew."' Bobbie?'

'Mm?'

'Do *you* think sex before marriage is a sin?'

I hesitated. It would be wrong, surely, to gainsay the customs and beliefs of Liddy's world. And I had a responsibility to Constance. Though she had expressed liberal views when discussing my relationship with Burgo she might feel differently about the sexual behaviour of her own family. But she had asked me what I believed.

'Well, that depends. Not being a Roman Catholic I don't see things in terms of sin and virtue, more as questions of kindness and unkindness or wisdom and folly. A sort of practical morality if you like, something quite fluid which I have to work out daily and be prepared to change my mind about. In principle I think it's actually a good idea for people to make love before they marry. They may not enjoy each other sexually, you see, and that would obviously be something of a disaster for both of them.'

'Would it? For the woman as well, do you mean? Granny says a woman liking sex is the sign of a sick mind. She says sex is the price girls have to pay for being married. Aunt Connie pretends to disagree but then she never has sex with anyone so what does she know? Of course the nuns and Father Bernard would burst blood vessels at the very idea that it might be nice. But *they*'ve never had it either. Sissy once told me that sex was worth risking going to hell for and that it was better than anything you could possibly imagine, but Sissy's cracked, isn't she?'

'Sex can be just as enjoyable for a woman as for a man. And I certainly don't think there's anything disgusting or wrong about it.

272

Sometimes the experience itself isn't good because of ignorance or not loving each other enough. And sometimes the circumstances aren't right.'

'What do you mean?'

'Well, people might be too young. Or too old, I suppose. Or the relationship isn't suitable. You wouldn't make love with your sister's husband, for instance, or your friend's—'

'Oh, you mean adultery,' said Liddy airily. 'I know all about *that*. Father Deglan said Dad and Sissy were in mortal sin and their behaviour set a disgraceful example in front of children and unmarried females. Aunt Connie got very cross with him and sent me and Flurry and Flavia out of the dining room but we listened behind the door. Granny stuck up for Dad. She said he was a proper man and had a man's *needs*. She said Father Deglan wouldn't be such a superstitious old fool if he didn't deny his own. There was an unholy row. I thought they were going to hit each other.'

'I can imagine.'

'Sissy said she loved Dad more than her own soul. Dad said he was grateful for everyone's concern but he preferred to mind his own business and perhaps they wouldn't mind minding theirs.' Liddy laughed suddenly. 'Dad's got a way of speaking that's really crushing. They all shut up after that.'

'I can see he might have been annoyed.' I wondered if public disapproval was the reason Mr Macchuin spent so little time with his children when they were so clearly in need of parental love and guidance. Presumably Dublin society was less censorious.

Liddy was silent for a time, continuing to ping her bracelet. '"Anyone who had a heart"', she sang, '"would know I dream a-r-ve you."'

'Do look at that.' I pointed to the lead-coloured mountains whose peaks were wreathed with clouds. 'Just like volcanoes about to erupt. So dramatic!'

'Can we walk along the King's Road?' Liddy asked dreamily.

'Not only can but must. It's only two streets from my house.'

'Not really? Oh, *joy*!'

'Look, a ruined tower! With a huge bird perched on top. It's a heron, isn't it?'

'Belville Sassoon,' murmured Liddy. 'Mary Quant.' A little later she said, 'It must be grim for you here. You must miss London like anything.'

'I did when I was living at home in Sussex. But here, it seems so far away as to be hardly relevant.' We had been bumping up the track through the walled garden when Liddy asked me that and now we reached the top of the hill from where one could look down on the turrets of Curraghcourt emerging from a sea of waving trees. 'Do you know, the strange thing is I find I don't miss it at all.'

TWENTY-FOUR

'Was there a miracle in Kilmuree?' said Constance as we unpacked the box of groceries in the kitchen. 'I've never seen Liddy so cheerful.'

I explained about the proposed London visit. 'I hope you approve. I ought to have asked your permission before promising.'

'God bless you! It's exactly what she needs. Something to look forward to. The poor child's been fretting for a change for a long time. I knew she was getting depressed but it's so hard to be fair to everybody.' She ran her fingers through her hair, making her fringe stand on end and leaving a smudge of ink on her forehead. She had spent much of the afternoon copying out Eugene's latest poem under his instruction, using a calligraphic pen on special handmade paper sent from Dublin. She had shown me the result with justifiable pride. Her handwriting was exquisitely neat, which was slightly unexpected when one considered her *distrait* appearance. 'I'd thought of trying to get away for a day to take Liddy to see the megalithic tombs in the Burren but a week in London'll be more fun. What a tonic you are, Bobbie!'

'Thank you. The meat and vegetables I ordered should be here any minute. They were promised by tea-time.'

'Good heavens!' Constance looked amazed. '*I* can never get anyone to deliver anything without several really ratty telephone calls.'

'They'd better. Otherwise I shall have to do something clever with sardines again and I for one am already sick of them. Speaking of telephones, do you mind if I ring home again?'

'He – whah.'

'Oliver? What are you eating?'

275

'Jutht a minute.' There was the sound of lip-smacking. 'Hello, Bobs. Ruby's homemade toffee. It's scrummy but extremely adhesive. The house has fallen silent but for the sound of mastication and the occasional burst of swearing as Mrs Treadgold takes out her teeth and prises them apart with the bread knife. It's put paid to Father's tirades and Mrs Treadgold's cheery quips about me turning into a vampire, for which I'm grateful.'

'Why does she think you're turning into a vampire?'

'Because she's one of those simple folk who think there's some virtue in getting up early. I don't see it myself.'

'What time did you get up today?'

'About an hour ago.' I looked at my watch. It was five o'clock. 'Ruby made me some maple syrup pancakes for breakfast – *she* doesn't bat on about sunlight and vitamin D – and gave me a plate of toffee to sustain me during my bath. I was just getting into it when I heard the telephone ring so I came scooting down to answer it.'

'I'm touched that you bothered to scoot.' I could not keep a little severity from creeping into my voice.

'I thought you might be Sherilee.'

'How's Mother?'

'She felt sick after you rang yesterday. No connection, I'm sure.'

'Perhaps too much sugar? Is she better today?'

'How would I know? I told you, I've only just got up.'

'Go and see, would you? I'll hang on.'

I heard a clunk as the receiver met the hall table. The smell of Ô in the sedan chair had been overpowered by oranges. Curls of peel lay next to a pile of crumpled paper handkerchiefs on the seat. I had glimpsed Flavia's face, tense with misery, through the window of the sedan chair when I had crossed the hall on my return from Kilmuree.

'You'd think,' said Oliver after what seemed like a long time, 'that one's mother would be accustomed to the sight of her only son in the raw. Surely she must have been present on occasion at bath-time, perhaps even have changed the odd nappy?'

'You mean you're standing in the hall without any clothes on? At five o'clock in the afternoon?'

'I told you. I was getting into my bath. And what difference does the time make? Ruby, thank God, was calm.'

'She saw you with no clothes on?'

'She's a sensible woman. She said I'd catch my death of cold and chucked me Mother's dressing-gown. Hang on, that's the doorbell.

276

No, don't hang on. I'd better answer it. Ruby's giving Mother an enema and is best not disturbed. Toodle-pip, old thing.'

'Oliver! Wait a minute! You haven't told me—' But the line was dead.

'This is it.' Flurry pulled the sacking from what looked like a row of metal boxes and tubes bolted together. 'It's called the *Flying Irishman*. This is the tender.' He pointed to one end. 'The driver sits here, in front of it. This is the boiler.' He indicated the other end.

'How does it work?' I asked.

'When you put coal in the furnace the flames heat the water in the pipes and turn it into steam. It builds up pressure and then it's forced into the cylinders which drive the pistons. Simple.'

'It doesn't seem simple to me,' I said. 'I'd imagined something much smaller when you said a model railway. You know, like a Hornby set.'

'Of course it's got to be big enough to sit on and take real passengers,' said Flurry. 'What's the good of it otherwise?' He looked enquiringly at me, his grey eyes magnified by the lenses of his spectacles, as though the idea of imaginative play was a foreign concept.

'Have you made it all yourself?'

'I've got this book by Bassett-Lowke. They made lots of railways. Thady O'Kelly, the blacksmith, makes the parts from my drawings.' He pulled away another piece of sacking. 'Here are the wheels. My next job is to get them on to the chassis.'

'It must cost a lot of money.'

'Dad gives me money for it. And I do maths homework for the boys at school. They pay me five pence a sum. Twenty-five pence for geometry because there's drawing and it takes longer.'

'Aren't the other boys going to be rather stuck when it comes to exams?'

'I give them coaching for sixty pence an hour. I'm good at it because I'm a boy and I know how they think.'

'It sounds hard work.'

'I like maths. And it means they leave me alone. Otherwise I'd be beaten up because I wear glasses and can't play games. They call me the Prof.' Flurry gave one of his rare smiles. 'I hate History and English. I can't see the point. As for Scripture . . .' He made a sick noise. 'It isn't true. How could it be?'

I did not feel myself qualified to answer this. 'What is it you want me to do?'

277

'See those sleepers?' He pointed to a huge stack by the barn door. 'They're real ones Dad bought in a job lot. They have to be sawn into three. My railway's going to be triple gauge. We're using a lot of old iron fencing for the rails. There's a tape measure and a bit of chalk by the saw-horse.'

'I want to strike a bargain with you, Flurry.' He pushed his spectacles further up his nose and looked at me expectantly. 'If I agree to spend some time every day – as much as I can manage – cutting up these sleepers, will you eat the vegetables I put on your plate?'

Flurry jumped backwards as though I had struck him. 'You mean turnips and things? Sprouts?' He shuddered.

'Not those two if you really hate them. I agree they've got a strong taste. But potatoes and frozen peas and carrots aren't difficult.'

'They are for me. Why?'

'The reason you get styes is because sausages aren't a balanced diet. You need vitamin C.'

'This one's nearly better.' He pointed to his eye.

'Yes, but there's one coming on the other eye. It isn't good to use the antibiotic ointment indefinitely. And you'll start to get other things.'

'Like scurvy, you mean. We did that in History.'

'Exactly.'

'How much of them have I got to eat?'

'Well, we could start with a spoonful.'

Flurry drew wide the corners of his mouth and screwed up his eyes in expression of absolute disgust. 'What size spoon?'

'Pudding size.'

Flurry clasped his hands behind his back and walked up and down the barn, thinking. Then he said, 'Tell you what. For half an hour's sawing I'll eat half a spoonful. For an hour I'll eat a whole one. Done?'

'Half an hour, one spoonful. An hour, two.'

'Half an hour, three-quarters. An hour, one and a half.'

I refused to negotiate. I was pretty certain that an hour's non-stop sawing would nearly kill me. After further argument we spat on our palms and closed the deal with a handshake. I took up the saw.

Neither the promised delivery of vegetables from Turlough McGurn nor the meat from Sean Rafferty materialized.

'It's the Irish way, I'm afraid,' said Constance. 'We're a gregarious lot and like to have everything on an agreeable footing. Sometimes truth seems less important than saying what we think will please.'

I made six tins of sardines into a fish pie with the last of the tinned potatoes. It was quite as revolting as it sounds but was received with rapture. I could not decide whether they were all masters of the art of concealing their true feelings or if poor Constance's food had been even worse than mine. We were only a few repulsive forkfuls through it when there was a commotion in the hall. The deep baying of the huge dog tethered to the porch set off Maria's shriller barking. Then we heard a scarcely human voice lifted in a roar of protest such as a lion might make on seeing another better-looking lion approaching his females.

Into the dining room, without ceremony, burst a giant red man. He was quite six feet six inches and his shaggy hair and full beard were flame-coloured. His complexion was fiery to match. Even his eyes seemed to be crimson with anger. He stood inside the doorway, screwing up his face in a ferocious glare and smiting his palm with his fist. Maria stopped barking and ran under the table to press herself against my leg.

'Michael McOstrich!' cried Constance in a voice of astonishment.

I liked the Irish way of referring to others by their full names. It gave a picturesque, biblical flavour to proceedings. Michael McOstrich was straight from a miracle play. He could have played Wrath without make-up. Then I remembered where I had heard the name before and my amusement ebbed.

'Where is he?' bellowed Michael McOstrich. 'Where's that blackguard? Where's that rogue and knave, Timsy O'Leary?'

'Now, Michael! You'll frighten the children if you shout like that,' said Constance, standing up to offer him her hand. The children looked interested rather than frightened. Ten minutes before, Flavia had entered the dining room, her tear-swollen eyes fixed on the open pages of *Watership Down*. She had scarcely touched her food, dabbing at her eyes and sniffing as she read. Now she was staring openmouthed at Michael McOstrich. Flurry was motionless with a tinned carrot on his fork prongs and Liddy was smothering a giggle behind her napkin. 'What has Timsy done?' Constance asked. 'Won't you sit down, Michael, and take a glass of something? And there's some delicious fish pie.'

'Thank you, Constance.' Michael McOstrich made a visible attempt to restrain his anger. 'I'm not hungry. How are you, Maud?' He favoured her with a stern glance before returning to his grievance. 'I've lost a jennet. I heard in Murphy's that it was Timsy O'Leary who cut her free from the hobble. I never interfere with other men's property and I don't expect anyone to interfere with mine. It isn't by stealing and defrauding that I've made Ballyboggin the biggest farm this side of Galway. Every acre's bought and paid for by hard work and honest dealings. Honesty's a weakness with me, if you like. And I won't stand for thieving.' He glared around the room as though some of us might be contemplating dashing over to Ballyboggin to steal his furniture. 'That ass is a champion. I reared her myself and there was a tag in her ear to say she was mine.'

'It wasn't Timsy who untied your donkey,' I said into the pause that followed. My courage almost failed as the scorching light from his crimson eyes fell on my face. 'It was me. Her legs were caught up in the rope. She might have been lying there all night, unable to move, without anything to drink or eat. I'm sure there must be a law against such cruelty. If you want to keep a donkey from straying you should put up fences.'

'Fences!' blared Michael McOstrich, coming round to me and putting his face so close to mine that his beard tickled my cheek. There was an overpowering smell of fresh cow dung from his shirt and trousers, which were held up by yellow braces. 'And what, miss, do you know about fences? There isn't a sturdier length of post-and-rail in the country than you'll find at Ballyboggin! I put it up myself. Fences!' He shouted the word, making my head ring. 'Who but a woman would think to fence the mountains!'

He struck his thigh a blow that would have broken the femur of a lesser man and then, to my surprise, his face cracked into a smile. He put his hands on his hips, leaned back from the waist to laugh with a volume that could have brought down the precious La Franchini plaster. Everyone else laughed too, no doubt relieved to see good humour restored. Everyone except Maud, who pressed a handkerchief to her nose.

'Now, Michael,' said Constance, 'let me introduce you to Miss Bobbie Norton. She's come over from England to stay with us and I want you to—'

'From England?' He nodded his great red head. 'I thought so. I said to myself, Michael, I said, this girl's eyes flash and her mettle's fiery. She's not one of our gentle Irish girls. There isn't much you can tell Michael McOstrich about women.'

There was something I did not like in the way he looked at me: as the cock of the yard might look at a young hen, newly introduced to the flock.

'Excuse me,' I said, getting up and finding the top of my head beneath his chin. 'If you don't mind I'd like to clear the table and bring in the pudding.'

Michael McOstrich stood his ground. 'You're a servant here?' He frowned.

'No,' said Constance.

'Yes,' I said, attempting to move past him. 'I'm the housekeeper.'

He looked down at me while stroking his wild wiry red beard. 'You're not my idea of a housekeeper. But then the Macchuins of Curraghcourt never did do things like anyone else. Too grand to dirty their hands, that's the long and short of it. Though there've been McOstriches at Ballyboggin nearly as long, give or take a hundred years.' He struck himself a violent blow on the chest. 'And the Macchuins weren't too proud to run to Ballyboggin for help when the O'Flahertys came calling with drawn swords.'

'Really, Michael,' said Constance. 'You do talk such nonsense. Our families have been good neighbours for centuries. And my great-grandmother was a McOstrich of Ballyboggin. Pride doesn't come into it at all. Of course we all know what a great success you've made of the farm.'

Michael grinned without taking his eyes off my face. 'It's true I could buy up any man in the county. I tell you what, Miss Norton. I've not been to England myself but likely property there's to be had for the taking if it's left lying around. You English have a habit of marching in and grabbing what you want without so much as a by your leave. I'm a fair man. Fairness is as natural to me as breathing and I defy any man here to say that's not so.' He looked sternly round the table. His eyes fell on Eugene, who nodded cravenly. Michael looked back to me. 'If you'll promise that you'll not interfere again with what's mine I'll let bygones be bygones. No man can say fairer than that.' He offered me his giant red paw.

The table collectively held its breath. I held mine in order not to be knocked unconscious by the smell of dung and put my hands behind my back. 'I'm sorry to be disobliging, Mr McOstrich, but if I find any creature kept in conditions I consider inhumane I shall do whatever I can to relieve its suffering.'

'Come now, Bobbie,' said Eugene. 'Shake the man's hand. I expect the animal was worth a few pounds—'

'I beg your pardon, Devlin, but I'll be obliged if you'll shush.' Michael bent his hot eyes on Eugene, who shushed at once. 'Now, miss,' continued Michael, with something almost wheedling in his tone. 'You're a handsome girl – I don't remember when I saw a finer – but you ought to consider a man's feelings. I've climbed down in the presence of these others and you ought to do the same and take my hand in friendship.'

'I don't mind doing that,' I said, 'but I won't promise not to do what I think is right.'

'What entertainment!' said Maud. 'Like a Greek play but more amusing.'

Michael scowled and jutted a scarlet lower lip through the forest of his beard. Then to my relief he let out a diabolical laugh that rang about the room. 'Ha, ha, ha! Lord save us, but you've as much pluck as I've ever seen in a female! You like to be ahead of the field and first over the ditch, I bet!'

'Not particularly,' I said coolly, though I relented so far as to hold out my hand.

He grasped it and shook it as though cracking a whip, nearly dislocating my shoulder. 'Well, anyway, I like your spirit!'

'There! Thank goodness that's settled.' Constance sounded relieved. 'Now, will you stay to dinner, Michael?'

'No, I'll be going, Constance. I've a new bull just arrived. A Charolais sent over from France. I don't believe there's a finer bull in all Ireland. And there are the accounts to check. I've the best steward in Galway but I make sure of that by letting him know he's under my eye and under my thumb. I'm as mild as milk if I'm treated right but cheating, lying and idleness I won't stand for. That's the character of the Master of Ballyboggin and I think that's well known hereabouts! Good evening, all. Goodbye, Miss Norton.'

The model of mildness reached the door in two strides and turned to rest his eyes on me with something of puzzlement in them.

'If it isn't Michael McOstrich!' said Sissy, coming in just then. She was wearing a bright red shawl over a full, flounced skirt and a black mantilla over her hair. 'Are you stopping?' She flashed her excellent teeth at him, raised one arm over her head, put the other on her waist like a flamenco dancer, wriggled her hips provocatively and stamped her feet. The effect was spoilt by Maria running out from beneath the table and fastening her teeth into the swirling hem. 'Get away, you little sod!' Sissy kicked out angrily and there was a tearing sound.

'Good evening, Sissy McGinty,' said Michael, not even glancing in her direction. 'No, I'm away.' He was as good as his word. He seemed to leave an imprint of his blood-red eyes on the air which faded seconds after he had gone.

'I don't know how you dared stand up to him like that,' said Constance as she helped me wash up after dinner. 'Everyone round here is terrified of him. A few years ago he knocked a man clean through a window for winking at his sister.'

'I think bullies ought always to be stood up to.'

I was wiping glasses with one of the half-dozen drying-up cloths I had bought in Kilmuree, having burned the existing ones, which were stained and ripped to filthy rags. Katty and Pegeen were slumped at the hearthside with the black bottle. Thanks to their efforts, the drawing room was now relatively clean, after the removal of the old newspapers, glasses, and scraps of food as well as sackloads of dust, so I had relented. Timsy had been made to wash the windows. He had worked his features through an extensive repertoire of grins, smirks and winks, in token of a wholly insincere admiration of me. Katty had observed this pantomime with a grim smile. He had eaten his supper and gone out again.

'Michael's a good man, though,' said Constance. 'When I was a little girl I used to sit next to him at school and he'd sharpen my pencils for me and protect me from the other boys. The McOstriches were as crippled, financially, as the rest of us until old Mr McOstrich died of drink and Michael took over the farm. He's worked tremendously hard and put the EEC subsidies to good use and turned the land to profit for the first time in a century. Now he's the richest man for miles around. It's just a pity that he's got a chip on his shoulder.'

'Perhaps it was lack of imagination rather than downright cruelty. The donkey, I mean.'

'All the farmers round here hobble their horses and donkeys. It's been the custom from time immemorial.'

I felt a moment's guilt at having interfered with an age-old tradition. But I was not an anthropologist bound to record unflinching the sacrifice of garlanded heifers or the circumcision of little girls. It had been customary at one time to throw Christians to lions but fortunately for Father Deglan there had been a change of heart.

I put down the spoon I was buffing. 'Think how miserable you'd be with your legs attached to a weight you had to drag about all the time.'

Constance walked over to the china cupboard with a pile of clean

283

plates, her gumboots making a soft clumping sound on the flag-stones. 'I've never thought about it before but you're right.'

'Constance . . .'

'Yes?' She turned and smiled sweetly. 'What is it, Bobbie?'

'That dog tied up on the doorstep.'

'Osgar? Is there anything wrong with him?'

'I don't know. He's so savage I can't get near him.'

'It's a family tradition to keep a black dog tethered by that door, from the bad old days of the O'Flahertys.'

'Does anyone ever take him for a walk?'

'Oh, yes. Every morning Timsy takes him for a run.'

'Well, he couldn't have this morning. I looked for him high and low before I left for Kilmuree to give him a list of jobs. Katty and Pegeen wouldn't tell me where he was but Flavia said he was asleep in the apple store until tea-time.'

'Oh dear. I doubt Timsy's the right person to have the care of him. He's so unreliable. But we're all nervous of Osgar, to tell the truth. So that's why the cow's complaining. The poor thing can't have been milked this morning. Now the milk'll be falling off again and she'll get mastitis . . . the vet's bills . . . Finn'll be so cross. Really, it's too bad!' She flapped her drying-up cloth with irritation and dashed a cup to the flagstones where it broke into two. 'Oh, damn! One of the pretty green ones. I'm so clumsy! I'm such a fool!'

'Let me have the bits.' I examined the fragile china shards that had so recently been a shell-shaped cup. 'It's Belleek. Worth restor-ing. If we can get hold of the right kind of glue I'll have a go.'

'Oh, would you? How clever! We've stacks and stacks of those cups in the attic. I just brought down a few because I love the little shell feet.'

'Would life at Curraghcourt be drastically changed if Osgar were allowed to run about occasionally?'

'Well, I suppose not. By all means, if you can rehabilitate Osgar, go ahead.'

'Will Mr Macchuin mind, do you think?'

'Finn? I don't suppose he'd even notice. But you mustn't take on too much, for your own sake. I'm frightened you'll get fed up with us and go away and I couldn't bear that. Bobbie' – she clutched my hand – 'sometimes I feel as though I'm struggling beneath an immense burden and every time I stumble I'm afraid I won't be able to get back up again. I go on a bit lower, a bit more helpless and hopeless each time.' Her eyes filled with tears. 'The children are neglected, I

quite realize. Violet's sinking gradually, Maud's getting more crippled. There isn't enough money to repair the house. We're going to
rack and ruin and there's no one but me to stop it.' She buried her
face in the drying-up cloth and began to cry.

I put my arms around her. 'Things'll look better in the morning.
You're exhausted. And a bit depressed. Let me take on some of that
burden. Really, I want to. There was never any chance to make things
different at home. My parents are resistant to change and my zeal
for reform was frustrated at every turn. If you'll promise to tell me
when you think I've gone too far—'

'You couldn't!' Constance lifted wet eyes to my face. 'I trust you
completely. Do whatever you think. I'll help you all I can though I
know I'm incompetent.'

I pressed Constance into a chair. 'Sit there and I'll make us some
Horlicks.' On impulse I had bought a tin of it in Kilmuree,
knowing perfectly well that my current insomnia owed nothing to
'night starvation' but surrendering none the less to an effective
advertising campaign. 'It'll take away the taste of sardines. And,
Constance . . .'

'Yes, Bobbie?' Constance wiped her eyes and smiled wanly.

I glanced over to the fire. Katty and Pegeen had slipped further
down in their chairs with their heads lolling over the backs, mutter-
ing as they dozed. 'About Violet.'

TWENTY-FIVE

I could smell disinfectant from the top of the attic stairs. Keeping my eye on the bowl of stirabout and the glass of water, so as not to spill them, I edged round the door into Violet's room. It was so dark that I walked into a chair left by the bed and only just managed to save the contents of the bowl and glass.

'Good morning, Mrs Macchuin,' I whispered, adapting my voice to the tomblike atmosphere. 'It's Bobbie. I've brought your breakfast.'

No answer, naturally.

'I'll help you to sit up.'

I slid my arm beneath her. She weighed almost nothing so it was easy to prop her against the stacked pillows.

'Good. Now if you'll open your mouth I'll put a little in.'

I offered the spoon. Violet moved her head and the stirabout dripped on to the bedclothes.

'Damn!' I said under my breath.

When Constance had deputed to me the task of giving Violet her breakfast Pegeen had declared that Mrs Violet hated strangers and would refuse to eat. Constance had asked Pegeen how she knew this as I was the first person outside the family to attempt it. Now it looked as though Pegeen would be proved right. I tried a second spoonful with the same result.

'I'm sorry,' I said, 'I can't see what I'm doing. I'm going to let in a little more light.'

I pulled the curtains back. The sun disclosed a carpet that was far from clean, ugly deal furniture and whitewashed walls now grey with strands of cobwebs. The fire had gone out and the room was cold as well as depressing. I returned to the bedside.

'Violet,' I said in my normal voice. 'I hope you don't mind if I call you that? It's a beautiful day. You can't see much through the windows from here but you can see sky and the dust whirling in the beams. It's really pretty. Apparently it's like that in the sea: billions of minute swirling specks.' I put the spoon between her lips. There was a movement of Violet's throat as she swallowed its contents. 'It's called marine snow and tiny creatures live on it. But perhaps I'm telling you something you already know?'

Violet's eyes remained closed. Her face was colourless, unlined and oddly flat-looking, as though the substance was gradually seeping out of her. Probably this was due to lack of muscle tone. Her lips were dry and cracked in the corners and her skin was flaky. I wondered if she was suffering from vitamin deficiency. As far as I knew her diet was unvaried. Stirabout, which was oats diluted with milk to a liquid consistency, four times a day. And always tea or water to drink.

'Do open your eyes and take a look. From my bedroom windows this morning I could see for miles. Mountains, fields, forests and clouds. I saw the heron again, looking for breakfast in the canals. I was out on the roof feeding the cats. They're starting to be quite friendly, the big ginger one specially. Flavia and I have called him Alexander as a tribute to his bullish desire for world dominance. There are thirteen of them living on the roof. When the sun warms the lead it's baking hot and there's plenty of rainwater to lap. I'm afraid there are rats. I discovered half a one beside one of the chimneys.'

While I was talking Violet swallowed until the bowl was more or less empty. Some of the porridge had transferred itself to my thumb. I licked it off. It was so bland as to be repulsive, like wet cardboard. I held the glass of water to her mouth. Some of it ran down her chin. A sound like a sigh escaped her and then a trickle of moisture, a tear, crept from the corner of one eye.

'Violet.' I took her hand in mine. 'Try to open your eyes so I'll know you can hear me. A blink'll do. Please try.' I stared intently at her face. Her mouth and nose twitched but the movement might have been involuntary. 'You're unhappy, aren't you?' I continued. 'I don't blame you. Anyone'd be depressed living up here in this gloomy room, away from everything and everyone. But the world is still as beautiful as when you last saw it. If only you'd open your eyes, you'd see the light pouring in. Perhaps even a bird flying by.'

No response. Slowly her head rolled away from me. I moved her so she was lying down. Her nightdress was wet over her thighs. Between her legs was a strip of sodden towelling. A smell of urine penetrated the disinfectant. I looked around. There was a washbasin in the corner of the room but no flannel or sponge. I would have to leave that to Pegeen. I relit the fire, putting on plenty of turves in case the open curtains made the room cooler.

'Goodbye, Violet.' I paused at the door. 'I'll come and see you this evening.'

Her head remained turned away from me.

'Just look at these!' I said a few hours later, holding up a carrot. 'I swear it's the one I bent in half in the shop. You could tie a knot in it, it's so old.'

I chucked it on the kitchen table and burrowed deeper into the box the greengrocer had just delivered. When I had complained that it was nearly twenty-four hours late he affected surprise and assured me he had rushed the fruit and vegetables to Curraghcourt the first minute he could, regardless of the inconvenience to other customers who were now rioting in his shop, clamouring for the premium articles he had gathered for my delectation.

'The whole box contains nothing but carrots!' I cried. 'There must be ten pounds of them. Wait a minute, what's this?' I extracted a brown paper bag from beneath them. 'Tomatoes, so squashed they're oozing seeds. What's more they smell of nothing except the bag they came in. Imported from Holland, I bet, when home-grown English tomatoes are ten a penny at this time of the year. Irish, I mean: it comes to the same thing.'

'Bejasus, but it does not!' flashed Sissy who was sitting at the table, sipping Horlicks. Having discovered the remainder of the Horlicks I had made the night before for Constance, Sissy had conceived a passion for it and was already on her third jugful. Her small face was prettily set off by a shiny yellow sugarloaf hat trimmed with a limp blue feather. 'An Irish tomato can't be bettered in all the world! It's the water that's black as treacle with the peat which makes them sweet. An English tomato is a poor anaymic little wizeny thing.'

'All right. If you say so. But how dare Mr McGurn make such extravagant promises and then send these withered objects! And a day late. There's no sign of the celeriac or the chicory. And where are the courgettes he described as still bathed with the morning dew?'

Constance laughed. 'I doubt if he even knows what they are! Certainly I've never seen such things in Kilmuree.' Seeing my face,

288

which must have expressed rage and amazement, she looked contrite. 'I told you. It's the famous Irish charm. It's all about making you feel happy then and there and be damned to the consequences! Maddening, I realize.'

'It *is* charming, most of the time. Don't take any notice of my temper. I'm disappointed that I still haven't got anything decent to cook with. I'll just have to pick out the best carrots and make soup with the rest. And the meat hasn't arrived yet. I suppose the butcher's standing guard over my order of prime cuts from a pedigree prize-winning herd, defending it against all comers,' I added sarcastically.

'More likely he's forgotten,' suggested Sissy. 'But speaking for myself I like sardines and you've a way with them, there's no doubt of that.'

She smiled, screwing up her flat little monkey nose, and the bright red and green glass jewels on her bodice trembled in the sunlight falling on us from the high windows. A farthingale skirt of the same yellow as her hat trailed in the crumbs of mud which had fallen from the sack of potatoes that had been sent with the carrots. Though gaudy, the dress suited both her looks and her mercurial temperament. She had been angry a moment before. Now she was cheerful again.

'Thank you. If I never see another sardine I shall be well pleased.' I picked up the bill to check that I had not been charged for the missing celeriac, chicory and courgettes. 'I'd be perfectly happy to make vegetarian food if only we had decent— I don't believe it! He's asking more than Harrods Food Halls!'

'They're apt to be pricey things, vegetables, in this part of the world,' Constance explained. 'They have to come a long way. Most of the land's too wet and stony for anything but grazing sheep.'

I opened the sack of potatoes. The first one I picked out had been tunnelled by slugs. I threw it down in disgust. 'What about the walled garden? That must have had fruit and vegetables in it once.'

'We gave it up years ago. It's too far from the house. A ten-minute brisk walk. I can remember picking raspberries there as a child when we still had two gardeners. And there were peaches in the greenhouse. But the money Grandpa got for selling off the rest of the estate wasn't well invested. A speculation in South America that went bust. He had to sell the house in Dublin to pay for Finn to go to school in England. A pity, really, considering how much he hated it.'

'What a shame – about the estate, I mean. If it's any consolation my own family seems to be going to the dogs financially too. Neither

Oliver nor I could possibly afford to keep up Cutham Hall even if we wanted to. But we've only been there four generations: just a hundred years. It's not at all the same thing.'

'Well, it *is* sad but it can't be helped. So many of the Big Houses have fallen on hard times. We're lucky not to have been burned down. The IRA tried to torch Curraghcourt during the Civil War. They gave Granny and Grandpa an hour to get all their things out and even helped them to do it. Some of them were local boys so they were quite respectful. Then they threw petrol everywhere but fortunately they'd forgotten to bring any matches. Apparently Grandpa seized the moment to give them a wigging about how he was as good a Republican as they only he knew better than to resort to violence which would simply alienate other people from their cause. While they stood politely and listened Granny and my father, who was just a little boy then, rang Scornach Mór. The soldiers came but not before the IRA boys had run away. Granny said it took a year to get the smell of petrol out of the rooms.' Constance sighed. 'Poor house. It's sheltered so many of us and withstood so much . . . but it does no good repining. I'd better get on with the ironing. There's a pile like one of the Twelve Bens.'

'I'll start lunch,' I said. 'But first I'll see how Katty and Pegeen are getting on with the hall.'

They were squatting inside the great fireplace playing noughts and crosses in the ashes. I promised them the black bottle half an hour earlier if they would only scrub the floorboards until they shone. They set to, fairly willingly. I was learning the art of compromise.

Lunch was a version of *pipérade*, with carrots substituted for peppers. Actually it was surprisingly edible. The freshness of the eggs helped, though their yolks were as pale as primroses. Everyone had second helpings except for Flurry who managed a spoonful with chattering teeth like a chimpanzee. Even while we ate the pudding – tinned mandarin segments and condensed milk; not a good combination – I was racking my brains for something to cook for dinner. It must have carrots in it but *not* sardines.

Here Fate was kind. After lunch I went into the library. I had decided that no fear of reprisals should prevent me from tackling a shelf a day in my war on dust and damp. I noticed that a cracked window pane was funnelling rain directly on to the spines of a set of Thackeray bound in crimson morocco. I already had a list of fifteen broken panes elsewhere that let in water and needed to be replaced. Running my hand downwards to detect the extent of the damage I came to a fat, flamboyantly pink book on the lowest shelf. I stopped to read the gold letters on the spine. *The Constance Spry Cookery Book*. Eagerly I took it out. Here was inspiration! One thousand two hundred pages of it. I looked up carrots. *Carottes Vichy, carottes à la poulette, carottes glacées*, carrots with a piquant sauce, braised, *veloutées, hongroises, galette*. I took Constance Spry back to the kitchen, feeling only a little guilty, and started to weigh out the flour for a carrot cake for the children's tea. I listened to Pegeen and Katty, who had made a good job of the hall floor, groaning out sentimental songs as they sipped, until they were nodding and snuffling with sleepiness.

'By the way,' I said, 'has anyone seen my new padlock?'

They had not.

I went up to Violet's room. It was again in darkness. New candles burned at the shrine and the atmosphere was thick with invalid smells. Impatiently I drew back the curtains and undid the window latch. 'Listen, Violet.' I leaned over the inert body. 'Listen to the wind and the birds.'

I had brought with me a cup of Horlicks made with creamy milk. I put a spoonful between Violet's lips. The tip of her tongue came out immediately and I gave her a second spoonful. Quickly she drank what was left, making little grunts between sips. 'Did you enjoy that? Shall I bring you some more tomorrow?' The smooth face was disappointingly unresponsive. Her chest rose and fell but there was no other sign of life. 'I'll go now. I'm going to make a telephone call and then help Constance clean out the hens. Goodbye.'

I had my hand on the doorknob when I heard a faint groan. Her head, eyes shut, had rolled towards me. It was not much, but it was something.

'Fleur? It's Bobbie.'

'Bobbie! Where *are* you? We've all been going out of our minds not knowing what had happened to you.' Fleur sounded half pleased, half angry to hear my voice. 'What an idi*otic* thing to do. When are you coming back?'

'Not for a while. I'm so sorry to have worried you. You can understand it's been difficult.'

'Well, yes, I suppose I can, but you shouldn't have gone away! *Why* did you? Burgo's been so furious. I've never seen him in such a temper.'

It was bliss to be able to talk about Burgo with someone who had seen him recently. 'Has he been down to Ladyfield?'

'He was here on Wednesday. He wanted to make sure Dickie and I weren't hiding you from him. As if I *would*!'

I knew perfectly well that though Fleur seemed to be fond of me there was only one person whose wishes, feelings and opinions mattered to her.

'Where is he now?' I asked.

'He's gone back to London. And that stupid Anna's there, too. Nasty superior thing! So stuck up. But she's terrified of horses. Refuses to go near them. And the last time she came to Ladyfield, when King Henry ran up to say hello she yelled to Burgo to take him away. She actually called him a brute.'

'Burgo?'

'No, you clot, King Henry. And I saw her lift her foot to kick him.'

I knew that Fleur was as impulsive and generous with her hates as with her loves so I could not assume from this dispraise that Anna was either arrogant or vicious, though I badly wanted to. 'I suppose not everyone likes dogs.'

'Only really awful people don't. Anyway, Burgo went to meet Anna at the airport on Thursday. Bobbie, what are you playing at, throwing him into the arms of that beastly woman!'

'Hardly that.' I felt sick, imagining them together, though the meeting could not have been pleasant for either of them. 'As a married couple aren't they already in each other's—?'

'You know what I mean.'

'She hasn't actually done anything wrong, has she?' I pretended to be reasonable, false, jealous creature that I was. 'I'm afraid Burgo and I have hurt her—'

'Oh, you needn't bother about *her*! She's incapable of suffering – hard and selfish – you're the one he really loves. And now you've left him! Why've you been so stupid, Bobbie! You've made him *so* unhappy!' I could hear she was getting angrier. We had rarely discussed her brother. Of course she knew that we were lovers and because she saw that Burgo was happy she approved of it. Dickie pretended ignorance of our relationship because he was a man and it was easier. When Burgo and I were with them we were discreet. We did not kiss or hold hands but then we didn't need to. Just being in the same room had been enough. 'It was stupid to run away!' Fleur continued to scold me. 'But it's not too late. Come back, Bobbie. Just say you will and I'll ring him straight away to say you're coming. Please, *please*, let me make him happy!'

'I can't do it, Fleur. This isn't a tussle between Anna and me for Burgo's affections. It's much more important than that. It's about what he wants to do with his life. We all need time to think, to make up our minds calmly and rationally. It would be a great mistake to rush into any kind of decision.' I heard Fleur groan with impatience. 'When did you last speak to him?' I asked.

'He rang last night. He sounded so depressed.' Fleur's voice changed. She was crying. 'Oh, Bobbie,' she sobbed, 'I can't believe you really love him – you couldn't hurt him like this if you did – wicked and *cruel* – I hope you're satisfied – thrown away all his love – and mine as well – forgive you for making him so unhappy – *ever* . . .'

'Fleur! Don't let's quarrel. Try to understand—'

But she had slammed down the receiver.

I grieved to have made Fleur miserable, to have made Burgo miserable, Anna miserable. I felt myself to be everything Fleur had accused me of and worse. I considered ringing her back, rushing upstairs to pack, returning at once to London. Part of me longed to do that. But Burgo was with Anna now. Ten years of marriage had to be examined, explained, repaired or . . . ended. If I ever wanted to like myself again I must not interfere with that.

'Where's Timsy?' I asked as Constance and I stood in the hen-run.

This was in the stable courtyard. One wall was the east front of the castle. Opposite and parallel was the coach house, a handsome two-storey building with a clock tower where Timsy and the girls slept. At right angles to that were twenty looseboxes, all empty at the moment as the Cockatoo and the two donkeys that these days comprised the stable at Curraghcourt were out in the paddock. The barn, the granary and the cow-shed made the fourth wall of the courtyard. The apple store, a small, free-standing structure with a gabled roof, was close to the door that led to the kitchen quarters. It was raised on stone pillars to discourage rats but these days instead of apples it housed the generator. In the centre of the courtyard was a strange construction consisting of two sections of wall perhaps four feet tall and twelve feet apart with a drain running between them. Constance explained that this was a carriage wash. The wide walls had been for the grooms to stand on so they could clean every part of the vehicle including the roof, important because it was the first thing to be seen by expectant hosts standing at the head of flights of steps as the visitors drew up.

The floor of the hen-run was cobbled like the rest of the yard but years of throwing down cabbage leaves and potato peelings combined with droppings had created several inches of noisome slurry. This was patterned with arrows from the feet of the chickens that were now clustering together as far away as possible from Maria who was prowling up and down outside the wire, licking her chops. They seemed to be in moult. I knew something about chickens as at one point in my childhood we had kept them at Cutham Hall. I had liked training them to eat corn from my hand and watching them establish a pecking order. It had been a great sorrow when one night a fox had squeezed beneath the hen-house door and dispatched every one of them to that bourn where all hens are equal.

'I last saw him coming out of the apple store,' said Constance.

'What's the big attraction in there? Every time I see him, he's going in or out of it. And he hasn't swept the front courtyard though I've asked him three times to do it.'

'He's hopeless, I know.' 'Hopeless' was the adjective most frequently on Constance's lips. 'The only thing is, he's absolutely loyal and that's worth a lot, isn't it?'

Though in general I heartily approved the easy, familiar relationship between employer and employee enjoyed by the Irish – particularly when contrasted with the chilly English equivalent – I was not convinced that in Timsy's case his loyalty absolutely compensated for his shortcomings.

'He needs taking in hand,' I said. 'Does he do what Mr Macchuin tells him?'

'I wish you'd call him Finn. It sounds so unfriendly and disapproving, calling him Mister.'

Actually I did disapprove of Mr Finn Macchuin, almost more than anyone I had ever met. Or, in this case, not met. How could he reconcile it with his conscience to enjoy himself in Dublin while his wife, mistress, sister and three children were struggling in poverty and discomfort at home? I forgave him his neglect of his mother-in-law. Though I enjoyed Maud's acerbic shots, I could see that as mothers-in-law went, she was not ideal.

'Only one egg again.' Constance had been searching the nesting boxes. 'These birds aren't worth their keep.'

'They don't look exactly in peak condition.'

'They're in their dotage, that's the trouble. Too old to lay and too stringy to eat. Perhaps I'd better ask Timsy to wring—'

'No!' Flavia burst from the hen-house. 'You *can't*! They're my *friends*! You can't wring their necks! I'll run away and I'll take them . . . all . . . with me . . .' She became inarticulate with grief.

'Darling!' Constance tried to put her arms round Flavia but she tore herself away.

'I won't *let* you kill them.' Flavia was standing in front of the hens, her arms outstretched, screaming, while Maria barked herself almost insensible. 'I've known them practically all my *life*. It would be *mur*der!'

'Darling, be reasonable,' pleaded Constance. 'Hens aren't pets.'

'What's *that* got to do with anything? Think what it would be like to have your neck wrung . . . twisted round so you . . . can't breathe . . .' Her sobbing drowned the rest of the sentence except for the words 'horrible', 'mean' and 'hate'.

Constance raised her eyebrows at me and lifted her shoulders and hands in despair.

'Listen, Flavia.' She tried to pull away from me but I held her firmly. '*Listen!* Nobody's going to do anything unkind to the hens. Aunt Constance and I solemnly give you our word on that. Don't we?' I looked at Constance.

'All right. Certainly,' she said.

Flavia continued to cry but more quietly.

'The ground in this run is sour,' I said. 'We'll get Timsy to build a new run and then we'll get some new, young hens to come and live with these and they'll all lay better eggs because they'll be on fresh ground. If you want deep yellow yolks the hens have to be able to eat grass.'

'Really?' said Constance. 'I never knew that.'

'You promise?' Flavia looked up at me with pink-rimmed eyes.

'I promise.'

'Cross your heart and hope to die?'

I made the appropriate gesture.

'Stick your finger in your eye?'

'My finger's rather muddy. Let's go and find Timsy now and ask him to do it.'

We discovered Timsy coming out of the apple store. When he saw us he hastily turned the key of a shining new padlock that fastened the door. My padlock.

'There aren't any posts,' he said when I told him the plan.

'You can use the old ones.'

'The fox'll be after them if the run's outside the yard.'

'We'll put wire over the top so he can't.'

'Then we'll be short of wire.'

'I'll buy some on Monday. I'm going to Kilmuree first thing in the morning to speak to the butcher. And the greengrocer.'

Timsy had run out of arguments. We went to mark out the new site in the field. I left Flavia and Timsy putting in canes and string and returned to help Constance.

The barrow was filled with ordure, apple cores and orange peel. The hen-house was evidently one of Flavia's regular reading haunts. 'What do you do with this?' I asked.

'Usually I dump it in the moat. That's where we chuck everything. One day I suppose it'll be filled to the brim with rubbish but not before I'm dead.'

'Why don't we make a proper compost heap? I saw just the place a minute ago near where the new hen-run's going to be. We can put all the kitchen and garden waste there too.'

'What garden? There isn't one, I'm afraid.'

'Well . . . never mind. We'll have two heaps and Timsy can turn them and water them regularly.'

Constance laughed. 'When you're planning things you get a particular look in your eyes. Such as I imagine Napoleon had as he disposed his troops about the battlefield. Sort of reflective but intensely focused at the same time.'

'It'll be well for me to remember that he overreached himself and came to a bad end.'

'Perhaps you're more like Constance Markievicz.'

'Who's she?'

'A famous Sinn Feinian, who was sentenced to death for her part in the Easter Rising. They let her off, I'm glad to say. I was named after her but I'm afraid I haven't the courage to be a revolutionary. There are several beautiful verses written about her. "Wild child of Lissadell, Not for thee the cool nights of virgin dreams, but contumely and fire, nights of hell . . ."'

I shifted from one leg to the other, sinking a little in the fetid mud while Constance recited what seemed a long poem. Little puffs of cloud raced across the heavens and cawing rooks came spiralling down and flopped on to the battlements. Sissy, still dressed as an Elizabethan courtesan, wandered through the archway of the coach house, her arms full of vegetation, and disappeared through the back door. Flavia and Timsy appeared next, arguing passionately. I began to worry about the carrot cake I had put in the oven for the children's tea.

'Miss Bobbie!' Pegeen's voice issuing from the larder window interrupted Constance's ballad. 'The meat's just here. Will I be putting it on to boil?'

Later, when all the meat – or one might more truthfully say all the fat and gristle – had been unpacked and examined and exclaimed at, in a rage, by me, and I had begun the task of scrubbing the sprouting roots from the potatoes, there was a tremendous row at the front door. Osgar, who had benefited from the butcher's inadequacies in the form of a dish mounted high with off-cuts, was baying hideously. Katty went to find out the cause of the disturbance and returned a moment later with a large bouquet of red roses, intertwined with honeysuckle and wrapped in newspaper.

''Twas left on the doorstep,' said Katty, a smirk wrinkling her hooked nose and grimy cheeks. ''Tis for Miss Bobbie.'

'What a lovely surprise!' I said, thinking at once of Kit. I took the note she held out to me.

'Who's it from?' asked Constance, Flavia and Liddy in unison. The last two had gathered in the kitchen in response to the smell of the cake that was cooling on a rack before it was iced.

Dear Miss Norton [said the letter],
Hoping this finds you as it leaves me, in good health. I trust some flowers from the garden will be acceptable. I am not much of a hand at letters but I would like to put it in writing that I consider you a handsome woman.
Yours sincerely, M. McOstrich

P.S. The ass has come home of her own free will.

'Silly ass,' I said aloud.
'Who?' asked the others.
'The flowers are from Michael McOstrich.'
'*No!*' said Constance. 'Why, he's never so much as smiled at a woman before though there are plenty of girls round here who'd like to get his attention. And a letter! That's tantamount to a proposal of marriage!'

297

'You won't marry him?' Flavia put her hand on my sleeve, looking worried.

'Of course she won't, you little idiot,' said Liddy, who was looking charming in the Peruvian jersey I had lent her. 'Why would Bobbie want to marry a clod-hopping farmer who goes to Mass every Sunday in a suit his mother made him twenty years ago? And often his clothes are splashed with blood because he does his own slaughtering. In the kitchen. So beastly! His sister Máire has to hold the pigs and chickens while he cuts their throats. She hates it but Michael's got such a temper she has to do whatever he says.'

'Oh, promise!' urged Flavia, holding my arm tight. 'You wouldn't like it, really! It would be better to be a nun.'

'I certainly *wouldn't* like it. I'll promise not to marry him even if I never have another proposal. But we're forgetting he hasn't actually asked me.'

'Who is it you aren't going to marry?' Sissy had come in. She sprang up on to the table and perched on its top, sticking her legs out straight in front of her and, seizing a knife, cut a large slice from the cake, cramming it whole into her mouth like a child.

'Michael McOstrich,' said Flavia. 'That cake isn't finished yet.'

'Michael?' Sissy spoke with her mouth full. 'He asked you? I don't believe it!' She looked thunderous.

'No.' I removed the cake. 'He wanted to tell me the donkey's come home, that's all. And he sent me some flowers.'

'Michael gave you those?' Sissy stared at the pretty nosegay of crumpled rose petals and trembling heads of honeysuckle as I unwrapped them. Before I had any idea of her intention she had jumped from the table, snatched them from my hands and thrown them into the fire. ·

'Oh, Sissy! That's too bad of you!' I seized the poker and rescued the flowers but most of them were spoiled. 'What a mean thing to do! Why did you?'

She was grinning fiendishly now and rolling her black eyes. Both hands were on the farthingale of her skirt so that her elbows stuck out defiantly. 'So what'll you say now when your boyfriend comes a'courting? Will you tell him Sissy McGinty sent them to perdition, you bold *Sasanach*?'

'That was a mean thing to do, Sissy,' said Constance. 'I think you should apologize to Bobbie.'

'I'd sooner the devil tore out me tongue!' shrieked Sissy, running out of the kitchen.

'Take no notice of her,' said Constance. 'She has a jealous nature and any attention paid to anyone else upsets her. She'll be over it in a flash.'

'I don't mind her being angry,' I said, 'but the flowers were so beautiful. It's a shame.'

'Are you going to ice the cake?' asked Liddy.

'In a minute,' I said absently. My attention had been caught by the newspaper the flowers had been wrapped in. Near the bottom of the front page was the headline: *Disgraced Tory Politician Pleads for Privacy*. Underneath was a photograph of Burgo and Lady Anna Latimer, arm in arm, smiling at each another. I looked at the date. It was this morning's edition of the *Daily Recorder*. I smoothed out the paper and carried it to where a shaft of light came down from one of the windows. '*My wife has forgiven me*,' said the article in quotes, '*and I consider myself a lucky man. My lapse of judgement has hurt her very much and it has also damaged the party to which I owe my loyalty. To them I apologize. I am enormously grateful to my wife for retaining her faith in me despite the recent episode of which I am now deeply ashamed. We would appreciate being left alone by the media during this difficult time.*'

When I went to bed that night after an evening that seemed interminable and during which the effort made to appear carefree had nearly broken down a hundred times, I was a little comforted to find in a tooth-mug beside my bed a bunch of wild flowers and a note which read: *From Flavia. To make up for the ones that were burned.*

TWENTY-SIX

'What are you doing?'

Sissy's voice behind me made me jump. I had been exercising great caution, stretching out my hand towards the ring to which Osgar's chain was fastened while keeping my eyes on his jaws that were beginning to slaver as he looked fixedly at my ankles.

'You startled me! I was trying to undo the chain to take him for a walk.'

'Were you now! And whatever for?'

'It's cruel to keep an animal chained up all the time.'

'It is?' Sissy gave me an oblique measuring look as though she suspected me of derangement. Certainly one of us was more than a little strange. But I was glad she seemed to have recovered her temper after her outburst over Michael McOstrich's flowers.

'*I* think so,' I said trenchantly, ready to argue my case.

'Likely you're right.' Sissy's concurrence was unexpected. 'I shouldn't like it meself. And he's a fine animal.'

We looked at Osgar, who sat up blinking, as though disconcerted to find himself suddenly an object of interest after years of being stepped over and ignored.

'I'm pretty sure Timsy hasn't taken him for a walk since I've been here.'

Sissy laughed, a shrill sound that made Osgar shrink back. 'He hasn't since I've been here and that's a year come Lughnasa. He's terrified of the poor beast.'

'That accounts for the state of the doorstep,' I said in disgust. 'Well, something must be done about it.' I reached across to the ring once more. 'Since I've been here I've been feeding him up to get him to trust me and I think it's working—' I snatched back my hand as

Osgar growled. 'Damn! The trouble is I'm terrified of him myself. He's such a big dog.'

As if in agreement Osgar showed us two rows of perfectly enormous teeth that were shining with saliva as though anticipating a good meal from my arm.

'Tish!' said Sissy. 'Sure he'll bite you if you're timid with him. He thinks you're going to hurt him.'

'How am I to pretend I'm *not* frightened of him?'

'A *diabhal*! Stand away, woman. I'll show you.'

Sissy began to make a peculiar noise, half-whistle, half-purr. It ran up and down between three notes and was, I must say, quite disturbing. It was an uncanny sound and made one think of remote forests, under-sea caverns, anywhere miles from the haunts of man. Her black monkey eyes took on an unearthly brilliance. Osgar's ears, usually flat to his head, pricked up and he stopped growling. Slowly he bowed his head and sank on to his forequarters. Calmly Sissy put her little hand to his collar and undid the clasp. Osgar continued to crouch, mesmerized, unaware that he was free.

'Come, boy.' Sissy backed away, patting her knee.

Osgar tottered to what would have been the length of his chain and stood there, his eyes fixed on Sissy. He refused to go a step further.

'Oh, come, you great *óinseach*!' Sissy walked up to him and took hold of his collar. She pulled the reluctant Osgar away from the porch towards the middle of the courtyard. Now I could see that his hindquarters were small by comparison with his head because of muscle wastage. 'There you are!' Sissy let go of him and immediately he dropped down on to his haunches, whining pitifully.

'Poor thing!' I approached cautiously. 'He's probably agoraphobic. Good boy! Here, boy!' I offered my hand, pretending to myself I was not frightened, but the minute Osgar growled the stratagem failed. 'Anyway it doesn't look as though he's going to run off.'

Sissy was laughing at me. I had been too preoccupied to notice before that she was wearing a matador's costume, complete with shoulder cloak. 'Sure he won't. You make a fine pair, feared to death of each other.'

'How did you do that? Make that noise, I mean?'

''Tis an old circus trick. Before I took to the trapeze I helped the lion-tamer. Five nights a week I put my head into the lion's mouth without even a puncture of my skin.'

I was impressed by this courageous, if pointless, accomplishment. 'What shall we do with him now?' I wondered.

Sissy shrugged. ''Twas you wanted to free him.'

My intention had been to take a delighted Osgar for a brisk run before chaining him up again but I realized now it was not going to be so easy. 'You wouldn't like to take him for a walk?'

'I would not. I'm going to check me snares.'

'Snares?' I could not keep disapproval from my voice.

Sissy lowered her voice. 'I'm after the *sidh*.'

'You mean . . . fairies?'

'Whisht! They don't like to be spoken of.' She lowered her voice to a hiss. 'I'm after a *fir darrig*. They're better tempered than the cluricaunes or the pookas. Not so likely to cross me eyes for catching them.'

'How will you know what sort you've caught?' I whispered back.

'The *fir darrig* wear red, of course.'

I had to admit that Sissy was refreshingly different. After only a little time in her company I was able temporarily to forget the cold-burning barb in the pit of my stomach.

'I feel such a fool,' I confessed to Constance when we were alone in the kitchen washing up after lunch.

Though I had read the newspaper article only once before screwing it up and throwing it on the kitchen fire I found I was able to recite the disagreeable paragraph almost word for word. Constance, her beautiful grey eyes suffused with tenderness, put down her drying-up cloth without speaking and kissed me gently on the cheek. Her quiet compassion, without exclamations of anger or disbelief or any of the indignant responses I might have felt the circumstances required, was exactly what I needed. It allowed me to unburden myself freely.

'I believed that our love was different from other loves. Well, I've got what I asked for.' My voice sounded strained and artificial even to my own ears. 'I stand convicted of conceit and stupidity before all the world.'

Constance shook her head. 'You're too hard on yourself. Love comes to us unbidden. We can only submit to its dictates.'

'I don't know,' I said. 'I could have resisted Burgo at the beginning. I didn't love him then, when we hardly knew each other. How could I have? I liked the way he looked. I was attracted by his voice and the way he talked about things. I was grateful for his attention. If I'd met him in London when I was happy would I have fallen in love with him?' I stopped polishing the battered lid of a copper pan to reflect.

'Well?' Constance asked in her soft voice. 'Would you?'

'I honestly think I'd have been put off by the negatives: the fact that he was married and a politician – Tory, at that. I wonder if love isn't in some ways a negative process. We're conscious of an emotional void, therefore we seek love. I was lonely and unhappy and it affected my judgement. Well!' I tried to laugh. 'I'll never trust it again.'

'Bobbie, I hate to hear you sound so bitter. You're hurt and rightly so,' said Constance. 'He ought to be ashamed of himself. If he loved his wife what was he doing with you? And if he doesn't, why is he going back to her?'

'The thing is, Constance, he wanted both of us. I offered the excitement of something new and forbidden. She was the career move. But he didn't care enough about either of us to give up the other until he really had to. Then he chose her.'

'You did run away. He must have thought you'd given *him* up.'

'He knew I'd read about it in the newspapers. If he'd really loved me he couldn't have done this. At least he might have played for time. Four days: that was all it took him to decide. A lapse of judgement! An episode he's now ashamed of! How trite! How . . . sordid!'

'You're taking too black a view. He probably didn't say anything like that. And if he did, who knows what pressure his colleagues and his wife put on the poor man?'

'Oh, Constance, don't speak kindly of him.' I put down the lid, by now burnished to a high sheen, and covered my face with my hands. 'Don't you see? I can only get through this if I can teach myself not to love him.'

Luckily, during the days that followed either the quantity of the tasks requiring my attention or the distracting presence of other people prevented me from feeling the full measure of my sorrow except as an ever-present, smarting wound. The nights were different. It was then, as I shifted restlessly on the lumpy mattress and tried to beat substance into my pillow, that I applied myself to the hard lesson I was determined to learn.

I had not been the love of his life, certainly; nor, perhaps, he of mine. We had been violently attracted to each other but the affair had fallen at the first hurdle, which proved it had not the makings of a lifelong passion. I felt myself crippled by the blow and perhaps he too was bruised, but he would soon get over it. And so must I.

There never could have been a happy outcome as long as Anna still loved him. I was wiser now and I would turn my present suffering to my own benefit. In future my course would be determined by prudence. When hope – that she might not be able to forgive him, that he might not be able to forget me – tried to worm its way into my thoughts, I resolutely crushed it. There would be no more lapses of judgement, no more shameful episodes.

As dawn broke I welcomed the gathering of the seven-toed cats. It was a relief to leave the hot, rumpled sheets, to go to the window and refresh my tired eyes on the beauty of the woods and mountains. I put dishes of meat and milk out on the roof and watched the cats as they ate. Afterwards, they would find places to sleep it off, the sagging canopy of the half-tester being a favourite place for a nap. The race to get breakfast ready for the dining room and trays sent up to Maud and Violet sufficed to rid my face of an appearance of woe. Constance was the soul of tact, never speaking of the past unless I did, which was rarely.

With Constance's full support, I had my way about giving Violet a more varied diet. To economize on time and labour we began every dinner with something like soup or a savoury mousse, food that was soft and easy to eat so that Violet could have some of the same. Puddings were things like fruit purées, custard or jelly. These changes meant that Violet's teeth must be cleaned, which was anathema to Pegeen and Katty. That they did not use a toothbrush was evident from their own sparse and blackened fangs so I took on the job myself. Violet quickly learned to open her mouth to facilitate the teeth-cleaning. I suppose the strong taste of toothpaste must have added savour to her monotonous existence.

Now we drew back the curtains each morning and they stayed open until dusk. Constance and I talked in loud cheerful voices and visited Violet as often as we could. Flavia was a ready convert to the new regime. She gave up several hours each day to reading, singing and talking to her mother. It was not long before we were able to convince ourselves that Violet was becoming more responsive. We could not understand the meaning of the noises she made but we agreed that she was groaning, grunting and sighing more often. Then she introduced a new sound into her vocabulary: a high-pitched wail, like a child's. It was actually quite distressing but we told ourselves that all change was for the good. It was Flavia's idea to bring objects to put into Violet's hand: ordinary things like marbles, pencils, buttons, petals and fir cones. After she had explained what the object was and cupped Violet's unresisting fingers round it, Flavia would gaze intently at the still face for signs of recognition. Her disappointment was so evident that sometimes I questioned the wisdom of what we were trying to do.

'Flavia,' I said one morning, perhaps three weeks after my arrival at Curraghcourt, 'let's move your mother's bed to the opposite corner so she can be near the window. She'll have much more light and she'll be able to feel the air on her face.'

As the bed was on castors and the floorboards bare – we had thrown out the existing carpet as being too dirty to clean – we managed this between us without much difficulty. Liddy came in just as we were manoeuvring the bed into place. She was by nature impatient, restless and easily bored and spent much less time with Violet than her sister. Also she was at a more self-conscious age and found it disagreeable to hold one-sided conversations. But at my suggestion she had manicured her mother's nails which Pegeen had cut into ragged points. After Liddy had massaged Violet's hands with cream they looked twenty years younger and you could see how beautifully shaped they were. We substituted a mild soap and a sponge for the carbolic and huckaback which Pegeen used to wash Violet's face and applied face cream twice daily to Violet's cracked lips and cheeks. The change in her appearance after two weeks was remarkable.

'Do you think she'll feel cold?' asked Flavia doubtfully as I opened the windows to let the breeze play on Violet's face.

'Could you find an eiderdown, do you think?'

'I'll go,' said Liddy, who was always keen to get away from the disinfectant smells and those they ineffectually masked.

She was back five minutes later. 'There aren't any spare eiderdowns so I brought this.' She laid a coat over the bed. 'It was Mummy's. It's real mink. I was wondering if I might have it, actually, since it isn't much use—'

'Look! Look!' cried Flavia.

We watched, holding our breaths, as the fingers of Violet's left hand uncurled at the touch of the fur. They trembled as they moved slowly across the shining dark brown hairs, not more than an inch either way, but the movement was unquestionably deliberate. I felt the back of my neck prickle.

'Liddy, you're a genius!' I said.

Flavia burst into tears.

305

'Flavia, this is your miracle as much as anyone's,' I said. 'You've been so good about spending time with her and—'

'I'm not crying about *that*,' sniffed Flavia crossly. 'I don't mind it was Liddy who thought of the coat. I'm crying because Mummy's alive. She's properly alive. Now everyone'll have to believe she's going to wake up.'

'Well, perhaps, but we mustn't assume too much . . .'

But Flavia was not listening. 'I'll go and find some more things for her to feel.' She was halfway through the door before she came back to kiss her mother. 'I won't be long, Mummy darling. Don't go away because I've got so much to show you.'

I felt afraid then. Afraid that Violet might be too severely brain-damaged to make further progress. That Flavia's hopes might be cruelly dashed. And it would be my fault.

'I suppose she'd better keep the coat,' said Liddy with a trace of regret.

'Are you absolutely certain?' asked Constance, whom I found in the granary. 'It wasn't just a tremor?'

'I'm certain. The thing is, until today we've been trying to stimulate her right hand. When we changed the position of the bed it was her left hand which was nearest. People who have strokes are always more paralysed on one side than the other, aren't they?'

'I know so little about it. I did question the nuns after it happened but they were unforthcoming. The Catholic view is that misfortune is sent by God as a cross to be patiently and humbly borne in atonement for sin. And I feel sure it would never occur to Dr Duffy to go against any counsels that came from Dublin, the fount of all medical wisdom. I feel so guilty now that I didn't try harder.' Constance's face assumed its habitual expression.

'You shouldn't feel that. For one thing you've had more than enough on your plate. And for another, how do we know this isn't going to end in disaster? Flavia's convinced now her mother's going to get better. It's quite possible Violet won't make any more progress and I shall wish I'd never interfered.'

Constance emptied a sack of chicken corn into a bin. 'We must risk that. Let's give it all we've got. I remember that coat. She looked so lovely in it. Poor dear Violet.' She lifted several empty sacks as though hunting for something.

'What are you looking for?'

'A hammer. My wardrobe door's fallen off again.'

'Will this do?' I extracted a mallet from the spokes of a bicycle wheel.

'Thanks. Everything's in such a mess—'

'Just a minute.' I interrupted her. 'How many bikes are there? Are they in working order?' I pulled upright the one that was on the top of the heap. It was rusty but had its full complement of wheels, saddle, handlebar and chain.

'They were left here by a ladies' cycling club from Japan. They'd pedalled all the way from Dublin – not in one day, naturally, but staying at B & Bs – and they were in the terminal stage of sanity. It had rained every day and by the time they got to Connemara the roads were roaring cataracts. Poor things, all you could see were glistening eyes and black topknots through the coating of mud. We took them in and gave them tea while they telephoned for a coach to take them back to Dublin and the next plane home. They were exquisitely polite but you could see that for them this was a far cry from the Emerald Isle as promoted by travel agents. Between November and March it varies from khaki through every shade of brown to the colour of dung.'

'This is a pretty good bike.' I hopped on and cycled slowly round the barn. 'Gears and everything. It just needs a bit of oil.' I came to a squeaking halt in front of Constance. 'I've just had an idea.'

Constance snapped her hand smartly up to her temple. 'I wonder how officers of the Imperial Guard saluted. Palms facing down or outwards, do you think?'

A little later I was crossing the hall on my way to the kitchen when I heard the telephone bell vibrating within the sedan chair. I leaned inside to answer it.

'Kilmuree five one seven.'

'Is that you, Bobbie?'

I climbed in and closed the door. 'Hello, Jazzy. How are you?'

'Darling, how are *you*? Feeling a little better?'

Since the news of Burgo's return to connubial bliss had hit the headlines Jasmine and Sarah had been kindness itself. They had rung so often to check on my state of mind and body that Maud had talked of having another line connected so that the family might once in a while communicate with the outside world.

'Oh, I'm not too bad. Doing my best not to think about it. So where are you?'

'Somewhere totally at the back of beyond but I've never lived in the country before and it's super to be able to hear birds singing and see butterflies. It's so quiet at night your ears hiss. We only moved three days ago. It took a while for Teddy to find something he thought I'd like.'

'And do you?'

'It's a little too soon to tell but I think I shall. Actually it's a perfectly foul bungalow. You never saw anything so *hid*eous: three-piece suite, swirly patterned carpets, a forest of giant plumy things in the garden; but we're so in love that nothing else matters. It's dirt cheap because poor Teddy's got to carry on paying *her* mortgage and the children's school fees.'

'Where is it exactly?'

'Enfield.'

'In Middlesex?'

'Yes, I think so. The back of beyond, as I say. And I'm being such a good little housewife. We had to let the Filipinos go. They cost an arm and a leg and besides there isn't room in the bungalow for them. It's lucky you taught me how to cook corned beef hash. Teddy says it's his most favourite thing to eat. Isn't that extraordinary, considering it's the only thing I *can* cook?'

'Miraculous. What do you do all day?'

'Well, as we make love practically all night long I get up quite late. Then I go for a walk. You never saw so many bungalows in all your life. And horrid little orange flowers planted in circles round the clumps of the same plumy things in every garden. There ought to be a law against them.'

'African marigolds and pampas grass, probably.'

'You're such a knowledgeable gardener, darling, I'm in awe. Well, then I come back and have lunch and read the newspapers. Then I have a little sleep. I may do some dusting. Before I know it, it's time for Teddy to come home so I have to really get cracking then. I get the gin and tonics ready and arrange the papers by the television. There's a special cricket match on at the moment and he likes to watch that, and we have supper and he tells me what he's been doing, just like an old married couple. It's such fun. And then we *dive* into bed for the best bit of the day.' Jazzy giggled and sounded so happy that I wondered if I had been misjudging Teddy. 'But you've hardly told me a thing about *you*, darling.'

'I know, but I ought to be peeling carrots for lunch. There's so much to do here. Let's talk again in a day or two and I'll fill you in then.'

'I hope you aren't wearing yourself out. And pining for you-know-who? Are you eating?'

'Yes. Really, I'm fine, don't worry. Every day I feel a bit more cheerful. Being busy is my salvation.'

'I must say I hadn't realized what fun it was being domesticated. Always something to see to. Let me see, what's the time?'

I looked at my watch. 'Twelve o'clock.'

'Right. In exactly six hours I shall open a tin of corned beef. It's been so marvellous to talk to you. Teddy's so heavenly to be with, he's so clever and wise, and noble, and of course quite indispensable for all the really im*por*tant things.' She giggled. 'But there's nothing like a girlfriend to really *talk* to, is there?' For a moment I thought I detected a note that was not quite unadulterated bliss in Jazzy's voice.

'No, indeed.'

TWENTY-SEVEN

'Timsy, where are the spades, forks and hoes?' I peered into the back of the Land-Rover. All I could see were the baskets, seed packets, balls of string and coils of hose I had stowed there earlier.

'Spades is it? Sure, you never give a man a moment to draw breath!' In fact Timsy had taken to puffing hard as though in the last stages of exhaustion every time I approached him, even if the second before he had been lying in a chair with his feet up and his eyes closed. 'But you could drive a pack of slaves without so much as a whip. Just one look from those sparkling eyes—'

'Would you mind getting them now?' I cut in ruthlessly. 'You can drive and we'll meet you down there. If you forget the spades and forks and things the cupboard stays locked.'

Timsy shot me one of his calculating looks, which sometimes cut through his obliging but dimwitted Irish retainer act, to check whether I was serious, then he went away in the direction of the barn where the implements were stored.

Constance, Sissy, the three children and I got on our bikes. Katty, who had declared she would sooner ride a broomstick, was to travel in the Land-Rover with Timsy. Pegeen was staying behind to look after Violet and Maud. Maria was excited by this departure from her humans' usual methods of locomotion and ran in circles round us, barking her head off. Osgar was on a lead, the other end of which was held by Sissy who said she could easily steer single-handed. He looked far from pleased to find himself in this maelstrom of whirring wheels and incessant noise – Flurry and Flavia being compelled by whatever strange impulses direct juvenile behaviour to ring their bells without pause. Osgar flinched and growled and tried to sit down and was generally uncooperative until Sissy shouted abuse at him after

310

which he settled into a depressed-looking lope alongside her, ears flat to his head, muzzle to the ground.

The children raced off and we grown-ups followed at a more leisurely rate. I found I needed to concentrate if I was neither to run over Maria, who was trying to bite our front wheels, nor be unseated by a pothole.

'Are you managing all right with Osgar, Sissy?' cried Constance as we came to a place where in less balmy weather a stream had crossed the track and large boulders had been washed down the mountainside to lie in our path.

'Sure, a baby could do it! I was one of Donovan's Flying Angels – bareback ponies, but it's much the same thing. Look at me now!' To our combined admiration and alarm Sissy attempted a handstand on the handlebars. This went well until the panniers of her Marie Antoinette costume fell over her eyes and she hit a stone. When we picked her up she was screaming with laughter despite a bloody nose. Poor Osgar had received a clout from the flying bicycle and was disinclined to get up again until Sissy hit on the expedient of biting his ear, after which he permitted himself to be dragged along by the neck. I began to have serious doubts about the wisdom of interference in all cases.

The walled garden restored my faith somewhat. Rose-bay willow-herb, ragwort and docks stood waist high. Every stone sheltered a luxuriant fern or two. In the centre was a dipping pond half filled with black mud. But despite years of neglect the fruit trees had continued to blossom and bear fruit in their season. Already there were tiny burgeoning apples, pears, plums and cherries.

Recently I had put my early waking to good use. I had risked Mr Macchuin's wrath by removing another book from the library – this time *The Golden Treasury of Good Vegetable Gardening* – and had boned up intensively on what everyone who aspired to call themselves a gardener should know. A programme of careful pruning would do wonders for the fruit crop next year. As it turned out July was the perfect time to prune fans, espaliers and cordons. I had studied the diagrams carefully and now I longed to take the secateurs from my bicycle basket and begin at once.

But first the others must be organized. The track ran through the garden in a wobbling curve to avoid the stone ramparts of the dipping pond. From an aesthetic viewpoint this was undesirable. The garden was divided into four by a wide path that ran at right angles to the track. An iron pergola covered the length of this path, bare now

311

but most of it in good repair and perfect for runner beans and sweet peas next spring. Probably I would have left Curraghcourt by then so that would be up to Constance. But even in late July there were plenty of things that could be sown at once.

'As soon as Timsy gets here we'll begin in this section.' I directed the attention of my troops to the south-facing side near the derelict greenhouses, which were bathed in sun whenever clouds permitted. 'First we'll clear away all the rubbish.' I indicated an old oil drum, an iron bedstead, a pile of rotting deckchairs and several car tyres. 'Then we'll mark out two crossing paths to divide each quarter into four. We'll have a programme of crop rotation. Brassicas here.' I pointed to the relevant piece of ground. 'Here roots, over there peas, beans and salad crops, and in the last quarter— Flurry, what are you doing?'

His head had disappeared inside a large galvanized tub on wheels. 'I'm seeing what this is for.'

'I think it's a watering cart. Where was I? Yes, we'll have permanent beds of artichokes and asparagus and perennial spinach—'

'Will I have to eat it?' asked Flavia. 'It makes my teeth go like chalk.'

'We'll see. Now each plot will have to be double-dug. Double-digging means' – I consulted my notes – 'that we mark out a two-foot-wide strip with a line of string across the end of the half-plot to be dug first.' I paused, then consulted them again. 'Wait a minute: that's after we've divided the plot down the centre with another piece of string.'

'Is that in the same direction or across?' asked Constance.

'Um, let me see. Parallel. Take the soil out of this trench to the depth of a spade's blade.'

'I know nothing about a trench.' Sissy looked about her. 'Where is it?'

'It's the trench you're going to make by digging,' I explained patiently. 'Marked by the lines of string.'

'A spade's blade,' murmured Constance. 'Blade of the spade in the shade of a glade made to fade by a jade palisade . . .'

I gave Constance a reproachful look and referred again to my notes. 'Heap the soil at the same end but on the path near the adjacent half-plot,' I read out.

'What's that?' asked Sissy.

'What's what?'

'An adjacent half-plot?'

'It's the other half of the bit of soil you aren't digging that's next door to the bit you are.'

'Begor, and it's confusing.'

'I like the idea of digging out the soul,' said Constance. 'As though this garden has a spirit crouching in the ground waiting to be redis-covered.'

'*Soil*, Constance. Let's all try to concentrate. Yes, well. When you've done that you break up the bottom of the trench to a depth of, let me see, ten inches with a fork.'

By this time only Constance was listening to me. Flurry was wheel-ing the watering cart away to the far end of the garden. Liddy was sitting in a deckchair, deeply absorbed by the copy of *Vogue* which had been delivered that morning and from which she refused to be parted. Flavia was attempting to walk the length of the garden on the stone rope-edging of the path and Sissy was hanging upside down by her knees from the pergola.

'Where's Timsy?' I asked crossly.

Three-quarters of an hour later, after Flavia and Liddy had eaten nearly all the sandwiches and Flurry had finished taking apart the greenhouse stove and Sissy's gymnastics had broken a section of the pergola, the Land-Rover arrived. Almost speechless with annoyance I handed round the spades to the four grown-ups, bidding them tersely to dig. I got busy with sticks and string and Liddy was deputed to hold one end. After she had several times let go of it at the crucial moment I set her to the task of fixing hoses to taps and substituted Flavia as string-holder.

Timsy complained volubly of his back and blisters and Constance was several times distracted by a particularly beautiful cloud forma-tion. Sissy and Katty dug like terriers. A quarrel broke out because the former had accidentally thrown mud into the latter's eye. They resorted to rolling on the ground and pulling out each other's hair before they were forcibly separated. I had an inkling of how Napoleon must have felt after the failure of his Continental Blockade. It ought to have worked and it was not his fault that it did not. But this must have been small comfort. I took myself off to prune an espaliered apple tree to recover my equanimity.

Several hours later, I was planting the last spinach seed. It was nearly seven o'clock and I was alone in the walled garden. Katty had walked back to the house soon after the mud-throwing incident. She refused to be shaken in her conviction that she would be forever-more blind in that eye. She had made a pathetic spectacle tapping the ground before her with a dead branch as she stumbled across the walled garden. I had gone to the gate a minute later to check that she had not fallen into a ditch and was relieved to see her give a little skip of pleasure like a week-old lamb as she ran up to the top of the hill.

Timsy had biked away an hour later saying that Siobhan's teats were giving trouble. Liddy had managed to soak herself setting up the irrigation system (that is, fastening two hoses to two taps) and had been sent to take a hot bath. Flavia had been constantly busy, burying with hymns and prayers each mouse's skull and pig's tooth that surfaced.

Sissy had continued to dig as though attempting to penetrate the earth's crust and get down to magma. She was remarkably strong for such a small woman and had tremendous stamina. Long after Constance and I were lying exhausted in deckchairs, blowing on the patches of stinging raw flesh on our palms and fingers, the sun was flashing on Sissy's spade as she hurled clods, stones, sticks and nettles into the sky. The ground looked as though a meteorite had collided with it but she would not be governed in any way as to method or result. I had some sympathy with this. None of us likes to be told what to do.

They had pedalled away at about five o'clock, Constance to act as amanuensis to Eugene's poetic needs, Sissy and Osgar to check her *sidh* snares and Flavia to groom and powder the verminous cats. As fast as we defleaed them they picked up new ones, presumably from the colony of rats that had previously been such an essential part of the roof's ecosystem. But their ears and necks (the cats', that is) were growing hair again and there was less scratching. Also they were putting on weight. The half-tester sagged a little lower each day.

I put down the rake and stretched to relieve my aching back. There was a great deal of simple satisfaction to be had from horticulture. The objectives were straightforward and their achievement, provided one was prepared to put in the work, presented no difficulties. So I thought then, in my state of prelapsarian innocence, not having read the chapter on neck rot, dry rot, white rot, smoulder, scab, rust, spraing, gangrene and club root, to say nothing of slugs, snails, caterpillars, flea beetles, wireworms, eelworms, leatherjackets and carrot flies. I wound up the hoses and put all the implements into the back of the Land-Rover. I had a glorious vision standing knee-deep in flourishing verdure in a few weeks' time, holding a basket laden with produce. As it was the second half of July I must not forget to buy onion and shallot seeds for planting next month.

The second half of July? Then today was – I made a mental calculation – yes, the twentieth. I had been so busy that for the first time in my life I had forgotten my own birthday. For nearly a whole day I had been twenty-seven without being aware of it. I leaned my elbows on the tail-gate and sighed. For a few hours I had also forgotten Burgo. We had made love for the first time three weeks after my last birthday. Not long ago he had said that we must remember to celebrate our anniversary. Such sentimentality is the glue of love affairs that lack reality.

'Bugger!' I fastened the tail-gate and kicked the rear tyre as I walked round to get into the driving seat. 'Bugger! Bugger! Bugger!' I slammed the door.

'What's the matter?'

I looked out of the window. 'Flurry! I thought you'd gone back with the others.'

He was standing beside the Land-Rover, his face, hands and clothes filthy with rust and cobwebs. I noticed that his latest stye was getting better. 'I've mended the greenhouse stove. It just needs a new top plate. Thady O'Kelly could make one. And the radiators need soldering.'

I had a brief pleasing picture of rows of seedlings, cuttings, tomato plants, a vine jewelled with grapes cloudy with bloom before I remembered that there was not a single whole pane of glass in the entire building.

'I'm afraid it would cost a lot of money to glaze it,' I said. 'It certainly couldn't be managed out of the housekeeping.' Flurry's expression became despondent. 'It *would* be lovely. Do you think your father might be able to afford to have it done?'

'Every time Dad comes home he says we'll soon have to move out and live under canvas with the tinkers. Once I went camping with the scouts at school.' Flurry shuddered. 'It was hell. So far we haven't had to but I'm working on a design for a tent with a chimney and drainpipes and a proper roof. And proper walls.'

'I suppose it wouldn't be a tent then. It would be a house.'

'Oh, yes.' For some reason this amused Flurry. He had a rich chuckle that was pleasant to hear. We were nearly back at the castle when he stopped laughing and said, 'What were you swearing about?'

'Oh, nothing.'

'It sounded like something.'

315

'I was cross with myself. But it's over now. I'm going to try to forget about it. We all do stupid things, I suppose.'

Flurry thought for a while. 'Dad says Timsy makes a profession of stupidity. What do you think that means?'

'I think he means Timsy pretends to be more stupid than he is.'

'Why would he do that?'

I thought for a while. 'I don't know. Perhaps because it amuses him. Perhaps he's bored.'

'When Liddy said she was bored Dad said it was because she had an empty mind. If she learned to think as well as feel she'd be much happier. Liddy said all she wanted was to fall in love and then she'd never be unhappy again. Dad said love was an overrated emotion, nearly always doomed to disappointment.'

As the possessor of a wife and a mistress conveniently under the same roof Mr Macchuin could afford to be disdainful of affection, I thought resentfully as I parked the Land-Rover in the old coach house.

'I think he must've said that because of Mummy being ill.'

My resentment was softened immediately.

The kitchen looked really rather attractive, I thought. Constance had washed up the picnic things and apart from Katty and Pegeen slumped by the fire everything was tidy. The flagstones were gleaming, the copper pans were polished to a high shine. The wild roses I had picked that morning and arranged in a lustre jug glowed against the snowy whiteness of the table. I could smell the fish pie cooking in the oven. Constance had unmoulded the egg mousses for the first course with only one serious casualty.

This did something to lighten my burden of self-reproach, which had weighed so heavily recently. I ought to check the drawing-room fire. I remembered to duck the chain on my way to the hall which further improved my mood. Flurry had run ahead of me. I was just in time to see the drawing-room door open and someone's arm come out – I thought it was Flavia's – to yank him out of sight. I followed him in. I was surprised to see not only the two children but Liddy, Constance, Maud, Sissy and Eugene as well. They were standing in a group before the fire with glasses in their hands, smiling at me. Except Maud, who looked irritated.

'Happy birthday, Bobbie.' Constance came over to kiss me. She put a glass in my hand.

'Happy birthday, happy birthday!' cried Flavia and then they broke into the traditional song, all except Maud who sank slowly on to the sofa with an expression of acute suffering. Eugene sang loudly with a great deal of vibrato.

I felt foolish as one always does on these occasions, but also moved. 'Thank you all very much. How did you know?'

'Several people rang this afternoon,' explained Constance. 'They sent messages wishing you a happy birthday. Just a minute.' She fumbled in her sleeve for a piece of paper. 'I wrote down the names. Sarah. Jasmine. Oliver. And David. I thought the occasion justified raiding the cellar for real champagne,' she went on. 'Besides, Finn did say last time he was home that they needed to be drunk. They were laid down by my grandfather more than twenty years ago and apparently some of them are already past their best.'

'How did you get in?' asked Flurry. 'I thought no one was allowed in the cellar.'

Constance's cheeks became pink. 'I found the key the other day when I was looking in Finn's stud box for a pair of nail scissors.' She grew redder. 'Perhaps we needn't mention it when Daddy comes back. Unless he asks, of course. Then I shall tell him, naturally. I chose one I hadn't heard of. I hope it's the kind he keeps for the Hunt Ball raffle.'

I took a sip from my glass. It was deliciously rich. I glanced at the label on the bottle which stood on a table nearby. Krug Grande Cuvée! One of the most expensive champagnes in the world! I felt immediately guilty. Such a prince of wines ought to be drunk at the correct temperature with concentration and appreciation. It was already much too warm.

'It was such a kind thought,' I said, pretending to examine the label and then putting the bottle down further away from the fire. 'The most marvellous treat.'

'Of course we didn't have time to get you anything specially,' said Constance. 'But I want you to have this.' She handed me a small black box. Inside was a pretty ring set with garnets and seed pearls. 'It's of no value but it was left me by my godmother so it truly is mine to give away. It doesn't belong to the family.'

'It's beautiful,' I said. 'But, Constance, I can't accept it.'

'Please take it. I shall be so hurt if you don't. I've never worn it. It's too small even for my little finger.'

Her soft eyes were pleading. I put it on the ring finger of my right hand and kissed her.

'It's much too generous of you but I'll wear it while I'm here anyway.'

'Constance would give a beggar her best coat,' said Maud. 'You may call it generosity. I call it folly.'

'And I would like you to have this.' Eugene bowed, presenting me with a clear view of his rather grubby parting, and handed me a sheet of paper. I recognized Constance's writing. 'My spring poem. I shall be happy to translate it for you.'

'Thank you. I shall treasure it.'

'Rubbish!' said Maud. 'You'll stuff it in a drawer and never look at it again.'

'I made this.' Sissy held up a crown woven from leaves and flowers. 'There's meadowsweet for fertility, wood sorrel for sexual pleasure, thistle to cure jealousy, milk vetch for prophetic dreams. You must wear it till the moon sets on your name day for the pishogues to work.'

'Gosh!' I bent my knees so that Sissy could place it on my head. 'Thank you so much. That sounds an explosive combination. I'm not sure I'm quite ready for all that.'

'Nonsense!' said Maud. 'Modern girls are little better than tarts.'

'I'm sending for your present,' Liddy informed me. 'I'm afraid you'll have to wait a few days.'

'Really, it's too kind of you,' I protested.

'You'll have to wait for my present too,' Flavia explained. 'I've taken a photograph of each of the cats. But I'll have to finish the film and then get it developed. Some of them wouldn't stay still and I only got their back views but I hope you'll be able to tell which is which.'

I kissed her. 'What a lovely idea!'

'I haven't had time to think of anything.' Flurry looked grave. 'I *could* give you my knife for good.' He took this sacred object from his pocket and looked at it doubtfully.

'I'd rather have a ride in the train when it's finished,' I said.

He looked relieved and put the knife away.

At dinner I was not allowed to do any fetching or carrying but had to sit at the head of the table and be waited on. The thistles in Sissy's crown were scratchy but after a while I managed to forget how ridiculous I must look. Sissy had gone to town with the table decorations. Despite it being still light outside there were as many as six three-branched candlesticks on the table and between them and above them, like a jungle canopy, were bunches of gunnera leaves, some of them more than a yard across, which shrivelled into holes where the heat from the candle flames scorched them. Earwigs and black beetles launched themselves from the leaves to fall on to our plates.

'I brought up some white wine from the cellar to go with the fish pie,' said Constance. 'It's in the fridge. I'll go and get it.'

'Why is Osgar hugging Maria?' Flurry pointed to the window.

Liddy and Flavia rushed to look. 'You silly baby!' said Liddy. 'They aren't hugging, they're mating.'

'Come away, girls,' said Eugene. 'The sexual congress of beasts is a barbarous sight.'

'You should know,' said Maud.

''Tis Nature's poetry,' said Sissy, going to look.

'Oh, damn!' I said. 'I never thought of that!'

'The tone of your mind is too exalted,' Eugene suggested gravely.

'Supposing Maria has puppies?'

''Tis a bucket of water that's needed,' said Sissy, evidently tiring of quite so much poetry during dinner. She lifted her panniered skirts to reveal slim strong hairy legs and plastic sandals and skipped out.

'If Maria does have puppies,' said Flavia in a voice of awe, 'it'll be the second time today that my prayers have been answered. And that's never, ever happened before, even when I've asked for really easy things like not having to do gym or Peg Loony not being foul to me in break.'

'Who is Peg Loony?' asked a voice from the door.

'Daddy! Oh, my darling daddy!' Flavia ran to fling herself at the man who stood surveying his own dining room, a range of expressions (but one of surprise predominant) on his handsome face.

TWENTY-EIGHT

I was immediately conscious that Mr Macchuin's arrival was ill timed. He had looked at me once and turned away but not before I saw astonishment in his eyes that his place at the head of the table had been appropriated by a perfectly strange woman. Matters would hardly be improved when he learned that I was his new housekeeper. I pushed back my chair and stood up, feeling horribly awkward.

'Finn! Darling!' Constance had come back into the dining room. 'How wonderful!' She embraced him as effectively as anyone can when holding a bottle of wine in each hand. Flavia was still clinging tightly to his waist. 'Why didn't you let us know?'

'I tried to ring as soon as I was sure I could get away but the line was always engaged.'

He was not at all what I had expected. I had imagined . . . what, precisely? A bon viveur, with his cellar, his appetite for urban life. Something of a rake too, keeping a mistress and a wife in the same house. I had pictured the expansive girth, flushed cheeks, perhaps even the red nose of an intemperate sensualist. This man was tall, spare and pale-skinned with short black hair turning grey. I guessed his age to be about thirty-five, perhaps even forty. He was wearing a dark suit and a plain blue tie. By contrast with the rest of us he looked tidy, respectable, conventional, almost ascetic.

'Sorry. That was me,' said Liddy, coming up to kiss her father. 'I was ordering something for Bobbie.'

He put his free arm round her. 'How was the end of term? I don't suppose you got the Latin poetry prize?'

'You know they don't teach Latin at our soppy girls' school, Dad.'

'And much you care about it. You're looking magnificent.' He turned her round so he could examine the skimpy yellow shift cut

320

low in the front and even lower at the back. 'Isn't it rather cold?'

Liddy giggled. 'I'm OK sitting near the fire.'

Mr Macchuin glanced at the chimneypiece. If he noticed the absence of the pile of old newspapers, shoes and a broken fan heater that had graced the hearth before and the brightness of the brass fender, tongs and poker that had previously been brown and sooty he gave no sign. 'Do we usually have a fire in July?'

'It's to dry everything out. Do you really like my dress? I put it on specially for Bobbie's birthday.'

'Is he the latest boyfriend?'

'Darling, you're hopeless,' said Constance. 'I told you all about Bobbie when you rang last.'

Mr Macchuin's attention was caught by the bottles Constance was clutching to her chest. He turned his head slightly to read the label. I thought he flinched but it may have been a trick of the light. 'Chevalier-Montrachet nineteen sixty-eight. Hm. You've taken to house-breaking, Con.'

Constance looked uncomfortable. 'I found the key in your room. I wouldn't have touched it normally, only it's Bobbie's birthday and she's worked so hard and I'm so grateful. We've been having lovely things to eat; she's such a marvellous cook and the house is so much cleaner. We've started to reclaim the old walled garden, the girls aren't drinking so much, we've ordered new hens; everything's different and so much better. Honestly, she's worked like a slave from dawn till dusk and you won't recognize the place . . .'

I could see this recital of my achievements was not having the effect Constance intended. Men are creatures of habit. They dislike change. Most of all, they dislike change that has taken place in their absence, without consulting them. Mr Macchuin's dark brows were drawing together over the bridge of his long, thin nose.

At that moment his attention was caught by the empty bottle of champagne. He walked over to the table to identify it. He opened his eyes wide and drew in his breath sharply.

'How do you do?' I said, walking forward with my hand extended. 'I'm Bobbie Norton.'

He shook it briefly. His eyes, grey and deep-set like Constance's but harder, met mine with a look that was not unfriendly exactly, but cool. He had a broad face with an angular jaw. It was easy to see, looking at him, that Constance would be a handsome woman if she lost a couple of stones. 'How do you do?' he said. 'It's good of you to put my household to rights so selflessly.'

'Not at all,' I said. 'It's good of you to pay me a salary.'

He continued to look at me. For a moment I feared he had recognized me but he only said, 'You're evidently a connoisseur of wine.'

'Oh, Bobbie didn't choose—' began Constance but whatever she was going to say was forgotten as Sissy burst in.

I felt a strong curiosity to see the modus operandi of this ill-assorted couple.

'Mavourneen!' Sissy's black eyes were bright with joy and she was undeniably fetching. She stood poised on tiptoe a moment before skipping in great bounds towards him, neck stretched up to kiss him on the lips. ''Tis burning like a fire in hell I've been to see you this long while. But in the dew this morning it was written that you'd be coming.'

He kissed her briefly then held her at arm's length, towering over her. 'We may all have to resort to writing in the dew if Liddy continues to run up the telephone bill. How are you, Sissy?'

'Pent up!' Sissy rolled her eyes in a way that would have made a tired man quail.

Mr Macchuin raised his eyebrows as he looked her up and down and said, 'Marie Antoinette was well known, I believe, for her excitable nature.'

'And who's she, I'd like to know?' Sissy's face darkened and she showed her teeth in a terrifying manner. 'Some hussy ye've been seeing in Dublin? Let this Mary Antonetty come here, tell her from me, and I'll scratch out her eyes and I'll roll her liver in oats and fry it in pig fat and I'll hang her by her hair from a tree . . .' She paused, panting with emotion.

'You stupid, ignorant creature!' said Maud. 'Marie Antoinette had her head cut off two hundred years ago.'

'*On diabhal!*' exclaimed Sissy. ''Twill teach her to lift her skirts to them that's above her.'

'I often think it has been a mistake to try to educate the peasantry,' Maud said to no one in particular.

'Hello, Maud, you're looking well.' Mr Macchuin went round the table to kiss the cheek she extended.

'I look terrible. You, on the other hand, contrary to the just deserts of liars, appear to be thriving.'

I saw, to my surprise, that she liked her son-in-law. Or rather, she could not help responding to him as a woman responds to a man whom she finds attractive. Her eyes shone as though a switch had been turned on.

He rested his hand on her shoulder. 'How's morale?'

'I'm irritable and bored. Bored half to death. I'd like to go the whole way. If I could get up to the roof I'd throw myself off.'

'You've never been a coward, Maud. Your resolution and will-power have always been an example to the rest of us.'

'I no longer wish to cut a fine figure. Even if I could.'

'Now who's a liar?'

Maud shook her head and smiled with an air of coquetry.

'Hello, Flurry.' Mr Macchuin walked over to his son who had been standing by the window, looking at his father with an expressionless face.

'Hello, Dad. Did you remember?'

'What?'

'The book about bridges.'

'Yes.'

'Is your case in the hall? I'll go and get it.'

'Wait a minute.' Mr Macchuin detained the departing Flurry by gripping his arm. 'How are you?'

'My styes are better. Bobbie bought me some ointment. I had a stomach ache last week.' He strained against his father's grasp but Mr Macchuin held on.

'It's a question that doesn't usually require such a particular answer, unless an absolute disaster has befallen you. You might say "fine, thanks" or "well, thank you". Then you ask me how I am.'

'How are you, Dad?'

'Much better for seeing you, my dear Flurry.'

Flurry's face broke into a smile. 'Really?'

'Really.'

'Can I go and find it now?'

'All right. Don't get my things in a mess—' But Flurry had gone.

'Hello, Eugene.' The master of the house approached his guest. 'How's the muse?' The two men shook hands.

'A little shy from time to time but it is her nature to be slippery. I subscribe to Yeats's view that in poetry it is the accident that charms and inspires. One must compose in an improvisational mode. The intention can never be more than merely admirable.'

'You mean you have to make it up as you go along?'

'Well . . . yes. I suppose that is what I do mean.' Eugene's eyes began to pop as he scented an audience. 'I could demonstrate the point by reading you my latest verses?'

'Thanks.' Mr Macchuin smiled. 'But you know what a blockhead

I am for that kind of thing. It would be casting diamonds before apes.'

Eugene demurred politely but did not press the point. I felt almost envious as I witnessed this nimble side-stepping of what was for me an almost daily duty: listening to the incomprehensible product of Eugene's spontaneity. Mr Macchuin was capable of diplomacy, it seemed, and this, too, was unexpected. Constance, with her frequent references to her brother's temper, had led me to imagine a man always flying in and out of moods, at the mercy of his own passions.

'Don't open that, Con,' he said pleasantly, as he saw his sister preparing to get to work with the corkscrew on the Chevalier-Montrachet. 'It won't be cold enough. What are we having?'

'Fish pie with frozen prawns!' cried Constance in accents of joy.

Whatever his thoughts, he kept them to himself. 'I'll find something that doesn't need to be too chilled.'

While he was in the cellar I busied myself at the sideboard, serving the fish pie, peas and purée of carrots, feeling embarrassed by this paltry demonstration of my much-vaunted cooking skills. I slipped into a chair beside Flurry at the far end of the table and encouraged him to eat the four peas I had given him while the others discussed Dublin and mysterious things which sounded like so many sputum-rich clearings of the throat and of whose nature I was ignorant except that I divined them to be assemblies of eccentrics, given to extreme opinions. This should have given me the clue. Now I know they are spelled Oireachtas, Dáil, Seanad and Taoiseach.

My silence went unnoticed. I was happy to amuse myself by studying the painting that hung over the fireplace. It was a portrait of a woman in the manner of Gainsborough, her hair elaborately curled and powdered, her grey dress edged with wonderful lace. In one hand she held a posy of flowers. Her other hand rested on the open door of a birdcage. The eyes were beguiling, the mouth open fractionally as though she was poised forever on the edge of laughter. It seemed to me a sublime piece of work. If there had been money to spare I would have suggested having it cleaned. I spent an enjoyable ten minutes repainting the horrible brown walls green in my imagination and cutting into small pieces the 1940s utility sideboard on which stood a hot-plate, a repulsive aesthetic movement vase decorated with storks and an equally horrible art deco chromed-metal lamp . . . I realized that the fish pie had been eaten down to the last anaemic rubbery segment of prawn and that it was time to fetch the apple tart.

Afterwards I made coffee and took the tray into the empty drawing room. I could hear laughter coming from the dining room. I decided to leave them to it and retire early to bed. As I crossed the hall towards the stairs my reflection in the looking glass made me jump back with a cry of dismay. I had forgotten that I was wearing Sissy's coronet of weeds.

'You mustn't take Finn's temper too seriously,' said Constance.

'Daddy didn't realize it was your magazine or he'd never have said anything,' said Flavia, who was sitting between us in the front of the Land-Rover as we drove back from a neighbouring farm, having collected the new chickens.

'Let's forget all about it,' I said politely. 'I have.'

This was a lie. I was still smarting. We had been at the breakfast table when Mr Macchuin had come downstairs, looking much more relaxed in an old jersey and corduroys. I was pouring coffee while Constance put butter and marmalade on a slice of toast for Eugene. Liddy was reading *Vogue* with rapt concentration and failed to notice her father's arrival. Smiling, he looked over her shoulder. Then his smile vanished.

'Liddy, really! After all we've said on the subject!'

Liddy looked immediately guilty and tried to close the magazine but Finn put his hand on the page. '"Summer's Super Diet",' he read aloud. '"For lunch the weight of an egg in raw fillet steak plus two glasses of juiced watercress and five asparagus spears . . ." Liddy, this is as absurd as it's dangerous.' He turned some pages. '"The step-by-step guide to flawless beauty." Honestly, why do you read such junk? The silliest novel would be better than this. Look at this woman!' He prodded a photograph of a girl advertising a nightdress. 'She's so thin, she looks as if she's dying of a horrible disease. This is a vile attempt to make women think that nothing matters but appearance.' His anger seemed to mount. 'How dare you women demand equality when your minds are swimming in this slush? I won't have such trash in the house!'

He walked over to the fireplace and held the magazine over the flames.

'If you burn it I'll never forgive you!' Liddy was large-eyed and tense with temper. I saw how alike they were. 'I don't *care* if it's trash. It makes me feel happy when I read it. Anyway, it isn't mine, it's Bobbie's and you *can't* burn her things. I'm going to stay with her in London and I shall read exactly what I like and if I choose to starve myself to death, that's my business. You can't go away for weeks and come here just when you feel like it and . . . and tell me what to do . . .' She was losing control now. 'You don't want me to be beautiful because you're afraid . . . you're afraid . . .' Whatever it was she thought her father was afraid of I never discovered for she burst into tears and ran weeping from the room.

Mr Macchuin turned to look at me, his eyes fierce, his lips drawn back in an expression that reminded me of Osgar. 'You'd better have this.' He threw it on the table. 'Perhaps you'll be good enough to keep such stuff in your own room. I don't want my children contaminated by it.'

I was immediately furious myself, though I kept my voice under control and spoke with a cool contempt I knew would enrage: a technique I had learned when dealing with my father. 'It's a harmless fashion magazine, hardly pornography or a manual for heroin users.' I laughed disdainfully. 'And there's little chance that Liddy will find watercress or asparagus in Kilmuree.'

The technique was more successful than I had bargained for. I thought for a moment he might explode with temper for his face grew dark and he clenched his right fist. 'Don't meddle, Miss . . . whatever-your-name-is. Or you'll be sorry.'

He walked out before I had time to think of a provoking reply.

'It's because he's had such a time with poor Liddy,' explained Constance as I steered between the potholes. 'A year ago she started dieting and she ended up almost a skeleton. Anorexia nervosa, Dr Duffy said. She's been so much better recently. But Finn's still worried about her. I'm so sorry he was rude to you. He flares up and then he simmers down almost at once. But I, for one, hate being on the receiving end.'

'It certainly isn't pleasant,' I said.

I was experiencing a disagreeable combination of resentment and repentance. However he might behave with members of his family nothing could excuse rudeness towards someone in his employ. But I could imagine the anguish of watching one's beloved daughter slowly starving herself.

'Liddy seems pretty well at the moment,' I said. 'She had two helpings of kedgeree this morning before your brother came down.'

'Oh yes. I've been really pleased to see how she's been eating up since you've been doing the cooking. I'm afraid my food would make a slimmer out of the fat lady at the funfair. Look out!'

I jammed on the brakes as we rounded a corner to avoid running into three men who were walking along the track. They scrambled up the banks and disappeared over the top.

'Who were they?' I asked. 'They seemed rather anxious to get away.'

'One of them was Mickey Joyce. And I think the other two were Padraig O'Conner and Cahir Roohan. They did look a bit alarmed to see us. I expect they're shy.'

Their faces beneath the peaks of their caps had looked anything but shy to me. In fact I thought they looked furtive and up to no good but Constance probably knew better than I.

'I don't believe *Vogue* could do anyone any harm.' I returned to the former, more interesting topic. 'Anorexia springs from deeper causes than the influence of fashion, doesn't it? Men *like* to think women are dangerously superficial and venial. It makes them feel less threatened and inadequate. Also they feel better about the hours they devote to cars, football and breasts. But all the same, I wish I'd known.'

'How many more?' I asked, throwing another section of sawn sleeper on to the heap. The barn was full of the resinous smell of sawdust.

'Only five hundred and forty-six,' said Flurry with sanguine calm.

'Good God! When's it ever going to be finished?'

Flurry looked surprised. 'We've sawn one thousand, two hundred and fifty-three already over the last year. We're two-thirds of the way there.'

'How are the rails coming on?'

'Thady O'Kelly's waiting for more iron. He's used up every bit of the old fencing.'

I flexed my aching fingers. 'I admire your single-mindedness, Flurry, I really do. But I can't saw another stroke. Let's go and see how the new hens are settling in.'

I watched with satisfaction as the old brown hens scratched and pecked among the long blades of brilliantly green grass. Timsy, under my direction, had cleaned out and deloused the hen-house and already its occupants were growing more feathers and putting on weight. This may have been because Flavia now had charge of feeding them and giving them fresh water every day. The new hens were huddled together, unnerved by the journey in the Land-Rover and finding themselves in strange surroundings. They were plump and fluffy with black and white feathers and crimson combs.

'I'll check the eggs,' said Flurry. A moment later he took his head out of the nesting boxes to say, 'Eight. That's fifty-five per cent up on yesterday.'

'Nine,' said Flavia's voice and a hand appeared from one of the boxes, holding an egg.

Flurry was silent, calculating.

'Gosh!' I said. 'At this rate we'll be selling them at the market in Kilmuree.'

'Could that pay for the iron for the rails?'

'I'm afraid not. If we gave up eating eggs ourselves and sent every single one to be sold it might eventually raise enough money for the screws.'

'What are we going to do?'

I was touched by his assumption that we were in the railway business together but I had no answer to the problem. I was anxious to find money for other things besides. An automatic washing machine was top of the list. Katty and Pegeen washed every Monday. This required laborious loading and unloading of the old twin tub, which squealed like a pig being slaughtered as it flooded the floor of the laundry room with soapsuds. Eventually the lake ran out into the corridor and, with the addition of mud from the yard, was trodden over the kitchen floor. Almost the worst thing about the operation was the prostration afterwards of Katty and Pegeen. With reddened arms, wrinkled fingers and ringing ears they could hardly find strength to crawl to their chairs and were fit for nothing for the rest of the day, despite my gradual reduction of rations from the black bottle. But during the rest of the week they were more wakeful and achieved much more. After I had poured their taggeens there was always grumbling about stinginess. But these days they showed me little outright hostility. I suppose my behaviour was in accordance with their presumption about English ways. We had been bossing and bullying for eight hundred years and by now they knew what to expect.

'We'll find the money from somewhere,' I said to Flurry.

In the kitchen I cut up onions to roast beneath a leg of lamb. No rosemary, of course. When I had asked for herbs the greengrocer, Turlough McGurn, had patted my hand sympathetically. After several stand-up rows in which I had done all the rowing and he had beamed and chuckled, he treated me as though we were old chums.

'Is it for decorating the food you're wanting them, Miss Norton? The stomachs of the Irish'll not take to that kind of fancifulness, you'll find.'

This was the formula he fell back on with every request I made for almost anything but cabbages, carrots and potatoes. I could grow herbs in the walled garden. But a time and motion expert would disapprove of cycling a mile in the pouring rain for a sprig of thyme. The answer came to me as I was putting the meat into the oven. The front courtyard was paved with cobbles that swooped up and down in waves like a stormy sea. Against the walls on three sides were borders edged with bricks. They were sparsely and unattractively planted with Hypericum and clumps of mustard-coloured golden rod. I had several times thought the borders would be better done away with. Now I saw how beautifully they would lend themselves to a herb garden.

In each corner I envisaged a neatly clipped yew buttress. Balls of box would give the scheme definition and look good all the year round. Then in between them at the shadier ends I could plant parsley, mint, lovage and fennel. And along the sunny wall rosemary, thyme, sage, tarragon and dill . . . I was so fired by the beauty of this scheme that I was compelled to go at once to the courtyard to visualize my plan in situ. A howling met my ears as I crossed the hall. Osgar was back on his chain by the front door. But whereas before he had endured captivity with the silent passivity of hopelessness, now that he had tasted freedom and more particularly Maria he was no longer disposed to take things lying down. He strained at the end of his chain and gave vent to his feelings. Mr Macchuin was standing just out of Osgar's reach, regarding him with blackened brow.

'Who let this damned dog off his chain, I'd like to know?' he demanded.

I was sorry to have to quarrel with my employer twice on the same day. But on this occasion I was confident that I was in the right. I squared up to fight.

'I did. It's cruel to keep a dog chained up.'

'He's supposed to be a watch-dog, not a *cavaliere servente*. If Maria isn't pregnant it's no thanks to Osgar.'

'That would be unfortunate,' I said coolly. 'But it doesn't change the fact that it's indefensible to keep a big dog like Osgar without allowing him any exercise. If you don't want Maria to have puppies you should have her spayed.'

His face grew darker. 'How I treat my dogs is none of your business, Miss Norton, but in fact Timsy walks Osgar several times a day.'

I felt myself growing hot, on my own behalf as well as Osgar's. 'Timsy hasn't walked him for months. He's afraid of him.'

'Nonsense!'

'It's true!'

'He's savage and unfriendly. He's not a lap dog.'

'That's because he's had such a horrible life.'

We glared at each other. Mr Macchuin's eyes were cold, his lower lip jutted, his nostrils were white. He stretched his mouth in a grimace, trying to keep his temper and match my froideur.

'No doubt, Miss Norton, other people's customs and traditions mean nothing to you.' He took a deep breath and I read in this pause his struggle to keep England and the English out of it. 'It may interest you to know, however,' he continued, 'that there's been a black dog tied up at this door since the twelfth century!'

The pathetic fallacy of this argument inflamed me to the point of nearly losing control. 'If you believe that tradition justifies barbarous behaviour perhaps you think we ought still to be burning people for heresy and sending children to Australia for stealing loaves of bread?' I smiled annoyingly. At least that was my intention.

'You equate chaining up a dog with capital punishment?' He spoke equally coldly, though his jaw was quivering with anger. 'I suggest, Miss Norton, that you're confusing ethics with sentiment.'

'Oh, so you think cruelty is a matter of degree? Pulling the wings off flies is harmless fun but you jib at cutting off a man's head?'

'I think it's a matter of intention. I don't accuse you of cruelty when you step on a beetle.' He bared his teeth and I saw that he would have liked to accuse me of anything and everything.

'Thank you. And what is *your* intention when you subject this dog' – I pointed to Osgar which made him bark more fiercely than ever – 'to a life of misery?'

'Sophistry, Miss Norton! I deny his life is miserable!'

'Look at his back legs! The muscles are wasted. Besides having no exercise he's been starved of affection, companionship, proper food, warmth, all the things any living creature has a right to have. Everything, in fact, but that disgusting fish-meal. You think that can be right?' I heard my voice tremble and felt tears rise. My recitation of Osgar's wrongs had brought me to breaking point. I could be cool no longer. 'In England you'd be prosecuted for cruelty to animals!'

'Ah yes, in England!' His eyes flashed. 'You're well known to be a nation of animal-lovers and sentimentalists though it's never stopped you marching into other people's countries, plundering them for

330

your own gain and subjecting the indigenous population to vassalage and poverty!'

I began to shout. 'I refuse to accept personal responsibility for the British Empire.'

'What's happening?' Constance came rushing out. 'What's the matter?'

'Oh, yes!' Mr Macchuin stabbed the air with his forefinger and shouted back. 'That's English all right! That's English to the core, isn't it? Lloyd George took exactly that attitude when he drew up the iniquitous treaty that brought civil war to the whole of Ireland and has caused nothing but trouble ever since! He threatened war if we didn't agree to remain part of the *damned* British Empire, then he just sat back and let us get on with it!'

'You can't blame the English because *you* chose to fight among yourselves!' My ability to reason had been defeated by a rush of emotion. 'Anyway Lloyd George was *Welsh*!'

'Do stop, both of you.' Constance stood between us with her hands over her ears. 'What with Osgar barking and you two shouting, I feel as though I'm in Bedlam! Finn, how *could* you shout at Bobbie like that! When she's done so much for us! She can't help being English. You must apologize at once.'

Mr Macchuin jammed his hands into his trouser pockets and pressed his mouth into a hard line. 'If it comes to that she lost her temper first.'

'I did *not*!'

'No, please, *dear* Bobbie.' Constance laid her hand on my arm. 'Don't let's have any more arguing. It upsets the children.'

I felt immediately ashamed. But damn it! They were *his* children.

'There's no need for an apology.' I put up my chin. 'I shall go and pack my things.' I turned on my heel and went into the house.

'Bobbie, *please*!' Constance ran in after me. 'Don't leave. I'll do *any*thing. Take a day off, take a *week* off. I'll bring you all your meals on a tray, the children will be your slaves, Eugene will read poetry to you all day long . . .'

When I heard the anguish in her voice and saw the tears standing in her eyes my anger evaporated immediately. 'It's all right, Constance. I won't go if you don't want me to – unless your brother insists.'

She put her arm round my neck. I could feel her shaking. 'Of course he won't. I tell you it doesn't mean anything when he gets angry. Really, it's over in a moment.'

I kissed her. 'I'm sorry I lost my temper. Don't be upset.' I took several deep breaths to calm myself and looked at my watch. 'Let's try and pretend it didn't happen. I'll go and peel the potatoes.'

'I'll come and help with the vegetables. And we'll have a drink. I made Finn bring up some bottles of something decent.'

We scrubbed and peeled and chopped and soon we were talking and laughing about other things and it was as though the quarrel had never been. But I was aware that I would not be able to forget it. And that each time I saw Osgar chained I would be angry and it would get worse, not better.

It was a beautiful evening of cloudless skies and balmy breezes. Drinks were on the terrace. I supervised the taking out of chairs and tables but remained indoors myself, using as my excuse the construction of a dish of *poires belle Hélène* with tinned pears and melted bars of fruit and nut mixed with condensed milk for the chocolate sauce. The ice cream I made with powdered milk as Siobhan's yield was down again. It would have been difficult to invent a more nauseating concoction.

In the dining room I treated the corporeal presence of Mr Macchuin as so much empty air but was more than ordinarily talkative with everyone else so that I should not seem to be sulking. Also I had taken a little extra trouble with my appearance in order to boost any flagging of morale, should there be cold looks or bitter words. This turned out to be a mistake. Our world at Curraghcourt was sufficiently restricted to make the least alteration of behaviour or appearance a matter of universal fascination.

'You're looking surpassingly well this evening, Bobbie.' Eugene sent an approving glance down to my end of the table as soon as there was a lull in the conversation. 'I wish I could think it might be for my benefit but alas! To paraphrase dear Byron: When the sun set where was she? He was a Celt on his mother's side, you know.'

'I was so sorry to miss the reading,' I said. 'I was busy in the kitchen.'

'And you were in the bathroom for absolutely ages,' said Flurry. 'I wanted to show you my drawing of the funnel.'

'I haven't seen that dress before,' said Liddy. 'It looks very expensive.'

'It's just an old thing I've had for years,' I said. 'How's the holiday project going?'

'It's staggeringly boring. I like that new way of doing your hair.'

'You don't usually wear that goldy-brown stuff on your eyelids,' said Flavia. 'Are you going to a party?'

'Has no one in this family been told that it's rude to make personal remarks?' said Constance.

'She'll be hoping Michael McOstrich will call.' Sissy was wearing a sort of Heidi costume of peasant blouse, black-laced bodice embroidered with edelweiss and red dirndl skirt. She had a circle of rouge on each cheek and her hair was plaited into clumsy braids with loops and strands sticking out, as though the long winter evenings in a hut up on the high pastures with only a grumpy old Alm-uncle to talk to had driven Heidi to drink.

'Michael McOstrich?' I heard Mr Macchuin say. 'What's he got to do with anything?'

'Michael McOstrich makes me think of a fox,' said Flavia. 'I like the tufts of red hair that stick out of his ears and nose.'

'Sure he and Bobbie are sweet on each other.' Sissy pulled savagely at a lock of hair that hung over her eyes. ''Tis bokays and love letters he sends. He wouldn't do for me.' She assumed a superior air. 'He's a loud, roaring kind of man. He's quite likely to smash you wit' his fists if you don't do his bidding. She's welcome to him for my part.'

I was unable to keep silent any longer. 'Mr McOstrich and I are barely acquainted. I'm sure he's a paragon among men but he's certainly nothing to me.'

'Of course she doesn't care tuppence about that ignorant turf-cutter,' said Maud. 'The finery's not for his benefit. It's aimed at someone else altogether.' All eyes were immediately fastened on Maud with expressions of intense interest. She paused to light a cigarette, evidently delighted to have created a stir. 'Don't tell me you didn't hear the two of them fighting like Kilkenny cats before dinner?'

'What a wonderful sky!' exclaimed Constance. 'The most stunning vermilion light, like a cooked lobster.'

No one even pretended to look.

'What *are* you talking about, Granny?' asked Liddy.

'It's plain if you take the trouble to observe, my child.' Maud smiled. 'Bobbie wants your father to know she doesn't care a stuff for his good opinion. She means to use every weapon at her disposal to make him sorry and acknowledge her power. She's banking on the fact that he, no less than other men, will be a fool when it comes to a good-looking woman.'

''Tis strange to me what all the fuss is about.' The breadth of Sissy's nose and the roundness of her nostrils was more pronounced in the middle of a great black frown. ''Tis a dull sort of dress, I'm thinking.'

'It's a wonderful dress,' sparked Liddy. 'Not everyone wants to look as though they've got a bit part in a play about Swiss prostitutes!'

'Girls, girls!' protested Eugene. 'Let us break bread together in a spirit of amity. Gross words ill become the lips of the gentler sex: "like blushing buds, like curls of rose, issuing their charge of honey . . ."'

'What the feck's he on about?' demanded Sissy.

'If everyone's got their particular fixation off their chests,' said Mr Macchuin, 'perhaps we might have a sensible conversation?'

The door opened and Pegeen announced in her screeching, whistling voice, 'Ladies and gents and Sissy McGinty, Michael McOstrich is come.'

TWENTY-NINE

'Just give each row a few minutes with the hose, would you,' I instructed Constance, 'while I shovel on the muck? I must say, Ireland's reputation for non-stop belting rain seems quite undeserved. Apart from the night I arrived it's been positively balmy.'

The sky was veiled with high, thin clouds; the air was fresh. I had pruned two more apple trees and discovered translucent red and black globes on the overgrown currant bushes. Already there was in the walled garden a satisfying suggestion of things being reclaimed, regenerated, a promise of fruition.

'I hate to destroy a happy illusion but I'm afraid this is something of a record. May was a deluge and June wasn't brilliant. Anyway, we'll enjoy the fine weather while it's here.'

Constance and I had cycled down to the walled garden to superintend the arrival of fifteen tons of manure, delivered by a farmhand who worked for Michael McOstrich. It had been the one good thing to come out of the previous evening as far as I was concerned, entertaining though it must have been for everyone else.

I had been conscious that everyone would assume Michael had come because of me. He looked quite different from the last time I had seen him. For one thing he was wearing a suit. It was made from thick brown tweed, speckled like a thrush's breast. His giant boots had been polished and his ginger beard trimmed. His aureole of flaming hair had been slicked flat, giving him the appearance of an exuberant red setter after a swim. As the evening advanced, I found it peculiarly fascinating to see first one clump of hair and then another break free of whatever unguent had restrained it and spring back into unruliness.

He had entered the dining room with a comparatively subdued, almost bashful air.

'How are you, Finn?' He had approached Mr Macchuin who had risen at his entrance. The two men shook hands. 'You're looking pale.' Michael McOstrich clapped his host on the back, making him cough involuntarily. 'Too much chasing the pen indoors, I expect.'

'I'm sure you're right, Michael. How's the prize herd?'

'You never saw a better sort of dairy cow than my Kerries. Some people say you can't beat Friesians but I say that's rubbish.'

'I'll take your word for it. How's the barley experiment going?'

'It'd make the hangman weep, the trouble we've had with it. The thin soil's the problem. But I'm not going to be beaten. It's not in my nature to buckle under. We'll be putting on a quantity of manure, rotted turf and seaweed in the autumn and we'll try the barley again. How are you, Maud?' He went round the table greeting each of us in turn. When he came to me he took my hand in his hot red paw and squeezed it until my bones crunched.

'Thank you so much for the flowers, Mr McOstrich.' I smiled at him through a mist of pain. 'Such beautiful roses.'

'You'd have to go a long way to find better roses than we grow at Ballyboggin.'

He stared at me with solemn bloodshot eyes until I was obliged to look away.

'Sit down, Michael,' said Mr Macchuin, drawing up a chair and placing it next to mine. 'I'll get you a drink.' It might have been my imagination but I thought I saw a sardonic light in my employer's eye.

Michael's great fist folded round the glass of whiskey Finn brought him as though it were a thimble, and while the others talked he sipped it without moving his eyes from my face.

Constance saw that I was discomforted by this unwavering examination. 'Bobbie, has Eugene told you about his new work? So exciting! He's thinking of writing a modern verse drama about Maeve. She was the queen of Connaught two thousand years ago. There are lots of poems about her, the most famous in the great Ulster Cycle, *Táin Bó Cuailinge*, written in the eleventh century.'

I tried to look intelligent and concentrate on what Constance was telling me but I could not manage to forget that I was the object of fierce scrutiny.

'Maeve was, I'm sorry to say, ah-hum . . . faithless. A Paphian,' said Eugene.

'What's that?' asked Flavia.

Eugene's eyes popped with disapproval. 'It means, dear child, a woman who enjoys the attentions of men – in their less cerebral moods.'

'A whore, you mean?' asked Sissy. 'Well, what of it? You're always so hard on us girls, Eugene. You want us to be locked up and put to hemming pinafores. What's wrong with a little bit of fun?'

'How well I remember when we had that frightful poetry festival.' Maud's eyes were shimmering with malice. 'You blacked that woman's eye because she asked Finn if he'd mind holding her book of lays while she took off her cardigan. Where was *your* sense of fun?'

'The dirty cow!' muttered Sissy.

This mention of his favourite subject jolted Michael from his reverie. 'Polled Shorthorns, now,' he mused. 'It's a breed for milking that can't be bettered, only by the Kerries.' As this remark seemed to be addressed to me I gave him a quick half-smile of acknowledgement. Perhaps encouraged by this Michael leaned sideways to put his face near mine and said in a confidential tone, 'We'll be putting the new bull in with the cows any moment, Miss Norton. He's bellowing fit to bust in the shed. There isn't an animal in Galway that has such stamina.'

I pretended to be listening to Eugene who was talking about dithyrambs to Flavia, who was reading a book. Michael took to chewing the ends of his moustache while he brooded on my face. Sissy sent me an angry glance. Surely she could not imagine that I was enjoying Michael's attentions?

'I'll make some coffee,' I announced, getting up. Again I caught Mr Macchuin's eye. I was almost certain that there was in it something annoyingly like amusement.

I was washing up peacefully to the snores of Katty and Pegeen when a shadow fell across the soapsuds in the bowl. Michael's shaggy head blocked out the light as he rocked gently in his boots. He thrust a letter into my rubber-gloved hand and bolted from the kitchen.

Dear Miss Norton [it said],
    Hoping this finds you, etc. Would you do me the honour of stepping out with me Wednesday next? It is said you cannot do better than Connemara women for eyes and figure but I admire your yellow hair more than I can express in words.
    Yours sincerely, M. McOstrich

P.S. I shall wait for your answer.

337

I sat down at the kitchen table to scrawl an immediate reply.

Dear Mr McOstrich,
Thank you so much for your invitation but my duties here
prevent me from accepting it. Could you let me have ~~ten~~ [I
crossed this out] fifteen tons of cow manure? I should be
very grateful.
Yours sincerely, Bobbie Norton

I took the coffee into the empty drawing room, propped my
answer on the tray and went to bed before the others came in.

'Poor Michael,' said Constance, absent-mindedly watering the path,
Maria and the trug full of red- and blackcurrants as she reflected on
the previous evening. 'He looked so crestfallen after dinner. He asked
me if I ever let you have the evening off.'

'What did you say?'

'I said the terms of our agreement strictly prohibited time off
except to go to church on Sundays. But I don't know whether even
that will discourage him. He's used to having his own way.'

'He's not the only one.' I was thinking of Mr Macchuin.

'You mean my brother,' said Constance with that quickness of
understanding for which I so often failed to give her credit. 'Ah, but
I was meaning to tell you. While you were making breakfast this
morning Finn gave Timsy a terrific ticking off for not walking Osgar.
He was so severe I was quite taken aback. And I'm to make an
appointment at the vet's to have Maria spayed. Sissy's out walking
Osgar at this moment on Finn's instructions.'

I felt a sense of gratification. It was enough to be acknowledged right. I would not expect anything so magnanimous as an
apology.

'Have you made the appointment? At the vet's, I mean. Because
we ought to take some of the cats at the same time.'

Constance looked surprised. 'Cats? You mean the ones that live
on the roof?'

'There was a litter born yesterday. Two tabbies and a black-and-
white. Adorable.'

I did not say that I had made a bed for their mother to give birth
in in the bottom drawer of my dressing table, in case Constance
thought I had taken leave of my senses. She was a poor old sack of
bones – the cat, that is – with a running nose and gummy eyes, but

we had put her on extra rations and she purred ecstatically most of the time. Flavia was now dividing herself between Violet's bedroom and mine, reading *The Phoenix and the Carpet* to her mother (which I had recommended, knowing it to be a cheerful story) and worshipping the kittens.

'It's such a pity that the drive runs through this garden.' I surveyed the potholed track with disfavour. 'It ruins the symmetry.'

'Until a few years ago everyone used the road through the woods. I still do, sometimes. I like driving through the tunnel of trees. It's just a bit longer that way.'

'But perfectly usable?'

'Oh yes. Actually in winter it's better because its surface has been stoned. This track's nothing but a bohireen.'

'What's that?'

'It means a path rather than a proper road.'

'Suppose we shut those gates at the far end? Then everyone would have to follow the old road.'

'What a good idea. But you'll never get Timsy to go all the way round. It was he who took to driving through the walled garden in the first place.'

'We could put a chain and padlock on them. And hide the key. And for now we can fasten them with twine.'

The gates were wedged open with tussocks of grass, stones and accumulated mud. It took us some time to dig it all away so we could close them.

'Look at that.' I pulled at a strand of ivy to expose the stone face of a man to the right of the gates. 'This is a fine bit of carving. Much too good to be hidden.'

We cleared away the rest of the ivy. The face belonged to a robed figure, roughly three feet high, standing in an arched niche in the wall. Carved in the smooth semi-circle of stones above were the letters S-T-F-I-A-C. The rest had been worn away.

'I never knew it was here,' exclaimed Constance. 'It's been hidden for at least thirty years.' She ran her fingers inside a circular hollow at the statue's feet. 'This is a stoop for holy water.'

'Perhaps it's a good omen for our project.'

'It can't do any harm anyway.' Constance bent to pick the flowers of the cinquefoil that grew by the wall. She placed them at the saint's feet, then laughed apologetically. 'Of course it's just superstitious nonsense but old habits die hard.'

I added some pink-splashed trumpets of bindweed. 'And we need all the help we can get.'

After tying up the gates with an elaborate system of knots we returned to the serious business of cultivation.

'When we go back I mustn't forget I promised Eugene I'd order him some books from Dublin about Queen Maeve.' Constance sprayed water on to the seed packets by mistake. 'I daren't ask Finn if he has anything in the library. There was what's known as an "ugly scene" a while ago when Eugene took some of Finn's books into the garden and forgot to bring them in. Of course it rained. Finn doesn't always understand what it means to have so much of one's psychic space taken up by the demands of creative composition.'

This reminded me that I still had in my possession the gardening book which must be returned at a suitable moment; that is, when its owner was elsewhere. I could rearrange the bottom shelf so that the absence of the cookery book, which I intended to hang on to, would not be noticed.

'You were going to tell me about Eugene; how he comes to be living here. If you think he won't mind?'

'Oh dear, no. He has the most open, transparent nature. And he writes poems about it all the time. Besides, he's so fond of you.'

'Is he?'

'He said only this morning what a delightful addition to our circle you are.'

'How kind of him.' I felt guilty immediately that I generally found Eugene either absurdly pretentious or annoyingly self-centred. But now I knew he liked me I was prepared to acknowledge that there was a gentle chivalry about him that was pleasing. He stood up when I came in even if he had until that second been fast asleep. He treated me to his views on life and literature and listened respectfully to my replies. Altogether he treated me with a careful courtesy that must rarely be a housekeeper's lot. He never shouted, raved, looked black or clenched his fists.

'He said – what was it exactly? – yes, he perceives that you have some secret sorrow. He's terribly sensitive to the pain of others, which is rare in a man, don't you think?'

'Certainly.' I smiled but secretly I was mortified to discover that my unhappiness had been so plainly written on my face that even a complete id— someone as introspective and disengaged from the world as Eugene had detected it. I thought I had been hiding it rather well.

'It makes it worse that a man of such rare qualities should have

340

been so let down.' Constance gazed into the middle distance, inadvertently watering my boots as she talked. I turned off the tap. 'Two years ago he fell in love with a pretty young girl called Larkie Lynch. She was Miss Potato Marketing Board of West Galway and all the boys of Kilmuree were after her. Eugene asked her to marry him, although he was quite a bit older and really they had nothing in common. It's clear now she wasn't at all in love with him. I don't like to think badly of people but I'm afraid' – Constance lowered her voice though there was no one to hear us – 'she was marrying Eugene for his money.'

'I didn't know he had any.'

'Well, it isn't much, just a cottage and a small allowance left him by an aunt a few years ago. It meant he could give up being a schoolmaster which he hated and survive financially by giving a few private lessons. The rest of the time he could concentrate on his poetry. I suppose it must have seemed like affluence to a girl like Larkie whose family has always been poor. Anyway, she agreed to marry him. The day was fixed and Eugene bought a new feather bed and had the kitchen redecorated.'

'Making no secret of his priorities.'

'What?'

'Never mind. Go on.'

'He planted his garden with love-in-a-mist and made a little house with his own hands for a pair of doves. He ordered a trap and a white pony to take Larkie to the church and had it garlanded with flowers.' Constance's eyes were full as she related these details. 'When the day came he put on the wedding clothes he'd had made specially, copying them from a painting of Aubrey de Vere, and walked down to the church. He waited by the altar for three hours but the bride never came.'

'That was cruel of her!' I made an inner resolve to be kinder about Eugene in my thoughts from now on.

'I knew you'd feel for him. When I told Finn he said what did Eugene think he was doing trying to marry a girl half his age who had no education and would bore him to death in a week. He said it was obvious that Eugene had his own libido to thank for getting him into such a mess and he'd had a lucky escape. You see, it's what we were saying, most men are incredibly unsympathetic.'

Certainly Mr Macchuin seemed to me the most unsympathetic man I had ever met but naturally I did not say this to his sister. 'So what did Eugene do then?'

'He made a little speech of apology to the congregation, half of whom had already got tired of waiting and gone away. It didn't help to have been jilted in front of everyone he'd ever known.'

'I'm sure it didn't.'

'Then he went home and stopped the clocks at the hour when the marriage should have taken place. He refused to see anyone and shut himself up alone with his grief. Every day since then he's put on his wedding clothes.' This explained Eugene's strange smell. 'It's to remind himself of the duplicitous nature of Eve. The wedding breakfast was left on the table until it was eaten by mice, down to the last currant.'

I wondered if Eugene had got the idea from reading *Great Expectations*.

'Did he ever find out what happened to the treacherous Larkie?'

'It's common knowledge that she went to America with the money Eugene gave her for her trousseau. With Sam O'Kelly, the black-smith's son. Apparently he and Larkie were sweethearts from child-hood. I don't know if Eugene knows. Naturally I haven't mentioned it.'

'So what put a period to his solitary existence?'

'It was Father Deglan's idea. He thought Eugene might accept an invitation from Finn. We're still shockingly feudal in these parts and dreadful though the food here is – was, before you came – some people still consider . . . You know, they like to be asked to the castle.' Of course she was not going to admit, even to herself, that pure snobbery had brought Eugene from his hermit's cell. 'Eugene came to dinner last November. There was a bad storm that evening and several trees came down across the drive. We were completely cut off so he stayed a few days. And somehow he never went back.' I thought I had kept my expression entirely neutral but Constance added, a little defensively, 'It's so convenient for us to have another man about the place with Finn away so much. We're so remote. Even in Connemara there's sometimes trouble.'

'Trouble?'

'Oh, you know.'

'You mean, the IRA?'

'We don't really like talking about it. But there are strong feel-ings. These days it's as much about territory and political power as religion and nationalism. I hate it! It's all wrong, so much killing and misery. But it's in the blood of the Irish. I sometimes wonder if we'll ever stop fighting. What would the lads do if they didn't have secret armies to belong to and guns to smuggle and ambushes and bombs to make? They wouldn't want to be clerks and bus drivers and insurance salesmen after all that swaggering. Ezra Pound wrote a very good poem about it.' Constance began to recite:

'The problem after any revolution is what to do with
your gunmen
as old Billyum found out in Oireland
in the Senate, Bedad! Or before then
Your gunmen thread on moi drreams . . .'

As I stood listening I tried to imagine Eugene protecting us against men in masks, with guns and evil intentions. It was not easy.

'"I've got the world on a string, I'm sitting on a rainbow,"' Liddy sang along with Frank Sinatra. We had brought the gramophone and a selection of records up to Violet's room. 'Mummy used to love this song.'

'What else did she like?' Flavia was sitting beside Violet, giving her spoonfuls of puréed strawberries.

Flavia remembered little about her mother. Though she had been four at the time of Violet's stroke she seemed to have blotted out most memories of her childhood before then. Her mother's sudden departure into an unreachable world must have been hard to bear.

'I don't know.' Liddy lifted her thin shoulders in a shrug. 'Cigarettes. Racing. Clothes. She had lovely things. I remember one particular dress: black lace, a tiny waist and a full skirt. It's still in her cupboard. I'll go and get it.'

She rushed away. Though her conscience forced her to spend time in her mother's room, even occasionally to tend to her physical needs, Liddy was an unwilling nurse and was reluctant to talk about the time before Violet's illness.

A sunbeam was falling directly on to Violet's face. Because of the washing and moisturizing her skin had lost its flakiness. Her hair, formerly lank and mousey, was shampooed frequently these days and was a shining chestnut, exactly the colour of Flavia's. I went to the window to pull the curtain across to shield Violet from the glare. Glancing idly at the view, my attention was caught by two men walking in the park far below. There was nothing to wonder at in this except that their behaviour was shifty. They looked about them and seemed to be keeping as much as possible to the shadows of the trees. But when I asked Flavia to come and see if she recognized them, they had disappeared.

'She likes this pink stuff.' Flavia had returned to the bedside and was watching her mother's face intently as she spooned in more strawberries. 'When she's keen on something she makes a special noise. Like *ga-ga*. Listen.'

I stood still for some time trying to detect it but could distinguish nothing particular from the usual groans, sighs and inarticulate cries. Again I had deep misgivings about the course we had embarked on. Violet had put on weight and as a result was more difficult to lift. But she must be more comfortable – if she was capable of feeling discomfort. When in the care of Katty and Pegeen she had been left in the same position, always on her back, arms crossed on her chest. Now we turned her from one side to the other every two hours during the day. The bedsores on her bottom, heels and elbows were washed and dried carefully and protected with a barrier cream. They were already looking a little less raw. I had bought bags of disposable incontinence knickers from the chemist. Instead of disinfectant we used rose water and baby oil.

All this had to be an improvement. But the day might come when we had to concede that Violet would never be any better than she was now and that our efforts to stimulate her were in vain. Liddy, I suspected, might be secretly relieved that she need no longer spend dull hours in the sickroom. Flurry rarely came anyway, preferring to work on his railway. But Flavia . . . I felt a sensation of dread as I tried to imagine Flavia's reaction to such a crushing disappointment.

'Mummy.' Flavia bent over the bed. 'See if you can move your fingers in time to the song. Then we'll know you can hear it.'

I turned up the volume a little and we both studied Violet's left hand.

'What's going on?' Because of the music we had not heard the door open. Mr Macchuin looked annoyed. 'I can hear this racket from the floor below.'

'Hello, Daddy.' Flavia put down the strawberries and went to take his hand. 'It's Mummy's favourite record. We're trying to wake her up. It was Bobbie's idea. That's why we've moved the bed, so she can feel the fresh air on her face. And look how much prettier she is now we're washing her properly.' She pulled him towards the bed. 'We put Bobbie's Elizabeth Arden Eight Hour Cream on her every night and lipstick every morning. Liddy found it in her drawer. It's called Red Ice. It's a nice bright colour, isn't it?'

I winced inwardly to hear this frequent mention of my name. I had moved away from the bed and was busying myself with the spirit kettle, boiling water for Violet's coffee. Now I decided to turn it off and go downstairs but in my haste to get out of the room I knocked over the milk jug.

'Feel how soft her skin is now,' Flavia pleaded while I tried to mop up the milk.

A regrettable curiosity drew my eyes irresistibly to the scene.

Mr Macchuin stroked Violet's cheek with a forefinger. 'Very soft.'

An indecipherable emotion, a mixture of pity and tenderness – or it could have been anguish? – showed briefly on his face. For the first time I felt the pull of sympathy towards my employer. Seeing them together, he healthy and vigorous, she torpid and insensible, I thought I understood why he spent so much time away from home. It must be like tearing open a slowly healing wound to see someone you loved in this perpetual sleep that might as well be death. Nor was it hard to understand why he had succumbed to the warmth of Sissy's embrace. Misery makes one vulnerable to temptations one might ordinarily resist, as I knew only too well. In judging him I had been hypocritical.

'See how much better she is,' persisted Flavia. 'I used to be able to make my thumb and middle finger meet round her wrist. Now look.' She demonstrated that this was no longer possible. 'Bobbie makes her nice things to eat. You can't see her ribs now. And Bobbie cleans her teeth twice a day. And we talk to her about what we've been doing. I *know* she can hear me. She can't say anything yet but she will soon.'

Flavia stared at her father with large, anxious eyes.

'Darling.' Mr Macchuin put his hand on his daughter's head and stroked her hair. 'It might be that the area of Mummy's brain that's necessary for thinking has been harmed beyond repair. You mustn't hope for too much. We must go on loving her just as she is and be thankful that we still have a part of her. Believe me, darling,' he added as Flavia backed away from him, shaking her head, 'life doesn't always turn out as we want it to. We have to learn to make the best of it—'

'*No!* I'm not going to give up! Don't you *see*, there won't *be* a miracle if we don't go on hoping and praying and believing? That's what we were doing wrong before Bobbie came. We'd just given up.' Flavia looked at the shrine. Candles, their flames pale now in the bright light of day, burned between two egg-cups of wild flowers before the statue of the Virgin Mary. 'For the last week I've been coming up here every night at bedtime to pray to the Blessed Virgin to help Mummy to come back to us. I wasn't going to say anything about it because I thought you'd all tease me but you've *got* to believe. Promise you won't laugh if I tell you something very, very important?'

Mr Macchuin sighed, then smiled, rather perfunctorily. 'I promise.'

'And do you promise, Bobbie?'

'Yes, I promise.'

Flavia's expression became tense with emotion and she lowered her voice almost to a whisper. 'Two nights ago the Blessed Virgin cried. Her cheeks were wet. I could see them winking in the candlelight. Honestly, Daddy, it was a miracle! And I know what it means! I *know* Mummy's going to get better.'

'Sweetheart.' Mr Macchuin took her by the shoulder and spoke seriously. 'What we call miracles are just happenings that we can't explain in scientific terms. You mustn't believe everything that the nuns tell you. They're good women, most of them, but simple-minded and superstitious. Why should God choose just to make Mummy better? Why not cure all the people in the world that are crippled or sick? What you saw on the statue's cheeks was probably condensation. The warmth of the fire reaching the cold of her china face. She's just a piece of clay, darling, nothing more—'

'I knew you wouldn't believe me!' Flavia's eyes were welling and her lips were quivering. 'I know you think it's all bunkum, Daddy, but you'll see I'm right – and never mind that you don't believe because *I'm* going to believe enough for both of us, and then you'll see – you'll see . . .'

Flavia was made speechless by weeping and ran from the room.

Mr Macchuin sighed and pressed his hands to his forehead. I felt despair. I knew the blame for this would be laid at my door and also, which was worse, that I deserved it. He dropped his hands to his sides and stared at the vase of wild white butterfly orchids beside his wife's bed and at the photographs of the three children we had pinned up on the walls, before turning to give me a long look through narrowed eyes.

'I suppose' – he cleared his throat and thrust his hands into his pockets – 'to be fair, I must assume that this meddling was begun with good intentions, Miss Norton, however ill conceived the plan.'

How prosy this man was! Not for him plain words like 'I expect you meant well' or 'Probably you thought you were doing the right thing'. He spoke in fluent rounded periods, like a mayor addressing his corporation. I was to be rebuked. And because he was paying me I was supposed to submit. I was damned if I would.

'Yes, you should assume that. What other motive could I possibly have?' I spoke calmly and mopped the wet table-top energetically to avoid looking at him. 'It would have been far less trouble to continue to feed Mrs Macchuin gruel and cold water and to ignore all but her most basic needs.'

I glanced up to see a gleam of anger on his face like a crack in the wall of a volcano. He pressed his lips together before speaking. 'You are no doubt unaware of the advice of the consultant in whose care my wife was placed after she became ill.' This was half-question, half-statement. 'In his experience the severity of the haemorrhage, combined with her comparative youth, led him to think that a second stroke would be fatal. He advised us to give her palliative care only.'

'Constance did tell me that, actually.' I went to the basin to rinse out the milky cloth.

'But, despite that, you could not restrain yourself from interfering?'

'Look at her. Can you deny that she has made a remarkable physical improvement?'

He turned again to stare at his wife. 'I suppose she does look a little better.'

'A *little* better?' I was incensed by the meanness of this. 'When I first saw her she was undernourished, dirty, neglected—'

'Don't dare to suggest' – he removed one hand from his pocket to point a finger at me – 'that I have in any way failed to provide Violet with proper care.' His expression was a grimace of painfully suppressed rage.

'I *do* dare.' I threw down the cloth. 'She was unkempt and starving! Left to lie in the dark in her own urine and – and worse. And quite apart from the physical ghastliness, her life must have been a purgatory of loneliness and boredom. I've no idea how much she understands, how much she hears or feels. But if you're capable of imagining what it must be like, if she's even vaguely conscious, to be paralysed and left to the care of two drunken, incompetent women, you *might* be able to understand why I wanted to change things. Now, at least, she's well fed and properly looked after by, among others, her own children in surroundings that are clean and cheerful. What can possibly be wrong with *that*?' I was no longer calm. I was breathing hard and prickles of heat ran up and down my body.

'The only thing wrong with that is that it might have killed her!' he shouted. 'Did that *ever* occur to you, Miss Norton?'

'Yes!' I shouted back. 'But if it were me I'd prefer to be dead than living in hell!'

Mr Macchuin's eyes grew wide and he actually snarled. He clenched his fists, then folded his arms tightly across his chest as though to restrain himself from hitting me.

'*You'd* prefer! What gives you the right—how *dare* you presume—'

'It's not a question of right but of obligation!' I yelled. 'You don't step over someone dying in the street because you haven't been introduced. You were all too afraid to take the responsibility—'

'That does it! That *does* it!' He walked round in a circle, his eyes closed as though the sight of me would be too much for his self-control. 'You're like all women! You're incapable of minding your own business! You've turned my house upside down, taken over my children, bewitched my sister into thinking you're divinely omniscient; you've got all the men in the district slavering like dogs and you've probably got Maria pregnant into the bargain—'

The imputation that I was a female temptress was like a blow in the face. I hated him at that moment. But it served to restore my self-command. 'If she is,' I said freezingly, 'I think you will find that Osgar is responsible.'

'And now,' he panted, 'you're trying to murder my wife!'

I bowed my head coldly. 'Oh yes, in my moments of leisure. You, of course, being a *man*, have been attending to much more important business. While your sister and I have been struggling to look after your house, your three children, your wife, your mother-in-law and your mistress, *you* have been preoccupied by things that really matter.'

'How I spend my time is absolutely *no* concern—'

'What do you think, Bobbie?' Liddy waltzed in to her mother's room as though in the arms of an imaginary man. She was wearing a black lace ballgown of tremendous elegance. 'It fits me perfectly— Oh! hello, Daddy. I didn't know you were here.'

She stopped twirling and looked self-conscious. He stared at her and then at me, his expression changing from disbelief to fury and finally settling into contempt.

348

'So this is the way you spend your extraordinarily valuable time. Liddy, you look like a high-class courtesan. It's much too old for you. Take the wretched thing off.'

'You *pig*, Daddy! It's a beautiful dress. You don't like it because it's Mummy's and you can't bear—'

'Shut up, Liddy. I've heard enough female voices raised in accusation today to make me sorry I came home.'

'It was a lot nicer without you!' Liddy flung back before exiting with her head in the air.

He sent me a look of concentrated loathing. 'I just – hope – you're – satisfied,' he spat out before following her from the room.

Satisfaction was the last thing I felt. I was furious. He was a bad-tempered, domineering chauvinist; idle, profligate, irresponsible and no doubt worse things besides. I hated him. I despised him. But it was his house and they were his family. If Curraghcourt was travelling rapidly to hell in a handcart it was not my business to try to stop it. In addition to rage and exasperation I felt – though it nearly killed me to admit it – something like remorse.

'I'm sorry, Violet.' I lifted the sheet at the end of her bed to check that the hot-water bottle against her feet was still warm. 'I'm going to have to go away. It's impossible, I just can't live in the same house with your husband. I'll try and get Constance and Flavia to— My God!'

This last exclamation was forced from me as I glanced at her face. Her eyes were remarkable, the colour of stormclouds touched with amethyst. I knew this because they were open and staring at me.

THIRTY

I went downstairs, in a state of high excitement, longing to tell someone what I had just seen. But by the time I reached the hall I had changed my mind. I decided to say nothing about Violet to anyone. After staring at me for several seconds she had closed her eyes. They had remained closed despite my coaxing and pleading. Supposing I got everyone's hopes up and it never happened again? It would be better to wait and let one of her own family make the discovery. But there had been such meaning in that look! I felt almost certain there had been a mind behind those eyes, conscious and thinking.

What was I to do now? Constance would be unhappy if I left Curraghcourt. Her brother would be unhappy if I stayed. I cared only about her happiness but presumably his were the feelings that counted. Whatever the decision I ought to finish preparing dinner for everyone else even if my own turned out to be a sandwich at the nearest railway station.

Katty and Pegeen were busy at the table, the former laboriously cleaning silver at the rate of one teaspoon every five minutes, the latter peeling potatoes. Together they were grinding out a sentimental song in cracked voices, something about Ireland being a little bit of heaven. Maria and Osgar sprawled at their feet. Osgar had won his freedom by howling non-stop whenever he was put on his chain. He did not seem in the least grateful for liberty and an improved diet, slinking away whenever Flavia and I tried to pet him. He lived only for Maria, whom he followed slavishly about, but it was enough for me that I no longer felt miserable on his behalf.

Constance was standing at the sink, washing something in a bowl. I went over to see.

'Hello, Bobbie.' She threw me a smile over her shoulder. 'It's

350

Eugene's shirt. I have to be awfully careful with it. The lace is falling apart after two years of wearing it every day. I expect it'll need a few more stitches. There are places where it's all darn. Goodness knows what'll happen when it's too bad to mend.'

I began to push cooked carrots through a sieve to make soup. 'What's Eugene wearing now?'

'He's shut up in his room in his dressing-gown.'

'If he can take it off to have it washed without being metamorphosed into a cockroach or a pillar of salt I don't see why the shirt shouldn't be thrown away like any other piece of clothing that's finished its useful life.'

'Ah, but don't you see,' she said in a low voice so Katty and Pegeen could not hear, 'it has symbolic meaning.'

'Symbolic of what, exactly?'

'Of . . . um, I don't know.' Constance stopped stroking and patting the shirt to think, unaware that a blob of foam was clinging to one eyebrow. She pushed her hair out of her eyes transferring foam to the other eyebrow. 'A broken heart, I suppose.'

'If anyone else mooned about for two years, flaunting their grief before all the world, you'd think they were being ridiculously self-indulgent.'

'No, I wouldn't.'

'You would.'

'Yes, I would. But Eugene's suffering has been exceptional.'

'I don't think so. Everyone has to suffer. Think of Maud with her arthritis. Think what the children have gone through because of Violet. Your brother,' I added a little coldly. 'Every day people are enduring bereavement, sickness, bankruptcy, bad luck and unhappy love affairs. While they try to come to terms with their misery the least they can do is change their clothes. Besides, I don't believe Eugene *is* suffering. Actually, now I think of it, he's probably the happiest person at Curraghcourt.'

'Oh, Bobbie!' Constance's face with her Father Christmas eyebrows was a charming picture of contrition. 'How awful of me! I'd forgotten for the moment your own situation. That's because you always seem so cheerful even though your heart is breaking.'

'Do I?' My spirits rose on hearing this. 'It's not as bad as that. In fact, often I'm too busy to think about it. And much of the time these days I'm more angry than sad.'

'And so you should be. He must have been crazy to go back to his wife.'

I shook my head. 'The thing was, Constance, he'd never really left her. I'm not angry with him particularly, but I'm furious with myself. Everyone knows politicians have egos like phagocytes and that their bodies are vats of testosterone. Power and sex are the only things that matter to them. After all, it's necessary for their careers to be adept at lying and deceiving.' As I said this I realized that my vehemence betrayed a still smarting wound. But I had no desire to burst into tears. Thanks to time and hard work I had moved on a stage from absolute wretchedness. Slowly, steadily, I was unravelling the ties of love and desire that held me to Burgo.

'I expect you're right,' said Constance.

'I know I am. But never mind all that. Eugene should have told himself ages ago that Larkie what's-her-name was nothing better than a designing jilt and not worth shedding a tear over.'

'I suppose I have to agree.' Constance looked at the shirt, a sodden mass in the bowl. 'But at least he's not like other men. You must admit it's remarkable that after all this time, nearly two years, he's refused to look at another woman.'

'He's been looking at you.'

'Me?' Even in the poor light of the kitchen I could see that Constance had turned the colour of the soup I was making. 'Oh no, Bobbie, you're mistaken. He thinks of me as a sister.'

'Men *never* think of women as sisters. Unless they actually are, of course. Does he behave towards you in any way like your brother?'

'Like Finn? Not at all. There's no one like Finn if you're ill or in trouble but otherwise, if you don't really need him, you might as well be invisible. But Eugene's not like other men.'

'So you said.' I allowed myself to look sceptical.

'Well.' Constance began to be flustered. 'I should be sorry if he *were* interested in me – it would be dreadful for him to be disappointed twice – though I know you're quite wrong and he never thinks about me at all in that way—'

'Constance. Dear Constance.' I stopped sieving, folded my arms and looked at her. 'I think you ought to examine your own feelings a little more closely.'

'What? You mean . . . Oh, no! You think I'm in love with Eugene?' Constance laughed as she squeezed unappetizingly grey water from his shirt. 'Because of our common interest in poetry we spend a lot of time together, and we like the same kind of things. And' – her tone became defensive – 'I enjoy doing things for him, to make him happy. Honestly, would you call that being "in love"? I wouldn't. It's just being good friends. When I'm low, being with Eugene cheers me up. And when I'm happy he sympathizes so well with my mood that I feel twice as good. And when I see him hurt it's like being cut to pieces. I feel it here.' She clutched the wet shirt to her heart with rubber-gloved hands. 'I know people sometimes laugh at him and I want to kill them! That's all it is, Bobbie, just friendship.'

I said nothing but continued to look at her, smiling.

'Well, it's an unusual kind of friendship, I admit,' Constance continued. 'But every relationship's unique, isn't it? And when a man's as attractive as Eugene it's inevitable that from time to time one might get a little carried away in one's thoughts. It's his voice, I think, probably. There's no one in the world with such a beautiful voice. It could make the trees and mountaintops bow down like Orpheus's lute. It makes me shiver sometimes, it's so noble and dear and . . . when I shut my eyes and listen to it I could bear to die right then at that moment because he's there and that's all I want in the world . . . Oh, Bobbie.' Constance stopped and looked at me with tragic eyes. 'Oh God, you're right! I *do* love him!' She made a sound that was between a laugh and a sob. 'Only – only – I didn't want to admit it to myself because I know he still loves that little *bitch*, Larkie.'

'Oh no he doesn't.'

'How can you be so sure?'

'Because I can see it's you he depends on for his happiness. Your praise, your help, your reassurance, your sympathy. Your love.'

'He's never even kissed me.'

Constance's voice had risen with the strength of her feelings. The warbling behind us had ceased. I turned to see Katty and Pegeen motionless, a spoon and a knife raised apiece, craning their necks to hear.

'Let's go and give the hens their supper,' I suggested.

We watched the new chickens, who were now displaying all the arrogance of youth, steal the plumpest grains of corn from the older birds. We checked to see that Flavia was not in residence in the hen-house before resuming our conversation.

'What am I going to do?' Constance marched up and down inside the wire-netted corral while Maria and Osgar did the same without. 'How am I going to look him in the face now? I suppose the best thing will be to try to pretend everything's the same.'

'It can't be the same, though,' I pointed out. 'You've been brave enough to recognize your true feelings. Now he's got to do that too. My guess is that he doesn't give a damn about Larkie but he's absolutely terrified of being rejected twice. He'd rather be celibate for the rest of his life than go through that again. And he's nursed his wounded pride until it's as precious to him as a baby at the breast.'

'The poor darling.' Constance shook her head sorrowfully as she paced. 'Doesn't it make you want to weep in sympathy?'

'Oh, certainly. But that won't do much good. Has he ever tried to . . . make a pass at you?'

Constance stood still, thinking. 'There *was* one time, quite soon after his arrival, when we were alone together in the drawing room. Everyone else had gone up to bed. He said – I remember it perfectly – "Would you be offended to be offered the admiration and affection of a heart that has been pierced and drained of its life's-blood, my dear Constance?" It was the first time he had called me by my Christian name. Wasn't it a beautiful thing to have said?'

'Well, yes.' I remembered that I had thought Burgo's most trivial remarks to be witty *aperçus*. 'What did you say?'

'I don't remember exactly. Something about treasuring such affection and admiration all the more. He said, "Why so?" And I said – Oh, what an ass I was! – I said I knew that what he was offering was in the purest spirit of friendship. I wanted to reassure him that I quite understood that he was in love with Larkie Lynch.'

'You can't be blamed for that. When he'd made such a parade of his broken heart—'

'Oh, no, not a parade! It was absolutely genuine!'

'I mean, you were so conscious of the violence of his grief that you didn't want him to think you'd got the wrong idea.'

'Exactly.' Constance looked miserable. 'He was a byword locally for suffering and constancy. It was more likely that Father Deglan would take up pimping in Galway than that Eugene could ever be interested in another woman. He spoke so often of Yeats's lifelong unrequited passion for Maud Gonne. It seemed to have a great fascination for him.'

'Yes, well, Maud Gonne has always seemed to me a thoroughly vain and rather selfish woman who enjoyed stringing poor Yeats along. Anyway, what did Eugene say when you talked about the pure spirit of friendship?'

'He bowed and kissed my hand and went to bed. He did look a little gloomy, but then in those days he often did.'

'Has he said anything else of an amorous kind?'

'Well, he's paid me compliments. Once he said I was the only woman he'd ever met who came near to understanding the complex workings of his mind. Wasn't that dear of him? But I've always been careful to let him know that I considered our friendship to be something spiritual and sacrosanct.'

'Hm. Somehow you've got to make him see that a little down-to-earth physical contact would be acceptable. You could, of course, take the direct course of walking naked into his bedroom.'

'I couldn't.' Constance shook her head fervently. 'I absolutely could not do it.'

'No, well, I see that. I don't think I could either. Particularly not after all that talk about purity.'

'Besides, supposing you're wrong? Supposing he isn't interested in me except as a bosom chum?'

'Men don't make bosom chums of women. If they don't fancy them, frankly they aren't remotely interested in them. A woman who has no sexual potential for a man could be devoured before his eyes by wild beasts and he still wouldn't notice her.'

'Darling Bobbie, sometimes I wonder if you aren't a little prejudiced against men.'

'Ah, well, if I am, it means that the wool can no longer be pulled over my eyes. And that you can believe me when I say that Eugene only needs to be shown the way to have him galloping up the path to your door, all past loves forgotten.'

Constance smiled and I thought how pretty she was. A stray beam of light caught the russet tones in her soft brown hair and turned her clear skin to gold. Her eyes, her best feature, were a wonderful shade of deep grey. The drab, droopy skirt, holey cardigan and gumboots did nothing for her figure and general allure. The bushy eyebrows needed attention; for a moment I was again inspired to imagine a transformation but then I remembered that I would probably not be there to effect it.

'I don't expect it will be too difficult, now you know what it is you want.'

'You'll help me, Bobbie, won't you? You're so much more experienced with men.'

I winced inwardly at this but I knew Constance was entirely without malice. 'I'd be delighted to, if I'm still here. I'm afraid your

355

brother and I have had another row. He disapproves of what we've been trying to do for Violet.'

'Damn! I was hoping to have a word with him about that. Was he really angry?'

'He accused me of trying to kill her.'

'Good God, he must be mad!'

'Certainly in the American sense. I'm afraid we rub each other up the wrong way. It's a clash of temperaments.'

'But you'll make it up. I'll speak to Finn; make him apologize. You *can't* go.'

'I don't want to.' I looked at the distant mountains, now patched with gold and copper, their frowning aspect effaced by the sun pouring down their flanks, at the forest of trees on their lower slopes, untamed, as green as parsley. 'I love it here. I love the wildness, the remoteness. I love being with you and the children. I love feeling useful, being able to make a difference. And I love this marvellous old house, every inch of its damp, crumbling magnificence.' I turned to look at the massive walls of the castle. 'When I think of the hundreds of people who've taken shelter here and lived out their lives, I feel linked to them, to the past . . .'

I stopped, conscious that I was sounding rather impassioned.

'When I think of all your hard work and the difficulties with supplies, Father Deglan's bullying and Finn's quarrelling, it's clear to me you've had a spell cast over you,' laughed Constance. 'I can't believe my luck!'

Flurry came through the gateway that led into the courtyard. He was holding the saw.

I looked at my watch. 'I'm sorry, Flurry. I said four o'clock, didn't I? And it's nearly half past. Constance, would you mind finishing off the soup while I do some sawing? It only needs simmering for twenty minutes and then three or four spoonfuls of cream stirring in. Don't let it boil after that. Stick in a couple of bay leaves, would you?'

'Bay leaves?' Constance looked blank. 'Are they in the larder?'

'It's that tree with shiny leaves by the back door.'

Flurry and I put in a good three-quarters of an hour's work on the railway. I found the sawing easier now I was used to it. But there was still a large pile of sleepers to get through. Flurry was bolting together some metal plates. It bore no resemblance to anything like a train but he was calmly confident.

'Right, that's it.' I hung the saw up on its appointed nail. 'I must go and finish the cooking.'

'What's for dinner?' Flurry spoke with his pencil clenched between his teeth as he paused in the process of jotting down calculations.

'Roast loin of pork with prunes and mashed potatoes.'

Flurry's mouth became letterbox-shaped with disgust. 'Ugh, ugh, ugh!' He stamped around in the sawdust, unable to express his complete horror.

'You could eat the pork.'

'I never eat pork.'

'You eat it every day. It's what sausages are made of.'

'Is it?' He looked astonished.

'Yes. What did you think they were made of?'

'I thought they came like that.'

'Sausages are pigs' intestines, washed, of course, and filled with bread and scraps of meat. These days some butchers use a synthetic material because people don't like the idea of eating intestines.'

'No.' Flurry looked thoughtful but said nothing more.

On my way to the back door, I met Timsy who was walking purposefully across the courtyard to the apple store.

'We're low on milk again.' I gripped him by his greasy collar, Ancient Mariner style, as he attempted to slide away. 'Did you milk Siobhan this morning?'

'She's drying up now.' He tried to break free but I hung on.

'Miss Constance told me this morning Siobhan ought to be giving milk for another four months.'

'Ah, well.' Timsy looked cunning. 'God bless her, what Miss Connie knows about cows you could carve on the knob of a shillelagh.'

I did not dare to ask what a shillelagh might be.

'Did you milk her?' I persisted.

Timsy's eyes were fixed on something over my shoulder and he jerked his head suddenly sideways as though afflicted by a tic. I turned in time to see a booted trouser leg disappear into the bushes that grew plentifully around the archway.

'Who was that?' I asked.

'Nobody at all. Sure I milked the old girl at six as always.'

'I don't believe you. And there *was* someone there.'

'That'd be my cousin coming to tell me about my aunt who's at death's door with consumption. God save her soul, she buried six babies—' I took a step in the direction of the bushes and now it was Timsy's turn to seize me by the shirt sleeve, pulling it hard until I thought its seams would give way.

'Let me go!' A short struggle ensued. By the time I had broken free and reached the bushes, the owner of the leg had gone.

'All right, Timsy.' I returned to the attack. 'What's going on? Who are these men that wander about the place at all hours? I saw two skulking about today. They didn't look as though they were up to any good.'

'This morning, you say? That'd be some other cousins coming to console me about me aunt knowing I was fonder of her than a broody hen of her eggs—'

'I don't believe you've got an aunt. Or any cousins.'

Timsy pretended to look wounded but I was practically sure he was laughing at me. 'Well, now, Miss Bobbie. I was hoping to save your blushes, but the truth of it is, these men you've been catching sight of, they've all heard rumours of your beauty and now they're coming to see for themselves whether 'tis true or not.'

A grin almost broke through his assumed seriousness.

'I wonder you're not ashamed to tell such lies.'

'Who was it as told Michael McOstrich she wasn't allowed any time off?' Timsy allowed me a glimpse of his native sharpness. 'I heard it from one of my cousins—'

'Well,' I cut in ruthlessly, 'make sure you milk Siobhan this evening. We're down to our last quarter of a pint.'

Timsy tapped the peak of his cap to indicate respect and compliance, both patently insincere.

In the kitchen Pegeen was pounding the potatoes to atoms and Constance was putting crisps and peanuts into little dishes to accompany drinks before dinner. Olives were an undreamed-of sophistication in Kilmuree. Discreetly I fished privet leaves from the soup. I made the sauce with the wine the prunes had been simmered in, boiling it with redcurrant jelly and cream until it was thick. I put on carrots and frozen peas; the fresh ones had, as usual, failed to appear. I had made a lemon mousse for pudding which Flavia had taken much pleasure in decorating with blobs of cream and hundreds and thousands, making up with gaiety for what it lost in elegance.

Turlough McGurn had had a shipment of lemons from a mysterious source the week before and was selling them ridiculously cheaply provided one took a whole box. I was running out of things to do with them. We had already had lemon soufflé, lemon jelly, lemon meringue pie, lemon syllabub and Sussex pond pudding.

Dinner seemed to be more or less organized. It occurred to me that this might be my chance to return the gardening book. The gap left by the two large volumes I had borrowed was bound to be noticed, and sooner rather than later. I ran up to my room and took the *Golden Treasury* from my bedside table with feelings of regret for it had cheered many a bleak dawn.

In order to replace the book undetected it was necessary to reconnoitre. I crouched beneath the library window in a thicket of weeds (my ankles being painfully stung by nettles), then lifted my head slowly to peer over the sill. Mr Macchuin was not at his desk. I stood up cautiously and saw that the room was empty. I dashed back indoors and went into the drawing room, pausing at the door to the library. The prohibition against trespassing on this sacred ground was held in such general respect that I felt some trepidation. It had been different when I knew the grand vizier to be far away in Dublin. A bird twittered as it flew past the window and made me jump.

I opened the door. The temptation to tiptoe was almost irresistible. I was immediately glad I had resisted it, however, for I had not taken three paces across the floor when a voice said, 'May I help you, Miss Norton?'

Mr Macchuin was standing on the library steps just to the right of the window, in one of the only two places that had been out of my field of vision. He had both the ethical and strategic advantage.

'Oh.' I had banked on meeting him again in the bolstering presence of Constance and the children at dinner. The memory of our last conversation made me extremely uncomfortable. 'Thank you. I came to return this. I found it in the drawing room.'

At once I regretted the cowardly lie. He descended the steps and came towards me, holding out his hand for the book.

'You found it in the drawing room?' He expressed surprise with his eyebrows.

'Yes.' I felt myself grow warm. 'I'd have knocked but I didn't know there was anyone in here.'

'Was it you outside the window looking in just now? I saw a shadow fall across the floor.'

'It wasn't me.'

'I see.' For a moment I thought I saw the beginning of a smile before he frowned, examining the book's spine. '*The Golden Treasury of Vegetable Gardening*. Now I wonder who might have borrowed it? As far as I'm aware, none of my family knows a buttercup from

359

a daffodil. But perhaps they've been inspired by your laudable efforts in the walled garden?'

'Perhaps.' I attempted to match his coolness.

'In that case it would be a pity to discourage them, wouldn't it?' He held out the book. 'I suggest you return it to the drawing room for the crypto-horticulturist to consult when the mood takes him or her.'

He did smile then. I was at a loss to account for this lightning change of attitude. But I was not ready to accept what might possibly be a flag of truce.

'Very well.' I gave him a look I flattered myself was dignified and turned to go.

'Miss Norton. I wonder if you'd be good enough to listen to me for one moment.' I looked at him enquiringly. He had stopped smiling. He was standing with his back to the fireplace. I was struck by his remarkable likeness to the portrait over the chimneypiece, presumably an ancestor. 'Will you accept my apology for some rough words this afternoon? I was already harassed by some news in this morning's post and then, when faced by what seemed to me at the time unwarranted and dangerous med— interference, I lost my temper. I've since had time to reflect and I've come to the conclusion that I was . . . wrong to speak to you as I did.'

Apologies cost nothing and may not be sincere but I realized that this obstinate and imperious man would have had to wrestle hard with his natural inclination to dictate in order to make one. I relaxed my froideur a fraction.

The man in the portrait had the same straight nose, high cheekbones, strong chin and firm mouth, above which was a clipped military moustache. This luckily Mr Macchuin did not have. Nor were the eyes the same. Those of the ancestor were satisfied, autocratic. Mr Macchuin's were – for the time being – conciliatory.

He cleared his throat. 'I'm sure you meant well' – he must have seen me stiffen for he added quickly – 'and I admit the possibility that your course of action may be the right one.' He walked away from me over to his desk and picked up a glass paperweight, which he passed from hand to hand as though relishing its coldness. 'I've been thinking about what you said about preferring death to a life of such . . . privation. Though Ireland is struggling to bring its ideology into line with the rest of Europe, ours is still a deeply religious culture and such a view, as you can imagine, is unorthodox. I may not be a practising Catholic but we are all, I suppose, influenced by the ideas that surround us from our birth. Our instinctive responses are the product of our early teaching however much we may strive to override them by rational thought.' He began to throw the paperweight from hand to hand as though weighing his words. 'When I asked myself if I would choose to live as Violet has lived for the last four years, I knew the honest answer was that I'd prefer to die.'

I was so surprised by this handsome admission that I nearly blurted out the news about Violet opening her eyes. But I thought better of it immediately.

'Yes,' he continued without looking at me, 'and in acknowledging that, I then had to ask myself what I might have done to alleviate a life that was worse than death.' He would have made a jolly good headmaster, I thought, able to deliver off-the-cuff lectures in well-constructed sentences. 'I ought to have appointed more suitable custodians for her care. Katty and Pegeen, though unquestionably loyal, were not fit companions. I ought to have done more. I make no excuses.' He screwed up his eyes for a moment as though even thinking of those extenuating circumstances – lack of funds, I supposed, and a typically male reluctance to face up to painful predicaments – grated on his nerves. He shook his head suddenly as though trying to throw off thoughts that tormented him and put down the paperweight. He leaned back against the desk, both hands gripping the edge. 'Everything that you can do for Violet, Miss Norton, I shall welcome. I accept full responsibility for the outcome. I wish you'd let me know if there are any additional expenses to be met.' He smiled again, rather sadly. 'I suppose Elizabeth Taylor's Twenty-Four-Hour Miracle Lotion doesn't grow on trees.'

'No.' I smiled back, forgetting hostilities for a moment. 'But Pond's Cold Cream will do just as well. What we do need, though, is an automatic washing machine.'

'An automatic . . . Don't we have a washing machine?'

'Yes, but it's ancient and hopeless and wastes hours of Katty and Pegeen's time. Violet's sheets need to be changed every day. Sometimes more than once. There are good ones on the market these days that will soak, wash, rinse and spin in the same drum at the push of a button in a tenth of the time.'

'The same drum? Really?' he repeated. I could tell he had no idea what I was talking about. 'How much might such a piece of engineering wizardry cost?'

'About a hundred pounds.'

His mouth twitched in what was nearly a wince. He ran his hand over his face to hide it. I supposed he was thinking how many dinners and bottles of claret he could buy with such a sum. But to give him his due, he walked immediately round to the other side of his desk, took a cheque book from a drawer and put his signature on the line.

'I'll leave it blank.' He handed it to me and smiled again, almost grinning. I thought he was rather overdoing the entente cordiale. He saw me courteously to the door, then closed it behind me. It was not until I reached the hall and I caught sight of myself in the looking glass that I discovered a long strand of goose-grass in my hair and another clinging to the sleeve of my shirt.

Mr Macchuin did not attend the ceremony of drinks before dinner. I guessed this was because he wished to be spared Eugene's recital. On this particular evening he was the loser. While we sat on the terrace enjoying the delicious refreshment of a light breeze as it ruffled the surfaces of the canals, Eugene recited poems by three young men who had been executed for their part in the 1916 Easter Rising. Sissy, dressed in Lincoln green complete with a quiver of arrows and a hat with a broken feather, sat cross-legged on a wicker chair and at the end of each poem waved her fists and muttered in Gaelic what sounded like maledictions. Constance was unusually withdrawn, not watching Eugene's face with her customary rapt look but staring at her own knees. Maud drank three glasses of sherry, chain-smoked and read the copy of *Vogue*, which had reappeared in the drawing room.

For me it was a further part of my education. I found it astonishing that I had lived for twenty-seven years just over the sea from Ireland without comprehending the nature of the bitter and bloody conflict waged between us. When Eugene read the beautiful, inspiring verses of Joseph Plunkett, who had been only twenty-nine when he was shot by a British firing squad – Constance was right, Eugene did have a beautiful voice – the wickedness of war and the wanton slaughter of intelligent, idealistic, passionate young men pressed sharply on my mind.

I felt ashamed of my preoccupations with washing machines and soup. I had too much cold, practical English blood in my veins. My ancestors, on my father's side at least, when not oppressing the Irish through every century since the Vikings had left off, had been busy oppressing almost every other nation they had had anything to do with. We were a bossy, ritual-loving race. Give us scarlet

362

coats and a brass band and we asked nothing more than a hostile climate, horrible food and a bout of dysentery to be perfectly happy. Where was our national fervour, our spontaneity, our love of life? I gazed into the distance where the mountains rose above the derelict garden and wondered why I had not asked myself these questions before.

All too soon I had to go in and grope my way, blinded by sunlight, into the bowels of the earth to get vegetables into tureens and plates into the oven to heat. We had only just taken our seats in the dining room when Pegeen flung open the door in the inimitable way she had, banging it against the wall to produce a shower of plaster flakes. 'Ladies and gents, and Sissy McGinty, 'tis Michael McOstrich,' she screeched. 'Will he have a place at table or shall I be putting him in the hall?'

Of course Constance had to ask Michael to stay to dinner. His copper-coloured eyes roamed the room until they found me, after which they remained fixed as though he were a hungry dog and my face a plate of mutton chops.

'Good God!' Maud gave Michael a look of cold contempt. 'You again. I wonder you don't think of moving in.'

''Tis like the gombeen man,' scowled Sissy. 'You can't rid yourself of him.'

If Mr Macchuin was surprised, on entering the dining room a minute later, to see Michael once more enjoying his hospitality, he hid it admirably. He asked tenderly after the cows and the barley, apparently having forgotten that only the day before he had asked exactly the same questions. Michael answered fully, undisturbed by this patent insincerity.

'What's a gombeen man?' I asked Liddy an hour later, as we were finishing the lemon mousse, which was quite good, though I say it myself.

'Haven't the faintest. I wish they'd pack in arguing.'

The crossfire of talk had, as so often, become a heated row by the main course. This time the quarrel was about whether Lady Lavery, wife of the famous painter, Sir John Lavery, had been the mistress of Michael Collins. Michael McOstrich gave it as his opinion that Collins had been a traitor to Ireland by treating with the British on any terms. At this point Sissy tried to stab Michael with her fork and had to be restrained by Eugene, but as Michael was looking at me he was oblivious to the danger. In a well-meant endeavour to promote peace Eugene volunteered to read a poem he had written some years ago called 'Beal na mBlath' which, for my benefit, he translated as 'Pass of the Flowers', the place where Michael Collins was killed – not by the British, I was thankful to learn, but by his own countrymen. Even Constance was too agitated to express enthusiasm for this idea and Eugene sat through the rest of dinner silent and offended. Mr Macchuin, who sat with his fingers interlocked, tracing the line of his jaw with his thumbs, seemed to be thinking of something else.

'Do you think I ought to dye my hair blonde?' Liddy asked me.

'I shouldn't. It's a very pretty colour already.'

'Do you think it's true that blondes have more fun than brunettes?'

'Not for a moment. Often people think you can't be very bright if you have fair hair.'

'I don't want men to think I'm clever. I want to make them weak at the knees with lust.'

'That sounds highly inconvenient. And quite boring.'

'Oh, Bobbie, you fibber! Of course it's boring if it's men like . . .' She rolled her eyes in poor Michael's direction. 'But what about if it was someone who made you want to give up everything in the world for them? Whose every touch thrilled you to screaming point?'

'I think you may be expecting too much. It might be like that for a short time but it could never last. A lot of the initial thrill is your imagination playing tricks. You get used to someone and the excitement wears off. Then, if you're lucky, you start to really love them. Much better than ungovernable lust are things like respect and having things in common—'

'Hark at her!' I had not realized that Sissy was listening to our conversation. ''Tis a nun you'd take her for. Butter wouldn't care to melt in her gob! When we all know she's been throwing out lures to every man that comes her way.' It was unfortunate that the others had quarrelled themselves to a furious standstill, each too angry to speak, so that Sissy's taunts were clearly audible.

'That'll do, Sissy,' said Constance.

'Is it doing now?' Sissy flashed back. 'And who are you to tell me what I'm to say and what I'm not to say? Just because you were born in a big house and you can tell the names of your grandparents and their parents before them makes you not a whit better than me!' Sissy spoke rapidly and angrily. She had had several sherries before dinner and quite a few glasses of wine during.

Constance looked dismayed. 'Of course not, Sissy. No one thinks that for a minute. But you mustn't be unkind to Bobbie who's done you no harm at all.'

'Maybe she has! Maybe she's put a spell on *all* the men here!' Sissy turned to point a grimy finger towards the head of the table where Mr Macchuin sat. His attention was caught by the gesture. He frowned. 'Maybe she'd like to get bigger fish than Michael McOstrich.' She was breathing hard now and leaning forward to glare at everyone in turn so that the hunting horn she wore round her neck dangled in the remains of her mousse.

'Sissy McGinty,' said Michael reprovingly, 'I believe you're drunk.'

'Drunk, coarse, illiterate . . .' said Maud.

'I take exception to you insulting this young lady.' Michael was talking to Sissy.

'We all know what you've got in mind for the *young lady*,' Sissy flung back. She put scornful emphasis on the last two words. 'And you're welcome to her, for my part. But when it comes to poaching on my ground, I beg to differ with her!'

'I don't know why you're so cross with Bobbie,' said Flurry. 'She's the only girl round here who can saw.'

'I wish people would stop shouting,' cried Flavia from beneath the table where she had withdrawn with her book. 'I can't concentrate.'

'Why don't we talk about something else?' said Constance. 'Eugene, do tell us about Maeve—'

'If you don't look out, Constance Macchuin,' snapped Sissy, 'that witch'll have *him* off you and all. Not that *I* think he's much of a catch but it's no secret that *you're* awfully stuck on him—'

'Sissy,' said Mr Macchuin quietly, 'you're making a fool of yourself.'

'Yes, but isn't it entertaining?' said Maud.

'Har-h-h! You take an Englishwoman's part against *me*!' Sissy sprang up from her place, her pretty face flaming. Osgar and Maria began to run round the table, exciting each other to a frenzy of barking. 'It's clear now what's been going on! I'm only good for walking the dog—'

She was interrupted by the whistling tones of Pegeen as she threw open the door. 'Ladies and gents, and Sissy McGinty. A Mr Randy's come to see you. He says he's a friend of Miss Bobbie's.'

'She had better start charging for her services,' said Maud.

Sissy pointed the index and little finger of her right hand at me, which I took to be some sort of ill-wishing. 'May the devil stick in your throat!'

'Good evening.' Kit Random, looking extraordinarily clean and smart by comparison with the rest of us, though he was informally dressed in an open-necked shirt and jeans, surveyed the faces round the dining table with an expression of friendly interest. 'I'm sorry to barge in in the middle of dinner. I'd have waited outside but this young lady' – he smiled at the simpering Pegeen – 'insisted on announcing me. Hello, Bobbie. How are you?'

THIRTY-ONE

'It seems to me you've gone native,' said Kit as I walked with him to where the Alfa Spider was parked on the other side of the draw-bridge beyond the gatehouse. The little red car looked new and dashing beside the rutted track and the moat, empty of water but half filled with rubbish. 'That's not a criticism,' he added as I made noises of protest. 'I'm fond of the Irish myself and I'm delighted to find you so at home. That means you must be happy. When I read about that man going back to his wife, I was worried. But it's all right, isn't it?'

'Yes. It's all right.' And I was relieved to find that this was true. It still hurt to think about Burgo so I avoided doing so most of the time. I was easily moved to self-loathing. But I was no longer wretched to be without him. I felt as though I had moved an immense distance away, much further than the geographical span that separated us. It was . . . all right.

'I thought of telephoning but it seemed better to wait until I'd finished visiting my authors so I could come and see for myself.' He crossed his arms, leaned against the bonnet and looked me up and down. 'And I like what I see.'

Kit had a charming smile. Apart from the colour of his eyes, he was without any of the attributes of conventional masculine beauty, yet I liked looking at him. His brown hair was nearly as curly as Maria's and his nose had a bump halfway down but his eyes were keen with intelligent curiosity; his mouth was too large but it was good-humoured. I remembered the way his ears stuck out, giving him the look of a bright undergraduate. He had told me he was thirty-five but at first glance you would have guessed twenty-something.

'Thanks. What a fool I've been, though.' I shook my head as I remembered my idiotic misconceptions. 'If only Constance had *told* me!'

'Told you what?'

'That my boss is a fully paid-up member of the working classes.'

'That Finn Macchuin's a senator, you mean? You really had no idea?'

When I had introduced Kit to the others he had shaken Mr Macchuin's hand and said, 'I've been following the progress of that bill for agricultural reform in the *Irish Times*. I hope you get it through. It's obviously going to benefit outlying districts like these.'

The annoyance caused by Sissy's behaviour had been instantly banished from Mr Macchuin's face and he had replied to Kit's questions at some length. I had not understood any of it.

'What are they talking about?' I had asked Liddy in an undertone.

'I don't know,' Liddy had shrugged. 'It's too dull for words. Ever since Dad became a senator he's been away nearly all the time. I wish the IRA would blow the Senate up but it's far too boring for them to bother with.'

I had spent much of the time in the drawing room afterwards turning over this astonishing piece of information in my mind, wondering quite why it had never occurred to me that my employer might be absent from home on legitimate business.

'I thought he was an irresponsible libertine, whiling away the hours among the fleshpots of Dublin while the rest of his family went to perdition,' I explained to Kit. 'I practically accused him of idle profligacy to his face!'

Kit laughed. 'That'll teach you judge us poor men so harshly.'

'You needn't make capital out of it. I'm afraid one lost sheep being returned to the fold isn't enough. Being a senator's pretty much like being in the House of Lords, isn't it?'

'Similar, yes, but they don't inherit the appointment. Senators are either elected or appointed by the government and serve for a limited term. It would be fair to say that it's a more intellectual, less conservative body, with fewer vested interests.'

'A politician. Think of that!'

'It *is* ironic. But not, I imagine, the same kind of man.'

'No, probably not. I don't know, really.'

'Was that funny little dark thing his girlfriend, though? I mean, oddly engaging, but not the sort one would have imagined such a reputable man – he teaches mediaeval history at Trinity College, Dublin, as well as being a senator, you know – to go for.'

'Does he, really? How amazing! I had no idea. Constance is a darling but extremely vague. I *wish* she'd put me properly in the picture. I suppose it was Sissy's existence that set me off on the wrong path in the first place. How did you guess they were lovers?'

'She seemed to be behaving in a proprietorial way after dinner. I saw her kiss his ear when she took him milk for his coffee. He looked awfully stern after that. And why the Robin Hood get-up? I can see it would be arousing to some men. That plus the little girl appeal and the athleticism. She certainly oozes a weird sexual magnetism. But the senator looked as black as Acheron when she did a back-flip in the hall.'

'She used to be in a circus. And after that she joined a company of travelling players. When they disbanded there was no money for wages so they divided the costumes between them. She told me she hasn't bought any clothes for five years.'

'So she does talk to you sometimes? It struck me you weren't exactly her cup of cocoa.'

'You seem to have learned more about the household in two hours than I did in two weeks. She was quite friendly at first but not any more. It's because Michael McOstrich is paying me attention. Sissy's terribly jealous of anyone being preferred to her, even by someone she affects to despise.'

Kit smiled. 'Poor fellow! He wants to carry you off to his potato patch.'

'He happens to be related by marriage to the Macchuins and an important local landowner in his own right. But even if he were King of Connemara it wouldn't be enough. Besides being bad-tempered and domineering, he's really only interested in cows.'

'Tell me about Constance. Has she something wrong with her feet?'

'I don't think so. Why?'

'Is it usual to wear gumboots at dinner?'

'I've got so used to it I didn't notice. Probably the gumboots are to save thinking-time. She's a prime example of an intelligent woman swamped by domestic tasks whose mind is longing to be elsewhere.'

'Like you?'

'No. I'm more practical. There's a part of me that really enjoys doing simple everyday things. Particularly when I can see results.'

'Clearly the poet with the smell like a troop train isn't burdened by domesticity. I saw Constance stir the sugar into his coffee and actually break into a run to fetch him his spectacles.'

I told Kit about the relationship between Constance and Eugene and the story of Larkie Lynch.

'Good lord! And Constance really likes him? With those bulging eyes he reminds me of a chameleon. When he sat down I quite expected his face to turn green to match the chair.'

'Constance is too high-minded to be swayed by appearances.'

'Everyone's influenced by what people look like. The truth is, she likes chameleons. So the household is pullulating with thwarted passion. Everyone in love with someone else. It seemed to me the senator would like to give the little circus tumbler the brush-off. Has he someone else in mind to be Mrs Macchuin?'

Though he asked the question lightly and continued to smile I sensed a sudden sharpening of interest.

'The post happens to be filled.' I told him about Violet.

Kit whistled. 'Poor woman! The sleeping beauty. I hope she *is* beautiful.'

'Oh, yes.'

'And you've come along like a good fairy to wake her up. Well, well. It's intriguing. I'm glad I've taken a couple of weeks' holiday just now. You won't mind if I stick around for a bit?'

Constance, with true Irish hospitality, had urged Kit to send for his bags from the Fitzgeorge Arms in Kilmuree but he had explained that a number of clients were expecting to contact him there.

'I'll be very pleased,' I said, meaning it. 'I could do with some help.'

Kit laughed. 'Practical indeed. You're not going to cozen me by pretending you'd like me to stay for my blue eyes alone.'

'What a conceited creature you are! They are a wonderful colour, I admit.'

'I'm delighted you've noticed.'

Kit soon fell as comfortably into the pattern of our daily lives as though he were a lifelong friend of the family. He worked all morning in his room, lunched at the Fitzgeorge Arms, then came every afternoon to Curraghcourt and stayed for dinner. He was the perfect guest and applied himself assiduously to getting on good terms with everyone. His considerable charm with women operated by identifying various idiosyncrasies of the one to be charmed and teasing them in a way that flattered because it implied a fascinating singularity. With men Kit dropped the teasing in favour of affability. He could converse on any topic, even on the subject of cows with Michael McOstrich, with what appeared to be enthusiasm.

Kit insisted on being allowed into the kitchen and was an excellent aide-de-camp, willing to turn his hand to peeling potatoes, chopping onions, stirring sauces and washing up afterwards. Katty and Pegeen, excited to find a man other than Timsy in their kitchen, were coquettish in Kit's presence and inclined to shriek. He soon acquired the bruised forehead that seemed to be a mark of initiation.

He stoked fires, repaired bicycle punctures and Liddy's hairdryer and changed the oil in the Land-Rover. He took over my sawing stints for Flurry's railway and managed to double the daily production of sleepers. Having trained several gun dogs in his youth, it was a simple matter for him to teach Osgar civilized behaviour. He was strict and consistent and Osgar, who had been filled with misgivings by our attempts to pet him, understood and respected the voice of command. In no time at all Osgar had learned to sit, stay, walk to heel and, best of all, stop barking when instructed to do so. Kit also proved invaluable at persuading uncooperative cats into baskets to travel in convoys to the veterinary surgery in Kilmuree.

Sissy's was the hardest heart to conquer because she suspected Kit of being fond of me. But a few days after his arrival in Connemara Constance and I were in the drawing room, discussing how best to rearrange furniture, when our attention was caught by unusual activity in the garden. We rushed to the window and were astonished to see Kit launch himself athletically from a tea chest to land on the end of a plank which was laid across a log. Sissy, who had been standing on the other end, shot into the sky spinning like a diabolo, chucked Kit under the chin with her flying feet and knocked him to the ground.

Bravely he picked himself up and they tried the trick again. And again. Each time it resulted in Kit being spread-eagled on his back on the grass with Sissy on top of him. Once she actually succeeded in landing on his shoulders. For a few seconds they swayed back and forth before slowly toppling like a dynamited chimney stack.

'I do like him so much,' said Constance. 'Don't you, Bobbie?'

Kit and Constance shared a passion for the poetry of James Clarence Mangan (or at least so he claimed) and during one of their conversations he had teased from her the information that she too wrote poetry. Only the day before he had persuaded her to show it to him. I had yet to learn his verdict.

'Oh yes,' I said. 'Who could fail to like someone so remarkably agreeable?'

'I can tell he likes you.'

I looked at Constance. She put on an appearance of innocence but there was no one in the world less able to conceal their thoughts. 'I know.' I smiled. 'You want me to fall in love with him and live happily ever after.'

'Well . . . that does sound rather appealing, doesn't it, after all?'

'Is there no limit to your talents?' I asked Kit after lunch the next day as we hoed and irrigated the ground in the walled garden. 'Oh, look! Surely that's a shoot!' I dropped on to my knees to examine a speck of something green thrusting up through the bare soil. 'A radish, I think. How exciting! Thanks be to St Fiacre.'

Eugene, when told of our discovery of the statue in the niche, had done some research and unearthed the information that St Fiacre was the patron saint of gardeners. Now we never left the garden without replenishing the offerings of wild flowers at the saint's feet.

Kit came and looked. 'A dandelion. Still, if that's what turns you on.'

'Nonsense! But, really, I'm awfully impressed by your ability to be all things to all men. You can discuss politics with the grand vizier, race meetings with Maud, steam engines with Flurry and hemlines with Liddy. To say nothing of your skills as an acrobat.'

'You mean to accuse me of falseness, I know, but are you never guilty of trying to please? I'm a gregarious animal and I like harmony.'

'Of course I try when the occasion demands but I'm just not so good at it.'

'Besides, to call me an acrobat is gross flattery. The number of bruises decorating my chin and chest testify to my lack of skill as a humble catcher. Are you planning to provision an army?'

I had finished sowing a third row of spring cabbage. 'I *had* thought of selling surplus produce on a roadside stall. But then I remembered that we'd be lucky to get twenty cars driving past the entire day. And not all of those will want vegetables.'

'Possibly none of them. They'll have freezers stocked with things already peeled and chopped into fork-sized pieces. Depressing, isn't it?'

'Very. And we do need money so much.'

'You're really taking it all to heart, aren't you? Trying single-handedly to put Curraghcourt back on its legs? I hope it's not Finn's manly jaw or his romantic melancholy that's inspired you to try to save him a few bob. Why do you always call him "Mr Macchuin", by the way?'

'He's never asked me to call him anything else. He always calls me Miss Norton.'

'Probably he thinks you ought to say first.'

'He's the boss, after all.'

'But you aren't the usual sort of housekeeper. I've noticed you avoid talking to each other.'

'Not particularly. We're both preoccupied. He's always shut up in his library with important paperwork and I'm busy with furniture polish and vegetables.'

'Hm.' Kit looked at me speculatively.

'It's better that way. We've a tendency to quarrel.'

'Oh, yes?'

'We rub each other up the wrong way. He's cross-grained, huffy and dictatorial. I like my own way, too.'

'Of course you do. And a very good way it is.' Kit put his thumb over the end of the hose to water with a fine spray the row I had just planted. 'But I've seen him watching you. And you're very aware of him, aren't you?'

'Honestly, Kit, you're like a spy at the Elizabethan court! I suppose you're taking notes and sending them off to your Spanish masters.'

Kit laughed. 'I told you. I find people's behaviour fascinating to observe. When you have to skim through several manuscripts a day and immerse yourself in other people's impassioned fantasies, you begin to see a plot in a dropped handkerchief and love under every thorn-bush. Also'– he put his hand lightly on my arm – 'if I can be strictly truthful for a moment, I'm inclined to be jealous. From the beginning I've entertained feelings for you that aren't brotherly. I know you aren't over that other business. I don't want to pester you and for the time being I'm not hoping for anything other than the purest friendship. But I shouldn't like to find that I've been stand-ing off politely only to find that a bolder man had rushed in where this particular fool had feared to tread.'

I looked away to the mountains, iron-grey against a sky suffused with pink as the sun began its descent. An arrow-head of geese flapped through the air above us beneath clouds of gold. The vast, unspoiled beauty of my surroundings corresponded with growing feelings of relief at being free from the complications of a love affair. I looked down, seeking inspiration for my answer from the soil.

'You're standing on the infant radish!' Kit pointed to my foot. 'You murderer!'

I jumped back and bent to brush the compacted earth from the dot of leaf. The seriousness that had threatened was deflected.

'Do you know,' Kit said, 'talking of stories, it occurred to me after I'd left you at the bus station in Kilmuree that you hadn't told me how the press got to hear of your romantic association with the minister. I've been wondering ever since. Would you be kind enough to put in the missing piece of the plot?'

'I'm afraid it was Mrs Slattery who ratted on us. If you remember, she was the wife of the inn-keeper at the Fisherman's Reel where we always stayed. Perhaps we ought to have spread ourselves more thinly but the fact was that I felt sure she wouldn't give us away even if she found out who Burgo was because she was more than a little in love with him. She used to stare at him in a sort of rapture while she was polishing glasses. Mr Slattery was short and bald, not really the stuff of dreams. But she must have seen Burgo's face on the television or in a newspaper and decided that money mattered more than love. The first time we went to the Fisherman's Reel after the Conservatives had got into power, she was different. Not so friendly, almost snappy. I didn't think about it much. I assumed she'd had a row with her husband but obviously she had a guilty conscience. Anyway, we had supper and went to bed as usual. In the morning Burgo drew back the curtains. Because of the sloping roof the window was at ground level. He bent to look out, yelled and fell back on to the bed. The orchard was packed with journalists waiting for their photographic opportunity. As Burgo was naked they all had more explicit pictures of the Minister for Culture than they'd bargained for.'

'I'm glad you can laugh about it.'

'I didn't laugh at the time, naturally. We left separately. Burgo went downstairs first, ordered a taxi and went straight back to London. I let an hour go by before I came down but of course they knew I was there and they were waiting for me. I had to push through the hordes in the bar with flashes going off in my face and people shouting questions in my ear. I ran out to my car. One man put his hand on my arm to stop me getting in so I kicked him hard on the shin. It was a miracle I didn't injure anyone. I simply had to put my foot on the accelerator and hope they'd get out of the way. They all piled into their cars and followed me. We did a lengthy tour of Sussex until I thought I'd lost them, then I went home. But someone must have been on my tail for they were all at the gates by evening. No one printed the nude studies of Burgo. I suppose it would have contravened some law of decency.'

'A sad end to a tempestuous love affair.'

'I didn't realize when we kissed each other before he rushed downstairs that I'd never see him again. Now I'm glad I didn't. It must be terrible to know you're saying goodbye for the last time to someone you love very much. Think of all those poor Irish mothers who had to watch their children sail away to America.'

'Yes, but remember, emigration was a fact of life for all European countries during the nineteenth century. If you're going to take the sorrows of Ireland on your shoulders you'll be beaten flat.'

A battered van rumbled into the walled garden.

'Aha!' said Kit. 'I've been expecting this. Only an hour late!' He went to speak to the driver. I heard him say something about following us up to the house. 'Hop on your bike,' he said to me, 'and you can see my surprise. It's a present to Curraghcourt as a thank you for hospitality received – and for hospitality to come, I hope.'

'How lovely! What is it?'

'Lovely doesn't quite describe it but I hope you'll be pleased. Wait and see.'

In the stable courtyard the driver opened the doors of the van and I looked inside.

'Kit! You genius!' Had it not been for that earlier moment of seriousness I would have kissed him. 'The perfect present! A circular saw!'

Timsy was summoned and the three men unloaded it.

'Was it very expensive?' I asked Kit as soon as the van had gone away.

'I saw it advertised in the newsagent's in Kilmuree. The farmer's bought himself a nice new chainsaw. He was glad to get rid of it.'

Kit jerked a handle on a length of wire and started the engine which was attached to the saw by a rubber belt. The tremendous racket brought Flurry from his shed where he had been closeted with the *Flying Irishman*. We watched with awe as Timsy and Kit guided a sleeper towards the spinning blade. It sliced into it like a penknife through balsa wood. Kit moved the sleeper along to the second chalk mark and in ten seconds it lay on the ground in three equal pieces.

'*Voilà!*' said Kit. He had to shout to make himself heard. 'Accomplished in a fraction of the time without raising a blister and no more than a comely glow on the brow of the operator.'

Timsy took off his cap in tribute. ''Tis better than anything in a film.'

'Let's do some more!' cried Flurry, approaching the saw.

Kit caught him by the shoulder. 'Repeat after me: "I, Florence Macchuin, swear on the soul of Isambard Kingdom Brunel that I shall not lay so much as a finger on this highly dangerous piece of equipment. For fear of losing it."'

Flurry looked disappointed. 'OK,' he muttered.

But Kit made him stand still, raise his right hand and solemnly pledge his word.

'Luckily Flurry isn't strong enough to start it up by himself,' said Kit later as we walked towards the back door, leaving Timsy sawing up sleepers and grinning with enjoyment. 'But I wouldn't put it past Timsy to leave it running unattended.'

'Talking of Timsy, he's left the apple-store door open. Let's see what keeps him so busy.'

The contraption that filled the back part of the little building behind a mound of rotting apples was unfamiliar to me. A large plastic barrel filled with a golden liquid lay upon a trestle with a corkscrew pipe winding down from it. Around it stood bottles and jars, most of them filled with the same yellow liquid.

'Is it a cider-press?'

'Not cider.' Kit unscrewed the cap of one of the bottles and sniffed it. 'This is poteen!'

'This is a whiskey still?' I stared at it, amazed. 'Well, I'm blowed! No wonder Timsy's been so amenable to my rationing of the black bottle! I can hardly believe it! Who'd have thought he'd have the energy and initiative?' I peered into boxes of sprouting potatoes and a bin of mudlike liquid, to the surface of which rose slow thick bubbles. 'You have to admit it shows enterprise. I suppose that explains those men who've been creeping about the place. He's been generating himself a nice little income.'

Kit pointed to a cable that led from the generator. 'He's been quite ingenious too, using the element from a kettle to boil up the water. I wonder how the senator will like his house being turned into a shebeen?'

I was silent for a while as I thought. Then I said decisively, 'He must never know.'

'You surprise me. I'd no idea you were so fond of Timsy.'

'Timsy be damned! As undoubtedly he will be. No, I want him to go on making the poteen. And charge more for it. As much as the market will bear. But he'll have to hand over fifty – no, seventy-five per cent of the dosh. I said we needed a source of income, didn't I?'

'Bobbie! You aren't serious?'

'Perfectly. It's not like dealing in drugs. We aren't going to lead the innocent into error. I remember you said yourself it's what the country people have always drunk.'

'Yes . . . but . . . if you get caught the penalty's a swingeing fine, possibly a term in jail. What'll you say to Finn as he's being hauled off to chokey?'

'I shall make it perfectly clear to the examining magistrate that Mr Macchuin knew nothing about it. Which will be true.'

'How are you going to make Timsy hand over the takings? Oh, blackmail, of course.'

'Exactly. Either he agrees to give me a high percentage of the take or I snitch.'

'Never let anyone try again to argue the case against the power of the cinema to corrupt.'

'If your conscience is queasy you'd better cut along now. But make it snappy. The saw's stopped.'

'If you're going to talk all the time like James Cagney I shan't be able to stand—'

'Shh! Stow your whids. Here he comes!'

We waited in the shadow of the open door. As soon as Timsy came in we closed it behind him.

'Mother of God! The devil's come down in a whirlwind!' cried Timsy, no doubt confused by being thrown unexpectedly into a darkness unrelieved by so much as a crack in the door or a chink in the brickwork.

'Nothing to worry about, Timsy. It's Miss Bobbie. And Mr Random.'

'Hello, Timsy,' said Kit's voice. 'Nice little business you've got here.'

'Oh, Mr Random, your honour. You wouldn't tell on a poor country boy that's forced to scrape what good he can from an evil stinking trade only because he's got two motherless orphans to support—'

I took charge. 'We haven't time to waste with all that, Timsy.'

'Jesus, Mary and Joseph!' Timsy groaned. 'And I'm only looking after this stuff for a friend. To think you do a poor soul in need a good turn and you get into trouble for it! Oh, mercy, Miss Bobbie—'

'I'll be more inclined to be merciful if you'll shut up a minute,' I cut in. 'Now listen to what I propose.' I explained the terms of the alliance.

'Begor, who'd have thought it! You'd withhold the last anointing from a dying man! And you with a face that'd make the blessed angels want to scratch out your eyes!'

'Do you accept or not?'

There was silence while Timsy thought. I could almost hear his brain ticking over in the darkness.

'I doubt you realize, Miss Bobbie, how little the stuff'll fetch. Likely it won't be worth your while—'

'Don't think you're going to cheat me, Timsy. I shall send Mr Random into Kilmuree to research the going rate.'

'Timsy's right,' said Kit's voice bitterly. 'You *would* deny a dying man his last spiritual comfort.'

'Either you play ball with me, Timsy, or I'm going to report you to Mr Macchuin. Is it a deal?'

Timsy dropped the fanciful similes and his voice became brisk. 'Thirty per cent?'

'Eighty.'

'Fifty!'

'Seventy-five!'

Another silence. Then I heard Timsy make a disgusting sound in his throat and spit noisily. 'Done, Miss Bobbie. You'll shake hands on it?'

As it was Thursday Father Deglan was coming to dinner.

When I came downstairs from giving Violet her supper Kit was standing at the sink peeling potatoes. He sent me a smile of complicity. Katty and Pegeen were enjoying a brew of tea by the fire, opening their eyes occasionally to check the progress of the stew that steamed in the black pot on the hook. After a week or two of eating my food Katty had complained that she was 'up all night with wind like a mare trying to drop a foal'. As Pegeen and Timsy always agreed with Katty, these days the three of them were left to cater for themselves.

Sissy, dressed in a pierrot's baggy white suit with a red ruff, a row of pom-poms down the front and a pointed cap, was pulverizing a heap of shining black berries in a mortar. She answered my greeting with a glower from cold black eyes. I offered her the plate of currant biscuits I had made to go with the banana ice cream. She crammed

378

three together into her mouth scattering crumbs over her front and continued to pound. In a moment of abstraction Flurry took one, too.

In the dining room, Mr Macchuin was standing by the fire listening to Eugene who was entertaining him with the story of Cuchulain's magic spear. Mr Macchuin was listening politely but something in his face led me to think his mind was wandering. Kit joined them and brought the subject round to politics.

'What did you think of Edward Heath's extremely drastic plan to redraw the border between North and South? You remember: he wanted to transfer those areas of the six counties that were predominantly Catholic to the Republic and create a Protestant sectarian statelet. Was it possible that it might have worked?'

Mr Macchuin's expression and posture changed immediately. He looked wide-awake. 'You mean at the time of Bloody Friday?'

Kit nodded.

'Well, it's the sort of thing that looks all right on paper. But it would have meant the compulsory rehousing of roughly five hundred thousand people. That would have required an increase in the number of troops in the province and there's no reason to think that would have brought about any lessening of bloodshed . . .'

Kit's social skills were to be envied, I reflected as I took my usual chair at the foot of the table with Father Deglan on my left and Constance on his other side. It was clear the priest was listening to the discussion at the other end of the table as he ate his soup, for he ignored our attempts to include him in our peaceful talk about the paintings of Degas.

As soon as Father Deglan had taken the keenest edge off his appetite he called out, 'Is it true some of yous is legislating for the introduction of sex education in schools?'

Mr Macchuin paused in the eating of his stuffed onion – really not bad, if a little greasy – to reply. 'That's right. It's pretty sure to get through. And not before time.'

Father Deglan made a sound like 'Ee-ach!' and put down his knife and fork. 'For shame, Finn! And to think we pay you people good money for such knavery!' His seeing eye sparkled like molten metal. It had to be acknowledged that Father Deglan truckled to no one. 'Power crazes, 'tis true. Between you, you'll be responsible for the undoing of our young women. There'll be a tidal wave of illegitimacy.'

'You don't mean to accuse the Senate, surely?' Mr Macchuin

379

pretended to be shocked. 'There are only sixty members and some of them are definitely past their prime.'

'You may mock, if you please. And who is it that's to impart such perilous stuff in the schools? Ye'll not expect the nuns to put such words in their mouths fresh after telling the Theological Virtues?'

'Provided they stick to the truth, in a comprehensible way, it doesn't matter much who tells them.'

'And you'd let yer own *garsúns* listen to such filth?'

'There's nothing filthy about sex,' interrupted Sissy. ''Tis as natural between men and women as between bulls and cows and pigs and sows that love to charver all day if they're allowed.'

Eugene looked pained by this frank exposition.

'Besides, we can't all be so fortunate as to conceive immaculately,' said Maud. 'Though most women would prefer it. If only men were less libidinous. It seems even the Catholic clergy cannot be continent.' There had been a scandal about a priest running away with a young woman in one of the newspapers brought by Father Deglan.

Pegeen flounced in as Father Deglan's face grew fiery. I hoped it was not to announce Michael McOstrich. And if it was, that Sissy would shut up about cows and bulls.

''Tis Rickeen O'Shaunessy, the fiddler,' whistled Pegeen. 'Come to see about lunacy.'

At least that is what I thought she said. I learned afterwards that this annual festival in celebration of St Patrick's victory over a heathen called Lug is spelled Lughnasa and pronounced LOOnǎsǎ.

'Oh dear!' said Constance. 'I'd quite forgotten. What's the date today?'

'It's the twenty-sixth,' said Kit.

'Oh, no!' Constance counted on her fingers. She looked at me. 'Bobbie, what are we going to do? The entire district will be expecting to come for supper and dancing. In six days' time!'

THIRTY-TWO

At half past six on the evening of the festival of Lughnasa I looked at my face in the bathroom mirror to check that it was clean. I had washed my hair and rinsed it with vinegar to banish any lingering odour of cows. To sugar the pill of having to share the profits of the shebeen, Constance, who had responded enthusiastically to the idea of turning the still into a source of income, had taken responsibility for the hens and I was learning to milk Siobhan, two jobs Timsy had always hated.

And it must be admitted that now Timsy had something to do that challenged his intelligence he worked hard. He had decided to diversify and to produce a superior poteen from grain as well as the less refined kind made from potatoes. To increase production we had invested in a second-hand immersion heater to replace the kettle element. The apple store was already filled to capacity with dustbins of bubbling fermenting liquid, leaving room only for Timsy and a single customer. The rest waited in the granary so as not to alert the suspicions of Mr Macchuin. Often I heard bursts of laughter and voices raised in song. It was fortunate that his visits to the stable yard were rare.

I was no longer afraid of Siobhan and was becoming more proficient at milking, though the muscles in my forearms were still weak and ached fearfully after each session. But there was something pleasurable about perching on the little stool up to my knees in clean creaking straw, something reposeful in the sound of the milk spurting into the white enamel pail and the grinding of giant molars as Siobhan steadily consumed the hay. Gradually we were learning to understand and trust each other. I was soothed by the flower-meadow smell of her silky skin, the turning and flicking of her soft ears, the occasional backward glances from the corners of her mild butter-scotch eyes. I enjoyed doing something that had been done in the same simple way by women like me for thousands of years. The very monotony of the task was agreeable. Rhythmically, methodically, one squeezed out, with the fine stream of frothing milk, the little frets of the preceding hours.

Turning the handle of the separator in the still room afterwards brought further satisfaction. The bluish-white skimmed milk gushed from one spout while the thick yellow cream flowed more slowly from the other. The milk was refrigerated; the cream was left to lie in large shallow earthenware pans. Only the topmost unctuous layer was skimmed off the next day for butter-making. Katty and Pegeen disliked churning so I offered to do it when I had time. If the atmosphere was humid the butter took a long time to turn and your arm ached appallingly but the satisfaction of hearing the sudden slap, slap as the cream parted into lumps of gold and whey was hard to beat.

I leaned over the basin to put on lipstick and mascara, then stood back to examine the result.

The problem of what to wear to the party had been solved for me quite unexpectedly. Naturally I had brought no evening dresses with me, having expected to spend my term of servitude behind a green baize door. Constance and Liddy had been indignant when I had suggested I should stay behind the scenes.

'Oh, all right then,' I had said as we discussed the matter during lunch on the day after Rickeen O'Shaunessy's visit. 'Of course I shall be delighted to come.' I had thought regretfully of one or two favourite things gathering moths and dust in my wardrobe at Cutham. 'I can wear the smartest of my sundresses.'

Liddy was shocked. 'You can't! I mean, all your clothes are chic and groovy but you ought to have something long and glittery and exposing lots of flesh. Lughnasa's the only chance we get. There's the St Stephen's Day dance but it's always so bloody cold.'

'Don't swear, darling,' said Constance in the sort of voice that does not expect to be listened to. 'And you know Father Deglan has strong views about bare arms and necks.'

'Bugger Father Deglan!'

Constance looked appealingly at Finn but he was staring out of the window.

'Ah, well. As you say.' Constance shrugged and returned to the question of what I was to wear. 'I'd willingly lend you something of mine but I'm twice your size. Perhaps we could take something in.'

'Three times would be nearer the truth,' said Maud. 'You'd have to remodel the dress entirely. Besides you have the taste of a provincial. Whatever her faults of character, Bobbie has an excellent figure and good style.'

'Thank you,' I said.

'I don't think Bobbie has *any* faults of character,' began Constance warmly. 'She's been perfectly angelic from the moment she arrived.'

'Rather too fond of the men.' Maud drained her glass of usquebaugh: a liqueur flavoured with coriander which she often drank instead of wine. 'I'll have another, Finn.'

Mr Macchuin stood up. His attention was drawn to the window. 'Why are those people wandering about in the garden?'

'They'll be bringing provisions for the Lughnasa supper,' Constance said quickly.

'They aren't carrying anything,' he objected.

'Don't fuss, Finn, but give Maud another glass. Bobbie's got it all in hand.'

Mr Macchuin did as he was told and then returned, frowning, to the window.

'This is a particularly good vintage. I can *feel* it doing me good.' Maud gave one of her rare smiles as she sipped the fulvous liquid. 'Now, Bobbie, I have an entire room of dresses that I shall never wear again and you may choose one.'

'Stone the crows!' said Liddy. 'This is more of a miracle than the liquefaction of St Gobnut's bloody blood.'

'Liddy!' said Mr Macchuin but as he did not remove his eyes from the garden the reproof carried little weight.

The next day I had knocked on Maud's door at the appointed hour. Her room was large and faced south. It contained some wonderful furniture but its beauty was marred by an enormous television: the only one in the house. Liddy complained about this continually for though Maud allowed her to watch it she would not compromise with other people's tastes, particularly when racing and show-jumping were on.

A cruel fate had denied Maud her greatest pleasures, hunting and dancing, at a comparatively early age. She was fifty-eight, but looked much older. A bottle of usquebaugh and an ashtray filled with cigarette ends were always beside the bed. These and the television were opiates to deaden pain and disappointment, not the least of which must be the condition of Violet. Maud never talked about her to me, or to anyone else as far as I knew, but she must often have thought about that attic room where her only child lay in a state of insensibility.

When Constance had tried to interest Maud in our scheme for the better care of Violet, Maud had turned white and said, 'You're a fool for your pains, Constance Macchuin. Nothing can be done for her.' She had struggled to her feet and gone out of the room immediately afterwards. When Maud was particularly hard and unpleasant I reminded myself what she had to bear.

'This is terribly kind—' I began.

'It certainly is. Get on with it.' Maud, who was lying on a sofa beside the fire, returned her eyes to the newspaper she was reading. But she added, without looking up, 'When you've chosen let me see you in it.'

Leading from her bedroom was a large dressing room in which stood several racks of clothes. The evening dresses were, I guessed, mostly from the forties and fifties and so had lost any appearance of datedness and become Art. Though they reeked of damp, the fabrics were still sumptuous, the cutting masterly. I tried on several before deciding on a dress of dark blue silk velvet with an overskirt of layers of tulle. It was strapless but over one shoulder was a trail of diamanté stars stitched to an almost invisible band of net. The stars flowed diagonally across the bodice to the waist from where they trickled down into the gathers of the tulle. It was supremely elegant and wildly romantic at the same time.

'Balenciaga,' said Maud when she saw me in it. 'I wore that to a ball at Castletown in . . . when was it? Nineteen forty-six – or was it forty-seven?'

'I can only just do it up round the waist. I'd better not eat anything for the next few days.'

Maud glanced down at her own bony frame with complacency. 'I don't suppose self-restraint is something that comes easily to a sensual nature such as yours.'

I repressed a smile. 'I can't say it does.'

'You'd better nip it in the bud or it will be your undoing. Never forget that men want to do the chasing. Throwing yourself at a man's head never did a woman any good.' I thought I saw a spark of something like curiosity in her glance before she added with her usual disdain, 'But you can please yourself about that. It's nothing to me.'

'Golly, I'm so envious!' said Liddy, coming into the bathroom. 'Why didn't she lend it to me?'

'Thank you,' I said. 'But you look lovely. You've no reason to envy anyone.'

This was true. Liddy had put on weight and her skin was free from spots. She was wearing a white silk dress of Violet's, which she had altered to fit her. Liddy had been taught by the nuns to sew and had only needed help with the cutting and pinning. She twirled across the floor towards me to display the full effect and then broke into a fit of sneezing.

'Crikey! You don't think you may have overdone the scent?'

'Most probably I have.' I had hung Maud's dress before the fire for a day and a night but it still smelt as though it had been unearthed from the family vault. I had poured half a bottle of salts into my bath water and immersed myself afterwards in Shalimar. 'You don't detect damp?'

'I'll never be able to smell anything again. My sinuses are in agony. Never mind. We both look absolutely beautiful. It's a pity there won't be anyone worth impressing. I suppose Kit won't dance with anyone but you.'

It had more than once occurred to me that Liddy was forming a crush on Kit. When he looked at her she became self-conscious and when he wasn't looking at her she stared at him with all her eyes.

'I'll be too busy to dance,' I said. 'I'll have the supper to see to. One more dab of Shalimar to be on the safe side and then we'll go and help your aunt.'

'Are you sure you like it?' The scent had been Liddy's birthday present to me and she asked me this at least once a day.

'*Love* it. Steel yourself and take a good sniff.' I lifted my chin and held my neck towards her. 'Can you detect anything resembling a cow? I don't want to inflame Michael into losing self-control.'

Liddy giggled, sniffed and coughed. 'Promise. Not the faintest hint.'

We went to Constance's bedroom. She was standing in her petticoat, looking in despair at the heaps of clothing on her bed. Her bare feet were beautiful: well-shaped, straight-toed and unmarked by corn or callus; one of the benefits of gumboots.

'How gorgeous you both are! Liddy darling, you've put on weight and how much better you look for it. And even Father Deglan's going to be guilty of impure thoughts when he sees you in that dress, Bobbie. Golly!' she added as I advanced upon her. 'You smell like a distillation of all the flowers in the world. But how is any man to dance with you without being knocked unconscious?'

'It'll be better when it warms up on my skin.'

'You'd better hurry up, Aunt Connie,' said Liddy. 'What are you waiting for?'

'I've tried on everything I've got and it's either too tight or too frumpy. Whatever made me buy such ghastly things in the first place? Was I off my head? Or under the influence of a mind-altering drug?'

'I thought you said you were going to wear your brown,' said Liddy.

'I put it on but it makes me look exactly like one of Siobhan's cow-pats. Unfortunately it's the only thing that fits. I must have put on at least a stone since last year.'

'This is pretty.' I held up a black dress.

'I can't do up the zip.'

'Put on the brown again and let's see it,' I suggested.

Liddy zipped it up for her. It was big enough but the ridges and bulges about Constance's hips and thighs made her look like a badly wrapped brown paper parcel.

'It would hang better if you took off your pants,' I suggested.

Constance looked startled. 'You mean go downstairs without any knickers on?'

'Why not?'

'I should feel indecent. Utterly wanton.'

'As no one else would know, would that matter particularly? You needn't *be* wanton.'

'I suppose not.' Constance felt under her dress and withdrew the article, which was waist-length and made from aertex.

'That's much better,' said Liddy. 'Wait there.'

While she was gone I went through Constance's jewellery box: a mess of unravelling cotton-reels and loose face powder. At the bottom I found a heavy Middle-Eastern-looking necklace, made from square gold beads alternating with round ones of turquoise. 'Put this on,' I said.

The gold lit Constance's face and the chunkiness diminished her broad shoulders. 'I think there are some earrings and a bracelet to match.' She examined herself in the looking glass. 'Finn brought the set back for me years ago from somewhere like Egypt or Syria but I've never worn them. I always thought they were too flamboyant for me.'

'On the contrary.' I rummaged through the box and found them. 'They are perfect for you. He has a good eye, obviously.'

'I expect Violet chose them. She always dressed so well, poor darling.'

386

Liddy reappeared with an armful of brightly coloured fabrics and some curling tongs. 'I've brought some of Mummy's scarves. You could knot them over your hips to hide the podgy bits.'

Poor Constance's self-image was so poor that she did not flinch at the brutal candour of youth but did as she was told.

'Here, try this.' Liddy picked up a lovely silk wisp, the colour of aquamarines. 'It'll go perfectly with that stunning jewellery and cheer up that horrible brown.'

The effect was everything one could have wished. The plainness of the dress was transformed at a stroke into understated sophistication. 'Now hair. Sit down.' Liddy pushed her aunt on to her dressing-table stool and got to work with the tongs. She smoothed Constance's untidy curls into an elegant series of waves, parted at the side to hang sexily over one eye. 'OK, let's have a look in your make-up drawer. Oh, heavens, Aunt Connie! The sort of mascara you have to spit on went out with flint axes.'

Liddy went away and came back with her own pots, pencils, bottles and compacts. She shaded, smudged, outlined, blended, brushed and blotted and the result was a triumph. Constance was an almond-eyed Juno, a tawny goddess, with flawless skin and red lips.

Liddy surveyed her aunt critically. 'There's still something not quite right. I know.' She took a pair of tweezers from her make-up bag. 'Those eyebrows. We haven't time to do them properly – besides they'll probably go red where I've plucked them – but I'll just take out the ones in the middle.'

'Ow-how, ooh-hoo!' protested Constance, but when at last she looked at herself in the mirror, she exclaimed, 'I can't believe that's me!' She caught Liddy's hand. 'Thank you, darling. It's too sweet of you to take so much trouble.'

'Any time,' said Liddy airily but I saw she was pleased.

'I'm sorry but I'm going to have to go to the lav again. It's because I'm nervous. When I was younger I hardly saw anything of the dance floor. I was always standing with crossed legs in the queue in the cloakroom.'

Liddy and I waited for Constance at the head of the stairs so we could make our entrance together. From the landing I could see through the banisters into the hall below where the dancing was to take place and probably had done every year since the building of the present castle some five hundred years ago. We had practically denuded the demesne that morning to decorate the panelling with branches of greenery. It looked luxuriant and bosky. In the absence of dance crystals Katty and Pegeen had grated candles and scattered the shavings on the oak boards to make it 'skeety'. The smell of wax wove in with the smell of burning turf and the sharper scent of sap from the birch, lime and larch.

Kit, Mr Macchuin and Eugene were standing in a group before the fire. The two former were wearing dinner jackets while Eugene had on his usual green frock-coat. As we descended the stairs, I was delighted to see Eugene's eyes fasten on Constance with an expression of acute interest.

'You look very pretty, Liddy.' Mr Macchuin stepped forward to kiss his daughter. 'Like a healthy young woman instead of a bag of bones.'

I almost tutted aloud at this typically masculine compliment that seemed to disparage as much as it affirmed. He turned to look at his sister.

'Good God, Con! I hardly recognized you.' He looked her up and down with brotherly impartiality. 'Your hair's different. And you're wearing lipstick. What's it all about?' I longed to tread hard on his uncomprehending foot. Then he said, 'It's a welcome change from the cardigan and boots.'

'Yes, indeed.' Eugene's nostrils flared as he breathed heavily and his eyes bulged. '"The shallop of my peace is wrecked on Beauty's shore."'

Constance blushed prettily.

'I can't wait for the dancing to start.' Kit took hold of me and waltzed me expertly round the room. 'My God! You're intoxicating! It's like drowning in a river of flowers. "Some day,"' he sang in a light baritone, '"when I'm awf'ly low – When the world is cold – I will feel a glow just thinking of you – And the way you look tonight." Will you promise to dance with me all night? Once I've done my duty by the wallflowers, that is?'

'I'd love to but until supper's been eaten and cleared away I'm strictly on duty.'

'It was a fine day for the Macchuins when you dropped in.'

I looked over my shoulder at Constance standing before the fire, her rouged mouth parted as she listened to Eugene. At Liddy checking her appearance in the punch ladle. At Flavia coming down the stairs in a charming blue dress, holding a book in front of her and feeling for each step with her toe. Behind Flavia came Maud in black as always but with a diamond necklace and earrings that blazed.

After Maud came Sissy, her usually lithe skips hampered by a strapless dress covered with flashing green and silver sequins that hugged her figure all the way down to her ankles. A net frill stuck out over her bare feet. Her breasts were covered (barely) by embroidered scallop shells. The mermaid costume suited her simian features and jagged black hair with its blood-red tips. She wriggled with tiny steps across the hall and put her hand on Mr Macchuin's arm. He had his back to the room and was prodding a sod of turf into flame with his toe. The expression on his face as he took in Sissy's appearance was worth any amount of dusting and potato-peeling.

'It was a fine day for me.'

'Well, Liddy,' I heard Maud say as we drifted by, 'that's a pretty dress. But you'd better not put on any more weight. At your age I had an eighteen-inch waist and so did your mother.'

I made Kit stop beside them. 'Liddy's just perfect,' I said. 'Don't you think so, Kit?' I squeezed his hand hard.

'What?' He gave Liddy a careless glance. 'Oh, a siren. The boys will be dazzled.'

Maud looked me up and down. 'How singular! Our housekeeper is better dressed than any of us.'

THIRTY-THREE

The musicians: three fiddlers, a banjo-player, a flautist and a man with a *bodhrán* (a sort of drum), positioned themselves on the landing which was large enough to be a sort of minstrels' gallery. Not long after their arrival the guests began to pour in through the open front door. Everyone, from Colonel Molesworth who had driven over in his Bentley from Annagh Park to Francie Synge who had deserted her post by the swing door of the Fitzgeorge Arms, was gorgeously arrayed in his or her best party clothes. Osgar, overwhelmed by the sudden influx of humans, retreated beneath the side table from where he maintained a sullen surveillance, unable to let himself go sufficiently to join Maria who greeted every visitor with barks or dribbles according to her view of them.

I went to check that all was well in the kitchen. Katty and Pegeen were handling the pans of food with unusual care, fearful of splashing their best clothes. They had been responsible for the traditional dishes. Crubeens, rated high by Timsy and the girls, were pigs' trotters (back feet only) pickled in strong vinegar then boiled. Drisheen was sheep's blood and mutton suet mixed with breadcrumbs and milk. Pudding was made from carrageen moss, a kind of seaweed. After it had been cleaned of molluscs and tiny worms, it was simmered in milk with lemon rind and sugar and poured into a mould where it set like blancmange.

I had poached a salmon, roasted three chickens and baked a large ham, and made a quantity of hollandaise sauce. There were potatoes, of course, and Turlough McGurn had promised cucumbers if he had to cross the Sahara with a team of camels to get them. Instead of the six I had ordered he sent six boxes, so I made not only cucumber salad but cucumber soup and mousse as well. For pudding I made crème brûlée using the eggs and cream which we now had in abundance.

As soon as I saw that there was plenty for everyone I relaxed. The Irish habit of talking to strangers as though they had known them for years contributed in no small way to the party spirit. Unmarried women were much in demand when dancing began again after supper. Several men with shiny suits and shinier faces, who had been too shy to ask before, were now emboldened by punch and inclined to quarrel about who should take me round the floor. But when Michael McOstrich appeared in the doorway, they melted away.

'You'll take a spin with me, Miss Norton.'

He looked magnificent in his evening clothes. There was about him a fierce manliness, which I might have found attractive had I been at all interested in agriculture. He was as determined in his dancing as in his wooing and made no concessions to other couples. As a result we left a trail of crushed feet, bruised shins and knocked heads behind us.

'I was getting in the cows,' he said in explanation for his late arrival. He marched me once round the circumference of the hall before saying, 'Won't you change your mind about refusing my invitations? I'll confess you're a trouble to me. I don't know when I've taken such a fancy to a young lady. Perhaps you don't realize that my intentions are honourable? I'm not the man to trifle with God's holy laws. I mean it all fair and square.' He stood still so suddenly that a couple ran into us. 'I'm offering marriage, Miss Norton.'

'Please call me Bobbie. This is so sudden. Of course I'm aware that it's a great honour . . .' We seemed to have strayed into Jane Austen. It would be wrong to seek safety in cowardly ambiguity. 'I'm afraid it's impossible.'

'I'm offering a good home. And there'd be nothing like the work there is here. Máire could wait on you. And no one would dare to look down on you. Just let them try.' Michael tightened his hold on my waist and scowled ferociously. 'There's not a man in Connaught I couldn't buy out if I chose. Finn Macchuin now, he's an embarrassed man. Likely he'll soon be selling Curraghcourt to make ends meet.'

'Oh, I hope not!'

The dismay in my voice struck Michael's ear suspiciously. 'What'd it be to you?'

'The family have been here such a long time.'

'The McOstriches have been at Ballyboggin nearly as long.'

'I should be just as sorry if you had to sell up.'

'No fear of that. Why, there isn't another farm with a brand-new spudding machine for twenty miles about. I've ordered a new bed.'

'Really? I'm so sorry,' I added in apology to the woman whose eye I had nearly put out with my elbow.

'The best in the shop. Headboard, sprung mattress, the lot. I'm not a man to spare expense where it's wanted.'

'I'm sure you're thoroughly generous.'

'As to that, there isn't a man in Connaught can drive a harder bargain. I make a pound do the work of ten of other men's. Now, say you'll come over to Ballyboggin and take a bite of supper? There'd be just the two of us. My brothers can eat in the scullery. Máire takes hers standing up as it is.'

'I should hate to put your family to so much inconvenience.' Through the gap beneath Michael's armpit I caught sight of Sissy dancing with a man who was already drunk. Her dress was split to the thigh. She did not seem to be enjoying herself. When she caught my eye she stuck out her tongue. This emboldened me to set in motion the plan I had been hatching. 'Besides,' I went on, 'I couldn't square it with my conscience to make another girl unhappy by accepting your very kind proposal. It might even drive her to do something desperate.'

'What's that? What girl?'

'A girl who, I happen to know, is almost broken-hearted because you never show her any attention.'

'Broken-hearted, you say?' Naturally he was interested. 'Over me? And who's the *cailín*?'

'I'm not sure I ought to tell you. It would be breaking a confidence.'

'A lady's feelings are sacred to me. I'm not the man to make free with a girl's reputation.'

'Well, in that case . . . it may surprise you to know that Sissy McGinty is looking at us right now and wishing with all her heart and soul she was in my shoes.'

'Sissy McGinty?' he bellowed. 'The tinker's bastard?'

'Ssh! Remember her reputation.'

'Why, it's known the length and breadth of Galway she's Finn Macchuin's bit of flash.'

'Do keep your voice down. A man of the world like you must know it's a woman's prerogative to change her mind.'

'It's true you're a fickle crew if not kept up to the mark.'

I wondered what methods Michael might employ to keep any woman belonging to him 'up to the mark'. But I thought Sissy could take care of herself.

'You wouldn't have any difficulty keeping a girl's attention fixed, I'm quite sure.'

'Oh, Bobbie!' He sighed sentimentally and pressed me to his capacious chest. 'Couldn't you find it in you to be that girl? I know I'm a rough sort of fellow. When my father died, God rest his soul, the bailiffs were at the door and I've four brothers and a sister younger than me. I had to set to and bring the place about or they'd have starved. I've not had time to cultivate the winning ways that ladies like. I've had to lie down in my mud last thing at night and get up before dawn to make the place pay. But I'd be good to you, no fear of that.'

At that moment I felt I had glimpsed the real man behind the boasting and self-assertion. I forgot that the sum of our acquaintance amounted to half an hour's conversation and was truly sorry to be the cause of pain.

'It wouldn't work, Michael. We have nothing in common. But thank you, anyway. Now I really must go and see to things in the kitchen.' I tried to free myself from a grasp like a cattle-crush. 'Why don't you ask Sissy to dance?'

'You don't mean it? A McOstrich and a McGinty? Why, her father sharpened knives for a living and her mother was out of the cat-house.'

'I call that ungallant of you. A McOstrich of Ballyboggin stooping to petty snobbery? I'm shocked. You could make a queen of a beggar-woman, if you chose. Sissy was good enough for Senator Macchuin, remember.'

'That's true.' This evidently gave Michael pause. If there was one man to whom Michael was ready to bend the knee it was Mr Macchuin.

'She's got a passionate nature, that's obvious. She's very pretty. And original.'

'Maybe.'

'And she's very fond of you.'

'Is she now?' Another pause. I felt his grip slacken. 'Well, I'm sorry for it. It's a sore thing to be in love and get no return for it.'

I slipped from his arms and went to supervise the stacking of plates and the soaking of knives and forks. When I returned to the hall I found Sissy standing alone with her back to the fire, warming her fish-tail and bare back. There was a cool wind blowing from the ever open front door. I scanned the bobbing crowd. Of Michael there was no sign.

'Hello,' I said. 'Are you enjoying yourself?'

'I am *not*. Have you seen Finn?'

'No.'

Sissy looked crosser than ever. 'I never saw such a lot of gobshites under one roof.'

'There's someone I know who'd be deeply hurt to hear you've a low opinion of him. He thinks a great deal of you.'

'So what! Don't care if he does.' Sissy's flat little nose went up higher. 'Who do you mean?'

'I'm not going to tell you if you don't care. It would be too cruel.'

'Ah, go on. I don't believe you know anything about it, cold-blodded as you are, you *Sasanach*.' When I said nothing she lowered her chin a little and said gruffly, 'Well? Do you want me to knock it out of you?'

'Promise you'll be kind to him?'

'Tell me or I'll pinch you.' She held her thumb and first finger against my bare arm.

'All right. It's Michael McOstrich.'

She pinched me hard and I jumped. 'Don't do that!'

'Liar! 'Tis yourself he wants to spoon with.'

'That can never be. I'm only the housekeeper. He's got his family honour to think of. He told me if there was one girl in Galway he'd like to make mistress of Ballyboggin, it was you.'

'If you're having me on I'll bite you!' She lifted her lip to show her teeth.

This was no time to be faint-hearted. 'He was telling me just now how pretty and original he thinks you are.'

'More likely he was thinking of his precious cows.'

'A man's all the better for having an interest. I'm told he's a rich man.'

'I care nothing about money.'

And to give Sissy her due, I believed her. 'He's taller than any man in the room by a head. And good-looking. And pretty passionate, I imagine.'

'That's what you think about in the night, is it?' She gave me another pinch but it was gentler than the first.

'Come on, Bobbie,' said Kit's voice in my ear as he put his arm round me. 'I've danced with every matron, maid and jade. Now it's your turn.'

The musicians, their faces dripping with their exertions, were playing jigs and reels, rhythm and melody pouring forth from their very souls. Neither of us knew the steps, of course, but nobody troubled to be accurate and we skipped, swung and cantered, too breathless to talk, for twenty minutes.

'Mercy,' cried Kit at last. 'I must have holes in the soles of my shoes you could put your fist through. Let's go to the library where I've hidden a bottle of champagne.'

'The library? Do we dare?'

'I asked Finn if he'd mind and he fetched the bottle himself.'

In the drawing room a card table had been set up. Maud, Colonel Molesworth, Lady Butler-Maddox and her companion, Miss Thrope, were playing bridge with furious concentration. The library was deserted but the fire was burning well. On the desk was a tray bearing a bucket of ice, a bottle and two glasses.

'Cosy, isn't it?' Kit handed me a glass.

'Not quite the word I'd have chosen. I can't forget I'm on forbidden territory. But this seems to be an evening of Bacchic intemperance when anything goes. I've never seen so many people so thoroughly drunk.'

'The Irish know how to enjoy themselves,' said Kit. 'It's forgetfulness of self that's crucial.'

I pushed back strands of hair that had fallen over my face. 'Whatever the formula, I'll subscribe to it.'

'Constance has asked me to come back at Christmas.'

'They're so hospitable.'

'Constance is a shameless matchmaker. That's the truth of it,' said Kit. I looked at the bubbles springing in my glass and smiled vaguely. 'Will you still be here?' he asked, walking about the room, examining the spines of books that caught his eye.

'I don't know. I might go home to see how my mother is. I'm rather worried about her. But if things are all right at Cutham, I'd like to come back if Constance still wants me. I've formed a scheme for the regeneration of Curraghcourt. Sooner or later I'll have to get a proper job now there's nothing to keep me out of England. But . . .'

'But what?'

'Nothing. Anyway,' I went on after a pause, 'you're a friend of the Macchuin family in your own right. My comings and goings needn't affect you.'

Kit smiled. 'It's rather too late for that.' When I didn't say anything he held out his hand. 'They're playing something quieter now. Dance with me.'

'What, here? In this holy of holies? I'm not sure I can. It's the equivalent of playing shove ha'penny on the altar of the Sistine Chapel.'

'Are you afraid of Finn? Or is it me you're afraid of?'

'Your Honour, Learned Counsel is leading the witness. Of course I'm not afraid of either of you.'

I put myself in his arms and together we drifted round the room to the distant strains of 'Too-ra-loo-ra-loo-ra, That's an Irish lullaby', beneath the indifferent gaze of Plato, Socrates and Augustus, whose busts adorned the bookshelves and who had no doubt seen it all before. Kit held me close, put his cheek against my brow and hummed gently in my ear.

'Isn't this nice,' he said after a while.

'Very nice.'

'When our headmaster said our schooldays would be the happiest of our lives he didn't know about you.'

'Or he didn't know what a smooth-tongued Lothario you'd become.'

'You mistake my character entirely. I am the soul of truth. Nanny always said with ears that stuck out like mine I'd only get a girl to love me for my noble nature.'

'And how have you got on?'

'If you really want to know: a handful of full-time girlfriends; one broken engagement – she broke it off; and one failed marriage. I was the one who fell out of love.'

'Really?' I lifted my head to look at him. 'You never told me you've been married.'

'It's never seemed particularly important. Is it now?'

'No. Though, naturally, as a friend I'm interested.'

I returned my temple to his cheek while I thought. The fact was that I knew almost nothing about Kit, though I felt so comfortable with him. He was well educated, amusing, charming. But he was more complicated than that.

'I can hear the hum of machinery, cogs turning, ratchets clicking. You're thinking about my having been married. Wondering what she was like. Why it went wrong.'

'I'm curious,' I admitted. 'Somehow I find it difficult to imagine you in the grip of dark emotions.'

'You think me superficial?'

'Not a bit. But too easy-going to quarrel.'

'Well, as it happens we didn't quarrel much. I married her because she was kind enough to fancy herself in love with me and, having taken Nanny's chastening words to heart, I thought it was too good to pass up. She was – is – a sweet, pretty girl. Devoted not only to me but to puppies, ponies, kittens, sugar and the colour pink. Romantic novels and musicals. Anything fluffy and soft. Then I discovered that I was horribly bored. Not her fault but mine. Luckily we hadn't had time to breed. I was twenty-three. Much too young. I'm not proud of it.'

'Poor girl!'

'Don't worry about her. She married again. A rich old lord who worships her.'

I contemplated this picture. 'I must say I think you're rather particular. She sounds attractive.'

'I've grown *very* particular. Particularly particular in the last few weeks, since coming to Ireland.'

'I'm fond of ponies and puppies and kittens. Nor do I scorn certain shades of pink if used judiciously. *Jane Eyre* is a romantic novel. As is *Pride and Prejudice*. I like *Top Hat*.'

'In that case I'm doomed to go on repeating my mistakes. I've already detected a regrettable habit you have of thinking well of animals and badly of men. Repeat after me: two legs good, four legs bad.'

I freed myself from his embrace. 'That reminds me, I must go and see if the tabby cat's had her kittens yet. I promised Flavia I'd keep an eye on her.'

Kit sighed. 'Can I come? There might be an opportunity for a spot of midwifery. I've had plenty of experience with puppies and it can't be all that different. That would put me in your good books, wouldn't it?'

'Certainly. I won't know what to do if anything goes wrong.' But in the hall Father Deglan, one of the few guests not completely drunk, was talking to Liddy in scolding tones. She looked sulky and mutinous. I put my hand on Kit's arm. 'Ask Liddy to dance, will you, and be kind to her? I'll come down when I've checked the cat.'

'I'd rather warm the runt in the bosom of my evening shirt.'

'Please.'

'Don't be long then.'

The light was on in my bedroom. Flavia was lying on my bed, fully dressed and asleep. I pulled the eiderdown over her. From the depths of the cupboard a very pregnant cat looked gloomily out. I assured her with specious cheerfulness that all would soon be well and gave her some milk. I wondered whether Pegeen, whom I had last seen in the drunken embrace of Turlough McGurn, had remembered to give Violet something to drink. Taking the jug of milk I went up to the attic floor.

Except for one candle burning before the Blessed Virgin, Violet's room was dark. I switched on the bedside lamp. She was turned towards the wall. I lifted her so that she lay facing me in the pool of light. Her forehead was puckered in a slight frown, her eyes closed as usual.

'Hello, Violet. How are you?'

Her forehead felt hot so I untucked the bed, put her arms over the blanket and smoothed back a lock of hair that had fallen across her cheek.

'I wish you were downstairs so you could hear the music. The party's going well, judging from the level of intoxication. There's a man clinging to the newel of the staircase, assuring it of his undying affection.' I began to spoon drops of milk into Violet's mouth. 'Liddy's dancing with Kit. She'll be safe with him. He's a decent man. And intelligent. And he makes me laugh. He's dependable. That should be enough, shouldn't it? Though somehow, Violet, I get the impression that wouldn't be a quality *you'd* put top of the list. Don't ask me how I know that. Perhaps it's your clothes, all the things you've chosen, that lipstick. I think you'd find Kit *too* nice . . . not dangerous enough. But I never want danger again.' I wiped her mouth and put some Vaseline on her lips. Then I patted cold cream into her face and neck. Her nostrils flared and her lips quivered as though she might be going to say something. But she remained mute. I stroked her hair. 'Oh, Violet, I wish you'd wake up and talk to me. Do try! If you could see Flavia lying asleep on my bed – she's been looking after that tabby cat I told you about – she looks so adorable. Flavia, I mean. It's so sad for her to grow up without you.'

No response. I walked out of the pool of light towards the basin to fetch her toothbrush. I pulled the cord that switched on the light over the mirror and then screamed aloud.

'Ssh! Don't get upset. I'm sorry. I didn't mean to frighten you.' Mr Macchuin was sitting on the window seat.

'You *terri*fied me. How could you *do* that: hiding there in the dark all that time. I nearly had a heart attack!'

His eyes were glittering in the hard light cast by the fluorescent tube. His bow tie and the top button of his shirt were undone. He had a glass in his hand and a bottle of what looked like whiskey on the seat beside him.

'I'm sorry. I came upstairs for a little peace. I was banking on your going away any minute.'

'I'm sorry to have disturbed you!' The shock had made me angry. 'If you can put up with me for another two minutes I'll go away as soon as I've cleaned Violet's teeth. Unless you'd like to do it?' I held out the toothbrush and toothpaste.

'I wouldn't do it as well as you. Don't be cross. Can't you understand that a man might want a little quiet in his own house?'

'You needn't sound so martyred. It wasn't *my* idea to celebrate Lughnasa. I'm by no means addicted to society. And I delight in silence.'

'Really? You can scream though. Any seagull would be jealous.'

'Ha, ha! Very funny.' I was trying to remember exactly what nonsense I had been telling Violet.

'Have a drink, Miss Norton.'

'No, thank you, Mr Macchuin,' I said coldly. 'I dislike whiskey. Besides, I'm interrupting your precious solitude.'

'Can't you get off your high horse for once?' He must be drunker than he looked. 'Why do the English have to be so stiff? Call me Finn, for God's sake.'

'It's nothing to do with being English. *You* always call me Miss Norton.'

'I'd be afraid to do anything else without an invitation.'

'Well . . . if you like you can call me Bobbie. It's a matter of complete indifference to me.'

'"It's a metter of complete indiff'rence to meah",' he mimicked in a high voice with exaggeratedly anglicized vowels. 'I can't imagine how you people ever get together to increase your race. It must be a ghastly embarrassment.'

'I like that! When you can't produce a sentence that doesn't sound like an instruction manual.'

He looked surprised, then laughed. 'Liddy says I'm getting pompous. The influence of the Senate, I suppose. All right, Bobbie – what a ridiculous name for a girl – let's have a drink and declare a truce between Ireland and England. It's not whiskey,' he added, 'it's Armagnac. A good one.' He stood up. 'Sit there' – he pointed to the window seat – 'and I'll get you a glass.' He went to the basin and rinsed out Violet's tooth-mug.

It seemed easier to comply. And I happen to like Armagnac. After Mr Macchuin (I could not think of him as Finn) had given me the mug filled to half way with amber fluid he made no move to sit beside me. Instead he walked round the room and paused beside Violet's bed.

'I was wrong, wasn't I?' He took his wife's lifeless hand in his. 'In my heart of hearts I can't persuade myself she'll recover. But one ought to try to hope. Wasn't it Wordsworth who said we live by admiration, hope and love? We can't survive in a bleak world of reason, common sense and duty.' He continued to hold Violet's hand but he looked at me. 'What do you say to that, Bobbie, sensible, industrious and rational as you are? Florence Nightingale to my wife, bosom friend of my sister, guardian angel of my children. Also doing sterling work in your subsidiary role as animal protection officer.' He raised his glass in a toast and smiled. 'Not forgetting the power you have over the wild mountainy men.'

I turned round as something tapped on the window behind me. A trickle of water caught the light as it ran down through the dust on the outside of the pane. 'It's the first time it's rained since the night I arrived.'

'Unusual for Ireland. As you'll find out. If you stay. We've made almost a virtue of our weather. It's a matter of national pride that most of the time we're up to our knees in mud.'

In the distance bright splashes of orange and red glowed against the blackness of the night. 'What are those lights?'

'Bonfires. It's traditional at Lughnasa to drink as much as you possibly can and jump over them. The *Garda* are trying to make it illegal because several people have been burned to death.'

I said nothing at that moment because I saw that Violet's eyes were open. She was staring up at Mr Macchuin.

'I'm going back to Dublin tomorrow,' he said after a pause during which Violet had closed her eyes.

'Will you be away long?' I asked just to keep him talking. It had occurred to me that it might be her husband's voice that drew Violet from her deep sleep. The first time she had opened them he had been standing beside the bed, arguing with me.

'I don't know. The implications of the legalization of the sale of contraception for bona fide family planning seem to require lengthy discussion.' Violet's eyes were open again. 'I think we'd do better to put our weight behind getting all restrictions whatsoever on the sale of contraception removed. The numbers of unmarried girls crossing to England for abortions grows by leaps each year.' The senator was frowning now. He returned Violet's hand to the bedclothes and began to stroll about the room. I was almost sure that her eyes were following him. Which meant that she could see. 'Who are we trying to kid, anyway? The black market in contraceptives is hurting the people who can least afford it: people with too many children already; young men earning a pittance as agricultural workers. Almost the only people who still believe in the *Humanae vitae* – the papal encyclical of nineteen sixty-eight – are the priests and the ancient die-hards who don't want sex anyway.' He stopped pacing to look at me. 'I'm not shocking you, am I?'

'Not in the least. It's obviously of crucial importance to people's welfare and happiness.' The moment he stopped talking Violet closed her eyes.

'I suppose Ireland seems extraordinarily backward to you?'

'I think it's charming.' He seemed to be waiting for me to say something else but I wanted him to talk. 'Life in Dublin must be quite a contrast to Curraghcourt.'

'It's a lovely city. Do you know it?' I shook my head. 'We used to have the most infamous slums in all Europe. Foreigners went on guided tours of the worst parts just to marvel at our poverty and degradation, but we've come a long way since then. Now we see ourselves as having something to offer culturally and historically and we're beginning to take pride in our architecture. I have a handsome set of rooms overlooking St Stephen's Green. But when I'm there I want to be here. I miss the children, the house, the quiet . . . the beauty of the mountains. The wildness.' He drained his glass, unaware that his wife was staring at him with unblinking intensity. 'Then when I get home there are so many . . . difficulties . . . that usually it isn't long before I'm yearning for the distractions of city life which leave one no time for reflection. It seems impossible to settle anywhere. Perhaps the truth is I don't know how to be happy any more.' He stood thinking for a moment and then shook his head and ran his hand over his forehead. 'I'm getting maudlin. I've had too much to drink. What about you? What keeps you here, wasting your talents in a job that's dull, dirty and repetitive—'

'Must you go immediately?' I interrupted because Violet's eyelids were fluttering and drooping now as though she were very tired.

He looked surprised. 'Yes. I think I must.'

'Because I really think . . . Do look at Violet.'

He turned his head. 'What?'

'All the time you've been speaking her eyes have been open.'

He went quickly to the bed and bent over her. 'Violet? *Violet*. It's Finn. Look at me.' From where I was sitting his shadow hid her face. After what seemed a long time but was, perhaps, a minute at the most, he straightened up. 'I'm afraid you've allowed yourself to be deceived by wishful thinking. Or the movement of shadows.'

'I didn't imagine it.' I tried to conceal my disappointment. 'I swear her eyes were open and she was looking at you. Do you think I'd risk raising your hopes so cruelly if I weren't absolutely certain?'

'No.' He smiled. 'I'm sure you really believe you saw it. Because, purely from disinterested kindness, you long for it to happen. But it was a trick of the light.'

'If only you could stay a few days longer. I'm certain it's your voice that draws her out of unconsciousness.'

'Miss Norton – Bobbie – I'm touched by your concern for Violet, truly I am. But for the children's sake, for everyone's sake including your own, I don't think it's a good idea to invest too much in the idea of her getting better.'

Men are stubborn creatures. It is a mistake to argue with them for it only encourages them to harden their theories to adamantine and makes it impossible for them ever to admit they are wrong. With a superhuman effort I controlled my impatience and composed my face to express compliance.

'I haven't offended you?' He was obviously nonplussed by my failure to respond with my usual acerbity.

'Not in the least.'

'It would be to a high degree ungrateful if I had.'

I made my voice brisk. 'Let's forget all that. In fact, I want to consult you about something else entirely. I'd like to stay on at Curraghcourt for a while if that's all right with you?'

'Do you need my permission? The boot is on the other foot, rather. Constance has threatened to tear me limb from limb if I quarrel with you one more time.'

'Good. But I do need your approval and co-operation. Because I have a plan.'

THIRTY-FOUR

'It was pretty good, actually.' Liddy leaned back against the window. We were in Violet's room. Outside massing clouds dripped moisture like swollen sponges. 'I've never danced properly before. With someone who could.'

She chewed a fingernail while she reflected. We had had this conversation or something along the same lines at least every few hours since Lughnasa, seven days ago. The party had been proclaimed a success by everyone except Sissy who was more furious with me than ever. The cause of her anger seemed to be Mr Macchuin's – Finn's precipitate return to Dublin, though I had had nothing to do with that. We had come down to breakfast late on the morning following the party to find a note from the master of the house lying on the dining table, addressed to Constance. Propped against one of the candlesticks were three brief messages for the children. When Constance read aloud her brother's apology for having left without saying goodbye Sissy had stamped her foot and hurled her piece of toast at me before rushing from the room. She was a good shot, having had a knife-throwing act at one time, and it hit me squarely in the face. The missile was too light to do me any harm but the butter was a nuisance.

'I suppose all English public schoolboys can dance and kiss without drowning you in saliva,' said Liddy, folding up her legs on the window seat where her father had sat a week before.

'Don't you believe it.' This was the first I had heard about kissing. I was feeding Violet porridge made with cream and brown sugar. The watery stirabout had gone by the way. Her ability to swallow had improved and food no longer ran down her chin. 'The best you can say about most public schoolboys is that they're proficient at

403

Latin. And playing girls' parts in Shakespeare plays. They live in hope of finding a woman who won't mind being called by her surname.'

'I suppose you're going to marry Kit?'

I stopped feeding Violet to look at Liddy. She had lost something of her bloom. That morning I had heard someone being sick when I walked past the bathroom. Liddy had emerged shortly afterwards, perspiring and pale. She attributed the attack of vomiting to having eaten something that had disagreed with her but I suspected she might have put her fingers down her throat. 'I'm not thinking of marrying anybody,' I said.

'Oh.' More chewing of the savaged nail. 'I should think it would be very boring to be married.' She examined the shreds carefully. 'Kit's so respectable. You'd have to open fêtes and be nice to the tenants.'

'You know more about it than I do, obviously.'

'He told me about his parents and their house in Norfolk. It sounds incredibly swanky.'

I began to feel slightly dissatisfied with Kit. What business had he to boast of his credentials and kiss sixteen-year-old girls?

'I should hate all that sort of thing,' continued Liddy. 'Having to be on my best behaviour all the time. Probably he expects to be an old-fashioned husband. You know, separate bedrooms and he knocks on your door in his dressing-gown and demands his conjugal rights.'

Evidently Liddy's imagination had been extremely active.

'Does anyone behave like that any more?'

'Haven't the faintest.' She wrapped her arms round her knees and was silent for a while, brooding. 'I'd hate to be married to a man who was a lot older than me,' she said eventually.

'There'd be obvious disadvantages. A long widowhood for one thing.'

'And he'd be terrifically masterful because he'd know so much more than you.' She stared out of the window, dreaming, while I washed Violet and cleaned her teeth. 'Bobbie?'

'Mm?'

'You're not in love with Kit, are you?'

'I'm not in love with anyone.'

'Because I don't think you're suited to each other, really I don't.'

'No?'

'No.' Liddy was unable to keep an eagerness from her voice. 'You need to marry a man you can boss about and organize.'

404

I could not help smiling. 'I'm sure you're right.'

'And someone taller. If you wore four-inch heels you'd be the same height as Kit. Honestly, I really think it'd be a bad mistake for you to marry him.'

There was a knock at the door. 'Bobbie? Are you there?' It was Kit.

I checked that Violet's face was clean and that the paraphernalia of invalidism was tidied away.

'Yes, come in,' I called.

'I've been looking for you everywhere.' He stood in the doorway, holding a bunch of wild red fuchsias. 'I stopped on my way from Kilmuree to pick these. I know how you love them. Hello, Liddy.' He threw her a smile, not seeming to notice her blushes. 'I must say, they look rather insignificant to me.'

I took the flowers. 'Ah, but though they're tiny, when you look into them they're exquisite. It seems so profligate of Nature to scatter something so exotic as carelessly as though they were nettles. You're early.'

'The weather's grim and the ms I'm reading is such tosh. I'm on the verge of cutting my throat. Say you'll come to my rescue and have lunch with me at the Fitzgeorge Arms?'

I telegraphed caution with my eyes. 'I can't today. There's too much to do.' I had my back to the window so I was able to mime the words 'Ask Liddy.'

'Surely you can take *one* lunchtime off?' Either Kit was obtuse or he was determined to ignore my signals. 'It's just conceit that makes you think you're indispensable.'

'None the less, it's necessary for my ego. Perhaps Liddy would stand in for me, if you ask nicely.'

Kit ignored this. 'But you're necessary to *me*. Think how horrible I'll look with my throat grinning from ear to ear. And the mess the landlady will have to clear up.'

'I'm going.' Liddy sprang to her feet and bounded to the door. 'Have a good lunch, you two. I only hope' – her voice broke – 'you don't get food poisoning.' She pushed past him and I heard her running down the corridor.

Kit lifted an eyebrow. 'What's up with Ireland's answer to the falling birth-rate?'

'Kit! How can you be so unkind!'

'That girl's too precocious for her own good.'

'Did you kiss her at the party?'

405

'Only a fatherly peck, I swear. I'm not used to being flirted with by someone young enough to be my daughter. I was brought up to consider it bad manners to reject a young lady's advances but the experience brought me out in a cold sweat. Any moment I thought I'd be clapped in irons by the *Garda Síochána* for molesting a minor.'

'I'm afraid she may be rather fond of you.'

'You needn't worry. I'm not remotely tempted to take advantage of a teenage crush. I have the Englishman's horror of adolescent storms. And I like a little intelligent conversation from time to time.'

'That wasn't quite what I meant.' I leaned forward to wipe Violet's mouth then stopped, surprised. 'Go on talking. Tell me about the manuscript you're working on.'

'It's about an accountant called Brian whose plane comes down in a jungle and he's the only one left alive. He's rescued by this tribe of Amazons who strap him to a ylang-ylang tree and insist on every permutation of sexual intercourse several times a day. I've no doubt it got a lot of things out of the author's system in the writing . . .'

I was watching Violet's face. Her eyes were open and turned towards the door where Kit was standing. I nodded to him and flapped my fingers to encourage him to continue. He looked puzzled so I pointed to the bed.

'What? Oh, Christ! I see! Ah . . . you want me to go on talking? . . . Yes, I've got to the end of the first chapter where one Amazonian – who I think may turn out to be the heroine – hits upon the merciful idea of a cold compress . . . It gets steamier. Not at all suitable.'

'Talk about the weather. Anything. Stream of consciousness.'

'It's too wet to work in the garden this afternoon but I'm sure you've got something back-breaking indoors lined up. I was thinking as I lay in bed this morning how I'm going to miss this place. It hasn't exactly been a rest-cure. In fact I've rarely worked harder but it's got under my skin, somehow, along with the dirt.'

'You're going away?' I kept my eyes on Violet's face. 'That's a great pity. There's so much to do and you've been so helpful.'

'I haven't settled on a day but I shall have to go back to London soon. I've resorted to the most ridiculous excuses to extend my trip as it is. Ferry strikes, enteric fever, shirts lost at the laundry . . .'

'Before you go will you give me a lesson on the circular saw? Timsy says he's too busy to help Flurry. And actually I think he's telling the truth. The queue in the granary never seems to grow less.'

'I'll finish the sleepers before I leave, even if I have to stay up all night.'

'You're marvellous, Kit.' I smiled up at him. 'Thank you.'

'I suppose it's something to be missed for my industry. Is it foolish of me to want to be missed for my own sweet self?'

I turned back to Violet. 'Go on talking.'

'Well, now. I had an interesting chat with Maud yesterday. She told me – as usual, not pulling her punches – that I was wasting my time drooling after you. She said you were the sort of girl who liked things to be complicated and difficult so you could see yourself as a romantic heroine. You preferred a man who'd look daggers rather than sheep's eyes. She wasn't complimentary about either of us. She obviously sees me as an effete Englishman of the type she trampled on in the days of her power. Except that they at least were engaged in manly occupations. Landowners, army officers, masters of foxhounds. She has all the contempt for the arts that people of that generation and class generally feel. My grandmother and great-aunts all walked with a limp, their right legs withered from having ridden side-saddle to hounds for forty years, and considered anyone who liked poetry to be vitiated and deservedly consumptive. Of all the differences that separate humanity, I think the Arts versus Philistinism the most divisive. Catholics and Calvinists all believe in God. Whigs and Tories believe in the power of politics. Both the rich and the poor believe in the desirability of money. But a hunting man is blind to the beauty of an iambic pentameter and fiction to him is claptrap. And what do we intellectual dilettantes understand of the pleasures of hecatombs of warm, dead creatures offered to the god of sport? How's that for loquacity? I think I've earned that lunch.'

'It *is* horrible.' Flavia stuck out her head from beneath the bed. 'That's what you meant, isn't it? That it's wicked to kill things for fun?'

'Flavia!' I said, startled. 'What *are* you doing under there?'

'I heard someone coming and I thought it was Pegeen so I got under the bed because she tells me off for disturbing Mummy and then just as I was going to come out I heard Liddy's voice and I thought she'd tease me for hiding under the bed and then—'

'Never mind,' I beckoned to her. 'Come and look.'

Flavia crawled out. I put my arm round her and turned her towards the bed. Violet's eyes, the colour of black grapes in the gloomy, rain-streaked light, were wandering restlessly about the room. Flavia sucked in her breath in a harsh whoop. Her body stiffened beneath my arm, then shook violently as though she had received an electric shock. Trembling from head to toe, she picked up her mother's hand

and pressed it against her cheek. Violet's eyes rested on her younger daughter's face with an expression of puzzlement that became alarm.

'It's all right, Mummy,' whispered Flavia, her tears falling fast. 'It's me, Flavia.' Her highly sensitive nature enabled her to interpret Violet's feelings instinctively. 'I've got bigger because you've been asleep a long time.'

I could not decide whether the moisture that filmed Violet's eyes before she closed them was a reaction to the swimming particles of dust or a response to the intense love in Flavia's voice.

I was ruthless in making use of Kit's energy and ingenuity now the possibility of his going away had been brought to my attention. Living within a ring of mountains in a remote area of unspoiled landscape did strange things to one's concept of time. It was easy to imagine that nothing that happened in the world outside had much relevance. But we had a great deal to accomplish in our own small sphere. The great plan I had proposed to Finn on the eve of his departure was to take advantage of the scheme set up by Hibernian Heritage to assist owners of large historic houses to do running repairs in return for opening them to the public for so many days a year. It had been in my mind since Constance had spoken to me about the impossibility of such an undertaking on my first morning at Curraghcourt. Constance had been at first doubtful about the size of the enterprise but I persuaded her that we could do it. She had written at once to ask for a representative of HH to call and already someone had telephoned to make an appointment for the end of January. Meanwhile we had Finn's permission to stir the castle to its foundations in order to present its most inviting face to scholars and tourists.

Constance and I spent a long time debating which parts of the house we would display and in what order. After an inspection of the first floor we decided to include the south tower room that was a grander version of my own and the room next to it which had the remains of a lovely Chinese wallpaper. I thought it would be a good idea to display the dressing room which led off it and was part of the fifteenth-century castle. Concealed within some fine early panelling was a jib door, behind which were the remains of a mediaeval garderobe.

'Can we make this interesting enough, do you think?' Constance surveyed the dismal furniture in the dressing room, a fake, badly carved Jacobean bed and some chairs upholstered in hideous mushroom Dralon.

'We'll make this into a bathroom. There's a marvellous old slipper bath in one of the attic rooms. We'll bring that down here.' I scribbled a note to that effect. 'And those old-fashioned scales. And the shaving table. There's that pretty blue-and-white lav in the mahogany box next to the still room that no one ever uses. We'll stand it against that wall. It'll be plumbing through the ages. Before I went into the auction house I worked briefly for the National Trust. There's nothing visitors like so much as kitchens, bathrooms and lavatories.'

Constance picked up a cushion and then threw it down as a large spider scurried out from its stuffing. 'I must say everything looks incredibly shabby. Ought we to get new curtains for the beds and recover the chairs?'

'We'll put the later stuff upstairs, but anything pre nineteen twenty we'll repair and clean. Shabbiness won't matter as long as we can restore everything to a sort of ripe old beauty. It's a pity we can't show your brother's room: it has the best view of the canals. Come to think of it, it would be a good idea to get rid of the weeds and regravel the walk between them. We might even trim those yews that have grown so massive.'

'I know where there are some photographs taken in about nineteen thirty. The yews were cut into Christmas pudding shapes sitting on drums. Could we copy that? Or are the trees too old?'

'Constance! What a brilliant idea! Yews are very good-tempered. You can cut them back as hard as you like and they shoot again from the trunk. What's more, August is the perfect month for doing it. It'll transform the garden and it won't cost us a penny. I don't know how I'm going to stop myself going out now with a pair of shears.'

We went into Finn's room. It was extremely tidy and smelled faintly of vetiver. The four-poster had a curved tester decorated with oak leaves, perhaps Chippendale. I admired the view from the window. Clipping the yews would reveal the smooth sheets of olive water that were now just flashes of light between the branches.

'It's going to look stunning,' I said with satisfaction.

'Won't it!' agreed Constance. 'We *must* include this room. We'll make it the last on the tour. Finn could always sleep somewhere else if he objects.'

'Well, you can suggest it. I wouldn't dare.' I admired the portrait of Liddy in red chalk that hung above the washstand, the pair to one of Violet that hung in Flavia's room. It would be a good idea to include a résumé of the family history in the guide book we planned to write to accompany the tour. There was a painting of Constance's grandmother hanging on the stairs among other Macchuin ancestors. Her expression was reproving and she was dressed in black relieved only by a crucifix on her large bosom. 'It *would* mean we could display four rooms in a row. We could put a rope across the corridor by yours so the visitors have to turn left by the linen cupboards. Then Maud won't be disturbed by tramping feet. They could go down by the back stairs into the kitchen without retracing their steps or running into people coming up.'

'You're going to show them the kitchen?' Constance looked astonished.

'No. You are. It'll be an added thrill for them to be given the tour by a member of the family.'

'Will we be able to keep the kitchen tidy enough?'

'It'll be good discipline. Besides, we'll have all morning to be untidy in. We shan't open until something like two o'clock.'

'What about Katty and Pegeen? Won't people think it odd to find two bodies slumped by the fire?'

'They won't have time to sleep. They'll be too busy helping in the tea-room.'

'A tea-room? Heavens! What'll Finn say about that?'

'Our visitors will need refreshment if they've come a long way. And lavatories. For the time being they'll have to make do with the downstairs cloakroom. If the project gets off the ground, we'll have to install a few more. Perhaps in the old tack-room.'

'Can there be anything you haven't thought of?'

'Oh, plenty. We'll be making it up as we go along, for the first few months at least.'

'I'll ring Finn this evening and ask him about including his bedroom on the tour.'

'Will you say anything about Violet?'

Constance hesitated. 'I think, in view of his reaction when you tried to tell him before, perhaps not. He's convinced himself she isn't going to get better so he'll probably think we're hallucinating and get worried. Let's wait until he comes back and can see for himself.'

Since Lughnasa Violet's condition had improved remarkably. It seemed that the deeper registers of the male voice were needed to rouse her from insensibility so Eugene had been deputed to recite poetry to her for as long as his strength held out. With exemplary devotion to duty he spent long hours between lunchtime and dinner in Violet's room, sometimes thundering in defiance, sometimes reducing himself to sobs by his own pathos. Violet watched him at intervals, her eyes tracking his movements. Each day she opened her eyes more often and for longer.

On one of these occasions Constance had taken Flurry up to see Violet. Mother and son had looked at each other impassively for a brief moment before Violet had turned her eyes back to Eugene and Flurry had asked if he could go downstairs and get on with the steam dome of his engine which was giving trouble.

'Poor Flurry!' said Constance later. 'He finds conversation difficult at the best of times. I suppose it's the autism. Dislike of change is characteristic, isn't it?'

'I believe so.' I gave the pastry for the onion tart I was making a quarter-turn. 'I know so little about it.'

'You can't know less than I do. Finn didn't seem to want to talk about it when he came back from the specialist in Dublin. He was sad and silent for a long while afterwards. I didn't feel I could raise the subject myself.'

'It must have made it more difficult that he couldn't talk about it with Violet.'

'Mm. I suppose so.' Constance helped herself to a biscuit. I made them often now as Flurry had decided that he liked them. I crammed them so full with currants that they were nearly black with vitamin C. 'Strange, isn't it, how you can live so intimately with other people and yet have so many subjects that are taboo. I adore Finn but there are lots of important things we never talk about. Violet, the children, money, the future. I suppose he thinks I'm too impractical to be worth sharing problems with. That makes me feel very inadequate. And I know he doesn't care for Eugene particularly but I'd like to feel we could at least acknowledge his presence in the house. He can't still be waiting for Eugene to go home. Not after nearly a year.' She took another biscuit. 'I'm a little afraid of Finn's temper. I suppose that's why I don't like to bring things up. And what's going to happen about Sissy? Can they still be lovers? I don't think she'd be so cross if they were. Was there ever such a household for misunderstanding and obfuscation?'

'That's family life, isn't it? It's just like that at home. My father and I rarely speak without quarrelling. He ignores my brother's existence except to express blighting contempt. And my mother never says anything to anyone except to complain. Curraghcourt seems relatively sane to me.'

411

'Does it?' Constance took a third biscuit. I put the lid on the jar and removed it. 'You really don't think we're all quite, quite mad?'

'I haven't enjoyed anything so much for ages as being here.'

'That isn't quite what I asked. Never mind.' She looked around vaguely. 'Where've the biscuits gone?'

'You know you said you wanted to lose weight? Those biscuits are made with lashings of butter. They must be more than a hundred calories each. You've just eaten a light lunch in a careless moment.'

'Oh, well, there doesn't seem much point in trying to improve myself. Eugene hasn't made a move towards me. If Lughnasa couldn't do it, nothing will.'

'Nonsense! He's terrified of rejection, that's all. Somehow, subtly, you've got to let him know you like him. Why not write a poem about your feelings – in the abstract, not mentioning names – and show it to him? Get him thinking.'

'He's never read any of my poems. I'm sure he'd think they were so bad that he'd be completely put off.'

I almost said nonsense again but realized that I was turning into a sort of Lady Bracknell figure. 'Kit thinks your poetry is good. What did he say? A command of imagery, passionate and subtle.'

'He was just being polite.'

'I don't think so. But if you won't believe him let me read some. I promise I'll tell you honestly what I think.'

Greater love hath no woman than that she read her friend's poetry. But then I truly did love Constance.

'Would you, Bobbie? I'd consider it a great favour.'

'Nons— I know much less about poetry than Kit. But, if it will help, I'd love to read anything you've written.'

Constance picked up a fragment of raw pastry and chewed it thoughtfully. 'I wonder . . . could I really?' Her eyes became unfocused.

I put the pad of paper I used for shopping lists in front of her and handed her a pencil.

When Liddy had been taken up to view the phenomenon of Violet with her eyes open she had stared at her mother for some time. Constance and I had stood sympathetically by, poised to offer reassurance.

'Golly!' Liddy had said eventually. 'I hope she isn't going to mind too much about that white dress.'

'She might not get well enough to mind,' Constance had said. 'We can't tell how much she's actually taking in. The message has to be sent from her eyes to her brain—'

'Flavia's got Mum's hair but I've got her eyes,' interrupted Liddy. 'I suppose they're Granny's really but mine are darker than either of them. I'd rather it that way round. I mean, it's easy to dye your hair any colour you want.' She nibbled a cuticle while she digested the altered state of things. 'If she does get really better she'll have to have all new clothes,' she said at last. 'I shall be able to tell her what's in. It might be quite fun.'

When Constance had told Maud that Violet was able to open her eyes Maud had said, 'I hope you don't expect me to be glad? What use will it be to her to be able to see the four walls of her room and the smirking, simpering faces of her attendants? She'd be better dead than in whatever limbo she inhabits. You're a sentimental fool, Constance.'

Pegeen and Katty were also far from overjoyed by the development. When Pegeen had first seen Violet looking at her she had screamed and fallen to her knees and Katty had crossed herself several times with a face of doom. They seemed to think that Violet's improvement was flying in the face of God's will, even to suspect it was the harbinger of some apocalypse. For days afterwards Violet's bed was damp with sprinklings from the stoop.

THIRTY-FIVE

'What's it all about?' asked Father Deglan as he came into the drawing room. We had gathered for drinks before dinner. We had not seen him for two weeks as he had been enjoying his annual holiday in Dublin, standing in for a brother priest who ran a shelter for drug addicts and prostitutes. For once Kit was not with us. He had set himself the task of getting to the bottom of his pile of manuscripts by the expedient of spreading them over his bed at the Fitzgeorge Arms, thus prohibiting sleep until they were disposed of. 'The talk's all over Kilmuree that Violet has been seen walking over the mountains. There are rumours that she rides a pooka. But it's all nonsense, of course. I can't get it into their heads that belief in fairies is just childish superstition.'

'Hark at the pot.' Maud almost slammed down her glass of usquebaugh as she perceived that chance had delivered into her hands a scourge with which to flog the priest. 'Roman Catholicism was devised as a means to control the ignorant masses by frightening them with fairy tales of pitchforks and purgatory. Don't you ask the poor dupes to believe a miracle happens every Sunday to a box of cheap wafers and a bottle of inferior wine from Dooley's?'

'What's a pooka?' I asked, in the interests of Father Deglan's cardiovascular system.

'It's a fairy horse that gallops away with you,' Constance explained, pulling a piece of red wool through the malodorous Persian carpet we were repairing. It was nineteenth century and good quality but in poor condition due to hard wear and constant damp. We could make it serviceable for tourists' feet by darning the biggest holes and putting a layer of felt beneath to absorb moisture. The floors were dark and sweating now because of the rain that for the last month had swept the lawns and thrown itself against the long sashes.

'Violet can open her eyes,' Constance went on, 'and we're almost certain she can see something. How much we don't know.'

'God's mercy is infinite.' Father Deglan crossed himself and even his sad eye seemed moved to something like joy.

'One might ask oneself, unless brainwashed to the point of idiocy, if it was merciful of Him to send her a stroke in the first place,' said Maud.

'It's been truly said you Protestants are like white blackbirds.' Father Deglan took up the gauntlet. 'At home nowhere. Resented by the Irish and despised by the English. You've a cold apathetic sort of religion. You look down your long noses at holiness and you can't give your hearts to God the Father Almighty because your souls are killed by pride. You have no meekness, humility or obedience and so you'll be cast into hell for eternity. I pity you from the bottom of me heart.'

'My family have lived in Ireland for three hundred years.' Maud's cheeks grew pinker with the pleasure of argument. 'I think that makes me as Irish as any brat from a bog. But I suppose you think the only true Irishman is Catholic, Republican and Gaelic-speaking.'

'Aye, I do and that's the fact. For one thing St Patrick established Catholicism here in the fifth century and anything else is nothing but tinkering. For another no true-hearted Irishman is content to suffer under the yoke of the tyrant oppressors – you'll excuse me, Miss Norton, if I speak plainly – and we'll fight till the breath is out of our bodies to rid ourselves of the Old Enemy.' He raised his fist in a salute.

Maud rolled her eyes. 'Oh, simple minds!'

'Is it guilt now for your kind's misdoings that makes you so unreasonable?'

'I've never felt guilty in my life,' Maud said scornfully. 'Guilt is extremely vulgar.'

'I do like hearing Gaelic spoken,' said Constance pacifically, 'but it's such a difficult language to learn.'

Father Deglan drained his glass of sherry and looked expectantly at the decanter. 'There was no difficulty in my day. We were taught in Gaelic and heard not a word of English.'

'I've heard Finn say that the predominance of Gaelic in schools is one of the root causes of Ireland's backwardness,' said Maud. 'Half the children's lessons are taken up with learning an archaic patter at the expense of maths and English and geography, while world history is scarcely touched on. We're insular enough without that, God knows.'

'*I* think censorship is as much to blame,' said Constance as she stitched in red part of a border that should have been blue. 'Eugene feels strongly about it, don't you?'

Eugene nodded energetically, with popping eyes. He had a sore throat from hours of reading to Violet and was resting his voice.

'Last time I was in Dublin,' continued Constance, 'I saw *Hay Fever* by Noël Coward. Hardly pornographic. But his plays were banned in Ireland until ten years ago. I mean, who in their right minds would consider "navel" a dirty word?'

'Sure, Constance, you're a victim of the newspapers and – hah – evil influences' – Father Deglan glared at Maud – 'with your harping on the ways of the world. What need is there to discuss the parts of the body at all, I'd like to know?'

I saw three men walk past the windows on their way to the apple store, with that indifference to rain that is so characteristic of the Irish. Business was booming. Someone had recently tipped off the *Garda* as to the whereabouts of the two shebeens that had been our only competition this side of Kilmuree. Timsy had publicly expressed his indignation at such treachery and threatened to 'puck the gob of the lousy scut' should the informer's identity ever be discovered, but no one, I imagine, was fooled for a moment. Soon we would have enough money to buy the washing machine. I had not been able to forget that flicker of dismay on Finn's face when I had asked him for a hundred pounds. I had not cashed the cheque.

'Do tell me about your schooldays, Father Deglan.' I liked the old man best when he was reminiscing. He was always willing to recall the hardships of his youth and his native facility with words made listening easy. 'It's a wonder you were able to learn anything at all,' I said when he paused to drain his glass. I was genuinely affected by his account of a remarkable dedication to learning despite poverty, aching cold, fleas, shortage of books and even of something to sit on, all of which deprivations had been accompanied by a relentless, gnawing hunger.

'It explains why the average Irish peasant is an illiterate dolt,' said Maud.

I saw a naked figure cartwheel past the window and whirl down the path between the *miroirs d'eaux*. Luckily Father Deglan was staring at the fire, rubbing his corky nose as he searched for memories in the ashes that flew like flecks of foam each time the wind blew down the chimney. Eugene strolled with a casual air towards the window, took up a position leaning against the architrave and stared pensively into the garden.

'Yet we were as healthy as the Proddies that dined on steak and jelly every day of their lives. Hah!' Father Deglan smacked his knee and gobbled down another generous handful of nuts.

'I suppose we shouldn't be surprised that an inadequate diet and squalid living conditions have done nothing to spoil the peasants' appetite for violence and drunkenness,' said Maud. 'Now I think I've had enough of Ireland's bitter draught. What's the news?'

'What was your childhood like?' I asked Constance as we washed up after dinner. The priest had been taken away by taxi and Maud had gone to bed. Eugene was dozing by the drawing-room fire. 'I imagine it was very different from Father Deglan's.'

Sissy, who was grinding berries and herbs, looked up sharply. Disdaining my cajoling smile she returned a stern gaze to her pottage. I made a mental note to buy an electric blender with money from the poteen fund next time I went into Kilmuree. It would be useful for both of us.

'Finn and I were brought up by my grandparents. I told you, didn't I, that the Republicans tried to burn Curraghcourt during the Troubles? Though my grandfather had converted to Catholicism and taught himself Gaelic he was still suspect in the eyes of the IRA because he was a senator. I was fond of my grandfather. Finn sometimes reminds me of him. His portrait's in the library over the fireplace.'

I remembered it. The man with the military moustache.

'My father went away to fight just after Finn was born in nineteen thirty-nine. I'm very proud of him for that. But you wouldn't believe how unpopular it made him with everyone here. Though officially Ireland was neutral during the Emergency – that's what we call the Second World War – half the country was actually pro-German. As a race we're incapable of neutrality. You'll not be offended, I hope, Bobbie, if I say that the only thing we've ever agreed on as a nation is our dislike of the English.'

I was not offended. I felt fairly confident that I had been excepted by the majority of these good-natured, generous-hearted people from the general prejudice against my kind.

'It was considered thoroughly unpatriotic to fight alongside the English. I'm afraid Ireland was shamefully ignorant about the persecution of the Jews. You have to understand that the majority of country people were still fetching water in buckets from wells.'

'Honestly, you needn't feel you have to make excuses. There's plenty I could apologize for on behalf of the English. I declare a détente.'

Sissy distracted us at this point in the conversation by pounding the contents of the mortar so violently that a sludge of berries and herbs splattered across the kitchen table. As we had finished washing up Constance invited Sissy to join us in the drawing room. She put down her pestle, folded her arms and stared at us with unconcealed animosity, so we went away, feeling obscurely guilty.

'Oh dear,' said Constance as we sat on the sofa together, the worn Turkey rug over our knees, and took up our needles. 'Sissy's so difficult these days. She seems so unhappy. I wish I knew . . . It's too bad of Finn. What was I talking about? Oh, yes, about Daddy.'

'Was your father killed in the war?'

'He almost got through it unscathed. But in nineteen forty-five, only weeks before the end, he was wounded by shrapnel. After months in hospital he was sent home. Granny told me later he wasn't the same man. He'd become an introvert. Silent and depressed.'

'I suppose he'd seen terrible things.'

'He was so isolated, that was part of the trouble. No one here understood or sympathized with what he'd been through. My mother found herself married to someone who preferred walking over the mountains alone to going to parties. They tried to patch things up. I was born in nineteen forty-seven. I have faint memories of a man with half his face crisscrossed with white lines from the shrapnel who was always clearing his throat and looking out of the window. He used to pat my head with a stiff hand when he saw me but he had a horror of noise so Finn and I were kept out of his way. Then, when I was five, something awful happened. I remember my mother and grandmother and all the servants weeping, and the *Garda* coming to the house. Finn was brought home from school. They told us that Daddy was missing and they were looking for him. A few days later they brought back his body on a hurdle. He'd drowned in the lake. Finn and I knelt down on the landing and peered through the banisters. We saw them pull back the coat that was over his body to show my grandfather. Daddy's face was a dark blueish-grey, like wet slate . . .' Constance's eyes filled with tears. 'It's silly of me to be upset after all this time.'

'Not silly at all.' I felt my throat tighten in sympathy. 'I had no idea. I wouldn't have asked if I'd known.'

Constance shook her head. 'It was twenty-seven years ago. But I see that face so often in my dreams. Well, Mummy hated Curraghcourt after that and went away to Dublin. She came back to see us occasionally but Granny and Mummy had never liked each other. Mummy died when I was eight. Granny said it was drink that killed her. They buried her next to my father. When Granny was dying she told me Daddy had left her a note before he went down to the lake but she'd destroyed it. Suicide's a mortal sin, of course. I can understand how she felt. But I'd so like to have had that note.'

Constance had forgotten about the carpet and was leaning against the arm of the sofa, her needle cupped in her hand, her thoughts far away. On the rug by the hearth Maria sighed and lifted her head to rest it on Osgar's large hairy flank. He licked his muzzle, speckled with turf-ash, and stretched a back leg. Outside gusts of wind chucked warm summer rain like handfuls of buckshot against the windows. Beyond stood the encircling mountains, their sides burnished with sluicing water, shielding us from the volatile mood of the Atlantic. All was wildness without, and warmth and safety within. Between us and the nearest cinema, café, amusement arcade and petrol station lay a vast, unpeopled, unfenced region of black lakes, sullen bogs, shuddering trees, crashing rivers and quaking cotton grass. Wild goats lay beneath dripping rocks while foxes stalked rabbits and birds clung to branches or nested among asphodel and bell heather.

'It's difficult to imagine being unhappy for long here,' I said. 'There's a sort of in-built self-righting mechanism in its peacefulness.'

'You'd think so, wouldn't you?' said Constance. 'But in almost every generation there've been Macchuin wives making tracks for the bright lights of Dublin. I suppose the men have always had things like hunting and shooting and fishing to distract them from the drumming rain. As a child I was never bored. I loved riding my pony and helping with the lambing and the harvest. Everyone was kind to me. But I still dream that I see my parents walking towards me, not dead after all, but only having been away on a long, long holiday, and I run towards them weeping with joy.' Constance put down her needle and rubbed her eyes as though weary. 'I wonder if Finn thinks about them; if he dreams of them, too? Do you know, we never talk about them at all?'

'Perhaps you're each afraid of upsetting the other.'

'I think it may be Granny's ghostly influence at work. She disliked

419

anything that interfered with the domestic comfort she put all her energy into creating. After the civil war, I think she was always a little afraid. When Grandpa was late, I remember, she used to pace up and down this room, up and down, up and down, until she heard his voice in the hall. Then she'd dart into that chair' – Constance pointed to the armchair that held the slumbering Eugene – 'and snatch up her sewing and smile as though she hadn't a care in the world when he came in.'

I let my eyes wander over the drawing room which had been created at a high point of civilization, at the lovely old furniture, at the portraits of dead Macchuins – the Cosway and the Kneller particularly good – at the fine ceiling, at the yellow damask walls, pigeon-grey in the shadows, and felt moved by something akin to love. Curraghcourt was my home in a way that Cutham had never been. I had work to do here. I could be useful. I could not imagine it as the background for a pacing figure, beset by fear in a turbulent world where observing a particular form of worship was enough to earn a bullet through the heart. The melancholy beauty of Ireland had got into my bones like the damp.

'Constance, are you there?' Father Deglan stood in the doorway, his greasy curls tumbled about his brow, excitement manifest in every feature. 'Have you heard it yet? I met Thady O'Kelly on the road; he says it's all over the wireless. So I turned round at once and came back, thinking maybe Finn would be on the telephone with the news from Dublin.'

'What is it? What's happened?' Constance looked bemused.

'Our boys have surpassed themselves, that's all. Not thirty miles away up the coast they've blown up Earl Mountbatten!'

THIRTY-SIX

At breakfast we were disinclined to talk much at first. We had listened to the early news bulletin on Maud's wireless, which did not tell us much more than Father Deglan had heard from Thady O'Kelly the evening before. An old man, an old woman and two fourteen-year-old boys had died when their fishing boat had been blown up in the bay of Mullaghmore. The IRA had claimed responsibility. Of course Lord Mountbatten had not been just any old man but an instrument of British imperialism and a member of the royal family. But I felt, as I'm sure Constance did, for the man himself, for the violence of his death and for the grief of those who had loved him.

'Those poor children.' Constance was the first to speak as she contemplated her untouched egg with wet eyes. 'Innocent young lives. Oh, it was cruel!'

'Cruel?' said Maud who, having been disturbed at an unusually early hour, had broken the habit of years and come down to breakfast. 'It was cowardly! Wicked! Disgraceful! In fact I can't think of words bad enough to describe it. This country groans and whines and licks its centuries' old wounds in public but in private it's sly, sneaking and vicious!'

'It was unfortunate about the boys.' Eugene crumbled his slice of toast and blinked mournfully. 'I'm afraid it will make us rather unpopular.'

'Do you think they felt . . . anything?' Flavia's book lay closed by her plate. She looked green. The proximity of the deed made it all the more harrowing.

'No, darling,' Constance said at once. 'It would have been very quick. They wouldn't have had time to register pain.'

'Why should those boys have been killed?' persisted Flavia. 'How

421

can it be part of God's plan? Father Deglan said that the mighty had been cast from their thrones. But those boys weren't mighty, were they? One of them was the son of a fisherman.'

'Don't forget, darling, they're in heaven now' – Constance paused in the process of cutting the rind from Eugene's bacon to smile tremulously at her niece – 'where it doesn't matter a bit what race or religion you are and they're much, much happier than they could ever have been on earth had they lived to be ninety.'

'Tchah!' Maud pushed away her plate of food untouched. 'It's no good that fool of a priest trying to make it into an act of national heroism. It was cold-blooded murder, that's all.'

'Murder? Who's murdered?' Sissy came in just then. 'If you mean those people up the coast, well, it's war, isn't it? What about all our boys shot by the British? The lads that were hanged after the Easter Rising? How many children was it died during the famine and none to help them?'

'Ah, you remember the poem by Lady Wilde on that subject?' Eugene smiled gently as he looked around the table.

'Bread! Bread! Bread! and none to still their agonies.
We left our infants playing with their dead mother's hand:
We left our maidens maddened—'

'Please, Eugene.' Constance looked stern. 'After yesterday's atrocity, I don't think things that happened more than a hundred years ago—'

'Why should we care because this lot were lords and ladies?' interrupted Sissy. She glared at me defiantly from beneath her stiff black fringe, seeming oblivious to anything but the aggravation of my English presence. 'Except it'll make the British more sorry.'

'I can't listen to any more of this.' Maud got up and hobbled out of the dining room.

'I agree with you, Sissy,' I said. 'Class makes no difference at all. And if the IRA thought blowing up an earl would make the English suffer more, they were mistaken. We're not particularly fond of our aristocracy. But the successful targeting of prominent people will make the British feel more vulnerable – and more determined to punish.'

Sissy raised her right hand. '"These Protestant robbers and brutes, these unbelievers of our faith, will be driven like the swine they are into the sea by fire, the knife or by the poison cup until we of the

Catholic Faith and avowed supporters of all Sinn Fein action clear
these heretics from our land." That's the oath of allegiance to Sinn
Fein. And we mean every word.'

But for the mood of gloom created by the tragic event of the previous day I would have been amused by this dramatic formulation
which sounded like the kind of thing we made up when playing
Robin Hood in the shrubbery as children.

Sissy put her face close to mine. 'That's three less of them.' She
held up the appropriate number of fingers. 'That's what.'

Her eyes were so close to mine that she squinted. For the first
time I felt alarmed by her antagonism.

'That's *enough*, Sissy.' Constance sprang up, looking furious. 'I
don't want to hear another word of quarrelling and feuding in this
house. No!' She held up her finger threateningly as Sissy opened her
mouth. 'I mean it! Not another word, from you or anyone else on
the subject of war or religion. Let us all try to behave like Christians,
at any rate!'

'I don't remember seeing you angry before.' Eugene stopped eating
to look at her while egg yolk dripped from his fork on to his plate.

'O Deirdré, terrible child,
For thee, red star of our ruin,
Great weeping shall be in Erin—'

Constance clapped her hands over her ears. 'I think I'm going
mad.' She rushed from the room.

Eugene turned puzzled eyes to me. 'What did I say?'

'I hope it hasn't made you hate us.'

Constance and I were in the kitchen, preparing lunch. We had just
been told by the boy who delivered the groceries from Dicky Dooley's
shop that the IRA had blown up eighteen British soldiers at
Warrenpoint only hours after the murder of Mountbatten and his
family.

'Not hate, no. I do feel sad. It's awful to imagine the grief of all
those families. Poor young men. What did they ever do to deserve
it? They probably went into the army to have adventures or to get
away from home. I am angry, I have to admit, but I also feel guilty.
The more I learn about Irish history the more ashamed I feel of the
way the British have behaved in the past.'

'*You* feel guilty? I can tell you, *I* feel as though my hands are dripping with gore. I wish I could stop thinking about it. I get a horrid pain in the pit of my stomach whenever I think of those boys . . .'

'Don't, Constance.' I looked up from the lettuce I was washing. 'We know neither of us would do such a thing to our worst enemies, no matter what the provocation. I don't believe it's anything to do with nationalism. It's everything to do with people feeling angry about themselves, about their disappointments and failures and weaknesses. And it says something about men. They enjoy being violent, that's all. Fighting and killing is much more fun than hard work.'

I plunged my hands into the water and swooshed the lettuce about furiously. Because of the rain every crinkle of every leaf was choked with mud. It was our first real crop after the handful of radishes the flea beetles had left us.

'There *are* female terrorists,' said Constance.

'Yes, but how many have been implicated in shootings and bombings? Perhaps one in fifty? If that?'

'I've no idea.' Constance was chopping the lettuces that had bolted and were too bitter to be eaten as salad into a saucepan to make soup *au père tranquille* for dinner. 'But for all we know there may be thousands of wives and mothers and daughters egging the men on. You know, Bobbie, I can't share your prejudice against men. Think of Eugene and Finn and Flurry.'

'Flurry's not a man yet. But I agree with you, he's entirely lovable at the moment and it's impossible to imagine him as a selfish brute.'

'Would you say Finn was selfish? Or brutal?'

'No, not brutal, of course not. Anyway, he's your brother. I wouldn't accuse him of brutality and selfishness to your face even if I could justify it.'

'I know you think he ought to be here doing his share of the work. You needn't deny it. I know you too well. But he does so much good as a senator. Besides, we need his salary.'

'If I'm prejudiced against men I'm even more so about politicians and their usefulness, but I expect you're right.' I decided to change the subject in case I was required to give Eugene a character reference. 'Isn't it annoying about the lettuces bolting? I've consulted the book and it says it's because they were transplanted later than April.'

'And Finn's been so generous to Eugene,' Constance persisted.

'Mm. Yes.' I had to admit that many men would have been annoyed to find a guest invited for dinner still there nearly a year later. Whether this was generosity or inertia I was not prepared to say.

'And think how good he's been to Violet and Maud.'

It was true that to Maud, not the easiest of mothers-in-law, Finn was unfailingly courteous and that before he left for Dublin he had given us carte blanche from what I knew were limited resources to buy for Violet whatever we thought might improve her lot. But there had been those years of neglect before. A man ought to be good to his wife without anyone thinking he deserved praise. And there was his mistress, possibly now ex-, but still beneath the same roof as his invalid wife. I realized that Constance could cite the presence in the house of Sissy, a penniless refugee from the harsh world of vaudeville, as yet another instance of his open-handedness. Constance was naturally inclined to take her brother's part. And I . . . well, I had to admit that Constance was right: my view of men had become jaundiced.

'And there's Kit,' Constance went on. 'Surely you can't hold anything against him? He's the perfect English gentleman. Well mannered, well educated, charming – and he adores you.'

Having dried the leaves in a tea towel I began to tear them into small pieces. 'Aren't you exaggerating?'

'It's obvious from the way he looks at you. Also – don't be annoyed – we had a little talk.'

I stopped tearing. 'What about?'

'There! I ought to have known better than to tell you. Now you're cross.'

'I'm not. What did he say?'

'Not much, honestly. Just that you've had a hard time from the press – of course I knew that anyway – and that that man, Burgo Whatshisname, treated you very badly. He thinks you need protecting. He's worried that you might react by starting another affair on the rebound that would be equally disastrous.'

'Is he indeed!' I felt my face grow warm with indignation. 'Listen, Constance, I got what I deserved. Burgo made no secret of the fact that he was married. I knew it before I allowed myself to fall in love with him. Contrary to popular mythology it's a voluntary state, *I* think. Anyway, I'd seen enough of the world to be certain that an affair with a married man invites more kicks than ha'pence. But I was bored and miserable and I told myself that this was different. Of course it wasn't. I admit it made me unhappy but it's over now and I'm quite all right. I don't need to be treated like a green-sick girl who's been jilted by an unscrupulous villain. Don't tell me he thinks I'm going to run away with Michael McOstrich? Though it would be none of his business if I did!'

Though I tried to speak mildly, I suppose my anger must have shown on my face for Constance's lip began to tremble.

'Oh dear! What an idiot I am! A silly blundering fool—'

'No, no! Of course you're not!' I stripped off my rubber gloves as quickly as I could, never an easy process, and threw my arms round her. 'I'm sorry I was cross. But I'm not cross with you at all. Honestly, Constance, we're both upset because of what's just happened and likely to get things out of proportion. I'm really sorry. Let's have a glass of wine. We need to cheer ourselves up.'

Once the dreadful Riesling from Dicky Dooley's had started to take effect and our equilibriums were on the way to being restored, I asked, 'So who did Kit think I might be about to make an ass of myself with this time? Do tell, just for amusement's sake. I promise I won't be angry.' I smiled in demonstration of this as I sandwiched chicken breasts between greaseproof paper in order to flatten them before bread-crumbing them and frying them in butter. 'I know. Turlough McGurn. What does it matter that he hasn't a hair on his head or a thought in it, other than how to flog rotting contraband vegetables?'

'Actually he thought – you'll never believe it, I laughed when he said it – he thought it might be . . . Finn.' Constance looked at me nervously, but when she saw I was calm she continued. 'I told him it was ridiculous. That you were more likely to quarrel than anything else. But Kit said that was often a sign there was a great attraction. Sexual tension, you see, having to be kept under a lid. I must say it sounded rather dramatic. It made me think of pressure cookers.'

'He did, did he?' I began wrathfully. 'I mean' – schooling my face to smiling tranquillity – 'perhaps he thinks I've only to see a married man to fall passionately and uncontrollably in love with him?' I took the rolling pin and gave the chicken breasts several savage whacks. 'As you say, I'm sure he only wants to save me from myself.' I was unable to prevent something of a hiss escaping in this last sentence and Constance looked at me again, more closely.

'No. It's more than that. I'm sure he's in love with you himself. He started to confess as much but I stopped him. I'm no good at keeping secrets. Honestly, I'd rather not know. Besides, I didn't feel comfortable talking about you behind your back, even though every word he said was in your praise. I did accept his card.' Constance fumbled in the pocket of her trousers. 'Here it is.' She handed it to me.

I whistled. 'Albany, Piccadilly. That's a very smart address.'

'Is it? I didn't know.'

'Oh yes. Why did he want you to have this?'

'I suppose . . . he thought I might let him know if something was . . . brewing. Naturally I'd never do any such thing.'

'Naturally not.' I took a block of fresh butter from the fridge and put a chunk to melt in a frying pan. By the time it was starting to melt to a glorious liquid gold I could look Constance in the eye with an expression that was serene.

'After all, it's meant in kindness,' said Constance pacifically.

'Of course.'

I began to compose a short sharp speech to deliver to Kit as soon as I could contrive to be alone with him after lunch. But this satisfaction was denied me for, just as we were sitting down to eat, the boots boy from the Fitzgeorge Arms appeared, soaking wet and sporting a streak of mud from the seat of his trousers to the crown of his head from his long bicycle ride, with two letters, one for Constance and one for me.

'Oh, what a shame!' Constance had opened hers first as I was busy serving the chicken. 'Kit's had to go away! How we're going to miss him! He says how sorry he is he had no time to say goodbye but his office has a flap on. He thanks us all for a wonderful visit. He wishes to be remembered to you, Maud, with deepest admiration and respect.' Maud lifted her eyebrows and stared out of the window as though indifferent to praise. 'And to you, Eugene, with thanks for many hours of pleasure and enlightenment.' Eugene held up both hands in a gesture of confutation and pursed his small mouth with mock modesty. 'Sissy,' continued Constance, 'his message to you is that he looks forward to further gymnastics at Christmas.'

'If you write back you can tell him some exercises to do,' said Sissy. ''Tis the building up of the shoulder muscles he must dwell on.'

'I don't think our relationship is of the kind that permits personal remarks about his physique,' Constance said. 'Liddy, he says he cherishes the memory of dancing with you at Lughnasa.' Liddy turned as red as the radishes in the salad bowl.

'Is there a message for me?' asked Flavia.

427

'He says will you carry on with the training of Osgar. And Flurry, he's going to send you a colour chart of heat-resistant paint for the *Flying Irishman.*'

'I hope there's a dark red. Or green.' Flurry wrapped his lower lip over his upper one while he pondered the question.

'Never trust an Englishman when he is charming,' said Maud. 'An Irishman is charming because he wants you to like him. But an Englishman hopes to bedazzle your wits so he can bend you to his will.'

'What rubbish, Maud!' Constance sounded quite cross for her.

'Read your letter, Bobbie,' urged Flavia.

I shook my head and put it aside. It was not until six o'clock that day, after I had given Violet a supper of lettuce soup, mashed potato and apricot purée, that I opened my letter from Kit.

'Listen, Violet.' We were alone in her room. She had opened her eyes as she always did these days when being fed. I was sitting on the edge of her bed, so she could easily see and hear me. 'Listen.' Her eyes rested on my face, jerked away, then came back. Her right eyelid drooped but it was not unattractive. It gave her a quizzical expression, as though she were always just about to wink. 'You remember Kit? I think you liked him.' Violet licked her lips, probably in response to the lingering taste of apricots. 'You seemed to enjoy listening to his voice anyway. He's gone away. Back to England.' I was holding Violet's attention at least. 'I'm going to read you his farewell letter. *Dear Bobbie.* That's me, Violet, remember?' I squeezed her hand. To my great delight I felt her fingers tighten around mine. *'I'm more sorry than you can imagine to have to leave without saying goodbye. But something's come up in London and I'm catching the overnight ferry.'* So he was already in England. I felt a depression of spirits that was disturbing. What a fool I had been to resent what had seemed to me to be oppressive interference. Now I would have given a great deal to see him walk in, with that air of his of finding life amusing.

It's been a remarkable few weeks. Out of the world, out of time. I can see you love the place and it seems to suit you. But don't lose your heart to it completely. That would mean cutting yourself off from many good things and remarkable experiences. Curraghcourt is perfect as somewhere to recuperate but you are too lively and intelligent to spend these crucial years when you ought to be making the most of your

*talents in a tumbledown castle in a dark forest by a black
lake, like a fair maid under a spell of enchantment. I expect
you will be annoyed with me for saying this. I know you
don't like to be told what to do. Particularly not by a man.
So I'll pipe down. Believe me, I only want to save you from
the bad fairy. I'll telephone soon,*
 Kit.

'Well, Violet, what do you think? Not exactly a love letter, is it?
No protestations of passion or assurances of undying devotion. I like
it much better for that. I was angry with him a little while ago but
now . . . Tell me, Violet' – I felt her hand tremble in mine – 'does
this volatility denote Constance's pressure cooker? Was I angry with
Kit because I'm more than a little fond of him? I bet you know a
thing or two about love, don't you?' Violet stared at me with wide
eyes and faintly dilating pupils. 'I wish you'd tell me about love.
Because I realize I don't know the first thing about it. I'm not even
sure I believe there is such a thing.'

'Bub,' said Violet.

I was so startled that I dropped her hand and sprang up from the
bed. 'What? What did you say?'

Violet pressed her lips together and one corner of her mouth quivered. 'Bub,' she said again.

'I can hear you. I'm listening. But I don't quite understand. What
is "bub"?'

In my eagerness to grasp what she was saying I leaned over her.
Violet screwed up her mouth as though gathering strength. 'Bub
. . .' she said distinctly and then let out a deep sigh. 'Bub-ba.'

'Bobbie! Is that it? You're saying my name? Bobbie?'

'Bub-bee.'

My skin came out in gooseflesh. 'Violet!' I took both her hands
in mine. 'That's wonderful! I can understand you very well. Now try
and say *your* name. Say Violet.'

Violet put her lips together and blew out air. 'Byle.'

'Yes! Put a *t* on the end. Tongue behind your teeth. T-t-t.'

'Byle-t.'

'Well done!' I was desperate to make the most of the moment.
'Now say your mother's name. Maud.'

'M-m-m. M-mum-mum.'

Here was proof, if I needed any, that Violet was capable of thought
as well as imitation.

'Now say Finn.'

But the F proved too difficult. Knowing nothing about speech training I was unable to explain how to make the sound. Violet became frustrated and tearful. She closed her eyes, turned her head away and seemed to sink back into her own world. But I was elated. I went downstairs to find Constance who wept when I told her what had happened.

'It's been such a ghastly day and I've felt so depressed and now this marvellous thing's happened,' she sobbed. 'It's a rebuke for lack of faith. God forgive me.'

Why Constance should at once assume that Violet's achievement was God-given, I did not know. But while milking Siobhan I gave it further thought and the conclusion I came to was that Constance's faith was as instinctive as a preference for light, warmth and hope over darkness and gloom and despair. However many covering layers were stripped away by reason, her religion was as intrinsic as skin and bone.

THIRTY-SEVEN

In the middle of September, the day after Flavia's ninth birthday, the children went back to school. This coincided with the arrival of autumn and the landscape becoming Fauvist with splashes of crimson, yellow and russet. Time gave the impression of gathering speed until the weeks were barely distinguishable one from another. When I look back to that period, I was, if not actually euphoric, at least no longer unhappy. I was too busy to think about myself during the hours I was awake and insomnia was a thing of the past. Now I slept from the moment I turned out the light until my alarm clock went off at six.

I continued to ring home each week but it was clear I was not needed there. These days it was Mrs Treadgold who answered the telephone. My mother was now well enough to bath herself and walk to the lavatory without help. Ruby gave my mother manicures, pedicures, massages, conditioning treatments for her hair and had made her a new nightdress and bed-jacket. According to Mrs Treadgold Ruby was a whiz with the sewing machine and a born nurse. My mother had put on weight. They all had. My father enjoyed five courses for dinner and afterwards played Scrabble with Ruby. These days he rarely went up to his club. Oliver had gone to live with Sherilee upstairs in the Red Lion. Mrs Treadgold's digestion had improved but she had a troubling rash on the backs of her knees. I tried not to give way to a feeling of pique that they were managing so well without me. I had to admit that I could not match Ruby's selflessness.

The beginning of the school year dictated changes to our routine. Constance, the children and I had an early informal breakfast in the kitchen. The children had to leave the house by eight to be driven by Constance to school in Williamsbridge. Eugene and Sissy had their more leisurely breakfasts later, in the dining room. Whenever I went in to replenish the toast or clear the plates, they would be sitting in silence, Eugene reading studiously while Sissy repaired her costumes. Having been sketchily made in the first place they were always coming apart and leaving beads or scraps of lace or wisps of marabou about the house. I pointed out to Constance that it would be more practical and economical, not least of time (*our* time, as Eugene and Sissy apparently had all the time in the world) if they took breakfast in the kitchen as well. Constance explained the peculiar delicacy of the situation according to Irish rules of hospitality. As they were guests she did not like to suggest a change that might imply they were in any way a burden on the household.

While Pegeen and Katty took trays to Maud and Violet I put the results of the morning's milking through the separator, skimmed the cream pans and collected the eggs. By the time I had finished tidying the kitchen Constance would be back and usually we spent the morning doing whatever was needed to restore order and beauty to the rooms that were to be shown off. Then for two hours every afternoon Constance and I gardened. In England everyone retires indoors when it pours. In Ireland you could be immured for weeks with such a spiritless attitude. So I learned to ignore the rain. I bought industrial quantities of things like derris and Bordeaux mixture to combat blight, wilt, aphids, beetles and mites. We sowed spring cabbages, lettuces, broad beans and peas and hoed up the weeds that grew like Jack's beanstalk.

We took a thermos with us and had our tea-break sitting in broken deckchairs beneath pieces of corrugated iron balanced across the glazing bars of one of the greenhouses. The rain had filled the dipping pond to the brim and there was always a gathering of birds on the rim, immersing themselves, shaking their feathers and preening. The greatest pleasure for me was to watch the red squirrels, with tufted ears and gleaming fur the colour of just peeled conkers, either frozen with clasped paws in attitudes of meditation or springing into the safety of a tree. A quarter of the walled garden had been reclaimed now and the more or less straight green rows running across the sticky black soil were a testament to our labours. When I took myself upstairs afterwards to change, my hair was stuck to my cheeks in ringlets, every stitch I had on was steeped in mud and drips hung from the tip of my nose and the lobes of my ears. I felt I was halfway to acculturation.

The most dramatic and radical of our horticultural improvements was the trimming of the two rows of yew trees that lined the avenue between the canals. Constance found boxes of old photographs of former masters, servants, children, horses and dogs with the garden as background. She remembered the huge stone urns filled with palms that had once marked the boundaries of the top terrace. They had been sold in the late fifties, as had the marble statues of Apollo and Aphrodite which had stood at the heads of the canals. The photographs showed an elaborate parterre on the west side of the house. Briefly I played with the idea of restoring it before common sense put an end to this fantasy. It would be much too labour-intensive. But the theatrical yews – in the photographs they looked like black cardboard cut-outs of giant acorns in cups – would need trimming only once a year.

It was much harder work than I had imagined. It took us several days to cut each straggling tree into a shape that resembled a ten-foot-tall steamed pudding. Each yew (there were twenty of them) had to be reduced to roughly half its size and some of the branches were as thick as my thigh. They would take several years to become dense and sharp in outline but it was possible to see, after only four were finished, the exciting contrast between the formality of the clipped yews and symmetrical canals with the wild woods and mountains beyond, just as the original landscaper must have intended.

At half past three either Constance or I went to fetch the children. Tea and then homework, the most disagreeable part of the day, took up all the time before dinner. Flavia adored writing essays but Liddy kicked her chair, groaned and grumbled through every sentence. Flurry was baffled by the requirement to imagine himself as a penny for a day or a monk in the Middle Ages. While we made suggestions and sketched out hypothetical incidents, he would stare at a blank page for hours, becoming mysteriously inkier without having written a word. Finally we resorted to dictation. Of course we knew this was thoroughly deceitful and certainly not in Flurry's best interests but it was essential to end everyone's torment. Yet when the homework was maths he could run through columns of figures faster than seemed humanly possible. Liddy and Flavia were practically innumerate and Constance and I little better, so we were dependent on Flurry to lighten our darkness.

The two younger children had supper early in the kitchen so they could be in bed by nine o'clock. By the time Constance and I had cooked and served dinner for the adults and washed up afterwards I could hardly climb the stairs to bed. But I was cured of love. The conviction that this was so came gradually. I found I could think about the past without pain. I suppose I deliberately made Burgo out to be a limb of Satan, or someone much worse than he really was, in order to speed the healing process. Whatever the truth of it, when I thought of him that autumn it was with a mixture of feelings – regret, shame, affection – but also detachment. I was myself again.

A speech therapist came once a week to spend an hour with Violet. She gave us exercises to do with her and though at first I felt impatient because the goals we were instructed to aim at seemed so paltry – a whole week practising the letters b and p – after a few weeks it was evident that Violet was making progress. By the beginning of December, after much hard work on everyone's part, she was able to communicate with half a dozen words or phrases, like 'drink' and 'lie down' and 'want sky out', which meant she wanted the curtains closed. Her right eyelid still drooped and her mouth was crooked but the speech therapist assured us there was every chance of improvement if not complete recovery of the paralysed muscles.

As Violet became increasingly conscious of her surroundings she often had fits of crying that were distressing to witness. Sometimes she was voluble but we could not understand what she was saying. Strings of syllables, meaningless to us, came tumbling out while she banged her clenched left hand furiously on the bedclothes. In such moods she would deliberately upset her food if she could and glare at us with hatred.

The advent of a physiotherapist improved things further. Miss O'Rourke's large frame and round face with upturned nose and large nostrils appeared to fascinate Violet. When Violet threw a tantrum and screamed, 'Bad pig!', Miss O'Rourke, who soon became known to us as Rosie, said, 'If it's wickedness you're in the mood for I'll go off and have my lunch. Maybe I'll look in later to see how you are. And maybe I won't.'

She once left Violet alone for two hours and instructed the rest of us to do the same. To my surprise when the time was up it was a chastened, conciliatory Violet who greeted us. We had been in the habit of treating Violet as though she were a cross between a sickly princess and a genocidal dictator.

434

'And we'll have none of this weakly lying about,' Rosie insisted. 'Pillows and more pillows. We'll sit you up so you can have a view of the world instead of that crack in the ceiling. Then in a while we'll swing you round so you can put your legs down and get the feel of a good solid floor beneath your feet. After that you'll be sitting in a chair in the blink of an eye.'

Rosie believed in the power of music to override blocked pathways in the brain. She had Violet shaking a maraca with her good hand, pressing keys on a toy piano, and hitting a gong in time to Frank Sinatra and Mel Tormé. She bullied Violet, shouted at her, once even smacked her, but Violet's face always brightened when Rosie walked in. Recognizing Rosie's worth we paid for a supplementary session of physiotherapy each week with money from the poteen fund, which was mounting steadily.

'The poteen's earned us more than a hundred pounds this week already.' I was painting the cloakroom floor with red cardinal to hide the white blotches caused by damp coming up between the tiles. Constance was sorting through a large chest that stood in one corner. 'What I find astonishing is people's unlimited capacity for alcohol. I see the same faces coming up to the stable yard three or four times a week. And sometimes the apple store vibrates with voices raised in argument. But you've got to hand it to Timsy. He's a natural venture capitalist. He was trying this morning to renegotiate the terms of our agreement so he could lend us money at a favourable interest rate—'

'Look! These gloves were Finn's when he was a little boy.' Constance had not been listening. 'I always admired them because they were such a lovely red. And this scarf was Granny's. Now who could have worn these?' She held up a pair of black lace mittens. 'I don't believe anyone's turned out this chest for centuries. It's like an archaeological site, layers of people's lives . . . Oh!' She took out an army cap, khaki with a peak. 'The Irish Fusiliers. It must be Daddy's. I'd no idea it was here.' She ran her fingers over the badge, her eyes dark, her voice a little tremulous. 'To think it's been here all these years.' She turned it between her hands, brushed the dust from the crown and stroked the leather band. 'Still, what use is it? I mustn't be sentimental.'

'Don't put it back,' I said as her hand moved towards the chest. 'We'll put it on display beneath that drawing of him on the landing. It's part of the history of the house.'

—'*Could* we? You can't imagine what it would mean to me.'

435

Looking at her face I thought I had an inkling.

The automatic washing machine had arrived. The day it was installed Constance and I shared a bottle of good Mâcon Blanc from the cellar as we watched the weekly load of fifteen white school shirts whirl in the drum. Predictably, Pegeen and Katty refused to use it. This was crafty of them as it meant that we took over the washing of practically everything but their clothes. But it was worth it for ease and speed and dry floors. Now we had our sights set on a tumble-dryer.

The rain kept up pretty steadily throughout the autumn but there came a time, three-quarters of the way through December, when the temperature dropped from the high fifties to the low thirties and in the mornings a light glaze of frost lay over the ground beneath a brilliant cloudless sky. At Cutham I had cursed the ancient radiators which were inclined to sulk in a barely lukewarm state because their circling waters were choked with particles of rust. But if you have never lived without central heating you can have no idea of the intensity of the cold that dogs you between fireplaces and crackles in every cubic inch of the bathroom, which is densely befogged the second you run the hot tap. I must have been less hardy than the others for I was the only one to get chilblains on my fingers and toes despite wearing gloves and several pairs of socks even in bed.

During the days of frost it seemed warmer out than in and I was glad of any opportunity for exercise which might improve my circulation. The ground in the walled garden was too hard to work and we had stopped cutting the yews for fear of frost damage but on the terrace below the canals was a wilderness of hornbeam surrounding a round, debris-filled pool, perhaps thirty feet in diameter. The photographs showed that the hornbeams had once been tightly clipped into a circular stilt hedge. *The Golden Treasury of Trees and Shrubs* having approved their pruning during the dormant period, I went most afternoons with a saw and a pair of secateurs to cut the lowest branches back to the main trunk.

Maria and Osgar accompanied me on these occasions. Osgar was now unrecognizable as the savage, ill-conditioned creature who had tried to take a piece out of my ankle on my arrival at Curraghcourt. Good food had made his coat shine and his eyes bright, and chasing Maria about the house and garden had built up his physique. He had several bad habits, the most tiresome of which was to clamp his jaws on any item of clothing or

436

furnishing to which he had taken a sudden and unpredictable liking. He would salivate like a rabid animal and refuse to let it go no matter how much we cajoled or threatened until we put a plate of raw meat under his nose. Father Deglan's soutane was peculiarly attractive to Osgar and Constance had to spend more than one evening darning the rents made by his teeth. Osgar ignored my efforts to make friends with him but I was fond of him as of a protégé who had, more or less, made good.

On one particular afternoon not long before Christmas I went down to the pool, carrying a tall stepladder. I had already finished the stilt part of the hornbeam hedge by exposing the trunks to a height of six feet all the way round the circle. Now I wanted to tame the upper parts to restore the disciplined shape of the original pleaching. I was standing, saw in hand, on tiptoe on the very top of the stepladder when Osgar bounded past and knocked it over.

I had felt it rocking beneath me before it actually fell so I had time to cling to the stoutest branch within reach. I found secure places for my feet and peered down through the leaves. The ladder lay on its side. The distance to the ground was a mere ten or twelve feet but the tangle of intervening branches made the descent tricky and the naked trunk offered neither handholds nor footholds.

'Hello!' I shouted. 'Is anyone about? Could somebody put up my ladder?' I was hoping to attract the attention of one of Timsy's customers who might be on his way to or from the apple store. I heard a rustling of leaves as the dogs romped in the undergrowth with heartless indifference. Then they dashed, barking, away. 'Hello!' I called again, feeling foolish. 'I'm stuck! Is anyone there?' No answer. I decided to climb down as far as I could and then jump. Hornbeam limbs grow close together and they are whippy. By the time I had wriggled down a little way my face was scratched and the secateurs in my pocket had sprung open and stabbed me viciously in the knee.

'Bloody hell!' I said aloud. 'Osgar, you're an ungrateful *beast*!' Without warning the spur on which I was standing snapped beneath my weight. For a few seconds I hung from a bough curved like a long bow under high tension. As I was preparing to let go I heard footsteps and a voice from below said, 'Hang on! I'll put the ladder up.'

I hung on for all the good it did me. There was a terrific crack and the outer end of the treacherous branch plummeted with me on to something yielding that partly cushioned my fall.

437

'You've killed him!' Sissy burst from the bushes and pushed me off the prostrate body of Senator Macchuin.

'I haven't.' I got to my knees and bent over him anxiously. 'He's just winded. Give him a minute, Sissy. How can he breathe if you keep kissing him?'

We watched with concern as he panted and grimaced and clutched his diaphragm. After a while he was able to draw enough breath to swear expressively.

'I'm terribly sorry,' I said. 'I couldn't help myself.'

He sat up. 'What – were you doing – up – the damn tree – in the – first place?'

'I'm pruning it into a stilt hedge. I hope you're not much hurt?'

'I hope not too. Stop that, Sissy. I'm all right.'

Sissy narrowed her eyes at me and displayed her bottom row of teeth.

'Let me help you.' I took hold of his arm. Sissy immediately grasped the other one.

'Thank you, I can manage,' he said grumpily, shaking us both off and scrambling up. He brushed dirt and leaves from his suit, felt his jaw tenderly and moved it experimentally from side to side. 'Nothing broken, no thanks to you.'

'I'm afraid you've got a cut on your cheek.' I offered my hand-kerchief, streaked with black from the secateurs, which I had oiled that morning.

He pulled out his own much cleaner handkerchief and wiped his face. Then he looked at me. 'For once the gods have been just. You have several. You'd better have this.' He gave me his hand-kerchief and stood frowning while I dabbed carefully. 'Does it hurt much?'

'It stings a bit.' Actually my right cheek was throbbing as though on fire.

'Good.' He looked at me, his expression grim. 'A stilt hedge? Well, I'd hate to have had my back broken for a trivial cause.'

'Aren't you making rather a fuss about a slight winding?' I spoke coldly.

He continued to look at me without saying anything until Sissy made a growling sound.

'Let's go up to the house,' he said. 'I've had an appalling journey. The clutch went on the Peugeot just outside Dublin. Every train was late. And the taxi had to drop me outside the walled garden. Some damned fool's padlocked the gates.'

'I'm the damned fool,' I said. 'Why didn't you make him follow the proper drive that runs through the woods?'

'Because another damned fool's left a pile of planks right across it. Not you, I don't suppose?'

'They're the new floorboards for the corner of the drawing room. I suppose the delivery man didn't know – we'll have to put up a sign – oh, bother! Now I'll have to fetch them myself in the Land-Rover.'

'Can't Timsy go?'

I looked at my watch. It was half past three. Between four and six was Timsy's busiest time when his customers needed fortifying after a day's work. 'I'll go down and wait for Constance and the children. They'll give me a hand to load them. It'll be dark in an hour. I'd better hurry.'

But when I took my first step, my right ankle, which had been throbbing in a background sort of way, protested. A pain like a nail being hammered into my leg ran up to my knee.

'I can hop.' I gave an experimental skip. Each jump forward was agonizing but I knew better than to seek sympathy. I reached the steps that led up to the canals but then my good, hopping leg gave out completely. Sissy, who had been walking backwards in front of me to watch my progress, threw back her head and gave a crow of delight.

'Give me your hands, Sissy,' said Finn. 'We'll make a chair to carry her.'

But Sissy shook her head and bounded away across the grass like a springbok, laughing gleefully.

'Fortunately I never try to understand women,' said the senator, with a great weight of meaning. 'That way madness lies.'

'Besides,' I said, with awful irony, 'as long as they continue to look after your children, clean your house, cook your meals and launder your clothes, why bother?' I wanted to include wife and mistress with the children but I did not quite dare.

'What a sadly splenetic nature you have. But isn't it ill advised, seeing as I'm the only means you have of getting to the house? And, if I'm not mistaken, it's starting to rain.'

I looked up. A grey cloud hovered overhead. Several drips landed on my upturned face.

'This is no time to stand on ceremony. I'll give you a piggyback.' Finn took off his tie, stuffed it in his pocket and undid the top button of his shirt. Then he turned round and bent gracefully at the knees.

'Won't I be too heavy? I don't want to get mud on your clothes . . .'

439

'Stop fussing and hurry up. I'm getting wet.'

I put my arms round his neck and jumped up clumsily, hurting my ankle very much in the process. The senator started off well, at a brisk pace. Halfway up the steps he began to pant a little.

'You might think . . . of giving up that extra . . . slice of toast.'

'I weighed myself yesterday as it happens. I'm eight and a half stone. No one could call that heavy.'

'We . . . must have those . . . scales checked.'

The rain came down in cataracts. I began to laugh.

'I'm glad you're . . . amused.'

'I'm sorry. But we must look so ridiculous.'

'*You* may. I refuse . . . to believe I look anything . . . other than my usual dignified . . . self. My God! What's happened to the yews?' He paused for a moment and lifted his head to look to left and right.

'Constance and I have been clipping them. It's how they used to look. Before the war – the Emergency, I mean. I hope you like the result?'

He shifted my weight higher on his back and staggered forward between them. 'Is there no end to . . . your appetite for improvement? As it happens . . . and luckily for you . . . I do . . . like it.'

Not surprisingly, I had not ridden piggyback since I was a child. In those days it had never struck me as a particularly intimate method of travel. Now I was very aware of his dark hair inches from my face, of my hands clasped beneath his chin and of my legs fastened round his waist. Rain trickled down my neck and face.

'Stop kicking!'

'Sorry.' I was by now convulsed with laughter.

'I'd like . . . to know . . . what's so funny.'

'Can't . . . tell you.'

'You're hysterical.'

'I think I am.'

'If you could . . . manage to remain . . . in possession of your . . . senses for the last . . . fifty yards . . . we'll have . . . done it.'

He completed the last bit at a run and dropped me without ceremony by the drawing-room French windows. He opened the doors and I hopped inside. He flexed his arms and arched his back and then mopped the rain from his face.

'Thank you.' I tried to subdue the *fou rire* that had overwhelmed me. 'I'm really sorry to have put you to . . . so much trouble.'

'I've rarely seen anyone look more penitent.' He handed me his handkerchief again, now wet as well as bloody. 'I know how Sinbad felt, poor devil!'

'If you're comparing me with the Old Man of the Sea I call that insulting.'

'It is rather,' he smiled. 'And unjust since you've climbed down of your own accord. You remember how Sinbad got rid of him, finally?'

'He made him drunk.'

'Exactly so. For the sake of the legend we'll have a bottle of something decent while we lick our wounds.'

'Daddy!' Flavia raced into the drawing room and flung herself into her father's arms. 'I didn't know you were coming today. Darling, *darling* Daddy! I've missed you so much. You've got to come upstairs with me at once and see Mummy. We've got a surprise for you . . .' She drew back to look at him. 'What have you been doing? Your face is bleeding and you're all wet.'

'Finn! How wonderful it is to see you!' Constance came in, followed by Flurry. 'Goodness, what's been happening here? You look as though you've both been in an accident. Bobbie, your face!'

Flurry examined us with interest. 'Have you been fighting each other?'

'Not quite.' Finn kissed the top of his son's head. 'I've never actually hit a girl though I've often wanted to. Apart from your aunt, but I don't count that because we were very young at the time.'

'I sprained my ankle falling out of a tree,' I explained. 'Your father was kind enough to carry me back.'

'It's lucky you weren't badly hurt.' Constance stripped off her hat and gloves to embrace her brother. 'There's a poem about the Countess of Desmond who was killed falling from a cherry tree. Mind you, she was a hundred and forty years old at the time. Apparently she renewed all her teeth twice.'

'Some people will do anything to be original,' said Finn.

'I'll get the children's tea.' I put my weight gingerly on my right foot. The pain was intense. Constance helped me to a chair close to the fire. She bathed my scratched face and brought a bag of frozen peas to strap to my ankle.

'Shall I take the leaves out of your hair?' she asked tenderly. 'Though they're really rather becoming.'

'I believe it's a look she deliberately cultivates,' Finn said on his way to the cellar.

The next morning the swelling had gone down a little and I found

441

that by binding my ankle tightly I could bear to put weight on the toe. Being obliged to hobble meant that it took me much longer to do things but fortunately it was Saturday when we always had breakfast later. I had planned to ask Timsy to drive me down to the walled garden to pick up the floorboards but to my surprise I found Finn and Flurry had already brought them up and stacked them in the kitchen corridor.

'It's good to be home,' the senator said, apropos of nothing in particular as we lingered over toast and marmalade at the table. He looked around. 'Everywhere looks unusually clean and tidy. And this coffee is quite drinkable. In fact, it's excellent.'

'Bobbie orders it from Dublin,' Constance said immediately.

He frowned, then made an obvious effort to smile as he glanced in my direction. 'I'm grateful for all the trouble you've taken.' He did not see Sissy, who was standing behind him, make the sign of the evil eye in my direction. In Ireland this is called the *Droch Hool*.

Flavia saw her, though. 'You'd better spit,' she whispered. 'It'll save you from being cursed.'

'What happens if I don't?' I whispered back.

'Anything from the milk going bad to dying horribly.'

'Even that would be better than spitting in the dining room.'

'But,' continued Finn, 'though it seems churlish to cast a damper on this admirable industry, aren't we counting our chickens before they're hatched? I suppose coffee from Dublin is a relatively small extra, and God knows the other stuff was bloody awful, but there must be a hundred pounds' worth of oak floorboards in the corridor.' Obviously the price of wood had gone up since he had last bought any for the bill for the floorboards had been nearer two hundred, even with a discount for more orders promised. 'The man from Hibernian Heritage may refuse to give us a grant. In that case where's the money to come from?'

'It's all right,' said Constance. 'They've already been paid for.' When her brother continued to look at her enquiringly she added, 'From a secret fund which we've decided it's best you don't know about. Because you're a senator.'

'I see. Something illegal.'

'It'll be better if you don't even try to guess. But it's nothing that will do harm to anyone.'

'Miss Norton's inspiration, I suppose.'

He seemed to have forgotten that we had agreed on the night of Lughnasa to call each other by our Christian names. He sent me

442

another look, less friendly this time. But when you have recently been carried on a man's back several hundred yards through a rainstorm it is difficult, if not impossible, to feel resentful. So I found, anyway.

'Well, yes.' Constance put up her chin and spoke boldly. 'Bobbie's responsible for the original flash of genius. But I can truthfully say that from the first I thought it was a brilliant idea. And if anyone has to go to jail for it, it should be me as head of the household during your absence.'

He winced as though he had come across a pip in the marmalade. 'Let's hope, Con, it doesn't come to that. I don't think you'd like slopping out in Galway prison nor having your hair pulled and your teeth kicked in by the other women. But perhaps you'll be able to share a cell with Miss Norton.'

He fiddled with his napkin, folding it into the shape of a sailing boat like the ones Oliver and I used to make from newspaper when we were children. I realized that he was trying to avoid the appearance of giving a lecture. 'You're both grown women. I can't dictate to you how you should spend your time. But I'd be grateful if you'd draw the line at turning my house into a gambling-den or a bordello.'

'Honestly, there's no cards or sex involved,' Constance assured him.

He smiled gently at her. 'I didn't really think there would be.'

'What's a bordylow?' asked Flurry.

'You're the wordsmith, Eugene,' said Finn. 'You explain.'

'Shouldn't we be making plans for St Stephen's Day?' Constance was transparently eager to change the subject.

Finn groaned. 'Mercifully, I'd forgotten that.'

'It's the day after Christmas,' Flavia explained to me. 'We always have a party for everyone. Like Lughnasa but bigger.'

'It's the best night of the year,' said Liddy, moodily crumbling her uneaten slice of toast. 'Not that *that's* saying much.'

'We have a piper,' said Flurry. 'He plays so loud it makes you want to scream.'

'And Daddy always makes a funny speech,' said Flavia. 'Last year Moll Flahey split her dress laughing and had to go home.'

Finn put his head into his hands.

The day having begun late, we spent the rest of the morning trying to catch up. At twelve I limped upstairs to give Violet her lunch. Rosie's predictions had been too optimistic. Violet could not yet sit in a chair without falling either forwards or sideways but with an arrangement of three pillows she was able to sit up in bed and was learning to feed herself with her left hand. She was steering a wobbling spoon of finely chopped sole and spinach to her mouth when the door opened and Finn walked in.

The evening before, over a delicious bottle of Sancerre that tasted of gooseberries, Constance had told her brother of Violet's wonderful improvement since he had last seen her four – or was it five? – months ago. Flavia had taken her father upstairs at the first possible moment to see Violet but to her intense disappointment her mother had been asleep and they had gone away without waking her. Finn's opinion of women, which he took little trouble to hide, was that we were histrionic, irrational creatures with little sense of reality. It was obvious from the gravity of his expression when he came downstairs that he thought that we had been guilty of at least wilful exaggeration, at worst mass hysteria, and I could hardly blame him. He had probably allowed himself a brief moment of hope and in that case his own disappointment must have been severe. Asleep Violet looked just as she must have done for the last four years except that she no longer dribbled and could turn herself in bed so she no longer resembled an effigy. But a man would not notice such details as these.

Now, when she heard the knock, Violet looked to see who it was. The next moment she had thrown her tray and spoon to the floor. Trembling with effort she stretched out her thin white left arm. From the corner of her mouth she croaked, 'H-inn! H-inn!'

Finn gripped the handle of the door as if to support himself and the blood drained from his face until he was as white as the walls. We who had cared for her had experienced Violet's restoration to life as an infinitely gradual process. For him it must have been as shocking as seeing an apparition, the ghost of the woman he had loved, whose death he had accepted as fact even if he had not ceased to mourn. I put down the cup I had been holding, stepped over the mess of fish and spinach and crept from the room.

THIRTY-EIGHT

Kilmuree offered nothing in the way of desirable Christmas presents so the day after school broke up, Constance and I took the three children to Williamsbridge, twenty miles away. In the interests of their pocket money and our own far from abundant resources we put an upper limit of five pounds on the cost of any present. This made it doubly difficult to find anything that might go even halfway towards satisfying either the giver or the receiver.

In addition to our own present-hunting we had to buy things on behalf of Eugene as there had not been room for him in the Morris Traveller. He had written out a list with minute descriptions of each item and for whom the present was intended so that we would be sure to buy exactly the right thing. He had enclosed a ten-pound note.

'Where am I to find a first edition of Goldsmith's poems for Finn?' Constance consulted Eugene's list as we took a break for fish and chips at the Come Inn. 'Even in Dublin there may not be such a thing. Williamsbridge has one bookshop. It sells things like *Making Merry with Macramé* and *The Christian Way to Health*.'

I examined the list. 'Essence of bluebells for Maud.'

'It *is* her favourite flower.' Constance looked apologetic. 'It was very thoughtful of him.'

I looked through the café window into the street of hardware stores and public houses, gloomy despite the light reflected in shop fronts and puddles. Williamsbridge smelt of rain and exhaust fumes and the local tannery.

'Thoughtful, yes. Obtainable, no.' I returned to the list. 'Eighteenth-century enamelled *étui* for Bobbie. How kind!'

'What's an et-wee?' asked Flavia.

445

'It's a little case for needles. Eighteenth-century *étuis* are much sought after. Eugene seems to be expecting rather a lot for his ten pounds. A hundred pounds would be more like it.'

'Actually it's my ten pounds,' said Flurry. 'He borrowed it off me this morning.'

Constance handed the two five-pound notes back to Flurry. 'I'm afraid Eugene, though the soul of generosity, isn't very practical. I'll lend him some money myself.'

Liddy, who was reading over my shoulder, laughed loudly in my ear. 'He wants to give you a baby marmoset, Aunt Connie. As long as he doesn't want to give you any other kind of baby! Ugh! Imagine being in bed with Eugene! You'd need a gas mask— That's my foot, Bobbie.'

'Sorry. It's these boots.' I had been forced to wear an unglamorous pair with zip fasteners, left in the house by a long-departed guest, to accommodate the bandaging of my sprained ankle. 'I feel a bit like a deep-sea diver in them.'

'They *are* hideous,' said Liddy. 'No wonder they make Osgar bark.'

Osgar had conceived a passion for the boots and had been maddened by his inability to seize both of them at once. Whenever I wore them he ran backwards in front of me snapping at each toe in turn. It quickly became irritating. Now, however, I was grateful to the boots for turning the conversation.

'A crocodile dressing case for Violet,' read Constance. 'You must admit, Eugene's highly attuned to other people's tastes.'

I admitted it readily. When we reached home after a long day comprising a variety of emotions, among which were hope, despair, gratification and frustration, even Liddy went early to bed without complaint.

Everyone offered to help with the additional cooking, cleaning, decorating and organizing created by Christmas and the party on the following day. This was kind of them but the results were mixed. Mince pies and puddings were allowed to blacken or boil dry: the watcher having wandered off to admire the Christmas tree or to experiment with a new hairstyle. Glasses were smashed by inexpert hands and precious belongings were tidied away to remain undiscovered for months despite frantic searches. The candle placed in the drawing-room window as a symbol of hospitality to the Virgin and Child set fire to a pair of handsome old curtains and had to be beaten out with a silk cushion.

On Christmas Day Maud was taken by taxi to the Church of Ireland in Williamsbridge and everyone else went to the Roman Catholic church in Kilmuree, except for Finn and me. His apostasy was too long established to earn more than a sigh from Constance and a few words of bitter rebuke from Liddy along the lines that if *he* didn't believe in all that crap why should he expect *her* to?

'Argue it out with your aunt and Father Deglan,' he replied. 'As far as I'm concerned your religious beliefs are entirely your own affair. But I would ask you to moderate your language when talking about other people's faiths. If I hear you calling it crap in front of Pegeen and Katty I shall be seriously annoyed.'

Liddy dropped her sunglasses from the top of her head to her nose to signify that she was shutting out an unjust world and followed the others out to the Land-Rover.

'Are you sure you don't want to go with them?' Finn asked me.

'No. Really. Thank you. There's nothing like knowing you have to produce a three-course lunch for eleven people to distract you from spiritual thoughts. Besides, I wouldn't know any of the hymns. It isn't any fun if you can't sing your head off.'

He smiled. 'Your religious convictions are of the profound, philosophical kind, obviously.'

'Is it so obvious?' I returned the smile and limped away towards the kitchen.

I expected him to retreat to the library but to my surprise he followed me down the dark sloping passage.

'I could do something to help, couldn't I?' He examined the bowls of peeled and chopped vegetables, the reduction for the *sauce bigarade* to be served with the geese, and the smoking pan with the clattering lid beneath which two puddings were steaming.

'Thank you. Everything's more or less under control.'

'It all looks impressively efficient.' He put his finger into the brandy-flavoured custard and licked it. 'Very good. And what's this?' He had put his finger into a pot of what looked like black jam and sucked it before I could stop him.

'That's one of Sissy's concoctions.' I smiled to myself as I watched shreds of orange peel pale in bubbling water. 'Flavia says it's a spell. Probably meant for me. What a surprise it'll be if you turn into a barren toothless hag.'

He withdrew his finger. 'I expect you must wonder . . .' he said, then stopped. I was sure he had been going to say something about

447

Sissy but had thought better of it. 'It's very good of you to do all this. I hope you aren't missing your own family too much.'

I strained the blanched peel over the sink and added it to the reduction of onions and red wine. 'I do miss my brother but he's got a new girlfriend so I wouldn't see much of him, anyway. To be truthful, I've never enjoyed spending Christmas with my family. My parents' marriage isn't happy and prolonged exposure to each other's faults invariably leads to rows. And my father disapproves of both his children. By Boxing Day everyone's sulking in their own rooms, brooding over their injuries. I'd much rather be here.'

'That relieves my conscience, if it does sound a little sad.' He helped himself to a raw sprout from the bowl and bit into it. His teeth were even and white, I noticed.

'Sad? Yes, but quite common, I imagine. I'm frequently enraged by my family, sometimes depressed, always critical, yet there's a part of me that loves them. At least I find I can't be indifferent to their sorrows. It's the same for everyone, isn't it?'

'I suppose it is. One tends to feel one's own family is superior only in being peculiarly deranged.'

Now I had him alone, in what seemed to be a sociable mood, I seized the moment. 'What do you think about bringing Violet downstairs this afternoon for an hour or two?'

'Violet? Downstairs?' He looked taken aback. 'Won't it be too much excitement for her?'

'She's so bored. Yesterday she made Pegeen cry by hitting her on the nose with her maraca. She was so pleased to get a reaction that she threw everything within reach: a book, a candlestick, a jar of face cream. Most unfortunately a cup of hot tea. Rosie O'Rourke says she needs more stimulation.'

'Well.' He took another sprout. 'If you really think . . . I suppose we shan't know until we try.'

'The only difficulty is Maud. She refuses to go up to see her, you know. She says the attic stairs are too steep. She's resisting the idea of Violet getting better. But she might listen to you.'

'You overestimate my powers of persuasion if you think anything I say will change her mind. I've never met a woman more stubborn and opinionated.' He looked thoughtful for a moment as though running through the long list of women who nearly qualified for first place. Outside, the wind sprayed rain against the high windows. Inside, the kitchen glowed with the warmth of a fresh coat of primrose-coloured distemper. 'From the beginning Maud refused to accept

448

the fact of Violet's illness. Maud considers ill health to be self-indulgence. In her eyes only the lower orders need to go to bed and be looked after. That's why it's particularly cruel of fate to have crippled her. When Violet was expecting Liddy, she was pretty unwell: sick, with terrible headaches. Maud's remedy was to take her to Dublin and throw her into a non-stop social round. In a way I suppose it worked, as a distraction. The day after Liddy was born Violet had to go with her mother to a dinner party and afterwards to a dance. There's no tenderness in Maud's character, no desire to protect, no sympathy. Nor does she ask for any for herself.'

'But she's lent me one of her own dresses.'

'I didn't say she has no good qualities. She's remarkably brave. I've seen her get on a horse I shouldn't like to be in the same stable with. She never complains of pain. I can't imagine Maud doing anything petty or sneaking. She's generous, and truthful to a fault, as you'll have noticed. But quite intolerant of weakness, fear, doubt . . . those perturbations of the spirit that make us human. I wonder if it has something to do with being Anglo-Irish.' I looked up and saw Sissy's face at the window, staring down at us. Because the sill was so close to the ground her neck was stretched out like a swan's. Given the wind and rain and the nettles, it must have been an uncomfortable perch. 'You're a minority living among those you've dispossessed,' Finn continued, unaware we were under surveillance. 'However arrogant you are, being universally mistrusted, often hated, can't be comfortable.'

I gave the potatoes a liberal basting with goose fat. 'But wasn't that all a long time ago? No one could blame the original landowners for feeling resentful that their farms and estates had been confiscated and handed over to strangers. But surely now, many generations later, Maud's accepted? She thinks of herself as Irish, I know. She's often extremely rude about the British. Not that I mind,' I added so he would not think I was allowing personal feelings to creep into this dispassionate socio-political discussion.

'You have to remember that the hatred the Catholics have for the Protestants was intensified a hundredfold by the popery laws that excluded Catholics from holding important political, administrative or ecclesiastical posts from the end of the seventeenth century to the beginning of the nineteenth.' Finn was in lecturing mode but I was glad of it because I wanted to understand Ireland better. He hoisted himself on to the edge of the table and spoke slowly and clearly as though to a class of first-year students, gesturing with his strong, broad-palmed hands to illustrate a point. 'They weren't allowed to teach. They couldn't vote or practise law. Or buy land. Protestant heiresses marrying Catholics were forbidden by law to inherit. It was an attempt by an insecure minority to crush the life out of Catholicism. The fact that it didn't raises all sorts of questions that would take too long to answer. But the point I want to make is that as the Protestants had all the plum jobs and all the influence and most of the money, there was a tremendous social gulf between the two religions. And distinctions of caste are felt more profoundly than any other division. It's often been said that though drink is much to blame for Ireland's problems nothing's been so disadvantageous to its advance as gentility.'

He paused to eat another sprout. I looked up and had a shock. For a moment it seemed that Sissy's face was grotesquely distorted. Then I realized that in order to facilitate her reconnaissance she was standing on her head.

I repressed a grin for the subject was serious. 'I thought the English were unparalleled in their snobbery and addiction to social-climbing.'

'There isn't a nation in the world that doesn't have its hierarchies based on birth or money or a harvest of shrunken heads.' Perhaps he thought he was being rather too lenient for he added, 'Of course you English can detect a ploughboy ancestor from the way someone buttons their waistcoat or holds their spoon.'

From the moment of my arrival in Ireland I had been eager, perhaps disingenuous, in my readiness to admit the criminal tendencies of Imperial Britain. This had been partly as a pacific in the face of hostility and partly because of a genuine conviction that we had behaved badly in the past. Now I felt a sudden desire to wave the flag, or at least to allow it to flutter feebly. 'It's true. But less so these days, I think. And we do have more or less complete religious toleration. I expect you'll say that's not a virtue. It's simply indifference. And you'd be right. But I'd say we are a fairly peaceful nation. Terrorism receives no support from the general population.'

Finn frowned. 'I admit I can't defend violence whether it's inspired by religion or politics . . . We seem to have strayed from the subject. Where were we? Yes: Maud. I remember Violet's father once broke his arm in a fall out hunting. He knocked up the nearest doctor and had the bone set without anaesthetic so he could be in at the kill. I expect Maud's opinion of the poor man went into irreversible decline when he finally broke his neck.'

450

'I suppose there's something admirable, if a little heartless, in that attitude. But we can't let Maud's prejudices get in the way of Violet's recovery. And there's another thing I wanted to consult you about. It's lonely for Violet and it's extremely inconvenient for the rest of us to have her shut away on the top floor. There's a large bright room on the first floor, which used to be the nursery, that we've just finished clearing out. Don't you think it would be more suitable?'

He laughed. 'Miss Norton, you're an irresistible force and I can no longer even pretend to be an immovable object. Everything shall be as you say. I promise I'll do my best to make Maud see sense. But she's like all women in that once she's made up her mind about something you can't budge her. It would seem like a humiliating loss of face.'

'Mr Macchuin, you delude yourself if you think that's an exclusively female characteristic. And if you eat one more sprout I'm going to have to fetch a new sack from the larder and peel some more.' He dropped it back into the pan. 'Besides, uncooked they're terribly indigestible.'

'Look here.' He pointed a finger at me. 'You may turn my house upside down, reclaim my garden, amend my bank balance and re-route my drive – in short you may revolutionize my entire domestic world – but my digestion is my own affair.' Before I could reply he added, 'Didn't we get on to first name terms last summer before I went away?'

'We only said we would. You left before we could get comfortable with it. It's that tiresome caste system again. I *am* your house-keeper, after all. If Mrs Treadgold, our housekeeper in Sussex, called my father Gifford, he'd probably faint with shock. And Timsy, Katty and Pegeen call you "sir" and "the master".'

He shrugged. 'Your father was in the army, wasn't he? I've always found ex-soldiers to be particularly keen on rank. As for Timsy and the girls, that's just tradition. I was Finn to everyone who worked here until my grandfather died. But I shouldn't mind in the least what they called me as long as it wasn't insulting.'

I thought this was probably true. He didn't seem to care for ceremony or deference. I should not have dared at Liddy's age to speak to my father with the casual insolence which she sometimes used to hers. But my father was jealous of his position. His first concern was to receive his due as the head of the household and a person of importance in the county. Having no competition Finn took it all for granted.

451

'Besides,' he continued, 'you know perfectly well that whatever the traditional housekeeper is, you aren't it. What does your house-keeper call you?'

'Roberta.'

'Very pretty – and democratic. But as everyone else here calls you Bobbie, so shall I.' He stretched his hand towards the pan of sprouts then drew it back as he caught my eye.

'I have to admit that however democratic we are superficially, we aren't as egalitarian in other . . .' I paused in the process of sharpening a knife on the steel. 'How did you know my father was in the army? I'm sure I haven't told anyone that.'

'We're back!' Flavia came running in. 'It was the longest, most boring sermon ever and we're starving! Hello, Maria! Hello, Osgar— Bad boy! Let go!' They began a tug-of-war with her scarf.

Finn folded his arms, perhaps as a gesture of self-protection. 'That's an impressive glare. It reminds me of the picture of Medusa in my Latin primer. I gave myself away there, didn't I? The fact is there was a lot about your father being a war hero in the newspapers.'

The mere mention of the horrible things brought back my old phobia. My heart began to race and I felt hot and sick. 'You read all that stuff about me?'

'Not in detail. It seemed like fairly unimportant gossip. But I could hardly have failed to recognize you since your photograph was on the front page of every English newspaper for several days running.'

'Are you fighting again?' Flurry, who had followed Flavia into the kitchen, looked from my face, probably flushed, to his father's, on which masculine superiority almost but not quite concealed what I suspected was amusement – or was it contempt? Flurry caught my arm. 'Why was your photograph in every newspaper?' When I did not reply he looked at the table on which lay a large salmon, locally caught and smoked, waiting to be sliced. 'When can we eat? Must I have some of that?'

'Half an hour if your grandmother's back.' I addressed myself to the children. 'And you must try a little: it's really delicious. Don't forget to hang up your coats and wash your hands. There are peanuts and crisps on the drinks tray in the drawing room if you're both hungry but leave some for the others. Flavia, Osgar's pulling your scarf into holes. Let him have it for a bit and perhaps he'll get sick of it. Will you run up and see if your mother has everything she needs? And, Flurry, check the fire in the dining room, would you?

'It didn't occur to you to say anything about it at the time?' I said when the children had departed to carry out these tasks. I intended to sound detached but there was an infuriating break in my voice.

Finn remained calm, arms still crossed, irritatingly aloof. 'I thought it was more tactful to refrain from mentioning it.'

'You mean because of the insulting things they said about me.' I approached the fish and began to cut slivers fine enough to see the blade through. I was angry with myself. How could the memory of those stupid articles still have the power to hurt after all this time?

'They weren't exactly complimentary, were they?'

I was thankful that my hair had fallen forward to hide my face. I applied myself with greater energy to slicing, not trusting myself to speak.

'Let me do that,' he said, standing up and coming round to my side of the table.

'I've started it now,' I said ungraciously, keeping my head down.

'I should have known at once, from the moment I met you.'

'*What?*' I was unable to make my tone anything but defensive.

'That everything they said was a lie.'

I was so surprised by this unexpected kindness that the tears rushed into my eyes. The blade, sharpened to an edge that could have cut leather at a stroke, slipped to one side and pierced the flesh of my left thumb.

'Now you've cut yourself. You should have let me do it. Is it deep?' I rolled my eyes expressively as I sucked the gash. 'You'd better have a plaster.'

I removed my thumb from my mouth to say, 'Top right drawer of the dresser.'

He stirred the contents of the drawer into a terrible mess while I held the cut under the cold tap.

'Here we are. Let's see.' We watched the blood bead and then disperse over the wet surface of my skin. 'Hm. You need a big one.'

He fumbled in the box, dropping plasters over the floor, while I held my arm above my head to stop it bleeding. Above us Sissy grinned from ear to ear, exultant at the success of her spellbinding.

'Does it hurt?' He extracted the plaster from its envelope and pulled the waxed paper from the sticky ends, cursing under his breath as they clung to his fingers and stuck to themselves.

'Yes, a bit. You're supposed to pull the bits of paper off *after* you've applied the pad to the wound. Try another one.' He took out a second plaster. 'Ow-how!' I cried as he pressed it over the cut.

'Think of it as punishment for excessive independence.' He tried to straighten the gummed sections which had folded into concertina creases.

I could not help smiling. Transgression and retribution. However much intellect and experience may shape our characters the teaching of our early years can never be entirely erased.

He glanced up. 'What amuses you?'

'Who was it who said give me a boy before he is seven and he is mine for life?'

'What? Oh, I see the cunning way in which your mind works. Probably someone like Ignatius Loyola. A Jesuit, anyway. I call that churlish after I've done everything I can to save you from bleeding to death. Hold still. I can't see.' Sissy's head and up-ended body were obstructing some of the light that straggled into the kitchen. He took my hand and peered closer, trying to smooth the ridges and crumples from the crooked plaster. 'There now.' He gave me a minatory look as though daring me to disagree. 'I call that a thoroughly professional job.'

For what might have been one second or a hundred we stared at each other. I felt the pressure of his hand, saw his pupils dilate. I heard Sissy heehawing in fits of laughter and then a faint thump as amusement got the better of her sense of balance. The sounds of the tap dripping, the ticking of the clock, the puddings rattling in the pan grew loud. The challenge in his eyes had been replaced by an expression that was aghast. This was probably mirrored in my own. We were transfixed like creatures in a flood of light. The glare revealed at a stroke something that, despite my best efforts, and no doubt his, had been growing since our first meeting from a suspicion, a disturbance of the mind, a sudden pressure round the heart into a condition that insisted upon recognition. It was inexpedient, indefensible, quite impossible; yet I was disarmed, helpless, deprived of motive power by it, unable to move or speak or even breathe.

'I've given Mummy a drink but she says she wants you, Daddy.' Flavia had come in unnoticed.

'Well . . .' he said at last, in a voice that had lost all its usual certainty. 'Well . . .'

I took my hand away. 'We'd better get on with carving the salmon.' My own voice sounded distant because of the drumming of blood in my ears.

'Yes. Hm, where's that knife?'

454

We looked around helplessly, dazed by the alarming and unwelcome revelation.

'What's happened to your thumb?' asked Flavia.

'I've cut it but it's not bad. You go up, Mr Macchuin – Finn. I'll be much more careful this time.'

'We don't want blood all over our fish.' He picked up the knife and approached the salmon. 'Particularly not English blood.'

'Daddy! You mustn't be mean to Bobbie,' said Flavia reprovingly. He lifted his eyes briefly to mine. 'Joke.'

Again I had a sensation of terrible danger. I looked away and smiled to show Flavia I was not hurt. 'The old grudges are the best.'

'Don't stand around idly, you girls. Bring me some plates.'

While Flavia and I took the smoked salmon, bread and butter and lemons into the dining room, Finn went upstairs to see Violet. A glass of champagne later I felt more relaxed. By the time we sat down to eat my pulse was more or less normal and the presence of Father Deglan and Colonel Molesworth was a welcome distraction.

After the roast geese I brought in a clear jelly, made with lemons and egg whites and set with carrageen, for those whose digestions might find the accompanying plum pudding too rich. I had made the jelly in a mould shaped like a castle and it had turned out perfectly.

'What do you think, Bobbie?' Finn said as I put the puddings on the sideboard behind his chair. 'I've a Tokay Aszú in the cellar that ought to be drunk. Or do you think the fruit will overwhelm it?'

'That would be wonderful!' I detected a note of hysterical enthusiasm in my voice and felt myself blush to my eyebrows. 'But shouldn't we drink it on its own to be sure of appreciating it properly?'

It was an attempt to be natural which to my ears failed completely. We did not look at each other and had carefully avoided doing so since the epiphany in the kitchen. There was an unaccountable pause in the general conversation as though someone had rung a bell for silence. Anxiously I sought for something to say to fill it but my thoughts scurried away like insects when a stone is lifted. I heard him clear his throat, then cough. To my relief, Constance asked Colonel Molesworth to tell us more about the monograph he was writing and Maud said, 'Good heavens, girl! Have pity. It's Christmas Day.'

I cut up the jelly and plum pudding and the children took round the plates. The awkward moment had passed and I wondered if I had imagined it. But when I sat down I saw that Maud was staring at me, her amethyst eyes inquisitive. I looked away and met Sissy's scowl. I turned eagerly to listen to Colonel Molesworth whose long nose and massive hoary head made me think of a polar bear. Luckily he was deaf in his left ear and had not heard Maud's rudeness. He launched without preamble and in a trumpeting voice into his favourite subject, ancient battles that had been fought on Irish soil. He was writing a short history of the Scottish mercenaries hired by the Gaelic lords during the sixteenth century (to fight the English, of course). They were known as Redshanks because they went bare-legged in kilts so their calves and knees were always scarlet with cold. The rest of lunch ran smoothly, if one discounted the usual spats between Maud and Father Deglan. I was careful to keep my eyes from the other end of the table.

In the afternoon Flavia, Constance, Eugene and I went for a walk. The rain held off obligingly for an hour or two so we were able to inspect progress in the walled garden. Eugene found a mole whose tunnelling days were over and laid it at the feet of St Fiacre as a Christmas offering. This brought on a poem, which silenced him for the rest of the walk and made him so abstracted that Constance and I had to take an arm each or he might have wandered away to the mountains instead of back to the house. Luckily there was a strong breeze, laced with the lavender water which had been Liddy's Christmas present to him. Eugene had thanked her most charmingly and politely doused his handkerchief upon receipt.

The problem of the recherché extravagance of Eugene's shopping list had been dealt with by a few words of tactful advice from Constance. The result had been surprising and a reminder that people are sometimes more gifted and resourceful than they appear. Eugene had produced homemade presents for everyone. To me he gave his own translation of 'The Lament for Art O'Leary'. Art O'Leary had been shot (by an Englishman, naturally) for refusing to sell his favourite horse for a pittance. Eugene had accompanied the poem, written in his own elegant calligraphic hand, by a pen-and-ink illus-tration of the widow throwing up her hands in grief as the mare returns riderless, covered in her master's blood. The drawing struck me as being really accomplished and I was touched by the trouble he had taken. Eugene had bowed his forehead almost to his knees in acknowledgement of my sincere praise.

I had given Constance a pair of yellow yachting boots I had found in a hardware store. She wore them that afternoon and pronounced them to be as light and flexible as silk, like walking barefoot. She had given me a magnificent electric mixer with beaters, a dough hook and a blender attachment, which I was certain must have cost nearer fifty pounds than five.

'Well, perhaps it was fractionally more,' Constance had admitted, 'but there didn't seem to be anything in Williamsbridge half nice enough to give you otherwise. Actually, Finn gave me the money but he said I wasn't to tell you. I'm hopeless at keeping secrets, aren't I? But I don't want you to feel guilty, thinking you've bankrupted me.'

'It was enormously kind of you both.'

'Not as kind as all that, considering we'll be the beneficiaries. I'm looking forward to tea.'

As it was Christmas Constance was allowing herself a slice of cake. She had been tremendously self-disciplined during the months before Christmas and was trimmer by a stone. I thought she looked marvellous during the walk, the sharp air colouring her cheeks and brightening her beautiful eyes. It was a pity that Eugene's were bent on the ground as he rolled syllables around his tongue and occasionally groaned aloud with the agony of composition.

We called on the *Flying Irishman* on our return. Flurry was hard at work with his new tool set, a present from his father. The engine was nearly ready for painting.

'Want to see it start up?' asked Flurry. 'Of course it needs rails but it can get up a head of steam and move a little way.'

We professed ourselves eager. Flurry set light to the turf in the fuel box. Soon rings of steam were puffing from the funnel and when he threw a lever the train moved slowly forward.

'Florence Finn Fitzgeorge Macchuin, you're a genius,' cried Constance, her eyes moist with pride. She swooped down on Flurry and kissed him.

'Don't.' Flurry took a filthy handkerchief from his pocket and polished his spectacles with it before wrapping it round his hand to shut off the steam. 'The trouble is the handles get red-hot. I haven't found a way to insolent them yet.'

'How fast will it run on rails?' I had had an idea.

'Six, or perhaps eight miles an hour.'

'Is it strong enough to pull anything?'

For answer Flurry found a particular page in his Bassett-Lowke manual and showed me a train about the size of the *Flying Irishman* with three carriages behind packed with people.

'That's it!' I said. 'We could offer something I bet none of the other houses open to the public will have. A model railway you can ride on! Think what a draw it'd be for families with children! Do you think you could do it, Flurry? Could you make little carriages like that?'

'Course.' Flurry was dismissive. 'They're only boxes on wheels. But I'll need wood and the wheels cost masses.'

'The thing is, Flurry, it's your train. What do *you* think of the idea?'

He stuck out his lower lip considering. 'It might be quite good fun,' he said solemnly.

We hauled Eugene from the pile of sleepers on which he had been reposing, lying on his stomach with his head propped on his elbows and one foot pointing to the roof, gazing dreamily at a drum of engine oil and dragged him back indoors.

'Won't it be fun!' Flavia's eyes, deep-set like her father's, looked fathomless in the subdued light of the kitchen. 'Imagine being able to ride on a dear little train. Where will it go? All the way down to the lake?'

'The train wouldn't be able to get back up the hill,' I pointed out. 'We'll have to work out a scenic route, perhaps through the woods. Will you fetch the cake from the larder while I make the tea?'

'I'll lay the tray,' said Constance.

While I was waiting for the kettle to boil I emptied the contents of the jar marked *Isinglass* where we kept the income from the poteen. I counted more than a hundred pounds in notes. There had been thirty-eight pounds two days ago. Timsy must have done excellent business on Christmas Eve despite the extra church attendance required by the celebration.

'It's the most beautiful cake I've ever seen.' Flavia had covered it with crisp waves of icing and decorated it with silver balls, sugar flowers, plaster robins and a snowman on a toboggan.

Liddy put her head round the door. 'What are you all doing?' She had forgotten to be sophisticated and cynical. Her expression was unusually animated. 'There's a surprise in the drawing room. Hurry up.'

Flavia went ahead of us bearing the cake in triumph. At the door of the drawing room she screamed. I grabbed the plate in time to prevent the cake sliding to the floor. Violet was sitting in the wing chair.

'Mummy, Mummy, Mummy!' Flavia raced to embrace her.

'Careful, darling!' Finn was bending over his wife adjusting the cushions that propped her up. 'I've had a job to get her to stay upright. Are you warm enough, Violet?'

The wing chair had been placed close to the fire and she was wrapped in blankets but her bare feet, like a child's in their unblemished smoothness, were tinged with mauve. Her rich brown hair coiled about her neck. Her useless right hand lay curled, a bird's claw, in her lap.

''Es.' Violet stared at us with huge, excited eyes. 'Bob-bie. Dow' stairs. Good.' She looked down at her daughter who was kneeling beside her with her arms as far round her mother's waist as she could reach. 'Drink, please.'

'I'll get you a cup, Mummy. Would you like some cake? You can have the bit with the snowman and the toboggan on.'

'Hell-o, Con.' Violet gave her lopsided smile. 'D'awing 'oom.'

'Yes, darling.' Constance bent to kiss her sister-in-law tenderly. 'Just like the old days.'

''Es. Old days.' Violet laughed with happiness.

Constance looked at her brother as he turned from stoking the fire. Her eyebrows rose. He responded with a half-smile, quickly lost as he pressed his lips together as though troubled. I tried to imagine what this moment must mean to them. Dreams of a return to a past life, perhaps. It was pretty to see Flavia put a cup into her mother's trembling hand and guide it carefully to her lips. The frowning concentration on the child's face as she fastened the ribbon of her mother's nightdress and brushed crumbs of icing from the corner of her mouth, like a proud parent anxious to display her offspring favourably, must have touched her father if he noticed it. But the expression on his face as he stood with his hands in his pockets gazing at his wife and daughter was absent, pensive. No doubt he was wondering what would happen if Violet remained an invalid, unable to walk or to voice her thoughts freely, dependent on others for the fulfilment of the slightest wish and fully conscious of her incapacity.

'I'll get something for her feet.'

I hobbled up to my room and found a pair of thick woollen socks. Coming downstairs I passed Maud's room, the door of which was fractionally open. I heard the tap of her stick as she walked up and down, exercising as her doctors had instructed, though it was Christmas Day. On impulse I knocked. 'Maud, it's Bobbie. Shall I bring you a cup of tea?'

The noise ceased at once. There was no answer. Constance told me later that she had mentioned to Maud the possibility of Violet's being brought downstairs at tea-time. Maud had said she didn't want to be a spectator at a freak show and there was a television programme she particularly wished to see. She remained in her room until dinner, long after Finn had carried a tired but jubilant Violet back to her attic room.

I found it difficult that night to slow my thoughts sufficiently for sleep to overtake them. As I turned restlessly in my bed beneath the weight of slumbering cats I asked myself whether the reckless indulgence of my inclination to meddle in other people's business did not deserve the severest censure. Considering the potential hazard to other people's happiness, I was inclined to think it did. Then I allowed that other matter – such a piece of folly, so dark a secret that I shuddered to confess it even to myself – to surface in my mind and considered stepping out through my window there and then to throw myself from the battlements.

THIRTY-NINE

'You both look marvellous,' I said.

It was the evening of St Stephen's Day. Constance, Liddy and I were on the landing, preparing to reveal our sparkling party selves to the world. Liddy was wearing a dress she had made herself from a length of tangerine-coloured silk found in the linen cupboard. It was cut extremely low in front, revealing edges of her black bra, and had a slit up to her knickers. It was the perfect colour for her and lent warmth to her pallor. Heavy make-up concealed the spots and dark circles under her eyes. I remembered with sadness how well she had looked at the festival of Lughnasa.

Constance wore a pretty blue dress which she said she had not been able to get into for at least ten years. Her eyelashes were sooty with mascara and her lips were crimson with the lipstick I had given Liddy for Christmas. But the greatest transformation had been effected by the plucking of her eyebrows. Liddy had begun the task five days before, tweaking out small areas at a time to minimize the swelling and redness. She had been much more ruthless than I would have dared. But the resulting fine dark bows emphasized Constance's good bone structure and the fascination of her eyes.

I had put on one of Maud's beautiful dresses with a sensation of pleasure, despite the unsuitability of bare necks and arms in temperatures close to freezing. It was pale pink taffeta, with a ruched strapless bodice and a full skirt. She had lent me some marvellous creamy pearls to wear with it. When I had tried to thank her she had said, 'I'm repaying a debt. Constance would undoubtedly have given me food poisoning before much longer.'

'You don't think I look tarty?' Constance asked anxiously. 'I've never worn such a bright lipstick.'

'It's Estée Lauder,' said Liddy with pride. 'It would make *any*one look a million dollars.'

'Though why I should worry, God only knows,' Constance sighed. 'If I went downstairs wearing nothing but a bra and pants Eugene wouldn't notice.'

'*What?*' cried Liddy. 'You can't *poss*ibly mean you fancy that smelly— Ow, Bobbie, that hurt!'

'Awfully sorry.' I lifted my right foot from Liddy's toes. 'I'm still so clumsy.'

'You aren't going to wear those dreadful old things this evening?'

I lifted my skirts to reveal the zippered boots. 'My foot's too puffy to get into anything else. Luckily they won't show beneath my dress.'

'You've overdone it,' Constance said reproachfully. 'I told you so. You wouldn't let me do the ham or make the salads.'

'You were finding glasses and polishing the dining table. I'll be all right. I'll sit about and take it easy and the swelling will go down.'

'But you won't be able to dance!' said Liddy. 'And you look fan*tas*tic in that dress.'

'I shan't mind a bit. I'll be able to watch you.'

'If *on*ly there was someone worth dancing with,' cried Liddy in anguish.

'Perhaps Colonel Molesworth's nephew will be good-looking.'

'Not if he's anything like his uncle. Besides, he's nineteen. Not nearly old enough to be interesting.'

'You won't remember,' said Constance, 'but the colonel's brother was a dish.'

'I don't think our tastes in men are the same, Aunt Con.'

'Anthony Molesworth was the most handsome man I've ever seen. But a complete cad.'

'Really?' Liddy began to sound interested.

'I hate this bit.' Constance seized my arm as we reached the head of the stairs. 'I always mean to hurry so I can get downstairs before anyone else. But somehow the time seems to run away with me.' Liddy and I had found Constance standing in her room half in and half out of her dress, sucking the end of a pencil as she adjusted the metre of a line of poetry. These days she was more absent-minded than ever but I loved to see the light of inspiration in her eye. 'However old I get,' said Constance, 'I'll never be mature enough to go to a party, even my own, without feeling panicky. I always imagine people are staring at me, criticizing my physical imperfections. Which is silly and vain. Just one last trip to the loo.'

We waited until she reappeared.

'I'll go in front,' Liddy said kindly to her aunt. 'They'll be too busy looking at me to notice you.'

The group of men on the hearth stopped talking as we descended into view. The young man standing next to the colonel had definite promise. I should not have called him exactly handsome but he was certainly attractive with dark wavy hair and a charming smile.

'Please God, don't let him be queer,' whispered Liddy as we crossed the floor.

Introductions were made. When I allowed myself to look at Finn, he turned away his eyes at once and bent to put another turf on the fire. I refused a drink and went almost immediately to the kitchen to superintend the dressing of salads. But not before I had heard the nephew, whose name was Nigel, murmur to Liddy, 'Hello, Phyllida. You're a turn-up for the books, I must say. Fancy finding a swinger like you in the howling wastes of Connemara. That's an awfully pretty dress. Heh, heh! What there is of it.'

Father Deglan's face, whose eyes had locked on to Liddy's near-naked chest from the moment of her entrance, darkened to a dangerous shade of mulberry.

Once I had satisfied myself that everything on the dining table was as near perfection as it could possibly be I allowed myself a glass of punch. Constance had insisted that the poteen fund should pay for three girls from the Fitzgeorge Arms to serve and wash up so I could rest my foot. I joined the others in the hall with a delightful feeling of freedom from responsibility, only partly curbed when I remembered a particular piece of meddling on my part, which at the time had seemed such a good idea and about which I now had second thoughts. These moments of horrid doubt are the ineluctable evils in the career of any busybody. The consequences would follow shortly. The musicians were tuning up, guests were arriving and soon the bench in the downstairs cloakroom was buried feet deep in beaver and musquash.

'Good evening, Miss Norton.' Michael McOstrich shook my hand.

I had not seen him for several months. His flaming hair and beard had been cut very short. A buttonhole and a daffodil-yellow waistcoat gave him the air of a dandy but his eyes were cold. I was not forgiven.

'Lovely party.' Colonel Molesworth bent his good ear close to my face. 'It's generous of Finn to keep up the old ways. There never was a better fellow. Will you allow an old man to tell you you're looking very lovely, my dear? I was never married myself – too shy to ask, you know. Better with my own sort. Soldiers now, you know where you are with them . . . but I can still appreciate the fair sex.' He smiled, baring a set of brown pegs. 'You're the best-looking girl in the room, in my opinion, but you'd better keep that to yourself. Invidious comparisons, you know, Miss Norton.'

'Thank you, Colonel. Do call me Bobbie. It *is* a jolly party.'

The noise level was rising fast. Liddy and Nigel were already dancing. She looked happier than I had ever seen her.

'Thanks, I will if you'll call me Basil. Pretty little thing,' said the colonel of Liddy as they skipped past. 'But too thin. And giddy. Hope she won't let my scamp of a nephew take advantage. He's like his father.' The colonel tutted and shook his head. 'Blood's thicker than water and all that but I shouldn't like . . . Young women these days are allowed a lot of licence but I don't know if it makes them any happier. You'd better put her on her guard.'

'I'll try if you think it's necessary but I don't suppose Liddy will listen to me.'

'Do that, my dear. I know what you mean. Whoever takes advice? I don't meself. I may not have been much good with women but I used to get into scrapes. Finn's father, now – we were the same age, you know, served together – there was this filly in Anzio, a stunner, all bosom and lips . . . Yes, well, we won't go into that. He was a good man. Ought to have stayed in the army, become a regular. Fools here didn't understand him. Tragic what happened . . . wicked waste.'

Colonel Molesworth – Basil – was in an unusually loquacious mood. I had drunk no more than a single glass of punch but I was feeling remarkably cheerful myself. I glanced over to the side table which bore the punchbowl. Timsy had been instructed by Constance to prevent any unauthorized additions. He lounged against the wall, his eyes fixed on Liddy's chest.

'His wife wanted him home,' the colonel burbled on, 'to dance attendance on her. No good comes of marriage as far as I can see . . . Greatest respect for the sex, of course, but she was a flighty piece if ever I . . . Still, *nil nisi bonum*. Better not speak ill of the— Good God! Did you ever see anything like that!'

The colonel's jaw dropped as he stared over my shoulder. Gradually a hush fell over the great hall as we all turned towards the staircase. Finn was coming down with Violet in his arms. Liddy and I had spent a long time preparing her for this moment. We had chosen the black lace dress as it had a high neck and wrist-length sleeves that

464

concealed Violet's wasted muscles. Liddy had curled her mother's hair to give an impression of abundance and applied rouge with a liberal hand so that she looked rosy with health. Violet, seeing the rapt assembly literally at her feet, reacted on cue. She stretched out her good arm towards them and said slowly, with her very best diction, the phrase we had been teaching her for the last twenty-four hours.

'Hell-o ev—one. *So* lovely – see you – all.'

There was a collective gasp, almost a groan. No heart could fail to be touched by this vision of Beauty awakened. A tide of excitement ran through the crowd, then everyone surged forward to kiss Violet, clap Finn on the back, exclaim, laugh, shake their heads and articulate their amazement in any way they could. A few brave ones dared to embrace Maud who was seated by the fire, holding court among her acolytes. Maud smiled though her eyes were stony. For a moment she was dumb, pale. Only the heaving of her chest, visible because of the flashing of her diamonds, betrayed her emotion. Then, with dignified hauteur, she pulled herself up on to her sticks and began to hobble towards her daughter. The guests stood back to make a path for her.

'Finn,' she said as soon as she reached him. 'You had better put Violet on one of the sofas in the drawing room. I shall take care of her. You will have other things to see to.'

I went ahead of them to organize wraps and cushions. When Violet had been laid tenderly down, supported behind her back and beneath her arms, her dress arranged to hide her stocking feet, Maud beckoned to one of the girls from the Fitzgeorge Arms and asked for two glasses of champagne.

'Honestly, Maud,' said Constance. 'I don't think it's a good idea for Violet to drink.'

'Nonsense. Of course she will drink. This is a party.'

'I'll open a bottle,' said Finn. 'But don't say anything or everyone will want it.'

The guests laughed good-humouredly at the little joke and pressed round the sofa. Violet gazed upon them with impartial affection, charming them with her sloping smile as they fought to get close enough to stroke her hand, pat her head and assure her of their devotion. It did not matter that her speech was slow and slurred for everyone talked and no one listened. Their warm hearts responded unreservedly to the romance and pathos of her condition. There were many tears as well as smiles. I saw Basil Molesworth's shoulders

465

shaking as he held his handkerchief to his eyes and several guests had to be revived with glasses of punch.

We were, most of us, a little drunk already, which may have accounted for the extravagance of the reaction, yet I still could not imagine this scene taking place in Sussex. The English are generally too afraid of making fools of themselves. We – myself included – would have fallen back on the old ploy of pretending we had noticed nothing out of the ordinary. But, swept along by the rip-roaring euphoria around me, I enjoyed the sensation as much as anyone and, possessing neither a handkerchief nor a sleeve, resorted to blinking hard.

''Tis a miracle,' said Father Deglan, his face glistening and his nose glowing with the thrill of the moment.

'Indeed, so it is,' echoed Dr Duffy. He recollected himself. 'But without speech training and physiotherapy it could not have happened.'

They glared at each other. Before battle could be joined, a young lady of bold demeanour and impressive size forced her way into the centre of the hall. I felt a flutter of nervousness. This was the piece of meddling I had both looked forward to and feared in equal parts. The stir created by her arrival could not compare with the furore caused by Violet's resurgence. It was altogether a lesser phenomenon but it sent a slight frisson through the company all the same. The musicians were taking a breather just then so I was able to overhear the exchange between the man of God and the man of science.

'I'll be blowed! Isn't that Larkie Lynch?' Dr Duffy peered over his spectacles at the young woman who was staring about her with an expression of defiance.

'May the good Lord preserve us!' said Father Deglan. 'Little Larkie! I'd heard a rumour she was back but I didn't expect her to show herself here.'

'Not so little now. She must have put on three stones at least.'

'Nor Lynch neither. I've been told that though 'twas in a benighted, heathen place, there was a ceremony in a Catholic church and the vows were taken before Sam O'Kelly laid so much as a finger on her.'

Dr Duffy sniggered. 'If you believe that, you'll believe the earth is flat.'

'Aye, well, it may be, for me. What matters is how you behave yourself when you're on it.'

'And can you tell me' – Dr Duffy's voice was condescending, as

466

from a savant to a credulous bigot – 'where exactly *was* this benighted, heathen place?'

''Twas in New Jersey.'

The news that Larkie Lynch had returned from America had not yet reached Curraghcourt. I had only discovered it myself two days before. I had been making a last-minute visit to Dicky Dooley's grocery in Kilmuree before the shops closed for the festivities. At the counter a young woman had been asking for tubs of marshmallow whip, strawberry-flavoured peanut butter bars and fudge-flavoured popcorn. Her voice was loud, her accent a mix of Irish and American, her manner dissatisfied. I sat on a chair to rest my throbbing ankle and waited.

'Ha, ha! Miss Lynch, bouchaleen – Mrs O'Kelly, I should say.' Dicky Dooley's voice was deferential. 'Without a word of a lie, we've the best selection of goods this side of Galway.' I leaned sideways to see round the young lady's well-padded shoulders and plump arms encased in a leather coat as tight as the skin on a black pudding. Dicky's good-natured freckled face was screwed into an expression I knew well: one of infinite regret at his inability to accommodate his customers' fantastical requests. 'Sure there'd be no call at all for that kind of thing. If I got it in for you I'd sell one out of the box and be left with the others on my hands until the mice nesting in them'd be of the tenth generation.'

This was what he always told me when I asked for things like olive oil and black peppercorns. I had supposed this was reasonable but Mrs O'Kelly disagreed with me.

'Will you listen to him, the old lazybones.' As I was the only other person in the shop Mrs O'Kelly turned to appeal to me. 'If a ten-pound note lay at his feet 'twould be too much trouble for him to stoop and pick it up. He has as much enterprise as a fly stuck in a web.' She had stamped her foot, making her round cheeks wobble and the floorboards shudder. Remnants of prettiness – fine blue eyes, a delicate nose and a rosebud mouth – were buried in curves of flesh. 'And here's me spending my savings to come back and pay my respects to Sam's mother in her last illness only to find the wake over and done.' She made a sound of disgust at this unlucky turn of events. 'Well, I'll not stay in *this* hole. Sam and me'll go to Dublin to earn our passage back to where the stores stay open twenty-four hours and you can buy things to eat that'd make your mouth water like the Niagara Falls.'

I had put on my most sympathetic face. 'Would your name be Larkie, by any chance?'

After introductions had taken place we exchanged views on the vibrancy and vitality of the United States, the pleasures of drive-in cinemas, big cars, efficient central heating, and the non-existence of Baskin Robbins ice cream in Ireland. Though Larkie seemed to have given her heart to America, she had retained her native sociability and readily agreed to accompany me to Katy's Kauldron to cement our new-found friendship. I just had a cup of tea but Larkie settled for coffee with whipped cream and a doughnut filled with custard and fluorescent pink jam. While she feasted I said how much I hoped she would come to our party on the day after Christmas.

'Up at the castle? And what for?' She put up her three chins. 'I'm much obliged to you for the invitation but the Macchuins are nothing to me nor me to them. I don't hold with some thinking they're better than the rest of us. That's not the way of the modern world.'

Larkie had espoused sound democratic principles during her two years in the United States. There was about her a forthright intelligence that was attractive. I decided to trust her. As soon as I mentioned Eugene she turned the colour of the jam.

'What you must think of me I don't know. 'Twas very bad, running off like that, but Sam and I were that desperate to get away. And we'd not a cent between us. I'll admit when I've thought what Mr Devlin must've felt when I didn't turn up at the church I've cried like a baby with the pity of it. I never meant any of it to happen, Bobbie. I didn't love him at all. I couldn't understand half what he said, with all those fancy words. He never stopped trying to better my manners and stuff my head with facts that wouldn't stay in. It wouldn't have worked. There wasn't a thing he liked about me but my face and figure. 'Twas lust he felt and there was no more to it than that.'

'I can see there's a great deal about you that any man in his senses might really love but men always make fools of themselves over pretty girls. They can't help themselves. I'm sure you didn't lead him on.'

Larkie wiped away a coffee moustache and stared at me with grave eyes. 'I did not. But I shouldn't have taken the money, I know. Sam says it was only sharing things out a little more equal between the haves and the have-nots but then men can always reason with themselves to justify a bad action, can't they?' She searched in her bag and drew out a purse shaped like the head of Mickey Mouse. 'To tell the truth, Bobbie, I can't be easy about it. Perhaps you'll oblige me and give him this, with my sincere regrets.' She put down

468

three twenty-pound notes. ''Tis only a tenth of what he gave me but it's all that's left of what we saved.'

'Come and give it to him yourself,' I suggested. 'I'll arrange for you to be alone with him if that would help.'

'No, thanks. Sam's a jealous man.' She smiled as though she liked this. 'He'd be wondering if there was something in it after all though I've swore to him I never loved anyone else. Which is God's truth. He knocked a tooth out of the last man that put his hand on me.'

'Well, then, bring Sam. It's important,' I hurried on seeing that Larkie was on the point of refusing once more. 'When you went away without saying goodbye Eugene was left with a dream of you which he's clung to ever since. I think seeing you again, a real flesh-and-blood woman, happy with another man, would force him to give up that dream. It would be a shock – the unexpectedness – but that would be good for him.'

Larkie's eyes filled with sentimental tears. 'The poor man! I understand you. 'Tis called making a closure. It's all the rage in the States just now.'

'I think you owe him that. More than the money, actually.'

Larkie had stared at me for a moment, biting her lip and tapping the table-top with pearly lilac fingernails while she thought. 'You're right, Bobbie.' She waved to the waitress. 'Let's have a rum truffle.'

Larkie had been as good as her word. At the appointed hour there she was in the great hall of Curraghcourt, dressed like a Hollywood star in a gold lurex siren suit stretched to tearing point over her large hips, her startlingly blonde hair bouffant, her lips gleaming with pink lipstick. She was on the arm of a very tall young man, who looked as though he wished himself elsewhere. I limped between the dancers to welcome them.

'Hello, Bobbie.' Larkie's voice was challenging as she returned the stares of the other guests. 'My, but nothing's changed here, has it?' She looked with disapproval at the panelled walls with their displays of weaponry half hidden by boughs of ivy, holly and yew, at the vaulted ceiling, blackened with the smoke of centuries. 'For heaven's sake! I suppose some folks like things old, with wind whistling through the cracks and a fire that smokes like the funnel of an ocean liner.'

I offered my hand to Sam.

'How are you, miss?' He knuckled his forehead then dropped his arm smartly to his side on catching Larkie's furious glance. His mien suggested a gentle giant but his nose was spread over his face and his ears were crumpled and torn so I guessed that when drunk he became a fighter. On the grounds of size alone I should not have liked to see poor Eugene on the receiving end of Sam's displeasure.

'Take your cap off, Sam,' Larkie instructed him. He whisked it off and stood folding it into quarters and eighths while Larkie and I conversed.

'I'm so glad you could come,' I said. 'I expect you know everyone here far better than I do.'

'That's true enough.' Larkie's head was high.

'Hello, Larkie.' One of the men who daily travelled the path between Kilmuree and the apple store came up to her. 'Heard you were back. You're looking swell, as they say. Hello, Sam, you old dog.' He punched Larkie's husband in the ribs. 'Ran off with the first prize under our very noses.' He leered at Larkie and Sam's brow knitted.

'Perhaps we ought to start supper,' I suggested. It was earlier than I had planned but I had noticed Eugene wandering towards the dining room five minutes before.

'I'm ready for a bite.' Larkie strode forward. 'This way, is it?'

Eugene was sitting on one of the window seats eating a large plate of smoked salmon. He looked up, waved a fork amiably then returned to his food.

'Hello, Mr Devlin,' said Larkie. 'Don't you recognize me?'

FORTY

It was then that the evening seemed to gather pace and an element of unreality took over. It may have had something to do with the punchbowl, which like the magic porridge-pot was able mysteriously to replenish itself no matter how much was taken out of it.

Poor Eugene. As his brain made the connection and informed him that this portly girl standing before him was the turtle-dove of his dreams, his *princesse lointaine*, his Maud Gonne, beyond reach but forever enthroned in his heart, his jaw dropped and the smoked salmon fell to the ground. I bent to catch the plate as it bowled across the room towards us. He tried to speak but could only make a gasping noise. He attempted to stand but his legs were enfeebled by shock and he fell back upon the cushioned window seat, cracking his head against the shutter.

'I've given you a bit of a surprise, haven't I?' Larkie walked over to him and held out her hand. Eugene offered her his fork, then collected himself enough to put it down on the cushion (where it made a greasy stain that proved difficult, later, to remove) and put out lifeless fingers. Larkie shook them vigorously.

'This is Sam. My husband.'

Sam smiled bashfully, no doubt conscious of the six hundred pounds, and lifted his knuckles to his forehead until another glare from Larkie encouraged him to drop them. Eugene's cheeks and forehead were changing from white to red and back to white again like the lantern fish that signals its desirability through dark waters with flashing bands of colour. There was a brief disturbance as Maria and Osgar quarrelled over the smoked salmon scattered on the floor.

'You're looking well, Mr Devlin.' Larkie retained her presence of mind admirably. She glanced round the dining room. 'Bobbie says you've been living here a long time. I expect it's just your kind of place. Antiquated, like those poems you was so fond of.' She sniffed. 'It's got a peculiar smell. Sort of fusty. Meself, I like things bang up-to-date. Contemporary. Picture windows, wall-to-wall carpets and a cocktail bar.'

Eugene stared at Larkie like a man with fairy ointment on his eyes, a useful preparation which permits the anointed to see things as they really are.

Constance came in with Eugene's spectacles. 'I've found them. They were in the fridge, as I suspected. How we're going to get the butter out of your waistcoat pocket I don't know. Do you think fuller's earth, Bobbie—?' She opened her eyes wide and let out a sound like 'pwhoof!' as though she had been winded, before saying in a weak voice, 'It *can't* be. It *is*. Larkie!'

I slipped away to check on Violet. She was surrounded by admirers. Her eyes were huge in her small face as she lisped her thanks for their kind attentions. Her good hand held a cigarette, her curled right hand lay hidden beneath a cushion. She had eaten little but had drunk two glasses of champagne. Her hectic gaiety overlaid what looked to me like exhaustion. Maud sat beside her, accepting compliments on her daughter's remarkable recovery with every appearance of satisfaction. I hesitated to interfere.

When Finn bent over the sofa and took Violet into his arms, there were protests from the circle that had gathered round the invalid.

'It won't do for Violet to tire herself,' he said firmly.

'You make a beautiful picture, the pair of you,' sighed Lady Butler-Maddox. 'And one I never thought I'd see again.'

Violet giggled and rested her head against her husband's shoulder, throwing her arm about his neck.

'You're a sentimental fool, Laura,' said Maud. 'You'd better come and play a rubber.'

'What do you think, Bobbie?' Basil Molesworth murmured into my ear, as we watched Finn thread his way through the crowd bearing his fragile burden, his dark head bent over her charming face. 'Make a handsome couple, don't they?' They certainly did. 'Yes, a romantic sight, there's no doubt of that,' Basil continued, 'but it's not quite the happy ending it appears, eh? There's the little circus girl, for one thing.' Sissy, standing by herself nearby, also watching Finn, was dressed fetchingly as a wood nymph with a green and gold dress, the sleeves and hem of which were cut into tatters. She wore a necklace of leaves and had made up her face and bare arms with green greasepaint. She looked like an ethereal being, an enchanting pixie, but her expression was demoniac. 'What's Finn going to do about her?'

'Come on, Basil,' called Maud. 'We need you to make up a four. You can have Laura as your partner and I'll take Miss Thrope. She's the perfect dummy.'

'I'd better go,' muttered Basil. 'I'd rather stay and talk to you but Maud's a terrifying woman. Keep an eye on those two, will you?' He pointed to Liddy and Nigel who were dancing, glued lip to lip and hand (his) to buttock (hers). 'I shall have to concentrate on my game if I'm not to be flayed by Maud's tongue.'

Should I intervene? Though Liddy's and Nigel's behaviour was indecorous it was hardly criminal. Before I could decide my view of the room was abruptly cut off. Someone standing behind me had put their hands over my eyes. The smell of expensive cologne filled my nostrils as a voice with a marked Irish lilt growled in my ear, 'Guess who?'

'Kit!' I struggled free and turned quickly.

'Damn! I hoped you'd think it was Michael McOstrich or some other lusty suitor. How are you, my darling?' Kit was grinning widely. I put my arms round his neck and pressed my mouth to his cheek. 'Well, you *are* pleased to see me!' For answer I kissed his other cheek.

He looked marvellous. His face was so intelligent and good-humoured; his evening clothes were of the finest barathea and lawn without a speck of mould; his patent pumps were well polished; everything about him was elegant.

'When did you? How did you? It's the most wonderful surprise!'

'I came over on the afternoon ferry. I've been driving ever since. I just stopped at the Fitzgeorge Arms to change and grab a drink and then came on. I'm ravenous.' He put his hands round my waist and looked at me hungrily.

'Come quickly into the dining room then, before everything's eaten.'

He pulled me closer. 'When you look at me like that, as though you were just a little fond of me, food seems unimportant. Let's dance instead.'

'I'm sorry, I can't. My foot.' I lifted the hem of my dress to display the bandaged ankle in its zippered boot.

'You mean I've driven like the wind to dance with you and it's all been for nothing?'

'I'm afraid you'll have to make do with my conversation.'

'I love talking to you but I wanted to able to hold you tightly in my arms all evening without causing a scandal. What happened?'

'I fell out of a tree. It's nearly better. Just a temporary deterioration because of Christmas.'

Kit frowned. 'They work you too hard.'

'Not at all. Constance begs me every day to go to bed and let her wait on me. Whenever Eugene finds me carrying anything he insists on relieving me of my load. It's highly inconvenient because he always forgets what he's supposed to do with it. This morning I discovered Maud's breakfast tray, untouched and completely cold, in the airing cupboard and the clean sheets on the desk in the library.'

'I'd like to take you away to a charming house where everything boring and sordid is done for you so you could do just as you liked. And when I came home you'd be able to tell me about the books you'd written, the music you'd played, the flowers you'd planted and the pictures you'd painted.'

'It sounds like heaven. But I haven't deserved it yet. I need to serve my apprenticeship on earth milking cows and cleaning ovens and unblocking drains. Besides, too much sweetness without alloy might make one ungrateful.'

'That just shows how long it's been since you wrote a poem or did any sketching if you think that composition is without its own pain and struggle. You should hear my authors grumble. You'd think they were personally responsible for keeping the world spinning on its axis.'

I laughed. 'It's sweet of you to want to save me from drudgery. Now come and have supper and while you're eating you can tell me what you've been doing.'

To protect our clothes we put a napkin over the smoked salmon stain on the window seat and while Kit ate cold roast beef and potato salad, I trifled with some delectable prune mousse, a recipe from the fat pink book to which I would be grateful until my dying day.

'We had the usual crazy stampede at the office to get things done by Christmas,' Kit said. 'As though December the twenty-fifth is some kind of apocalyptic watershed, beyond which the universe will metamorphose into something unrecognizable. Then I had to hotfoot it to Norfolk. Mama had invited no fewer than three families with marriageable daughters. I engaged each one in exactly fifteen minutes' talk before moving on to the next, in strict rotation. If I offered one a drink, I took the next one nuts and pulled out a chair for the third.'

'It was kind of you not to excite false hopes.'

'Now, Bobbie, don't get sarcastic. Of course I didn't suppose the girls gave a damn whether I noticed them or not. It was because Mama's eyes were everywhere, measuring, assessing, divining. I wanted to save her the bother of scheming, as tiring as it would be futile.'

'You don't sound as though you like your mother very much.'

'I wonder if Boudicca's children liked her? Or Livia Drusilla's? They probably admired their mother's industry and her refusal to admit defeat. But we have nothing in common. Neither of my parents read books or look at paintings or do anything which might make them question the absolute rightness of their views. Their lives are exactly what they would have them be. They're terribly spoilt, in fact.'

'What's made you different?'

'Aha! Perhaps I delude myself that I'm different. But don't let's talk about me. Much too dull.'

'No one really thinks that, do they? The truth is, you're secretive. Evasive, even. Like those birds – plovers, aren't they? – that lure predators away from their nests by trailing a wing and pretending to be injured. I think you're hiding something: a wife and six bonny children; or perhaps you're a bigamist or a train robber.'

'What a romantic you are, though you pretend to be so practical. That dress is perfectly stunning.' He ran his finger from the point of my shoulder down to my elbow. 'And you in it.'

Now it was my turn to divert the conversation from myself. 'We've all made terrific efforts to do Curraghcourt credit. I'm sorry you missed Violet's grand entrance. You'll be astonished when you see her: she's so much better. And Liddy looks bewitching. Where *is* Liddy?' From where we sat I had a good view of the hall through the open double doors. I had been keeping a check as she rotated slowly past at regular intervals in the arms of Nigel. 'I'd better go and check on her.'

'Surely your duties don't include nursery-maiding?'

'It isn't duty. It's affection. Have another drink. I shan't be long.'

During an interval to allow the musicians to slake their thirsts the younger guests were sitting on the stairs. I spied Nigel among them, talking to Francie Synge, the golden-hearted girl from the bar of the Fitzgeorge Arms. This was reassuring but where was Liddy? There was no sign of her in the drawing room, the library or the kitchen. Finn was standing in what was apparently his favourite place, by the fire, between two women. They seemed to be vying with each other for his attention. His expression of profound boredom would have amused me if I had not been concerned about Liddy. I walked over to them.

'I'm looking for Liddy,' I said. 'Have you seen her?'

'Probably in her room.' Finn crossed his arms. I had noticed that he often did this in reaction to me. 'Let me introduce you. Grania Lake, Helen Fitzpatrick, Bobbie Norton.' He began to slide away from us, no doubt with the library in mind.

'How do you do?' I said, detaining him with a look. 'What's the matter with Liddy? Is she unwell?'

'I told that stupid boy she was dancing with that he'd better remember that she was sixteen and there were laws against what he had in mind. He said *she* said she was nineteen.'

'Poor Liddy!'

'I objected to the way he was trying to tear off her frock. Daughters are expensive to clothe these days.'

The two women giggled like schoolgirls. The one in red with false eyelashes, to whom I had taken an immediate dislike, put her hand on his arm in a custodial way. 'Finn, darling, you can't fool me with such cynical talk. You *adore* Phyllida.' She pouted coquettishly. 'No man is good enough for your precious little girl. When the day comes to take her down the aisle you'll be weeping like a baby.'

Finn tried to disengage his arm. 'I hope common sense will prevent me from making such a nauseating spectacle of myself.'

She took a swig of punch and tightened her hold. 'They're very . . . *very* lucky children to have such a handsome father to take care of them. It's what all we girls want, really, whatever those women's libbers say. They're all so unattractive, poor things, they have to have *some* bows to their strings.'

'How cruel you are, Grania.' The other woman leaned her full weight against him and staring up adoringly with unfocused eyes. 'I'm sure Finn admires impe . . . inpependent women, don't you, darling?'

Finn pushed her gently upright. 'I like women who can stand on their own two feet.'

'Was Liddy upset?' My voice may have been a little sharp.

'Isn't this young lady your housekeeper?' Grania's eyes beneath the false lashes were hostile. 'Don't you have washing up to do?'

The band began to play again. Finn frowned at me. 'Before you tackle those dishes, Cinderella, we'd better have that dance.'

'What dance?' I asked. 'Besides, my foot . . .'

'Yes, come along.' He put his arms round me and swept me into the middle of the floor. I repressed a cry of pain when he trod heavily on my toe. 'Sorry. I had to escape those harpies.'

'You could have invented an urgent telephone call.'

'I didn't think of it.'

'You may be responsible for serious damage. Think of the hospital bills.'

'It was you or me. Naturally I chose me.'

We danced further away from the fireplace and the furious stares of Grania and her friend.

'You've just made me two enemies for life,' I said reproachfully.

'All good-looking women have enemies.'

A pause during which we danced to the farthest point from the fire.

'That was a compliment.'

'Yes. It was stupid of me.'

We circled for a while in silence in our dark corner. The band was playing 'The Londonderry Air'. The candles burned brightly, with a mysterious halo. I wondered if they needed snuffing or if I was just hopelessly drunk.

'Timsy's been doctoring the punch, you know.' My voice sounded faraway even to me. 'I feel rather . . . unlike myself.' I seemed to be on fire and yet I was ice cold at the same time. The room had become enormous and echoing as though it had expanded to a vast cavern and the other dancers had withdrawn to an immense distance, leaving us to revolve slowly in isolation.

'I'm afraid that won't do as an excuse.'

'An excuse for what?'

He did not reply immediately. Then he said, 'Does your foot hurt much?'

'It's agony, actually. You've already trodden on it several times which hasn't helped.'

'I'm a rotten dancer.'

I smiled at his starched shirt front. 'Hopeless.'

We turned slowly on the same small piece of floor.

'This isn't a good idea, is it?' he said after a while.

'No.' I dragged my thoughts from a succession of fractured dreams. 'You've just kicked my bad ankle.'

'Sorry. Oh God, I'm sorry!'

I felt his left hand tighten round my right one.

'I'm sorry, too.'

'What a pair of fools!' He looked down at me and I saw that expression which had so alarmed me the day before.

I shut my eyes, knowing it was in my own. 'Speaking for myself, nothing could have been further from my intention.'

'You don't think *I* wanted this? I'm in enough trouble as it is.'

'We can behave like sensible, rational people and put a stop to it right now.'

'Of course we can.' He pulled me closer and I felt the warmth of his hand on my neck. 'That's reassuring, isn't it?'

I leaned against his heart. '*Wonderfully* reassuring.'

'Daddy. Daddy!' A voice was buzzing like a bumblebee in a foxglove somewhere on the edge of the world.

'What is it, Flavia?' Finn released my hand in response to the tugging on his sleeve.

'Osgar's got his teeth into Lady Butler-Maddox's fur cape-thing and he won't let go.'

For what seemed like an age he stared down at his daughter. 'I'd better come,' he said at last.

He let go of me. I felt as desolate as if I had been shut out on a dark and wintry night.

In the drawing room Kit was wrestling manfully with a growling Osgar and the tippet before a gathering crowd.

'That dog ought to be put down,' said Grania, who had pushed herself forward. She clutched Finn's coat. 'You shouldn't keep such a dangerous animal. Look what he's done!'

Kit's wrist was bleeding.

'Stand back,' Finn commanded Kit. 'Dogs are pack animals. He knows I'm his master. He won't bite me.'

Several women screamed as Osgar sank his teeth into Finn's hand.

'You bloody little—' He collected himself. 'You damn well *should* be put down.'

'Daddy! Promise you won't!' Flavia pulled at his coat. 'Bobbie, you won't let poor Osgar be put down! He can't help it. He doesn't know any better.'

'My tippet!' moaned Lady Butler-Maddox.

'My hand!' said Finn.

'A lot of asses you are!' Sissy strode into the circle around Osgar. 'Will you shut your noise?' she addressed Grania, who was clinging to Finn and wailing.

'Be careful, girl.' The monumental bulk of Michael McOstrich loomed over Sissy. 'You'd better keep away. 'Tis man's work.' He leaped back as Osgar lifted his lip and snarled savagely.

An unnatural brilliance came into Sissy's eyes. From the back of her throat issued the unearthly half-whistle, half-purr over three notes that was her lion-taming song. As soon as he heard it Osgar dropped the tippet and crouched down, whining. Sissy picked up the fur and handed it to Laura Butler-Maddox. 'Sleep, sir,' she instructed Osgar, who rolled over on to his back and allowed her to rub his stomach with her foot. Despite her small stature, she looked Olympian, a warrior-goddess with her prize at her feet. The apple-green greasepaint that had run into streaks hardly detracted at all.

'How did you do that?' Michael asked while people exclaimed and applauded and Lady Butler-Maddox examined her foxtails minutely. 'I've never seen not'ing like it. A pishogue, was it?'

'No! 'Twas just a trick.' Sissy looked pleased to have caused a sensation. 'I can make all animals obey me. I could make your cows give double the milk if I liked.'

'You could?' Michael stared at her with new interest.

'Let me tie that for you,' I said to Kit who was trying to bind his wound with his handkerchief. 'You look rather white. Is it painful?'

'There's some cognac in the library,' said Finn. 'Help yourself. I'm going to find some lemonade for the punchbowl.' He levered Grania from his arm and gave her into Basil Molesworth's keeping.

In the library I poured Kit a glass of brandy and stoked the fire. 'How is it? I could get you an aspirin.'

'What? Oh, my hand. It's nothing.' He went to stand with his back before the flames. 'This cognac tastes most peculiar. Like cherry-ade. That's odd. Finn's usually so fussy about what he drinks. Or at least his grandfather was.'

I went to examine the decanter. Round the rim was a slick of black.

'That's Sissy's special jam. You mustn't drink it! It might make you ill.'

Kit looked astonished and put his glass down quickly. 'That girl's trying to poison him? Nor Hell a fury, eh? I've already had two mouthfuls.'

'Do you want some salt and water?'

479

'No, thanks. That punch is stronger than stomach acid. Wait here. I'll get two more glasses.'

When he returned I examined him anxiously for any sign of ill effect.

'You still look pale.'

'Do I? If so it's nothing to do with the cognac.' He wiped the neck of the decanter carefully, then poured a glass for each of us. He took a sip, rolled it around his tongue then looked at his glass reflectively. 'I saw you dancing together.'

'What? Oh, you mean with Finn just now? Yes, it was an excuse to escape two rather awful women.' I turned away to put the stopper into the decanter. 'He's a hopeless dancer. My poor foot's been trampled to a pulp.'

'You're in love with him. I saw it.'

'Oh, what rubbish! What are you talking about? Of course I'm not! Don't be ridiculous!'

'If not, why are you angry? Look at me.' I turned to face him and met his eye squarely. He smiled. 'You can tell me, you know. We can still be friends, can't we? Even if my own hopes are dashed.'

'I'm sure I could.' I made myself speak calmly. 'Tell you. If there was anything to tell. But there isn't.'

He continued to look at me speculatively. 'I hope that's true. For your sake as well as mine. You've some experience of the mess that results from loving a married man, haven't you? And this time there are three children in the case.' When I didn't say anything he laughed without enjoyment in the sound. 'How ironic! No one but priests or prudes could blame Finn for consoling himself with another woman when his wife lay in a coma. What's more, he'd probably have been forgiven for ditching girlfriend number one – not very suitable, after all – for his beautiful, superior housekeeper. But now that Violet's been restored to the bosom of her family, people will think the very worst of a man who could abandon a pretty, defenceless woman just when she needs all the help she can get.' He shook his head pityingly. 'And it was you who woke her up.'

'I quite agree. It would be base treachery to desert her. For any reason. And I'm sure he has no intention of doing so.'

'Come here, Bobbie.' I went to stand next to him on the hearth rug. He took my hand. 'Tell me the truth. You can trust me. I want the best for you. Of course I'm horribly jealous – it can't be a surprise – I'm not good at hiding my feelings whatever you say about my duplicity – I'm in love with you. And that means I'd hate you to be unhappy.'

'Kit!' I was moved by this confession and the gentleness in his voice, so different from his usual joking manner. 'Oh Kit! I'm so fond of you—'

'Are you in love with Finn Macchuin?'

'No!'

'Prove it. Kiss me.'

I was so eager to deny the accusation that before my fuddled mind could work out the sophistical reasoning behind this request I lifted my face to his. He put his glass on the chimneypiece, put his arms round me and looked hard into my eyes. When he put his lips on mine I knew I had passed the test.

'Bobbie, Bobbie!' He kissed me harder. I forced myself to respond with enthusiasm. I liked Kit. I wanted to love him. It would be the perfect solution. So often I had declared with cold certainty that love was a matter of will. Now I must put my theory to the test. 'Darling Bobbie!' He pressed me closer and groaned. 'I want you so much!'

What had I been thinking of? That a few kisses would be enough? When his hand began to travel from my neck across my bare shoulder-blades and down to my waist I leaned back within the circle of his arm. 'Kit, I'm so sorry. I'm not sure I'm quite ready – it was such an awful experience, Burgo and I . . .' I felt myself grow hot with shame.

'It's been six months.' I could hardly blame him for a slight incredulity in his voice.

'But it was so traumatic having the whole thing blown apart in public. It's ridiculous, I know. I just have to take things slowly. I can't explain.'

'You don't have to.' He shrugged. 'It's whatever you want, darling. I have no rights.'

This was true. But if so, what on earth did I think I was doing? I dismissed the idea that there had been some *arrière pensée* on Kit's part which had led to this disturbing situation. But I felt at every moment more deeply committed to something I did not want.

'You've made me so happy already.' He ran his finger lightly down the naked part of my breastbone, stopping at the top of my dress. 'Kiss me again. I won't ask for anything else until you give the word.'

I was so grateful for this concession that I complied willingly. I heard the library door open and Kit stopped kissing me to look up. By the time I had turned my head, whoever it was had gone.

'I really must go to bed. My foot's killing me. It's been an exhausting day.'

'Of course, my darling. I'm just being selfish, wanting to prolong the glorious moment. There'll be lots of other times. It's just that I've wanted to do this for an age. In fact, ever since I saw you doubled over the rail on the ferry, feeding the fishes. Naturally I wasn't in love with you then. That was plain lust. It took a night under the stars to convince me that my feelings for you were not merely lubricious.' He laughed and I was a little reassured by the return of his usual facetious style. 'I'll see you to the foot of the stairs.'

As we walked through the drawing room Basil looked up from his cards and waved. Maud glanced from Kit's face to mine. Her mouth twitched. Then she jabbed Basil's arm with her pencil to make him concentrate on the game. There was no sign of Liddy anywhere. Nor of Nigel. Michael McOstrich and Sissy were dancing together, the top of her head just reaching his watch-chain. I felt too distracted to register more than a passing gratification at this advancement of my scheme. Finn stood by the fire, with Grania by his side. She was talking earnestly. I saw him nod his head then turn to stare into the dark recess of the chimney.

We had reached the staircase. Kit gave my elbow a discreet squeeze. 'Up you go. Sweet dreams, darling. I know mine will be.'

He made no attempt to kiss me again. His manners were too good for a public display of private feelings. He was in every way eligible: intelligent, witty, charming. There was no end to his virtues. I felt his eyes on me as I crept up the staircase but I did not look back. I limped along the landing, pain shooting through my ankle with every step. There was a light under the door of the south tower room. I put my head round the door. Nigel and Francie Synge were testing the bedsprings of the four-poster. I hoped, rather bitterly, that they were enjoying themselves.

As soon as I reached my own room I sank on to my bed and clutched my head. 'Oh, damn and blast and *hell*!' I exclaimed aloud.

'Bobbie?' A figure rose, blocking from view the red embers of my fire. I switched on the bedside light.

'Liddy! What are you doing here?'

'I must have – fallen – asleep,' she said between yawns. 'I wanted to talk to you so I thought I'd wait. I was playing with the kittens and I must have drifted off . . . Oh, Bobbie.' Her voice rose to a wail. 'Dad's such a *beast*! I'm so miserable!'

FORTY-ONE

During the days that followed Christmas a cloud came over the demesne. It rolled in from the Atlantic ten miles away and settled in the valley. After a week of staring out at the fog which left trickles of condensation on every window pane outside and in, we all became a little tetchy.

'For heaven's sake, Liddy, do stop grumbling,' said Constance, quite snappily for her. We were having drinks in the drawing room before dinner. 'I don't know what's got into you these days.'

'I'm incredibly bored,' said Liddy. 'That's what's got into me. There's nothing to look forward to. I'm sick of everything.'

'What about a trip to Williamsbridge?' Kit suggested. 'I've got to go to the library there. You could buy that dress you've been on about.'

'Oh yes,' said Constance. 'Do go, Liddy darling. That'll put an end to the daily inquisition about whether we *really* think pistachio will suit you or not. As though you cared tuppence for my opinion.'

'I don't know why *you're* so stroppy these days.' Liddy turned her sunglasses on her aunt. 'I suppose at your age it must be sexual frustration.'

'Liddy.' Finn, who had been hidden behind a newspaper, lowered it to look severely at his elder daughter. 'This is the drawing room and you are in the company of your luckless family and their unfortunate guests. Moderate your conversation to suit.'

It was only when he spoke that I judged it safe to look at him. I always regretted giving in to the impulse for the shock of longing, followed swiftly by guilt, made me absolutely wretched. Guilt because I knew that I must do everything in my power to crush that longing and by looking at him I knew I was feeding it. Guilt because of

Violet. Guilt because of the children. Guilt because I accused myself of deceiving Kit.

I could not understand quite how it was that I found myself daily – hourly – more compromised. When Kit rested his hand on my arm it had a distinctly proprietorial feel. When he kissed me goodnight I felt as though a pact had been sealed. Since the party I had managed to arrange things so that we were hardly ever alone and never for more than a minute or two. This was cowardly and stupid. I knew that before long he would suspect that I was deliberately avoiding him. I had the suspicion that he watched me closely. He might already have noticed that Finn and I rarely spoke to each other and then only with exaggerated coolness. I think it was Aristotle who said that in order to be brave you must first act in a brave way. I intended to apply this prescription to my present difficulty. I tried to behave as though I were indifferent to Finn Macchuin, hoping that genuine indifference would follow. Or if not indifference then at least an ability to be near him without a sensation that was one quarter joy akin to delirium and three-quarters acute pain.

To my everlasting shame it was not only guilt I felt towards Violet. When I saw her cling to Finn, saw her rest her head against his shoulder and look up at him with adoring reliance I was horribly jealous of her right to do it. When he put cushions behind her back and took the hand she held out to him I felt sick with heartburning and was disgusted with myself. What could his feelings be? For four years he had taught himself to believe that his wife was forever beyond reach. Now, though Violet was still physically feeble and partly paralysed, the strength of her personality was manifest. Weak and incapacitated as she was, she had become again wife, mother, daughter, sister-in-law and, to me, friend. She had been drawn once more into the centre of the circle and for this at least I heartily rejoiced.

The day after the party Maud had given orders that the room next to her own should be made ready for Violet. She insisted that her daughter needed no further therapy as she was now capable of recovering unaided. She treated Violet as though her disabilities were caprices. She needed only to try harder and she would be able to sit up and walk and move about like anyone else. Maud did not cosset Violet or sympathize with her and was scathing about her tears and tantrums. She snapped at her when she forgot words or could not pronounce them clearly. She was disgusted by the sight of Violet's curled hand and ordered Pegeen to strap it to a splint so that it lay straight. It was all very far from the recommended methods of rehabilitation but Violet did not seem upset by the harshness of this new regime, nor cowed by her mother's tyranny. Perhaps there was the comfort of familiarity.

'I wonder if Eugene's back from his walk?' Constance looked concerned. 'In this fog it would be easy to get lost. I'll just run up and see if he's in his room.'

'For God's sake!' muttered Liddy as her aunt left the drawing room. 'She'll be running up a mountain with his slippers next.' No one answered her and for a minute she sat and brooded. I was repairing a lampshade and Kit was looking at a manuscript. 'You used to tell us when we were kids to speak the truth and shame the devil.' Liddy, obviously still smarting from his reproof, addressed her father's newspaper. 'Now you're always trying to get me to shut up. That's just hypocrisy. Why shouldn't I say what we all know to be true? Aunt Connie hasn't had a man for as long as I can remember.'

'If that's the case then I think she's shown excellent sense.' Finn folded his paper with the air of a man much put upon. 'You'd do well to remember, Liddy, that when you talk of things you know nothing about, you're likely to make a fool of yourself.'

'What about that dress?' said Kit tactfully as Liddy screwed up her fists.

'Can we go tomorrow?' asked Liddy. I could see hope reborn as she registered Kit's apparent willingness to take her. Since the party she had been appearing only at lunch and dinner, several times with swollen eyes. 'I've got to go back to school the day after.'

Kit pulled a face of regret. 'I'm going to see an author in Kerry tomorrow. It'll take me all day to get there and back.'

'Shit!' Liddy kicked the footstool hard. 'And I've got stupid play rehearsals on Saturday. The dress is bound to be gone by next week. It's the only cool thing in the whole of fucking Connemara.'

'Must you swear so extensively, Liddy?' asked Finn. 'You're frightening the mice.'

Oh, how I envied the arm of the chair on which his hand lay! Constance and Eugene came in then. He had evidently only just returned from his walk. His hair had escaped from its ribbon and hung damply about his face which glistened with moisture. He threw himself into a chair as though exhausted and I bit back a remonstrance about his wet coat being bad for the upholstery. It was Constance's chair, after all.

'Did you say you've already tried the dress on?' said Kit. 'If so, Bobbie could come with me and pick it up for you.'

'Would you?' Liddy turned her lenses towards me and clasped her hands beseechingly.

I could not avoid being alone with Kit for ever. Perhaps it would be better to stop resisting, to give in to his wishes. I liked him. I had enjoyed being with him before there had been talk of love. Transforming this liking into something stronger would be the best and quickest way to conquer that other madness. 'The day after tomorrow? Well, yes, I suppose I could. I shan't be able to garden if this weather keeps up.'

Liddy looked delighted. 'I can't give you the money until I've paid in Granny's cheque, that's the only thing.'

'I'll lend you the money willingly,' I said.

'No,' said Finn. 'I will.'

Our eyes met briefly. He looked away a second before I did. I wondered whether these continual rushes of adrenaline, the short-ness of breath, the racing of my heart might ultimately shorten my life.

'I need some sewing threads.' Sissy, who was sitting with her feet up on the window seat, plying her needle but also, I was certain, observing the scene closely, sent me one of her hatchet glances.

'I'd be delighted to get them for you,' I said, hearing in my tone the false brightness that was always in my voice when I spoke to Sissy, and which I seemed unable to disguise. Though we had little in common, I would have preferred a semblance of friendship. I suppose efforts of this kind are always detectable, but some people will give credit for good intentions and forgive the insincerity. Sissy did not seem to be the forgiving kind. She bent her eyes to her work and stabbed the needle in, viciously.

'That's settled then,' said Kit. 'I'll pick you up the day after tomor-row, Bobbie. Two o'clock be all right?'

'I'll look forward to it.'

He rewarded me with a smile of such sweetness that my courage almost deserted me. Whatever else I did, I must not hurt him.

Eugene coughed to attract our attention. 'I should like to accom-pany you to Williamsbridge.'

Eugene had been unusually silent since St Stephen's Day. When

486

addressed he started as though his thoughts were elsewhere. We had been denied poetry readings. Instead he had taken to pacing the drawing room, his hands fastened behind his back, his gaze bent on the ground. If I had not understood that here was a man suffering some dark night of the soul I might have protested at this excessive wear of an already fragile carpet. When he was not pacing the drawing room he was pacing the mountains. The relentless drizzle had caused the toes of his shoes to curl up like cup hooks. Constance's most recent effort to scrub his shirt collar had resulted in its partial separation from the rest of the cambric and every day a larger expanse of pale flesh was visible. Even the ribbon that tied back his hair had begun to fray. He was a discouraging sight but the stoniest heart must have pitied his state. Constance watched him with compassionate eyes.

There was just the briefest perceptible pause before Kit said smoothly, 'Of course. Do join us.'

I was both disappointed and relieved.

'Rather warm, isn't it?'

I wound down the car window. In fact everything one touched was damp and dripping, the air was soft and sodden, and even beyond the valley the fog was thick enough to require headlights. The landscape was exquisite in tones of grey, like a drawing in Indian ink.

Eugene sat in the tiny space behind the front seats of the little red Spider, his knees drawn up to his chin. 'I was thinking it was rather cold.'

'Ah, but with the window down you can smell the heather.'

Inevitably we had caught up with a truck full of sheep. As the road was single track with passing places every few hundred yards, Kit was forced to idle along in third gear. 'Look at those poor creatures.' Eugene leaned further forward and Kit opened the window on the driver's side. Eugene pointed a finger over my shoulder at the faces of the sheep, who did indeed look woebegone. 'They are going to have their blood spilt by the butcher's knife. I think I will become a vegetarian.'

Kit became uncharacteristically annoyed by the slowness of the lorry. I spent the rest of a comfortless journey admiring the mountains and loughs and musing on meatless dishes I could cook for dinner. I finished my shopping in Williamsbridge in two hours and returned laden with parcels to find Kit sitting in the car, flicking through one of the books he had borrowed from the library.

'Darling!' He threw the book into the back when he saw me peering in through the window. 'You're silvered all over with droplets like my old golden retriever. Come and warm up.'

'I'd better put my bags in the boot.'

'I'll do that later. Hurry up.'

The moment I had squeezed myself inelegantly into the passenger seat Kit took me and several carrier bags into his arms and gave me a lingering kiss. 'I've wanted to do that for such a long time. Have you any idea what it feels like to see the object of your desire for several hours every day and be unable even to hold their hand?'

I confined my answer to a smile.

'Why are you always surrounded by other people? You'd think just once in a while they'd want an early night. I thought you'd be angry with me if I gave the game away. Would you?'

'Not angry, exactly. But uncomfortable. I'm not sure why.'

'Is it because you don't want Finn to know?'

I remembered that Finn had come into the hall as Kit was helping me to put on my coat, lifting my hair so that it lay outside my collar. There had been something intimate and possessive in the way Kit had fastened the buttons as though I were a child. Instinctively I had glanced at Finn and seen, or thought I had seen, something like extreme distaste on his face before he looked away.

'It isn't any one particular person.'

'Oh, how I love you, you little liar.' He gave me that penetrating look I was beginning to dread. But it had the power to awaken the spirit of rebellion that guilt had effectively crushed.

'Kit, I wish you wouldn't cross-question me. It almost makes me feel I'm being bullied into—'

'I don't believe it!' This exclamation had nothing to do with my objection to being quizzed. Kit's finger was pointing to the street. 'Do look!'

Walking along the pavement towards us was a man in a pale velveteen suit with a pink silk scarf knotted at his throat. What made him specially noticeable was his air of self-conscious dandyism. He stopped at every shop window to admire his reflection in the glass and to tweak his clothes or brush back a lock of his hair which had been trimmed to just below his ears and was frequently blown into his eyes by a fitful north-easterly.

'It can't be!'

'It is!'

'He really looks quite handsome! What are we going to say? Ought we to pretend we haven't noticed?'

'You can pay him a nicely turned compliment,' said Kit. 'I'll concentrate on the driving.'

Eugene's expression became diffident as he minced up to the car.

'Hello.' I scrambled from my seat to let him into the back. 'How very elegant you look.'

'Do you really think so?' He smoothed the fabric of his lapels and brushed an imperceptible speck from his sleeve before bending to peer into the back. 'Oh dear.' He withdrew his head. 'I am disturbed by the propinquity of that case of wine. It is made of a rough kind of wood. It may snag my trousers.' He smiled charmingly. 'Would it be too troublesome to remove it to the boot?'

'Yes,' said Kit with uncharacteristic sharpness. 'It's too big. I've already tried it.'

In the end I crouched in the small cavity behind as there was no danger of my jeans coming to harm. All the traffic seemed to be going the other way so Kit was able to drive very fast and my spine was fairly tortured by travelling over potholes at speed, but I judged it better to say nothing. Eugene sat very still in the passenger seat, having adjusted his new clothes with infinite care to prevent them crumpling. Whatever unguent the barber had put on his cropped hair was asphyxiating. Despite Eugene's complaints that he was becoming windswept Kit insisted on having the windows down again. I guessed from Kit's silence and the way he drove that he was cross that I was not sitting next to him. I knew how significant such trivial things seem when you fancy the world well lost for love. As we were coming towards the foot of the hill that separated the demesne of Curraghcourt from the rest of the expendable world I rested my hand discreetly on Kit's shoulder and felt him relax immediately.

'Aren't those trees marvellous?' He pointed to a row of ancient sweet chestnuts that had once been part of an avenue. Their trunks were six feet in diameter and the grooves of the bark swirled like barley sugar.

'Marvellous!' I said.

'Sometimes I think there really are fairies here, hiding in trees and under the ground, ready to play tricks on us if we antagonize them.'

'They undoubtedly will,' said Eugene solemnly.

Kit lifted his shoulder slightly beneath my hand and I understood the shrug to mean that he enjoyed the dottiness of certain aspects of Irishness and knew that I did too. Suddenly I felt happier and more hopeful than for some time.

Constance happened to be standing in the hall as we came in. She was carrying a basket of chestnuts for roasting after dinner. Eugene sauntered towards her, trying but not altogether succeeding to look insouciant. He paused beneath one of the great lanterns which were switched on all day because of the fog, so she received the full effect of the suit, the cravat and his shingled head. With commendable presence of mind she dropped only a few chestnuts. They skidded across the floor and disappeared beneath the side table from where Pegeen vacuumed them up the next day, jamming the cleaner and causing much bother until it was taken to pieces by Kit and the troublesome nuts removed.

'Allow me.' Eugene removed the basket from her hand with a gallant bow. I reminded myself to keep an eye on it if we were to see it again before the winter was over.

'*Thank* you!' breathed Constance with what might have seemed excessive gratitude, considering the basket could have weighed no more than a few ounces. She cleared her throat. 'How . . . well you look!'

'Do I? I was about to say the same to you.'

Constance did look particularly attractive in a black dress with a high neck, put on for Father Deglan's benefit as he was coming to dinner, with her thick curly hair swept over to one side as Liddy had taught her. They stared at each other and slowly each darkened to a shade of strawberry which made their eyes sparkle brilliantly by contrast.

'Shall we . . . Would you like to resume our readings this evening?' asked Eugene. 'I found a new edition of Patrick Pearse today. There are one or two poems with which you may be unfamiliar.'

'Yes,' Constance almost whispered.

'*À bientot*, then.' Eugene flourished his free hand, bowed and swept upstairs with the basket of chestnuts.

Constance drifted back to the kitchen, her eyes fixed on some invisible point far, far away.

Kit looked at me. 'What she sees in that vain, deluded ass I can't think.'

'I don't believe he is vain, really. The posing is to cover a terror of rejection, poor man. Besides, Constance loves him and he loves her and that's enough. If only they can find a way to declare their feelings and not waste any more time. That seems to be the hard part.'

'Don't let *us* waste time, Bobbie.' Kit put his hands on my shoulders and turned me to face him. 'I shall have to get back to London soon. I want you to know that I love you. I'm telling you again so you've no excuse to doubt it. I'm not expecting you to commit yourself or to allow me to make love to you. But you ought to know what I feel.'

There was a manliness about this that drew me into sympathy with him.

'Dear Kit. I hope I—'

'Did you remember my cottons?' Sissy had pattered silently up to me.

'Oh, yes. Here they are.' I rummaged in one of the bags and brought out a spool of red and another of green. 'What are you making?'

'A tam-o'-shanter.' Sissy spoke coldly. She was dressed as Flora Macdonald in a white dress and a tartan sash fastened with a large plastic cairngorm.

'Did you get it?' Liddy came running down the stairs. She saw the bag with *Modiste* printed on it and screamed with delight. 'I've been praying you would. It was the only thing that kept me going through a day of total boredom. The French Revolution and hop, skip and jump in the gym. Could anything be more stupid?' She ripped apart layers of tissue paper and held the dress up against her. 'What do you think, Kit?'

'You'll knock them dead in Kilmuree.' He spoke with a studied indifference which I suspected was largely for my benefit. 'I'll take your shopping down to the kitchen, Bobbie.'

Liddy widened her eyes as she watched him cross the hall. 'I don't give a *fuck* about Kilmuree. The whole place could be burned down tonight for all I care.' She turned to me. 'Do you think I can wear this in London?'

'You'll outshine everyone I know.'

'Will I?' Her eyes shone and she slipped her arm round my waist. 'It was nice of you to get it for me, Bobbie. Oh, yes – Dad said I was to let you know he's had to go to Dublin. Something about preparing for some seminars he's giving next term. He'll be gone for several weeks. He said I was to give you this: a late Christmas present.'

She took from the side table a small green book, stamped with gold. I had a feeling beneath my ribs as though I had just been sawn in half. He had gone. I tried to persuade myself that it was a good thing, that I was glad. I turned the book to look at the spine. *The Collected Poems of W. B. Yeats.*

'He asked me to be sure to give it to you,' continued Liddy. 'Actually he said he'd stop my dress allowance if I forgot. But I think he was joking. It's not much of a present, is it?' Liddy looked apologetic. 'He got it out of the library. But he hates shopping. Aunt Connie's shirty because he hadn't let her know he was going today. He just appeared with his suitcase. He only spent five minutes saying good-bye to Mum. You can consider yourself privileged to be remembered.'

Sissy let out a slow hiss. I guessed she was among those over-looked in the leave-taking.

'It was so thoughtless of Finn,' grumbled Constance in a low voice as we sat together at the kitchen table later that day. Turlough McGurn had failed to make a promised delivery so, being sick of apples which we had eaten baked in pastry, turned-over, scalloped, as a filling for pancakes and puréed for a charlotte, we were destoning an ancient bottle of damsons we had found in the still room. Katty was sitting at the other end of the table, nodding and mumbling over the brass fire-irons from the dining room, which she was cleaning.

'I'm not upset for myself,' Constance continued *sotto voce*. 'Well, only a little because I do miss him; but it was so sudden. I'm sure he said he was staying until Sunday. Violet's been crying ever since. Maud told her to pull herself together and threatened to box her ears. I'm inclined to think a little firmness does Violet good but Maud carries things to extremes.' She paused to scratch her nose, staining the tip purple. 'Finn was in one of his silent moods, which didn't help. Men do hate scenes, don't they? Violet's always been demonstrative and now she's tremendously dependent on him. I suppose for her it's like starting all over again.' She leaned her head on her hand, empurpling her cheek. 'Imagine beginning a love affair with a man you've been married to for sixteen years. It could be very romantic.'

'You've got damson juice—' I began before I was interrupted.

'Romantic!' Sissy had come into the kitchen. I noticed subliminally that she was carrying a suitcase. 'It's a fool you are for all your clever way of talking! You can't see nothing that's going on under your stuck-up nose. You think you're better than anybody else because you live in a big house and your family's been ordering other people around for centuries but you're blind!'

At the sound of Sissy's angry voice Katty dropped the poker she was polishing. It clattered on the flagstones.

Sissy rounded on her. 'And you and that Pegeen can go to the devil, the pair of you: nasty, mean-minded sots! You're jealous of me for catching the eye of the master! You'd like to do me harm, I know, but you'll not have the chance now!'

Katty blinked in the face of this outpouring of venom.

'Really, Sissy!' protested Constance. 'Must you shout?'

'I've as much right to shout as anybody else!' Sissy yelled. She made the sign of the evil eye and so ferocious was her glare that I found myself sinking down into my chair. 'I curse you all! May love never flourish in this house! May passion grow cold and sweethearts hateful! May there be no babies born here but bastards! Then you'll know what it is to have folk look down on you through something that's no fault of your own.'

Katty crossed herself several times and tiptoed out of the kitchen. Sissy spat contemptuously after her.

'Sissy!' Constance seemed stunned by this outburst of malevolence. 'You sound so bitter – angry! What have we done? I thought we'd made you welcome, that you were happy here . . .'

'We! Yes, that's it!' Sissy laughed, screwing up her dark monkey face in hatred that was charged with a sort of ecstasy at being free at last to speak of the injuries which she had nursed and brooded over for so long. 'It's us and them, all right! You've treated me like a beast that's to be humoured. Like that dog.' She indicated Osgar with a jerk of her chin. He was lying on his back in his customary place on the hearth, pedalling his paws as he dreamed. 'You've never made a friend of me. When *she* came' – Sissy turned her eyes on me – 'you were as thick as thieves in a trice. *She's* to be included in all your talk and thanked and made much of. *She's* a person in her own right. I'm a tinker's bastard and your brother's whore, who you've to be kind to for *his* sake.'

In her confusion Constance upset the bowl of strained damson juice as she sprang from her chair and approached her with outstretched hands. 'Sissy, *please*! If I've made mistakes, I beg your pardon. I never meant to hurt you.'

'*Hurt* me! It'd take someone with more brains than you to do that! It's nothing to me what you do. You can make a fool of yourself over that Eugene Devlin that's as much spirit as a thrashed donkey while all the time *she*' – Sissy directed a finger of scorn at me – 'plots and schemes. She's going to make a nest for herself in despite of you, Constance Macchuin, and then you'll find yourself playing second fiddle and see how you like it!'

Constance, surely the gentlest, kindest, least proud-hearted woman of my acquaintance, looked justifiably amazed to find herself at the receiving end of so much animosity. She abandoned her original purpose of putting her arms round Sissy and stood humbly with slightly bent head. 'I really had no intention of making you unhappy.'

'It's *me* that makes me unhappy or not,' Sissy said witheringly. 'You're incidental to me life. I'm going now. I expect you'll worry that I've pinched the silver. But you'll be astonished to hear that I don't give a damn about all that stuff you and she' – another angry glance in my direction – 'set so much store by. Where I'm going I shall have knives and forks that'll cut and pick up and that's good enough for me.'

'You're leaving?' Constance looked genuinely sorry though I knew that Sissy had been, if not a thorn in her flesh, then a hair-fine splinter from the day she had moved in. But a dislike of things unresolved that is natural to all of us prompted her to say, 'Won't you think again? I'm sure Finn would be very sorry if you left like this, after a quarrel.'

'He cares nothing about me.' Sissy tossed back her locks of red-tipped hair. 'I was the fool that time. He was sad and wanted comfort. I thought he might come to love me just because I loved him. But that's not how it works. I might as well have loved the moon. You can tell him from me . . .' Her voice broke and various emotions, ranging from loathing to grief and finally anger, ran quickly over her face. 'I don't care to be hanging on, receiving kind words out of manners. Here!' She put the pot of black jam that she had put so much effort into making on the table in front of me. 'You'll have more need of this than I. I've read in the dew that you've a great misfortune coming to you and I'm glad!'

I regarded it doubtfully and then said gently, for I was sorry for her and rather admired her proud defiance, 'Thank you, Sissy, but I hope I'll never be so desperate that I'll want to poison anyone.'

Sissy threw back her head and laughed. 'Eejit! A baby could eat the whole pot and not come to harm. 'Tis a love philtre. Where I'm going I shan't need it. I've charms enough.'

'Sissy!' pleaded Constance. 'Don't let's part in anger.' Timidly she put her hand on Sissy's arm.

Sissy threw it off as though it scorched her. 'You can go to hell!' She walked out of the kitchen, her head held high, her grubby

494

white dress trailing across the floor through the damson juice that had been spilt there.

That night, after I'd fed the cats and brushed my teeth I got into bed and opened the little green book at random. I read:

A mermaid found a swimming lad,
Picked him for her own,
Pressed his body to her body,
Laughed; and plunging down
Forgot in cruel happiness
That even lovers drown.

FORTY-TWO

After a day or two I got over the worst unhappiness of knowing there was no possibility of meeting Finn by chance on the stairs or of accepting a glass from his hand in the drawing room. The pleasure of stealing a covert glance from the other end of the dining table had been so intermingled with pain that it was as well, I told myself, it was no longer possible. As one gets used to doing without the sun in winter I accepted that the matter was out of my hands.

Surprisingly, I found I missed Sissy too. She would have been pleased to know that our circle seemed diminished without her. Constance was inclined to punish herself for a failure of sensitivity. 'I ought to have realized how she felt.'

At the time of this conversation we were in the morning room. This was to the left of the dining room and had not been used for a long time. After her grandmother's death Constance had gathered all the cases of stuffed birds and animals in the house, stacked them in the morning room and shut the door. Occasionally, over the last ten years, the door had been opened and another unpopular article had been chucked in. Unlike the morning room at Cutham, this one faced east so it caught the best of the early light. It had a pretty blue-and-white delft-tiled fireplace and was exactly what we needed as a sewing room where we could spread out curtains and carpets as we repaired them. We had emptied the room of its lumber and brought a large table, a sofa and several comfortable chairs down from the attics.

The disposal of the stuffed creatures had presented a problem. Damp had got into their cases and destroyed them beyond the point of being resaleable. Their sad little eyes hung down on rusty wires;

496

their fur and feathers were grey with mould. Flavia had been adamant that they should be neither burned nor thrown away. In the end we had given the glass cases to the rag-and-bone man, loaded the bodies into the back of the Land-Rover and driven them down to the grave-yard by the lake for burial.

The graveyard was on a promontory, so marshy at this time of year that it felt like walking on water. The graves from the mid-nine-teenth century were particularly sad. There were so many headstones with the names of entire families who had perished of famine fever within days of each other.

'At least there weren't any evictions on the estate,' said Constance. 'My great-great-grandparents set up a soup kitchen and fed every-one who came for help. But sometimes I think Ireland'll never get over that time. It fanned such a blaze of hatred. I'm so glad we don't own it all now. I'm not sure that we ought to have even as much as two hundred acres. But most of it's bog and I suppose no one else would want it.'

She laid a group of stuffed balding squirrels into the hole that Timsy had dug. Flavia led brief (it was raining again) but fervent prayers for the souls of the creatures, and we covered the bodies with leaves gathered from the woods to dignify their pitiful condi-tion until Timsy should return to fill in the hole. Constance put little wreaths of scarlet spindle-berries on the graves of her parents and grandparents. We drove home with that feeling of satisfaction and completion a well-conducted ritual always gives.

Because the morning room was smaller than the other ground-floor rooms at Curraghcourt the fire produced a fug quite quickly and Constance and I positively looked forward to retiring there once the chores were done. We were repairing my bed curtains when the conversation about Sissy took place. Inevitably the canopy above my head had given way beneath the weight of increasingly heavy cats and I had been woken in the middle of the night by a faceful of rotting fabric, spiders, flies, one dead mouse and a hundred years of dust. The cats naturally had gone from deep sleep to alacrity in the time it had taken for the canopy to rip and had jumped clear. In one of the linen cupboards we had found some old curtains of yellow chintz sprigged with lilies of the valley. Constance was unpicking the seams while I stitched them into bed-hangings.

'Ought we to scrap this bit?' She held up a length of chintz that had been bleached by sunlight of long ago. 'Do you know, it never occurred to me to wonder whether Sissy might think we looked down on her because of her birth.'

'We'll just take off the really faded part,' I said. 'The rest will do for the gathered heading. It didn't occur to me either. In England most people – of our generation, anyway – would scoff at the idea that there was anything shameful about being illegitimate.'

'Really? I can't say that would be the case here. I suppose, because contraception is still against the law in Ireland unless you're married, there has to be some kind of stigma to prevent us being overwhelmed by unplanned babies. It's ridiculous, I agree. If I really believed God wanted unmarried girls to go through all that misery and the poor babies to be punished, I'd have nothing more to do with Him from this moment on. But, you know, I hate the idea that Sissy thought I was despising her.'

'Her prickliness meant that she saw slights where none existed. The fact is we didn't share the raw materials of friendship: similar attitudes and tastes, that sort of thing. And there's a chemistry you can't overrule. Real friendship isn't that common, after all.'

'That comforts me a little. But I still feel as though somehow I've behaved badly. Do you think Michael McOstrich will be good to her? He's the kind of man who expects to be boss and have everything done for him. I admire him no end but I've always thought he was a bit of a bully.' We had seen Sissy in Kilmuree on Michael's arm that morning. She had a swing in her step and a haughty expression. He had looked pleased with himself and there had been something proprietorial about the clasp of his huge hand over her small one. Each party had pretended not to see the other.

'I can't imagine Sissy letting anyone order her about.'

'There's one consolation: it'll be a terrific weight off Finn's mind. With Violet getting better poor Sissy could only have been a difficulty. Do you think this room smells of mice?'

I sniffed. 'I should say the predominant smell is damp coming out with the warmth.' I sniffed again. 'But perhaps mice as well.' Carefully I restitched scallops of silver thread, a process called snailing (perhaps because it took an age to do) to the head of a tassel that was part of one of the tie-backs.

Constance stood up and began to prowl about the room, looking for nests. 'I expect you thought them an odd couple from the start. Finn and Sissy, I mean.'

'Well, yes,' I murmured.

Constance turned over a chair to examine the base. 'You have to understand how it began. Finn was so depressed at the time, poor darling. To be fair, he's had enough problems to try the patience of a saint. And Finn certainly isn't that. He'd already had a fling with some woman in Dublin. She used to ring him up here all the time until he got fed up. And I've a feeling there may have been one or two others. I think Finn's quite attractive to women.'

Constance paused as though expecting me to say something. I frowned, concentrating on fastening off my thread.

'It's hard for us to understand what a driving force sex can be for some men,' she went on. 'Although,' she added quickly, as though correcting herself, 'women have strong needs, too, of course, and just as much right to gratify them. Anyway, it was at our party for Lughnasa that Finn and Sissy met. That was the year before you arrived. Sissy looked so attractive. Alive and warm – different, you know, from the other girls. Not nervous and giggling like the village girls, who were shy of him. Or putting on airs like the daughters of the gentry, who'd been warned by their mothers not to have anything to do with married men. Finn could have had his pick of the older ones who were bored by their dull husbands. But he's not the type to get a thrill out of cuckolding a man under his nose.'

'I suppose not.' I peered more closely at the galloon (a sort of braid) that had edged the old torn hangings, wondering how much of it could be saved.

'Sissy was wearing something dramatic in her usual style, with bunches of flowers behind her ears. She made him dance with her. Put her arms round him and dragged him on to the floor. After a while he started to enjoy himself. She can be very engaging if she wants.'

'I've seen that.'

'They got rather drunk, the two of them. She stayed the night. I hope you're not shocked?'

'Not in the least.'

'He was lonely, you see. And she made it plain she wanted him. Sissy was right, she *did* comfort him. Only, sadly for her, she wanted more than that. I acquit her entirely of any mercenary motive. She really fell in love with Finn. I'm probably biased as he's my brother but I think he's good-looking.'

'Yes.'

Perhaps there was a coldness in my tone which encouraged Constance to sing her brother's praises.

'And he's clever and well educated. By comparison with what she'd always known he might even have seemed well off. The romance of the Big House. Who could blame her?'

I gave a half-smile that might have been acquiescence.

'She'd had such a hard time.' Constance seemed eager to win sympathy for Sissy, and by association for her brother's cause. 'Her father was a drunkard who beat her and she joined the circus when she was fifteen. The trapeze artist wanted to marry her but he had a terrible temper too so she ran away with a travelling theatre company. When that folded she lived a hand-to-mouth existence selling medicines and spells and living in a deserted bothan halfway up a mountain, miles away from anywhere. But men were always hammering on the door wanting something else besides a cure for rheumatism. Once she was raped. Apparently she put up a good fight and he has the marks on his face to this day. Here's the nest!' She pulled out handfuls of cotton wadding from the back of the sofa. 'The entire thing seems to be a lying-in hospital for mice. Luckily the last lot of occupants have gone.'

'We'll have to get it reupholstered, I think. Poor Sissy! Did she report the man to the police?'

'That would have been a waste of time, I'm afraid. In this part of the world a girl of Sissy's reputation would get no sympathy from anyone. They'd say she'd asked for it by living alone and wearing her hair long and dying the ends red. It's wickedly unfair. They'd never say that about a man.'

'Did she tell you all this?'

Constance looked sad. 'You've seen for yourself, she's never trusted me. Or even liked me, it seems. No, Finn told me. He wanted me to understand what she was doing here. He was dismayed to wake up with a terrible hangover and find her in his bed. He expected her to leave at once. But when she begged him to let her stay he didn't have the heart to send her back to that kind of life. It was weakness, perhaps, but also the right kind of generosity, to my mind. I don't think they slept together much after that. He felt he was taking advantage of her, knowing that it could never come to anything. You don't think too badly of him, now you know, do you?'

'No,' I said. 'I don't think badly of him at all.'

When the children went back to school for the Lent term Constance and I redoubled our efforts to get the house into good order for the visit of the Hibernian Heritage inspector. I was too busy to brood

500

much on the unsatisfactory state of my heart. It was almost as it had been last autumn when Finn had been in Dublin and I had not yet learned to think of him in any other light than as a cantankerous employer, unfaithful to his wife and neglectful of his paternal duties. But had I not even then begun to change my idea of him? I could not say exactly when the disarming of my prejudices had begun.

Kit made himself extremely useful during the days he remained in Kilmuree. He and Timsy moved furniture to our dictation and carried down treasures from the attic storerooms. We decided to repaint the dining room. Constance said she had always hated the brown paint chosen by her grandmother, a horrible colour applied thickly over every detail of the plasterwork except for the ceiling. If Constance was right in thinking that the La Franchini brothers were the original *stuccatori*, then the room could be dated to the middle of the eighteenth century. We tried to scrape back to the original paint but damp had destroyed the layers beneath. As the drawing room was lined with yellow silk damask and the bits of the hall that weren't panelled were painted a sort of buff, the dining room had to be something quite different. The Georgians were fond of colour and would have found the prevailing taste for magnolia from cellar to attic an extraordinarily joyless and uninspired style of decorating. We decided on Dutch pink, in vogue from 1750 onwards. Joyfully we took down the ugly brown rep curtains. In a trunk on the top floor we had found what we thought might be the original silk ones, frail and faded at the edges where the sun had scorched them but still a beautiful grey-blue.

Kit drove to Williamsbridge and had gallons of paint mixed to match the sample I provided with the help of Flavia's paintbox, and we got down to it without delay. It was not as easy as we had imagined. So few things are. In the middle of each wall was a large roundel depicting a scene from Aesop's Fables bordered by swags of flowers, fruit and birds, which had to be undercoated, then picked out in three shades of white. The work required concentration and a steady hand. The frieze was to be given the same time-consuming treatment. The manticores were barely distinguishable from the chimerae beneath their overcoats of brown paint. One day there might be enough money to remove the earlier layers and restore the plaster to its pristine sharpness. After the first day Constance, Kit and I had paint on our clothes, hands and faces and in our hair. Our nostrils were filled with the smell to the point of nausea, our tempers were in rags, and we had undercoated less than a tenth of the area. Constance went to the telephone and the next day Dicky Dooley's brother, Eamon, who was a decorator and handyman, came to help.

Further assistance came from an unexpected quarter. Flurry proved capable of long hours of painstaking brushwork. What is more he actually enjoyed it. It was a useful incentive to get on with his homework so he could get to grips with the twirls and arabesques of intertwined leaves, flowers and fruit, the fine detail of pelts and feathers and the plump limbs of the putti. He was more accurate and disciplined than any of us.

'I would help,' said Flavia after tea on the first day of decorating, 'but I've been given this lovely book to read for homework.'

She held it out to show me. It was *A House of Pomegranates*. Clearly in the opinion of Flavia's English teacher Oscar Wilde's Irishness outweighed any corrupting moral influences. But I was doubtful of the wisdom of this choice.

'Lovely stories,' I said, 'but some of them are terribly sad. Why don't you ask her to give you *The Canterville Ghost* instead? It's so much more cheerful.'

'Oh, but I *must* read it. I'm the only one in the class who's been given a proper grown-up book. All the others are still on kid's stuff. If I don't read it she'll think it's because I can't.'

It was not long before the sound of sobbing accompanied the smell of oranges issuing from beneath the dust sheets covering the dining table. We all, Kit included, remembered weeping over the death of the faithful swallow in 'The Happy Prince' so it was not surprising that poor Flavia, whose sensitivity to the pain of others was so finely tuned, was devastated. 'The Nightingale and the Rose' was too harrowing to finish. Flavia's eyes became so swollen she could hardly see. The book went back to school the next day accompanied by a note from Constance which was untypically sharp.

'What persuaded us this was a good idea?' Kit surveyed the one wall we had finished after four days' hard work. 'I hate this colour. It's old ladies' vests, tinned salmon and elastoplast. I bet the man from the ministry will say it's got to be changed. I'm thankful I'm leaving tomorrow. I'd rather drown myself in the lake than paint another inch!'

'My grandfather drowned himself in the lake,' Flurry called from the top of the ladder.

Kit looked aghast. He was generally so socially adroit that he must have felt his blunder acutely. Perversely, when I saw that he could be vulnerable, I came nearer to loving him than at any other time. 'Oh, Constance! Did he? I'm so sorry. Naturally if I'd known I'd never have made a joke of it—'

'Of course you wouldn't.' Constance waved her paintbrush at him. 'I know that. Don't give it another thought. I *think* I like this colour,' she continued hastily to cover the awkwardness. 'I've never done anything in the least what you might call creative without being tortured by hideous doubt. I try to tell myself that there are no aesthetic absolutes and the only thing that matters is whether *I* like it. But that's nonsense, of course. If a tunnel-visioned, colour-blind psychopath with delirium tremens happened to pass by and said it was a bad choice I'd be immediately convinced he was right.'

''Tis a pity you wouldn't listen to me, Miss Constance,' said Eamon Dooley, who was washing his brushes and drying them on his cap. 'Didn't I say to paper the whole thing in woodchip and hide all them mounds and hollows? 'Twould make it modern and bright and ye could paint it a nice neutral shade. I wouldn't be painting the outside toilet this colour, not if it was the last pot of paint in Galway.'

'I suppose you'd like to get rid of the mouldings as well,' said Constance in a nettled tone.

'I would. It's old-fashioned. And not decent, neither.' Eamon looked disapprovingly at the fat little boys tripping along the frieze with nothing but a swirl of plaster to conceal their nakedness.

I stood back to view the pink. I also was experiencing indecision. 'I like the way it changes with the light. It's almost blue in the shadows and sort of pale apricot in the lightest parts.'

Eamon Dooley looked at me pityingly. 'I'll be off. Back at eight-thirty tomorrow. Goodnight all.'

'That means ten o'clock,' said Constance after Eamon had shut the door behind him, 'but at least he comes.' She looked at her watch. 'Time for Eugene's tea.'

'There's some chocolate cake in the tin,' I said. 'Or there are meringues.'

'Better be the cake. Meringues tend to make a mess.'

These days Eugene bore himself as though he were made of valuable porcelain. He hardly bent at the joints for fear of making the elbows of his coat and the knees of his trousers baggy. A speck of soup landing on his shirt front made his eyes bulge with distress and sent Constance running for a cloth.

'Have a look at this,' I said as soon as Kit and I were alone. From the pocket of my jeans I took a sheet of paper on which were written several verses.

'"The Well-Tempered Love". What's this?'

'Constance's latest poem. It's about Eugene.'

'I think it's good,' Kit said when he had reached the end of five stanzas. 'Sensitive but strong. Original.'

'I wanted her to let Eugene read it but she says she's afraid to. I'm certain he's crazy about her but it's so difficult after a long period of friendship to broach the subject of love.'

'It *is* hard to tell people how much you love them. There are so many words for hatred: repugnance, loathing, abhorrence, hostility, abomination, disgust, enmity, revulsion, execration. One could go on for ages. But love? There's adoration, devotion – not quite the same thing. I can't think of any others.'

'Fondness, sympathy, affection . . .' I began.

'I'm fond of my dogs. I sympathize with junior doctors and single mothers. I have some affection for my old headmaster. None of these feelings comes anywhere near what I feel for you. I'll be leaving in a few hours, Bobbie. Let me love you a little.'

I shut my eyes, willing myself to blank out the image of . . . someone else.

'Darling!' he murmured. 'I really think you're just beginning to—'

'Do you really like your headmaster?' We had forgotten that Flurry was up the ladder, painting a pineapple. 'Mine spits when he talks. Right into your face. He blew me up once because I wiped my face on my sleeve. I didn't know I shouldn't have.'

I could not decide, when Kit and I kissed each other goodbye in the hall after dinner, whether the regret I felt was due to the departure of a competent pair of hands or to something altogether more significant.

The visit of the inspector coincided with a miraculous drying of the atmosphere. The veils of rain evaporated to reveal a sky bright with high, white cloud and we saw the mountains for the first time for weeks. On the morning Mr O'Brien was expected to arrive we whisked away the strings that conducted the rain into the buckets and, on second thoughts, the buckets, too. We hoisted out of harm's way the turf chain that dangled into the stairwell, intending to stun him only with our charms. With my hairdryer we got rid of some of the blotches of damp on the damask on the drawing-room walls. We mopped up the puddles in the hall and the basement corridor.

'I'm so nervous,' said Constance. 'Just one more trip to the lav and then I'll try and see it through.'

I was pretty nervous myself. But when Mr O'Brien arrived he turned out to be jolly and friendly. He was a little round man in a green tweed suit with a waxed moustache, spectacles and a hearty laugh. I expect he was used to being fêted by hopeful owners. We sat him in a chair beside a roaring fire in the hall and pressed him to drink sherry and eat devilled nuts and cheese *sablés*, baked that morning. His forehead glistened with heat and consumption as he patted the dogs and laughed at our jokes. But all the time his eyes were roving about the hall, fastening on the vaulted ceiling, the panelling, the longcase clock by Thomas Sanderson of Dublin, the wonderful side table, the Irish delft chargers.

'Come, ladies,' he said when he had eaten the last *sablé*, 'let us view the ancestral pile.'

While Constance rushed to the lavatory, Mr O'Brien walked around and scribbled things in his notebook. I followed meekly behind, ready to point out any treasure he might have missed. But his eye was sharp and when it fell on anything good it glinted with pleasure. Even the marvellous chased brass lock on the front door was recorded. As we conducted him round our prearranged circuit he peered, stroked, tapped, sniffed and wrote busily. All the precious things we had brought down from the attics – the four chairs covered in gold Genoese velvet; the Chippendale green-lacquered chest of drawers; the George II mahogany drawing table; the pair of giltwood mirrors; even the fruitwood tea caddy in the shape of a pear – drew him like iron to a magnet and merited at least half a page each.

'Charming, charming!' he said of the drawing room. 'All of a piece and wonderfully lived in.' He touched the wall delicately. 'Mm. Damp, of course. Of course.' He looked up. 'A very fine ceiling indeed!'

We had left the dining room until last.

'Oh, my dears!' cried Mr O'Brien as we opened the double doors. 'It can't be . . . it *can't* be.' He walked about in circles on tiptoe, swinging his arms, gazing up at the ceiling.

I had schooled Constance carefully. 'It's believed in my family to be by the La Franchini—' she began.

Mr O'Brien cut her off with a bellow of joy. 'I thought so, I hoped so, I prayed it would be so! Of course if possible it must be

505

authenticated but' – he made upwardly thrusting movements with his fat little hands – 'this is precious, precious, *precious*! Good heavens! What . . .?' He stared at Sissy's repairs in the mouldering corner. 'How . . . An octopus. Yes, hm.'

'It's a mermaid,' said Constance.

He turned away from her and I saw in the looking glass his face contorted with pain. Then he resumed his survey of the room. With a cry he ran to the fireplace and stared at the painting of the woman in grey. 'Is it . . . Could it be – a Gainsborough?'

Constance and I exchanged excited glances.

'My dears, the jewel in the crown! And Dutch pink! *What* a joyous colour! Perfect! Absolutely perfect!'

And suddenly I was quite sure that it was.

The three of us sat at one end of the dining table for lunch and ate off the beautiful Berlin service with the best silver. After three courses, with wine, coffee and cognac, Mr O'Brien wandered along the path between the *miroirs d'eaux*, burping gently, pencil in hand, making further extensive notes. We told him of our intention to make a flower garden and to restore the octagonal dairy. We showed him the granary and explained our plans for it. Four men waiting inside looked up from their game of cards, touched their caps to us and murmured polite greetings.

'It'll make a capital tea-room!' Mr O'Brien rubbed his hands. 'And isn't that little building on stilts an apple store? Just the sort of thing to appeal to visitors.' He took a step or two towards it.

I placed a detaining hand on his arm. 'Unfortunately the key is missing. Temporarily.'

'But I saw two men go in not five . . . Oh, well, as you say, my dear.' He watched three youths scuttle along the wall and slide out of sight into the granary. 'It must be expensive to maintain such a large work force,' he said sympathetically. 'Loyal family retainers, no doubt.'

'The men you see walking about are visitors.' I had embarked on this explanation without thinking it through. I stared at a rake propped against the coach-house door, seeking inspiration. 'They are applicants for our new gardening school.'

'A gardening school!' Mr O'Brien's tone was jubilant. 'I must say, the resourcefulness of you ladies is seemingly limitless. Were you planning to make it residential?'

'Yes,' I said, just as Constance said 'No.'

'That is, not at first, perhaps,' I added while Constance muttered something about being only too willing to reconsider.

'Well, I'd advise it, if you think you could manage it,' said Mr O'Brien. 'Good hotels are rare in these parts. It'd be the most tremendous draw.'

After we had exhibited the *Flying Irishman* to his delighted gaze and explained our scheme for entertaining the public thereon, we put him into the Land-Rover and drove him down to the walled garden where we treated him to an exhaustive tour of the vegetables.

'You may need to be selective about your students for the gardening school,' Mr O'Brien murmured as two men wandered through, arm in arm, waving bottles and singing 'That Old Irish Mother of Mine'. By the gate they broke into loud cursing and started to black each other's eyes.

We gave Mr O'Brien a lavish tea of whiskey cake and brandy-snaps filled with cream before waving him goodbye.

'My bladder!' exclaimed Constance, breaking into a run. 'What a darling!' she said on her return as we repaired to the kitchen to wash up. 'If only he'll be good enough to give us some money! I think I'd better say a prayer. In fact in the spirit of Henry of Navarre I'll go to Mass on Sunday.'

'You might as well,' said a voice behind us which made my face flame and my insides dissolve. 'Though when he said Paris was worth a Mass he was being entirely cynical, whereas you, my dear Con, are a genuine votary.'

'Finn!' She went to kiss him. 'We weren't expecting you! How lovely!'

He looked a little tired, stern, formal in his town clothes. He bent his head to allow Constance to kiss his cheek. The light above him threw a beam on his dark head and cast the planes of his face into pale curves and his throat beneath the strong jaw into shadow.

'I thought I'd come and see how you were getting on. Just for the weekend, you know. Hello, Bobbie.'

He looked at me briefly and then turned back to Constance. An observer might have thought his greeting cold.

'How lovely!' Constance patted his arm fondly. 'Violet will be thrilled. And the children. You must be exhausted after the drive. Tea or a drink?'

'A drink. I'll change first.' He smiled, the merest twitch of his mouth. 'I never feel I'm truly home until I've swapped exhaust fumes for turf smoke.'

'Well, that's extraordinary!' said Constance as soon as he'd gone.

'He hasn't been home just for the weekend since . . . for a very long time. I wonder . . .' She was silent for a moment, thinking. 'Perhaps this means he and Violet . . . it's going to be like the old days. Wouldn't that be wonderful?'

'Wonderful,' I echoed.

FORTY-THREE

'Hand me that spanner, would you?'

It was Saturday morning. Finn and I were standing in the bowl of the round pond below the canals. A couple of inches of black water lay in the deepest part but the rest was filled with rotting hornbeam leaves. Flavia had been sent up to the house to fetch a monkey-wrench.

'This one?'

'That'll do. I'm not at all sure this is going to work.' There was a minute's silence while Finn fought to undo a stubborn nut that held the perished rubber hose in place. Then he said, 'You and Constance seem to have transformed the house. The dining room, particularly.'

'What do you think of the colour?'

'I'd never have chosen it myself. But' – his face flushed as he applied extra force – 'it gives the illusion of warmth. Mm, yes, I like it. Oh, bugger!'

'What's the matter?'

'The thread's gone.' He clasped the hand he had grazed in the process. '*Now* what, I wonder. Perhaps I could saw it off.'

He kicked the old pump with his toe as it lay rusting and useless among the heaps of dead leaves. The new pump I had ordered from Galway sat in its cardboard box beside me at the stone edge.

'We might ask Thady O'Kelly to look at it,' I suggested tentatively.

Finn folded his arms and frowned. 'You were just humouring me, weren't you, when you accepted my offer of help? You have no faith in my abilities as a practical man.'

'I dare say Thady O'Kelly doesn't know the first thing about legislature or the Hundred Years' War.'

'Now you're trying to salvage my pride. Will the coffers swollen by whatever nefarious activity you're all engaged in support Thady's prices?'

'Oh, yes. Money seems to be flowing in.'

He looked at me with narrowed eyes. He was wearing his holiest jersey and his hair stood up slightly at the crown, like Flurry's. 'Whatever it is, it seems to involve an extraordinary amount of undercover activity. Every time I look up I meet the bloodshot gaze of someone skulking in the undergrowth. The minute they catch my eye, they shoot off, like a rabbit anxious to escape a stoat. I am the stoat, I take it.'

I smiled. 'Honestly, you don't want to know.'

He returned my smile and for a while we stood looking at each other. The song of a blackbird in a nearby tree grew loud and piercingly sweet. The trilled notes seemed to throb with ecstasy as he told his chosen mate what good things he had in store for her. The breeze whisked the dead leaves into a spectral frolic and the sun appeared briefly at the edge of a cloud like a diamond in the icebound heavens.

The harsh call of a crow circling above us broke the spell. Finn closed his eyes and shook his head. 'No. No, I don't want to know. Things are complicated enough. If you've a spark of decency, Roberta Pickford-Norton, you'll take pity on a poor imbecile who not only can't replace a simple electric pump but who's powerless to keep himself from putting his hand into the flame. All the way home I told myself to turn round and go straight back to Dublin. Three times I drew off the road and called myself a fool for wanting a sip of the cup that fires the blood and intoxicates the senses. But here I am. Did you ever come across such a crack-brained idiot in your life before?'

He kicked the pump again, this time savagely, and the hose flew off, emitting a spout of water that drenched our knees. We looked at each other again and the air around us seemed to shiver with words unspoken. Nothing could be gained by pretending not to understand him.

'If it will help I'll go away.'

'No. You're needed here. *I'll* go. And make myself stay away.'

He put the back of his hand to his mouth and sucked a bleeding knuckle.

'Should you do that? Stagnant water is host to some extremely unpleasant bacteria.'

510

'Oh, you termagant!' He pointed a filthy finger at me, his eyes fierce. 'You'd nag a man to death! Why is it that I'd willingly—'

'Daddy!' Flavia was running along the path between the canals waving the monkey-wrench. 'I've found it. It was in the Cockatoo's stable.'

'Thank you, darling.' He took it from her. 'I've done the tricky bit. Now watch your father give a dazzling display of technical wizardry.'

By lunchtime Thady O'Kelly had been summoned. It took him fifteen minutes to gather the component parts that had been hurled angrily to the ground and fit the new pump. We filled the pool, which took all afternoon. The sun, invisible all day except for that one brief shining, had gone down behind the clouds and all about was dusky blue. We put on coats, scarves and gloves and brought out a bottle of champagne for the grown-ups and cocoa for the children to celebrate the restoration of the fountain. The pump had been wired to a switch in the dairy, which was the nearest source of electricity. Finn signalled with a torch to Flurry who was waiting there. There was a brief pause, the sound of spluttering and gurgling and then a rod of water shot into the sky.

'Look, Mummy!' Flavia cried, though her mother, seated in the window of the drawing room, was too far away to hear. Flavia flashed her torch beam to catch the plume of water, which had generated cries of wonder from the house party and quite a few encouraging shouts from concealed watchers around the demesne.

'I want to cry,' said Flavia.

'Please, *no*,' said Liddy.

'It's as though everything's coming right,' Flavia persisted. 'The fountain's like Mummy, isn't it? Shooting up. When we thought it couldn't be done. It's a . . . What are those things that mean something else?'

'A symbol,' said Finn, putting his arm round his younger daughter as she pressed herself to his side.

'Your coming home this weekend makes it perfect.' Flavia rubbed her face against his sleeve. 'Last night Mummy and Granny were having a row. Granny wants Mummy to learn to walk but Mummy said there wasn't anywhere to walk *to* so she might just as well sit in a chair and stare at the wall and everything was beastly. When I told her you'd come she stopped crying and said, "I was praying he would. Give me that silly old stick then and I'll try." So now you see you've got to come home more often so Mummy will get better.'

511

This artless little speech pierced my heart as sharply as the breast of the nightingale was pierced by the rose thorn.

'The tumbling water makes the most glorious sound,' said Constance. 'Flavia's right. It *is* a symbol. Of life and vitality. The promise of spring.'

'I was thinking the same,' breathed Eugene. 'Growth and renewal. Cuckoos, primroses, celandines, speckled eggs in feathered nests.'

'I was thinking about my electricity bill,' Finn said in the tone of one intending to repress excessive flights of fancy.

'What are you thinking about, Bobbie?' asked Flavia.

'I was thinking how much I love it here,' I said slowly, 'and how sorry I'll be to leave.'

'But, Bobbie' – Constance took my arm – 'surely you're not thinking of going away now?'

'I'll stay another couple of months until the opening. I can't deny myself the pleasure of seeing our plans put into action. And of course I'll wait until you've found a suitable replacement. But then I certainly must. It was only ever supposed to be a temporary thing, you know. I have to think about my career.'

'Why can't you have a career here?' asked Liddy. 'You could write a book about Irish houses or how to mend carpets or something, couldn't you? And go on being our housekeeper. We could have holidays in London when you got bored. I mean, we'll never find anyone we like half as much.' Liddy was touchingly in earnest. 'Dad, you're always so hot on telling everybody what they ought to do. Why don't you tell Bobbie she's not to leave?'

Finn was silent. Then he said, 'Where's Sissy?'

'Really, Finn!' Constance sounded quite cross. 'Do you mean to say this is the first time you've noticed Sissy isn't here? How hurt she'd be if she knew! Men are so careless of anything not affecting their immediate comfort.'

'That's no doubt true, Con, but it doesn't answer my question.'

'She's gone to live with Michael McOstrich,' said Liddy. 'And good riddance, *I* say. She was a pain in the arse, particularly recently when she got all moody and neglected. I think you ought to promise to consult the rest of us the next time you take a mistress. As soon as you were sick of her you buggered off to Dublin. But we've had to put up with her for *ages*.'

'Oh, what a bad child you are,' said Finn. 'Feckless, idle and insolent, with the vocabulary of a sergeant major. None the less, there's a particle of truth in what you say.'

'What is Sissy mistress of, exactly?' asked Flurry. 'Don't laugh at me, Liddy. I hate it when you do.' Flurry turned his back on her and pulled his coat over his head to block out the sound.

Flavia put her arm round him. 'It means a girlfriend. For old people. But Daddy doesn't need one any more. I'm going back to the house to make sure Granny isn't making Mummy cry.'

We followed her. As soon as Violet saw Finn she waved her good hand in his direction. 'F-hinn. F-hinn. Lovely f-hountain!' It was one of her new words for the day. 'Remem-ber – you said – gar-den bad. Remember? I said – pretty.' She struggled to bring the words to the surface of her mind. 'When you brought – I – came here.'

'You mean when Daddy brought you here to be married?' Flavia was better than any of us at making sense of her mother's speech.

'Yes! Yes!'

'I don't remember.' Finn took Violet a glass of champagne and sat beside her on the window seat. 'But I'm sure you're right. It just shows what a young ass I was.'

'When I hear men admit to being in the wrong,' said Maud, who was sitting beside a nearly empty bottle of usquebaugh, 'I always suspect them of contemplating mischief.'

'F-hinn is good as – good,' Violet patted his arm. 'Kiss me.'

Obediently Finn bent to kiss his wife's brow.

I took my jealous heart away to see to the stewed haricot of mutton with onions.

Finn left for Dublin early on Monday morning. I had avoided being alone with him. He seemed to be doing the same and such was my confused state of mind, I both approved this discretion and was wounded by it. Again I had to accustom myself to wintry despair after he had gone. I hoped he would be able to resist coming back. When I found that he could, I was desolate.

As February flew past and then March, I told myself that I was beginning to conquer my unlucky *Schwärmerei*. I applied my much vaunted theories about passion and lust to my own case. The idea that I was in love with Finn was nothing more than over-heated imagination. It was up to me to check it and apply some common sense for all our goods, not least my own. I told myself this every day as I planned, supervised, improvised, shopped, cooked, milked Niamh – we had put Siobhan out to grass for a well-earned rest – sewed and washed up. Yet every night before I fell asleep I read the poetry of Yeats, that most ardent of romantics who knew what it was to love without reward, from the book *he* had given me, knowing that I was undoing all the good work of the daylight hours.

We sat as silent as a stone,
We knew, though she'd not said a word,
That even the best of love must die,
And had been savagely undone
Were it not that Love upon the cry
Of a most ridiculous little bird
Tore from the clouds his marvellous moon.

It was a relief to fill my mind with simple, straightforward things, such as the cheapest way to construct a basic kitchen in the granary that was to be the tea-room.

We had heard nothing from Mr O'Brien. He had warned us that the wheels of Hibernian Heritage ground slowly and that our application for funds was one of many. But, whatever the verdict, Constance and I were determined to go ahead and open Curraghcourt to the public. Timsy's customers shifted their quarters to the loose boxes. We got Eamon Dooley to put plumbing and a sink in one corner of the granary. We bought a second-hand propane cooker and a small fridge. On the newly whitewashed walls we nailed up boards and covered them with photographs of the house and family, going as far back as the 1880s.

We found ten tables of assorted sizes in the attics and more than enough chairs left over from the poetry festival to go round them. At Sullivan's, the draper's, I drove a hard bargain for ten seersucker tablecloths, luridly checked in pinks, blues and greens. We gathered a miscellany of what Pegeen and Katty called 'delph': cups, saucers, plates, milk jugs and sugar bowls. Their assorted sizes and patterns added interest to the naked rusticity of the granary. Jam-jars of wild spring flowers would ornament the tables.

Eugene drew a family tree and illustrated it with miniature portraits taken from the paintings about the house. He put together a guide book, covering the history of Curraghcourt and the locality. The life of an isolated demesne in the west of Connemara impinged little on national affairs so we included pages from the diaries of long-dead chatelaines of Curraghcourt; recipes for soap and pound cake; advice on the governing of servants; the order of household prayers; pastes, powders and tinctures to cure that most prevalent and dread disease, tuberculosis, all of which must have been sadly unavailing. How to

514

prevent moss growing on leather-bound books. A suitable dinner menu for a hunt ball. What to do in cases of lice, fleas, ticks and worms.

Eugene illustrated these counsels with drawings that were as amusing as they were accomplished. I had never heard him make a joke or even a wry remark but his sketches of people lying drunk against a table leg at an important dinner or being dragged by one foot in a stirrup across the path of fanatically intent riders-to-hounds had a delightful humour about them. This hitherto unsuspected facet of Eugene's personality reconciled me all the more to the idea of Constance being made one with him at some point in the future.

So far there was no sign of this scheme being brought to maturity. I had at last persuaded Constance to show Eugene several of her poems about love. He had read them carefully and kindly given her the benefit of his advice as to how she might improve them. He admitted that for a beginner she had a talent for expressing nuances of mood. He had handed them back to her with a bow and the recommendation to study the great ones of the past if she wished to improve.

'Short of throwing myself naked into his arms I despair,' Constance said afterwards.

'I really thought the poetry might do it.' We were painstakingly removing the black sediment of damp from the glazing bars of the dining-room windows with cotton wool dipped into a solution of bleach. 'I suppose most men are pretty hopeless at picking up subtle hints.'

'Why are humans driven to seek love all the time?' Constance frowned as she rubbed. 'It would be so much better if we concentrated all our strength of mind and body on producing great art and nurturing the state of our souls. Of course we could love one another in a friendly way. But how much better it would be if sex were as unimportant as brushing one's teeth. Simply a mechanical process for engendering children, if you were certain you really wanted them. It would solve so many problems.'

'Is everyone capable of great art, do you think?'

'Well, perhaps not. But at least we could improve our characters. Instead of fussing about whether someone has noticed the sparkling of our eyes and bothering about the liquidity of theirs we could devote ourselves to the attainment of spiritual perfection. It's got to be more worthwhile.'

'Like being a monk or a nun, you mean?'

'Well, yes. But with less emphasis on mortifying the flesh. At school the nuns whipped our hands so hard for the smallest offences we couldn't straighten our fingers for days afterwards. My knees have never recovered from hours of praying on damp stone floors.' Constance paused in the process of wiping away the bleach with a sponge and looked pensive, her grey eyes reflecting the light from the misted windows. 'The worst thing of all was we went to the lavatory after breakfast and weren't allowed to go again until before lunch. My bladder's always been temperamental. I was so frightened of Mother Superior that one glance from her mean little eyes made me desperate to go. Golly!' Constance rolled her eyes. 'Those hours of *tor*ture, unable to concentrate on anything but keeping my legs pressed together until finally the agony became unbearable and I wet myself.' Constance closed her eyes and shuddered. 'We weren't allowed in the dormitories until bedtime so I had to walk around the rest of the day slowly drying out, the elastic of my knicker legs rubbing my thighs raw, smelling of pee. The other girls used to bribe each other with sweets to get out of sitting next to me. I was known as the Stink Bomb.'

'Oh, Con!' I was inexpressibly moved by this confession. Now I understood why she too was terrified of rejection. 'How dreadfully children suffer and how helpless they are to help themselves! Surely the anguish we feel as adults is light by comparison? Mostly we can take action, and even if we can't we have, or ought to have, some command of our minds.'

'As for my mind, I hope I can manage to put on a cheerful face, if that's what you mean. And I tell myself not to be such a dolt, every hour of every day, almost. But as to taking action, that's just what I can't do.' Constance's face became gloomy. 'Eugene hasn't said a word to me about Larkie but he's stopped writing about love and betrayal and is working on a prose-poem about Wolfe Tone and the seventeen ninety-eight rebellion. I've never seen him so cheerful. He asked me yesterday if I thought he ought to move back to Kilmuree. He was worried that he might have outstayed his welcome.'

'And you said?'

'I muttered something polite. He offered to stay until the opening if I thought he could be useful. Then, when my mind was doing a double somersault wondering what the hell I could say to stop him going, he said perhaps he'd better give his tenants notice to quit by the beginning of May. I'm a fool! Because I couldn't bring myself to risk rejection and humiliation he's going to go away and it's all my fault!'

516

Mindful of Constance's painful condition of suspenseful love I tried to be positive. 'I think that's only good news, really. That he's stopped thinking of himself as a victim. As to moving away, well, it might bring things to a head.'

'I suppose it might. Anyway, that's enough maundering for now.' Constance stretched her limbs and exhaled noisily. 'Let's have a drink. You can't *think* what a luxury it is, having someone to talk to. Granny was the only other person I've ever dared to tell about the peeing problem. She said I should pray. So I did. But apparently God was too busy absolving sinners and beatifying saints to bother to send me a larger bladder. I've never had a close female friend of my own age before. You know how I feel about Eugene' – she blushed – 'and I'd cut off my right hand if it would do Finn or the children any good, but you're the only person I feel I can say absolutely anything to.'

Dear Constance. I felt conscience-stricken, knowing how much I was concealing from her. 'I'll open a bottle of Dicky Dooley's special-offer champagne,' I said. 'Its comparative nastiness will mean we can drink to friendship without feeling guilty.' I fetched a bottle from the fridge, popped the cork and poured two glasses. 'Here's to the resolution of all our difficulties.'

'And to the power of the mind to resist becoming an enfeebled, man-oriented cipher,' Constance declared robustly. 'There are so many other things in life worth thinking about.'

She was quite right. It was pathetic to moon about, like green-sick girls, dreaming of love fulfilled. We drank to that.

'If only' – some of the vigour departed from Constance's tone – 'something would happen to change our lives, something from outside that would make us stand in a different relation to each other. Eugene and me, I mean. But nothing *ever* happens at Curraghcourt so it's no use wishing for it.'

As it happened, she was shortly to be proved wrong.

FORTY-FOUR

We had broadcast the opening of Curraghcourt as widely as we could among newspapers, magazines and Heritage pamphlets. According to these publications the tourist season began officially at the beginning of April. For three weeks beforehand shrieking winds and fierce rain hurled themselves against the walls. Beside every water-logged sheep lay a tiny sodden lamb. Birdsong was drowned out. Bog myrtle and cotton grass bent their buds beneath the onslaught. Only the gorse came bravely into bloom.

In the walled garden there was no sign of the lettuce, onion, carrot, broad bean and pea seeds I had sown four weeks earlier. The potatoes lay in a sludge as viscid as melted chocolate. The asparagus crowns I had ordered from Dublin had been washed out of the soil. Lashed by rain that flowed like glass ropes from my knees, elbows and nose, I had replanted them. This resulted in a heavy cold that ran round the entire family.

The day of the opening came. After a night of coughing myself into a feverish headache I dragged myself from my bed to face a blushing dawn. I opened the window. Puddles lay on the roof, smooth but for the occasional ruffling from a light breeze. The rain had stopped. The extraordinary beauty of the forests and mountains thrilled me as much, perhaps more than the first time I had seen them, for they were now familiar and dear to me. My fever cooled; the headache began to ease.

I picked my way across the floor among a sea of cats, all of whom had moved into my bedroom in protest at the unrelenting weather. The new canopy above my bed heaved with bodies. Alexander, Paudeen and Dervla, the most domesticated of the tribe, worked their giant paws in ecstasy as I rubbed their bronze-coloured ears and striped fur. Reproduction had been brought to a standstill and good homes had been found for some of the kittens but fifteen cats were still too many for a smallish room. I had caught more than one squatting in a corner when the weather howled inhospitably beyond the improvised cardboard cat-flap.

Osgar was now the chief obstacle to their living downstairs. These days he roamed the demesne terrorizing, by a lift of his lip and a resonant growl, rats, squirrels, sheep and even the Cockatoo. Some people – probably most – would blame my foolish sentimentality for this unsatisfactory situation. Anyway, I had to sort it out before I left.

By a quarter to two, the hour of our debut, the dogs had been shut up in the boot room, the signs for the tea-room and lavatory were in place and the areas not open to the public had been roped off. Each of us was poised, strung with anticipation, at his or her appointed post. I took a last glance, trying to see the house with the critical eyes of a stranger. It looked, perhaps, a little shabby and dilapidated but undeniably well loved. It smelt of furniture polish and flowers, mostly daffodils with a good deal of mahonia and skimmia. My heart swelled with affectionate pride as I swept turf ash from the side table with my sleeve.

I took my place in the niche of the gatehouse where in feudal times servants had spent long days training their eyes upon the road that snaked down the distant hill, in expectation of English soldiers coming to lay siege to the castle or of local squireens coming to dance and dine. I had a rickety table before me, a book of cloak-room tickets and a bowl of loose change. Constance was stationed by the front door on the other side of the courtyard, ready to embark with the first-comers on the tour. There had been some argument about this. Constance thought that as I knew more about the furniture, paintings and decoration I would be the better guide. But I was positive that the visitors would prefer the cachet of being shown round by a true daughter of the house to details about veneers, gilt-bronze and hard paste porcelain.

Pegeen and Katty, in clean aprons, were waiting in the granary – that is, tea-room – behind the piping-hot urn we had bought, second-hand, from Turlough McGurn. The children were at school, furious to be missing the excitement. Maud and Violet were closeted upstairs in their rooms with an electric kettle, the television on and the blinds down. Maud was apprehensive of the tramp of proletarian feet but Violet was disappointed to be shut away. Timsy was harnessing the

Cockatoo. We hoped visitors would be charmed to be taken down to the walled garden in an authentic horse-drawn Irish car. Timsy had been forbidden to drink on pain of instant dismissal. Of course we all knew this was an empty threat.

Only the previous day Eugene had been visited by inspiration. Weeks before we had discovered in one of the attics a collection of eighteenth- and nineteenth-century silhouettes, bust-length, full-length and groups with lithographed backgrounds, consigned there by Constance's grandmother when such things had gone out of fashion. They were all of good quality and three were signed by Augustin Edouart, the most famous 'scissorgraphist'. Together they made a striking group in a corner of the drawing room where the mildew on the yellow damask was particularly bad.

Eugene had offered to set himself up with easel, paper, pen and black ink, to dash off a head-and-shoulders silhouette of anyone willing to pay five pounds for the privilege of sitting. He had practised on the children and we had been impressed by the result. He was able to produce a good likeness in about fifteen minutes. Only experience would tell whether this would be a profitable exercise but if nothing else it was a welcome sign that Eugene was prepared to see himself once more as a contributing member of the human race.

I sharpened my pencil in case teething troubles needed to be taken note of, tidied the change in my bowl, placed my book of tickets at a neat right-angle to my jotting pad and again fixed my eyes on the (almost) blue horizon. After a long hour during which I had written out my grocery order for the week, made a list of repair jobs indoors and sketched out a cutting border for the walled garden, I went indoors.

'I suppose we were expecting too much.' Constance was sprawled in one of the hall chairs with *Castle Rackrent* in her hand. 'Perhaps there aren't any tourists this far west so early in the year.'

'Or not enough other kinds of entertainment nearby,' I said gloomily. 'Probably they can't be bothered to come this far just for one castle.'

'There's Clerenshill and Glassenough within sixty miles of us. They both open at Easter. I wonder what these beastly trippers want,' she added, bitter in her disappointment. 'A funfair and lions, I suppose.'

'Oh, Constance, I can't bear it to be a failure! We've worked so hard!'

'It's only the first day. Come on, Bobbie. It's not like you to be downhearted.'

It was true that my nature was generally optimistic. But it had been my idea to open Curraghcourt. We had spent something like two hundred and fifty pounds on paint, specialist cleaning things, ingredients for the tea-room and, most expensive of all, two signs directing people here: one for the centre of Kilmuree and the other to indicate the road that led to the demesne. The total of man-hours put in was incalculable.

Constance flexed her arms above her head. 'Perhaps the Heritage people will give us some money regardless of how many people do or don't come to see us.'

I shook my head. 'They won't. These boards are run by hard-headed accountants. If they give money to us why not to every large house with a leaking roof and rising damp? Of which there must be thousands in Ireland. We have to prove to them that we're an asset to tourism. But, as you say, it's only the first day. Perhaps the word hasn't got around yet. Where's Eugene?'

'Lying down in the library. He says he hardly slept last night for excitement. I promised to call him if anyone came.'

'It's a miserable anticlimax. We'd better check on the others.'

Timsy was stretched along the seat of the outside car, his eyes closed, reeking of whiskey while the Cockatoo pulled him slowly about the courtyard in search of the stunted grass that grew between the cobblestones. In the tea-room Pegeen and Katty were huddled together over a pot of tea and a game of noughts and crosses. Their aprons were not looking quite so clean. Katty whisked something out of sight as soon as she saw us. I had no doubt it was a black bottle. I lacked the spirit to protest.

'Now look.' Constance threw back her shoulders and put on her bossiest voice. 'What sort of impression will this make? Someone might come at any moment. We must continue to hold ourselves in readiness.'

Pegeen grinned up at her with bleary eyes. She had lost another tooth.

Half an hour later Constance and I let the dogs out and joined Pegeen and Katty at their table which now looked as though a family of ten had wiped their hands and faces on the tablecloth every day for a week. To cheer ourselves up we had a glass of poteen and some chocolate biscuits. Constance of course was familiar with the taste but I had to hold my nose to get it down. It must be admitted, things looked much more cheerful afterwards. I taught the others how to play Hangman and for some reason this simple game was a smash hit. Pegeen and Katty, by now hiccuping and periodically slipping from their chairs, screamed with excitement whenever they hanged anyone or were hanged themselves. They winked and cackled and nudged me with their elbows and for the first time I felt they had forgiven me for being English and were willing to include me in the sisterhood, so it was not an entirely wasted half-hour. At four o'clock I went back to the house to fetch the lunch trays from Maud's room. My foot was on the bottom stair when I heard the tooting of a car horn. I raced towards the gatehouse.

'Ho there, postern-keeper! This is a slack outfit and no mistake.'

'Kit!'

He emerged from the shadow of the archway. 'Hello, my darling Bobbie.' He drew me to him and kissed me soundly. 'You're looking marvellous. If a trifle flurried. Is that chocolate on your chin?'

I rubbed my forearm across my face and tried to pull myself together. The effects of the poteen were long-lasting. In the context of a day spent idling away hours that felt like years, Kit looked bright-eyed, dynamic and fit, like an advertisement for vitamins. His elegantly waving hair was streaked almost white at the front and he was sporting a tan that made his teeth gleam.

'It's our first day open. Did you remember? If so, you're a friend in a million. Not a soul's been near us. It's discouraging, to say the least.'

'Of course I remembered. That hideous Dutch pink is burned on my retina. Every time I close my eyes I think of Curraghcourt and the smell of paint. And you. Not necessarily in that order.'

'It's wonderful to see you. Why are you so brown?'

'I got back from three weeks in Gstaad yesterday. Lovely weather, excellent snow.'

'Being a literary agent has other rewards than the merely cultural, evidently.' After I said this I thought it sounded rather grudging so I added, 'You mustn't mind if we're all a little flat. We've slaved to get things ready and I quite thought we'd have some customers our first day.' I sighed. 'Another of life's cruel lessons.'

'What would you say if I told you there was a bus-load of eager culture-vultures cresting the hill at this moment,' asked Kit. 'And another not far behind?'

I stared at him wonderingly. 'Are you teasing me? Because if so I think it's a rotten joke.'

'Look!' Kit pulled me through the archway and pointed to the hillside. Rolling down it, at this distance about the size of a liquorice

522

comfit, was a bright red single-decker coach. 'Some of the Kilmuree wits thought it would be amusing to redirect your signs. The roads of West Connemara are congested with disgruntled pleasure-seekers, thoroughly lost. I happened to meet the two buses on my way over. I set them on the right path and I've turned both signs round. Then I put my foot down to get here in time to warn you.'

'Kit! You're an *ang*el!' I hugged him. 'Oh, you excellent man! Words can't express my heartfelt gratitude—'

'It's not words I'm particularly interested in.' Kit put his arms round my waist but I was too distracted to respond.

'Oh, no! Pegeen and Katty! And Timsy!'

FORTY-FIVE

At half past five Constance and I stood by the front door to watch the last vehicle lurch away over the ruts. I felt as though my eyes had contracted to pinholes with weariness.

Constance rubbed her hands over her face and fastened back with a kirby-grip the strands of her hair that had worked loose. 'I don't know about you, but I've got to have a big, big glass of something wholly intoxicating.'

'Come on, you two.' Kit appeared in the hall with a bottle and several glasses on a tray. 'Time to unwind. Oh, Constance, I've got something for you.' He gave me the tray and felt in the pocket of his jacket. He brought out a thin booklet and handed it to her. 'Page five.'

Looking bemused Constance turned the pages as directed. Then her face became fiery and her hand flew to her mouth. 'My poem! Oh, Kit! How did you . . . It isn't nearly good enough. I feel over-whelmed . . . Did you have to pay somebody?'

'Not a penny. It's a very reputable magazine. The editor likes the poem very much and wants to see what else you've written. It may be the beginning of something. Poetry's as hard a way to win fame and fortune as busking outside the chip shop with a harmonica but keep writing.'

She kissed his cheek. '*Thank* you.'

Eugene came in then and I saw Constance hesitate, then put the booklet behind a cushion. I wondered if she wished to show it to him when they were alone or whether she was afraid of making him jealous.

'It was so good of you to do that,' I said to Kit in a low voice. 'To send it to the magazine. It ought to do wonders for Constance's morale.'

'It was a little thing.' Kit took back the tray, put it on the table and filled the glasses. 'But if it pleases you, I'm glad.'

I felt I really loved him at that moment. 'Would you do one more thing for me? Usually I ask Eugene but so often he gets as far as the landing, then forgets what he's supposed to be doing and goes off to his room. Would you bring Violet down? She hates being shut away from all the excitement. Then we can spend a pleasant hour or so congratulating ourselves.'

'Oh, Jesus, Mary and Joseph!' Constance threw herself on to a sofa in the drawing room. 'I have never *ever* in my entire life felt so thoroughly undone! And it was only part of an afternoon and two tours! What will it be like tomorrow?'

'It's because it's all new to us, that's all. Naturally we've felt anxious and there's nothing more tiring. But, joy, oh joy! It was a triumph! They absolutely *loved* it!'

'They did! I'm blessed if I know why.' Constance grasped the glass I held out to her. 'Despite Osgar taking a shine to that woman's mink-lined mackintosh. Thank goodness Kit was here!'

I took out my jotting pad, already covered with notes. 'Tonight Eugene must make a notice to put by the front door, inviting all women to leave their furs under lock and key in the cloakroom.'

'Won't they think it odd?'

'It'll be part of the eccentricity. It seems that's the appeal.'

'It's true.' Constance looked puzzled. 'When I explained about the tradition of keeping a black dog tethered on the front-door step and how we'd decided it was time to break with custom in the interests of animal welfare but we were still trying to teach him acceptable manners, they all melted, including the owner of the coat. They took photographs of Osgar and the English visitors tried to give him mints and toffees when they thought I wasn't looking.'

'You must be sure to include the story in every tour from now on. We'll have to do something about the chain in the kitchen passage.' The fact that it had escaped its moorings and returned to dangle at head height had been unnoticed by Constance who had continued to dodge it instinctively. 'It gives a new meaning to the word brow-beaten. Several people came out looking rather bruised and that poor bald man was running with blood.'

'Perhaps Timsy could take it down?'

I began to scribble busily. 'I think it would be better to fix a large notice to it and you can explain what it was for and how you're all used to dodging it. More local colour. What was the story you told

525

that made all the men laugh? I heard them chortling when I took Maud and Violet some tea.'

'I'm sure it's apocryphal and does the rounds of all the old Irish houses. I don't think I'd have risked it if I hadn't had the poteen. In the old days the master of the house was in the habit of choosing one of the maids to warm his bed each night. I'm sure that much is true. Apparently one night the girl smelt so strongly of tallow and armpits that he got up in the dark, took a bottle of cologne from his dressing table and sprinkled it all over her. In the morning he found the poor girl covered with ink.'

'What are you – laughing – ab-b-bout?' asked Violet, clinging to Kit's neck as he carried her in, followed a few minutes later by Maud. 'How many – people – c-c-came? Did it go – well?' Maud had been persuaded to allow the speech therapist back and during the last few weeks Violet had made tremendous progress. She still spoke slowly, slurred her words and often forgot them altogether but it was now possible to have proper conversations with her. Though she still sometimes wept with frustration she tried to be patient and was always sweet-tempered with me. I had grown really fond of her.

'Rubbish!' said Maud, when the story about the ink was repeated. 'Of course they all reeked of sweat and horses and the pox, he probably worse than she. This modern coyness is all of a piece with the current passion for tasteless and misleading euphemisms. A man had the effrontery to open my bedroom door and ask for a *rest room*. I instructed him on no account to get on the beds but to lie down in the garden if he was tired. Violet says he was asking for a lavatory. What, I should like to know, is restful about excretion? Violet, you're slouching. Sit up!'

Violet had been leaning on the arm of the sofa looking at the latest copy of *Vogue* which had arrived that morning. Apart from Finn coming home, it was the event she most looked forward to.

I made another note. *Sign for lav on landing.*

Flavia came running in and went at once to kiss her mother. 'Did anyone come? What happened?' She sat beside Violet and took her mother's crippled right hand on her knee, stroking it gently because she knew the splint made it ache. 'It's taken us ages to get home!'

Constance had arranged that Sam O'Kelly would do the school run in return for an appropriate fee. He and Larkie were still kicking their heels in Kilmuree, lacking the funds to return to America.

'I gave him strict orders not to go faster than forty,' said Constance. 'The Morris won't take the strain of high speeds and we must have the Land-Rover here in case of emergencies. It's all been very exciting and, to put it conservatively, a howling success. But you'll see for yourselves on Saturday. In fact I'm hoping you'll all lend a hand.'

'Oh, yes!' cried Flavia. 'What can I do?'

'Do you think you and Liddy could be waitresses?' I asked. 'Pegeen and Katty were rushed off their feet.'

'I'd adore it!' said Flavia. 'I could have a little book to write things down in and I'd be very careful not to slop the tea in the saucers. Mummy gets so cross about that, don't you?' She rested her head against her mother's shoulder.

'I'm never cross with you – my sweet – b-baby.' Violet caressed Flavia's hair with her good hand. The smile faded almost immediately from her face as she turned back to *Vogue*, keeping her place with her finger as she struggled to read the words.

'Where *is* Liddy?' asked Constance.

'She's gone to the kitchen to find something to eat,' said Flavia.

Liddy seemed to be eating more sensibly these days, though it was too soon to be sure that the starving and bingeing were things of the past. I would have liked to have put this improvement down to Liddy's satisfaction at having her mother restored to her but the truth was that though she and Violet shared a passion for clothes and the fashionable world Liddy frequently found her mother's presence an irritant. She was impatient of the time it took Violet to express herself. Seventeen, I remembered from my own relationship with my mother, was a supremely ungracious age and there was more than a little of Maud in Liddy's character.

Just as I was thinking this, Liddy put her head round the door.

'Do you want the ham that's in the fridge?' she asked me, ignoring everyone else.

'Do you see that Kit's here?' said Constance crossly. 'If you can't be bothered to say hello to the rest of us you might at least have the courtesy to acknowledge his presence.'

'Sorry. Hello, Kit, how are you?' Without waiting for his reply she switched her attention back to me. At least she had got over her infatuation, I was thankful to see.

'Yes, I'm afraid I do want it. But there are scones left over from the visitors' teas and some jam and cream. You can finish them if you like. They have to be made fresh every day or they taste like cardboard—'

'Bags I!' yelled Flavia and the two girls raced each other for the door.

'What about you, Flurry?' asked Constance. 'Would you be able to help us on Saturday? You could take the coats and umbrellas and put tickets on them.'

'I've got to get on with the railway if I'm to finish it by the summer,' said Flurry. 'Besides' – he pulled down his mouth – 'I don't much like strangers.'

'I thought I didn't, either,' said Eugene, returning from a prolonged session in the kitchen with the Dabitoff. A spot of ink had fallen on his trousers. 'But they were all so polite and complimentary that I rather enjoyed myself.'

Eugene's silhouettes had been a *succès fou*. We had stationed him and his easel near the staircase where the visitors debouched from the kitchen at the end of the tour. Having seen how elegant the silhouettes looked in the drawing room people liked the idea of giving their own houses a dash of country-house style. A queue had formed which interfered with the progress of new arrivals so Kit introduced a system of tickets for the portrait sittings. This meant the visitors could wait their turn in the garden or spend more money in the tea-room, where they were entertained by Pegeen and Katty who were as good as Laurel and Hardy with the trays of tea and cakes. There had been a number of breakages but it was to be hoped that from now on they would be too busy to have time for more than an occasional 'supeen' to keep up their strengths.

'One knows one ought to resist the idea of racial stereotypes,' said Constance, 'but superficially there *are* characteristics that seem to run through. The Americans were the friendliest. They asked questions about everything.' She sipped her champagne with a happy smile of recollection. 'And they gave the biggest tips. I haven't counted yet but I think there's something like twenty-five pounds. The Japanese were very polite and extremely serious. They wrote down practically every word I said and didn't laugh at my jokes. I expect they thought I was mad. The French and the Germans were more inclined to be snooty about the crumbling state of things. But they were the best informed about the art and architecture. The English spoke in hushed voices as though they felt they oughtn't to be in someone else's house and didn't tip at all. But they came into their own in the garden. They cross-questioned me about propagation and pruning and soil types and I felt a complete fool not knowing.'

'I met a delightful couple who'd just flown in from Colorado.' Kit poured himself another glass of champagne. 'Irish-Americans in search of their roots. They want to buy a romantic old wreck of a Georgian house and do it up. They asked me if it was true that it rained a lot in Ireland. I hardly knew what to say. On one hand it would have been cruel to mislead them. On the other, there's so much wonderful architecture here that needs to be saved by philanthropic foreigners as the Irish themselves are so indifferent to it.'

Maud threw down a glass of usquebaugh in one draught. 'Why parvenus think it romantic to live in a gloomy ruin with donkeys for neighbours, hysterics for servants and the constant drip, drip, drip of things decaying all around them I shall never understand.'

'What did you say to them?' I asked Kit.

'I confessed that it did rain rather frequently but asked them if they didn't agree that romance requires fitful beams, lowering skies and muted shades?'

'A very good answer.' I held up my glass and smiled as he brought the bottle over to me. 'Thank you for coming today. We should never have managed without you. I had no idea you could drive a horse and cart so expertly.'

He sat down beside me and put his arm along the back of the sofa, resting his hand on my shoulder, and said softly, 'We don't know everything about each other yet, by any means. By the way.' He tugged gently at a lock of my hair. 'I've just been into the dining room. I take back everything I said about the colour. Now it's finished and hung with pictures it looks superb. So who's a clever girl then?'

'Speak up, you two,' said Maud. 'This is not a bedroom.'

During dinner, as everyone else was inclined to be noisy and jubilant, I allowed myself to become reflective. I had made my weekly call to Cutham an hour before. Oliver had been walking past the telephone. He had been unusually forthcoming. My mother was allowing Ruby to wheel her about the house. She and Ruby planned to make sorties into the garden when the weather became mild enough. My father had put on a huge amount of weight and his mood was uncharacteristically mellow. Oliver and Sherilee were thinking of taking on the lease of the pub. His novel had been shelved for the time being. When questioned he admitted he had not written a word during the nine months of my absence. No, there was no need for me to come home. Everything was ticking over nicely. Sherilee was a girl in a million. She was the only woman he knew who could drink a pint of beer in ten seconds flat and who could burp the entire chorus of 'Land of My Fathers'. Her mother happened to be Welsh.

As I served the *crème de riz à la Connaught* – in this case rice pudding with dried apricots so old they had required soaking for two days and a dash of poteen instead of kirsch – I acknowledged that where my brother was concerned, as with so many things, I had made a mistake. My zeal for reform, my seeming uncontrollable impulse to meddle had blinded me to the fact that darling Oliver was not cut out to be a novelist. He had obligingly gone along with my demands because he was lonely and grateful for my attention. But he had not the will to succeed. This misreading of character made me angry with myself. But I hoped I had learned my lesson.

I looked down the table to where Violet sat. She was talking to Kit, looking up at him with a coquettish smile, her drooping eyelid and lopsided mouth hardly noticeable by candlelight. True, she could not yet walk and she was entirely dependent on others. But the chances were that she would continue to improve. It had to be better than that long sleep of groans and mutters and dimly perceived dreams, didn't it?

She had told us that during the first part of her illness she had often been awake and could hear people whispering but it was like rolling about under water. She could not get her head above the surface to make sense of anything. Later when we had talked to her and tried to get her to respond she had begun to have moments of clarity when she understood perfectly well what we were saying but answers had slipped away from her before she could quite grasp them. That had been the worst time and she had almost been driven mad by frustration until the fateful day when she had managed to say my name. By comparison with the feeling then of abject helplessness the annoyance now of sometimes not being able to find the right words was as nothing.

This was all extremely satisfactory. But what was it about Violet that made one anxious? She was restless, which was natural in the circumstances. Maud had her so fiercely in thrall that there was bound to be rebellion before much longer. And once I had gone, Finn might spend more time at home . . . Oh, the guilt! I must stop thinking about that.

I pushed grains of rice about my plate, waiting for the others to finish. As soon as things were ticking over steadily with the visitors I must return to London and find a job. I could work for an auction house again, or do something with historic buildings. There were so many possibilities. I was twenty-seven. Old enough to know my weaknesses and young enough to do something about them. This sense of deprivation, of longing, that I carried permanently about with me must be uprooted and shut out.

I looked again at Kit and Violet. He had said something to make her laugh. Tenderly he patted the right-hand corner of her mouth with his napkin. It was a curiously intimate gesture. Maud, who was sitting opposite them, glared at her daughter and rapped on the table with her fork. Violet laughed again, her beautiful eyes brilliant. Kit sent Maud a look that was more flirtatious than contrite.

So he liked women. That must be in his favour. It was kind of him to try to entertain Violet. He could be relied upon to do the right thing. Kit and I were perfectly matched. We had similar backgrounds, tastes in common and found the same things amusing. We were both unattached – that is, single. We saw each other clearly without the distorting glass of illicit love that makes passion so exquisite and tormenting.

I got up to make the coffee. I shook my head, smiling, when Kit offered to help me.

'I want to go to bed,' said Violet, in the little-girl voice she sometimes adopted. 'Carry me up, K-Kit.'

'Nonsense!' said Maud. 'It's only five to ten. You're not ill.'

'It's all that – beastly – walking you made me do. I'm sleepy.'

'Nonsense!' said Maud again, as though Violet were a child instead of a woman of thirty-seven.

I left them arguing. It was peaceful in the kitchen. Pegeen, Katty and Timsy lay like logs on the hearth, the extra ration of poteen having taken its toll. The two dogs slept beside them, Osgar's chin on Timsy's rising and falling stomach. All around them pieces of paper fluttered in the draught from the chimney. I picked up a handful. They were covered with drawings of gallows and stickmen. I made the coffee, took the tray into the drawing room and revived the dying fire. Then I took a bucket of turves and some shortbread fans upstairs to stoke up Violet's and Maud's fires and replenish their biscuit jars. Pegeen and Katty had been too busy or too excited to make their beds. It was the work of moments to tidy Violet's bed but Maud's top sheet was stained with what looked like tea. It frequently happened that her hands were too stiff and weak to manage her breakfast tray. I took off the sheet and went to the linen cupboards. As I searched through the piles of linen for those with Maud's initials stitched in red on the corners I heard voices coming from below.

'You're a b-b-bad – boy.' Violet giggled as Kit carried her slowly up the stairs. 'I'm a married – woman. You shouldn't – s-say those things.'

They were clearly visible in the light cast by the brass lantern that hung above the stairwell but the linen cupboards, which lined a recess leading to the kitchen stairs, were dimly lit. I had no wish to spoil Violet's fun, so I stepped back into the shadows.

Kit paused near the top stair. '*You* shouldn't be such a little flirt! But, if you like, I'll put you down here and Eugene can take you the rest of the way.'

'Please – don't! He's such a – b-b-bore. I don't know why Con wants him to – wants him to – what's the word?'

'Make love to her, do you mean? There are less polite words but I'm sure you weren't thinking of those.'

Violet laughed again. 'It's – fun with you here. The others are so – d-dull. Oh Kit, say you like me – a little t-too?'

For answer Kit put his mouth on hers and they kissed lingeringly. I watched with a feeling that was mostly surprise. It occurred to me that I ought to announce my presence in some way but it would have embarrassed them. And, more importantly, me.

'Don't – s-s-top,' breathed Violet. 'I want – You m-m-must—'

'It's too public here,' murmured Kit. I shrank back against the shelves, hoping my feet were not visible beneath the open door. 'Where can we go? Your room?'

'Mummy'll be on the war-thing – any m-minute. She's such an old – beast. But we can lock the – thingy – door. Lucky she takes – long time to get up – stairs.'

'You're a wicked temptress. All right. But we'll have to be quick.'

I heard his footsteps hurrying by, then a door open and close. I asked myself what I should be feeling. What did a few kisses mean? It seemed more like a game than a betrayal. I resumed my search among smooth bed-linen, cool to my hot hands. It took me a little while to find what I was looking for. I turned out the linen cupboard light and stood for a while in the darkness, trying to decide what I ought to do. I didn't want to spy on them. But Maud's bed had to be made, and quickly too. I tiptoed back to Maud's room feeling like an incompetent thief, terrified of being caught. Passing Violet's door I heard her voice raised in a long moan of pleasure, which became gasping cries, higher and louder each time. There was a rhythmical knocking as of a bedhead hitting the wall. Kit began to groan and Violet to yodel. Not just kisses then.

I hurried into Maud's room and closed the door in an unsuccessful attempt to shut out the sound. Hastily I tucked in the sheets and blankets and threw on the eiderdown. I wanted to put my fingers in my ears when I heard a bellow from Kit but that would have made it impossible to fling the counterpane over the top. Minutes later I was thankful I had taken the precaution of turning off the light before opening Maud's door. Kit was standing just feet away, outside Violet's room. He was leaning against the opposite wall, wiping his mouth with his handkerchief and grinning all over his face. Had he not been absorbed by what were evidently pleasurable thoughts he must have seen me. I sprang back into darkness and waited until I heard him walk towards the main staircase. Then I ran like an Olympic sprinter down the back stairs and shot into the hall just as he reached the drawing-room door.

'I wondered where you were,' he said pleasantly as I advanced with a bonbonnière of chocolates I had snatched from the table as I hared through the kitchen.

'Oh, just tidying up a bit.' I tried to match his leisurely tone.

'You seem awfully out of breath.'

'Do I? It's been a long day. I'm rather tired.'

'You must be. You're gasping like a landed fish.'

'I'll get to bed as soon as I can.'

'O lucky cats!' He sighed as though he really meant it.

As I poured coffee and listened to the others making plans for the next day I wondered why I had felt so anxious not to be caught skulking, an unwilling witness to that brief unzipping of trousers and lifting of skirts. It was true that I had eavesdropped dishonourably but surely that was a venial sin compared with making love to one's host's wife?

I looked at Kit who was leaning forward in his chair, discussing something with Constance. As though he felt my eyes upon him he turned his head and smiled at me, an affectionate smile telegraphing approval, tenderness, even longing. He might have spent the last quarter of an hour talking sympathetically to Constance about the Gaelic League instead of screwing Violet to the mattress. I almost laughed aloud as I thought this and then it came to me in a flash that I felt guilty because I had not suffered a moment's jealousy or even hurt pride. I had not given a tinker's damn. The reason was simple enough. I had felt nothing but gratitude that it had been Kit making love to Violet and not Finn.

FORTY-SIX

'Bobbie! Thank heavens!'

'Jazzy!' I sat down in the sedan chair and closed the door, cradling the receiver beneath my chin as I took the weight of a stack of clean plates on my knees. 'What a lovely surprise!'

'Can you talk?'

'For a minute or two. I've got to get over to the tea-room before they run out of plates. Now the house is open to the public—'

'Oh, Bobbie, I've got to tell you, it's so awful . . .' Jasmine began to cry. 'I've never been so miserable in my – entire – life!'

Though naturally distressed to hear this I was not particularly surprised. During my telephone conversations with Jasmine over the last few months I had detected a distinct falling off of rapture with Teddy, though she had done her best to hide it; not, I thought, to deceive me so much as herself.

'Oh dear!' I said. 'What's happened?'

It seemed that Teddy's wife, Lydia, had telephoned to say that their daughter had been rushed to hospital with suspected appendicitis. Could Teddy come at once? Of course Teddy had gone and had remained in London for several days. He had admitted during a hasty call to Jasmine that he was staying with Lydia in the 'marital home' in Canonbury. Jasmine had decided that rather than allow loneliness and the yellow Formica in the Enfield bungalow to drive her out of her mind she would go up to town. She had taken a cab to Canonbury. The au pair had answered the door and informed her that sir and madam had gone out to lunch. *Lunch!* When Jasmine hadn't been able to eat a thing for days! Apparently the child had come back from the hospital that morning and was quite better. It was only a stomach bug. The *bastard*!

Pretending she was still at death's door and making Jasmine feel guilty as hell!

Jasmine knew the restaurant well. It had been one of their favourite haunts in the early days of her affair with Teddy. She had whizzed round to Les Lapins Sous Croûte. Teddy and Lydia had been sitting at *their* corner table! As Jasmine stared in disbelief through the window she had seen Lydia lean across to straighten Teddy's tie. And Teddy had taken Lydia's hand and *kissed* it! Before she had even thought about what she was doing, Jazz had rushed into the restaurant, seized the first thing that came to hand, which happened to be a Dover sole from the plate of an astonished customer at the next table, and brought it down on Teddy's head. She had been escorted back into the street by the head waiter, but not before she had managed to hit Lydia on the cheek with a *boule* of tomato sorbet.

'Can you be*lieve* it?' wept Jasmine. 'After I've given up everything for him – and lived for all those months in that hell-hole – and if I ever see another pampas grass thing again I shall cut my throat. I mean it!'

'Where are you now?'

'Back in Paradise Row. But my room's let. Sarah says I can sleep on the sofa for a while but the new girls are cross because they can't entertain their boyfriends. I feel horribly in the way. I'm thinking of going down to the river and ending it all. The doorstop ought to be heavy enough if I tie it round my neck.'

'Jazz. Please. Put the idea right out of your head. It's ridiculous to think of killing yourself because of a louse like Teddy. He isn't worth a tear. Stupid, shallow, selfish and debauched. Besides, he has the sex appeal of a putrescent worm. I'm sorry for his wife.'

'I thought you liked him.'

'No.'

'Bobbie, I couldn't come and stay with you, could I? I feel so desperately lonely and I don't know where to go or what to do. Just for a couple of weeks until I feel a bit better?'

I pulled a face of alarm and perplexity to myself in the privacy of the sedan chair. As housekeeper I was hardly in a position to extend invitations to my friends. But supposing I said no and Jasmine sped straight down to the river? 'Darling, I wonder if that's the best plan? Of course I'd adore to have you here but I'm not sure it would be the right thing for you. We're miles out in the wilds and there'd be nothing for you to do.'

'I could help you. You're always saying there's more than enough work. I'd be willing to *slave*. I wouldn't want any money, natch. I just have to be somewhere that doesn't have any memories of Teddy. I still love him, you see, despite everything.'

'That'll change in time. You ought to find a flat and get a job to distract yourself.'

'You don't want me either.' Jasmine let out a heart-wrenching wail of despair. I felt my throat tighten at the sound.

'Don't cry, Jazz. Of course you can come.'

'I'm so glad you said yes.' Constance's generous heart was touched by my description of Jasmine's misery. We were in the kitchen, unwinding with a glass of wine after the second day of being a stately home. Tour organizers throughout Ireland had been so thrilled to hear of virgin territory that they had dropped down on us in their hundreds and we had been run off our feet. Constance's mascara had moved to her chin. Every trace of mine had been transferred to my hands in the process of wiping the perspiration from my brow. '*Poor* girl! What a rat!' I understood Constance to be referring to Teddy. 'We'll have to think where she can sleep. When's she arriving?'

'I've booked a ticket for her on tomorrow afternoon's ferry to Dún Laoghaire. She'll get a train from there. I thought if you wouldn't mind I'd go and meet her at Williamsbridge. I'll get dinner ready before I go.'

'Of course I don't mind. We must make a fuss of her and keep her occupied mentally and physically so she has no chance to pine. Liddy darling, leave a few brandy-snaps for the others. They're Eugene's favourites.'

Liddy, who had been helping herself from the cake tin, looked guilty.

Constance looked at Liddy's plate. 'That must be all that was left of the chocolate cake. I'm delighted to see you eat, darling, but wouldn't it be healthier to have something like toast and Marmite?'

Liddy looked uncomfortable. 'There's no more bread.'

'There's at least half a loaf,' I said. 'I'm making fried bread for the *oeufs pochés soubise*. That's this evening's first course.' This elegant sounding dish, as recommended by Constance's namesake, was less glamorous in actuality: poached eggs with fried onion rings on a bed of onion sauce on the aforementioned fried bread. We needed to finish the sack of onions fast as they were beginning to rot in the middle. I went to the bread bin. 'But you can have a slice if you're starving . . . Oh!' The bin contained only crumbs. I glanced at Liddy. I was reluctant to make a fuss. It was good that she was eating, even if she seemed to be going to the other extreme. I dreaded to discover that she was making herself sick again. 'Never mind,' I said. 'I'll get another loaf from the freezer. And after dinner I'd better make *two* ginger-and-pineapple upside-down cakes for the visitors tomorrow. It was more popular than anything.'

'No, Bobbie,' said Constance with unusual firmness. 'You've enough to do. I'll make the cakes if you'll check I'm doing it properly. I wish I was a better cook. Perhaps the girls could help. Liddy, do you think you might—' But Liddy had already left the kitchen. 'Is it too much to hope that your friend Jasmine likes cooking?'

'As far as I know the only thing she can cook is corned-beef hash. Not much good for the tea-room. But she must have learned to do other things when living with Teddy. Hello, Kieran.' Turlough McGurn's delivery boy was lugging a sack into the kitchen. 'I hope that contains carrots.'

Kieran's round blue eyes expressed heartfelt regret at having to disoblige me. 'No carrots t'is week, Miss Bobbie. T'em's tornips.'

'Turnips! Oh no! We don't want them. You must take them back—' Kieran had disappeared at a run into the stable yard.

'How are we going to use up an entire sack?' Constance looked at the turnips with dismay. 'The children hate them and I must admit I'm not too keen on them myself.'

'Let's consult the oracle.' I riffled through the pages of the fat pink book. 'Hm. Turnip soufflé is all she can come up with. That sounds faintly disgusting to me.'

'I think it sounds interesting.' Kit had come in from picking up litter in the new car-park which was the field next to the Cockatoo's. 'I like turnips.' He came over to see what I was stirring, resting his hand on my shoulder as he peered into the pan containing the *soubise*.

'You're thinking of delicious little purple ones the size of golf balls,' I said, smiling, but keeping my eyes on the thickening sauce. It was annoying that now I found it impossible to look at him without the memory of Violet's cries of pleasure rising unbidden. 'These are a dirty grey and as big as mangel-wurzels, more suitable for cattle-feed. In fact that's what we'll do with most of them: give them to Siobhan and Niamh. Pour me another glass, would you, if you're having one yourself?'

'If you girls are determined to drink the profits I may as well join you. You'll have to get some proper litter bins, you know, clearly marked. I've got a sackful of crisp packets, sweet papers, pork-pie wrappers and Coke cans. In addition a fur glove, one copy of Shaw's *Plays Pleasant*, a broken umbrella and a used condom.'

'No!' Constance looked scandalized. 'In *our* car-park? Well, *really*! I can't believe any of the kind, polite, cosmopolitan people I showed around today could have zoomed back to their car after a heavy tea and – and had a quickly in the back. They just didn't seem the sort.'

Kit laughed. 'It's called a quickie. Even the civilized copulate, Constance.'

I guessed, from his satisfied expression, he was remembering making love to Violet.

'Yes, but not in the backs of cars.'

'Perhaps they were Timsy's customers,' I suggested. 'Though that's worse, isn't it? What will visitors think if they find drunken couples fornicating on the grass just where they want to park?'

'What a pair of spoilsports you are!' Kit laughed again in a way that was beginning to grate. 'Too much feminism takes the fun out of a girl, remember.'

'Would we have begun a movement for emancipation in the teeth of derision, imprisonment and force-feeding if the fun for women hadn't been taken out ages ago?' I kept my tone light-hearted as I briskly stirred the contents of the saucepan.

'If you're not getting enough fun, you might let me try to do something about it.'

Kit was standing at my elbow. I looked round to see that Constance was no longer in the kitchen.

'How conceited you men are. You think any problem can be solved by getting into bed.'

'I'm not conceited. I'm begging you to take pity on me. Bobbie,' he murmured, putting his lips close to my ear and speaking in a low voice, 'I don't think you women understand how wretched a man feels being within sight and sound of the object of his desires and not being allowed to touch.'

'What makes you think women don't feel quite as unhappy in the same situation?'

I knew as soon as I said it that this was a mistake.

'Well, you certainly aren't feeling like that about me,' he said with some asperity. 'It's Finn, isn't it? I saw the way you looked at him when you thought no one was noticing. Why can't you be honest enough to admit the truth?'

'Because – because – I wish you wouldn't bully me. I'm not obliged to tell you what I think and feel. You must stop spying on me. I'm not in the mood to have a love affair with anyone . . .' I hesitated. By making love to Violet he had inadvertently done me a good turn. I need no longer waste time and energy trying to persuade myself that I could love him. It would be better to end all speculation for him too. But I was reluctant to wound him. I looked at Kit's face, on which were written both anger and unhappiness, and felt thoroughly ashamed of myself for my cowardice. My head gave a preliminary throb. 'Do let's talk about something else.'

Kit sat on the edge of the table, his arms folded, looking at me. 'You've changed. Yesterday you were pleased to see me. You were warmer to me than you've ever been. Now you're cold.'

'I don't know what you mean.'

'I know you better than you think. And you're hopeless, as it happens, at concealing your thoughts. Now, let me see, when did it begin, this coldness?' He looked up as though thinking. 'Yes, you were chilly this morning at breakfast.'

'Oh, rubbish!'

'You were. I felt a boreal blast over my porridge. You were all soft-blowing sweet breezes before dinner last night. A-ha! I see! It's obvious now I think about it. You thought I was flirting with Violet. Shame on you for thinking the worst. Though I'm flattered you were jealous. What a silly girl you are! I was only being polite, trying to cheer the poor girl up. She means nothing to me. She's pretty but pretty dim, too.'

'Don't say another word! I can't bear to hear you talking like that— Oh, damn!' I added as I smelt burning. Flavia came in as I was hastily transferring the sauce to a clean pan before the taste of burned butter and flour could permeate the roux.

'What's the matter?' she asked. 'You look cross.'

'No, I'm fine. Have you finished your homework?'

'There wasn't much. I've been helping Mummy.' Flavia went up to Kit. 'She said to tell you she's ready to come down. She says to go up at once because Granny's having a bath which takes her ages and Mummy's all on her own and bored. I offered to stay but she said she wants you. She's put on a specially nice dress and spent ages doing her hair. It's good she's feeling happy again, isn't it?'

'Very good,' I said, as Kit frowned. 'Well?' I looked at him. 'Why don't you go?'

Kit seemed about to say something but in the face of Flavia's innocent hopefulness he evidently lacked the brutality. He left the kitchen without another word.

'I can't wait until Saturday,' Flavia continued. 'Did lots of people come today?'

'It felt like thousands. I haven't counted the ticket stubs yet. Will you stir this for me while I poach some eggs?'

'Everything seems to be coming right.' Flavia stirred industriously. 'Mummy's going to be quite well and I'm going to be a waitress. We're going to make money and Liddy's in a much better mood than she usually is.' Now that Flavia had pointed it out I realized this was true. 'If only Daddy would come home things'd be perfect, wouldn't they?'

'I expect you miss him a lot.'

'All the time. You like Daddy, don't you?'

'Of course.'

'Because I can see he likes you. Not as much as Mummy, of course, but I know he does. You mustn't mind when he's cross. Often the crosser he is the more he likes someone. He's very polite to people he hates. Once I saw him looking at you and he looked really fierce.'

It seemed I was surrounded by Argus-eyed observers, possessed of the wisdom of Solomon.

During dinner my headache developed into a blinding migraine. But not before I had seen that Kit met all Violet's attempts to flirt with him with a pontiff-like gravity. By the time I served the Norwegian cream, which would have been much nicer could I have laid my hands on a pot of apricot jam instead of the so-called strawberry preserve filled with woody pips that was all Dicky Dooley offered, Violet was downcast and inclined to be petulant. Primed by Flavia's remarks earlier I also noticed that Liddy was in a state of ill-concealed excitement. She slipped away from the table the moment she had finished her share of the pudding. When I went to the kitchen to wash up I found that every trace of the remnants of the three courses and half a truckle of cheddar had disappeared.

I stood on the platform at Williamsbridge station the next evening, searching the onrushing crowd for signs of Jasmine. An elegantly gloved hand was raised above the throng.

'Bobbie, Bobbie! My heart's broken! I shall never be able to love anyone again!'

I was enveloped in fur and Mitsouko. Jasmine's make-up was streaked with tears. She wore a full-length mink coat and her thick black hair was fastened up into a knot stuck with large tortoiseshell pins. Behind her a porter struggled with three large matching suit-cases.

I took her vanity case in one hand and tucked my other hand under her arm. 'I know the end of an affair feels like the end of the world at first. But I promise you, the misery will go.'

'But I'm not like you, Bobbie.' Jasmine's eyes continued to drip tears. 'I'm not strong and clever. I haven't any self-control. Teddy always said he liked that. It made me uninhibited in bed, you see.'

'Yes, well . . .' I saw we were attracting attention. 'We'll talk about it in the car going home. Come on, we'll have to run, it's simply pouring.'

'I'll try, darling.' Jasmine's mouth was a pout of misery. 'But I'm not very good at running.'

Certainly the five-inch heels of her red shoes did nothing to help whatever athleticism she may have possessed.

'Get in.' I hurled the vanity case into the back of the Morris Traveller, tipped the porter and threw myself into the driving seat.

'What a funny little car. It's like a toy. Are your people awfully poor?'

'They certainly aren't rich. That's why we've applied for a grant. To get the roof mended.'

'Sort of social assistance or whatever it's called, do you mean? Oh dear, how sad. Well, I shan't cost them a thing. I've sold the diamond bracelet Teddy gave me and I've tons of money. I shall buy them something nice to cheer them up.'

I heard a brighter note in Jasmine's voice at the prospect of present-giving. Naturally she could have no idea what Curraghcourt was like because our telephone conversations had dealt almost exclusively with the progress of her relationship with Teddy. 'It's a kind thought but you may not find it that easy to find something desirable in this part of the world.'

'Oh, I don't mean luxuries, darling. If they can't afford to mend their roof they'll be grateful to have something quite ordinary like cashmere bed-socks or handmade chocolates, don't you think?' She leaned forward to peer through the arcs made by the windscreen wipers. 'When will we reach the town? Perhaps I could get some-thing in Williams-what's-it. I didn't have time to shop before I left.'

'That *was* Williamsbridge.'

'No! But it was hardly a town at all. Are we coming to some-where bigger soon?'

'I'm afraid not. Everywhere gets even smaller from now on. What's the matter?'

Jasmine had given a faint scream. 'It's so dark. All the lights have gone out!'

'This is the country.'

'You mean there aren't street lamps?'

'Nothing but the moon and stars.'

'How peculiar. Even in Middlesex there's street lighting.'

She screamed again, louder.

'What's the matter?'

'Eyes. Glaring. In those shrubs. I hate shrubberies. Enfield is full of them.'

'It's a hedge, Jazzy. Don't worry. It was just a cat. Or a fox.'

'I'm absolutely terrified of them.'

'Foxes are timid creatures, really.'

'Not foxes. Cats.'

At least, I reflected, Constance need not be concerned that Jasmine would have nothing to occupy her mind during her stay at Curraghcourt.

FORTY-SEVEN

'I can peel potatoes,' said Jasmine with simple pride on seeing me drag a sack from the larder. Then she looked sad. 'Teddy taught me.'

Jasmine had been at Curraghcourt for several days now and the family circle had expanded to include her as comfortably as though she had been born and bred there. That was the way of the house. This is not to say that she herself felt like a native. Her body was in Connemara but her thoughts were all the time in Canonbury. Everything reminded her of Teddy.

When I had brought her in through the front door of Curraghcourt on her first evening she had looked at the vaulted ceiling, the magnificent fireplace, the sedan chair and the suit of armour and said with a heartbroken sigh, 'Teddy would have loved this! We took his children to Warwick Castle once and Teddy enjoyed it more than they did.' She looked at the swords and daggers and battle-axes and said, 'How lovely,' with an obvious lack of conviction. The giant elkhorn antlers had provoked a silent shudder.

When I showed her the drawing room she said that yellow was Teddy's favourite colour and when I took her up to her bedroom she said that Teddy had always maintained it was healthier to sleep in a cold room but she herself liked it hot enough to be able to walk around without any clothes on. On hearing this I had begged her to wear at least a nightdress as her room had a large window and the grounds were filled with sex-hungry men.

'Really, Bobbie?' She had looked at me with questioning eyes. 'Aren't there any girls for the poor things to make love to?'

'This is a Catholic country where sex outside marriage is considered sinful.'

'That's *so-o-o* sad.'

'Of course it goes on but not as frequently and uninhibitedly as in England. And there's no contraception so the price to be paid is not only hell-fire for eternity but hell on earth as well. At least for the girls.'

'Extraordinary!' Jasmine thought about this for some time before saying, 'Teddy wouldn't like that!'

It was not long before I could happily have rowed Teddy, bound and gagged, into the middle of the lake and dropped him overboard.

I had thought I knew Jazzy pretty well but I had been surprised to discover how many aspects of life at Curraghcourt were terrifying to her. When she had seen a small spider in the hall she had shrieked so loudly that I had dropped her cases in fright. In the dining room Jasmine had yelped and leaped from her chair on seeing a man peering in through the window. I explained that he was on his way to see Timsy and had looked in out of mere curiosity, but for the rest of dinner Jasmine's eyes roamed continuously between the window and a speck of damp on the ceiling which she thought she had seen moving. A brief power-cut provoked a bloodcurdling screech of terror and made Eugene spill his glass of red wine over his trousers.

But as a guest Jasmine made up for these slight imperfections in several ways. For one thing she was soft-hearted and amiable and charming to everyone. And for another she proved to be a star in the tea-room. She was so eager to oblige that the visitors easily forgave any muddles with orders and so pretty that half of them – the male half, naturally – would have been content to starve and thirst as long as they could watch her tripping about the granary in her apron, short black leather skirt and red high heels.

Even Pegeen and Katty fell under her spell when she quickly became as addicted to Hangman as they were. I had several times found the three of them bent over a game when they were supposed to be getting the tea-room ready for the onslaught of coach-weary customers. Timsy was the only member of the household who regarded Jasmine with suspicion verging on hostility. He was clearly frightened by her Eurasian looks, which spelled a blatant but sophisticated sexuality, not at all the same thing as Francie Synge's reasonably priced availability and reassuring quantities of body hair.

'Surely I could peel those potatoes for you?' Jasmine persisted. 'I shall feel I'm just in the way if you won't let me.'

'What you bring in, in tips alone, makes your presence thoroughly desirable,' I said. Seeing that her beautiful black oriental eyes were

545

beseeching I gave her a knife, a saucepan and the bowl of turnips. 'Be careful, it's sharp.'

'I'm not a child,' Jasmine said reproachfully.

She plugged the electric fire she carried round with her into the nearest wall socket and moved a chair next to it. The fire enabled her to take off her fur coat. The second Osgar had seen the coat he had advanced on her, saliva dripping from his jaws. Only the pitch and volume of Jasmine's screams had deterred him from attacking it. She was unused to animals and it was a pity that this first encounter was likely to put her off for good. Maria, usually the friendliest of dogs, was displeased by the screaming and disinclined to wag her tail.

Flavia had the good idea of giving Osgar the fur glove Kit had found in the car-park. Osgar was a changed animal from that moment. He licked it and nibbled it and shook it and nudged it along the floor with his nose. He slept with it under his chin and carried it about with him wherever he went, like a devoted parent or, as Timsy said, 'like a just-whelped bitch, begging the ladies' pardons'. Provided no one attempted to take it from him, Osgar was much better tempered and even put up with being petted by the visitors.

'There's mud on these potatoes.' Jasmine's tone was querulous.

'Did you get those shoes in Bond Street?' asked Liddy. From the moment of their introduction, Liddy had cross-questioned Jasmine minutely as to the source of her undeniably glamorous wardrobe.

'New York, sweetie.'

'New York.' Liddy was silent for a moment, imagining this metropolitan treacle well. 'I'd give anything to go there. Brooks Brothers, Bonwit Teller, Saks, Fifth Avenue; and, of course, the States have been immensely loyal to the Republic,' she added. 'The IRA couldn't have survived without American funding.'

'Are you feeling quite well, darling?' Constance looked at Liddy with concern.

'Yes. Why?'

'It's not like you to be interested in politics, that's all,' said Constance. 'Your father will be pleased. He says women can't expect to be treated as equals if they can't be bothered to take an interest in the judiciary system, the exchequer and the government of their country.'

'If that's the case I don't want to be treated as an equal,' said Jasmine. 'I should hate to have to think about laws and taxes and interest rates. It would bore me to death.'

Neither Constance nor I were quite honest enough to admit that on the whole this was our own view.

'I bet there've been plenty of men – poets, artists, musicians – who weren't interested either,' said Constance, 'but you wouldn't say they were inferior, would you?'

'I used to be bored by politics,' said Liddy, 'but now I think they're interesting. So many thousands of brave men have given their lives in the cause of Ireland's freedom.'

Constance and I exchanged glances. 'You haven't been talking to Father Deglan?' she asked.

Liddy looked indignant. 'The Church is run by power-hungry sadists, intent on keeping their flock poor, uneducated and voice-less.'

'Please, darling, don't say anything like that outside the family,' begged Constance. 'You'll upset so many people.'

'Dad says it in front of hundreds of people and it gets reported in the papers. So why shouldn't I?'

'Well, it's your father's job . . .' began Constance hesitantly.

'You mean it's because I'm a girl. So much for the equality for women you're always preaching about, Aunt Con. You're just pretending to be liberated. Between them priests and politicians have got your mind in a vice-like grip. I think I'll go for a walk.'

Constance was too stunned to think of a riposte.

'Shut that door, will you?' called Jasmine. 'There's a draught like a tornado. I've finished the potatoes, Bobbie.'

I took the saucepan of marble-sized turnips. Some of the peelings were larger.

'What's got into Liddy?' said Constance. 'Perhaps she's got a new history teacher?'

'What's got into Liddy is a boy.' It was rare that Maud entered the kitchen. 'I hope not literally, though these days . . .' She looked around critically. 'You seem to have cleaned the place up quite a bit. Not the usual slum of stinks and slops. When I was a girl some of the kitchens in the big houses had a gallery up there' – she pointed to the ceiling – 'so the mistress of the house could give orders without having to set foot in the place.'

'Wouldn't it put you off your food, though?' suggested Constance mildly. 'I mean, if the kitchen was too dirty to walk into?'

'We were too busy having a good time to worry about that. Dirt gives you immunity. These days we're all too soft.' Maud's eyes fell on Jasmine who was trying to remove mud from her fingernails with the pin of her diamond brooch. 'Some of us are nothing more than pampered, empty-headed fools. Violet's hysterical. She's refusing to eat. I want some arrowroot to settle her stomach. She seems to think there's something wrong with her and that the only cure would be several days in Dublin shopping, going to the theatre and lunching at the Shelbourne with some amusing people.'

'In that case,' said Constance, 'do you think arrowroot will be an adequate substitute?'

'Of course it's all self-indulgence. We've spoilt her between us. I wish Finn would come back and give her a good thrashing. That'd do more good than anything.'

Jasmine looked horrified. 'You mean her husband beats her?'

'Finn never has.' Constance rushed to her brother's defence. 'Not so far as I know, anyway.'

'More's the pity,' said Maud. 'It would have done her a lot of good.'

'Teddy liked to be beaten, 'said Jasmine thoughtfully. 'But I could never bring myself to hit him as hard as he asked me to.'

I could see that the turn the conversation had taken had aroused interest from the hearth. Pencils had ceased to draw stickmen. It was a pity because I longed to ask Maud something. I gave her the arrowroot and followed her from the kitchen into the hall.

'When you said a boy had got into Liddy, what did you mean, exactly?'

'I've tried to tell the girl to safeguard her market value but she's as silly as the rest. For the last week she's been talking like a trashy Republican newspaper so it's obvious that some man's filling her head with such stuff. Let's hope that's all he's filling.' Maud gave her bark of a laugh and lit a cigarette. 'Cherchez l'homme.' Leaving a trail of smoke she shuffled across the hall, her head sunk between her shoulders, like Carabosse surrounded by wisps of dry ice.

I pondered on her words as I unfroze three packets of fish fingers (Sean Rafferty, the butcher, having failed to deliver). I could hear the shade of Constance Spry tut-tutting in the background but I ignored her. I made a *beurre noisette* to smarten them up, sautéed potatoes, mashed the turnips and made *petits pois à la française*. The fish fingers were received with such rapture that I asked myself, with the exasperation familiar to housewives the world over, exactly why I *bothered*.

While Kit and Constance did the washing up, I made a walnut cake and kept Liddy under surveillance. From the corner of my eye

I saw her load a plate with the leftovers from dinner. She glanced about to see if she was observed. I beat butter and sugar vigorously. Liddy cut a slice of bread as thick as a dictionary, then drifted towards the back door. I followed at a discreet distance. Outside rain was drifting against my face like folds of silk. She crossed the yard and disappeared into the barn. Inside, the *Flying Irishman*, painted dark green with gold coach lines, was glorious in its finished state. Flurry was busy with hammer and nails constructing the sides of the first carriage.

'That seems to be coming on well,' I said. 'Have you seen Liddy?'

'No.' Flurry continued to hammer without looking up.

A wooden staircase led to the loft from which came a faint glow. I heard whispered voices before I was more than halfway up it.

'Thanks, Liddy,' said a male voice with an enthusiasm that suggested youth. 'I'm famished. You've been an age.'

'I couldn't help it.' This was Liddy's voice. 'I had to do my fucking homework. And dinner took for ever.'

'I don't like to hear swear words from that pretty mouth.'

'Don't you?' Liddy sounded surprised.

'I do not. It's ugly in a woman. Let me eat first and then I'll kiss that foul language away. Bejesus! Fish fingers! I thought your folk'd be too grand for peasant food.'

'Oh, we aren't grand at all! We're just farmers who've lost all our land. Our housekeeper's posher than we are.'

'Having a housekeeper at all's posh, isn't it? My ma did everything in the house and looked after the pigs and chickens as well.'

'My mother can't do that because she had a stroke,' Liddy said disingenuously, as though there were a possibility that Violet might have tended pigs had she been well enough. 'That was five years ago and she's only just getting better.'

'Ah, poor lady.' The teasing tone left his voice. 'There's none so high they don't know what suffering is. Dad always said that when my mother used to carp about upper-class people like you.'

'I'll go away and leave you to starve if you're going to be mean. Anyway, our housekeeper's more of a friend than anything. When she goes back to London, I'm going to stay with her. She's beautiful and has lovely clothes and knows about things that grand people know about. We're all quite ignorant.'

'You mean she's English? Curse them all, may they rot in *hell*!'

'Danny, no! I forbid you to curse her.'

The man laughed. 'I like it when you're angry. Come here and give me a kiss.' There was a silence of some ten seconds. Then he said, 'Liddy, Liddy! I don't want to take advantage of your sweetness. Have you ever been with a man?'

All this time I had been poised on the ladder, trying to make up my mind what to do. Now I shot up to the top and showed my head above the trapdoor.

'Mind if I come up?'

Before they could answer I had climbed into the loft.

'Damn!' said Liddy. 'I suppose you're going to tell everyone.'

I looked around. The light of two candles burning in saucers was enough to show me a pillow and a heap of blankets, an enamel jug and a Belleek second period cup among a pile of dirty plates. The young man who had been sitting in the straw with his arms round Liddy scrambled to his feet as soon as he saw me.

'How do you do?' I held out my hand. 'I'm Bobbie Norton.'

He hesitated, then reluctantly took my hand. He was perhaps twenty years old, with a face that was attractive despite its scowl and several days' growth of stubble on his chin. His other hand was hidden in a sling fashioned from a scarf I recognized as Violet's. 'With that voice you'll be the housekeeper.'

I looked enquiringly at Liddy.

'This is Danny,' she said sulkily. 'He's on the run from the IRA.'

'Tst!' Danny looked angry. 'Will you hush now! You'll get me killed yet, you crazy girl.'

'Is it true?' I asked.

Danny's eyes glittered and he shook his head but I saw by the twitching of his mouth that he was moved by some strong emotion, perhaps fear. 'I'm a travelling tinker, just looking for a place to lie up. I'll be moving on now so you needn't trouble yourself about me.'

I picked up a book that was open on the floor near where he had been lying. '*Metamorphoses*. Hm. I wonder how many tinkers read Ovid? Or know Latin at all.'

'I was in training to be a priest.' Danny held out his hand for the book. 'But I took it into my head that the open road would suit me best. Besides, the translation's on the opposite page.'

I stood looking at him, wondering what I ought to say or do.

He returned my stare. 'I'll take myself off, then.'

'No!' Liddy took hold of his sleeve and looked up at him. 'You're not well yet. You'll get caught if you go out there. You told me—'

'Whisht, Liddy!' He spoke sharply but he took her hand gently enough. 'You know nothing about it and that's how it should be.

550

You've been very good to me, darling, and I'll never forget you, but there's no future in it. I'll slip away now while it's dark. I'll be all right.'

Liddy bit her lip and tears filled her eyes.

'How did you hurt your arm?' I asked.

'I fell into a ditch.'

'It's not true.' Liddy rested her head on his shoulder and put her other arm round his neck. 'He was shot. He's had a fever all week until today.' She pleaded with me, her large drowning eyes just like Violet's. 'Bobbie, you *can't* let him go out in the cold and the wet. Please let him stay a few more days. I'll do anything for you, if you will. I'll waitress until I drop. Please, *please*!'

'It's not up to me, Liddy. I'll fetch your aunt and she can decide what ought to be done.' I looked at Danny. 'But if you've any sense, you'll tell Constance the truth. We won't be able to help you otherwise.'

'It'll be best I should go,' he said, but I heard a note of irresolution in his voice.

'I won't be long,' I said. 'Finish your supper. You look as though you could do with it.' Though the light was poor I had the impression of someone weary and downhearted.

'Can she be trusted?' I heard him ask as I went down the ladder. 'Supposing she rings the *Garda*?'

'She won't,' said Liddy. 'I can tell she feels sorry for you. Bobbie likes rescuing things.'

If I had not been troubled on Liddy's behalf I would have smiled at this.

'Con?' I put my head round the kitchen door. 'I want to consult you a minute. About the tea-room,' I added, seeing that Kit was looking at me with curiosity.

'Goodness!' Constance gave him the drying-up cloth. 'How flattering to be asked for my views on something domestic.'

'There's something I want to show you over here first.' I steered her towards the barn.

'Is it something to do with the *Flying Irishman*?'

'Yes,' I said in case the stable yard had ears.

'What on earth?' she said as I led her past Flurry, who was still hammering and ignored us, over to the wooden stairs.

'Just come and see.'

'I haven't been up here in years. It used to be where the farm-workers went with their sweethearts for a little— Liddy!'

Constance looked in amazement at her niece who stood with her arms around Danny, looking defiant. 'Who's this?'

'I beg your pardon for trespassing, ma'am.' Danny put Liddy to one side and took a step towards Constance, standing with his good hand on his hip in an attitude of one squaring up for a fight. 'Liddy's been kind enough to take care of me when I needed it but I'll be more than sorry if she gets into a row because of it.'

'Who are you?' asked Constance. She stared at the blankets and plates. 'How long have you been hiding here?'

'My name's Danny Quill. I've been here the best part of a week. My father was the schoolmaster over at Ballincarn. I'm . . . It's a bit awkward . . .' He ran his hand through his hair, brushing it back from his forehead. 'The truth is I'm on the run. I'd be grateful if you'd give me shelter one more night. I'm still weak from loss of blood and I could do with another twenty-four hours to rest up. Then I'll go, tomorrow night when it's dark.'

'On the run?' Constance seemed dazed. 'Who from?'

'Well, ma'am, from the *Garda*. And from the lads.' He gave a short uneasy laugh. 'Both at once. The devil's in it and no mistake.'

'From the IRA? My God!' It was interesting that Constance seemed unimpressed by the forces of law. 'What . . . Tell me how it's happened.'

'I'll tell you it straight.' Danny seemed to sway a little. 'But I'd be obliged if you'd let me sit down.'

'Of course! I think I need to too.'

We all sat on the hay except Liddy who positioned herself, cross-legged, at Danny's feet.

'I was at the seminary in Williamsbridge until a year ago. But I couldn't see my way to being a priest. There were too many things that didn't add up. The Church is buried up to its eyes in the past. If Ireland's ever going to be free we need to move forward and beat the English at their own game.' His eyes flickered towards me and then back to Constance's face. 'But' – he laughed again, a tired sound – 'you don't want to hear about all that. To cut it short I joined the IRA six months ago.'

'Is your father Bryan Quill, the poet?' asked Constance.

'Was. The old fellow died just before I joined up. And Ma's been dead three years now. I've none to shame.'

'I knew your father. He was a good man and a fine poet. I'm so sorry he's no longer with us.'

'Yes, well . . .' Some of the curtness went out of Danny's voice.

'I was telling you how I got shot. I expect you know, the IRA's finances come from donations from abroad – the United States, mostly – and one of the ways we help ourselves is by robbing banks. I don't apologize for that. You can't conjure guns out of thin air. The end justifies the means.'

'I don't think your father would have agreed with you.' Constance sounded indignant.

'I don't suppose he would.' Danny grew fierce in his turn. 'He'd have taken any blows anyone cared to give him rather than lift his hand against another man. But that's not *my* view of things. Though to tell the truth, I'm not sure any more what to think.' He sighed, letting his head drop back on his shoulders and closing his eyes as though unbearably tired.

'All right,' said Constance. 'You'd better go on.'

'So I was with the lads and we were robbing a bank in . . . it doesn't matter where, and some other fellows drove up and started shooting. I recognized one of them. A member of the INLA. He had a whacking great Kalashnikov rifle. The INLA get a lot of dosh and weapons from the Middle East. He shot my friend Joe in the mouth. He fell dead on the instant.'

'I'll never understand what you men really want,' said Constance. 'Aren't you all Republicans? On the same side?'

Danny laughed sardonically. 'It's not that simple. There are countless divisions and splinter groups, mostly feuding, some bitterly opposed. The INLA are close to the Provisionals but they hate the Official IRA. You have to understand that besides bank raids and foreign money, the IRA and the others are funded by protection rackets and drug-running. Dirty business means bad blood that's got nothing to do with the just cause of freedom. Joe'd been campaigning lately against choosing civilian targets. He always was a big talker: I suppose that's why they shot him in the mouth. Joe's idea was we should only pick off military targets. Soldier against soldier, see? The INLA were responsible for the assassination of that politician, Airey Neave, last spring. Joe said that was cowardly.'

Constance groaned. 'You're all as wicked as one another. What you men need is a lot of guns filled with blanks and then you can take pot-shots at each other all day long without doing any harm. You're like silly children, spiteful and selfish. I don't believe in your cause. It's just an excuse to play war games.'

Danny shrugged. 'I can't argue with you now. I'm too tired. And . . . I'm pretty disillusioned myself. The truth is I'm not the man I thought I was. For a while there in the bank, after they shot Joe, I was so shocked. I'd never seen a man killed before. A woman was wailing like the *caoineadh*. I saw out of the corner of my eye something red that was spreading. It was Joe's blood. Then one of our lot moved quicker than a snake striking and kicked the Kalashnikov out of that murdering bastard's hands. It flew up into the air and landed behind the counter. He yelled at me, "Finish the bugger off!" I was standing the nearest, see? Well, we weren't so well provided for. One rifle between three of us. I only had a knife. I lifted it high. I was going to ram it into his heart. For one second, perhaps less than that, I looked into the fellow's eyes. That piece of sh— that bastard had blasted my mate's head into a unrecognizable mess not a minute before . . . but still I couldn't – stick – a bloody – knife in him. I couldn't – do it!' Danny spoke jerkily, through gritted teeth, emphasizing each word with a nod of his head. 'I guess the things you're taught in childhood go deep. I turned and ran. I deserted rather than kill a skunk who wouldn't have hesitated to blast me more full of holes than a tea-strainer. I've been running ever since. I'll be running for the rest of my life probably.' He made a noise between a gasp and a grunt, then rested his forehead on his hand, shuddering throughout his frame. Liddy held tight to his knees.

'You were quite right!' Constance was blazing. 'You ran from violence and murder and everything that's stolen the innocence out of Ireland. You're still a part of the decent rational world and you ought to be praising God for your deliverance!'

Danny kept his face hidden. 'I can't get the sight of blood out of my eyes.' He gave a sigh that was almost a sob. 'Or the smell of my own fear out of my nostrils.'

Constance looked at me questioningly. I lifted my eyebrows and shoulders, a gesture of indecision. I had no idea of the consequences of befriending an IRA deserter.

'You'd better come into the house,' said Constance. 'It's cold here and you need proper rest and food. And we'll look at that arm.'

'As for that, it's nothing. Someone took a shot at me as I got into the street and the bullet grazed my arm. It's healing already. But I won't come in, though I appreciate the invitation. If you'll just let me stay till tomorrow night I'll take myself away after dark. They'll be looking for me, see.'

'Surely people leave the IRA all the time? They can't chase them all. They'd never get any robbing and killing done.' Constance was sarcastic in her anger, prompted in part, I suspected, by sympathy for this man who was still half a boy.

'They let most go without much struggle, that's true. But I'm in possession of more information than is healthy. Since seventy-six we've been organized into cells. Anything between five and ten men. The OC knows the Brigade Adjutant who gives him his orders, that's all. That way the Brits can torture prisoners until the next ice age and it won't do them any good. My nickname was "the scholar". That doesn't mean much. Half the lads can barely read or write. I was trusted with drafting reports for key members and not long ago I was given the job of compiling a detailed log of weapons dumps for all of Ulster and Connaught. Highly privileged information. I was proud of it at the time. Now it'll get me executed, probably.'

'The whole business makes me want to weep.' Constance stood up. 'If only all that energy could be put into something constructive!'

'It's all right for you,' said Danny, assuming some of his former belligerence. 'You're very comfortably situated with a fine castle to live in and a senator for a brother.'

'For goodness' sake!' Constance was fuming. 'It isn't my brother or Curraghcourt that's keeping Ireland ignorant and destitute. If you want to help the poor, why don't you start a business and create jobs? That'll do more good than hiding in alleyways and killing husbands and fathers. And sometimes the wives and children as well.'

Danny was scowling again. 'I'll go now.'

'Oh, give me strength!' Constance was magnificent in her fury. 'Will you stop being so *bloody* embittered and come along before I wash my hands of you entirely?'

'Don't swear, Aunt Con,' said Liddy. 'Danny doesn't like to hear it from women.'

Constance ignored this. 'Either you come into the house or I'll go this minute and ring the *Garda*.'

FORTY-EIGHT

'Who is this young Daniel among the lionesses?' Kit asked later when Danny had had his arm cleaned and bound and then been sent away to bath and bed.

'A friend of Liddy's.' I had emerged from the cloakroom with a selection of umbrellas and outer garments forgotten by the visitors. Thanks to the demands of the stately-home business, I had managed to avoid anything like a row with Kit. Not only because I hate them but also because he had been so helpful, so generous, so resourceful and everyone at Curraghcourt was fond of him. I was still quite fond of him myself. He had made love to Violet because he liked sex and perhaps had felt sorry for her. Most men, finding themselves in such circumstances, would have done the same.

'Is he the reason she's been so dreamy-eyed this last week?'

'Probably.' It seemed I was the last person to notice anything. 'Now who could have left these?' I picked up a pair of black suede high-heeled shoes with ankle straps, which were lying at the bottom of the stairs. 'They seem too frivolous for any of the sensible, serious, middle-aged people who came today.'

'I didn't hear the boy arrive. What's he done to his arm?'

'He's quarrelled with his family and we're giving him temporary shelter.' I held up the bottom row of a set of false teeth. 'I think these must belong to that poor old man who was being pushed around in a wheelchair by his bad-tempered daughter.'

'Isn't he a little old for so much cosseting?'

'Surely old age is the time when cosseting . . . Oh, you mean Danny. I don't think he's much more than twenty. But all men require cosseting, in my experience. Whether they should get it or not is a matter for debate.'

Kit looked at me narrowly. 'Why am I being cast into outer darkness?'

'What are you talking about?' I stood with an armful of caps, gloves and pleated plastic rain-hats, staring at him rather stupidly.

'Not long ago I was your confidant and almost best friend. Now you treat me as though I've got leprosy but you're too polite to let on you know.'

Kit was tiresomely acute when it came to subtleties of mood.

'You're imagining things. We're all exhausted by this new regime. I think I'll go to bed.'

'Just a minute.'

Kit took me by the shoulders, turned me round and steered me into the dining room. After we had cleared away the last traces of supper Constance and I had put the best china and silver on the table to impress the visitors and I had arranged five small vases of the flowers that grew semi-wild in the garden – anemones, grape hyacinths and narcissi – down its length. Despite Kit's grip on my arm, I found myself casting a critical eye over the result and made a mental note to get the wax off the candlesticks in the morning. It was amazing how much time – at least an hour a day – was saved by all of us, apart from Maud and Violet, having breakfast and lunch in the kitchen. We had bought a dishwasher with money from the poteen fund and so far everyone had abided by the rule to put in their own plates, cups, knives and forks. Even Pegeen, Katty and Timsy, usually resistant to any change initiated by me, had complied with the new policy as it gave them extra time in which to play Hangman. The time we gained was easily swallowed by the daily necessity to transform Curraghcourt from a chaotic muddle into a showplace.

'I want to talk to you,' Kit said.

'Couldn't it wait until morning? I'm practically dropping.'

He took the remains of the day from my arms and dumped them on a chair. 'You're still cross about Violet, aren't you?'

'What about Violet?'

'About me flirting with her – I admit that I did – the other night. I told you! I was sorry for her.' He looked injured. 'Have I so much as glanced in her direction since?'

'I should say not. Though I've no idea how you behave with her when alone. Nor do I care. It's none of my business.'

'If that's true why this chill in the air? This brisk smiling that doesn't touch the measuring eyes?'

'I've been too busy to do my sparkling, head-on-one-side Doris Day imitation.'

'I'm surprised a beautiful girl like you is so insecure. Though perhaps I ought to be flattered.' He let his hand run from my shoulder down to my chest and started to trace the zigzag pattern of my Fair Isle jersey across my breasts.

I took a step back. 'Don't!'

'Look, the poor woman's crippled by illness, bullied by her mother and neglected by her husband! Everyone flirts. It's a social duty. It doesn't mean a thing. I only wanted to cheer her up.' Kit put on an expression of contrition but the picture of him standing outside Violet's room grinning with satisfaction bloomed in my mind. Suddenly I was angry.

'From what Maud said this evening about Violet's state of mind you seemed to have failed signally. Perhaps it was a mistake to take on quite so many of Finn's connubial duties.'

He looked taken aback. 'Meaning?'

'I was standing by the linen cupboard when you brought her upstairs. I couldn't help overhearing. I was changing Maud's sheets while you and Violet were . . . flirting next door.'

Kit's face changed. 'My God!' He struck his forehead with the heel of his palm and groaned. '*Now* I understand.' He walked over to the window, then came back. 'Bobbie, I don't suppose you'll believe me if I tell you I didn't particularly want to – to make love to her, but it's the truth.'

'I don't care whether you did or not. You can make love to whom you please. Since your sense of social duty operates so strongly perhaps you'd better pleasure Violet again.'

He looked downcast. 'I don't blame you for being upset. It was a stupid thing to do. But she wanted it so badly. It would have been cruel to refuse.'

He appeared so dejected I almost felt sorry for him. But then I remembered Violet's unhappiness that evening. 'You don't seem to mind being cruel now. That's why I'm angry: not because you so nobly sacrificed yourself to Violet's needs but because you've made her miserable. Now you ignore her and make transparently lame excuses to avoid carrying her up- and downstairs. You must have seen that she's been on the verge of tears for the last two days. You won't believe me, I know, but I consider how you're treating her now is much, much worse than making love to her.'

Kit looked away towards the window and pressed his lips together, thinking. Then he spread his hands in a gesture of culpability. 'You're right. I've behaved badly. But I could tell you were angry, though I never guessed . . . I must say, in the circumstances you've put a good face on it. I didn't want to dig myself in deeper with her. I'm sorry, very sorry to have hurt her but it's you I love. You have such power over me.' He put up his hand and caressed my cheek with his finger.

'That would be unfortunate – if I believed it.' I forced myself to smile. 'Don't let's quarrel. It's all very unimportant. And you've been so generous with your help. We wouldn't have managed without you.'

'When I was making love to her I was thinking only of you.'

'I hope that's not true. It's insulting to Violet and makes you seem . . . well, never mind.'

'Do you think I'm a liar?'

I thought for a moment before replying. 'We all lie when it suits us.'

'There you are, Bobbie!' Liddy was standing in the doorway. I was grateful for the interruption. 'I've been looking for you every-where. Danny's asleep. I'm dying to talk. Oh, good! You've found my shoes. They're Mum's really but obviously she'll never be able to wear them again so she gave them to me.' She took the suede shoes from the pile and balanced one on her hand, lifting it high, admiring it. Then she kicked off her school loafers, buckled on the shoes and walked round the dining-room table, hands in the pock-ets of her grey school skirt, hips thrust forward in imitation of a mannequin's walk. 'Aren't they ace? They'll be perfect for London.' She giggled. 'I wonder what Danny'll say when he sees them. I expect he'll think they're shockingly decadent. He's so strait-laced. But really he'll be massively turned on by them. Men can't help themselves, can they?'

She slouched over to Kit and stood close to him, lowering her chin so that she was looking up at him through her eyelashes. Despite the school uniform she looked suddenly ten years older and irre-sistibly magnetic. It was inevitable that he should think of Violet, as I did. He sent me a glance in which I read the message that he was only as other men, defenceless before the tyranny of women. Seeing that she did not have his full attention, Liddy threw back her head and pouted provocatively.

'Oh, no, miss!' Kit pretended to look stern. 'I'm proof against your wiles. Schoolgirls are out of bounds.' She frowned. 'However alluring.' She smiled. 'Now stop trying to pretend you're a *femme fatale* and tell me: who is Danny? How did he hurt his arm?'

'Wouldn't you like to know?'

'I certainly should.'

'Well, then.' Liddy lifted her chin. 'You must promise on everything you hold sacred that you won't reveal what I've told you to another soul!'

Kit made a fist and lifted two fingers. 'Scouts' honour.'

'He's on the run from the IRA.'

'You're having me on!'

'It's true!' Liddy seemed delighted to have Kit's full attention at last. 'And from the *Garda*!'

'No!'

'Yes!'

Liddy gave Kit the details of Danny's story. 'He's most tremendously in love with me,' she declared triumphantly at the end of the recital.

'Of course he is.'

'And I'm in love with him!'

If she expected Kit to be jealous she was disappointed. 'Naturally you are. A good-looking, sensitive, high-minded boy, in danger every minute from deadly enemies, wounded by a bullet: what could be more romantic? I'm practically in love with him myself. I'm sure Bobbie's heart is already given to young Danny. Isn't it?'

He smiled at me.

Liddy looked uncertain. She dropped her seductive manner. 'You always tease about everything. I suppose because you're English you don't understand the trouble he's in.'

'Perhaps not. But if it's that bad I'm sure he won't involve you in it a minute longer than he can help. When's he planning to leave?'

'He's talking about going tomorrow but I shall persuade him to stay longer.'

'We must hope he won't be as persuadable as you think.'

'He will be.' Liddy smirked. 'I'm going to make it impossible for him to drag himself away.'

'Ah, I can guess just how you're going to do it.' Kit laughed and pinched her chin. 'You little minx! What a treat he has in store!'

'I'm sorry to bring you down to earth, Liddy,' I said sharply, 'but have you done your homework?'

The moment Liddy had departed, grumbling, Kit stopped smiling. 'I think someone should have a word in Danny's ear before Liddy releases her battery of charms. Or it might be simpler just to ring the police.'

'You promised you wouldn't!'

'Don't be naïve, Bobbie. The people who'll be looking for Danny are far more dangerous than she or you realize.'

'You seem to know a lot about it suddenly.'

Kit ignored this. 'They'll shoot him if they catch him. He'd be safer under lock and key in prison, though even there he can be got at. But the important thing is to get him out of here as soon as possible.'

I felt alarmed when I saw Kit was deadly serious. 'He's not strong enough to go on the run. I suppose one of us could drive him to Dublin and put him on the ferry tomorrow?'

'Don't be a fool. If they found out we'd helped him we'd be in trouble ourselves. Violence comes as naturally to these people as brushing their teeth.'

'We can't just throw him out to what may be his death.'

'You'd prefer to have the house burned down? Or to be taken prisoner yourself? Tortured for information, perhaps?'

I began to feel afraid. 'How do you know these things?'

Kit shrugged. 'I read the newspapers. I talk to people. You'll have to believe me when I say it's not safe to have that boy here.'

'I agree he must go as soon as possible. For Liddy's sake, if no one else's.'

'Liddy?'

'You heard what she said about persuading him to stay. I suppose she means to sleep with him. We can hardly chaperon them every minute of the day.'

'Don't tell me you're worried about Liddy's virtue?'

'I'm worried about her happiness. She's just a child.'

'A very precocious one. She's seventeen. How old were you when you lost your virginity?'

'Well . . . older.' Truthfulness compelled me to add, 'The same. Seventeen, nearly eighteen, actually.'

'There you are.'

'But it was much too young. I didn't know what I was doing. I want something better for her.'

'She's not your daughter. She won't thank you for interfering. Anyway, we needn't waste time discussing Liddy's maidenhead. I'm just concerned to get rid of the boy.'

'We *can't* ring the *Garda*. We invited Danny into the house. Implicit in that invitation was a guarantee that he could trust us.'

Kit sighed impatiently. 'Quixotic notions of hospitality don't apply.

This isn't a game of tennis. It was a bloody fool thing to do. I wonder at Constance. You, of course, could have no idea of the implications. But she must be fully aware of what these people are capable of. Unless she plans to get Eugene to recite them into a stupor.'

'She feels sorry for Danny. So do I. He's as anxious not to cause trouble for us as you could want. And no one knows he's here.'

'You hope. The grounds are crawling with IRA sympathizers.'

'Are they?' I turned to look out of the window but it was too dark to see anything. 'Let's wait until the morning. Danny needs a good night's sleep. Then we'll make plans.' I was on the point of asking him to promise that he would not take any action without telling me when I remembered that as far as Kit was concerned promises could be broken in the name of expediency.

'All right. But it's against my better judgement.'

'There's nothing to keep *you* here. You could go back to London tonight.'

'That's where you're wrong. There's everything to keep me here.' His face, which had been cold and hard while we were talking about Danny, softened. 'I've got to make you see that that business with Violet wasn't important.'

Before I could tell him I knew it, but that it made no difference, the door opened again.

'Bobbie! There you are.' Jasmine's shining black hair hung loose over a pale yellow silk dressing-gown which hung open to reveal a nightdress dripping with expensive lace. Teddy had been generous with underclothing during the first months of their relationship. Jasmine's bare feet displayed toenails polished gold. Her face, with its high cheekbones and exotic slanting eyes, was enchanting. Suddenly I saw the solution to several problems. 'There are birds in the corridor outside the bathroom.' Jasmine's expression was appalled. 'They're flying up and down, swooping over my head. I'm afraid to go to the loo.'

'Not birds, Jazzy,' I said mercilessly. 'Bats!' I put my hands over my ears as Jasmine exercised her lungs. 'Kit, would you escort Jasmine to the bathroom? I've got some clearing up to do.'

'Listen, everyone.' Constance was sitting at the kitchen table, a letter in her hand.

We were hurrying through breakfast to get on with our allotted tasks. At least, some of us were hurrying. Others were complaining about the necessity of wasting the best hours of the day at stinking school.

'Shut up, Liddy. Of *course* you're going. Listen, it's from Mr O'Brien!' Constance's eyes grew bright. 'He's going to give us seventy-five per cent of the cost of a new roof! I think I'm going to cry. I never thought I'd live to see Curraghcourt put on its legs again! He estimates twenty-seven thousand pounds in total. Such generosity! The darling's going to give us twenty thousand pounds!'

'It's not his money,' Kit pointed out. 'But I agree it's munificent. Where's the other seven thousand to come from?'

'I don't know.' Constance scanned the letter. 'Oh! Oh dear! I hadn't quite taken that in. We've got to come up with that much to qualify for the grant. Hell and damnation! Where are we going to get it? It's a bit late in the day to find you've got a stomach ache, Liddy.'

'Let's see what there is in the poteen fund.' I got up to find the jar. 'How long have we got to raise the money?'

'It doesn't say.' Constance referred again to the letter. 'But if it was five years we'd never do it. No, Flurry. Hell and damnation is *not* acceptable and I never want to hear you say it.'

I was counting the muddy, crumpled notes that had been stuffed into the jar marked *Isinglass*. 'There's nearly a hundred pounds here! Yesterday there was less than twenty.' I looked across to the hearth but it was unattended. 'I wonder . . . suppose we started up another still? Or several? The idea of rivalling the Guinesses suddenly seems more than attractive.'

'Remember, their business is legal,' Kit pointed out. 'You can hardly hope to start a thriving distillery without attracting attention.'

'Why shouldn't we get a licence to brew?'

'The existing breweries will have a cartel.' Kit was laughing at my earnestness. 'And you wouldn't be able to compete even if you could get one. Think of transport costs all the way from the land of bogs and mountains. You need to be near a busy port. And where would you put the machinery? You'd have to build a factory. You'd need capital. Which brings us back to the lack of seven thousand pounds.'

'Oh, you're right, of course. It was a stupid idea. But I can't bear to be beaten for such a comparatively paltry sum.'

'What about another poetry festival?' suggested Constance. 'If it hadn't been for having to pay for the missing chairs we'd nearly have broken even last time.'

'Morning, ladies, gents.' Sam O'Kelly's bony bashful face appeared through the back door looming over a large box. 'Here's Dicky Dooley's goods. Is the childer ready?'

'This is extraordinary!' I examined the contents of the box. 'What's come over Dicky? Almost everything I asked for. And look how neatly the box has been organized! Jars on the bottom, packets on the top! What's this?' I picked up a note written in tidy capitals.

Dear Bobbie,

No more arrowroot but we expect it by Thursday. Ditto whole blanched almonds. I'm after ordering black peppercorns, remembering you said you couldn't get them for love nor money. If there is anything else you require urgent a telephone call will suffice.

Yours affec.,

Larkie

'Larkie's taken a job at Dooley's,' Sam stated with an air of pride. 'First thing she did was throw out everything that was growing whiskers. Dicky made a whillalu at first but when he saw the customers liked the shop the way she'd set it up, he quietened down. She's making him send for a refrigerated unit to keep the flies off the dairy and cakes.'

'If you ask me, Dicky's in luck,' said Constance. 'Tell Larkie we look forward to calling in next time we're in Kilmuree. Run along, you children. Liddy, if I hear one more word about that stomach ache I shall lose my temper entirely. No, Flavia, there's no time to kiss the cats goodbye. Besides, supposing they have worms? You've given them pills? In that case Bobbie will say goodbye on your behalf. Flurry, have you got all your things? What note? Oh, damn! I remember you saying something about it but I was busy icing buns. Give it to me, quickly.' Constance cast her eyes over the note. 'What does Miss Coogan mean? A Chinaman costume by Monday? Does she imagine I have nothing else to do but comply meekly with her caprices and make elaborate— International Week, I see. Most praiseworthy, of course, but how I'm to . . . All right, darling, don't worry. I'll manage somehow. Goodbye, darlings, be good, and don't forget to— Goodbye!'

Constance sank down into her chair and poured herself another cup of tea. 'Really, it's the absolute limit. It couldn't have been anything simple like an angel or a ghost. A Chinaman! I've no idea where to begin!'

'Why not cut down an old dressing-gown?' I suggested. 'We could make a mandarin hat out of cardboard and long moustaches from strands of black wool.'

'Oh, yes! That sounds fine! My trouble is I panic too easily. It's just as well I've no children of my own. I'd be the most hopeless mother.'

'I don't agree.' Eugene, who had been sitting reading at the end of the table, seeming oblivious of the conversations going on around him, lowered his book. 'You seem to me an admirable surrogate parent. Kind, thoughtful, loving: what more could a child want?' He looked a little uncomfortable in the silence that greeted this remark. 'I shall go and prepare myself for a day at the easel.' He departed with dignity.

Constance was moved. 'I don't remember anyone paying me a nicer compliment.' Then she looked gloomy. 'I do hope it doesn't turn out that Liddy has appendicitis.'

'This is the section recently restored to fruit.' I waved my arm over an area planted with young currant bushes. 'On the wall behind we have fan-trained apricots, peaches and morello cherries, and espaliered apples.'

I turned my back on Timsy who was winking at me as he rested on his spade a few yards away. He was pretending to spread manure on the beds. Usually he could not be enticed from his still but the influx of new audiences for his 'Irishness' had proved irresistible and often I found myself in direct competition with him. As soon as he caught anyone's eye he became loquacious and the visitors were distracted by the demands of civility, which required attending to us both. Timsy wore a filthy Aran jersey and told anyone who would listen that it was his grandmother's pattern. Before they could nod politely and look away he would fix them with his bloodshot eyes and expose grimy teeth in a nauseating smile while explaining that the different patterns had evolved because the fishermen of Aran needed to be able to identify their kin when the drowned corpses were brought ashore. Dangling over the jersey Timsy wore a pendant in the shape of a shamrock and without pausing for breath he would go on to describe how St Patrick on first arriving in Ireland had plucked the three-leafed plant from the ground and used it to illustrate the doctrine of the Trinity. On his finger Timsy sported a claddagh ring. He embellished with rolling eyeballs the story of the Galway girl who had fallen in love with a Spanish sailor, a survivor of the wreck of the Armada. The sailor had made a ring with two hands holding a heart surmounted by a crown, symbolizing love, loyalty and friendship, which sentiments were cherished in the bosoms of all born and bred Irish as demonstrated by the ubiquity of the ornament. Timsy happened to have a cousin who was a craftsman in gold and who could sometimes be persuaded for an insignificant sum to hammer out a tasteful high-class version. Likewise of the shamrock pendant.

When Timsy sensed he held his audience in his palm he would fetch an ancient set of bagpipes from the greenhouse and set up a hideous wailing containing not one true note to conclude the performance. Since Timsy had a louder voice, a ferocious geniality, an unstoppable flow of talk and absolutely no sense of shame I was usually obliged to wait until he had finished his act and had been round collecting praise, orders and tips, bent double with simplicity, gratitude and bogus charm.

'Over here we have gooseberries—'

'What steps have you taken to prevent peach leaf curl?' interrupted a woman with a large bottom and the penetrating vowels of a well-bred English accent.

'Top of t'e morning to ye all,' began Timsy.

I cut in quickly before more than a few had turned their heads. 'I've been spraying with Bordeaux mixture at fortnightly intervals since January. Over here raspberry canes—'

'Which varieties?' It was the Englishwoman again.

'Um . . .' I turned my head on one side to read the nearest labels. 'Malling Jewel. Glen Cova—'

'*Érin go brágh!*' cried Timsy, advancing. 'Which means, yer honours, Oireland for ever!'

The Englishwoman was not to be distracted from important business. 'And which do you find most resistant to cane spot?'

'Oh . . . er, Malling Jewel.'

'Really? You do surprise me.' She gave a superior smile. I sensed some sympathy for me among the other visitors. They were bored by the catechism and the accent sounded excessively sharp in the open air.

'Now here we have strawberries.' I indicated, with pride, six perfectly straight rows of exquisitely green rosettes.

'Oh dear.' Oxford accent gave me a pitying smile. 'Mildew already, I see. I don't think *they*'ll come to anything. Naturally with such a damp climate you can't hope for much.'

'Irish strawberries are second to none for flavour,' I said, perhaps a little too combatively. The crowd stirred, sensing war.

'Obviously you have never tasted our English strawberries' – the Oxford accent became rebarbative – 'or you would not make such an assertion.'

Timsy was resorting to desperate measures. 'If ye peep round now in t'at corner where shtands t'e *speal* – t'at'll be a scythe to yer honours – ye may be fortunate enough to glimpse a wee maneen, no bigger t'an a dog, t'at is a leprechaun.'

As was to be expected the group swivelled as one but I was so thrilled to be taken for Irish that I conceded the battle at once.

'Does it mean I've picked up the brogue?' I asked Constance later as we sat in the drawing room with a well-deserved glass of wine.

'Not quite that, perhaps. But a certain lilt. It's unavoidable. I'm sure you'd lose it after five minutes of being in England.'

'I hope not.'

'You don't mean you want to sound like a mackerel-snapper?'

'I've never heard that term before.'

'Oh, pejorative names for the Irish are legion. Barks, bog-trotters, micks, salt-water turkeys – that's American, meaning just off the ship – flannel mouths – meaning insincere, you know – dogans, teagues: oh, I could go on and on.'

'None the less I'm delighted to be mistaken for one of you. I do so love it here.'

'Goodness knows why when we've worked you almost to death between us.' She held up her glass. 'Let's drink to the day I put that advertisement in the newspaper. I could never have guessed then that you would come and put us all right.'

'That's rather overstating it. For one thing, we aren't right, we're short of seven thousand pounds.' And, I thought but did not say, of all of us in the house only Flavia had been made undeniably happier by anything I had done. Tidying drawing rooms is comparatively easy. Lives are intractable, unmanageable things.

'We'll find it somewhere. We'll sell something, put up the prices in the tea-room, run that gardening school you told Mr O'Brien about. Why not?'

The setting sun gleamed faintly, throwing cloud shadows across the yellow damask. The silver threads of a spider's web hanging from a lustre of the chandelier drifted into view. Constance perhaps was happier too. She was certainly more optimistic. Our friendship was a reward out of all proportion to the work I had put in as housekeeper. I was going to miss her terribly.

'I've had a marvellous time.'

Constance who had been in the act of raising her glass to her lips, looked at me over the rim. 'That has a valedictory sound.'

'I'm afraid I *must* hand in my notice – and soon.'

'You couldn't think of staying just as a friend? I could try to get another housekeeper. You say you're happy here. I know it's selfish of me but I *dread* the idea of your going.'

'I'd love to stay but . . . there are things . . . Of course we'll keep in touch. You could come and stay in London.'

'That would be lovely. But it won't be the same.' She ran her finger and thumb up and down the stem of her wine glass several times, her expression thoughtful, before saying, 'Bobbie, I hope you won't think me impertinent, but is it Kit? Are you going to marry him and live in Norfolk and have beautiful children and breed dogs?'

'No.' We looked at each other. She smiled briefly then glanced away, obviously afraid of seeming inquisitive. 'It isn't that I don't trust you, Con. I do, absolutely.'

'Well, then I must say it, if you'll forgive me. I really hope it isn't. Kit, I mean.' Constance took a deep breath and spoke rapidly, her face flushing. 'Because all day he's been paying a great deal of attention to Jasmine. Flirting's hardly the word for it. Seducing would be more like it. And I've just seen them walk past the window together. Arm in arm!' I looked at Constance's indignant face and could not help laughing. Constance laughed too, with relief. 'I'm so glad you don't mind. I've been feeling really furious with him. I was afraid you'd be hurt. And that would be so cruel after that last awful man— Oh, Bobbie, I've just had a thought. You're not going back to England because of Burgo?'

'No! That's well and truly past. I hardly ever think of him. And when I do I'm neither angry nor unhappy. I feel an affection for him still, and for the good times we had, but that's all.'

'Thank goodness! I know you consider yourself equally to blame for the affair but *I* think he treated you badly. Honestly, I don't know why we bother with men at all. They're almost all of them so selfish and faithless. Their loves are as insubstantial as gossamer. An efficient sperm bank would be much more satisfactory.' Her attention was caught by two figures at the French windows. Kit and

Jasmine had cupped their hands round their faces to see in, smiling roguishly. Kit rattled at the handle. 'The key isn't here,' mouthed Constance. She gestured energetically. 'You'll have to go round. I suppose I'll go to hell for that lie,' she muttered as they went away. 'Actually it's in my pocket. But they looked so pleased with themselves I couldn't stand it. The bare-faced effrontery! When only the other day he was on his knees to *you*. Does he think you won't notice?'

'I rather think I'm supposed to notice. It's my punishment. But I'm hoping they'll like each another.'

'You never were even the smallest bit in love with him?'

I sighed. 'I tried hard to be. But efforts of that kind never work, do they? I remember you said that love comes unbidden. The trouble is it seems to have a thoroughly malign sense of humour, selecting the most unsuitable people possible.' I stopped and pulled my thoughts into line, seeing that Constance looked puzzled. 'I hope Kit'll be good to Jazzy and put the ghastly Teddy out of her mind before he gets bored with Lydia again.'

'If it's your career that's the problem, I can understand it. You're not using your intellect as you should be, there's no denying that. But you could get a job in Dublin and come back here for weekends. Or write a book.'

'Mm. I'm afraid that wouldn't be . . . the solution.'

'So you're going back to England because you feel you need a rest. Or a change of scene?'

'I'd enjoy a weekend in London certainly. But taken all in all I prefer the country to the town.' I saw that Constance was perplexed but reluctant to press me further. 'Con.' I took a deep breath. 'If I let you into a great, great secret—'

'Hello, Aunt Connie, Bobbie.' Flavia came in and kissed us both. 'Friday. At *last*. I can't wait for tomorrow. I've made a string so I can hang my order pad on a belt round my waist, look!' She showed us a plait of red wool. 'I'm going to put my pencil behind my ear.'

'That will be very elegant, darling,' said Constance. 'Do you think you might scrub your fingernails? People might be put off by so much inkyness.'

'I'll do it at once. I'll just put back the book I borrowed about Japanese tea ceremonies. Oh, I forgot, I've got to have a Japanese costume for Monday.'

'I know, don't tell me,' groaned Constance. 'It's that *wretched* International Week.'

Flavia looked surprised. 'I thought it was the sort of thing you like. You're always saying we ought to be citizens of the world.'

'Yes, well, in principle I do approve.' She looked at me as Flavia disappeared into the library. 'What were you going to say?'

'Perhaps this isn't the moment—'

'Do look!' Flavia returned from the library, carrying an empty Coca-Cola bottle, a plastic bag containing crusts and a tube of paper that had once held Garibaldi biscuits. 'Someone's had a picnic on Daddy's desk. There's cheese squashed into the carpet and crumbs everywhere!'

'Would you believe it?' said Constance, exasperated. 'And everyone seemed so nice! Though there *was* that man who sat on Finn's bed and bounced up and down to see if it was comfortable. And a woman who opened the linen cupboards and inspected the sheets. I didn't quite like to ask them not to. After all, they've paid to look round.'

'I'll get a dustpan and clean up the mess,' I said. 'We don't want to encourage people to treat the library as a cafeteria. They might start cooking sausages on the hearth.'

'I'll fetch it.' Flavia ran off.

'I'll lay the dining table, shall I?' asked Constance. 'It's already seven o'clock.'

'Oh, yes, do. I hadn't realized it was so late.'

The library, being west-facing, caught the last of the day's light. The sky was gold and red, promising a fine morning to follow. Before the opening Constance and I had repainted the patched and flaking fronts of the shelves and the fluted pilasters in the original dark sea-green. It had taken days as we had stopped frequently to browse among the books but the improvement was dramatic. A blue opaline vase of primroses stood on the desk beside the blotter and inkstand, which had been pushed aside to make room for the picnic. I heard Flavia return with the dustpan and brush.

'Look. A squashed currant on the cushion.' I was bending over the sofa which had loose covers of blue linen that had faded to grey. 'I can scrape it off with my thumbnail, I think, without it leaving a mark. I dread to think what your father would say if he knew. It's a good thing he isn't here—'

'Ah, but he is. How does it feel to be caught red-handed?'

The shock of hearing his voice so unexpectedly made the blood rush inwards to my heart. I turned round quickly. There he was, exactly as he had been in my thoughts and dreams almost every minute of every day since he had gone away.

How could it have been otherwise? I had been living in the place where he had been born and spent most of his life. I had sat at his table, walked through his rooms, seen the same mountains, fields and trees, smelt the bog myrtle and the gorse and, when the wind was in the west, the salt of the ocean that must all be as familiar to him as the turf smoke that infused every lungful of air we breathed. Every day I had seen his likeness in the faces of his children and his sister and in the portraits of his ancestors. I had stood in his bedroom looking out across the demesne as he must so often have done, wondering what the future might hold, what was best to be done. I had dusted his books, which had told their own tale of the man to whom they belonged. I had taken care of everything that was his and, because they were his, I had loved them with passion. All my reasoning, all my attempts to assert my will, to be master of myself, had come to nothing. It had been futile to try to protect myself from the unhappiness that must come.

The angles of his face were sharp; his eyes beneath dark brows were deep-set, intelligent and storm-grey. There was a smile in them which disappeared as we looked at each other.

I tried to joke. 'It feels criminal.'

'How are you?'

'All right. The same. What about you?'

'Things are just the same with me.'

Thus we confirmed our love for each other. It was all we allowed ourselves and it was pointless – yet precious.

'Constance telephoned me last night about the Quill boy. I thought I'd better come.' This was an explanation, an apology for his presence. 'Where is he now?'

'Asleep up in Violet's old room.'

'And Liddy? Is she back from school?'

'Ten minutes ago. I don't know how serious it is, Liddy's attachment to him.'

'His being here is serious for all of us. He must be got away to a place of safety. I knew his father. A good man. And the boy's young enough to make a new beginning.' He looked down, then back at my face. 'A new beginning,' he repeated. 'How many must one make in this life, I wonder?'

There was a pause. Then I said, 'You left me a book. Yeats. I've loved it.'

'It was an impulse. Foolish. But I'm glad you like it.'

'It has your bookplate inside the cover. Perhaps I ought to return it before I leave.'

'No. Keep it. It isn't much, after all.'

To my dismay, I felt my eyes fill with tears.

'Finn, darling.' Constance had entered the library. 'I wasn't expecting you until tomorrow at the earliest.' She put up her face to kiss him. How I envied her that polite brotherly peck. 'I'm awfully pleased you're here. Aren't you, Bobbie?'

'Awfully.' I knelt to sweep the crumbs into my hand.

FORTY-NINE

While Constance and I cooked dinner Finn and Danny talked in the library. Liddy walked round and round the kitchen, getting in everyone's way, eating the cheese as fast as we grated it and taking spoonfuls of the raspberry jam reserved for the canary pudding.

'Darling Liddy, leave it alone,' I said, exasperated. 'There won't be enough for the rest of us and it's Colonel Molesworth's favourite. It'll be a stretch to make it go round as it is.'

'Oh, damn! Is he coming to dinner?'

'Yes, and Father Deglan. I thought you liked the colonel.'

'I do but if we have visitors it means Danny can't eat with us. Can Danny and I have supper on our own in my room, Aunt Connie?'

'I think we'd better ask your father.'

'I keep telling you, it's nothing but a sham, your feminism. As soon as there's a remotely important question to be answered you drop right back into female subservience. Why should Dad decide everything? He's always so strict. I bet he'll say Danny has to go tomorrow.'

Liddy grumbled on while nibbling at anything we took our eyes off for a second. I remembered how hungry being happily in love makes one and how the reverse is true. I looked at the grey sludge that was the beginning of a turnip gratin with disfavour.

'All right, it's settled.' Finn came in and helped himself to a glass of wine from the bottle of which Constance and I had already drunk half. 'Danny's going tonight.'

'No!' wailed Liddy. 'You can't be so mean! Please, Dad!'

'Sweetheart, I'm sorry.' Finn attempted to put his arm round his elder daughter but she shook him off. 'You must understand, it's for his sake as much as anyone's that he gets away at once. This isn't a game, Liddy. This could have serious consequences for all of us.'

'You're afraid people will find out and blame you,' said Liddy accusingly. 'They might even unfrock you or whatever they do to senators.'

'Don't be a fool.' Finn looked seriously annoyed. 'Danny knows too much. Men have been shot by the IRA for far less. If you care anything at all about him, you'll do everything you can to get him away now.'

'Where's he going to go?' Liddy's lower lip was trembling.

'To France. He speaks good French apparently and it'll be easier to lose himself there than in England. I've already arranged with a man I know in Paris to get him a room and some kind of job.'

'Paris!' Liddy was silent for a moment, presumably contemplating running away to join Danny, perhaps modelling for the Paris shows, becoming a muse for Yves Saint-Laurent.

'How's he getting there?' asked Constance.

'As soon as Father Deglan and Basil Molesworth have gone I'll drive Danny to Rosslare. There's a ferry to Cherbourg tomorrow morning.'

'But it's six or seven hours to Rosslare! And you've just driven from Dublin! You'll be shattered!'

'I'll be all right. I'll get a couple of hours' sleep in the car before going back to Dublin.'

'Dad, can I come with you?' Liddy clutched his arm and looked up at him with pleading eyes. 'I'll do anything you want if you'll let me. I'll – I'll – clean your shoes for a year. I'll give up swearing. I'll . . . I can't think of anything. You say and I'll promise to do it, whatever it is.'

'I hope you realize now, Liddy, how little your father asks of you.' Constance sounded cross. 'But you're asking a great deal of him. If he takes you he's got to drive all the way back here and then again to Dublin on Monday morning.'

I looked down at the breadcrumbs I was making, in case my eyes were also pleading.

'I know. But, Dad, darling Dad, I'll love you for ever if you'll do this for me. I'll work hard at school and get those foul exams. Please!'

Liddy was gazing up at her father with just Violet's way of turning her head so that she looked at one sideways through her lashes.

'All right,' he said. 'If it means so much to you, you can come.'

'*Ang*el father!' Liddy hugged him and kissed him. 'I promise I'll slave all the rest of this term and next.'

'I'd rather you worked hard because you realized that it was in your own best interests.' He put her a little away from him. 'You little idiot!' he said. 'Don't you know I'd do a lot more than drive a few extra miles if it would make you happy?'

'Would you?' Liddy looked amazed. 'In that case, I'm sorry if I've been a pig. I'll try much harder from now on to be nice to you.'

Finn laughed. 'I look forward to that. But for now, let's concentrate on getting through the next twenty-four hours. Danny had better go back to bed until it's time to leave. He needs all the rest he can get. Be as discreet as you can be. The fewer people who know where Danny is, the better. Don't even tell your mother. Certainly don't tell Timsy or the girls. I saw Kit's car outside. Does he know about Danny?' Liddy nodded.

'Yes,' said Constance. 'But surely you trust him? I look on him as a member of the family.'

'It's important you don't tell Kit that Danny's leaving tonight or where he's going.' Finn looked briefly at me. 'Kit works for the British government.'

'I don't believe it!' Constance stopped stirring and turned to face him, drips of the béchamel sauce she was making for *oeufs mollets Maintenon* falling from her wooden spoon and spotting the flagstones.

'What? You don't mean he's a spy?' Liddy gave a scream of delight.

'Well, you could call it that if you wanted to be melodramatic, but only in a very small way. He's not going to be parachuted into the Soviet Union to infiltrate the KGB or sabotage the latest nuclear submarine. All he does is supply information.' Finn put down his glass and helped himself to some of the grated cheese, spilling a few shreds down his shirt front and adding to the mess on the floor. I wanted to protest but my mind was in revolt. I continued to push stewed onions through a sieve as I tried to take in what Finn was saying. 'The business of intelligence on both sides of the Irish Sea is a web of conflicting gossip, lies and wishful thinking. There are thousands of informers – touts, as they're known – and there are those whose job it is to collate the information, extract the bits that might be true or at least useful, and feed them back to HQ. Handlers, that's what they call them, isn't it? I expect Kit was recruited at university.' Finn sent me a quizzical glance. 'That's the strange way the English do things.'

'I thought . . . He said he was a literary agent!' Constance rubbed

575

the back of her hand across her forehead, streaking it with soot. 'Bobbie, had you any idea?'

I shook my head dumbly.

'So he is.' Finn tried to brush away the cheese that had fallen on his trousers. 'It's the perfect job for getting about the place, ostensibly to speak to publishers and authors and incidentally picking up useful knowledge to send back to base. It's not as you see it in films. The FBI won't be bugging the Fitzgeorge Arms. Nor will Kit have an armoury of lethal weapons disguised as fountain pens and wristwatches. All he does is follow a lead that's given him and report back if anything comes of it. It's a sideline, quite lucrative, I imagine, and lending a certain glamour to a young man's existence.'

'How do you know?' I asked. All the time Finn had been speaking I had been revolving ideas in my mind and coming to hazy and implausible conclusions.

'I rang up a man I know in Whitehall. He confirmed my suspicions that Kit was a tiny but useful cog in British Intelligence.'

'But what made you suspect in the first place?'

'Oh, several things. He's remarkably well informed about Irish politics. Most English people, even politicians, don't begin to understand the complexities. And he mentioned the change of boundaries between North and South that was proposed under the Heath government. Remember? He talked about it at dinner one night. It was top secret, yet Kit knew more about it than I did. That made me extremely curious. And you recall how he was off like a shot the minute Mountbatten was killed? His comings and goings seemed to be adventitious yet they coincided with external events in a way that aroused my interest. That's why I decided to investigate. I even wondered, vaingloriously, if it was me he was checking up on. But now I think not.' He glanced again at me.

'Are you going to expose him, Dad?' Liddy sounded excited. 'Can I be there?'

'I'm not going to tell him I know about his cloak-and-dagger work if that's what you mean by exposure. Why should I? Kit's done me no harm, nor anyone else here as far as I know. It's not a crime to assist the government of your own country. On the contrary, it shows a laudable patriotism. Intelligence is an essential part of the administration of every nation in the world. Kit is merely the modern equivalent of a messenger with a cleft stick.'

'In that case' – Constance waved her spoon – 'he'd be the last person to want to help the IRA, surely? So why shouldn't he know about Danny?'

'It's not as straightforward as that.' Finn poured himself another glass. 'For one thing, Danny has information that would be extremely interesting to the British. You don't think Danny would tell the Old Enemy what they'd want to know without persuasion? My guess is he'd rather be tortured by his own countrymen.' I winced as I heard this. Surely we English didn't go around beating the soles of people's feet and electrocuting their genitals? 'Besides,' Finn continued, 'politics is a dirty game. Sometimes it's useful to have pawns to exchange. You can't get the enemy to co-operate unless there's a face-saving trade-off.'

'But Kit's a friend!' Constance looked distressed. 'He's been so good, so helpful. And he loves our family! He's often said so. I can't believe he'd do anything we didn't want him to.'

'No one in politics can afford to be sentimental, Con,' Finn said gently. 'It's better not to put friendship to the test.'

'Bobbie, you haven't said anything.' Constance turned to me. 'Isn't this just the most disillusioning thing you've ever heard? Though of course I realize that Kit's on your side – that is, if you had a side, darling Bobbie, for I've never felt for a single moment that we weren't on the same side – but what I mean is, that as far as you're English then he's on your team but . . . Oh dear, I *hate* the idea of him not being utterly frank and open with us. Did he really say nothing about it to you? Not even hint if there was something he was investigating locally? Oh no, of course that's ridiculous. He came here because of you.'

When she said that I felt an additional smart of pain and sorrow because without intending to Constance had put her finger exactly on the bruise. Oh yes, he was here because of me. I was certain of that. I felt rather than saw that Finn was observing me. He had carefully exculpated Kit as far as was possible, had presented a fair, neutral picture. He wanted me to believe that this unsuspected, possibly perfidious facet of my fellow countryman need make no difference to my future plans, should they happen to include Kit. It was extremely chivalrous of Finn, I thought with a feeling that amounted to savagery.

I tried to decide how to play it. Shocked? Amused? Indifferent? Suddenly a smell of burning reached my nostrils. 'Con! The sauce!'

'This canary pudding is just like our mess cook used to make it,' said Basil Molesworth. I took this as a compliment. 'There wouldn't happen to be a spot more jam?'

'I'm afraid it was undeservedly popular. I don't suppose marmalade would do?'

The colonel shook his head. 'Not to worry. Look at that young woman now.'

My eyes travelled round the dining table, wondering whom he might mean. Jasmine, sitting opposite me, looked delicious in a Schiaparelli pink silk suit. Next to Finn was Constance in her becoming black dress. I leaned forward to see Liddy on the other side of the colonel, in my pin-tucked shirt from Mexicana – Liddy, of course, not Basil – worn with black trousers tucked into high-heeled boots in the style of a sans-culotte. All of them were worth looking at. 'She's come on a lot since Christmas. More substantial, though I know you ladies don't like to hear that. But she no longer looks as though a cold winter would do for her. And she's talking fairly fluently now too. I don't go in much for miracles – leave that sort of thing to the competition, eh? – but I've got to admit it's the nearest thing to one *I've* ever seen.'

Violet was sitting at the foot of the table in the place that for a season had been mine. She was looking bright-eyed, pretending to listen to Eugene, her spirits quite recovered now her husband was home.

'I remember when Finn brought her back here for the first time. Pretty as a fairy then, quite in your own style, my dear, but something of a pussy-cat. Mischievous, you know. That must have been' – he rolled his eyes upwards while he calculated – 'over seventeen years ago. Finn's grandfather – the Master, we all called him – was alive then. It was Finn's birthday. A good party, bonfires all over the estate, plenty of liquor, the usual black crows in attendance' – he glanced at Father Deglan on the other side of the table – 'disapproving of youth and high spirits. My, but there were some shenanigans that night! Violet was the belle of the ball. Of course we had pretty enough local girls, splendid teeth and good riders to hounds, but they didn't have Violet's winning ways. She could charm you off your perch like a fox charms birds from the trees. She made me shiver in my shoes! I've never gone for women you couldn't call a friend, but most of the other men there would have given their right hands for a smile from her. But she only had eyes for Finn.' The colonel shook his head then laughed at some sudden memory. 'It was about nine months from that night that little Phyllida put in an appearance. They'd married hastily in Dublin a few months before. The Master was furious about it but I said to him, "What are you bellyaching for, you old fool? She's as lovely a girl as you could want and Finn's a fine man. They make the handsomest pair in Connaught and they're in love. Who cares about a few months either way?" But the Master was a Catholic so he thought it was a sin, the silly old . . . I hope I'm not speaking out of turn? You'll be a Protestant, I take it.'

'I am, if I'm anything, and no, you're not.'

'That's good. Religion's throttled the life out of this country. When they got hold of the schools that put the lid on it really. Still, no use moaning about it now, the harm's done and there's change in the wind. We're beginning to feel the influence of the rest of the world now and by golly it's a damned good thing.' The colonel drained his glass of a superb Château Yquem which I was sadly aware was entirely wasted on the canary pudding. 'Do you know, I can't remember when I've enjoyed a conversation so much for a long time. You must allow me to say, my dear, that not only are you a strikingly beautiful woman but you've the brains to match.'

'Thank you.' I had spoken barely a dozen words throughout but the colonel had been too busy enjoying his own loquacity to notice. 'Are you sure you won't have any more pudding?'

The colonel patted his stomach and shook his head. 'Love to but—'

Whatever he was going to say was drowned by a screech from Jasmine. Most of us remained calm, piercing screams having become part of the pattern of our lives since Jasmine's arrival. Basil and Father Deglan looked thoroughly alarmed and Finn glanced around uneasily.

'There's a man looking through the window,' cried Jasmine. 'A hideous creature with a deformed face!'

'Nonsense!' said Maud. 'You're hysterical. Pull yourself together.'

'I saw him!'

'I once had a Malay girl in the kitchen,' said Maud to no one in particular. 'Never again. She could only cook rice and she had the morals of a whore.'

'Don't worry, Jazzy,' said Kit, who was sitting next to her. 'It's just one of the local lads. Too much in-breeding—'

The dining-room door was flung wide and in rushed Timsy, Katty and Pegeen, their eyes wide, their mouths gaping.

'What is it?' asked Constance. 'What's the matter—'

She stopped in mid-speech. Behind them came three men whose

appearance was terrifying. Their features had been distorted by stocking masks. One of them carried a gun. I had seen guns before. During shooting lunches at Cutham the hall had resembled an arsenal. But I had never seen a gun pointed at anyone. As its owner waved it round the table at each of us in turn, I felt real fear. Jasmine, temporarily checked by surprise, gave vent to a long penetrating shriek at full volume that made all of us, including the intruders, jump.

'Shut your mouth!' said the gun-toter, aiming it at Jasmine. 'Or I'll shut it for you with a bullet!' His accent seesawed between American and Irish.

Jasmine sensibly did as she was told, contenting herself with hiding her face against Kit's shoulder and uttering the occasional protesting sob. Flavia, who was whiter than the tablecloth, threw her arms about her mother.

'All right, ladies and gentlemen,' said the gunman with fine sarcasm. 'Don't trouble yourselves to get up. No one's to move. Just give us Danny Quill and we'll not disturb your banquet any longer.'

For a while no one spoke. Liddy stared down at her plate and looked as though she was going to be sick.

Then Finn said, very calmly, 'I'm afraid you've come on a wasted journey. Quill left the house this morning.'

'Oh, no, I'll not buy that. He was seen coming into this house last night. There's been a watch kept on the gate since dawn. No one's been in or out except Sam O'Kelly and the kids and you, Senator. We caught up with O'Kelly later. He knows better than to lie to us. Quill's here all right.'

'What makes you think he went out by the gate?' said Finn. 'There's a channel from the lough that runs out to the sea. He was picked up by motorboat long before dawn and taken round to Westport. By now' – Finn looked at his watch – 'he should be somewhere in the North Channel. Poor fellow, apparently he suffers badly from sea-sickness.'

It was a good performance, unhurried, relaxed as though it was nothing to Finn whether anyone believed him.

'You're lying.'

Finn shrugged his shoulders. 'Why don't you search the house?'

The one in charge turned to his minions. 'Do as he says. Get going.'

'Where shall us begin, Terry?' said one with a sweep's brush of black hair sticking up through the top of his mask. He had a high, almost girlish voice. 'I don't know me way round at all.'

'Sean Donoghue!' said Katty. 'I thought it was you! You should be ashamed of yourself!'

'Gobshite!' Terry cuffed the unfortunate Sean with the barrel of the gun.

'Hoo-hoo,' bleated Sean, nursing his ear. 'There was no call for to do that!'

'Wait till I tell your ma of you, Sean Donoghue!' said Katty.

Terry pointed his gun at Katty's aproned bosom. Her little black eyes were fierce, her hooked nose haughty as she crossed her arms and glared at him. She could have been taken as a model for Madame Defarge. I was impressed, being quite sure I could not have put on such a show of courage myself.

'You do any tale-bearing,' said Terry, 'and I'll blast out yer brains for ye, sure as a monkey likes bananas.'

Pegeen dropped on to her knees, closed her eyes and began to move her lips silently. Timsy bit his lip and looked at Finn for guidance. Finn remained calm, leaning back in his chair and folding his arms but saying nothing.

'Talking of monkeys,' said Katty bravely, if unwisely, 'you make a fine one yerself.'

'Is that so?' The face beneath the stocking mask underwent some sort of upheaval – I guessed a lowering of brows and a thrusting out of the lower jaw. There was a click as he cocked the trigger. 'I'm not sure you haven't just bought yerself a one-way ticket to purgatory with your big ugly mouth.'

A collective intake of breath could be heard from those sitting at the table.

'Think what you're doing, man!' urged Father Deglan. ''Tis *your* soul will go straight to hell for eternity if you kill a helpless woman.'

'Ha! Ha!' jeered Terry. 'You can't frighten me with your bugaboos of hell-fire and imps of darkness. All that's crap to keep the people under your great greasy thumb.' He took a step nearer Katty, who lost some of her defiance.

'You'll not shoot a priest, I'm thinking.' Father Deglan got up from his chair. Terry jerked the gun in his direction but Father Deglan continued to walk towards him until he stood in front of Katty. The gun was no more than two feet from his chest. 'And if you're so far cast out from the love of God as to commit such a sin, I took Communion this morning and I'm ready to meet my maker.'

He began to count the beads of his rosary and to pray aloud with his good eye turned up to heaven and his sad pearly eye looking at his persecutor.

'Well *done,* old chap!' called Basil. 'A gallant action if ever I saw one.'

'Shut it, you stupid old fool!' snarled Terry, looking at Basil. 'And you can shut it, too!' he addressed Father Deglan. 'I can't abide your whining to heaven. I had enough of it as a kid. It makes me sick to my stomach to hear you with your beggings and bargainings. *Shut* it, I say!'

Father Deglan did shut it. He stood with his flushed, shining face perfectly tranquil but continued to turn the beads between his fingers.

'All right, you two.' Terry turned back to his helpers. 'What are you waiting for? Go and find Quill.'

'You heard the senator,' grumbled the other man, who wore a black knitted ski hat pulled down to his eyebrows. 'He ent here. T'is is a fecking castle. However should we search it?'

'For crying out bloody loud!' yelled Terry. 'One of you start at the top and work down, and the other start at the bottom and work up, you useless cods. Christ! That I was given you two eejits to be working with!'

His henchmen departed, their hobnailed boots clattering on the oak boards. I hoped Danny would hear them coming in time to take evasive action.

'You three' – Terry waved the gun at Timsy and the girls – 'can go and sit over there and we'll wait and see what little fox my lads'll flush out.'

'I pity your poor mother, that's all,' said Katty and so far forgot herself as to spit on the dining-room floor. But to my relief she did as she was told. The three of them sat in a row on the window seat.

'Sit down, Father, will you?' Terry sounded frustrated. 'And don't give me any more trouble or begob it'll be a pleasure to blast you to kingdom come.'

Father Deglan returned to his place and for several minutes we were all silent. Glancing at Liddy's face I saw she was close to tears. It was a terrible strain, thinking of Danny, praying he would not be found.

'I've had enough of this.' Maud groped for her sticks and stood up.

'Sit down, old woman,' threatened Terry.

'It's obvious you were brought up in some bogside hovel or you'd have learned how to address your superiors.' Maud shuffled round the table and approached Terry without the smallest sign of fear.

'Get back, I tell you!' Terry cocked the gun again. 'Don't think your age'll save you.'

'I shan't trouble myself to think anything about it.' Maud moved slowly on her sticks towards the door.

'I'm warning you!' Terry growled. 'One step more and I'll fire!'

'Maud!' said Finn. 'Be careful!'

'Listen to me, you ignorant peasant!' Maud turned her head with difficulty to look at Terry. 'I've arthritis in my spine, my neck and my knees. It's coming into my wrists now and soon it'll be in my fingers. I shan't be able to hold a glass or a cigarette to my lips. I'll be a helpless cripple, dependent on the do-goodery of those with queasy consciences. I'd rather be dead. If you want to, shoot me. Otherwise I'm going to my room.'

She continued to the door. I admired her enormously at that moment.

'Splendid woman!' cried Basil. 'I take my hat off to you, Maud. You're a champion!'

'Damn you to hell!' Terry raged. 'All right, go on then, you old streel. But don't think you'll call the *Garda*,' he shouted after her. 'We've cut the bleeding wires!'

Maud's departure seemed to inflame Terry's temper fearfully. He muttered and cursed, taking aim at each of us in turn and making exaggerated movements of his trigger-finger to frighten us. In my case he was extremely effective. I was terrified. 'Stupid old bitch,' he groaned. 'Cripple! Huh! There's little enough she can do. It'd take her a year to hobble to Kilmuree! Let her stew! The old bitch!'

After five minutes of this our nerves were pretty much at snapping point.

'Excuse me.' Constance raised her hand politely as though about to ask a question of a visiting lecturer. 'I'm afraid I need to . . . answer the call of nature.'

'Sit down!' Terry bellowed.

'Please! I really must!' She pushed back her chair and took a step away from the table. As she had been sitting on the side nearest the door, the step brought her very close to Terry.

'Move and you're dead!' Terry aimed the muzzle at Constance's heart.

What happened next seemed to take place in slow motion. Constance crossed her legs and made an awkward wriggling movement.

Terry must have thought she was preparing to spring at him. 'You've asked for it, bitch!'

Finn jumped up and shouted, 'Con!'

Eugene launched himself in front of Constance half a second before Terry squeezed the trigger. A brief flash was followed by a crack louder than any sound I've ever heard, which brought down a section of plaster from the ceiling smack into the middle of the dining table. Eugene dropped like a stone.

'Eugene!' Constance threw herself on to her knees beside him. She pushed his hair from his forehead and stared at his white, still face. 'Oh, my darling! No! No!' She fell forward on to his chest and broke into a paroxysm of weeping.

Terry hesitated and I saw that the hand which held the gun was shaking. I wondered if in fact this was the first time he had fired to kill.

'Shut that row, for God's sake,' he yelled at Jasmine who was wailing like a factory siren.

Kit put his arms round Jazz and murmured words of comfort but she was hysterical. I did not blame her. I felt on the verge of hysteria myself. Violet and Flavia were crying only a little less noisily while the rest of us were voiceless and ghastly with shock. Flurry was sitting with his face screwed up, his eyes closed and his fingers in his ears.

While we remained more or less unmoving, horror having suspended our capacity for reason or action, a clatter of hobnailed boots could be heard in the hall. Liddy put her hands over her mouth and her eyes became enormous. I knew she was dreading seeing Danny between them.

Sean and his companion came in alone. 'Boss, we been up and down and in and out and we ent found—' They caught sight of Constance weeping over Eugene's lifeless body. 'Bloody hell!' The black-hatted one had to shout because of the din Jasmine was making. 'Boss, is it kilt he is?'

'I didn't mean— The gun fired wide! I was only going to frighten her! What's that, in the name of blazes?'

We listened in amazement to a sound that, though some way above us, split the sky with reverberating strokes.

'What the hell is it?' moaned Sean. He gripped Black Hat's arm. 'Lord, have mercy! 'Tis the Day of Judgement!'

Finn smiled suddenly, an electrifying sight in the context of our panic-stricken petrifaction. 'It's Scornach Mór, the alarm bell. Who'd have thought Maud would have had the strength to pull the rope? She's a wonderful woman, my mother-in-law.'

'Big Throat' smote the air with increasing volume as if in confirmation of this rare encomium.

'Well, boys,' said Finn. He continued to look amused, which seemed a little heartless, considering that Eugene had just been murdered. 'You're in a spot now. In ten minutes not only the *Garda* but the Fire Service and the Ambulance – and everyone else who decides to come along for the ride – will be here. And they're going to find you with a corpse on your hands and more than a dozen witnesses who saw you kill him. It'll be twenty-five years, at least. And you two' – he smiled pleasantly at Sean and the man in the black hat – 'are accessories.'

'Oh, feck! Boss, I'm going!'

Sean suited his behaviour to his words and was swiftly followed by his companion.

Terry hesitated for no more than a few seconds while Scornach Mór shook the heavens. 'May you rot in hell, every one of you!' he hurled at us as he ran from the room.

'Every man, be he ever so bad, thinks of salvation in a crisis,' said Father Deglan in a voice that trembled as he made the sign of the cross over Eugene's head. 'Ah, my son, my poor brave boy! *Nunc dimittis servum tuum, Domine—*'

'Quiet, everyone!' shouted Finn. 'Will you women stop crying this instant! That includes you, Con. Father, your offices are premature. I doubt if it's possible for a bullet to pass through a body and be deflected upwards with sufficient force to dislodge a lump of plaster twenty feet above. Eugene's fainted, that's all.'

Seizing a glass of water from the table Finn threw it over Eugene's face. We all stopped screaming, crying, moaning or whatever means we had found to express our acute terror and gathered round the body. Almost immediately our self-restraint was rewarded as Eugene fluttered his eyelashes and groaned.

'Eugene!' Constance lifted his hand and cradled it against her cheek. 'Speak to me!'

'Ohhh . . . Ahhh . . . Who . . . What . . .?' He gazed in an unfocused way at the circle of faces above him. 'What's that noise? Constance . . . My dear, you're crying!'

'I thought you were dead! You did it to save me . . . It was the bravest thing I've ever, *ever* . . .' A sob rendered her momentarily inarticulate. 'You sacrificed your own life for me . . .'

'I did?' A gentle smile played over Eugene's plump lips. 'Really?'

'You threw yourself in front of me and took the bullet!' Constance kissed his hand. 'My . . . *hero!*'

A look of concern clouded his gibbous eyes. 'Am I very badly hurt?'

Constance opened his jacket to expose a shirt front unblemished but for a few spots of egg. 'I don't think so. Do you feel pain anywhere?'

Eugene sat up and felt himself carefully. 'I seem to be all right. Except' – he touched his collar – 'I'm soaking wet. Has it been raining? I must dry my jacket at once in case it shrinks.'

'Never mind, darling.' Constance beamed at him. 'If it does we'll get you another one from the poteen fund. You've earned it.'

'Did you just call me . . . darling?'

Constance nodded, her cheeks suffused with emotion.

'Well, that's very agreeable. Do you think you could . . . say it again?'

Constance leaned forward and kissed him on the lips. '*Dar*ling!'

'Darling,' he reiterated, rolling the word round on his tongue as though savouring a new taste. 'Constance . . . darling.'

'Yes, *dear*est Eugene?'

'Would someone help me up? My legs have gone to jelly.'

Kit pulled Eugene up by his armpits as Scornach Mór fell silent. My ears throbbed in the absence of noise. After Eugene had flexed his limbs and smoothed down his hair, he became aware that we were staring at him, as enthralled as a circus audience watching a high-wire act.

'Constance.' He held out the crook of his elbow. 'Come with me. I have something to say to you.'

Eugene and Constance left the room, arm-in-arm, as though they were stepping on air.

'I'm shafted!' growled Timsy.

At the time I wondered why Timsy was so annoyed. Just then the *Garda*, accompanied by every person of importance in Kilmuree, including the bank manager and the undertaker, swarmed into the hall. For several minutes everyone talked at once. Maria and Osgar, having been released from the cloakroom where they had been incarcerated by Terry and his friends, dashed round barking their heads off. It was pandemonium. Finn drew Colin McDaid, the chief of the *Garda*, into the dining room and closed the door so they could hear themselves speak. He pre-empted the policeman's laborious questioning by giving a concise account of recent events.

'So no harm was done,' he concluded. 'We were lucky to get away with nothing worse than a hole in the ceiling.'

I contemplated with sorrow the eighteen square inches of lathes in the La Franchini brothers' masterpiece.

'Were any of them local, would you say, Mr Macchuin, sir?'

'I couldn't tell. They were all wearing stocking masks.'

'One of them was,' said Kit who stood nearby, sharing a cigarette with a trembling, tearful Jasmine. 'Sean Donoghue, Katty said.'

'Well, Katty Kicart?' Colin McDaid turned to her. 'You knew the lad, then?'

Katty glanced at Finn. He gave the tiniest shake of his head, unseen by the policeman.

'No,' she said. 'They was none of them from these parts.'

'There's a Sean Donoghue lives over at Ballygortin,' said the policeman. 'Are you sure now, Katty, what you're saying?'

Katty pursed her lips as if to spit but thought better of it. 'None of them.'

Colin McDaid turned back to Kit. 'What made you think, sir, that that was the name?'

Kit made an angry sound. 'I damn well know it was.'

'But there are at least ten witnesses here to say that you misheard.' Finn folded his arms and returned Kit's look coolly.

Colin McDaid frowned. 'Did anyone in this room hear mention of a name like Sean Donoghue?'

'I was here all the time.' Father Deglan's eyes were watering with shock but he fixed his good one on the policeman without wavering. 'And I can say for certain that name was never spoken.'

Colin McDaid looked at the rest of us. We all murmured denials except the colonel who blew his nose hard.

Kit ground out his cigarette in Maud's ashtray, looking not so much angry as contemptuous. 'I must have made a mistake then.'

'In that case' – the policeman's tone was regretful – 'we'll pursue our inquiries for three persons unknown. I doubt we'll catch them. You know how it is round here, sir.' He gave Finn a reproachful look. 'Everyone's related and so dashed shy of talking. I'll put out a message on the radio. You're sure now no one was hurt?'

He glanced across the table at Flurry who was sitting patiently with his eyes closed and his fingers in his ears.

Liddy pulled his hands away. 'It's OK, you dolt. They've gone.'

'Is Eugene dead?' asked Flurry in a dispassionate voice.

'Finn,' called Violet in a faint voice. 'I've been so frightened. T-take me upstairs.'

'Nonsense!' Maud stood in the doorway. 'What you need is a stiff drink. Carry her into the drawing room, Finn, and I'll see to her.'

'Mr Macchuin says it was you, ma'am, that rang the alarm,' said the policeman, looking respectfully at Maud. 'That was quick thinking.'

'No doubt it seems so to you,' said Maud, with deeply unfair rudeness, turning her back on him. 'We are not all imbeciles. Come, Violet. And you, Basil.'

Violet held Finn's neck tightly and buried her face in his jersey as he carried her out. Flavia followed them with her mother's cigarettes and fur wrap.

'I've never been so scared in all my life!' said Jasmine in a squeaking voice. 'It's been perfect heaven, Bobbie, and I've loved coming to stay in a real castle and everything, but I think I'll go home now.' Her mouth was quivering.

'Poor Jazz. I'm so sorry. I was absolutely terrified myself. But we'll feel much better after a good night's sleep.'

'I couldn't spend another night here. I positively *could*n't! If someone would be an angel and run me to the station?'

'I'll do better than that,' said Kit. 'I'll drive you back to England. I was planning to leave soon, anyway. We can go tonight, if you like.'

'Oh, *thank* you! That is . . . Bobbie, you won't be hurt?'

'Not a bit.' I kissed her. 'Of course I'll miss you and you've been a marvellous help but I quite understand.'

'I'll go and pack at once. I'll only be half an hour.' Jasmine skipped out of the room, restored to cheerfulness by the prospect of escape.

'Are you all right, Flurry me boy?' asked Father Deglan kindly, seeing the child sitting so pale and immobile. 'Wouldn't it be a good thing now for us to offer up a prayer of gratitude for safe deliverance?'

Flurry got up hurriedly. 'I'm going to saw.'

He was almost mown down in the doorway by Timsy, Pegeen and Katty all rushing to leave the dining room. Liddy had run away some minutes before, presumably to find Danny. Only Kit and I were left, two Protestants, worse than heathens in Father Deglan's eyes.

'Arrah!' He was philosophical. 'When they need the Lord's help

588

they'll not be slow to ask for it. 'Tis always the way. I'll take me leave of Finn and go now. God bless you both.'

The priest hurried out. Kit and I gave each other nervous, insincere smiles.

'That was a shattering experience.' I leaned over the table to take a spoonful of canary pudding from the serving dish to calm myself.

'Interesting to see everybody's reactions, wasn't it? Rebellion is in the blood, sinew and bone of the Irish. I judged discretion to be the better part of valour. The only thing more terrifying than a psychopathic killer with a gun is a witless idiot with one.' Kit picked up his wine glass, fished out a scrap of plaster and drank. He made a face.

I wondered if he felt ashamed because he had not been a conspicuous hero like Maud and Father Deglan. 'I was in too much of a funk to be able to command a single thought,' I said with absolute truth. 'Have a clean glass.'

'Better not. I've got a long drive ahead.' He looked at his watch. 'We'll have to find a hotel in Dublin. I'll ring the Shelbourne before we leave.'

'It's goodbye then,' I said. 'Thank you so much for everything you've done for Curraghcourt.'

'I did it for you. But that's all over now, isn't it? You've finally made up your mind and decided against me. Of course I know why.'

'It's very good of you to take Jasmine back to England.'

He smiled. 'She's my reward for being a good boy and not making a fuss.'

'Oh, Kit! Don't!' I saw to my dismay that I had finished off the pudding.

'That's what you planned, isn't it?' He watched me blush. 'I know you so well, Bobbie.' He made a little bow. 'Thanks very much for the consolation prize.'

I was angry with Kit and even more with myself. He made me feel that I had been less than a friend to Jazzy. 'I've a good mind to take her to the ferry myself,' I said.

'Only you haven't a car. Sam's got the Morris and I imagine Finn will be spiriting Danny away in the Peugeot as soon as the coast's clear. I wouldn't advise going all the way to Dublin in the Land-Rover. The brakes are practically useless.'

'All right, then, I'll take her on Monday.'

'Don't be ridiculous. For one thing nothing you could say would persuade Jazzy to stay another three nights. And for another, I like

Jazzy and I'm not going to vent my spleen on her. I'll look after her, don't worry.'

We looked at each other, he smiling, me frowning.

'Are you going to say anything about what happened tonight?' I asked.

'I expect I'll dine out on it for the next few weeks.'

'That wasn't what I meant. Are you going to report to whoever you report to? British Intelligence? Is that the same thing as MI5?'

Kit stopped laughing. I saw various expressions flitting across his face – puzzlement, duplicity, annoyance – before finally it settled into rueful lines.

'It's a fair cop, guv. I suppose I owe this to Finn?'

'Yes.'

'I gave myself away, didn't I, talking about that border business? I realized as soon as I'd said it that I'd blundered. But he didn't bat an eyelid. I hoped I'd got away with it. So he did some research and let you into my little secret. He must have been delighted.'

'What do you mean?'

'Bit of a body-blow to the competition, wasn't it? Particularly as you've gone native. Patriotism wouldn't make any difference in your case.'

'Oh, Kit, that's all rubbish. I don't give a damn which side you're on. What matters to me . . .' I paused and poured myself a glass of wine. I still felt unsteady. 'You were on that boat to check up on me, weren't you? You'd been given orders to make sure that Burgo's inconvenient little peccadillo would have no further consequences for the Tory Party. It was all a lie, your professed friendship.'

'That's not true and you know it. All right, I was supposed to find out if I could whether Latimer was planning to do a runner with you. But that was all I was supposed to do. It was just a casual assignment.' He laughed. 'I nearly didn't make the ferry. If I hadn't you'd have sailed away to a new life, the government would have shrugged its shoulders and hoped for the best and we'd never have met. I came back here because I wanted to make sure you were all right. No one in England knows I've been at Curraghcourt with you. They've never even heard of the place. They think the Fitzgeorge Arms at Kilmuree is a useful outpost for picking up tips about IRA activities. I came back because I'd already fallen for you. From the moment dawn broke on deck I was on *your* side. I fell in love with you then, Bobbie. You believe me, don't you?'

I looked at him without saying anything. I had been very fond of

Kit. I felt pretty sure the espionage stuff was nothing more than boyish posturing, just the sort of thing my brother Oliver would have exulted in doing, had anyone thought of asking him. But I did mind being made a fool of. I could do that so effectively for myself.

'Oh, come on, Bobbie!' Kit came round the table and took hold of my free hand. 'Say you'll forgive me. I'm sorry to have made you angry. It doesn't mean anything really, compared with how I feel about you.' He took my glass from me and put it on the table and seized my other hand. 'Friends?'

He looked so contrite that I found I could no longer be angry. Suddenly I felt almost sorry that he was going. I remembered the times I had been so delighted to see him, how grateful I had been for his help. And still was. It was better to part amicably. 'Friends.' I smiled.

'Give me a goodbye kiss.'

I offered my cheek. He turned my face to kiss me on the lips. I felt his tongue pushing against my teeth. I thought of Violet and stopped feeling sad. There was an undignified struggle before I pulled away.

'Honestly, Kit, you seem to think of women as nothing more than sexual provender, to be binged on at every opportunity. Why don't you just pick one and concentrate on her instead of grazing at every kerbside patch of grass?'

He looked wounded. 'Considering that you and I have never been lovers I consider the accusation unfounded.'

'Here I am.' Jazzy came in wearing her fur coat, her hair fastened back with jewelled butterfly clips. She looked very pretty.

I detected a gleam in Kit's eye.

'What do you think of him?' I whispered to Jazzy as I picked up two of the four pieces of luggage stacked in the hall to carry them out to the car.

'Kit, you mean?'

'Shh!' I pointed to the sedan chair. He was inside, telephoning for a hotel reservation. 'Yes.'

'Gorgeous, darling! Just like Bing Crosby, only more hair. You're quite sure he's divorced?'

'As sure as I can be without having seen the judge's signature.'

'That's all right, then. Nothing, absolutely nothing' – Jazzy's voice rose higher with the force of her conviction – 'could persuade me to have anything to do with a married man ever again. Bobbie, I've done with them! I hope Teddy's having a horrible time with Lydia.

He used to grumble that she refused to make love in anything but the missionary position. Well, now he'll need physiotherapy on his elbows. I just hope they've got a padded headboard.'

The week at Curraghcourt seemed to have been a crash cure, I reflected as I waved away the little red sports car, at least for Jazz.

FIFTY

'I hope Danny caught the ferry,' Constance said for at least the tenth time.

It was six o'clock the following evening. She and I were tidying up the tea-room after the busiest day yet. Jazz and Kit had been much missed though Flavia had worked hard and charmed the visitors with the obvious pleasure she took in her role as waitress.

I scraped cream from the tablecloth before folding it to be washed. 'If Danny missed today's ferry, will there be another tomorrow?'

'I don't know. I've never been to France. I've only been to England twice.' Constance was replenishing the sugar bowls, rejecting the grains that had become stuck together and were brown with tea. 'Once, when I was a little girl, we went to visit Finn at school. It was a dreadful place, stuck in the middle of a moor where the wind blew at ninety miles an hour. The monks – it was a Catholic school naturally – were so solemn and severe by comparison with Irish ones. I think that school's one of the reasons Finn doesn't like the English. He pretends it's a political prejudice but I know he was unhappy there. But he did say the other day when we spoke on the telephone that it was a pity the Irish didn't have the energy and perseverance of the English. I think, though he didn't mention your name, that might have been a compliment to you.' When I didn't say anything she went on, 'Fancy people using spoons they've stirred with to help themselves to more sugar. I thought *I* was slovenly but I draw the line at that.'

'Would it be a good idea to have cube sugar instead of loose? More expensive to buy but less wasteful. But then I suppose everyone would help themselves with fingers. So unhygienic.' I sighed. 'I'm shattered. I absolutely *must* have a drink.'

'I'm afraid we've turned you into an alcoholic by overworking you. Personally I could scream with tiredness.'

'You'll have to advertise for help. When I go.'

Constance clapped her hands over her ears. 'I refuse to even think about it. Not now when I'm so happy. I won't let anything interfere with that for at least twenty-four hours.'

Constance smiled down at the lumpy sugar. She had been like a creature under enchantment all day, absorbed by the realization of the wonderful thing that had happened to her: the euphoria of love returned. Whenever she and Eugene came across each other, bearing trays of bread and butter or rolls of paper and pots of ink, they seemed to bound towards each other on springs, transported by joy.

'I can still hardly believe it. Eugene said he *never* loved Larkie as he loves me. He realized quite quickly after she ran off that it had all been a mistake, that he'd desired her because she was young and pretty, that was all. But he felt he'd made such a fool of himself it seemed better to go on pretending that it was a great romantic tragedy. He couldn't think how to leave off gracefully. Once he saw Larkie again he knew no one would go on believing he was in mourning for his lost love. He was forced to give up the pretence.'

'That shows a surprising self-knowledge,' I said, rather thoughtlessly. 'Surprising for a man, I mean,' I added quickly.

'Oh, yes. Anyway, he thought I'd never care for him. He felt he wasn't good enough for me.' Constance sighed tenderly. 'He's such a dear, modest man. He was convinced he was fated to love unrequited. He comforted himself with the idea that torment was more productive for writing poetry. He says he may never be able to compose another line but it'll be worth it to know I love him. Wasn't that adorable of him?'

'Adorable. You know, Con, I think Eugene's more likely to be successful with drawing than with poetry. I expect he'll say he writes only to please himself but generally artists want to communicate, don't they? And in my experience they all want praise. When I go, the membership of his fan club will be halved immediately. And Gaelic's a bit of an acquired taste outside Ireland. Perhaps even inside it. I think he draws exceptionally well.'

'Do you? Really?' Constance looked astonished, then thoughtful. 'Well, you may have something there. Perhaps I ought to push him – gently – in that direction. As a matter of fact' – Constance reddened – 'he did say he'd like to draw me with no clothes on. He wants to worship my body.' She looked amazed. 'Can you believe it! I've never taken my clothes off in front of a man. Even when we were little Granny wouldn't let Finn and me share the bath in case it gave him what she called "thoughts". I'm afraid he had them anyway, though not about me, of course.'

'But, Con, surely you've had lovers?'

'Never.' She looked across the room at me as I emptied dying primroses and fetid water into a bucket. 'You have to remember, we didn't swing in Connemara as you did in England in the sixties. I had romantic fantasies about some of the boys I used to meet at parties but they weren't interested in me. I suppose they thought I wouldn't let them.' She sighed. 'And they were probably right. Bobbie?'

'Yes?'

'Eugene wants me to . . . go to bed with him.' Constance gazed into the middle distance while pouring sugar from a blue bag into a bowl. 'Granny said sex was so awful only a woman with a diseased mind could find it pleasurable. And that men always despised women who did. But in books and films the suggestion is that women enjoy it like mad.'

'With the right person it *can* be madly enjoyable. But don't rush into it before you feel ready.'

'I *do* want to, like anything. Only as soon as I try to imagine what it might be like I see Father Deglan's shocked face and hear the voice of Sister Veronica John talking about sex outside marriage being a terrible sin. Damn! Now I've made a mess with the sugar.'

I threw her a cloth. 'Speaking for myself I don't think it's a sin, married or not.'

'You don't?'

'Absolutely not.'

'Well, then, neither will I. I want to give myself to Eugene completely, to prove how much I love him. And if it does turn out to be a sin after all, I shall still feel it was worth it.'

It was on the tip of my tongue to mention contraception but I thought better of it for fear of putting her off. By the law of the land she and Eugene were prohibited from acquiring condoms legally and it was unlikely that they would be prepared to undergo the embarrassment of bargaining for them on the black market. I made a mental note to send her a box of something for the bedside cupboard as soon as I was back in England.

'Poor Liddy!' Constance abandoned her attempts to clean up the sugar and threw the cloth into the basket with the others to be washed. 'She'll be so sad when she gets home. How I sympathize with lovers who can't be together! I do hope Danny caught the ferry.'

I looked at my watch. 'Shouldn't Finn and Liddy be back by now?'

'They *are* late.' Constance looked worried. 'Of course they can't ring to let us know what's happened because the telephone hasn't been mended yet. Finn will be exhausted, poor boy. It was so good of him to take Danny. I'm prejudiced, I expect, because he's my brother, but I *do* think, despite his faults, Finn's an exception among men. I hope he and Violet will be happy. Of course, they're not very well suited: he's so cerebral and she's so physical. He thinks about everything and she about nothing – except flirting and being admired.' I wondered then if she knew about Violet and Kit and, if so, how. 'Poor girl, I mustn't be unkind. She's suffered so much. One thing I do know, she adores Finn and always has done. If he can only manage to play up to her a little. And not get sarcastic when she says silly things. You appreciate Finn better now, don't you, Bobbie? I know he can be grumpy but there are so many things to worry him. I wish I could feel that you really liked him.'

Again I found myself on the point of telling Constance everything. I hesitated, wondering if confiding in a third person would be a relief or an added complication and then Flavia came into the tea-room and the moment was lost.

'Bobbie, I've just been up to see the cats and there's one inside the chimney, miaowing like anything. I think she's stuck.'

'Oh dear! It's Dervla. She was up there last night, sitting on a ledge. I think Scornach Mór frightened her. I was sure she'd come down on her own.'

'I tried standing on a chair to reach her but I'm not tall enough.'

'I'll cook some fish and you can take it up to her. She won't refuse to come down then, I'm sure.'

We delayed dinner for half an hour and then went ahead without Finn and Liddy. Flurry was unusually talkative, excited because he had taken delivery of the first bundle of rails from Thady O'Kelly. He wanted to go out after dinner and start laying them but this Constance would not allow.

'Have a good night's sleep then you can get up early tomorrow and start as soon as it's light.'

'All right.' Flurry got up.

'Finish your pudding, darling.'

Flurry ate it at express speed standing up. 'Can I leave the table now?'

'What's the hurry?'

'You said to get a good night's sleep. I'm going to do that.'

Constance sighed. There were no half-measures with Flurry. 'Don't forget to do your teeth.'

Flurry felt in his pocket. 'I forgot. Thady gave me this note for you.'

Constance looked pleased when she had read the scrap of paper. 'It's from Thady's wife. She wants to know if there's a job for her here. What a stroke of luck! She's giving up working at the school because the children are so cheeky. Now, you two.' She looked at Flavia and Flurry. 'Mind you're polite to Mrs O'Kelly. We don't want her saying you're as bad as the Kilmuree children.'

'Is she a teacher?' I asked.

'No, much better than that. She's the school cook. We could put her in charge of the tea-room, couldn't we?'

For a moment I felt relieved that Constance would have reliable help when I had gone. Then came a pang of misery, imagining them managing perfectly well without me.

'I wish F-finn would come – back,' said Violet. 'The house is so d-dull without him.'

After everything had been washed up and put away we all went to bed early, anticipating a long night of sleep and a leisurely rising. The house was closed to the public the next day in accordance with the third commandment which instructed us to refrain from servile works on the Sabbath. I took several tins of cats' meat and a jug of milk up to my room and found Flavia there. Having had no success before dinner, despite the fish, she was trying again to coax Dervla down from the chimney with whistles and kissing noises. I stood on the chair and reached up as far as I could. Tantalizingly I felt fur against my fingertips but could not get hold of it.

'Perhaps if I put some books on the chair?' I looked around the bedroom. Only the copy of Yeats's poems lay on my bedside table, too precious to be stood on.

'I'll get some.'

Flavia ran downstairs. I climbed back on the chair to woo Dervla with soft words. Just as I was beginning to wonder where Flavia had got to, a voice I recognized immediately said, 'That cat only understands Gaelic, you know.'

I came down rather fast, bringing plenty of soot with me and banging my elbow. While Finn, with the advantage of extra inches, rescued Dervla easily, I stood wiping my hands and dusting my clothes, feeling vaguely foolish.

'Ungrateful animal,' he said as Dervla hissed and sprang away from him to disappear through the open window.

'What happened to you? Did Danny catch the ferry? We thought you'd be back earlier.'

'It was delayed by several hours. So I took a room in a pub and the three of us spent the time trying to sleep on a double bed with me in the middle as chaperon. Yes, he's gone. Poor boy. Half excited and half terrified. Such is the general condition of youth, though, I seem to remember.'

'And how is Liddy?'

'She stopped crying after about five hours.'

'You look tired.'

'You look sooty.'

'Where's Flavia?'

'Gone to console her big sister. I told them both to go to bed.'

He was standing with his hands on his hips. Through a hole in his dark blue jersey I could see a smaller hole in his pale blue shirt. His chin was shadowed with a day's growth of dark beard. He was standing close enough for me to put out my hand and touch him. Oh, how I wanted to! I clasped both hands together to prevent myself doing anything so foolish.

'Have you recovered from last night's adventure?' he asked.

'Oh. Yes. I was terrified at the time but I'm all right now. Are you going to say anything to anyone about Terry?'

'No one was hurt. I prefer to let sleeping dogs lie.' When I did not say anything he added, 'I expect it seems strange to you that I allowed three men, one of them armed, to break into my house, threaten its inhabitants, and then get away without recourse to the law.'

'It does seem odd, yes. But I long ago stopped expecting to understand Irish ways by looking at them from an English point of view.'

'The difference is that England hasn't had a civil war since the seventeenth century. Our last was in living memory. During the Troubles people went crazy with the thrill of violence, father against son, brother against brother. They forgot what they were fighting for. And there's been an aftermath of hatred and mistrust that's continued to this day and kept us from moving forward. There was talk of civil war again four years ago. We *can't* let it happen again. I don't want to do anything to inflame the situation. Accusations bring arrests, imprisonment. There are reprisals, then counter-reprisals; whole families are caught up in misery. I don't believe Terry intended to shoot any of us. His mouth is bigger than his courage and he frightened himself badly. As for the other two, I'll have a word with Sean Donoghue myself.'

'I wish I could understand why there's so much hatred in a country that's so beautiful and where the people are so warm and generous. But I can see that if you've been colonized and treated unfairly by another nation, then you might think it your duty to resist. And the IRA, who seem like monsters to the English, are your own people. Your next-door neighbour, your cousin, your parish priest even.'

He nodded. 'You must always put politics into its historical context. Central to the issue is a widespread feeling of ancestral grievance. Two classes, one with hundreds of thousands of acres, the other with scrapes among rocks.'

'Yet we have the same unfair social divisions in England. Since I've been here I've sometimes asked myself why English people from slum dwellings haven't got together to burn down mansions and castles.'

'Perhaps they have more sense.' Finn laughed. 'Three hundred big houses burned in Ireland during the civil war. But probably twice as many farmsteads, cottages and hovels belonging to members of the IRA were burned in reprisal by the Black-and-Tans. Sometimes when I sit in my library here looking out on to the woods and fields that are mine and think of Timsy, who by the merest accident of birth has inherited nothing but a place by my fire and a right to clean my shoes, I feel ashamed.'

'You could give him a patch of ground perhaps?' I suggested hesitantly.

Finn looked amused. 'As a matter of fact, I gave him the lodge, which wasn't derelict then, and half an acre round it as a twenty-first birthday present. He was very grateful, I remember. He did live there for a few months but when the winter came he moved back into this house without a word. So you see, an easy conscience isn't to be had for the asking.'

I could not help laughing at this. For a moment we shared the joke, more relaxed together than we had ever been. Then a look came into his eye that was alarming and I have no doubt that it was also in mine. My heart leaped into my throat and beat there, until I could hardly breathe. I dropped my eyes and he turned away.

'So this is your room. I haven't been up here for years.' He looked about him. 'It's rather primitive, isn't it? What possessed Constance? You ought to have had somewhere more comfortable to sleep.' He pointed to the canopy, as usual sagging with the weight of its dozing occupants. 'What on earth's that?'

'Cats. It's a *lovely* room.' My voice sounded odd, I thought, unnatural, the result of tension, probably. 'The view. The mountains.'

'But you can see mountains from every room in the house.' He went to stare out of one of the windows though it was completely dark outside. 'You ought to have had better treatment from us. We've made use of you. Taken you for granted.'

'Have you?' I said idiotically.

He shook his head. 'No. Not a bit, really. I'm just . . . making conversation.'

'I see.'

'It's going to be a cold night. The stars are bright. There's a full moon.'

'Is there?' I tried to pull myself together. 'That's another good thing about this room. Having four windows means you always get a good view of the moon whatever the time of year. And it seems much brighter in Ireland. I suppose that's the lack of pollution.' I remembered how often in the last few months I had looked up at the great silver globe and imagined it shining down on Dublin.

'It's easy to forget that the moon itself doesn't emit light. Moonshine is merely a reflection of sunlight. The moon's a lifeless, lightless rock but every culture in the world as far as I know has invested it with mythology and symbolism. The Egyptians believed the moon was the left eye of a great celestial hawk, whose right eye was the sun. Strange, isn't it, that we try to interpret the world by making up elaborate fables? I used to wonder about that during Mass, as a boy. And yet' – he put his hands in his pockets and looked down – 'there are times when truth and logic can be cold, comfortless things.'

'The beauty is real. One can always be comforted by that.' I heard something too heartfelt in my tone. I tried to laugh. 'And, at least if you can see it, it means it isn't raining.'

He turned from the window.

'Ah, yes, you've had the full Celtic baptism by immersion. You'll never be able to forget the drumming of water against the window, the squelch beneath your feet, the damp that gets into your clothes, almost under your skin.'

'I shan't forget it.'

'You're going then,' he said, after a pause.

'I must.'

'I'll be leaving for Dublin tomorrow morning. Early. I won't come back until you've gone.'

I felt a sick dread steal over my body. He walked away from the window and came to stand in front of me. I was afraid I might be going to cry. I gritted my teeth and dug my nails into the palms of my hands. It did not seem to help much.

'So it's goodbye,' he said. 'I'm not going to try and thank you for what you've done. If I began . . .' He bit his lip. 'I'm no good at this sort of thing.'

'What sort of thing?'

'Oh, I'm not very polite, you know.' He looked angry, suddenly. It was an expression familiar to me. I felt reassured. I had been disconcerted by this polite conversation-making stranger. 'I ought to say how good you've been.' His voice became sarcastic. 'Saving my family from ruin, single-handedly restoring my house and fortunes, all that sort of thing. Instead I want to curse you for being a tiresome, interfering English girl, who's cut up my peace, turned my life upside down, obsessed my thoughts night and day, killed sleep, tortured me every waking moment . . . Bobbie, God help me! You've practically destroyed me!'

He seized my shoulders and shook me until my teeth rattled then pulled me into his arms. We held each other as tightly as though demon hordes were coming to wrench us apart; as indeed they were, in a sense. 'Bobbie,' he whispered. 'I can't make myself do this. I can't make myself walk away as though you were not more important to me than life itself.' He kissed my forehead, my cheeks, my lips. The stubble on his chin grazed my face painfully but I would willingly have endured the pain for eternity just to have that moment.

'Don't walk – away then,' I said with what breath remained from the violence of his embrace. 'At least not yet.'

We kissed again. I put everything I had into that kiss, in case it was all that was left to me of happiness.

After a while he drew back. 'You know what I want.'

'I want it too.'

Finn went to the door and turned the key in the lock. 'You're quite sure?'

For answer I pulled off my jersey.

He smiled. 'You English. So intrepid, so direct, so certain. We shall never be free from the Old Enemy. At least I never shall be now.'

We kissed again long and wonderingly.

601

'Darling!' He drew away to look at me. 'Even now I can't believe
. . . I've tried so hard not to think of this, and ended up thinking
of it all the time.'

'I know . . . I *know*. Seeing you, hearing your voice, telling myself
it mustn't be . . . like shutting out light and air and warmth . . .
everything I need to live.'

Suddenly we were tearing off our clothes as if we had finally
convinced ourselves that what we had both wanted so much and for
so long was within the bounds of possibility. Before I could pull off
my jeans he picked me up and carried me over to the bed. That
made me think of Violet but I pushed the idea of her away. For a
little while he was mine alone.

Whatever priests say, there *is* perfect happiness on earth. I experienced it then as we told each other over and over again how much
we loved each other, as he joined his body to mine and we climbed
to paradise.

Afterwards, as I lay with my head on his arm, I asked him when
he had first begun to dislike me less.

'That came as a great shock. Of course the minute I saw you I
wanted to do this' – he laid his hand on my breast – 'and this' – he
moved it to my thigh. 'But that made me dislike you even more
because, you know, I felt you had power over me. I disliked you
particularly because I was so sure you'd never dream of letting me
do it. So cool, so superior, so unfriendly, so – English, in a word.'

'You, of course, were full of warmth and humanity.'

'Ah, I was a bastard, wasn't I? You made me aware of how unhappy
I was. Your beauty, your grace, your style and what I knew of you
from the newspaper reports: you seemed to represent a world in
which people enjoyed themselves, took what they wanted and didn't
have to pay the price. There was I, bitter, full of self-pity, with an
unmanageable house in a rundown demesne, three children about
whom I felt constantly guilty, a mistress I no longer desired, a wife
. . . whom I thought would be better dead. You know, I actually
wished sometimes that Violet would die. Does that shock you?'

He moved himself a little down the bed so he could look directly
into my eyes. I stroked the black whiskers on his chin. 'No. Not at
all. It must have been terrible to have her there but . . . not there.'

'I felt guilty. Guilty because I was able to see and feel and walk
and talk, while she . . .'

'I understand. Even though it wasn't your fault.'

He shifted again to stare up at the canopy. 'Do those cats ever

602

take it into their heads to jump down unannounced? I feel a little vulnerable imagining their claws . . . No, it certainly wasn't my fault. Until I went to see Violet in the hospital, after they carried her off the ferry more dead than alive, I hadn't set eyes on her for six months. And for the six months before that there'd been only the briefest of meetings when she came to Curraghcourt to see the children.'

'*What?*' I sat up on my elbow to look at him. Black shadows lay across his throat. As he moved his head to return my look the right-hand side of his face fell into darkness.

'I'm surprised Constance didn't tell you. I suppose she thought it would be disloyal. Violet ran off with Anthony Molesworth, the colonel's brother, six years ago.'

'She *left* you?'

'I'm flattered that you sound so flabbergasted. Yes. She left me with three young children. Liddy was eleven, Flavia and Flurry were three and five respectively.'

'But why? *Why?*' That Violet had willingly given up what I would have sacrificed everything for seemed a mystery beyond all understanding.

Finn laughed. 'Violet gets bored easily. She hates bogs and mountains and rain. Like all women.'

'Not all.'

'You've been here less than a year. If you had to spend the rest of your life at Curraghcourt—'

I put my finger on his lips. 'If I had to live on a tiny island with one tree and eat bananas three times a day and drink rainwater from my shoe I'd do it gladly as long as you were there.'

Finn looked at me with softened eyes. 'Thank you for that, my darling. Well, Violet isn't made of such stern stuff as you. Life is to be pleasure, that's all, no matter what the consequences. Of course, I'm prejudiced. Take no notice of that. I stopped hating Violet long ago. A part of me was only too glad when she went. The marriage was a mistake from the beginning. I was just as much to blame. I didn't want to marry her but she was pregnant with Liddy and I was pretty sure it was my baby. We had no ideas in common. Violet's never read a book in her life and can't see why anyone might want to. Once I knew she had slept with other men I no longer desired even her body. Violet likes sex. It doesn't matter with whom.'

I remembered Violet and Kit. 'You mean she's a nymphomaniac?'

Finn shrugged a naked shoulder which I bent my head to kiss. 'Is a nymphomaniac someone who wants sex more often than you do?'

he said. 'I don't know. It was as hard for her as it was for me. Perhaps harder. She tried, poor girl, to be faithful and I tried to love her. Flavia and Flurry represent our attempts to repair the marriage. But she couldn't keep away from other men. I learned not to care.'

I wanted to weep when I heard that, imagining a younger Finn, hurt, unhappy, but I restrained myself. A man doesn't want to be cried over when he has just made love to you.

'So she left you. Why isn't she with Anthony Molesworth now?'

'What would he have done with a comatose girlfriend? He likes racing and hunting and parties. In the circumstances Violet would have been something of a drag. And, to be fair, Anthony hasn't any money. He lives in a small flat in Dublin. Basil, being the eldest son, has the estate and what little money the family has left. When the convent that had been looking after Violet closed Basil offered to pay for a nursing home but it would have bankrupted him if she'd lived more than a couple of years. The obvious place for Violet was here. She was – is – the children's mother.'

'I don't think it was obvious. I think it was . . . noble. It's why I love you. One of the reasons. If there are reasons. Constance is right, you *are* good.'

'Constance said that?' Finn laughed again. 'No, my fierce little *cailin*, not good but weak. When faced with an insoluble problem I take no action. I let things take their own course. It's the Irish way.'

'You didn't have to take in Maud as well. Or Eugene.'

'I've always been fond of my mother-in-law. As one is fond of a buffeting wind on a north shore. We understand each other. And she was adrift. No money, no husband, effectively no child. If she could stand the draughts, the damp and the appalling food – that was before you came, my brave girl – I could put up with her. As for Eugene, well, he's not a man I love but I don't hate him either and my sister seems to think he's an angel briefly visiting earth.'

'They'll probably marry.'

'Will they? Well, I needn't fear the abrupt removal of my chatelaine, that's one thing. Eugene knows where he's well off.'

'I think he'll make her happy.'

'Good.'

'You haven't answered my question. When did you begin to like me – a little?'

'When I saw how much effort you were putting into things my idea of you began to change. You worked so hard, looking after the children and the animals as well as the house and the garden. I could

see how strange, how intractable, sometimes plain awful the circumstances were, so different from what you were used to, but you struggled on. That made it difficult for me to go on thinking of you as
– forgive me – an arrogant, spoilt beauty. I've never known a woman
like you. So determined, so anxious to do the right thing, so . . .
admirable. I was compelled to respect you. I fought against it, naturally. And then, there was that moment . . . Yes, that was it. You
remember Lughnasa? You came into Violet's room. I was sitting on
the window seat. You didn't know I was there. You were so kind to
her, talking to her, feeding her. So beautiful, so generous, so loving.
It was that moment when I felt your power steal over me.' He kissed
me. 'Yes, I fell in love with you then, though I wouldn't admit it to
myself.' He kissed my eyebrows, my nose, my chin and finally my
lips. 'I fear I'm always going to love you.'

'I wish I deserved it. The truth is that I'm horribly bossy and I
adore the feeling of power that comes from imprinting myself on
things. Curraghcourt has been the answer to a dream. It wasn't saint-
liness that motivated me but the satisfaction of putting things right.
Sheer egotism. It's actually a character defect.'

'Then we're both in love with an illusion, a coinage of the brain.
Is that why I feel as though I would happily go mad and be carried
raving from the room if only I could remember making love to you
for ever and have everything else blotted out?'

'Let's go mad together.' I returned his kiss. 'It's the only way. I
don't want to be sane and sensible and go on living without you.'

'Well, then.' He ran his hand from my armpit down to my hip.
'Let me love you, darling, *darling* Bobbie, while I have you.'

We made love again, more fiercely than before because a horrible, cold certainty that this happiness would not be ours much longer
began to intrude itself however desperately we pushed it away.

'I love you,' I said for the thousandth time that night, as we lay
quiet in each other's arms, later. 'I'll always love you.' But he made
no answer. His slow breathing told me he was asleep.

I woke once towards dawn. I remembered everything immediately
and sat up to lean over him, to watch him sleeping, to learn every
line and angle of his face so that I should never forget it. Then I
dozed. Dreaming of him, seeing him, tasting him, feeling his body
inside mine. When I woke again I found his face was turned towards
me and he was looking at me intently.

'What time is it?' I asked.

'Seven o'clock.'

I felt tears threaten but managed to keep them back. 'You ought to go now.'

'Yes. Don't get up. I want to think of you, lying there, so beautiful, when I'm on the road to Dublin, feeling as though my heart's been torn out of me . . . Oh, Bobbie!' he groaned and rested his head on my arm, 'Say you'll stay! I can't send Violet away. There isn't anywhere for her to go. And I can't divorce her because of the laws of this strange backward-looking land. But you and I could live here together and no one will know. And if they do, so what?'

'Every cell, every atom of my body wants to say yes to that.' I felt as though I was struggling in the grip of a terrible illness. 'And half my mind. But let's look into the future a little. When I imagine Flavia's face as she discovers that Violet is wretched because of me, I feel . . . I feel ashamed. What good is experience unless we learn from it? I know what it's like to be the secret part of a man's life. The guilt. The jealousy. I can't bear to think of Violet and the children hating me. I love your children. I love them for their own dear selves as well as because they're yours. And I'm very fond of Violet. When I see her talking and laughing I feel so proud of my part in that. She needs you so desperately. I don't want to be the reason that your marriage fails again, when this time it might work.' I thought of Kit and Violet then but stifled the sneaking, ignoble impulse that prompted me to save myself by telling him. It was not a lifebelt, anyway. If Finn had been there she would not have been interested in Kit. And Finn had not been there because of me. 'When your children have grown up, with the example before them of two people who worked hard to make a life together, you'll know I'm right. Sex isn't everything; nor, I think, love. It's doing the decent thing, putting the interests of other – innocent – people before one's own. A good conscience is a continual feast. I can't remember who said that but I know it's true. And you, of all men, will feel that. I couldn't bear to see you disillusioned with me. I don't want us ever to look at each other and feel . . . regret.'

'You've decided then. We must part.' Something of bitter weariness in his voice, of the man who yet again faces what he hates made me hesitate. But it was possible that Finn and Violet might yet be happy. I made myself think of Burgo. I had convinced myself then that the world was well lost for love and it had turned out not to be true. I had been thoroughly punished for my selfishness. This time I must get it right.

Finn was silent for a while, staring up at the canopy that bulged and rose here and there with the pressure of paws and haunches. 'I haven't much to offer any woman, encumbered as I am. I fear' – he screwed up his eyes as though in pain – 'you might come to hate me if I could only give you half-measures. Very well. We'll do the decent thing. Behave like good citizens. What the hell, I'm nearly forty-one. Half my life is gone and a fine mess I've made of it. Probably one cares less about one's own happiness as one gets older.'

'I shall always care about your happiness.' I turned his face towards me so I could look into his eyes. 'Always. Whatever you're doing, whether you're elated or in despair, I shall care. I won't know but I'll go on hoping that you're happy.'

He took a lock of my hair, wound it round his finger and pressed it to his lips. 'You're only twenty-seven. There's time for you to build something marvellous for yourself. A good job in which you can use that sharp brain, that instinct for beauty, all that remarkable will-power. A husband. Children. A place in society where you're honoured and respected.'

I smiled. 'That all sounds rather old-fashioned to me. I don't know that those things matter very much. If at all.'

'I'm an old-fashioned man, I suppose. This is an old-fashioned place.'

'It's another world. And it will almost kill me to leave it. But I know it's the right thing to do.'

'Could we meet sometimes? Just so I can be sure I've remembered you right?'

'Perhaps. After a long time. When we've got over missing each other.'

'As long as that? I'll be grey and toothless and in a wheelchair. But even then I'll still want you.' He gave a shuddering sigh. 'Let me make love to you one last time.'

I pressed myself to the length of his body, tried to lose myself in desire, felt again the sensation of wild joy . . . that this time turned to grief before it had ebbed.

Finn kissed me gently and then slid out from the bedclothes. I memorized his body as he dressed, determined to forget nothing. The scar on his rib cage – I would never know what caused it – the way the hair grew on the back of his neck, the breadth of his shoulders, the graceful hands. He buttoned his shirt, pulled on his disgraceful old corduroys, worn smooth on the knees by rough usage, picked up his jersey, gave me a last, long look and went to the door. I was hanging on to tears until he should be through it. He turned the key in the lock. He was going out of my life. The pressure on my throat was intense. He fought with the door handle.

'I can't undo the bloody thing,' he said. 'It just turns round in my hand. What are you laughing at?'

'It's despair. I know what's happened. The screw's fallen out on the other side. We're locked in.'

I got out of bed and ran over to rattle the handle, ineffectively.

He laughed too and held me, in my naked state, tightly against him. 'God! I want to make love all over again. This is cruel of fate. I don't know how many more times I'm capable of tearing myself away.'

'What are we going to do?'

'We could hammer on the door? Shout from the window. Ring Scornach Mór.'

'And have the fire brigade break in to find you locked in my bedroom. That would give them something to talk about in Kilmuree.'

I started to throw on my clothes.

He folded his arms and leaned against the door. 'Is it impolite of me to stare? Because I'm going to, anyway.'

'Put your mind on our predicament.'

'You're asking too much of any man, let alone a man who's so desperately in love.'

'Think, darling, do!' I urged. 'Can't you do something masculine and splendid with a nail file?'

I stopped at the sound of knocking.

'Bobbie?' It was Flavia's voice. 'Can I come in? I've got something for you.'

Finn and I looked at each other, our eyes signalling dismay.

'Just a minute, sweetheart,' I called while making frantic gestures to Finn to get under my bed. 'I'm in the middle of dressing. Won't be a minute. Just putting my jersey on. Com-ing,' I said as I saw Finn's foot disappear beneath the valance. 'I think the screw's fallen out again,' I called through the door. 'Can you find it?'

A moment's silence before Flavia said, 'Here it is. Hang on a mo.' Then the handle turned and Flavia came in. 'It was lucky I came up, wasn't it? I thought Timsy mended it.'

'Not well enough it seems. It *was* lucky.'

'Did Daddy get Dervla down all right?'

'Yes, straight away. What is it you've got for me?' I added, seeing that she held a piece of paper in her hand.

608

'The postman brought it. It's a telegram. Is it something important?'

'Probably not. The telephone still isn't working, that's all. I expect it's the colonel wanting to know if we're all right after our ordeal.' I tore open the envelope.

'Where's Wee Willie Winkie?' Flavia looked around for the white kitten that was her favourite though she tried to be stern with herself about loving them all equally. 'There he is! Come here and be stroked, you bad little cat!'

The kitten ran over to the bed and disappeared beneath the valance. In a trice Flavia was on her knees beside the bed stretching out her hand to find him. She gave an exclamation of astonishment.

'Daddy! What on earth are you doing under Bobbie's bed?'

'I came up to – make sure there were no cats up the chimney. Then the door blew shut. I was looking for the screw.'

It was not bad for split-second thinking.

Flavia began to giggle hysterically. 'You do look funny lying there. Come out. Laughing a lot always gives me a stitch. Mummy wants you to bring her down specially early.'

Finn crawled out and wiped his hands on his shirt. 'I found several dust-balls under there, Miss Norton.' He shook his finger at me. 'Make sure it doesn't happen again.'

Flavia bent double holding her side. 'Stop it, Daddy! I'm in agony! Don't you want to know why you're to bring Mummy down early?'

He smiled down at her. 'Tell me.'

'She wants to show you her walking. She managed last night to take two steps with Granny's sticks. Isn't it *wonderful*? Aren't you so terrifically glad?' She pressed her face against her father's stomach.

Over Flavia's head Finn sent me a look of love blent with hopelessness.

'I've got to go home,' I said. 'At once. Today. My father's had a heart attack.'

FIFTY-ONE

It was perhaps a good thing that the leave-taking was necessarily brief. I went up to Maud's room first. Violet cried so much and clung to me so tightly that my conscience was only appeased by the knowledge that I was about to plunge myself into hell on her behalf.

'I'm so grateful to you, Bobbie! Thank you, thank you!' she wept. 'I'll miss you so badly! And you haven't seen me walk!'

'Don't delay her,' said Maud. 'She has a long journey ahead. Go, Bobbie. I'll see to her.'

She stood over Violet, bidding her wipe her eyes and stop behaving like a waterspout. I wondered whether I should shake Maud's hand or even kiss her but before I could make up my mind she had shuffled away. 'I don't expect your father has much wrong with him.' She turned her back to me. 'Men always make a ridiculous fuss about nothing. But you'll be glad to get back to civilization. I suppose *we* have Constance's stew to look forward to. Goodbye.'

I went down to the kitchen. Pegeen threw her apron over her head and cried even more than Violet. 'May the good Lord bless you, love you and keep you,' she wailed. 'Who'll do everything now?'

'Mrs O'Kelly's coming to help,' I said.

'Is it Thady O'Kelly's Nellie?' asked Katty. She sniffed. 'Bejasus! How are the mighty fallen! *She*'ll not like scrubbing and dusting and cleaning that fecking separator!'

'Goodbye, Katty.' I offered her my hand. 'I shall always remember you with affection.'

To my surprise tears began to trickle down Katty's ash-speckled cheeks and she set up a wail that must have rivalled the Irish cry in volume as well as sincerity.

In the hall, where the rest of the household was gathered, Flurry shook my hand several times, hard. 'Thank you for helping me with the railway. I'm *very* sorry you're going.'

I bent and kissed him on the cheek. 'Goodbye, darling Flurry. I know you hate being kissed but I'm so fond of you.'

He straightened his spectacles, looked not actually displeased and said, 'That's all right.'

'My best wishes go with you, Bobbie.' Eugene stepped forward. 'May I?' He kissed both my cheeks with courtly grace, then seized my hand and squeezed it until my blood supply was in danger of being cut off. 'Very sad to see you go. Very.'

'Thank you. Now, Flavia, darling.' I addressed the top of her head as she had thrown her arms around me and was weeping. 'You'll make me cry too if you go on like that. Look after the cats and the dogs and make sure Timsy milks Niamh properly.' I turned up her face so that I could kiss her. 'I'm relying on you.'

Flavia, her eyes swollen with tears, nodded. 'I promise faithfully.'

'Goodbye, Liddy dear.' Liddy clung briefly to my neck. 'We'll have that week in London as soon as humanly possible.'

Liddy's dark glasses hid most of her expression. 'I bloody well wish you weren't going.' She sloped away, nibbling her fingernails.

I looked at Constance. I had to bite my bottom lip to stop it from quivering.

'Well now, Bobbie,' she said in a determinedly cheerful voice, her soft eyes bright. 'We can't have you going away thinking we're all a lot of cry-babies. I hope you'll change your mind and come back as soon as your father's better. I'm not going to try to tell you what your being here's meant to me because that would upset me and we want to end on a note of uplift. So, here's to a safe journey, darling . . . Ohhh!'

We both cried heartily as we embraced. An impatient tooting came from the other side of the gatehouse. 'That's Finn now getting angry. You'd better go, *dear* Bobbie. Write to me the minute you can. I won't come out.' Constance put her handkerchief to her eyes. 'I'm a fool, I know, but I can't bear to see you driving away.'

'Goodbye, dearest Con. Thank you for everything.'

She buried her face and flapped her hand. 'Go! Go!' she sobbed.

'Oh dear,' said Finn when he saw my face. 'As bad as that?'

I nodded and got into the ancient Peugeot. I turned to wave goodbye to Flavia who was standing by the ticket table in the gatehouse, her face contorted, her chest heaving. I waved goodbye to the house, bathed now in a freak ray of sunlight, old and beautiful and infinitely dear. We drove by the walled garden. I prevented myself from breaking down altogether by reciting the alphabet backwards.

I had got as far as O when a figure broke from the trees and came running alongside the car. 'Goodbye, Miss Bobbie,' called Timsy, leaping energetically over ruts and bushes and stones to keep up with us. 'Goodbye, you lovely creature.' He waved his cap as tears flowed from his blue eyes into his mouth, round with emotion. He ran for half a mile behind us and stopped just short of the gate where he lay down in the road to recover from the unaccustomed exertion.

'Will he be all right?' I was more grateful to Timsy than he would ever know for making my last sight of the demesne comical as well as sad.

'Timsy's the one person I never worry about. We'd all do well to take some lessons in living from him.'

'If anyone had told me ten months ago as I was coming along this road, lit only by the odd burst of moonlight, soaking wet, in the donkey cart with Timsy lying dead drunk among the cabbages, that I'd actually be truly sorry to say goodbye to him I'd have thought they were pitifully insane.'

'Well, that's the old Irish charm for you. Thoroughly fraudulent, just like Timsy. Look at those mountains!' The sunlight had turned the rock to silver and the gorse to gold. 'However often I see them, they seem to me one of the most beautiful sights on this earth.'

'Didn't your family own them once?'

'Yes. But only by a flight of fancy. No one could own them really. They comfort me mightily. One's petty concerns shrink to nothing before them.'

'Tell me about you as a little boy – what it was like to be brought up here.'

I folded my coat and put it over the handbrake so I could lean across and rest my head against him, my hand on his knee. He described playing in the woods and building camps and hunting on his pony, Duff. 'You wouldn't like that, I know. You'd be sorry for the fox. Well, so am I now, but then I never thought of it. Hunting is so much a part of the Irish way of life.'

'Only above a certain social level. I don't suppose people like Timsy go hunting, do they?'

'Ah, now, you mustn't take issue with me over the state of the world. Isn't that true in England as well?'

'Yes,' I admitted. 'Actually the division is greater if anything.'

'Let's not go too far the other way. Your trouble is you're a help-

less victim of fairy glamour. You see Ireland through rose-tinted spectacles. You'll be saying next you like drisheen and rain.'

'That black-pudding stuff? No!' I shuddered. 'But there is something extraordinarily beautiful about the rain when it slants across
the landscape and sparkles in every imaginable colour. I'm hopelessly
in love with some things Irish, that's true.'

He bent his head to kiss the top of mine. 'Tell me about your life
in England. I want to know everything.'

We talked about ourselves happily for two hours. This unexpected
time alone together seemed such a bonus, a blessing, that without
actually admitting to it, we conspired to pretend that the future did
not exist. Though I had a sick feeling that burned in the pit of my
stomach I could be superficially gay and almost forget where this
journey was taking us. We left Connemara behind and came to the
Midlands, flat, featureless, dull but for me still an enchanted place
because he was there. The hundred and fifty miles took three and a
half hours. As we drew nearer to Dublin, the gaiety became more
elusive, the sick feeling became a hard knot.

'You're worried about your father,' Finn said when I became quiet.

'Well, yes. I am, of course, though the telegram said he was in no
danger but asking for me. I can hardly believe that. I've never felt
that my presence gave him any pleasure.'

'I find that equally hard to believe. Bobbie?'

'Yes.'

'Do you mind if I stop the car? Just for a minute. I want to say
goodbye to you without other people around.' He pulled into a lay-
by. 'I want to kiss you for the last time.'

I felt a rush of tears in the back of my throat; my nose prickled
and threatened to run. A pain stabbed between my shoulder-blades
and ran through to my breastbone. We kissed, long and passionately.

'Right,' he said at last. He pushed me away almost roughly and
started up the car. 'We'd better hurry if you're to catch the two
o'clock ferry.'

After that we drove in silence. From time to time I turned to gaze
at his profile and each time received a violent jolt to my heart. I
found myself almost wishing he had gone out of my life when he
was meant to, that morning. How would it be when we had to say
goodbye? How could I stop myself howling like a child? We came
to the outskirts of Dublin and turned south for Dún Laoghaire. How
grim the back streets looked, though in reality they were no worse
than any other suburbs. When I saw the signs for the harbour, my

heart beat fast, the blood roared in my ears and my limbs trembled. He drove on, looking stern, saying nothing. I almost hated him for taking me willingly to that place of separation.

We entered the port. He found a space in the car-park.

'Here we are,' he said. His face looked grey.

'Yes.' I was thinking frantically. Whatever the consequences might be, this felt very wrong.

'I'll get your cases.'

He had got out of the car before I could detain him. He took the two big ones and I picked up the small one. He found a porter and a trolley. They said things I could not understand because my brain was seething with protest.

'There she is.' He pointed to the boat. 'You're in luck. The sea's pretty calm.'

Every rib, every bone ached. I was in agony, physically as well as mentally. I decided to tell him that I'd changed my mind. That I couldn't leave him. I would take a flat in Dublin, get a job, be his mistress, see him when he could spare time from his family. I would never ask him for anything and the moment he was tired of me I would go away without a word of reproach. I opened my mouth to say all this but a man came out of nowhere and said, 'Senator Macchuin, isn't it?'

Finn started. 'Yes.'

'I'm Roddy Clarke. *Irish Recorder*. I heard your speech on education. It was a fine one, very thought-provoking.'

'Thank you.'

'Are you going over to England, sir? I'm travelling myself. We might have a drink and a chat.'

'No.' Finn seemed to be speaking very slowly. He did not look at the man. 'No. I'm not going. I'm seeing this young lady off.' Roddy Clarke's eyes rested curiously on my face. 'My housekeeper. Miss Norton. She's been looking after my house in Galway.'

'Really?' Roddy Clarke looked me up and down and I knew exactly what he was thinking. Of course, we could not hope to fool him. Finn looked quite ill and I could feel myself trembling uncontrollably. 'And you're going home now, Miss Norton?' I nodded. 'Have you enjoyed your stay in Ireland?' I nodded again, clenching my hands inside my pockets. He was stealing the last precious moments. Why couldn't he leave us alone? In desperation I opened my mouth to beg him to go away but a siren wailed, drowning my words.

The reporter took hold of my arm. 'We'd better hurry, Miss Norton. The boat'll be leaving in five minutes. We'll get aboard so we can choose a decent seat.' He pronounced the word 'daycent' as Timsy and the girls did and I was filled with such a longing to be back at Curraghcourt that to my horror a tear ran down my cheek. 'I see you're apprehensive, Miss Norton. No need to worry. These tubs are as safe as houses. I'll look after you.'

Still he had hold of my arm.

'Goodbye then.' Finn held out his hand. I put mine in it. I felt a brief pressure then he had turned away and was walking back to the car.

'This way.' Roddy Clarke was pushing me through the throng of hurrying passengers. It was as well he did for I was almost blinded by fast-falling tears. We were going up the gangplank. I felt the throb of engines beneath my feet. I turned, blinking, rubbing away tears with my hands to see Finn, a distant figure, walking rapidly away through the crowd. He did not look back. Then he turned a corner and was gone.

'Steady now, Miss Norton. Are you not well? I'll get you to a seat.'

We climbed steep stairs to the passenger lounge.

'Sit here. I'll fetch you a drink.'

I was sobbing openly now and shivering as though in the grip of fever. I was being knocked about by elbows and cases but I was unable to protect myself. My eardrums were splitting with the noise of talking and laughter.

'Get this down you.'

I drank it. I had no idea what it was. As fast as I swallowed it, it threatened to come back into my mouth.

'Is the young lady sick already?' A woman's voice, kind, close to my ear. 'Why, hello! I remember you! Wasn't it this time, last summer about, that you crossed?' I looked into the sympathetic face of the waitress who had been so motherly on that terrible voyage out. 'My goodness!' she said. 'It's plain to see your stay with us hasn't done you much good. Will I fetch you a nice piece of Battenberg?'

FIFTY-TWO

My father's funeral took place a week later. Ruby, who had sent the telegram, had wanted to save me from a distressing journey home so she had lied about the gravity of his condition. I was grateful for this kindness. On reaching London I had telephoned Cutham Hall and Brough had been sent in the Austin Princess to Blackheath station to meet my train. We had driven straight to the hospital. I hardly recognized the large mound of inert flesh that had been my small, trim, energetic parent. There was no time to do more than hold his hand and kiss him before he died. He was unconscious so probably he did not even know I was there.

'I'm ever so sorry, dear. But it was nice that you were with him at the end.'

Ruby's plump, powdered cheeks were streaked with purple where tears had washed away her make-up and exposed broken veins. I looked no better myself. During that last embrace with Finn in the lay-by, some of the contents of my bag had spilled out and I had made the long journey home without benefit of comb or make-up, my hair in knots and my face speckled with grains of mascara. Under the hospital strip-lighting, which made our faces livid, we must have looked like a pair of clowns.

'What you need, dear, is to come home and rest. I'll make you something nice to eat and that'll buck you up. Poor dear Gifford! I'm so glad we were both there when he passed away. Your mother would've liked to be with us, I know, but she's not strong enough for all this upset and Oliver, bless him, doesn't like hospitals. I can understand that. You can't go against your nature, dear, can you? Now, you have a good cry, Roberta love, that's right. He was your dear dadda, wasn't he, and now he's gone and it's very sad. There, there! Auntie Ruby'll take you home.'

The next few days and nights seemed to have no shape, no purpose that I could understand. Mrs Treadgold's knees had inconveniently given way beneath the shock of my father's death. She valiantly 'came in' because she wouldn't let us down in a crisis but she could do little more than sit on the old kitchen sofa and receive cups of tea and cake from Ruby, who was unfailingly sympathetic in the intervals between making beds, washing floors, bringing down cobwebs and scouring the scullery sink. I did my best to help though Ruby was anxious that I should rest.

'You look peaky, dear,' Ruby said two days after my father's death. 'Just leave that basket of ironing to me and I'll get through it in a trice after I've got the towels in the wash and put an elastic waistband into your mother's black skirt.'

Mrs Treadgold shifted expansively to accommodate on the troublesome knees the plate of custard tart she was nobly eating as she couldn't stand by and see it go to waste. 'It's nerves, Roberta, and no wonder. What with the Major going off so sudden and your mother not getting any better it's a wonder we don't *all* look like death warmed up. When I got that telephone call to say he'd gone, I shook like a jelly for an hour after. I haven't been to the toilet properly – you know – since. The doctor says my bowels are a mystery beyond the skills of medical man.'

I did not leave the basket of ironing to Ruby, nor did I allow her to sit up till midnight with the waistband, but I was more exhausted than I could have believed possible. People wrote, telephoned and rang the doorbell to offer their condolences and to ask if there was *anything* they could do. Sometimes I wondered what they would say if I asked them to do a little light housework.

The undertaker came to show me photographs of coffins, accompanied by little square samples of brilliantly varnished wood in various shades of brown, called things like the Balmoral, the Regal and the Prestige, all at astonishing prices, except the Fundamental, which I was too cowardly to choose. I selected ridiculously expensive brass handles and dutifully turned the plastic-covered pages of a catalogue with pictures of ugly flower arrangements, my mind anywhere but on the virtues of the five-pound 'carnation tribute' as opposed to the fifteen-pound 'lilies only'.

We walked to the church behind the coffin and sang the hymns I had chosen with the assistance of the vicar who said that in his opinion what he called 'Guide me, O' struck a nice balance between regret for the departed and confidence in the everlasting.

Everlasting what, I wondered, as the bravest shrieked, 'Feed me now and evermo-hor-hor-hor-hore,' very high while the rest of us mouthed the words, frightened our voices might crack.

Everlasting grief. I thought I was learning about that. At the graveside, where there was what Mrs Treadgold called 'a good turnout', Ruby and I were conspicuous by our weeping. One could not expect friends and relations to be particularly sad. My father had not bothered to disguise the contempt he felt for them. My mother, sitting in her wheelchair, remained abstracted, gazing up at the rooks nesting in the dying elms. No doubt she subscribed to the view that it is vulgar to cry at funerals. Oliver looked greener than ever. I was sure he felt my father's death deeply, though he could not be said to mourn. I saw him tweak Sherilee's prominent bottom, tightly encased in black leather trousers, when he thought no one was looking. But you cannot lose a parent without pain of some kind.

Ruby cried, I think, because she felt she had lost someone of whom she was truly fond, though Oliver told me that my father had treated her as the next best thing to a slave. But Ruby's nature was soft and she had no intention of going against it. I cried because my relationship with my father had been so far from ideal and that must have been at least as sad for him as it was for me.

Mrs Treadgold had equipped herself with mourning clothes of the deepest hue and a packet of paper handkerchiefs but in the event she was so interested in the service and what everyone else was wearing that she remained dry-eyed. Brough was, surprisingly, the only other member of the funeral cortège to show emotion. My father had bullied him to the point of cruelty for thirty-five years but when the coffin was carried to the grave Brough held himself erect and saluted while tears slid down the side of his nose.

We gave a lunch for the mourners afterwards. Ruby had refused my help, saying that she could see I was all in and would be better resting. People got very jolly on South African sherry and bridge rolls filled with egg and cress, sausages on sticks, chocolate sponge and iced fruitcake, pulling solemn faces from time to time when they remembered that this was a wake.

I drifted through the days that followed. I wandered round the house and garden, tried to read, watched television without any idea what the programmes were until my mother said couldn't I pull myself together? My gloomy face and restless fidgeting were unsettling her. Now Mrs Treadgold's knees were on the mend, my mother and Ruby had a comfortable routine reading their favourite novels, with breaks to listen to *Woman's Hour,* Franklin Engleman coming *Down Your Way* and Alistair Cooke's *Letter from America.* They ate large quantities of sugar-laden food. They seemed happy. Oliver pulled pints at the bar of the Red Lion, told bad jokes, polished glasses, grabbed the prominent parts of Sherilee whenever she was in reach, and topped up the bowls on the bar with a fresh layer of peanuts each morning.

I could not acclimatize myself to my own country. It was so tidy, so organized, so crowded. Everything seemed diminutive. Though this was supposedly countryside, around every bend in the road there was a house, a lamp-post, a privet hedge with a man in an argyle jersey trimming it into a neat shape. Clean cars stood on herring-bone-bricked drives in front of diamond-paned windows sparkling with fresh applications of Windolene. Every roadside tree had the shape of a double-decker bus carved from its canopy. Beyond the gates of Cutham people seemed stiff and introverted, intent on presenting a respectable face that revealed nothing of their real selves. Knowing of my recent bereavement they took pains to keep contact with me to a minimum lest they should accidentally provoke me into losing self-control. If anyone more closely connected with me was surprised that I was taking my father's death so hard they kept their own counsel. Only Ruby tried to show me by pats on the arm, sympathetic sighs and little plates of biscuits that appeared mysteriously at my elbow that she knew I was going through some sort of emotional turmoil.

A letter from Constance arrived a few days after the funeral. I opened it eagerly and scanned the lines of copperplate for mention of his name. There it was. *Finn came home last weekend. That's two weekends running!! He seemed awfully tired, poor boy, but made valiant efforts to mend the generator which has packed up again. In the end of course I had to get in Thady O'Kelly . . .* That was the only mention of his name. I ran over the letter again as disappointed as a starving man offered a few stale crumbs, then read it properly, chiding myself for being a weak fool.

Apparently Liddy had had a letter from Danny which had sent her into transports. The visitors were continuing to come in droves and on the whole it was a terrific success though there had been a distressing incident when one of the visitors had tried to walk out with a silver sugar caster. He had thrown himself on Constance's mercy and explained that he was an illegal immigrant from Eastern Europe and had hoped to sell the caster to get money to send to his starving children so she had given him a five-pound note and let him go round Curraghcourt for free in exchange for the caster's return. There had been an article in the local press about Eugene's silhouettes. *Remembering what you said*, Constance continued, *I put out of my mind all thoughts of sin and took the GREAT STEP. I must admit I was nervous, we both were, but Eugene was so sweet, so kind. Bobbie, I'm so lucky. I know I don't deserve him. Naturally I'm not going to confess to Father Deglan what we've done. That means I can no longer take Communion but I don't care! Nothing so wonderful could be wrong!* There was a lot more about Eugene, which I read patiently, taking pleasure in the happiness that was apparent in every word. Flurry had put down several feet of track with the help of Sam O'Kelly, who had turned out to be a railway enthusiast. Flavia had started to bring the kittens downstairs, one at a time. Maria had taken a shine to Wee Willie Winkie, licking his head until the kitten was nearly drowned by saliva. Osgar had behaved well, only growling if the kittens approached his beloved glove. Violet sent her best love. Mrs O'Kelly had started work at the castle and was proving reliable and willing though unfortunately it was back to mince and boiled potatoes. How they all missed my wonderful cooking! In fact they were all missing me more than they could say and were looking forward to my return. *Surely you could come back soon even if only for a while? Of course your mother will be needing you just now. But it's not the same without you, dear, dear Bobbie.*

I read the letter through again, despite the shooting pains in my breast. Then I put it away in a drawer. I lacked the strength of mind to answer it immediately. I was frightened by my own inertia, unable to make plans, to contemplate what might lie ahead. I was standing in the hall looking out through the streaming window by the front door at the rivers running down the drive and wondering if I would ever again be able to see rain without thinking of bogs and mountains when the telephone rang.

'Bobbie? It's Fleur.'

'Fleur! What a surprise!' I saw several pictures in my mind's eye in rapid succession: Fleur's charming face and dark, cloudy hair; Dickie laughing amiably; the beauty of Ladyfield; and, of course, Burgo – not necessarily in that order.

'A nice one I hope. Dickie saw the notice in *The Times* about your father so we guessed you'd be home. I'm dreadfully sorry.'

'Thank you. How are you? How's Dickie?'

'We're both well. Dickie was saying just the other day how much he missed your guiding hand in the garden. So when we read about your poor pa, he said to ring you. I was a bit doubtful . . . I thought you might be . . . Oh, Bobbie, I'm sorry I was such a beast. That horrible telephone call! I was so mean to you! I regretted it the minute I'd put the phone down but I didn't have your number so what could I do? I'd no idea how to get in touch with you to say I was sorry. I telephoned Cutham but your father – I think it must have been your father – said he was going to inform the police if anyone else rang up asking for your telephone number.'

'I expect he thought you were a journalist. Don't worry, Fleur. I quite understood that you were upset about . . . someone else.'

'I was but that's no excuse. Do you forgive me, really?'

'Completely. Absolutely. Don't give it another thought.'

'It's more than I deserve. Where were you in fact? Or is it still a secret?'

'I was in Ireland.'

'Goodness! I never thought of that. I imagined you somewhere exciting. Rome or New York. What on earth made you go to Ireland?'

'I saw an advertisement for a housekeeper.'

'Curiouser and curiouser. Did you like it there?'

'I loved it.'

'Oh good. Then you're quite . . . happy again?'

How to answer this? 'Well, you know, with my father dying . . .'

'Oh, yes, of course. I'm sorry. I'm the most tactless person in the world. Poor Bobbie! Look, will you prove to me once and for all that you *have* forgiven me and come over and see us?'

I hesitated. I wanted to reassure Fleur that I felt no ill-will. But the prospect of being sociable filled me with gloom. It seemed to demand an effort that I was incapable of making. But this was feeble. I *must* make efforts. 'That would be lovely.'

'Marvellous. If you're not busy come to tea tomorrow. I'd ask you to supper but Dickie's got some golfing friends coming and you'd be bored to death. Oh, Bobbie, I've got this most extraordinarily beautiful foal! He's like a prince, the way he steps out holding his head in this wonderful curve. You'd *adore* him.'

As I heard the girlish excitement in Fleur's voice I remembered why I had liked her. She was guilty of nothing except possibly loving her brother a little too well. But that was all past and had no power to hurt me. And perhaps Dickie's cheerful face and transparently benevolent character might be just what I was in need of.

'All right. Thank you.'

At four o'clock the next day I turned into the drive beneath the immaculate rows of pleached limes that led to Ladyfield. I remembered the excitement that used to grip me at the thought of seeing Burgo. How strange that I had so completely forgotten him that he might have been part of someone else's life. I recalled his face more clearly as Fleur came running out, followed by her dogs, and threw her arms around me when I got out of the car.

'It's so lovely to see you! You must come and admire my new foal straight away.'

'Bobbie!' Dickie came limping out, beaming, flannelled and blazered as usual, smelling of soap and clean laundry, the epitome of a decent man. 'It's been much too long!'

'It has. I quite agree.'

'Yes, aha!' I saw that Dickie was embarrassed, remembering what had created the hiatus in our relationship. 'You're looking well. Very well, my dear.' I did not suppose this was true. I had thought, getting ready to go out, that I looked terrible. 'But a little thin. You must come and have some of Mrs Harris's delicious cake to fatten you up.'

'Don't fuss, Dickie,' said Fleur impatiently. 'Bobbie looks fine to me. All right, we'll just look at the foal over the stable door and then we'll come and join you in the drawing room.'

'And afterwards I'll show Bobbie the garden. Mostly it's still buds but there are some gorgeous tulips.' He looked at me anxiously. 'Now I know your refined tastes. What do you say? Are tulips too bright and stiff for you?'

'Not a bit,' I laughed. 'They're one of my favourite flowers.'

'By golly, it's good to see you!' Dickie gave my arm a squeeze. 'What have you been doing with yourself? I must say you're a sight for sore eyes.' Then his face grew solemn. 'But I was forgetting. Very bad luck about your father. An awful blow, these things. Knock you back a bit, don't they?'

'Yes. Yes they do, rather. But it was peaceful.'

'Good. Good. I'm glad to hear it. Now, you two go and look at that horse and mind you don't slip in the mud.'

'Isn't he beautiful?' asked Fleur. We leaned over the door of the stable and watched the mare and foal nuzzling each other, moving gracefully about inside the loose box. They were elegant, slender-limbed beasts, quite different from the Cockatoo with his barrel body and stocky legs.

'Beautiful!' I praised them until Fleur seemed to feel that I had done them justice.

Then I admired the dogs, trying not to think of Osgar and Maria until Fleur said, 'Come on, we'll go and have tea.'

If I had had any doubts about going back to Ladyfield they were dispelled as I walked into the house and saw the familiar rooms full of lovely things, well cared for and scented with the hyacinths that stood in deep bowls in every room. Dickie and Fleur seemed genuinely pleased to see me. I realized that apart from Oliver they were the first people I had encountered since my return to England for whom I felt real friendship.

Over tea we talked a little about Ireland. I tried not to be reserved but there were so many things I could not mention for fear of betraying myself. I described the scenery, Constance, the children, the animals – this for Fleur's sake – and the perception I had of Irish life, necessarily a narrow view as I had spent the entire ten months in one small part of it. I think I sounded cheerful enough but it was a relief to turn to Fleur's dogs, Dickie's golf, his presidency of the local fine arts society, the party they were planning in June to which I must be sure to come.

Dickie took his stick and stood up. 'Come on, Bobbie, the sun's out. We'll go and look at the garden and then you can admire my orchids in the glasshouse. Fleur thinks they're revolting.'

'I do! They have horrid brown bags instead of petals.'

'Only the paphiopedilums. The phalaenopsis are as pretty as anyone could wish.'

We went into the garden. Fleur took my arm. Dickie walked ahead. Listening to them arguing as in the old days I felt obliquely comforted. I saw that despite the difference in age, temperament and ideas they were reasonably happy together. As perhaps Finn and Violet could— No. I was not yet ready to think about that. Most people's lives were imperfect yet they rubbed along somehow. Perhaps for me also there would be some good times ahead. If I could just lose this feeling of extreme emotional fragility and buckle down to getting on with things (which things I could not quite formulate) I should be all right.

The garden was perfect, the lawns emerald and weedless, the borders mulched, the roses pruned to military neatness. Between the exquisite pink, white and purple tulips flowered mauve perennial wallflowers already smothered with bees, low mounds of violas, anthemis daisies and the pea-like *Lathyrus vernus*. Birds hopped about, piping of spring and parenthood. I admired everything including the muck-heap. Who was it who had said that Ladyfield was a Garden of Eden with its own serpent? Ah, Kit, of course, and that was typical. Everything was a game to him. How I wished I could take things more lightly and turn them into slightly cynical jokes! But he was wrong about Ladyfield. It was peaceful and ordered and beautiful, without a flaw. This was the aspect of England I could grow to love again. The discipline, the shaping hand, the goals set and the standards reached. I felt, for a moment, almost hopeful.

'Come and see the China House garden,' urged Fleur. 'Dickie's spent millions of pounds putting in everything you suggested.'

If I hesitated it was only for a second. 'Yes. I must see that.'

When we reached the narrow gap in the hedge, Fleur said, 'Dickie, I'm cold. Will you run in and fetch my coat?'

'That's too bad of you, darling, when I begged you to put on something warm before we came out. I want to see Bobby's face when she catches sight of my improvements.'

'All right, come in, see it and then go,' said Fleur. 'But hurry up. I'm feeling quite shivery.'

This made Dickie anxious. He barely glanced at my expression of delight before hobbling away. I had forgotten the enchantment of the China House with its up-flung eaves from which hung irons bells that chimed with the wind. A narrow red fretted bridge spanned the pond.

'*Sharawadgi*, indeed!' I ran on to the bridge. 'Truly a delicious and unanticipated surprise!' I admired the glossy veined pads of the water lilies floating on the still water. It was too early for flowers. 'And look at this cherry blossom!' I gazed into the delicate pale pink blossoms. 'This little garden has the most wonderful atmosphere: dreaming, timeless. And those cloud-pruned box! How clever Dickie's been!'

'He's made some changes inside, as well.'

Fleur opened the door. I stepped into the cool, dark chamber. The bed had been moved to the opposite wall and there was a new sofa with elegant scrolled ends – and there was someone sitting on it. I saw among the shadows a long leg uncross itself from its fellow as he stood up. The door closed behind me. I turned to see, through the window, Fleur hurrying back across the bridge.

'Hello, Roberta.' Burgo moved forward so that the light fell on his face. 'Don't be angry with Fleur. You know she always does what

I tell her.' He smiled. I had forgotten that smile. Also how dark his eyes were. Now they seemed alight with some secret enjoyment, though his mouth was solemn. I fought the temptation to run. Once before I had run away from the China House, from him, and by doing so had told him as clearly as if I had spoken the words aloud that he was more to me than other men. 'I'm sorry about your father,' he said.

'Yes. Thank you.'

'He'll be much missed by the Worping Conservatives,' he added with every appearance of gravity though I was not deceived.

'How are you?' Though I was troubled to find him there I was determined to appear calm.

'As you see.' He held out his arms from his sides to display himself. He was not altered in the least. Why should he be? It had only been ten months. It was my idea of him that had changed so entirely. The hair was the same thick, untidy white-blond. He had evidently just come down from London. His double-breasted suit was elegant, his tie a model of restrained good taste, his shoes burnished. It was the public man who stood before me but his face was recast second by second into the man I had loved.

'You're just the same,' he said.

I shook my head.

'I had to see you.' Burgo took a step nearer. Now I could see every line on his face clearly: that curved upper lip, the pinched-in corner of his mouth that made one suspect he was suppressing laughter. 'I wanted to tell you how sorry I am about what happened between us, the way things turned out. It wasn't at all what I'd intended.'

'That's very considerate of you.' I tried to keep sarcasm out of my voice so he should not think I still minded. 'But we've had time to get over it. And I was equally to blame. Let's agree to forget all about it.'

'Well, yes, if it's possible. Somehow I doubt it. I don't know how it's been for you but for my part I haven't found it exactly easy. I thought you should know that. Perhaps you think I let you down. You thought it was lack of love on my part. Yes, I see that's exactly what you did think.'

I tightened my facial muscles. I was not going to allow myself to be deciphered.

'I tried to find you.' As Burgo talked he moved closer. 'As a matter of fact I tried damned hard. But you'd disappeared as completely as though you'd dropped through a hole in the ground. I rang up everyone I could think of who might know where you'd gone.'

'I'm sorry to have been such a nuisance.' I smiled but he was not deceived.

'Oh, you're angry still. You frighten me.'

I did not think he looked particularly frightened, more as if he were enjoying the tension I was unable to defuse. I saw again in those dark eyes the light of amusement I had once so loved.

'You won't forgive me because I went back to Anna. You think me a manipulative, ambitious bastard. Don't deny it,' he said sharply as I schooled my features into a softer expression. 'All right, I did want the job. Desperately. But if you'd come to me instead of running away, if you'd allowed me to choose, I'd have chosen you. You believe that, at least?'

'Yes, I think you probably would.' I gathered my wandering thoughts and took myself in hand. 'But, you see, I didn't want to be "chosen", as you put it. Yes, I *was* angry, but not with you.' He did not speak as I paused to steady my voice. I guessed that he was disconcerted so I carried on before he had a chance to interrupt. 'I was angry with myself. I made a terrible mistake and even while I was allowing myself to fall in love with you I knew it was a stupid thing to do. I was quite aware of the danger and I went ahead because I imagined I'd be able somehow to cheat my way out of the consequences.'

I saw that he was taken aback. I could not mistake that look of doubt, so rarely seen but so clearly recalled now that he was there, in front of me, near enough to hear him breathe.

'Roberta. You make me feel ashamed.' I felt compunction then because the old feelings of love were sharp in my mind.

'As far as *I'm* concerned you did nothing wrong. If your conscience is bothering you, I exonerate you completely. You can go away and forget— No, you're right, that isn't possible. Well, we might remember it as an episode of glorious folly, with moments of great happiness for which we both paid very dearly. You, perhaps, more than I. I don't suppose your wife is going to forget it either. And she has no pleasurable memories to compensate for the misery.'

'Yes, it was glorious.' He took my hand in his. It felt familiar, warm. 'Roberta. Darling. It's been torture, not seeing you, not knowing where you were. Couldn't you at least have let me know you were all right?'

'I sent a letter.'

'Two lines. They weren't reassuring. You just said you were going

626

away. How was I to know what that meant? I've imagined everything. I was afraid you might be ill, that you might have married someone you didn't love on the rebound, even – oh, I know it sounds conceited – perhaps even have tried to kill yourself.'

'I'm sorry.'

'Don't be so cold. It's killing me. If you knew how many times I've wanted to send everything to hell – comb the country for you – get those bloody journalists to put a notice in the papers begging you to come back to me.'

I tried to remove my hand but he held on to it. 'That would have been very rash.'

'Would you have come back if I had?'

I thought I could afford to be truthful with him. 'Yes, I expect so. I'm sure I would have – in those first few weeks, anyway.' I was rewarded by an increased pressure of his hand.

'Fleur says you went to Ireland. Why? Did you have friends there?' He paused. 'Another man?'

'I didn't know anyone. That's why. I wanted to make a new beginning.'

'That isn't possible, is it? Neither of us can forget.'

'I *had* forgotten until today. Not you, of course; I shall always remember you. But I'd forgotten why I thought it worthwhile to ignore everything that experience and whatever intelligence I possess had taught me for the sake of . . . love.'

He held my hand more tightly. 'All right. You're punishing me. I'll take it if I must but have some pity, for God's sake!'

'How can I convince you that I hold myself entirely responsible? I don't want you to feel guilty about me. I don't want you to feel anything at all about me.'

'I don't believe you. You're still unhappy, aren't you? Don't deny it. I know you too well. And I know what it's like to live with regret, with longing. Loving someone I can never see, never hold in my arms. Roberta! There's only one way for us to make peace with each other.' He took hold of my other arm and drew me close. 'Kiss me.'

I allowed myself to look directly into his eyes. For a moment the scent of cedarwood and earthy smells stealing in from the garden operated on my senses to revive the memory of what I had felt at the height of our hunger for each other. But it was cold, poisoned, ashes in the mouth.

'I should have known you wouldn't have set this up and rushed

627

down here just so you could say you were sorry. You fancied a little variety. I suppose Anna's away? Or busy? Or perhaps unwilling.'

He let go of me abruptly and stepped back, as though I had threatened to bite him. 'Don't be a fool, Roberta!' He looked away from me, took a pace or two, thinking. I watched him, feeling a detached sympathy for his predicament. 'Of course, you're jealous of her.' He leaned against the arm of the sofa, stretched out his legs in front of him and sighed: the picture of reasonableness in the face of intransigence. 'That's understandable. I'd probably feel the same in your place. I suppose you want me to undergo some ordeal by sword or flame to prove my penitence. I didn't think you were like other women, wanting your pound of flesh.' Evidently Anna had laid down stringent terms. 'That's why I loved you. You were generous, unselfish, above wanting to possess, to parade your spoils.' He looked at me searchingly. 'And you haven't changed, have you? I've hurt you. I regret that more than you'll ever know. But you're the same woman I loved then. Just the same. And I'm the same man, helpless in the face of beauty. You have all my love, Roberta.' He looked at me, his expression serious, his dark eyes mournful and yet I saw in them a gleam of something. Was it amusement still? Or certainty?

'Goodbye, Burgo. I'm sorry you went to so much trouble for nothing.'

I went to the door. It opened easily. Dickie had cured the damp problem. I walked over the bridge and passed through the gap in the hedge. I made my way between the long borders, the greenery fresh and sappy, seductive with the promise of a brilliant summer. I crossed the lawn and skirted the house to reach the drive where my car was parked.

Dickie came dashing out through the front door, as fast as his leg allowed. I got into the driving seat and wound down the window. He came galloping round to my side of the car and bent to look in as I started the engine.

'I'm so sorry,' he said. 'I had no idea. Fleur's only just told me Burgo's here. Please don't go away like this.' His good-natured face was creased with anxiety.

'It's all right, Dickie. It really doesn't matter. Don't be cross with Fleur. She can't help herself where he's concerned.' I put out my head to kiss his cheek. 'I won't come again, but please remember how awfully fond I am of both of you.'

I let out the clutch and drove off. In my rear-view mirror I saw Dickie standing on the drive, looking after me with an expression of forlorn perplexity. Near the front gates Burgo's – or rather Simon's – car was parked among the trees, at an angle that hid it from anyone driving in. I was annoyed with myself for feeling agitated. My heart was racing and I felt almost dizzy with anxiety to get away. But of one thing I was certain. Though Burgo's outward attractions were not a whit less than they had been I had not been tempted for one moment to respond to them. Poor Burgo! How patiently he must have waited, anticipating a blissful reunion on the Chinese daybed. I shuddered, then was sorry that I had, for I had loved him once. The journey back to Cutham was long enough for me to do some serious thinking.

Ruby was in the kitchen taking a lemon meringue pie out of the oven when I reached home.

'Not bad, though I say it as shouldn't.' She looked with satisfaction at the crisp billows, touched with gold. Brough, who was sitting at the table eating a sandwich two inches thick, looked at the pie appreciatively. His neck was bulging over his collar, his uniform straining at the seams.

'It looks delicious,' I said. I waited for Brough to finish his sandwich and go out. 'Now, Ruby.' I detained her forcibly from returning to the cooking pots by placing my hand on her arm. 'Tell me the truth. Are you quite happy here?'

Ruby looked puzzled. 'Why, Roberta! As though I could be anything else. Naturally, we all miss your dear dadda, but I'm ever so fond of your mother and it's such a lovely old house. And Oliver, bless him, he's a dear boy. And I was afraid, dear, you'd resent me but instead you've shown me nothing but kindness. When you're all so good to me, how could I not be happy?'

'I think the boot's on the other foot but we won't argue about that. The thing is, I want to go back to London. To live, I mean. I can only do that if you'll stay and look after my mother.'

'Bless you, dear, I'd like nothing better. It's good of you to trust me with such a precious duty. I know how much she's going to miss you but like all mothers she thinks more of her children's happiness than her own.'

I kissed Ruby warmly. 'You must let me know if there's anything you want.'

I went away to make telephone calls.

FIFTY-THREE

'You can't think what a re*lief* it is to have you back,' Sarah said as
we ate scrambled eggs and smoked trout for supper in the kitchen
of the little house in Paradise Row. Five days had passed since I had
been to Ladyfield and met Burgo in the China House. 'The last girl
who had your room was even worse than the others. She always left
her knickers soaking in the basin. And she left the lid off the fucking bread bin with boring regularity. Every day I came back to stale
bread. And the one who had Jazzy's room ate curry every night. The
whole place stank like an unwashed armpit.' It can be seen from this
that Sarah ran a tight ship but I was, of course, used to that. Her
language reminded me of Liddy and thereafter of other people. It
could not be helped. I was in the same condition that poor Jasmine
had been in when she came to Curraghcourt. Associations would be
made however hard I tried to divert my thoughts. 'Anyway, that
apart, it's terrific to have you back.'

'It's lovely to be back.'

Sarah stared at me through horn-rimmed spectacles, her round
brown eyes serious. 'I hope you've put it all behind you. It was an
almighty cock-up but you've lived to tell the tale. I only hope his
wife is making him pay by demanding constant attention to her tiniest whim during the day and turning the cold shoulder to him at
night. He's probably a shadow of his former self.'

I realized she was talking about Burgo. 'Actually I saw him just
the other day and he looked buoyant and flourishing.'

'*What?* You idiot! You *mad*woman!' Sarah put her hands to her
temples and opened her mouth wide as though about to scream.
'You actually agreed to meet him?'

'I didn't intend to. Burgo and his sister arranged it between them.

Don't worry, I wasn't in the least tempted to start it up again.'

'You mean the bastard wasn't content with nearly wrecking your life once but wanted to do it all over again?'

'He isn't really a bastard, you know.' I saw Sarah's nostrils flare. 'Honestly, all he wanted was to recapture that first fine careless rapture. He's used to having what he wants. Luckily, I wasn't interested. But I won't hear him abused.'

Sarah put down her fork and looked at me accusingly. 'You're still in love with him!'

'I promise you, cross my heart and hope to die, stick my finger in my eye, I'm not.' This made me think of Flavia. 'I swear I no longer love him. But I wish him well. There's nothing wrong with that.'

'No-o-o.' I saw that from now on Sarah would regard me as someone who needed to be protected from her wildest excesses. Well, perhaps she was right.

'In fact meeting him again provided the impetus for moving back to London so I'm grateful, really. I was in a state of hopeless indecision.'

'Oh?' Sarah pounced like a stoat on a rabbit. 'So what's the state of play, Bobbie? In my experience a girl only really gets over a man she's been desperately fond of by spotting a better one waiting in the wings. Does this immunity to the charms of Burgo Latimer MP have anything to do with Kit? I dread to think of the complications, if so.'

Having sacked one unsatisfactory lodger in order to make room for me Sarah had decided she might as well get rid of both. I had learned, to my great pleasure, that Jasmine was coming back to live in Paradise Row. In fact we had only just missed seeing each other. She had departed, twenty-four hours before my return, for three weeks in Portofino with Kit. I presumed MI5 was bearing the brunt of the cost of an expensive hotel. This meant that for a while Sarah and I had the tiny house to ourselves. Sarah had met Kit when he came to pick up Jazzy and take her to the airport. I imagined the little red car bursting with matching luggage.

'I swear I'll be only too pleased if Jazz and Kit make a go of it. It was my intention that they should . . . delight in each other's company.'

'Get off with each other, you mean? What on earth was this Irish place like? From what Jasmine said it sounded like a cross between *The Celtic Twilight* and a film by Buñuel.'

'It was . . . very beautiful.' I saw that Sarah was waiting for me to go on. 'A castle dating from the thirteenth century, though most of what you saw was Georgian, set in two hundred acres of semi-wild parkland.'

'Sounds idyllic if you like that sort of thing.' Sarah looked unenthusiastic. She was town-born and -bred and disliked the country. 'But what about the occupants? From what you said on the phone I got the impression they were rather dull. But you were always so cagey.'

'I was afraid of being overheard. The telephone was inside a sedan chair with a door that didn't fit very well.'

'A sedan chair?' Sarah laughed. 'But of course. Fancy me not guessing that. Well, Jazzy was a little more forthcoming than you. She gave me a thumbnail sketch of the major players. Constance was the name of the maiden aunt, as far as I remember. Jazzy said she was kind and vague and madly intellectual and in love with someone Jazz thought was possibly gay.'

I stood up to check that I had turned off the grill. I knew I had but remembering Constance with sudden sharpness, and knowing it was unlikely I would ever see her again, threatened my composure. I felt like a beetle pinned to a board beneath Sarah's magnifying glass. 'Certainly sensitive and intelligent. Perhaps intellectual, too. She became a great friend.'

'Of course Jazzy thinks anyone who reads the words of bra advertisements in the underground is a serious bluestocking. Tell me about the lover.'

'Eugene isn't gay, just a little self-centred and thin-skinned.' I remembered Eugene throwing himself between Constance and the bullet. 'But not without courage. I came to be very fond of him.' Sarah frowned. 'But not fond in the way you're thinking. He and Constance are now deliriously happy.'

'There were three children, weren't there? From what Jazzy said they sounded difficult.'

'Difficult? No, I don't think so. Liddy's the eldest. Bored, restless, teetering always on the edge of depression. Eating problems, rebellious, the usual teenage identity crisis. Flavia's the youngest. She feels everything acutely, overflows with affection – the girls were suffering from lack of attention from their parents. And Flurry, the boy, he's clever but finds relationships baffling. He lives in his own world. Perhaps he's the happiest because of that.'

'Well, that adds up to difficult in my book.'

'I can't tell. I haven't had much to do with children. All I know is I loved them dearly.' I felt a shiver of pain, and concentrated on scraping a blob of scrambled egg from the cloth with the blade of my knife.

'Goodness! The place seems to have been charged with emotion.' Sarah's tone was sarcastic. She mistrusted expressions of affection, though I knew this was nothing more than a defence. She pretended to be tough and cynical because she was afraid of being hoodwinked by other people's insincerity. 'Presumably you didn't extend this devotion to the neglectful parents?'

'Their father was away a lot in Dublin. Their mother was in a coma. But she got better.'

'Ah, yes, Jazzy did mention the pretty waiflike wife.'

I explained about Violet's stroke and her gradual recovery. Sarah grew sympathetic despite herself.

'Poor woman! What a cruel thing to happen! I can hardly bear to imagine what it must have been like. But I'm beginning to understand why you were happy in Ireland. The situation was tailormade for you and you for it. I can see you rushing round righting wrongs and setting things in order. It was exactly what you needed after that bastard' – she caught my eye – 'after you'd managed to get your psyche into a double clove-hitch and convinced yourself you were personally responsible for the Fall of man and his expulsion from the Garden of Eden.' This made me think of Kit and as though on cue Sarah said, 'Kit was there quite a bit, wasn't he? Before Jazz arrived, I mean.'

'He spent several weeks at Curraghcourt during the ten months I was there. What did you think of him?'

'Charming. Intelligent. Friendly. Perhaps a little too charming. He said sensible things about the law and barristering. But I noticed that when Jazz told him you'd lived here too, before you went to Ireland, Kit responded like a pointer spotting a still-warm feathered corpse. He stiffened all over – well, the parts I could see, anyway – and he grew mighty thoughtful. He was having a good look at everything, much more interested than he had been. So what gives?'

'Nothing gives. I swear Kit and I were friends, never lovers.'

'You mean he tried to get into your pants but you wouldn't let him.'

'Kit wants to make love to every woman he sees. That's the only thing that bothers me. I hope he's not going to make Jazz unhappy by being unfaithful to her.'

633

'I'm not worried about her. She'll bounce back all right. She got over Teddy in less time than it takes to jug a kipper, didn't she? It's you I'm worried about. Why do you look as though you've seen a ghost and it's dogging your footsteps and tugging at your sleeve?'

'I'm all right, Sarah, really. I'm delighted to be back here. I just need to get my teeth into some work and then I'll be able to slip back into my old way of life before I met Burgo. It's what I long for. To have everything simple and straightforward and to be fancy-free.'

'Mm.' Sarah took a wedge of treacle tart. She was a hearty eater and scornful of both hemlines and waistlines. 'There's something you're not telling me. You don't trust me.'

'I do. Absolutely.'

This was true. It was myself I didn't trust. I saw that she was not satisfied but I had no desire to take her into my confidence. I thought it would be easier to pretend to myself that I was not miserable if I did not have sympathetic eyes following me about the house.

Sarah had been called to the bar during the last year and had also taken up real tennis and Italian lessons; a defence, she said, against the grimness of the previous tenants and their horrible habits. She had a new boyfriend, a stocky, jolly Welsh barrister who was a bachelor, so she was out a good deal. I had nothing to do. I went to art galleries and sat for hours before masterpieces, then went away having seen very little of them. I took myself to the cinema and the theatre but would have found it difficult to explain the plots. I walked the streets of London, trying to adjust to the noise, the dirt, the smells, the crowds. The hardness of the pavements, the glare of the lights, the constant blare of noise acted on my feelings like an abrasion of nerve-endings. The Thames flowing nearby was a great comfort. I spent many hours gazing at its ever-changing expanse, watching the ships sail up and down it, imagining it flowing out to the sea, to wild places.

'Here's something that'll interest you,' said Sarah about three days after my return to Paradise Row. She threw *The Times* across the breakfast table. 'Fourth or fifth item down in the personal columns.'

I read it quickly. *Latimer. On 22 April, to Anna and Burgo, at the Princess Alexandra Wing, St Edward's Hospital, a daughter (Isobel Helen). Thanks to all staff.* On the opposite page, in the society column, was a photograph of the parents, holding something tiny swaddled in shawls. Anna looked happy, Burgo looked amused. *Minister celebrates happy event,* said the caption. I did not bother to read on.

'Surely that was about the time he was trying to get back with you?' Sarah's brown eyes were indignant.

'It was the day before.' I paused, wondering what I really felt. 'I suppose the attention wasn't on him and he didn't like that. He was bored so he thought of me.'

'Don't put yourself down.' Sarah was severe. 'More likely the baby is a sop to his career.'

'Poor little thing, if so. *She* looks pleased, anyway.'

'You don't mind, Bobbie, do you?'

'No. I'm glad, really. It seems to put a very positive full stop to everything. I expect he'll be devoted to his daughter once she's old enough to admire him. Perhaps a nursery was what the marriage needed, after all.'

In my third week of being back in London, I was lucky enough to get a job working at the Victoria and Albert Museum. It was a more lowly position than I might have expected, given my qualifications and experience, and the pay was not particularly good, but I needed a reason to get up in the morning. And being surrounded by beautiful things was an abiding solace and a compensation for the lonely hours before dawn when I lay awake and tried unsuccessfully to keep my thoughts within bounds.

I was doubly glad to have the job when Jasmine returned because she and Kit spent much of their time in Paradise Row. Kit was working unpredictable hours as usual. Jazz was not working at all. He was superficially friendly, embracing me warmly, asking me about my work and talking about his authors, but beneath the boyish charm was an extreme coldness. We rarely talked of Ireland because when we did a disagreeable tension crept in, which we were powerless to prevent. I suppose there were certain things that we were both anxious to forget.

When Jazzy wound her beautiful golden arms around him or pressed her lips to his cheek or nibbled his ear he would steal a look at me, a look of triumph that had an edge of accusation. I did not blame him. I was determined to work my way out of my misery. Kit seemed to have decided to copulate his way out of his. I was not remotely jealous but the walls of Paradise Row were thin and I did not particularly enjoy hearing Kit and Jazzy making love with noisy exuberance. I always thought of Violet and in this context the idea of her was literally agony.

Constance wrote regularly with the latest news, always as though she believed I was about to return and take everything up where I had left off. They were busier than ever with visitors. Scaffolding was going up round the east tower, ready for work to begin on the roof. None of our extravagant plans had been necessary to raise the additional seven thousand pounds. Finn had simply gone to the bank for a loan. He had found out, as he was bound to eventually, about the poteen fund and had forbidden its continuance, so Timsy had set up the still in the lodge which Finn had given him years before. This was much more convenient for everyone and meant that the demesne was no longer crawling with seekers after oblivion. Finn had also discovered that Timsy had been running a betting shop, taking bets on everything from the length of the present Pontificate to the chance of a dry spell lasting five days. Constance had been annoyed to find that long odds had been offered on the chance of her and Eugene ever making a match of it.

Liddy and Danny wrote letters little short of novellas to each other every week. Liddy no longer talked of going to London. Paris was the summit of her desire. She was eating quite well, Danny having said that he liked busty girls. Violet had managed five steps with only one stick. She would be grateful for the Harrods catalogue. Constance hoped I wouldn't think her conceited for mentioning it but I had given her so much encouragement that she thought I might be pleased to know that two more of her poems had been published. She had been invited to join the Galway Poets, a fascinating group of people who met monthly for readings in Williamsbridge. Constance would be *extremely* (underlined three times) grateful for another present of *you-know-whats*. (I had sent her a box of forty Durex Fetherlites my first week in London. I presumed life with Eugene was proceeding satisfactorily.)

The railway was getting on well. A hundred yards of track had gone down. Dicky Dooley's wife had come to sit at the table in the gatehouse and sell tickets. She was sulking because Larkie O'Kelly was running the grocery store in Kilmuree practically single-handed. *Tins of artichoke hearts, Bobbie! And French mustard, chestnut purée and lumpfish roe!*

Flavia had trained Maria and Osgar to respond to the whistle, five times out of ten. The demand for handmade butter that they were selling in the tea-room was so great they had bought another cow from Michael McOstrich and a second-hand milking-machine. Sissy and Michael McOstrich had married. The reception had been at the Fitzgeorge Arms, a lavish spree according to gossip but no one from Curraghcourt had been invited, which was not surprising.

Kieran, Turlough McGurn's delivery boy, had quarrelled with his master and come to work in the walled garden. They had harvested the broad beans, carrots, potatoes and spring cabbages I had sown. The cauliflowers had come to nothing and most of the peas had been eaten by slugs but they had so many courgettes they were selling them in the tea-room. Mrs O'Kelly's cakes were all right but nothing like so good as mine. (I tried not to be ignobly pleased to hear this.) They had put glass into a small area of the greenhouse for seed-sowing. They planned to restore the whole, section by section, as the money became available. Maud had said she could not hear an English accent without thinking of me. She had not said what it was she thought, but Constance felt it was near enough a compliment, coming from Maud, to be worth passing on.

I read and reread Constance's letters until I knew them by heart. But afterwards I felt so unsettled and miserable that I accused myself of masochism. I found it difficult to reply because it was essential that she should think I was too busy enjoying myself to return to Ireland. Every word I wrote, therefore, was a lie. Occasionally I was tempted to unburden myself to Sarah for the pleasure of speaking about the one person who was always present in my mind though I tried so hard never to think of him. Later I was always thankful I had resisted the impulse to confide. What good could it possibly do? I must get myself over it as best I could.

At first I was reluctant to go out. The effort of putting on a good face and being an amusing companion seemed more than I was capable of. But as time passed, as we moved from a cool windy spring into a hot airless summer, I forced myself to behave with circumspection and at least to look as though I was cheerful. We gave dinner parties, went to other people's, attended first nights, private views, drinks parties: the usual enjoyments of town life. My heart felt like a stone.

The months passed. I was given a salary increase and greater responsibility. Sometimes I went out with Sarah and the jolly bachelor barrister. I joined groups from work in restaurants and wine bars. Harriet Byng, who had been responsible for my going to Curraghcourt in the first place, telephoned to ask me to meet her new husband, who turned out to be artistic director of the English Opera House, and exceptionally handsome and clever. It became my chief pleasure to go with them to sit in soothing darkness in that lovely auditorium, to listen to sublime singing and watch the playing out of other people's dramas and tragedies. I refused all invitations from men who I suspected might have ideas about extending the evening beyond talking and eating. There are not many men who are satisfied with conversation and the sight of one stuffing one's face at their expense. For my twenty-eighth birthday ten of us went to see *Così Fan Tutte* and afterwards to Annabel's. I danced with everyone and went home alone.

Gradually I became inured to unhappiness. There were days when I hardly noticed the pain in the region of my heart that was grief. I tried to put back the weight I had lost since leaving Ireland. I cut back on the drinking; I stopped taking headache pills. I began to sleep longer and deeper. Encouraged by Sarah I replanted the tiny garden of Paradise Row and redecorated the sitting room. This gave me real pleasure. But when I heard an Irish accent in the street I was immediately transported back to that other world and I could not read or listen to news about Dublin, Belfast, Stormont or the activities of the IRA without a wholly inappropriate feeling of nostalgia.

Constance, who had remained a loyal correspondent despite the fact that it took me weeks to reply with letters that were short and unsatisfactory, wrote to say that she and Eugene were getting married. *Now, Bobbie, I know it's a long way and you're busy now with your job and your gay life in London but you must know that the day won't be the same if you aren't there to see me off. As for going away, we're having one night at the Grand Hotel in Williamsbridge because we have to be back for the visitors but we won't mind that. We're so lucky to be together. But I must have you in the congregation. It's a lot to ask, I know, but it means so MUCH to me.* This was underlined several times. There was more about wedding arrangements. Eugene's watercolours, displayed in the tea-room, merited an entire page to themselves. An American had bought the lot and ordered another set of Irish beauty spots.

The Galway Poets had moved their headquarters to Curraghcourt and last week they had had an inspiring reading from a visiting Russian. No one had understood a word but they were all used to extracting meaning from the sounds and rhythms of Gaelic so this hadn't really mattered. A local newspaper had referred to Curraghcourt as a new centre of Irish culture, reminiscent of the great days of Coole Park and Renvyle.

Maud had reduced to trembling wrecks a couple she had found sitting on her bed, eating biscuits out of the tin. Liddy was working hard for her exams and driving everyone quite mad by lecturing them continually about the wrongs of Ireland. Flurry's railway was progressing well. It would be ready to take passengers by the start of next season. Flavia had begun to read *David Copperfield* and was crazy about it. She carried it with her everywhere and was planning to write a novel herself with Agnes Wickfield as the first person narrator.

Finn and Violet were going to stay for a week with old friends in Kildare.

Violet is so looking forward to it that she's been as good as gold, practising her walking and talking all day long. You would not believe the improvement. Yesterday she managed ten steps with only one stick. It gives me real pleasure to see them together. He's remarkably patient and good with her. Once or twice I've seen him angry because, you know, she's not the brightest star in the sky, but he tries very hard to suppress sarcastic remarks. He must feel grateful for this second chance. As for her, I have no doubt that she will do everything she can to make him a good wife. She adores him and always has done. The past ought not to be remembered by anyone. They were equally to blame, you know, for I must say that Finn neglected her and she, poor thing . . . Well, as I say, they have forgiven each other and that's all that matters. I'm secretly hoping they will have another baby. Wouldn't that be just perfect? That's if Violet's strong enough. I suppose they will consult doctors in Dublin first. God is very bountiful and forgiving, one can only feel, though I must admit to doubts about the way we've interpreted His intentions. Father Deglan is bullying me about taking Communion before the wedding and I've an idea he's twigged what my problem is. It will be a relief to be married and have a clear conscience. But I can't be quite happy until I've had it in writing that you're definitely coming. I've so much to tell you, dearest Bobbie.

I sent back an apologetic note, explaining that because of the pressure of work I could not spare the time to see her married. I knew my words lacked warmth though I tried to infuse them with enthusiasm for the ceremony to come. I sent a first edition of Samuel Ferguson's poetry, which I could ill afford. After that Constance wrote less often and more briefly. I knew she was hurt and I was truly sorry for it. But I had come to dread the pain that her letters unwittingly inflicted. They disturbed the smooth surface of common sense and prudence I was spreading over my sensibilities, like dead leaves over freezing soil.

Jazzy and Kit's wedding was a different matter altogether. To our relief Sarah and I were not asked to be bridesmaids. At the ages of twenty-nine and twenty-eight respectively we considered ourselves too old and Kit had more than enough female relations who were willing. The marriage took place in Norfolk as Jazzy's parents were between wives and husbands and never in one place for more than a few months at a time.

Random Hall was a magnificent pile of Tudor red brick surrounded by acres of parkland. Kit's father, Lord Random, was a tired old roué who was now reaping what he had had such a good time sowing. He was appallingly rude to the woman who was apparently his mistress, who in her turn behaved with offensive arrogance to any woman under fifty, in case they tried to steal her winnings. Lady Random did not trouble to hide her conviction that her son's marriage was a mistake. She spoke of Jasmine as "the bride", never looking at her without an intake of breath and a lifting of eyebrows. Nevertheless Lady Random intended to make the most of this opportunity to put on an impressive show. Elaborate marquees stretched over baronial lawns, everything was served on ice, including the wedding cake: a confection of pistachio and persimmon, which had been flown over from Maxim's. The flowers were green euphorbias and dark red roses that dripped like blood from every swag and pole and across every table.

Jazzy became tearful beforehand but not as tearful as her mother, an English rose whose petals had crumpled and who had stopped on her way to Norfolk for a fortifying drink or two. She must have had a flask in her bag for after the service she had to be supported down the aisle by Kit's father and one of the ushers. Jazzy's Chinese father seemed determined to pander to the reputation of his race for inscrutability. He was immaculately kitted out in morning coat and accessories and retained his top hat squarely on his head for the entire day. He sat alone, refusing to eat or drink or talk to anyone. He disappeared after the speeches and was discovered hours later meditating cross-legged in a grove in the baronial woods, naked to the waist, still wearing the top hat.

Jazzy looked extraordinarily beautiful and Kit delivered the responses in ringing tones, but I was disturbed by the way he looked at the chief bridesmaid, a buxom girl of eighteen. By the end of the day Lady Random was only slightly less drunk than Jazzy's mother.

She seemed to gravitate towards Sarah and me, perhaps because we were the only sober guests. We had tried to become intoxicated (weddings are only supportable when braced by a large intake of alcohol) but our spirits were low and we were victims of that hideous clarity of vision which is the result of the combination.

'The worst thing is,' protested Lady Random, 'the girl is a slut. You can see it in those slitty eyes. My grandchildren will all be baskets. Any passing fishmonger or knife-grinder that fakes her tancy. I've always hated the Japs. Ever since the last war.'

Sarah and I, who were standing on either side of her, held grimly to an arm each as Lady Random tried to sink into a gilt chair that someone had removed five minutes ago. In vain we assured her that Jazzy's father was Chinese and probably hated the Japanese even more than she did.

'Why couldn't my darling boy have fallen for one of you?' whimpered Lady Random. '*Any*thing would have been better than that half-caste. Life is *too* cruel. I'm going to die lown upstairs. I may be tome sime.'

There is no saying what Lady Random's feelings might have been had I been her daughter-in-law. I suspected that any woman, even a princess of the blood royal, would have been resented.

Not long after this nadir Sarah's and my fortunes revived. Sarah became engaged to her jolly bachelor and he moved into Paradise Row. I was head-hunted for a job at twice my current salary as assistant to a rich art dealer. I accepted his offer because I was aware that two bright, competent people were before me in the queue for career advancement at the museum and because I longed for change of any kind. The rich art dealer travelled the world in search of ever rarer and more beautiful paintings and antiques and he needed someone reasonably knowledgeable to keep his business running in England. The job was fascinating, never the same two days running, always challenging, sometimes rule-breaking.

The best thing about the new job was that I was now paid enough to begin a collection of my own. The house at Paradise Row began to fill with my purchases. I decided to specialize in Irish silver and Irish Chippendale. I justified this to myself on the grounds that these were still undervalued and would therefore be a good investment.

Time passed. I spent Christmas at Cutham. Ruby was thrilled to see me. She was knitting matinée coats by the dozen as Oliver was about to become a father. He complained to me several times *sotto voce* that Sherilee seemed to have gone off sex. She wore black leather dungarees over her distended stomach, ate pickled walnuts compulsively and called me 'Auntie Bobs'.

As spring came round once more I felt a resurgence of that egoism which is the kernel of survival. I enjoyed my job. The rich art dealer, whose name was Myles Boughton, was attractive, intelligent and appreciative of my efforts. He had an excellent sense of humour and an Irish grandmother. And a wife. He asked me to have dinner with him. I refused. When he asked me to go over the accounts with him after hours, this also I refused. I would not even share sandwiches and tomato juice with him at lunchtime when the office was empty. After a while I found it necessary to explain that I had made it a rule never to go out with married men, even in circumstances when I could be perfectly sure that nothing more than the purest friendship was offered. He confessed, then, that he remembered reading about Burgo and me a couple of years before. He said now he knew me it had made him thoroughly glad to be a champagne Socialist.

Despite my determination to keep a distance between us he continued to be a generous employer and found several pieces of silver and furniture for my collection at giveaway prices. When I became suspicious that he was subsidizing these bargains, he laughed and told me not to be an idiot. After he discovered that Sarah and I also had champagne tastes but insufficient incomes to indulge them he sent round cases at regular intervals. He claimed that they were presents from grateful clients and as he only drank Louis Roederer Cristal himself he would be grateful if we would take them off his hands.

I had learned my lesson. I felt proud of my own sagacity. Sarah thought I was taking things too far. She liked Lord Bountiful – as she always called him, even to his face. Luckily he was tolerant and was amused by her. Sarah said (not to his face) that anyway his marriage was on the rocks. This was probably true, I had to agree. I had met Mrs Boughton once. She was suffering from religious mania, had joined a cult and was attempting to give it pots of Lord Bountiful's money. Sarah told me at least once a day, in unsparing terms, that I was a fool to turn my back on this chance for happiness.

'You've been bloody miserable for so long, Bobbie,' she said to me one evening. 'Now you've got to seize this gift from the gods.'

'I don't know what you're talking about.' I was – justifiably I thought, after all my efforts – annoyed. In my own opinion I had come close to rivalling the Spartan boy, famous for concealing a fox within his shirt and not letting on, though it was gnawing at his entrails. Quite why he had done such a thing I could not remember.

'All right, you've gone through the motions,' said Sarah, 'but anyone with half a brain can see your heart isn't in it.'

'Isn't in what?' I asked, perhaps waspishly.

'In this life you've constructed so carefully. Being a single woman, independent, successful, hard-working, self-sufficient. Like an iceberg that's put out into the chilliest part of the Arctic Ocean.'

'I enjoy my work. My brain is pulsating with newly acquired wisdom. I have a circle of friends. Engagements almost every night of the week. I bind up the paws of any limping creature I meet. This house is filling up with beautiful things. Why does everyone think happiness always has to involve love and sex?'

'Because, my dear sweet simple girl,' said Sarah with great emphasis, 'it just bloody does. That's all I can say. You need a companion. Someone whose happiness is more important to you than your own. Well, of course, that's utterly unrealistic, but at least someone whose happiness matters nearly as much. You can't live alone and be happy. You ought to be able to, I freely admit, but you just bloody well can't.'

I acknowledged Sarah's common sense. Lord Bountiful – Myles – became pressing. I withstood the pressure, which made him more eager.

'What more do you want?' cried Sarah in exasperation. 'You're nearly twenty-nine. You're no longer a timid ingénue. He's good-looking, intelligent, well educated, kind to animals and likes gardening. For heaven's sake, let whatever happened in Ireland go the way of all flesh!'

'What do you mean?'

'All right. You want it in plain language. Jazzy says there must have been something between you and the master of Curry-what's-it. That place you lived in. It's the only thing we can think of that's made you into a wraith imprisoned behind a glass wall, condemned to watch life pass you by. We haven't dared say anything because you've been so strung up we were terrified of precipitating something worse. I've deliberately let the knives go blunt and stopped buying paracetamol just in case.'

I laughed. 'Honestly, Sarah! You and Jazz are hopeless romantics! Your fevered imaginations are running away with you. You're both in the toils of love and naturally you think everyone else should be, too. I just happen to like running my own life in my own way. I like Myles very much but . . .'

'But what?'

'I burned my fingers badly and naturally I'm reluctant to put my hand back into the flame.'

'Oh, for heaven's sake! You're not still thinking of that bloody old minister! He's probably got a paunch and bouncing twins by now.'

'I'm not still thinking of him.'

'Well, then! Are you going to make yourself a martyr to men's failings or are you going to seize life by the scruff of the neck like an intelligent woman and make of it what you want? You've got to think what your future's going to be. Do you want to be a lonely, embittered spinster or a paid-up member of the human race?'

I sighed. 'Put like that, there's only one answer.'

I began to go out with Lord Bountiful – Myles. We attended operas, plays and concerts. We went for walks, exchanged books, talked about beautiful things. We enjoyed each other's company, laughed a lot. A few weeks after our first dinner he separated from his wife. I hoped it was nothing to do with me. Myles and I were happy together. I had to admit that his companionship added something to my life that had been sorely missed. I felt much more cheerful. Until it was time to say goodnight when I refused to let him into my bed and he departed, disgruntled.

'For crying out *loud*!' yelled Sarah. 'What *more* will you demand of the poor man? He must have the patience of a saint! If I'd treated Bryn' – this was the jolly Welsh bachelor barrister – 'like that for a week he'd have been off. This poor man's been held at arm's length for *months*. Have a heart, Bobbie! Think of the future.'

It was now May. More than a year since I had left Curraghcourt. I had not heard from Constance for two months. I had put the past behind me. As Sarah said, if women wished to be accepted as equals they must behave in all ways as superior beings and not like mawkish, maundering slops. I saw the truth of this. When at breakfast one Saturday morning I received a letter from Lord Bountiful, now in Jaipur, I opened it with feelings almost of eagerness.

Dear Roberta [said the letter],

I'm going next to New York. I've decided to set up a base there. Will you join me? And run the place for me in your own inimitable style? For six months at least. Longer if you like it. I'm getting a divorce, by the way. I would appreciate it if you would help me over this hurdle. All expenses paid,

of course. If the answer is yes, you might like to order some
travelling thing: clothes, suitcases and whatnot. Stick them on
the account.

All my love, M

'Bloody *hell*!' said Sarah to the jolly barrister. 'New York! New clothes! New luggage! All expenses paid! All *you* ever give me is books and theatre tickets.'

'You said that was what you liked!' Bryn protested. 'You said you didn't want to be bought with female flimflams.'

'What a fool you are to have believed me.' Sarah was scornful. 'Well, Bobbie? I hope you're going to say yes?'

New York. I had never been there but I had seen it in films. It looked good. What was the word people always used about it? Buzzing. Americans were enthusiastic. They adored antiques. Much of the best stuff was already over there. I might be able to buy some of it back. It would be a new beginning. I would be an idiot not to go.

'If you don't go I'll think you're a complete—' Sarah began.

'I know, I know,' I said. I was silent a moment longer. 'I think . . . perhaps I will.'

Sarah let out a profound sigh. 'Phew! Bryn, you can go and bed down in Jazzy's old room tonight. I'm going to sleep the sleep of the just and I don't want to be disturbed. After thirteen months of walking on eggs, measuring every word I've said, tiptoeing round anything that might be a delicate subject: welcome back to the land of the living, Bobbie!'

'I'm so sorry to have been such a nuisance,' I said humbly.

I rang Myles in India and told him I would come to New York. He sounded pleased. He said he had rented a nice old house in Turtle Bay, a quiet part of Manhattan. I could have the ground-floor flat. Katherine Hepburn, who lived next door, was reputed to be something of a recluse and would therefore be an ideal neighbour.

For several days I went about my work in something of a dream, trying to imagine what my new life in America would be like. I failed completely. I would have to live it and see. I rang Cutham and told Ruby. She was excited for me.

'Your mother'll miss you, dear, no end, but I expect it's for the best. Sometimes I think you haven't been a happy girl. And I can't think why. With a lovely face and figure and so clever as you are, the world ought to be at your feet. If I've said that once to Oliver and Sherilee I've said it a thousand times.'

I could imagine how well that would have gone down with Sherilee, who had made it clear from the moment we met that she considered me a stuck-up bitch.

'Ah, well. Thank you for that. I'll come down tomorrow to say goodbye.'

'New York!' My mother looked up from her book. She was lying in a deckchair on the terrace at Cutham, her feet on a stool, a rug over her knees. 'I hear the crime rate is very high there. They have a lot of negroes and Puerto Ricans, of course, which would account for it. I only hope you know what you're doing, Roberta. I suppose there's a man involved. No, spare me the details.' She lifted a hand in protest as I opened my mouth to tell her about Myles. 'Just try to avoid getting into the newspapers if you can.' She rang the little brass bell that stood next to a plate of homemade Turkish Delight on the table beside her to tell Ruby that it was time for tea.

I went to see Oliver and Sherilee at the Red Lion. Sherilee was nursing a pink scrap. 'Poor Auntie Bobs,' said Sherilee as I held my nephew in my arms and kissed his dear little screwed-up face. 'It's a shame, it really is. Seeing other people's babies when you're not likely to have one of your own. I'm ever so sorry for you. I hear New York's a nasty dirty place. I hope you won't be lonely.'

Oliver walked out with me to the car. 'If business picks up I might come out and see you later on.'

'That would be lovely. Will you bring Sherilee and Marlon?' This was my nephew.

'Probably not. She's still off sex, you know.'

'Give her a chance. It's only six weeks since the baby was born. You must be kind to her and try to be patient. Now you're a father you've got to think about other things.'

'Like what?'

'Well . . . making a good home for him. Perhaps saving up for his education. Um . . . developing interests he might be able to share with you.'

'Mm.' Oliver kicked a bit of gravel about with his toe and looked gloomy. 'Perhaps. I don't remember our father ever sharing any interests with me.' He brightened. 'At least I'm not married to her. To tell you the truth, I'm not sure if Sherilee and I've got that much in common.' He put on his wise face. 'It'll be better if I don't get too involved.'

The word went round of my imminent departure for America. Jazzy, now living in a flat with Kit in Holland Park, came over at once to cry on my shoulder. 'I can't bear it that you're going! I've relied on you *al*ways to be there. And you *keep* running off.' She looked at me reproachfully through smudged eyes.

'But, Jazz darling, you don't need me now. You've got Kit.'

'Yes. Well, of course, he's marvellous and I *could*n't be happier. But recently he's had so much work on. He's been out nearly every night this week, entertaining authors, and he says I'd be bored and in the way while they talk business. Last night he didn't come home until two. It can be very lonely. I don't know a soul in Holland Park.'

I felt despondent when I heard this. Luckily Jasmine adored New York.

Harriet also was sad. 'I'm going to miss you like mad!'

'No, you won't,' said Rupert. 'I'm going to be flying over all the time, doing a season at the Met. You can come too.'

I was immeasurably cheered to hear this. Though I knew it was exactly what I needed I could not rid myself of a fear of being uprooted. It had cost so much in time and effort to re-establish myself in London.

'Stop worrying, you lily-liver!' cried Sarah. 'You'll adore it. And you'll adore him. I pretty much adore him myself on your behalf. What generosity! I *like* that in a man!'

Poor Bryn looked rather blue and that evening brought home an expensively beribboned box, containing a pair of Janet Reger knickers.

'You ass!' said Sarah. But I saw her kiss him in the kitchen later, quite tenderly for her.

An airline ticket, one way, arrived the following Saturday morning. The flight left the next day.

'Concorde, no less!' Sarah screamed. 'All *I've* ever had is a second-class ticket to New Street, Birmingham. I should have played harder to get. My goodness, Lord Bountiful's impatient! But wise, I think. He knows what a ditherer you are. Now you've got to get moving.' She looked at her wristwatch. 'In just over twenty-six hours you'll be airborne and winging your way to a new life!'

'But what about all my things?' I felt anguished. 'My furniture. The silver. The creamware dessert service I've just bought.'

'Goodness, but you're materialistic!' Sarah looked shocked. 'You can leave them here. I'll be delighted to look after them for you. Then, if you decide to stay for good you can have them shipped out.'

Bryn was sitting at the breakfast table in a towelling robe and socks, so brotherly was our intimacy at this stage. 'This is just like a rags-to-riches musical. Any minute men wearing white tie and twirling ivory-topped canes are going to shimmy in through the front door, singing about heaven. Can life offer more?'

'The girl's going to be lapped in luxury and she fusses about a few old bits of wood and metal.' Sarah spread butter lavishly on her toast. 'I feel like an ugly sister.'

'Now who's being materialistic?' I said.

I picked up a letter which had arrived in the same post as the airline ticket. It had an Irish stamp but the writing was crooked and wandering, not Constance's elegant hand. I opened it and looked at the signature. It was from Maud.

I got up from the table and went over to the window to read it.

Dear Bobbie,

You'll be surprised to hear from me. I hate letter-writing so I shan't bother with the usual courtesies. I don't know when you last heard from Constance. The girl is in a dream of love with that fool so perhaps she has not written to tell that my idiot daughter has left Curraghcourt and gone off to Dublin with Anthony Molesworth. There is no reasoning with fools. I cannot tell why I should have been saddled with a halfwit for a daughter. God knows I've tried to keep her straight. Anyway, she and Anthony have gone. Basil Molesworth, a fool of a different kind, is selling Annagh Park so he can buy a house in Dublin where we can all live in a no doubt uncomfortable ménage à quatre. He has the idea that the drier climate will help my bones. And that Violet may need us. As to that, I cannot say. Anyway, I do not feel I can stay on at Curraghcourt in the circumstances.

Of course I saw how it was going to be. After Violet left I asked Finn why he had been what we used to call a complaisant husband. He said he knew the marriage was going from bad to worse but his heart had not been in it. He was talking about sex naturally. If we women took that attitude the human race would cease to reproduce itself. Still, I dare say you disagree with me. The modern girl is a different sort of creature.

I suggested in that case he might as well go where his heart was. Or better still get you back here. I suppose you

*thought you had been discreet but for anyone with eyes to
see it was obvious. I cannot altogether blame you. Finn is
less of a fool than any man I know. His reply was that you
had a new life now and he had nothing to offer you but
financial difficulties, troublesome children, a life in a
wilderness far from all the things a reasonable human being
has the right to expect. This may be your view also. I don't
know. But because you were good to us, I have thought it
right to let you know. Apparently after his term as senator
ends, which it will do next year, he plans to write a book
about Charles Parnell. Who wants to read about a fool like
Parnell? Being English you may not know that he was a
nineteenth-century Irish politician who destroyed his career
by having an adulterous affair with a minx called Kitty
O'Shea. I leave for Dublin tonight. You can do as you like,
of course.*

   I remain, yours sincerely,
Maud Crawley (No reply expected.)

'That's a pretty stamp.' Sarah picked up Maud's envelope and
examined it. 'The Republic of Ireland. That reminds me. Someone
telephoned yesterday while you were out. A man. A good voice,
deep, educated, not quite English. It might have been Irish. Or Scottish.
I'm no good at accents.'

'When we met you thought I was Australian,' Bryn reminded her.
I looked up from the letter. 'What did he say?'

'I explained that you were tidying up loose ends at work. He
said he might ring back and I told him he'd better make it snappy
as you were leaving for New York soon. He asked if you'd be away
for long. I said, at least six months, possibly for good. He said . . .
what was it?' Sarah snatched the marmalade spoon from Bryn before
he could put it in the jam. 'In that case he wouldn't trouble you
when you were obviously busy and to wish you good fortune. Or
was it every happiness? But before I could ask his name he rang
off.'

'Bobbie! You haven't heard a word I've said.' Bryn was accusing.
A minute had gone by during which I had folded the letter, put it
back in its envelope and gone to the desk to find my address book.
'What I want to know is when we're going to be allowed to come
over and see you? Steerage, naturally. But I've always want to go to
New York. What do you say, old girl?' He winked at Sarah. 'Shall

we have our honeymoon there? Provided we aren't *de trop*, of course.'

Sarah was looking at me hard, with an expression that was severe. 'I hope I haven't done the wrong thing, telling you about the phone call. I assume he was someone from the episode that's history now. You're over all that. Think of the future, my girl. Now is not the time to be dreaming about the past.'

'Sorry,' I said. 'Yes, of course. I'm afraid I wasn't listening properly. The future.' I stood still for a moment, trying to collect my thoughts. 'Yes. Where's that address book? I'm going to ring the removers and tell them they must come and crate my things. Then I'm going to pack.'

'At last!' Sarah clapped her hands. 'I detect genuine enthusiasm. I see the martial gleam in her eye. I'm going to open a bottle of Lord Bountiful's champagne.'

'But it's nine o'clock in the morning!' Bryn objected.

'Don't be so puritanical,' Sarah reproved him. 'This isn't a chapel and we aren't miners whose only legitimate pleasure is a weekly bath and lot of sloppy singing.' She popped the cork, poured out three glasses and handed me one. 'Now drink deep, everyone. To the future!'

'To the future!' Bryn and I echoed dutifully.

FIFTY-FOUR

The windows of the departure lounge at Heathrow were clouded with circles of condensed breath from the open-mouthed spectators as Concorde was towed to her loading bay. The plane had the allure of a famous film star. However indifferent you might consider yourself to such things, you could not take your eyes off her. Inevitably the dipped beak, the lean body, the swept-back wings prompted comparisons with birds of prey: beautiful, noble, outlandish. Mounting the steps to the cabin, the drabbest of her passengers seemed to take on something of Concorde's self-conscious glamour. As she skimmed down the runway with formidable grace and a roar that made one's blood sing, even a woman as unmoved by machinery as I could not but be impressed by her elegance and the originality of her design. She positively screamed of the future. I saw her take off without the slightest regret.

The plane to Galway was, by contrast, a cigar-case with wings. I quite expected them to flap as we lumbered into the air. The neat fields and tidy villages of the English Midlands dropped away beneath us. As we reached cruising height the nun sitting next to me continued to count the beads of her rosary but with diminished fervour. In order to rid myself of the conviction that the plane was kept in the air by the rigidity of my stomach muscles I bought a minuscule bottle of champagne. It was too sweet and too warm but a glass and a half was enough to relax the tension which over the last twenty-four hours had been screwed to a pitch that made operating telephones, writing letters of apology and explanation, wrapping treasures and zipping suitcases more than usually difficult.

As we flew above the Irish Sea I saw what I was almost certain was the ferry, though it was no larger than a grain of wheat, ploughing the smooth waters on its way to Dún Laoghaire. I wondered if the motherly waitress was aboard, tending some sickly, miserable passenger. The coast of Ireland, outlined by a white frill of breaking waves, slid beneath us. Dublin, a condensed town plan of roads and squares neatly divided by the Liffey, petered out into the green crinkled plains of Kildare and Offaly. I must have dozed for a while. During my last night in England my sleep had been continually disturbed by the resurgence of emotions, floating up like bubbles to break on the surface of my mind, an uncomfortable mixture of hope, doubt, anticipation and fear. When I opened my eyes and looked again we were crossing a strand of pewter that must be the River Shannon into Galway. Now the colours became more varied. Every shade of brown and grey mingled with the green that was divided by the fingers of great lakes. We descended into Galway airport with breathtaking suddenness.

After Heathrow it seemed small and friendly. All around me people were speaking with the soft consonants and extravagant inflections which had given rise to a painful nostalgia whenever I heard them in England. I collected my luggage, found a porter and was taken to the bus station. I changed buses at Oughterard. The green and cream vehicle, twenty years old and in need of a coat of paint, set off twenty-five minutes late, for no good reason that I could discover except that the driver was enjoying a conversation with the conductor.

When the ground became hilly, my heart, already agitated, began to pound against my ribs. Behind the hills rose the mountains. Their beauty inspired such joy and terror that I was forced to eat the barley sugar the stewardess had given me on the plane to keep myself calm.

The woman sitting beside me wanted to talk. She was from Limerick, visiting her childhood home after several years' absence. She hated the harshness of the Connemara landscape, the brown bogs thick with cotton grass, the wind that blew summer and winter, the lack of human imprint.

'I love it,' I said. 'I can't think of anywhere else I'd rather be.'

The woman gave me a doubtful look.

As the bus descended the steep road into Kilmuree I had to pinch my arm to convince myself I was awake. I listened to the woman grumbling about the lack of an ensuite bathroom at her old home, the terrible television reception, the way her sister's husband went to bed at nine o'clock and expected the house to be silent thereafter.

I sympathized as well as I could but I heard scarcely one word in ten. Through the smeary window the woman's eyes grew round as she saw my luggage being taken off the bus. I suppose four large suitcases did look opulent. I thought of Jazzy and smiled to myself.

'Taxi, miss? Well, shite and onions! If it isn't Miss Bobbie!'

'If it isn't Sam O'Kelly!'

I kissed his cheek. He looked surprised but pleased.

'Bless me sainted mother but I never thought to see you here again. You're looking a picture. What brings you to the back of beyond on this fine day?' Before I could reply he picked up two of my cases. 'Sure 'tis the castle you'll be wanting. 'Twill be a pleasure to take you.'

Outside the bus station was a battered car with *O'Kelly's Kabs* written crookedly along its side. I got into the passenger seat while Sam fetched the remaining cases and put them in the boot.

'I'm awaiting delivery of a Fort Cortina,' he said proudly. ''Tis a pity you couldn't have come next week. But never mind, you'll be wanting to get on. Would you like me to step on it or do you fancy the scenic route?'

'Step on it, if you wouldn't mind, Sam.'

'You see Larkie's taken over Dooley's?' As we drove past it Sam pointed to a shop front forgotten for so long but now almost shocking in its familiarity. *O'Kelly & Dooley* was written above the plate-glass windows. 'The man's so idle he rarely puts in an appearance these days.' There was an arrangement of tin cans in a large basket. I thought (but perhaps I imagined it) the name of *Fauchon* leaped out at me as we drove past.

'I'll put a bit of boot behind it so you can see the castle before it gets dark,' said Sam. I appreciated what seemed a miraculous piece of mind-reading. 'You know, Miss Bobbie,' he added as we left Kilmuree and drove between craggy mountains that glistened after a recent shower like chased silver, 'there's many that knocks it but still, speaking as a man that's as familiar with the United States of America as with the back of me hand, I never did see a finer stretch of country than this.'

'I agree with you, Sam.'

'You do? That's good to hear.'

At the turn that was the beginning of the drive I saw the sign Constance and I had had installed fourteen months before. It said 'Curraghcourt 1 mile'.

This time I bit my thumb hard to convince myself I was not dreaming.

The ruts in the track had been filled with stones. We climbed the hill. Sam had stopped talking for which I was grateful. I wanted to take in every detail: the rusting wire of the fences, the sagging gates, the heaps of boulders, the sandy courses that marked rivers of recent rain. The woods greeted us, cool and dark. I recognized the shapes of trunks, the twists of individual branches. We came to where the track skirted the walled garden. I thought of asking Sam to let me out so I could go in and walk round it, examine the rows of vegetables, the espaliered fruit trees, the statue of St Fiacre, the compost heap. But that would have been cowardly. At the top of the hill we left the trees and began to roll downwards, the tyres skidding where the new layer of stones was thickest . . . and there was the house.

'Stop a minute, Sam, if you wouldn't mind.'

He obligingly pulled up.

Whenever Curraghcourt had forced itself into my mind during the last year it was this view of it I saw most often. Its four round towers, pierced by lancet windows, stood proud of the woods that crowded the east and west fronts. From this angle the eighteenth-century façade which had been built round the ancient core was largely concealed by trees and the gatehouse. One saw only the battlements and the ten great chimney-stacks from which drifts of lilac smoke vanished into the white sky. I wound down the window and breathed in the scent of bog myrtle. There seemed to be an extra ingredient in the air that refreshed me. My blood was careering through my veins, invigorated, as though my mind and body had been for a long time in a state of apathy.

'A fine place.' Sam spoke softly as though to himself. 'Something to be proud of. You won't find anything like it in New Jersey even if the shops do stay open all night.'

'Let's go on now.'

There was a new sign which separated coaches from cars by means of arrows. Another directed visitors to the Model Railway. 'Adults, 50 pence; Children, Free'. In the field to the left of the drive a girl with brown hair was taking a pony over a series of striped jumps. I recognized Flavia on the Cockatoo. She was too far away to hear me call.

'Here we are.' Sam drew up outside the gatehouse.

My courage almost failed at that point. My legs seemed disinclined to obey me. Sam opened the car door and put a steadying hand under my elbow.

'I'll bring them,' he said as I made an effort to pick up the smallest of the suitcases.

We crossed the drawbridge. The moat still smelled slightly of rotting vegetation but the rubbish had been cleared away. The holes in the planks had been newly patched with lead.

The ticket table stood untenanted beneath the archway which was cold and gloomy as usual. As it was Sunday there were no visitors. The front courtyard, north-facing and never particularly sunny, seemed brilliantly lit by contrast. I had forgotten the ringing sound one's shoes made on the undulating cobbles. Someone had planted little bushes in the borders that edged the courtyard. Roses and paeonies. They would be unlikely to do well in such thin soil. I remembered my scheme of a box and herb parterre for which there had never been enough money.

The great pedimented door was before me, newly painted a good dark green. It was ajar as always. I climbed the five steps, put my hand on the knob, passed through it. Now I was terrified this might be a dream. The hall smelt as it always did of turf smoke. I shut my eyes, opened my mouth and drew it deep into my throat.

Sam coughed discreetly. I must have been standing with closed eyes and parted lips for some time for he had brought in all my luggage. I searched in my bag for my purse.

'Did you leave your wits in England to think I'd take money from you at a time like this? It's been a treat, Miss Bobbie.' He wrung my hand. 'Larkie'll be tickled to death to hear you're back. I'll be seeing you.'

After Sam had gone I leaned against the door jamb and took in the details of the hall. In front of me, at the far end, were the stairs with the gallery above. There was the sedan chair and the suit of armour. The longcase clock still ran slow. A shaft of light from the window above the gallery made a path across the floor. I walked along it looking from side to side. To my left was the great fireplace with its stone chimneypiece. I remembered Lughnasa. And then St Stephen's Day. I went to stand beside the fireplace. I put my hand on the lintel and prodded the smoking turves with the toe of my shoe.

Constance came through the archway that led down to the kitchen quarters. She was carrying a vase in one hand and flowers in the other. Because she was concentrating on not spilling the water she did not see me. She went to the side table. I watched her putting the flowers into the vase: red tulips, bronze wallflowers and forget-me-nots. Her hair was shorter now, and she wore a blue cardigan and a flowered skirt that stopped at the knee. On her feet were neat court shoes.

'Oh, damn!' she muttered as water splashed on to the mahogany. She rubbed it away with her sleeve.

Maria and Osgar ran in. They saw me at once and rushed, barking, towards me, their nails scrabbling on the boards. Halfway across the room Maria changed her bark to a high-pitched whine. She flung herself at my knees, her body shaking with excitement. Osgar approached more cautiously, then ran back to fetch the ragged piece of fur he had dropped in order to bark.

'What's the *mat*ter with you, you silly creatures?' Constance turned from her flowers. She gasped and her hand flew to her mouth. 'Oh! It can't be— Surely not—!' Hurling aside the flowers she ran towards me. 'Bobbie! *Darling!*'

I threw my arms around her. 'Oh Con! It's so good to see you!'

'I'd given up all hope of ever . . . Oh, this is too wonderful! I'm going to make a fool of myself. I can't help it, the shock.' She stood back and took my hands. 'Let me look at you. It's been such a long time. More than a year!' She examined my face, then wiped her eyes with her sleeve. 'Not changed at all! Oh, be *quiet*, Maria! I can't hear myself think!'

'I'm so sorry for not writing, for not coming to your wedding. Do forgive me!'

'Oh, I'm so happy I just can't take it in. I thought you'd forgotten all about us!' She embraced me again. 'I'm not imagining it. It *is* you. This is *glor*ious!'

'It is. But I'd understand if you were angry.' I put my arm round her waist. 'It wasn't because I'd forgotten. It was because . . . it was difficult.'

Constance smiled and shook her head. 'I never was angry a bit. Disappointed, I admit. But you're here now. You've come back to see us. We won't even *think* about the past. I was so sad that we'd lost touch, but of course I understood. You've been having such a good time in London, so busy with your new job and your friends—'

'Constance.' I stopped her. 'That's not true. No one matters more to me than the friends I have here.'

'That's like you to say so! Oh, how *glad* I am you came! Can you stay a little while with us?' Her eyes took in the four large suitcases.

'If you'll have me.'

'*Will* we?' she laughed. 'I'll get the best room ready. You can have

Maud's— Oh!' Constance's smile faltered. 'Of course, you don't know. I hardly know how to tell you. Violet – oh, it was very bad, the poor children— Reliving the past, you see – only this time I'd hoped— It was foolish of me but I thought she'd changed. We mustn't think too badly— It's almost like an illness with her. Bobbie, Violet's *gone*.'

'I know. Maud wrote to tell me.'

'Maud? Wrote to you?' Constance looked her amazement. 'But whatever for?'

'She thought I'd be interested.'

'That's very strange, that she should have thought of telling you! But, there! Maud's an original. And you had so much to do with Violet getting better. That must be why. Poor little Flavia! The child's heartbroken. Cried every minute of the day her mother left. But I hope she'll get used to the idea in time. And she's going to spend the summer holidays with Violet and Maud and that horrible man. Ah, well, I suppose one shouldn't judge. I don't think, between ourselves, Liddy minded as much as she ought. And Flurry – you know how he is. When we broke it to him he went straight out and laid several yards of railway track with Sam. He doesn't seem to notice his mother's gone. I suppose he's grown up not needing her. *Poor* Violet! I can't feel she'll be happy for long with Anthony. And Maud's so *furious* with her! But why am I talking of sad things when you've only just this minute come? I must run and find Eugene. He'll be *thrilled* to see you!'

'Yes, but Constance' – my mouth was so dry I could hardly speak – 'is Finn here?'

'Finn? Oh yes. He comes every weekend now. He's in the garden, trying to mend the fountain. It's blocked with leaves again. It's such a pernickety thing, you wouldn't believe. As a matter of fact I'm waiting until he's given up to telephone Thady O'Kelly. Did you want to say hello to him?' Constance put her arm through mine and together we walked across the hall into the drawing room. 'I'm sure he'll be very pleased to see you. You know how he is. He doesn't fuss much over people. But he had a fondness for you, Bobbie, though he'd never have shown it. Men are so odd about letting you see what they feel. I'm afraid he's much better tempered now that Violet's gone, but I don't want you to think badly of him. He did try, you know. But there I go again, dwelling on past things that are best forgotten.' She patted my arm and looked at me with affectionate eyes. 'Finn asked me once if I'd heard from you. And then, when I was halfway through telling him, he said, "Don't tell me any more.

It's another world. I prefer to remember her as she was when she was here." I thought that was quite emotional, coming from Finn. Shall we walk down and see him?' She put her hand on the handle of the French windows.

'Con. Darling. Would you mind very much if, just this once, I went on my own?'

'You'd like to see Finn alone?' Constance looked surprised. 'Of course, if that's what you want.' She continued to stare at me. 'Bobbie, you look so white. There's nothing wrong, is there?'

'I don't know.' I bit my lip to prevent it trembling. 'I must go and see.'

'Well, how mysterious . . .' Constance's large grey eyes held mine, bewildered. I saw that ideas were forming in her mind, superseding one another, contending for place until finally they were supplanted by a look of absolute astonishment. '*Bobbie!* You don't mean – you *can't* mean – you and Finn?' She seized my hands and clasped them between her own. 'Oh, what a *fool* I've been! A fool! Was there ever anyone so *blind*? Oh, my *dar*ling girl! And all this time . . . *Now* I see why he's been so sad. I knew he didn't love Violet: the marriage was hopeless right from the start; but I wanted so much – for the children's sake – and there he was, shut up in the library when he ought to have been . . . What am I saying? Bobbie.' Constance gripped my hands until they hurt. 'I understand it all now. That's why you stayed away! You didn't want to stand in the way of it. That was good of you, that was like you! Now I'm going to cry again but don't take any notice of that. Oh, my poor brother! And he never said a word! Go quickly now. *Go!*' She pushed me through the French windows.

I stepped into the garden. The cloud that had been across the sun moved slowly away and the yew trees cast deep shadows over the gravel path. I walked between the *miroirs d'eaux*. The scintillating light dazzled my eyes. Birds flew low over the water, snatching at insects. A lark ascending poured out its song. I paused on the top step at the end of the first terrace and looked down.

The round bowl of the fountain had been drained, leaving a sediment of mud and leaves. Finn had his back to me. He was bending over the jet, doing something with a spanner. I looked hungrily at him, at the shape of his head, the way his dark hair grew down the back of his neck. He wore the same disreputable clothes. I recognized the holey blue jersey, the threadbare corduroys. He was there before my eyes. Real. Flesh and blood. I clenched my fist until my nails dug into the palm to reassure myself that it was really him. I watched him for a long time, relishing the angle of his shoulders, the breadth of his back, the occasional glimpse of his hands. A plane passed overhead, miles up. He straightened to look at it, shielding his eyes from the glare, his back to the steps. Then he swore savagely and hurled the spanner into the bushes.

'If I were you,' I said, 'I should give it a good hard kick.'

He started; froze; remained motionless, his back still turned towards me. There followed what seemed a long silence. Then he said, 'I don't dare turn round.' Oh, how I loved the sound of his voice! 'I'm afraid the *sidh* may be playing a trick on me.'

'Not that you believe in them.'

'I wouldn't mind saying I did if I could go on with the deception.'

'Say it then.'

'I believe in them, in all of them: roanes, grogans and gruagach, pookas, firbolgs and' – he turned and looked up at me – 'cluri-caunes.' He closed his eyes briefly and then looked again. 'Still there. If you're a good fairy, come down. Come down anyway. I daren't approach in case you disappear.'

I walked down the steps and stopped by the edge of the fountain. We looked at each other. His face, so infinitely dear to me, was the feast my famished heart had yearned for without ceasing since I had seen him walking away at Dún Laoghaire. I had to steel myself to look into his eyes and blink away the tears that rushed into mine. It was like looking at the sun. I saw a question there.

'I heard you were going to America,' he said eventually. 'Is this— Have you come to say goodbye?'

'Maud wrote to me. About Violet. I got the letter yesterday. I came at once.' I stepped into the bowl.

His eyes softened. 'Then you've come because . . . Are things still the same with you?'

'Still the same.'

'My love!' he said in a low voice. He took hold of my arms to draw me to him. 'My love! My *love*!'

Around us the birdsong faded, the leaves ceased to rustle, the earth seemed to fall away beneath our feet and the clouds to rush upwards and outwards. The air beat like a giant wing in sympathy with our great longing. The sound of hoofs on gravel broke the stillness and Flavia on the Cockatoo came skidding into the circle of hornbeams.

'Bobbie! Sam said it was you but I didn't believe him! Timsy! Hold the Cockatoo, please!'

Timsy, looking hardly embarrassed at all, rose from the bushes and stepped grinning into the hornbeam circle to take the mare's bridle. ''Tis a grand day, Miss Bobbie, that's brought you back to light us with your loveliness like a moonbeam pinned against the velvet sky with stars!'

'Oh, Bobbie! I have missed you!' Flavia threw her arms round me. She was at least three inches taller and looked more like Finn than ever. 'Why've you stayed away so long?' Before I could answer she said, 'I've got some new jumps. Daddy gave them to me for my birthday. Do you want to come and see?'

Finn put his hand on her shoulder. 'Just a minute, darling.' I saw he had to make an effort to command himself and I felt sick with love. 'Bobbie's only just arrived after a long journey. She'll have plenty of time to look at them later. Let's go up to the house.'

Flavia took my hand. 'Are you staying?'

'Yes.'

'For a long time?'

Over her head my eyes met Finn's. 'Yes.'

'Good-ee!' Flavia put her other hand into her father's and the three of us walked up to the top terrace and along the avenue between the canals. 'Will you do the cooking? Mrs O'Kelly's all right but her food's awful.'

'I shall have to be tactful,' I said.

'Oh yes. I'll try and think of something. Perhaps we could say that you can't eat Irish food without getting sick.'

Finn laughed. 'If that's your idea of tact, I don't advise a career in diplomacy.'

'I wouldn't dream of anything so boring! I'm going to be a writer. Bobbie, I've begun my novel. I've got to page one hundred already but I haven't been able to get David Copperfield into the story yet. There's so much to say about Agnes's dog. He's a really beautiful Newfoundland and my own invention . . .'

As Flavia talked Finn and I looked at each other and I saw what was in his mind as clearly as though he had spoken the thought aloud.

'Oh, Lord! A reception committee,' he said as we approached the drawing-room windows.

Constance, Eugene, Flurry, Katty and Pegeen had assembled to greet me. As Flavia led me in, Liddy rushed into the room and pushed between them to hug me.

'Bobbie! I can't believe it! Aunt Con says you're going to live here again! For good!' She let go of me to examine my appearance. '*Amaz*ing clothes! You look fabulous. Danny says I oughtn't to think about such trivial things but sometimes it's more than one can help. You haven't changed a bit!'

'But you have!' I saw with pleasure that Liddy was clear-skinned and bright-eyed. She was slender without being too thin. Her hair was fastened into a pony-tail and she wore intellectual black from head to toe. But there was about her a new confidence, a new poise. She was eighteen, on the threshold of adult life.

'I'm going to Paris next week! Dad's given me the airfare. I'm so excited! I've bought some new things to wear. But of course they're just tat, really, from Williamsbridge.' Her eye fell on my black alpaca coat from Chloé which I had bought to take to New York.

I took it off and handed it to her. 'Go and try it on.'

'You don't mean it? *An*gel Bobbie!' She skipped from the room, clutching her prize.

Eugene stepped forward and kissed me on both cheeks. 'The pleasure of seeing you again, my dear Bobbie, is only enhanced by being, by me at any rate, unanticipated and . . . Allow me to say how delighted I am to learn from Constance that you may soon stand in a nearer relationship.'

He straightened the lapel of his coat, which had been crumpled by the embrace. Luckily the children never bothered to listen to anything Eugene said but Katty and Pegeen looked interested.

'How are you, Katty?' I shook her hand.

'Very well, Miss Bobbie. Timsy and I are betrothed. I've took pity on him for he's been very faithful—'

'Oh, tell the truth and shame the devil, Katty Kicart,' interrupted Pegeen. 'You decided to take him just because I've got myself engaged to Des Toomey, the dentist in Kilmuree.' She beamed, exposing a complete set of brilliantly white, perfectly even teeth.

'You could signal to the man in the moon with them things,' said Katty. 'When you've finished blinding our eyes we'll get back to the kitchen before Nellie O'Kelly burns the rashers.'

She and Pegeen made a dignified departure.

'How are you, Flurry?' He too was taller and his face was less round. I did not dare to kiss him.

Flurry shook my hand and looked at me solemnly. 'Very well, thank you.'

'I'd very much like to have a ride on the railway later on.'

'Oh, yes.' He smiled cautiously. 'And you can see my plans for the new generator I'm making. It has a proper filter so it won't cut out if there's dirt in the fuel.'

'I look forward to that.'

'I've been very daring, Finn, and taken it upon myself to bring up something from the cellar,' said Constance. She showed him the bottle which stood in a bucket of ice. 'I thought we might drink Bobbie's health. What do you think? Will this be suitable?'

'Good idea,' said Finn. It was much to his credit he did not protest when he saw it was a Veuve Clicquot La Grande Dame, though it could hardly be chilled enough.

'To dearest Bobbie.' Constance lifted her glass when we all had one. 'Welcome back, darling!'

I looked at their faces through something of a mist.

'What do you think of the ceiling, Bobbie?' asked Constance. 'We've had it cleaned. A man from An Taisce – that's our equivalent of your National Trust – came with a team of men and spent two weeks on it. He says he's only done a rough job to halt the decay and he's coming back next month to do it properly.'

I looked at the drawing room, so beautiful with all its imperfections, and was lost for words.

'While we're on the subject of decay,' said Finn, 'there's a patch of damp on the ceiling of my bedroom I'll like your opinion of, Bobbie.'

'Daddy!' Flavia looked shocked. 'You aren't going to make Bobbie work the minute she's come back? You've got to be kind to her.'

'I intend to be very kind to her.' Finn took my hand. 'And I hope she's going to be very kind to me.'

'Oh, goodness!' grumbled Flavia. 'If I hear anyone else mention plasterwork again I'll probably scream. All right, I'll come with you.'

'No, sweetheart,' said Constance. 'I particularly want you to help me count out yesterday's takings. You know how hopeless I am at adding up.'

'Can't Flurry? He's much better at maths than me. Oh, all *right* then,' she said, seeing that Flurry was drifting towards the door, no doubt with his thoughts full of the generator.

'Come along, Bobbie.' Finn put down his glass. 'What I want to show you won't wait.'

Constance and Eugene smiled understandingly as we left the room. I caught sight of someone's apron whisking away as we mounted the stairs. 'I suppose there soon won't be a soul in Kilmuree who doesn't know exactly where we're going and what we're going to be doing.'

'Do you care?'

'Not a bit.'

We went into his room. It still smelt of damp and vetiver.

'Let me look at you,' he said after he had locked the door. We stood smiling at each other. Then he drew me into his arms. I felt his heart beating fiercely against mine. 'You know what I want.'

'Ah, yes. I want it, too.'

'I think you must after all be a good fairy, come to release me from the terrible spell an English girl put on me so I could never stop loving her no matter how I longed to be free from the torment.'

'Oh, no.' I put up my face to kiss him. 'I mean, if I can, to keep you spellbound for the rest of your days.'